THE
DANCER
AT
THE FEAST

THE DANCER AT THE FEAST

The Chronicles of Tyr-shan the Seer

G. IAN SMITH

Cookies and Oxygen PUBLISHING

Cookies and Oxygen Publishing
www.cookiesandoxygen.co.uk

Originally self-published in Great Britain by the author in 2011.
This fully revised and updated version first published in Great Britain by
Cookies and Oxygen Publishing in 2020.

ISBN
978-1-912403-07-3 (Paperback)
978-1-912403-06-6 (Ebook)

Printed and bound by Severn
severnprint.co.uk

Our forests give us many things like books, tissues, furniture, and so much more. The Forest Stewardship Council (FSC) helps take care of forests and the people and wildlife who call them home. FSC is an international, non-governmental organisation dedicated to promoting responsible management of the world's forests. Find out more at fsc.org.

This book was typeset in Adobe Caslon Pro and Lucy Rose

Cover Design by Steve Hall
Cover Illustration by G. Ian Smith
Stock Photograph © Andreykuzmin (dreamstime.com)

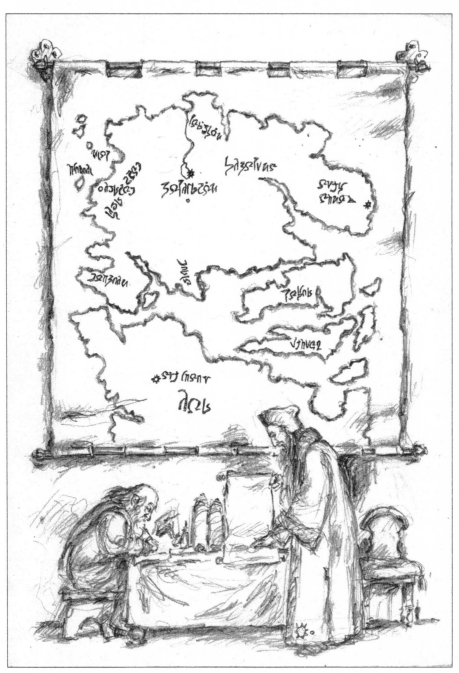

Tapestry of the Two Continents hanging in the Shrine, Valderthaan

If you like to pronounce character and place names the same way the author does, you will find a pronunciation guide at the end of this book on page 611.

However, Ian encourages you to work out your own pronunciation from the *look* of the word or in line with what you enjoy saying or hearing.

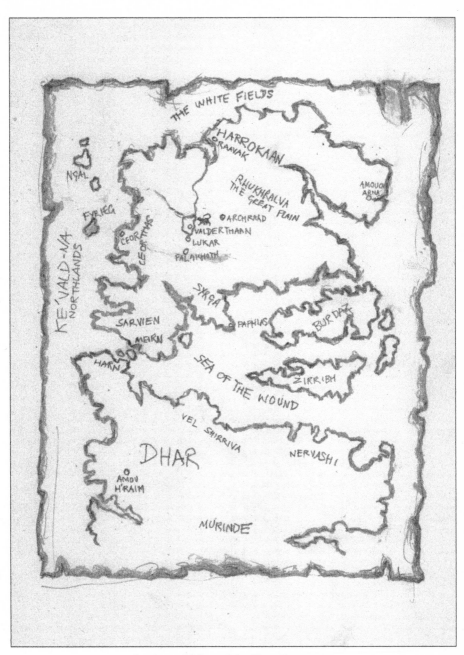

Anglicised Map of the Two Continents

CHAPTER 1

Storms

THE STORM SWEPT SUDDENLY from the north, from the mountains. Great, grey bulwarks of cloud trailing tattered banners of snow and hail. The land darkened, the shadow dipped, long, dark waters stirred and fretted under the gales funnelling down between the crags that hemmed them in. Howling storm-breath tore at a lake beneath the precipices, hunting its craft to the shore and the jetties of the high-backed island rearing from the swell. It seemed the city-crowned mass would break loose from the bridge that tethered it to the lakeside to founder on the southern shore. In the city beneath the storm, the burnished walls grew dim, gold sank to grey, and shrieks were swallowed in the thunder's maw. Almost to the pinnacles of the great coruscated towers came the black bending clouds, racing over and throwing their lightning-spears stabbing and blazing along the streets. Banners strained, tore and swirled away, the glimmer of a golden roof faded and died, and the sunlight fled to the south. The island-city and its lake, and all the life of man that lay beyond fell swiftly under the shadow.

Speeding south for many miles, the tempest lashed towns, roads, and pastures until it bore down upon a little figure who stood watching the grey curtain close over his green land. The lad gave a delighted shout, like a fighter accepting a challenge, and ran towards his sunlit valley. Leap of breath under his ribs, the stretch-pull, stretch-pull of muscles in his legs, the strength of bone and will that drove the earth under his feet. For the sheer delight of it, he whooped as he outran the storm.

He mapped out his route: a few hundred yards to the field's edge, jump the wall, scramble down the dip through the trees to the healer's house—there, the smoke swirling in the gust, the healer Wyrdha waved him on towards shelter.

The runner paused breathless in his wind-whipped field, glanced behind, then laughed again as he threw his lean body back into the unequal race. He saw others outside. Not far away on his left was a man running and stumbling, shouting and waving, his black cloak caught in the gale. He glimpsed a bearded face before the howling gloom surged over them and rain fell like stones. Near the wall, the healer was trying to move someone who stood with his hands spread out to the fury in the sky as if he was welcoming it. The bearded man had run out to help, and the pair manhandled the fellow down to the house before the youth could reach the wall. Their charge staggered like a dazed man and almost fell as he was hauled inside.

The lad flung himself over the wall and half-slid down the little slope through the trees to the healer's home. Instead of rushing inside he braced himself against a tree, drenched, breathless, and thrilled by his own awe at the wrath and power of the storm. Light and dark made war above the green slopes and the sun was in rout. The vast, grim, overwhelming cloud swallowed the green and gold, sinking everything into twilight. Trees blurred and faded into each other, the highest hills merged with the cloud, and the sun, despite brilliant stabs through the roiling armour, retreated down the valley. There were still small, bright fields and the flash of a silver river, but the vale below was sunk in night. It was like standing on the bed of some shadowed lake on whose surface a vast ship slid by; the hills were no longer hills but the backs of sea-monsters against faraway blue and white. Snow and hail and bitter rain streamed from the swirling sky, their long lashes, white and grey, flailed at the valley as trees leapt and thrashed. And over all moved the juggernaut of cloud, the belly of a huge, cold dragon whose wings shadowed all the world.

The worst fury over, he heard a voice above the wind.

"Tyr-shan? Tyr-shan, are you there? If you're not washed away, get inside!" The healer flattened himself against his house wall, pulling his coat around himself.

"I'm up here, Wyrdha! Don't wet y'self!"

The storm dragged its rain-curtain along the valley. It made a long, ragged shape like claws mauling the hills. For one superb instant, a line of white fire struck down before the voice of the thunder roared in. The boy ran over to the sparse shelter under the eaves of the house and stood leaning on Wyrdha's shoulder, drenched, staring down the valley in the hope of another lightning flash, but the great violence had left only gloom and rain behind.

"I would have thought," said Wyrdha tersely, "that wetting oneself was rather beside the point at the moment."

"Aye, very funny. Did y' see that?" gasped the lad. He punched Wyrdha's arm. "Do y' think it hit anybody?"

"It could have hit you, and no more than you deserve. Why didn't you come inside? You'll be ill!"

"Y're a healer, y' would cure me! Y' needn't be angry."

"I am not angry."

"Y' are that. Y' called me Tyr-shan and y' always say Tyr, so y're angry. Dead giveaway."

Wyrdha's heavy, frowning brows and thick beard made him look even more serious than usual. Conquered, he gave a slow, deep laugh. "Ah, you'll never be ill, Tyr. Your mother put too much life in you." He slapped the boy's shoulder. "But remember, I gave up thrills for a quiet life." His eyes smiled into far distances of the rain-pummelled valley.

Thinking about his travels? wondered Tyr. *Has he remembered something? Never tells us much.*

"It was a wild thing, though, wasn't it?" said Wyrdha suddenly.

"Oh, aye. It were like… alive," breathed Tyr. "It were—it were just…" He searched for a word and found none. He settled for a snorting puff of amazement and pulled the hanks of dark, wet hair from his face and shrugged them behind him. "You ever seen a storm like that? Y' got about a bit."

11

"Sometimes," said Wyrdha, peering into the greyness. "Sometimes."

Tyr squeezed water from his hair, or tried to. "Mam says Arna whips up storms like that and it means things. Y' can tell the future and that."

"That may be, Tyr—"

"Gizhurthra says that kind of thing's a por—wha's name? — por-tint, or somethin'. Says there's bad spirits that ride in the storm clouds and drop on the towns with the rain. He'll be goin' round for ages sayin' spells now, daft bugger."

"I do not listen to Gizhurthra," said Wyrdha in a hard voice, but he could not suppress a smile.

"Ey, that's good," said Tyr. "Folk like it when y' smile."

A laugh escaped Wyrdha. "Well, I'm not a complete stranger to excitement, you know. Never lose your sense of wonder, Tyr. Too many people—" He struck Tyr so hard he knocked him to the ground. A clatter of metal as something glanced off the house-wall where Tyr had been standing.

"Leave!" cried a coarse voice. Wyrdha froze as he stooped for the fallen dagger. A man stepped out from the trees, crossbow raised. The man who had flung the dagger was beside him, arm still stretched from the throw. A third emerged from the shadows under the leaves, slowly and carefully like a stalking cat, a long hunting knife held ready. All three were tense and deadly. Tyr tired to get to his feet, slipping in mud.

"Stay in dirt, valley-boy!" hissed the man with the crossbow, watching Wyrdha. "One of you move, I shoot."

While the others advanced cautiously, the knife-man ran to Tyr, dropped his weapon, then knelt on him, hauled his arms behind his back, and bound his wrists cruelly tight with a thong from his belt. He tugged the thong round Tyr's neck. The lad cried out as the man wrenched his arms up and his throat pressed tight. Still, he was alert, sharply aware: there was no room in him for fear. The rain hissed and whispered as if to soothe him as the predators advanced. They must have been waiting for them in the thickets. It was all so real, these men picked out in needle sharpness, so vivid, so strangely enthralling. He watched the men as he would a swaying snake.

The leader gripped his crossbow tighter, spoke sharply in a guttural tongue to the others and jerked his head towards the closed door. This could only be an instruction to burst in on the men inside. Tyr gritted his teeth. A call of warning from either himself or Wyrdha would see a crossbow bolt tearing through one of them.

The leader's companion unslung a round wooden shield from his back. Leather-covered, with bronze studs, it bore in red and white a crude ox-horn emblem. Harrak Plainsmen grabbing what they could from better folk to take back to their tribe. Those who sank to brigandry were merciless.

Their broad, heavy faces burned into Tyr's memory: the leader's scar, a white channel for the rain; the low, straight brows and broken teeth of the man staring over his shield; wide-set eyes and twisted mouth of the one who had bound him. They meant to loot the house and, later perhaps, make an offering of part of their spoils to their grotesque ox-god. It was hopeless.

The crossbow wavered.

"You stop," grunted the leader. "What you do? Stop!"

"What do you mean?" asked Wyrdha cautiously. "Stop what?"

"Black curse, you do something to me. Stop, or this in your throat." Wyrdha said nothing. The men stared at their leader, terrified now.

"Sorcerer," said the man with the twisted mouth. He snatched up his knife. "Spirit-man, vraakhin. The eye is on you."

"Don't look," said the leader. "Go inside, I watch him." They hesitated, fearful.

"V'karra stronger," said the other man, but his voice shook.

"V'karra not here, curse him. You go in, kill if you must," the leader snapped.

Before the men could move, the house door opened and a man lurched out. The leader swung the crossbow round, but his men blocked his aim. He swore at them and stepped to the side. There was a sound like a sharp breath: a rapid shape shot from the trees opposite and the man screamed as his fingers clenched and the bolt flew. The man in the doorway cried and fell back while the Harrak leader fell to his knees, clawing at an arrow in his side. Wyrdha gripped Tyr and dragged him away as more arrows flew.

Crashing from the trees came a swift swordsman, blade sweeping. He brought his blade down on the ox-shield and shattered it into the mud. The Harrak tried to swipe with a short sword but slipped and fell. Another stroke swept away his blade and fingers. With two of his group down, the other man panicked and fought badly. He ended up pressed against the wall of the house with a forearm gashed and a sword-point under his chin. With a feral howl, the leader lurched to his feet and pulled out a sword of his own. One of the hidden archers stepped out from the trees, crossbow over his shoulder and sword in hand. He easily dodged the Harrak leader's mad swings and lunges, knocked his guard aside and with an upward thrust sliced under his ribs. The leader fell, jerking and gasping in the mud like a fish on land. Blood welled up and spattered from his mouth, his limbs spasmed, and the clash was over.

The soldiers bound the surviving plainsmen hand and foot. Archers came from behind the trees on the far side of the house to retrieve their arrows. They shared relieved smiles and congratulations, along with tasteless jokes as they eased their helmets off. Someone laughed.

It shocked Tyr to realise that he had been joyfully running over the pastures not even ten minutes ago. He had since skirted death, seen a man killed, and two more had lost their freedom. And now here he sat, plastered with mud, and leaning against the house wall amid a wet, muddy anti-climax.

A tall soldier walked over to Tyr and cut his bonds. "All right, son?" the tall soldier asked.

"Aye, course I am," answered Tyr. He heaved himself to his feet, before realising he was very far from all right.

"Always shake like that then, do you?"

Tyr suddenly found himself seated again, this time on the bench attached to the outer wall of Wyrdha's house.

The soldier smiled and examined the marks flaring on Tyr's wrists. "Sod them ox-kissers," he said, and spat. "Don't care who they hurt." He shook his head and rubbed Tyr's wrists, the skin sore from the belt that had bound him.

Tyr glanced over at the brigands as an involuntary precaution. The man who had taken a blade to the hand crouched in the mud beside his dead leader. The corpse lay with limbs splayed out and eyes glaring up. A gout of blood was thickening in the beard, and the mouth was open. The captured plainsman swayed back and forth on his haunches, staring at the ugly thing and moaning to himself as he held his coat where his fingers had been. It was grotesque, dismal. Tyr looked away to find Wyrdha kneeling by his doorway. The healer's fingers were bloody, a crossbow bolt protruding from his visitor's leg. The man moaned. Wyrdha looked up as a soldier laid a hand on his shoulder; the healer made a gesture of thanks and Tyr noticed the bearded youth he'd seen while running ahead of the storm was crouching in the doorway too, bundling his black cloak under the wounded man's head.

"Could've got me," Tyr gasped to himself.

The sky's magnificent wrath was plain grey drizzle now, with a flush of brighter sunlight appearing. The tempest had swept to the south and the deadlier storm that had broken in a lightning of swords was also spent: the world was dull again.

The tall soldier was stooping over him, leaning on his knees. "Well, you'll live," he said. He jerked his head towards the captives. "Real animals we've got there. You're lucky, son, you really are." He patted Tyr's shoulder and leaned close, mock-confidential. "Mind you, they never had a chance: not against me and me stout lads here. Not a hope." Tyr smiled and trembled a little less, warming to the easy smile and quiet brown eyes. The man had seen about twenty-five summers; they all seemed to have been good ones. Another slap on the shoulder. "Come on then, let's be having you." He hauled Tyr to his feet. "You managing?"

"Think so," said Tyr, holding onto the wall and the soldier's arm. "What was they doin'?"

"Bit of business, I'd say. They'd get a nice little bag of silver bits for you in Archraad, my lad."

"Silver bits? Ey! Y' mean sell me?"

"Aye. All quiet like, of course. You'd be chucked in a wagon with two dozen other poor sods and whipped off down to Burdaz or somewhere. They like northerners down there."

Tyr shuddered, appalled by the vision of what he had escaped. He seldom thought of life beyond his own valley, far less about remote kingdoms. Being taken there by force, alone… He shook himself and looked up at the soldier. "I thank y'," he said formally. "I'm Tyr." He made as good a bow as he could manage, making his rescuer smile broadly.

"I'm Tharval," the man replied. "Captain Tharval to you. It's my pleasure." He laughed as Tyr flopped back onto the bench.

"Y've got the red on," said Tyr, acting as if he'd meant to sit down again. "Are y' the city Guard?"

Tharval sat down on the bench next to Tyr. He pulled off his helmet causing sandy-coloured hair to fall about his shoulders in the northern fashion. He smoothed his deep red uniform. "That's us. We're a bit far from home down here. Been following them ox-kissing sods three days. They tried stealing a little girl at Braldhar—"

"They never! Dirty buggers!"

"They are that. Nice, sweet, little place is Braldhar. Got a well in the middle. We got on their trail there. That storm was brilliant though. Let us sneak round and meet them. They never seen nor heard us coming." Tharval glanced round at the plainsmen, Tyr tried not to. "Right then, let's find out how your mate is."

"He's not me mate," said Tyr. "Dunno who he is. He were up in the fields, and that other feller brought him down here. He stumbled out and gave them all a shock. Then you came."

"Aye, he gave us our chance," said Tharval. "We could have come at them quicker, but your friend might've got the bolt in him."

Wyrdha glanced up briefly after finishing an impromptu dressing. "The hip," he said. "Not so bad as it might have been, but bad enough. I've removed the bolt."

Tharval peered at the injured man and grimaced.

Wyrdha sat next to Tyr and gripped his hand. "Thank the Lady," he said. "Thank the Lady. Let me see your wrists. And neck. Ah, all's well. Stretch a bit if you can." He put a strong arm round his friend and held him tightly against his side. "Now," he said, "get inside: get washed, get dried, lie down." He withdrew his arm and Tyr stood up and shuffled toward the door. Wyrdha crouched back down over his unexpected patient. "We're going to move you, my friend. Are you ready?"

"Eh? What's happened? What you doin' to me?"

16

"Thank the Lady."

Tyr looked down at the fellow's face as he stepped over him. He was a few years older than himself, with large wild eyes and a tangle of yellow hair. Terror and utter confusion filled his expression.

"I just come down to see Master's Mount. I was goin' to say rituals in the cave. I even brought a little figure of the Lady me Mam gave me."

"I was going there myself. A very sacred place, the cave," said the young man in the black robe. "Azhur va-Kherzir, at your service."

"My pleasure to meet you Azhur," said Wyrdha. He turned to the injured man. "I'm a healer. Your leg has been hurt by a crossbow. We're taking you into my house."

The injured youth raised himself up on his elbows, looking wildly about, speaking through rapid gasps. "Where'd. They. Go?"

"Quite safe now," said Wyrdha. "Lie back, please."

The fellow slumped flat and stared up at Azhur kneeling at his head. "What'd I do? I never did nothin' to them. Like wolves!"

Azhur gripped the fellow's hand in both of his. "Not your fault," he said. "An accident. You were just in the way of what they wanted."

The patient looked at Wyrdha. "I'm cold," he said faintly. "Am I goin' to die?"

"You certainly are not. Why, that wound could have been far worse."

"Wound?"

"You'll be all right," said Azhur. "Just lie still." But he failed to reassure.

"Here, you takin' my leg off? Oh, don't, please. I heard how they do that!"

"Your leg will remain firmly attached," said Wyrdha. "I will bandage it, but I will not add it to my collection."

"Collection?"

"My attempt at humour, your pardon. Captain? Will you assist me?"

"Pleasure', said Tharval. "Here! Think I know you, mate!"

"Don't expect an answer," said Wyrdha. "Shock, and I gave him something."

"Wait, I do know him. His step-dad has the *Golden Carp* at Lukar. Yauva's his name, harmless sort of feller. Knew his actual dad when I was a lad." Tharval shook his head. "Arna's wings! Fancy him getting shot by

Harrak!"

"Well, I prefer to close my door at night," said Wyrdha, "so inside he goes. Now, if we support him at waist and leg, Captain, and you do the same at the shoulders, master priest."

"Priest? Ey!" exclaimed Tyr from the fireside within, but Yauva of the *Golden Carp* cried out as the three men lifted him and no-one heard him.

CHAPTER 2

Ilissos

IN THE GLITTERING FRESHNESS of the afternoon, a horseman left the homestead which had sheltered him from the storm and took the narrow southern road through the storm-scourged moors where his host's sheep grazed. The land behind him lifted to a series of rough hills and sweeping vales of bracken and yellow grass. He had sent his horse speeding through their coarse pelt with the racing black clouds in pursuit, but now they moved at a slower pace through pasture and belts of tilled or wooded land. The colours of the moorland stretched around him, fresh and hard, washed by the rain for nature's festival and decked with glinting, shimmering moisture.

The rider halted. To his left the ground rose over a mile or so to a jagged line of pines that made a dark border against the sky. On the right, marshy, broken ground led his eye to a sweep of hills that marched in line with the road. Behind them, as they diminished, was the sharp crown of a solitary mountain, and beyond the blue of slopes farther still. There would lie the long valley the shepherd had described to him, carrying the river and the broad road from the city. The horseman smiled a little. He had been right to miss that road. The extra miles of the detour over the high farmland had been worth it. His reward had been the stillness of the early mist, the light like drifting pearl. Budding trees and the lichen of the rocks had flared up for him as great swathes of yellow light fell across the land from the rising sun. Birdsong thrilled away every thought of the clamour of the broad highway.

At the tail end of the morning he had found himself in a wild place of rock, stubby heather, and gnarled hills above long, grey scree slopes. There, as he looked around with delight, the storm had come upon him. Looking back to see how the sunlight lay on a vast cascade of a hill, he had seen the grim, roiling cloud rushing towards him. Blizzard and dark rain trailed after, throwing before it a single lightning shaft as a challenge. The horseman had stared transfixed; he felt like a man menaced by a host so terrible and magnificent he could not flee for the thrill of it. When the storm was almost upon him, he had turned his horse and begun, like another that day, an exhilarated race for shelter. Now he carefully relived the experience in his thoughts. He must remember it exactly, not only what he had seen but what it had felt like to find the awesome thing bearing down upon him. Neither he nor anyone in his warm homeland had encountered anything like it before, and, in his land, poets and storytellers had a high standing. He wanted his traveller's tales to outshine the best.

Now he wondered what the glorious darkness meant. Everyone knew when the elements of the world convulsed they pointed to something beyond themselves. It was the poets' task, and those gifted to see beyond things, to find out what. He pulled off his cap, ran his fingers through his dark curls and let his head fall back, moving his neck in slow circles to ease his muscles. He drew the sharp air into his body and felt his mind clear.

"Ah, Northland," he sighed. "*Ke'vald-na*, who would not love you, wild beauty? Who could tame you, strong creature?" He smiled to himself as he realised he had inadvertently begun a song. He would make one before the day was out. It might follow the trajectory of the storm's significance, or at least buy him a few meals here in the Northland.

The traveller sent his horse forward. He had taken his time on this lofty road, savouring its miles and letting the stillness refresh him while he shaped words and music. Perhaps the newness of the surrounding

21

lands would put something fresh into his songs. One reason he had fallen in love with *Ke'vald-na*—the Northland—was its unfamiliarity and otherness. It was harder, harsher, and wilder than his home. Deep foreign green of pine forests climbing the piled-up, jagged mountains. Rivers racing on the huge, brown plains to the broad valleys slung between the hills. Ragged coasts that held back the vast western sea. The traveller drew in a sharp, cold breath and rubbed his face. The olive tint of his skin placed him from the warmer south and his worn travel clothes had an uncommon look, except for the heavy fur-trimmed cloak he had bought for winter and still wore against the chill of a northern spring. He let the cloak fall back from his body so he could know the bite of the wind. It whipped about him like a lash, searing his face with a caress of needles, stinging his soul awake. *See, see,* it sang, *your mother's beauty, the queen's majesty, with beauty she brings forth all, with glory she is crowned, and of glory she sings.* The wind's song swirled up from the moors and swept down from the mountains. The voice of the whole earth telling him he was part of all that is made and brother to all things. He was a gift for them as they were for him.

The young man gently drew up his horse. He looked about him, suddenly astonished. The beauty was intense: the colours, the light, the deep, deep sky. A longing rushed up in him and seemed to burst out and draw him with it so that, rising beyond himself, he could delightedly look back and see himself. He longed for the mountains and for the massive beauty *in* them. He ached for the trees and for what made them what they were, reaching in his mind for branch and intricate leaf full of unending colours, more able to shine and glow against the eternal light. He longed with a beautiful pain, though he could not call it that, for the spring of life, for glory, for the brilliance that kindled the sun....

There was a pause, and the earth seemed poised in light. The traveller knew he was on a horse, on a moor, but everything around him seemed to have become more than a mere place. He felt it, not as an area but as an essence. A gateway to what it truly was, to the source and definition of its existence and to a bright, clear, happy being who was behind and beneath it all; but it was still itself, and more so for being experienced thus, rock and tree more hard and sharply real than ever.

A curtain was drawn quietly in his mind, and the brilliance from the casement behind shone through but softly to the shadowed chamber as things settled back to their soft, everyday realness. *So,* he thought, *it has happened again. I never thought it would. I thought when this came upon me on the hill above the world at Agoras such a thing could enter a life and divide it in two only once. I have never known how to speak of it. Now these northern firs, the moors, the hills are as lovely as before, but though I think I am content with them I am not. The longing remains.*

For a while he watched a bird wheeling about its endless heaven and thought of his home, Syrga—Northmen called it the Green Jewel—the little land of the green hills and the cypress trees sitting by the sea's edge. There was beauty there too: wild in its way, but softer, kindlier, and it would grow as the spring advanced. But he had reached out to beauty and found himself grasping for he knew not what. He knew no more of the definition of his experiences than he did of the meaning of the storm. He had promised himself he would seek for it, but that quest hardly seemed to matter at this moment. A quietness had come to him and though there was no understanding in his mind, he was aware that his heart grasped the knowledge, held the truth. The words, the understanding of the mind, would come later. Whatever *had* happened, he would try to rest in it and let it rest in him. Gently he flicked the reins and the horse moved off.

He had not gone far before he had company on the road. Horsemen were cantering towards him, coming up from the valley with the sun behind them; they had the bearing of soldiers. As the column came up to the Syrgan a shout and raised hand brought the riders to a halt. The traveller found himself under the tired, dutiful stare of the captain. The quietness in him persisted, so he smiled and said nothing. The men were relaxed, showing a friendly interest in the foreigner.

"Blessings of day to you, master," said the captain in the tired but dutiful voice of a man who would rather be at home. "You're a stranger here," he added, smiling a little at his own unnecessary statement, and was rewarded with a broad grin.

"A stranger, yes, and happy I am here."

The soldier allowed himself an affable little nod in return: this fellow wasn't edgy like they usually were. "Tharval's my name," he continued, speaking slowly for the foreigner's benefit, "I'm captain of this troop. Leader: I command."

"Yes, yes, this I see."

"Right. Well, I serve the Valgraav, the emperor—*em-per-or*—in his guard, his soldiers at the city. The big city on the island. Valderthaan." The other's face lit up. "You know that, eh? Now, I've got to ask you why you're on this road, master. There's been bad men in these parts, you see, and we've got to know who uses the lonely roads."

This made the foreigner very serious. "Ah, yes, yes, I have heard of your troubles. You think perhaps I am a Harrach—"

"Harrak? Aye, bad lot, we've got some here."

"Harrach, yes. But no, I am Ilissos of Syrga, and my city is Agoras on the Seventh Hill, and I wear the amulet of Cynathé—see?" He displayed the bronze design bound to his left wrist. "She is goddess in Syrga, and that is her sign, trees by the river, but you should see this, I think." He delved into a saddlebag and brought out a folded parchment. "This they gave me to let me cross the great bridge to Val—valt—"

"Valderthaan," said Tharval helpfully. "You been there, then?"

"Yes, forgive me, a hard city to say. But look, we have the same mark!" Ilissos pointed to Tharval's helmet and the bronze image of the rayed sun. The same sign, over the figure of a lion, was on the parchment's seal. "Your king's mark, I think. You will trust me now?"

"I might," said Tharval. He scanned the parchment. "You came up to the city from the east, through the pass at Mardokhal." He looked a little more serious.

"Does it say that?" asked Ilissos. "I did not try to read it. Yes, I was very far in the east, beyond the plain, but I kept to the south where there are the towns and soldiers, and I did not cross it. Even in the Far Lands they talk about the Harrach who seek gold and blood on your Plain. They will not have mine! And people say Harrach hate your king, and would kill him if they could and they say a sorcerer lives on the Plain in Arc...."

"Archraad."

"Arcrad, yes. It is very bad. I am sorry you must live with men like this."

Tharval, about to return the parchment, drew back his hand. "Where'd you hear about Harrak, exactly?"

"Why, everywhere. Even on the road and in the city too where the king is."

"How do you live, master Ilissos? For interest's sake, I mean."

Ilissos missed the intention of the question entirely. He gestured widely. "Oh, it is not too hard. I buy something, perhaps, and sell it again. I work, I hunt. There are many ways." He patted the saddlebags with a broad smile. "In Agoras I am a trader. You have a lady in the city? I have perfumes in my bag, and spices. Shall I show you? Herbs and scented oils she cannot find in the north. Or there is eye salve—"

"Go on, Captain," called a soldier. "I wouldn't mind my Gildta smellin' a bit better."

"Don't bother getting the eye salve," returned Tharval. "Then at least you won't have to look at her." He turned to face Ilissos again, "No, sorry, master Ilissos, but there're matters as won't wait, and we've got prisoners, so no sales."

Ilissos gave an understanding nod. "It will be beautiful in Syrga when I return," he said. "The light, the green! You must come to my land in the spring."

Tharval folded the parchment and returned it. "I might at that. I like the sound of Syrga. Everybody does up here. But that's the Bridge Seal from Valderthaan on your parchment, Master Ilissos, so you can go freely in the north. It'll speak for you if ever you can't say enough for yourself, though I doubt it'll ever come to that. Safe journey and Arna shine on you."

Ilissos returned the nods of the soldiers as they rode past, thinking no doubt of insufficiently fragrant ladies in the city. And then his smile faded away. Near the end of the column rode two sullen-looking men with hands bound and heads bowed. Another man's body was slung over the horse behind them, a trail of blood seeping down the saddle-cloth. The Syrgan watched the column for a while, sorry for this grisly stain on the day. But the wind blew, the clouds and grasses moved, and in time his mind moved on. He thrust his precious parchment deep into a saddle-bag, gathered his cloak about him and went on towards the valley.

Ilissos descended the valley's side for a while, shaking his head occasionally over the captive Harrak. The belt of trees that had marched alongside him to the west ended and the moors became a long, green slope into the valley. He reined in his horse to take in this new sight before he began the descent. Below, a glinting river twisted among tilled fields and pasture that rose on the valley's farther side into the shadow of long, brown hills dense with fir and pine. Along the valley floor and near the river was a contrasting grey line running straight north to south. It was almost a mile below, but Ilissos realised that this was the great highway, the King's Road as it was called, that ran from the island-city Valderthaan, the seat of power, through all the dominions of the Valgraav, the lord of the north. Even from this viewpoint it was obviously busy, and the Syrgan congratulated himself once more for taking the long, quiet road over the moors. He flicked the reins and allowed the horse to amble into the valley at its own speed. The outlines of the hills crowded away behind him, revealing the broad, dark, sentinel mountain that reared, snow-speckled, from the valley.

The first indications that a town lay below, were trails of wood smoke wandering up from behind a wooded slope to be caught in the brightness of the afternoon sun. Across the slope of land about half a mile away, along the valley's curving lip and almost level with him, Ilissos saw a broad, flat grazing land and its animals. On the slopes below were a few wooden houses and people moving down towards the road; several were wading across a stream that ran from the moors to the river on the valley floor. Ilissos wondered if some kind of welcome was preparing, his blue Syrgan coat made him a most visible stranger. There was shouting: brief, urgent calls that were worryingly close. If these people were running to intercept him, a friendly meeting looked unlikely. Something had happened here. Perhaps the soldiers travelling north on the moors with two bound men and a body had started from this place. Ilissos squared his shoulders and rode on.

The situation was soon clear. Well into the valley Ilissos brought his horse round a sharp, narrow bend and faced a knot of grim-faced men gripping sticks and tools. A few were holding long knives. Directly in front of him a large, sweating man in a leather apron was holding a business-like sword in both hands. Ilissos pulled the horse up sharply and glanced around. More men were moving up the valley to block his escape. He wondered whether to bolt but realised that would be as good as an admission of guilt, and the men with knives no doubt threw them very well. The visiting poet of Syrgan was utterly disadvantaged. He therefore smiled and remained silent.

This confused the men. They glanced anxiously at one another, then looked to the big man in the leather apron who glowered through his tangled hair and growled, "Who're y' then?"

Ilissos felt he understood things. "Already I am asked this," he said. "A soldier asked, and I told him I am Ilissos of Syrga, from Agoras on the Seventh Hill." No reply. "That is where I am going. It is beautiful now in Syrga." Shuffling and muttering.

"Syrga's all right, isn't it?" mumbled someone.

Ilissos tried again. "So sorry, masters, I am making you afraid—"

"Why do y' think that is, then?" snapped a stocky man with a wood-axe.

"What soldier?" barked the big man.

Ilissos cautiously dismounted. Grips tightened, men stepped closer.

"Don't you go for no knife, now," said the big man, "or you'll get this in you." He was directly in front of Ilissos, sword ready.

"Only a little knife, master," replied the Syrgan evenly. He slowly opened his coat, showing the rabbit-skinning blade at his belt. "There is a bigger one in the pack, on the horse, but he cannot use it."

"Don't be bloody funny," shouted the axe-man. "What do y' want here?"

"Well, that is easy. Some food and an inn. A shepherd on the moors, he says an inn is here."

"What shepherd?"

"A man named Ver-Var-Ah! Var-dis, is it? I cannot say it, but his beard is black and his wife will have another child soon." There was a murmur at this.

"That'll be Vardthaz," said several.

27

Ilissos seized the advantage, "These two, they told me there was a good inn at Falakhoth—I can say it! I had to try often—and the soldier, Tharval, he says I am not a bad man and the seal of the Bridge at Valddertan says the same." This was better, Tharval's name got a good response. Ilissos pressed on, "But masters, I think three men from the Plain wanted something here." That got them.

"What do y' mean?" asked the big man. The sword lowered a little.

"Well," Ilissos said, "Tharval and his soldiers keep them. Two were bound—" he put his hands behind his back for a moment "—and one, he was dead." This had the desired effect. Weapons became tools again.

"That's them, Tyrmar," said one. "He's all right."

"Knew it by the look of him," said another heartily.

The big man, Tyrmar, let the sword-point rest on the ground. "This Tharval feller," he said. "He's got a red beard, hasn't he? Big scar on his right cheek, like that." He drew a finger from eye to jaw.

Ilissos stared at him, mystified. "Why, no," he stammered, anxious now. "No beard, no scar. Another soldier has his name?" He stopped as loud guffaws burst out.

"That were just a precaution," said Tyrmar. "Y're an honest man, master Ilissos. Come on down to town and have a bite. I'm Tyrmar and I'm headman here. I've good reason to be thankful to them soldier lads, but y'll hear about that."

The men shouldered their tools, glad they had not been needed as weapons, and the whole group walked down to the town. Ilissos led his horse along and, true storyteller that he was, launched into a vivid saga of his meeting on the moor.

"We have the same sign, Tharval and I," he said, touching the amulet of the sun at his breast. "I think he let me pass for this also."

"What's that, then?" asked Tyrmar, tapping the amulet on the Syrgan's wrist.

"Well, Cynathé. She is goddess in Syrga and this is her sign. The great ones of the sun and moon, they brought her forth, and she begged them for the beautiful land at the sea's edge to be her own, to care for."

"I've heard of that." said Tyrmar. "She looks out for y', then?"

"Ah, she does. Is any land praised for beauty like Syrga? Where is

28

there so much of fruits and corn, vines and oil? Where are such skies? Where warmer air?"

"In my forge, most like," Tyrmar told him, slapping his leather apron.

Ilissos chattered on, "Cynathé, she is like the mother of us in Syrga, but we remember that once it was said that Hra'im—oh, it is hard to say—Hra'im was the name of the spirit men bowed to in the southern deserts. Listen now, I am a teller of the oldest memories and when the Lord of the South took your Northlands into his kingdom, he said you must worship Hra'im, only you called him Arna. So I am in Arna's land and I wear Arna's sign."

"Oh, aye," said Tyrmar, a little flatly, Ilissos thought. "Aye, we know all that. What vegetables do y' like?"

Tyrmar's men and their guests, human and equine, trudged through a gaggle of low, wooden houses, cutting a swathe through alarmed chickens and welcoming dogs, before arriving in the centre of Falakhoth. More of the wooden houses squatted, leaned, or otherwise huddled round a large square of trodden earth, their timbers still glistening with rainwater. Among them, Tyrmar's forge smoked and glowed within. A large group of women, close together for safety and comfort, clustered round a cairn of stones on which was set the carven figure of a woman, hands uplifted in the sign of blessing. A plaintive, thin-voiced song drifted over.

> Lady bless your daily breath,
> Lady give you happy death,
> Give you joy and sweet relief,
> Save you from the one beneath.

Tacked or tied to the figure were a host of small objects, moving and personal: a child's shoe, a bunch of ribbons or flowers, a piece of cheap jewellery, a scrap of parchment bearing some heart's secret need. The women were talking quietly, soothing each other with word and touch, as women do who wait together to see if their men are safe.

Tyrmar shattered the gentle scene at once. "Right, me dears!" he roared. "Here we all are, safe as houses. What about a kiss?"

With delighted shrieks of relief, each woman rushed to her man and a hugging, laughing, kissing, tearful festival of welcome began. A few

29

couples immediately rushed off to their houses, hanging on to each other like limpets as they ran. A few very elderly men, too frail for combat, clapped and shouted.

Ilissos, disinclined to hug or kiss his horse, enjoyed the happy melee but stood rather awkwardly on the edge until Tyrmar noticed and remembered his manners.

"Ah, beggin' y' pardon, master Ilissos! This here—" he swung a squealing, dark-haired little woman through the air "—is me goodwife, mistress Iethen." The woman landed in front of Ilissos and stared brightly up at him, fascinated at once by his exotic looks.

"Ooh," she exclaimed. "Hello, then."

"Ieth, this here's a feller from Syrga. We met him on the road. Weren't no bandits after all, but we give him a fright, so I brought him down for a bite."

"Syrga, eh?" said Iethen, arranging her hair around her head-cloth. "'Tis nice down there, isn't it? Well, blessin's of day, very happy to welcome you." And she was. Her voice was honest, soft and clear, as if she was thanking Ilissos for not being Harrak.

The Syrgan gave her a courteous bow as her deep, bright eyes flicked back to her husband. "*Aiyana va,*" he said. "*Sei seph'hona aima la meithon.*"

"Eh?" said Iethen loudly.

"Oh, we say it in Syrga."

"What's it mean, then?" Ilissos hesitated. "Come on, I don't like not knowin' what folks is sayin' to me!"

The Syrgan juggled words in his head. "Ah… it is difficult. Well, it is not close, but I think it is: *Your faces are happiness to me.* Does it have a meaning for you?"

"Ooh, yes!" exclaimed Iethen. "I like that! I'll give y' a good tea now, I will! Get y'self over to that forge."

"Where's Tyr?" asked Tyrmar, suddenly and seriously. "He all right?"

"He is," said Iethen. She locked eyes with her husband for a moment before he gripped her in a tight hug.

"Bloody bastards," he said, throat tight. "He could a—"

"He didn't though," said Iethen quietly, staring into realities with her head on his chest. "That's all about it, my love."

"Aye," agreed Tyrmar huskily, moist-eyed. "Aye, y're right." He coughed unnecessarily loudly and drew a hand surreptitiously across his face. "Right then. Master Ilissos here's wantin' the inn, Ieth."

"Oh. Well it's not bad, and it's decent scran, long's y're not used to banquets in Valderthaan."

"Oh, I do not worry for comfort," said Ilissos airily.

"Y'll be all right there then," Tyrmar told him. "Might even get a place to y'self, like."

"Well, don't put him off, love," scolded Iethen. "Thal's got to make a livin'." She clasped Ilissos' and Tyrmar's hands. "Tea first though, come on."

Iethen tugged the two men, with the horse in tow, across the muddy square towards the wide door of the forge. She made a small detour by the wooden figure. Pausing, she and Tyrmar made a little bow.

The headman looked up at the carved, kindly face. "I thank y'," he murmured, between his deep breaths. "I do."

Ilissos made a respectful little bow also, feeling he should be decent enough to honour other people's deities, whose territory he was in after all. Perhaps he could get an amulet of the pleasant Lady.

Arriving at the forge's open door, they found a dark-haired lad leaning against the frame with arms folded. He peered at them with the bleary, scowling look of someone who has just woken but still wishes to avoid the world.

"Weren't it Harrak, then?" he said.

"Nothin' like it, Tyr," replied Tyrmar heartily. "Just this feller here. Y' all right now?"

"Bit wobbly, Dad. Had a lie down though. Wyrdha made me."

"Y're too pale," said Iethen, stroking the boy's face.

"Give over, Mam, I'm all right—hey, you're foreign, y' are! Where y' from?"

"This here's Ilissos," explained Tyrmar, "and he's on his holidays from Syrga. He's havin' a bite with us, then he's stayin' at the inn."

"Is he? Utha'll fancy him somethin' rotten!" Tyr gave a weary but coarsely heartfelt guffaw.

"Tyr! Behave y'self!" said Iethen. "Utha's a nice respectable girl!"

"Chuck it, Mam. I'm not weddin' her."

"Well, I don't know why y' won't, Tyr, she's—'

"I'm not weddin' no fatty, I told y'."

"Now then, Ieth," said Tyrmar gently but firmly. "Leave it for now. The lad's had a shock."

"I'd have a bigger one if I snogged Utha."

"Tyr!"

The lad lurched off the doorpost. "I think I'll just have a walk," he said meaningfully. "Come on, Iliwotsit, I'll show y' the inn."

Iethen admitted temporary defeat on what was clearly a major issue for her and disappeared into the forge. Tyr, Ilissos, and the horse crossed the square, the lad ambling in a hunched, self-protective posture, hugging himself.

"You are not well, master Tyr?" asked Ilissos.

"Just had a fright."

"Oh. It is a big fright, I think. I also had one."

"Nearly got shot. Three of them Harrak buggers had a go at me."

"Oh. I am very sorry." Ilissos decided not to mention his sighting of the defeated Harrak until later. For now, a change of subject. "What is its name, the inn?"

"Not got one. They never bothered."

"We will give it a name, then. Think hard, Tyr-shan. Now, there is an inn at Agoras, and its name is the Olive Grove."

"What's an olive?"

"It's like a fruit. It's beautiful to eat, and it gives us oil."

"Y' don't get them round here. Call it something else."

"But olive is its name: *Shelou*—"

"No, y' daft bugger, the inn." But the mistake was funny enough to put a grin on Tyr's face and straighten his shoulders a little.

Less amusing was the man who sat hunched on a bench outside the nameless hostelry. The sagging figure irresistibly reminded Ilissos of a sackful of something that had gone very stale. He thought it might make an amusing song, but the man's face flung the idea from his mind at once. There was nothing amusing about Bardcha of Falakhoth. His hard features were bunched into a scowl and tugged down by a sheer weight of sourness. Thin, tight lips held in the bitter things revolving in the mind. Stony eyes stared out under red, puffy lids.

"Somebody wantin' lodgin'," announced Tyr. "Where's Thal?" The grey head lifted a little.

Ilissos peered at the bleak, disinterested face and sensed a challenge. "A beautiful day, master."

Bardcha sucked air into his lungs as if he resented it. "Better than it was." A pause as he regarded the ground once more. "Some storm, though, that'll mean somethin'. I've been through hard things in me time but never had a portent like that." This dire pronouncement was spoken without real interest.

Ilissos remained doggedly cheerful. "Yes, so sudden, the storm, but I found shelter. There are strong, warm houses in the north."

"Daren't get caught in somethin' like that," said the sighing voice. "Finish me off that would. Dose of fever'd end me."

"Bardcha?" said Tyr, used to this.

"I heard y' young Tyr: lodgin's. Just hang on a bit." He looked up at Ilissos. "Won't let an old man talk. They don't care, these young'uns."

"Y're not that old," said Tyr, irritated by this ritual.

"Y're not from round here," observed Bardcha.

"No, I am Syrgan. I travel."

"Ah. Syrga's a good place, eh? I'm stuck up here, of course. I'd go down there, but the journey'd kill me. How long y' stayin' for?"

"Y' needn't worry, we've plenty of room. There's a real priest stayin' here and all." A plump, fair-headed girl was standing at the inn door.

Ilissos beamed and gave a little bow.

"Hello, I'm Utha," she cooed, twirling the ends of her braids in pink, practical fingers. "That's me grandad. Are y' feelin' better, Tyr?"

"Rotten," said Tyr curtly, avoiding the blatantly appreciative gaze.

"Ohh. Shall I bring some hot milk for y'?"

"No, y' can't. Wyrdha says I've not got to be disturbed. I'll probably collapse when I get back."

"Inside, girl, and do some work. Don't interrupt y' elders," wheezed Bardcha. "And put a headscarf on. Be decent for once."

"Well, if y' must know, grandad, I've been helpin' watch the little'uns

33

in case it were more Harrak comin'. I think that's very important, don't y', Tyr?" No reply. Utha scowled and went inside but relented enough to send back a final winsome smirk that seemed unable to decide whether to land on Tyr or Ilissos.

"Young'uns," said Bardcha. "No respect. Goin' up north, then?"

"Going down south, master. I am going home."

Tyr scraped the ground with his foot, frustrated. The horse gave a little start.

"Now then, have a bit of patience," wheezed Bardcha. "Look at that, frightnin' the horse! Let us have a chat, will y'? I've not got much pleasure in life—"

"Don't be a miserable sod, dad!" Thaljhaz the innkeeper was ambling back from the welcome gathering with his arm around a sturdy-looking woman who laughed as she tried to push her yellow hair under her head-scarf. "Look, Verdje's right happy her husband never got shot by a Harrak. That should give y' plenty of pleasure in life, eh?"

Bardcha quickly turned away with an air of such crushed sourness it was clear the innkeeper had said something very wrong, or was meant to feel he had. The woman's mirth dried up at once. She broke away from her husband and went into the house, not even glancing at Ilissos. Thaljhaz called after her, but there was no answer. He took the reins of Ilissos's horse, embarrassed. "I'll see to him," he muttered. "There's a stable round the back. I'll get y' stuff inside." He paused, angrily struggling with the confusing guilt Bardcha had flung at him. "There's a space with a mattress or y' can sleep at the fire. Y' want a meal?"

"We're havin' him," said Tyr. A glance at Bardcha. "Y' shouldn't put up with him. Verdje looked right happy."

Thaljhaz managed an awkward half-grin merged with a frown. "Aye, she did. She does when she gets the chance. Well, master Ilissos, glad I didn't have to stick a knife in y'." The innkeeper's chin went out as his simmering anger threatened to take over. "Not that I wouldn't mind doin' that sometimes. Anyroad, I'm sorry for our little scene. Y' have a good meal at the forge. Good folk there, very *friendly* people who enjoy others *laughin'*." If Bardcha got the point of this, he gave no sign, nor any satisfaction to his son-in-law. "Right. I'll make your acquaintance later."

Thaljhaz abruptly began to see to the horse.

Tyr and Ilissos made for the forge on the other side of the square. The innkeeper's furious voice sounded behind them. "Y' like it, don't y'? We've all got to be as miserable as y'! Y' can't stand Verdje bein' happy, can y', y' unnatural sod? Y' own daughter! Arna should of sent that lightnin' through y' and given us all peace."

"They don't get on," said Tyr.

~

Tyrmar and Iethen did everything they could to satisfy Ilissos' ravenous curiosity about life in the Northland, but they failed to explain why Thaljhaz and his father-in-law didn't get on.

"Families," Tyrmar said vaguely. 'Y' know."

"When's that young priest comin' down from Wyrdha's?" asked Iethen by way of rescue.

But Tyr had his own tales of local life. "When I were a sprog," he announced, "there were this feller and his mates come in from the city—supposed to be royal or somethin'—"

"That's water under the bridge, Tyr," said Iethen firmly.

"Aye. Anyroad, they stops at the inn and gets drunk as weasels and the feller says he's in love with Verdje's sister, Antha, and he's goin' to wed her—"

"Ilissos isn't interested in all that, Tyr."

"He is, look at him. So he pulled her on his horse and off they goes. Course, he chucked her about a month later. She's livin' in Lukar now, dyein' cloth or somethin'."

"Well, she's made a good life for herself, so that's all right," said Iethen briskly. "Shall we just leave it now?"

"Tell y' what I think—"

"That's the taters nearly ready, so y' better—"

"Well, everybody knows, like, but Bardcha fancied himself related to rich nobs in the Stone Houses. He were hoppin' mad when Antha got chucked. When Verdje wedded Thal, Bardcha were right sick about it cos he knew he'd not get money nor nothin' with an innkeeper in the family. Hated Thal's guts, he did. Can't stand him and he hates Verdje for weddin' him."

"Ah, it is sad," said Ilissos, who had been listening fascinated with his chin on his hand. "It should be a song or something to laugh at, I think. I will give it a happy ending."

"Best of luck then," said Tyrmar. "It needs one. Bardcha makes their lives hell in that inn."

"Don't encourage them," his wife told him. "Now, get y'self ready: vegetables is done and I've got bread and some cold meat. Hope that'll be all right for you, sir."

The middle-aged man at the fire made a weak but reassuring noise.

"*Anthu*, Mam," insisted Tyr. "Y' call a priest, Anthu."

"Oh, beg y' pardon, sir—Anthu Jher-val, I mean, sorry," trilled Iethen, over-jovial with embarrassment. "The things our Tyr knows!"

"One marvels," replied the Anthu Jher-val. He smiled feebly with one side of his mouth and forced another sip of village wine into himself. "I, er—I was thinking, I shouldn't create work for you. I can eat at the inn just as well."

"Y'll do no such thing," exclaimed Iethen. "It's an honour, sir, havin' y' on the very day our boy—"

"Mam!"

"And we've got two priests as well," said Tyrmar quickly. "Y' never see them round here, and now there's two! Y' and the young feller can have a good chat. Dunno what priests talk about, mind. Goes all over me head." He gave a heartfelt guffaw that betrayed the fact that he presumed priestly conversation to be largely a waste of time.

"I have food in my saddle-bags," said Jher-val weakly, but he knew it was useless. His lame horse had to rest, which made him the victim of village hospitality. The honour of Falakhoth's once-in-a-lifetime encounter with one of Arna's priests had therefore descended upon him. He was painfully reminded of Valderthaan's civilised standards by the very fact of their absence. It was too much. He shifted somewhat into shadow and discreetly transferred a ring from his finger to a concealed pocket where the Golden Sun, a priest's insignia, was already safe. Tyr, lounging on a mat on the other side of the fire, squinted at him and scowled. So distrustful, the peasants. The priest sighed, his inward fuming intensifying with every taste of the horrid wine.

Jher-val's morose reflections were disturbed by a quiet knock on the rattling door that led to the forge.

"It's open!" called Iethen. No response.

"Will y' get in, we're starvin'!" roared Tyrmar. Thus persuaded, the new arrival pushed the door open and stood tentatively in the doorway. There was the bearded, dark-haired young man Wyrdha had addressed as 'master priest.' His lengthy hair fell over the shoulders of a long, belted coat, and his cloak was over his arm, but, unlike the priestly red of Jher-val's attire, all his garb was black. He was young, perhaps a year or two over twenty summers, though his dark, neat beard let him appear a little older. He stood awkwardly checking the buttons of his long, black tunic.

"How do, Anthu?" ventured Tyr.

"Ah—*Baranthu*," corrected the young man. "I'm not really a priest yet, not properly. Just a novice. Hence the black, you see." Tyr noticed how he wound his fingers together and shifted from foot to foot.

"Right. Well, how do anyway."

"I, ah—I hope I'm not late. I was helping your healer with his patient." He caught sight of Jher-val, started, and made a deep bow, hands crossed on his chest. "Ah—Azhur va-Kherzir, Anthu. Arna shine on you."

Jher-val grunted and nodded. "Glad you remember your novice's manners," he remarked.

"Yes," said Azhur, embarrassed. "Ah—master Wyrdha asks to be excused. His patient, you see, and, er, understandably he feels the need for some rest himself."

Tyr smiled lazily at the young man. His hesitancy and courtesy made it easy to like him.

"Get in then, there's a draught off that door," said Tyrmar. He made all the introductions and they arranged themselves around the fire. Tyr remained sprawled where he was, Ilissos was happy on the rush matting on the floor, Jher-val, naturally, took the big wooden chair with the cushion, and the others perched on high-backed stools or benches. Iethen handed around stew and vegetables in large, wooden bowls and

Jher-val, naturally, took the big wooden chair with the cushion.

set a platter with slabs of bread on the floor between them. Jher-val, on receiving his bowl, refrained from grimacing but did not trouble to feign a grateful smile.

"Well, thanks to the Lady for all earth's fruit," said Iethen briskly, glancing at the figure over the fireplace. Tyr saw how Jher-val, priest of Arna, showed that he despised this by his sour glance at Azhur. The young novice, caught between his hosts and his superior, was deeply discomfited and glanced anxiously about, hoping no-one had noticed the priestly conceit. A muscle jerked in his cheek and Tyr liked him even more.

"I say thank you to Cynathé also," added Ilissos brightly.

"That's nice," remarked Iethen, but Azhur took care not to look at Jher-val.

The talk took in this and that but focussed mostly on the marvellous events at Wyrdha's house and the elemental violence that had preceded them.

"That were a bugger of a storm, that," said Tyrmar. "Getting' attacked *and* rescued with that goin' on around y'! That'll mean somethin', that will. That's a por-tint, isn't it, Anthu?"

"Portent," replied Jher-val, seizing the chance of a moment's superiority. "Yes, the senior lore masters by now will be consulting the Scrolls and giving serious thought to the meaning of such an unusual storm."

"They certainly will, Anthu," added Azhur with intense interest. "*On The Interpretation Of Turbulent Skies* will be well used tonight. You know, Ar-brau'achtid's two volumes—"

"I am well aware of the standard texts," said Jher-val in a voice like a cudgel. "As you well know. Keep your place."

"Yes, of course," mumbled Azhur, staring crimson-faced at the food in his bowl.

The senior priest seemed entirely unaware of the paralysed silence that followed. "I could explain the general principles that the priests use in interpretation," he announced, "but of course I shall not bore you." The silent shock persisted.

At last Iethen rose and, in a trembling little voice, said, "Any—anybody for more vegetables?"

"I have eaten my fill, goodwife," replied Jher-val, still perfectly at ease. "I shall require a short rest soon."

"Bloody hell," murmured Tyr into his bowl. His mother stared at him in horror, but Jher-val's hearing was not sufficiently acute to take in the reaction he had inspired.

Iethen determinedly handed out the remaining vegetables as the company desperately sought a new avenue for conversation. No-one succeeded until Tyr said, "Ey, Ilissos! What y' starin' at?" Ilissos jolted out of a wide-eyed daydream.

"Oh, I am thinking. Something has happened and I do not understand it."

"Ah," said Jher-val, wielding his status like a battle-axe. "An issue of interpretation, I think?"

"I do not know 'interpretation,' master."

"I can tell you what it means. We have great learning in the north."

Ilissos' grasp of the language was fortunately insufficient to enable him to understand the Anthu's slight. "Oh no, it is not like your storm. Your priests would not be thinking to explain it."

Jher-val seemed to swell: whether from pride or wrath was not clear. "Come, now," said the priest tersely, "Arna's priests are well known for their ability to penetrate mysteries. Let's have your story."

"Are y' not needin' y' rest, then?" asked Tyrmar with a somewhat dark shading to his voice.

Jher-val waved him to silence. He would at least enjoy flaunting his knowledge if nothing else. Tyr, he failed to notice, was looking at him dangerously. "Not yet. Now, let me hear this. Out with it, fellow."

Tyr and his father exchanged glances; Azhur stared doggedly at the floor.

"Well, master priests, a question for you," Ilissos began, still missing Jher-val's rudeness. "It is very, very big, this question."

Jher-val raised his head somewhat. It was a movement which had, he felt, the right degree of condescension and pride of office. A movement to express the reaction of one who graciously permits a foreigner to ask him a very big question. "Go on," he said.

"Well, today—no, not only today—another time this has happened to me." He paused, trying to say in their language what he knew was beyond words. There was silence. Iethen twisted her apron. A priest was actually being consulted under her roof, and by an exotic foreigner.

"Yes?" said Jher-val.

Ilissos waved his hand desperately. "It is—it is, well, I will tell you. Today I rode on the moors above the town, and the storm was passed, and the air was clean like the mountain pools, and I looked out across your valley to the hills and the mountains in the West, and—how can I tell it?—such beauty! *A, ve'sastos se a le meira se arché!* There are no words, no words and I, a maker of songs!"

"Know what y' mean, it's lovely up there," said Iethen.

"Yes, lady, yes, but I do not speak of that. The beauty is in the hills, yes, but it also comes from beyond them, from a far place, and it pierced me with longing like a spear. What I longed for is not the hills or the bright air. I have them always, and I cherish them, but my longing goes out past them and leaves them. And what I long for I do not know, but I think it is something given to the earth to make it glorious. It is in the beauty of the mountains, but that is not what it is. Often, I have heard the voices of the hills and the great earth and I have listened to the songs of the rivers and the trees and my heart has answered them in love, for what they have said to me I understand. But this is a voice that speaks from another place. I hear it from afar and I do not understand it. It speaks and wakes such a desire that I would be torn off from my body if I could not go to that place and possess that thing it tells me of and love—love what? Master priests, can you tell me? What is this that happened to me? Is there more in the north of this thing? Is it found anywhere?"

No-one moved, the noises of the square came from far away. Tyr and Tyrmar stared with open mouths, Azhur looked within, and Iethen dabbed at her eyes.

"I thought there weren't any words."

Ilissos laughed quietly. "Ah, they came. Maybe it is because I make songs. But tell me if you can, what is it? In all my travels I seek out those who are wise, or deal with sacred things, but no-one understands me. Is there any answer in the north, master priests? These things have happened to you?"

Jher-val looked into Ilissos' eager face and then, quite without warning, realised desperately and furiously that the young man had encountered glorious things that had not been on even the most distant horizon of his knowledge. It occurred to him for the briefest, light-filled moment that something greater and more wonderful than anything his mind had so far grasped had just been described to him. He felt small, tiny even, and in a way that was oddly secure. A faint longing for this unknown thing to be his own trembled inside him. He felt a minute sense of his own reality, of who he truly was, or had been before he encrusted himself with knowledge. And then he was terribly afraid. The self he had carefully built was threatened. It angered him, and remembering who he believed he was, he said, "As far as I can see, you've been enjoying the scenery and got carried away. You're making far too much of it." It was a dreadful moment. Jher-val failed utterly to disguise what lay behind his forced off-handedness. His reply was a dreadful crudity after Ilissos' words of numinous joy, and he knew it. Against all the refined instincts of his rank he turned to the novice Azhur for defence. "Perfectly obvious, it must be a Syrgan thing," he said. "I have never come across it before, have you, lad? Never seen *that* in the Scrolls, have you?"

The Scrolls: voices of centuries, minds of myriads; words of priests, emperors, statesmen, scholars, holy men, soldiers; thoughts, prayers, letters, edicts, poems, liturgies, predictions, treatises, histories, homilies, and more that made up the accumulated resource of wisdom and indispensable knowledge of all who acknowledged Arna. Thousands of manuscripts that together gave the final, unopposed word on anything that concerned the kingdom of the north, stored and guarded with a trembling awe in the Holy Archives of Arna's great Shrine at Valderthaan. Priests should know as many as they could master, some giving their lives to their interpretation. But no-one knew them all. And now a novice-priest was being asked if they reflected the poetic excitement of a travelling Syrgan. Azhur ran his fingers round the rim of his bowl, trying not to look at anyone. "Well, Anthu," he mumbled, "I – I wouldn't presume—"

Jher-val waved a hand. "Speak up, lad, no need to be afraid of me.

Azhur ran his fingers round the rim of his bowl, trying not to look at anyone.

What do you think? Have you ever seen this stuff in the Scrolls?" He laughed anxiously. "Come on now, I insist."

"Well," repeated Azhur.

"Yes? Come on, come on."

Azhur took a breath. Eyes fixed absurdly on the bowl, he said, "Well, there's the forty-third scroll, Anthu, and the ninth and five thousandth and eighth. And Uhr-sarrak's *Lives of the Priests* has a fair number of passages which sound very like the sort of thing our friend was describing. I'd have to go back and read them again, of course, compare carefully... And then one or two passages in the Founding Scrolls referring to Ar-ven's experience on Fyrieg—it's the choice of words, but, as you know, Anthu, they're difficult passages, meaning's debated. Then again, Anthu, I can't say, not in all honesty, that I've had this sort of, ah, experience." Having addressed this speech to his wooden bowl, Azhur glanced up at Ilissos. The Syrgan's eyes were shining with amazed delight. Azhur smiled faintly. He looked over at Jher-val and his smile withered at once.

"You're very quick to correct your betters," said the priest in a voice like a grindstone.

"Oh no, Anthu. No, no, not correct. You simply asked—"

"Don't you tell me what I said! Do you always contradict your seniors, boy?"

"Ey!" said Tyrmar. "Give him a chance!"

But Azhur was crushed. "Forgive me, Anthu," he stammered, "it's only what I've read in the Archives—"

"Really? And when were novices given access to the Archives?"

Ilissos sat up like a dog about to catch a biscuit. "This is from your god's Scrolls? Read them to me!" said Ilissos.

"You keep out of this!" snapped Jher-val. To Azhur: "Well, I'm waiting. Explain yourself."

"It is unusual, Anthu, yes—"

"Highly unusual."

"But in this case, I'm permitted." Azhur took a breath. "I am assistant to Lord Galdtchav, the Senior Lore Master."

What Jher-val would have said next was never revealed, though the colour of his face was eloquent enough, for Tyrmar was suddenly on his feet. He leaned over the priest like a bear over a trusting sheep. "Y'll have y' rest now," he said. "And I'll tell y' why: I'll not have y' in my house one bloody second longer than I have to."

Jher-val gaped in utter shock, then managed, "I *beg* your pardon?"

"Beg all y' like, y'll not get it." The headman grasped the priest's arm and hauled him from his chair.

"How dare you! I am a priest of Arna!"

"Well, I'm sorry for Arna, then." Tyrmar lowered his head like a bull until his eyes were level to Jher-val's. "Dunno why he lets sods like you work for him, but perhaps it weren't the gods and it were bigger sods that let y' in. Y' see that lad?" He pointed at Azhur, who was sitting with eyes closed, apparently in extreme pain and gripping his food bowl till his knuckles whitened. "Y've been lookin' at him like he were dirt since he come in here. One of y' own fellers and y' show him up in front of folk he don't even know—"

"After all he's been through!" faltered Iethen, finding her courage.

"Now, look here, goodwife—"

"Don't y' talk to me mam like that, she's not lookin' nowhere!" Tyr unfolded his long limbs and rose to confront the priest. "Y' never even asked how I was, or Azhur, or anybody! Never y' mind him, Mam!"

"He could've got shot!" cried Iethen as Tyr stood in front of her, fists clenched. "They could've all got shot!"

Jher-val shook himself free of Tyrmar's grip. "How dare you!" he hissed. "I don't have to stay and listen to this!"

"No, y' don't," agreed Tyrmar. "I'm throwin' y' out, and don't think I didn't see y' slippin' them little trinkets in y' pocket. My hospitality's not much, but if that's all y' think of us y' can bugger off back to Valderthaan. Now there's the door. Off y' go!" And he landed a whack on the priest's back that sent him tottering out of the room.

Jher-val staggered into the square, stunned by Tyrmar's view of him and by the fact he had expressed it. Peasants didn't, they simply didn't, but these had, and they were now gathered at the forge door, letting loose upon Jher-val's head the emotions they had been nursing since the morning.

"People might as well not be there, far's y're concerned," cried Iethen,

45

now filled with bravado. "Terrible it is, terrible!"

"Y' tell him, Mam!" yelled Tyr. "What're y' a priest for anyway, eh? What's the good? What's it for?"

Jher-val had now recovered, and he had had enough. "What's it for?" he howled, absurdly shrill. "Arna's glory, that's what it's for!"

"Well, what the hell's that, then?" Tyr shot back.

"Something you little valley people never understood," spat the priest. He was neither willing nor able to control himself now, all his punctured status howled in pain. "He made this kingdom in spite of you. He rules you and your Lady and I serve his glory!"

"If Arna's glory means treatin' folk like muck, y' can shove it!" Thus Tyr summed up the discussion and reinforced his point with a gesture that the priest was unlikely to see very often.

Nonetheless, the priest grasped the lad's intent. "I declare an execration of the Fourth Intensity against you! May you—"

Tyrmar stepped forward. "I'll not tell y' again: sod off!"

At last, Jher-val's mind was illuminated by the realisation that even he was well advised to remove himself from the company of a large, wrathful metal-worker who was about to advance. He reached the inn in seconds and leapt inside.

"Oh, well done," said a voice. "And very well said, my young sir."

In the square stood a tall, powerful-looking man whose long, brown coat swung about him in a way that was both regal and comfortable. Beneath his fur hat, lengthy copper-brown hair swept down past a short beard onto his chest. He came forward, walking with an assured confidence that shamed the arrogant style of Jher-val.

"Good day, sir," said Tyrmar gruffly, as the fire of his anger died down.

Iethen curtsied involuntarily. "Arna shine on y' sir," she said, still flushed with victory. The man regarded her quietly and intently.

"Yes," he said, then reached out and put a hand on Tyr's shoulder. "Tyr-shan. I believe you understand Arna's glory very well."

"Better than him, anyway," replied Tyr. "I hope, that is."

"Oh, hope will not disappoint you," said the imposing man. "I, ah, know what happened to you: be restored quickly."

"Thank y', sir," replied Tyr. Now that the man was close, he noticed the gold that shot through his brown hair and the bronze earring hanging half-hidden. There was a scar on his cheek, deliberately made as an insignia.

"Mistress Iethen," he said, smiling down at Tyr's mother. "You see far, do you not? You see what truly matters."

"Oh, I don't know about that, sir. I just got angry with how that feller was treatin' our guests."

"Of course," said the visitor. "That's just what I mean."

"Can we do somethin' for y', master?" asked Tyrmar, puzzled by the man.

"Oh no, the reverse in fact. I happened to meet a group of players a little way along the road and, knowing the trouble you've had today—" the man's brow became lined with genuine distress, "—I felt some good entertainment was just the thing you needed. They're an excellent troupe, Eorthas' Men. Oh, and you needn't worry about paying them. I've seen to that."

"Well, bless y' heart, master!" exclaimed Tyrmar. "That's right decent of y'."

The man smiled and looked at the ground for a moment. "Well, some people have had narrow escapes today and I think we should celebrate. Don't you, Tyr-shan?"

"Oh, aye," said Tyr. "Long's that Jer-whatsit stays away."

The man made a wry face. "Ah, yes. Well, I certainly would not have chosen *him* for the Shrine. But I must meet the players and guide them up here. Blessings of day to you all." He turned and began to stride away.

"What they doin'?" called Tyr after him.

"Comedies, naturally," came the reply over the regal shoulder. "And *Shivara and the Black Emperor*."

"What's that?"

"A history play. Very exciting."

"Does it rhyme? Is it one of those?"

"Just enjoy yourself, Tyr-shan!" called the fellow, and he disappeared onto the little street that sloped down to the highway.

"Well!" gasped Iethen. "What do y' make of that?"

47

CHAPTER 3

Visions of the Past

THEY FOUND ILISSOS CONSOLING Azhur over Jher-val's behaviour. The novice leapt to his feet as Tyrmar and his family returned to the fireside.

"I'm most terribly sorry," he blurted out, anxiously winding his fingers together. "I really don't know what to say."

"What's up with y'?" asked Tyrmar. "Y' never did nothin', it were his fault."

"All the same, I feel rather responsible."

Tyr whacked his arm. "Shut up and sit down, will y'? Give him a bit more meat, Mam."

"With pleasure," said Iethen as Tyr flopped back down in his spot by the fire. "We just love havin' y'. There, get that into y'."

"Well, I—oh. Thank you." Azhur took the bowl of food as if he were receiving stolen goods.

Tyr sat up, determined to improve the situation. "Shall us have a proper introduction, seein' as I've hit y'?" He placed his right hand over his heart and jerked forward in a formal little bow. "Tyr-shan va-Tyrmar, at y' service. Now you."

Azhur stared for a moment, then replied with an easy, instinctive bow. "Azhur va-Kherzir, at your service, and honoured to be in your home."

Deep, large eyes full of thought regarded Tyr from beneath dark,

48

broad brows. There was a kind of melancholy searching in them, he felt, as though Azhur hoped for something from him, and a small, tight smile appeared on the wide, intelligent mouth, as if to offer the hope that he also had something he wished to give. "I'm goin' to get on with you," said Tyr, instinctively, and the smile eased and broadened.

"And I with you, I think." Azhur looked oddly serious. "Thank you," he said from somewhere within, and the smile settled quietly into place.

"Ahh, this is so good," exclaimed Ilissos. "Our priest is happy again."

"Not *quite* a priest," Azhur reminded him.

"That why y' got black on?" Tyr asked.

"Yes. Lord Arna's sign is the sun, you see, and it is in the sun that he rises over the world—"

"Never understood that bit," said Tyr.

"Well, I could explain later, if you like."

"Aye, all right, I'd like that."

"Well, when one becomes a priest, we say that he has entered into a fuller service of Arna, that Arna has risen upon him, like the sun. Which means that novices, the learners, are still, in a sense, in the night: Arna, the Sun, has not 'risen' on them yet. We are waiting for the dawn."

"Ohh," cried Iethen, "the dark just afore the dawn! Oh, I see now. That's what the black means."

"Ey," said Tyr. "That's brilliant, that is. I never knew all that."

Ilissos was fascinated. "And, master not-quite-priest, when your Lord Arna rises, will you see the beauty? Will you understand the great thing that I felt today?"

"Aye, will y'?" asked Tyr eagerly. "That sounded brilliant, that did." But Azhur seemed very perplexed.

"Well, I... I don't know. I never expected to. There's no suggestion that we will, that we ought to. And I don't know anyone that has. I'm sorry."

Ilissos was undeterred, "Ah, but you told us there are things in your god's Scrolls."

"Yes, but... but that was about other people—ancient people—the great Ar-ven, who began Arna's cult in the north. There's nothing about, well, nowadays."

"Your priests are... not the same in these days?"

"Well, priests—ah, what would you say?—they run the kingdom, make it work. Revenues, buildings, laws. They help the Valgraav to govern."

"Oh, your kingdom is ruled by the priests of the gods!"

"No, no, only the priests of Arna, the Priests of the Sun. There are priests of other gods, but this kingdom was created by Arna, so only his priests can help rule it. They perform Arna's worship rites too, of course, but their service to him is mostly the rule of the north."

"Then they do not see the great beauty? They do not know where it is from?"

"I don't know. Some of them might, but I don't know. I haven't heard of any."

"That's a pity, that," said Tyr. He was gazing dreamily through the window to a patch of blue. "What if that happened to all the priests? What would happen then, Azhur?"

The young novice was silent, his eyes misty. He rubbed his chest absently, then hugged himself with one arm and looked down at his food. "I have no idea," he said. "None at all." He seemed, for a moment, very sad.

Tyr frowned across at the young man, wondering. He searched for something to say, but as he opened his mouth—

"Ey! Y' hear that?" Tyrmar stood up, listening to the shouts and laughter outside the window. The sound of a pipe and timbrels drifted to them, mixed with singing and children's cries.

"The players!" cried Tyr and launched himself off the floor and through the forge door, suddenly very much improved. After him went the delighted Ilissos, and the rest followed.

As they came out into the square, they found themselves confronted with the big painted wagon that was the stage, home, and storehouse for the players' company. Men and women in bright clothes walked or danced beside the wagon as it creaked into the square. Even the sturdy old horses were decked out with bells and ribbons. A crowd of children were running and jumping around the players already and the villagers were stopping work and coming out of their houses, attracted by the cheerful sounds. For added emphasis, a bagpipe began to drone out a popular dance tune. Some people immediately began clapping and jigging where they stood, and a few seized a partner and broke into a dance. A thin young man with a wild mass of yellow hair flying out from his huge, shapeless hat jumped down from the lead wagon and gave an absurdly exaggerated bow as Tyrmar marched up.

"Stand up, y' fool, I'm not the Valgraav!" exclaimed Tyrmar, greatly amused.

"Not yet, but am I right in thinking you are the worthy headman?"

"I am. And y'll be the players."

"What on earth gave you that idea? But as a matter of fact, we are. What perception!" The young man pulled the worn red object from his head, releasing even more hair, and waved it wildly towards his companions. "Eorthas' Men: best in the land. Tragical, comical, musical, illusionary, comical-illusional, musical-comical-tragedy, with a song and dance thrown in, whatever you like, whatever you wish, we are your men and women!" This speech alone got a round of applause. "Now, we are here to request your permission for our gifted yet ironically impecunious players to perform in your most worthy community."

"Impy-what?" said someone.

"We need the money," the fellow explained. "I myself am Eorthas and I understand from a traveller on the road that Falakhoth is one of the few places in this province that appreciates culture, skill, and the mimetic art."

"Oh, aye," said Tyrmar. "That'll be the feller as paid y' for us."

Eorthas' startlingly wide smile slackened a little. "Ah… yes, that will be he."

"*What* kind of art?" asked Tyr.

"The mimetic art: our gifting and calling."

"Y' what?"

"We do plays. We make you laugh."

"That's all right then," said Tyr happily. "We could do with a laugh today." The surrounding crowd gave a murmured agreement.

"So I understand, and you shall have one. Nay, you shall have a multitude of them." Eorthas turned back to Tyrmar. "We have permission then?"

"Course y' do! Get on with it, quick as y' can!"

"Most certainly, sir." He looked sideways and twisted his hat in his hands. "Um… at this point, I'm really, usually, generally speaking, supposed to show you our license."

"And what's one of them?" demanded the headman.

"Well, we'll take that as read then. All right, if we may station our travelling palace of delights just up there, you'll have a show in an hour. All you need do is gather the audience."

"Brilliant!" said Tyr.

"Oh, that's nice, isn't it?" crooned Iethen as the wagons, trailing children, creaked to the further end of the square and the people dispersed to spread the news. "Finish y' dinner, Azhur, there's a love."

"Oh, sorry," exclaimed the novice, still absently clutching his food bowl.

'Y're lookin' a bit more perky, young Tyr," remarked Tyrmar.

"Oh, aye. I fancy a bit of a celebration." Tyr actually bounced on the spot a little.

His father laughed, then became thoughtful. "Do y' know, that's an idea."

"What is, love?" asked Iethen.

"A celebration. We could have a right good time tonight. Them players'll do music, and we could have dancin' and stuff to eat and all sorts."

"And celebrate me and Wyrdha not gettin' shot!" cried Tyr. "And Azhur as well," he added quickly.

"That other feller got shot," said a little, rat-faced man.

"Aye, but not bad. He'll be all right."

"How do y' know?"

"He will, I just know."

"Never mind it, Verrik," said Tyrmar. "We're havin' a celebration. There's plenty left from winter and we can put that old ox of Laughar's out of its misery."

"What, a feast? Like Midsummer?" Verrik said. "Y' can't have a feast just like that! What put that in y' head?"

The headman stepped up close to Verrik, who found himself staring up at the human equivalent of a very dangerous cliff face. "We're havin' a feast, Verrik," he said quietly but with a hint of distant thunder, "And if y' can't work out why, I'm not tellin' y'."

And that was the end of that. Tyrmar's enthusiasm spread like wildfire and soon the whole town was vigorously alight. Cooking fires flared up, people came running up from the fields across the river and began hauling out chairs, benches, trestles, and mugs, plates, and bowls of all kinds. Firewood was piled in the centre of the square and Laughar said his farewells to the ox which, though less than massive, was still able to render a final service to humanity as the main feature of the evening's menu.

With these feverish preparations around them, Eorthas' players transformed their wagon for the play—a process which, from the villagers' point of view, was almost as exciting as the performance coming later. One whole side, hinged, came down to form a platform, with its area almost doubled by the floor inside. Thus revealed, pots and pans, bundles of clothes, children, and some beds were whipped away from the exposed interior, and from an unexpected recess, a bright canopy unrolled to cover the stage. A sheet of painted canvas accidentally flapped down and there was a glimpse of palaces and southern skies, but Eorthas, acknowledging the gasps of admiration, hurriedly rolled the canvas up, calling, "You'll see it all and more, good people! Sooner you're ready, sooner we start." An elderly curtain of what had once been a rich, embroidered cloth swept across the stage and no more splendours were seen. Falakhoth was furiously busy: the townsfolk spurred on by the prospect of the play and the (rather hungry) players by the prospect of the feast.

As the predetermined hour drew to a close, people drifted to the space in front of the newly created theatre. There were cheers and clapping when drums and a trumpet sounded from within and those who were still busy quickly joined the audience already trembling with anticipation.

Eorthas seized the moment. The unseen instruments blared and rattled, and he flung the curtain aside—a maddening glimpse of scenery—to stride up to the platform's edge. At once there was a roar of welcome. They were more than ready for him in his colourful costume and painted face, for that meant a comedy was about to begin. The absurd hat, enhanced by ribbons, flailed through the air in a wildly flamboyant bow. More cheers.

"Worthy citizens of Falakhoth!" cried Eorthas. Laughs and catcalls. That was how speeches began in Valderthaan. "Worthy citizens!" Eorthas repeated, "Today our players bring you, as always, music and mirth, the highest comedy and the deepest tragedy. And indeed—" he suddenly became deadly serious and raised his hands for silence, "—indeed, tragedy came perilously near to you today. Perilously near." Mutters of agreement, with not a few glances over at Tyr. Then Eorthas' flung up his arms. "But it passed you by!" Cheers and applause. "I wonder where it went, then? Arcorath? What about Arcorath? Has Governor Var-hrothga had a tragedy? Maybe his larder burned down!" That went down well. The oversized governor's appetite was legendary. "He might have to cut down to *one* sheep a day!" Cheering. Eorthas' quick mind raced on. "Or Valderthaan?" Loud moans. "Why, for all you know there's been a tragedy in the palace itself!" More groans, mock cheers, and a shout of, "That'll wake 'em up, then." A thunder of applause which Eorthas made the most of. "Has tragedy struck the Master of Revenues?" he yelled above the din. "Perhaps even in the room where he decides the taxes! But no, come to think of it, tragedy strikes there every day! Could we not even say the Master of Revenues is a tragedy?" This brought such an outburst of cheers, applause, and just plain yelling that Eorthas knew he could say almost anything and have them laughing helplessly for as long as he wanted, and so he did exactly that.

At last the curtain drew aside for the players' first offering. The whole town crowded around the wagon ready to laugh itself helpless. Eorthas gave them a well-known comic piece about an absurd nobleman and his attempts to marry off his only daughter to an obnoxious foreign ruler. The daughter won every heart by her astonishing beauty and abundant virtue. Tears flowed and there were heartfelt cries of, "Get out while y' can, love!" When she confided that she secretly loved a handsome stable-boy—and it was mutual—there was almost a riot. Falakhoth agonised as the old nobleman's sister, an amazingly ugly widow who had neglected to shave that morning, tried to force the stable-boy to marry her instead.

After much hilarity, rudeness, and ingenuity, the stable-boy turned out to be heir to a distant kingdom. The lovers were blissfully wedded, and the widow made the best of a bad job by hauling Verrik onstage and marrying him instead.

Having roared themselves to near collapse at Verrik's embarrassment, the townsfolk showed their riotous appreciation and began to get their breath back.

"Y've got a cheek, you have, you lot!" said Verrik loudly, tottering at the edge of the stage. "I were right put out. What'd y' go for me for?"

"Here, don't flatter y'self," said the unshaven widow. "Y're not my type, mate." And Verrik was swiftly dumped back on the ground.

At the height of the renewed frenzy of preparation, Tyrmar discovered that Thaljhaz had opted out. He and two other men were hurrying across the square to the street that led down from the town. They carried bows and quivers on their shoulders and had long hunting knives at their belts. Thaljhaz' fury was almost visibly crackling around him.

"Ey, ey, ey," called the headman. "What y' up to?"

"I'm collectin' firewood," snapped Thaljhaz.

"Oh, right, y' goin' to shoot the trees first, then, are y'?"

"Goin' to watch the sheep. If y' have to know, there's been wolves about."

"There's folk arranged for that," said Tyrmar. "Anyhow, that's huntin' gear and a pack of food for the night, or I'm blind. What's goin' on?" He folded his arms and stood with his feet apart, a familiar sign that they would not move him without an explanation.

Thaljhaz glanced sullenly around, while his companions shuffled their feet and kept quiet. Verdje and Utha came running from the inn, eyes red and swollen.

"It's him and grandad," wailed the girl. "They've fell out again."

"Tell us somethin' new," said Tyrmar.

Utha gasped out the story between racking sobs. "He's always sayin' Dad's good for nothin' and it's woman's work runnin' an inn and Mam shouldn't have wed him. Then Dad goes off ragin'—y' do, Dad—and look at all them knives and arrows! What y' goin' to do this time?"

Verdje pulled her shawl tight about her as if it was armour. She was quieter that Utha, being well used to this, but her wet face was tight and drawn, and taut lines clustered over her high cheekbones. A strand of yellow hair hung in front of her ringed eyes. She looked at the ground and when she spoke it was in a strained, husky voice. "He won't come out, and he won't say sorry. If y'...." She raised her eyes hopefully, but her husband's furious glare crushed her hope. "No? But love, it's not true, all he says. Y' shouldn't let it—I mean, everybody knows it's not true. He's a stupid old man, that's all he is. Y' don't have to do this, love." Now her eyes were full of fear. She turned to Tyrmar and silently begged him to do something.

"What y' goin' to do, Thal?" demanded Tyrmar.

Verdje gripped Thaljhaz's arm. "He's goin' to kill that wolf. The big one that come down from north."

"Y' bloody fool!" gasped Tyrmar.

"I've killed wolves afore," countered Thaljhaz grimly.

"Not this kind, Thal! It had an ox's throat out, down by Arcorath. One bite, folk said as saw it. It's near as big as an ox itself!"

"Y're well up on it," said Thaljhaz defiantly, but his voice faltered. Utha and Verdje took hope.

"I hear things when I'm on a job," said Tyrmar. "They're sayin' it's been movin' back up north, followin' the river for a few nights." He tugged angrily at Thaljhaz' pack. "Y've heard that and all, haven't y'? Y've worked out where it'll be and y're gettin' an early start. Y're goin' to try and meet it. Enough food to get y' there and back—Broad Fields at Braldhach, is it? Good shootin' from the rocks at the falls, eh? Is that it?"

The muscles of Thaljhaz's jaw worked furiously. He tightened his lips and kept silent, more determined than ever now that Tyrmar had guessed the plan.

"Dad!" begged Utha.

Verdje tugged her husband's arm and began to cry.

One of Thaljhaz's companions sighed and began to take off his pack.

"C'mon, Thal," he said wearily. "Y' might be just a little feller, but that don't matter, we all know y've got guts. So no good gettin' eaten and leavin' Verdje a widow just to spite that old sod—beggin' y' pardon,

Verdje."

"It's only sense," said the other man, unslinging his bow and quiver. "Best stay and enjoy y'self. I don't want me wife a widow neither. We was only comin' to try and look out for y' and if y' want to know, we was hopin' we'd talk y' out of it on the way. If we met that thing, I'd be no good to y'—me heart's not in it and that's the truth. There's no killin' a thing like that with just three men. It's a mad one, I've heard. Hunts by itself and don't run with a pack. Kills things and don't even eat them half the time. Y'd want twenty men to get it, at least. Stay here, Thal, it's best." He fidgeted with the flights of an arrow, then blurted out, "I've not many friends, not really good ones like y', Thal. I don't want to lose y' this way." He sniffed and looked around awkwardly.

Thaljhaz stood like a melting wax statue, then his shoulders relaxed as his outraged pride slipped away and he bowed his head. A half-smile began on his tight lips and he heaved a great sigh, said, "Ahh!" and turned to go back. Tyrmar clapped him on the shoulder, while Verdje and Utha gave little cries of relief.

And at that moment, Bardcha came shuffling from the inn. He caught sight of Thaljhaz, stopped, then eased himself onto his bench with a look of mingled disgust and triumph. The little man's fury flared up at once, but the old man slowly turned his head to gaze in the opposite direction.

The innkeeper's eyes bulged, his face went white.

"No," whimpered Verdje. "No." Her father's simple movement was, she knew, meticulously planned and honed to perfection. The measured slowness, that angle of the head, that twist to the lips, all executed with a precision that exactly expressed Bardcha's contempt for his son-in-law. It was calculated, too, to justify itself by provoking Thaljhaz into worse outbursts still and so, in Bardcha's eyes, demeaning himself even more.

The enraged little man rose to the bait and bawled across the square, "That's right, I'm stoppin'! Y' disappointed? I'm not gettin' eaten to please y'!" And Thaljhaz laughed heartily, mightily pleased with his decision.

"Y'll enjoy the feast, then," said Bardcha, face still averted.

"Aye, I will. Y'll not be rid of me that easy!"

Bardcha looked around abruptly, his eyes narrowed. "What did y' start off for then, if y're not goin'?" Thaljhaz faltered.

"Thal, love," said Verdje. "Stay, now. He always does this, y' don't have to prove anythin'. Everybody knows y're brave." He hardly heard her.

"I'm gettin' away from you, y' snake!" he roared. "I've more sense than y' think. I'll not give y' the satisfaction of knowin' I've missed the feast!"

"That's all right, then," said Bardcha, unmoved. "Safer here anyhow. Y' can help wash up."

Thaljhaz's eyes cleared. He shook his arm free.

"Bardcha, leave be," warned Tyrmar.

"Leave be?" said Thaljhaz. "Not him." He stood for a moment, breathing hard, as if he had a decision to make. "We've all to suffer because of her, eh? Y' darlin' daughter."

Bardcha's head whipped round as though he had been slapped.

"Oh, Thal, no!" cried Verdje.

"Leave it, Thal," said Tyrmar. "We don't speak about that."

"Don't we? Y' should hear it in that inn some nights. He's never forgave her for goin' up to Stone Houses, nor for bein' what she is."

Bardcha rose, trembling with rage. "Y' take that back! I've no honour 'cause of her!"

"No, nor money! She never wed him, did she? And now an innkeeper's not good enough for y'!" Thaljhaz flung his words like barbs. Bardcha stepped back as though forcibly struck. The little innkeeper pressed his attack home. "One look at that white horse and his gold rings and y' had it all worked out, eh? Marryin' into money and gettin' y'self into high families in the city, eh? Y'd have had y'self the bloody Valgraav!" Thaljhaz laughed, swinging his terrible sword of words. "She got the heave, though, eh? Lost y' all that money y' was hopin' for and that's what y' can't forgive her, so don't give us y' speech about honour— y'd none to start with. What's the matter if she's no better than the trollops in Lachresh market?"

Verdje wailed. Bardcha gave a horrible cry and flung his staff, striking Thaljhaz longwise across the body. One end caught his jaw, but he was unhurt. The innkeeper leered in triumph, enjoying his hate.

Verdje had no more strength, she was on her knees sobbing. "Thal,

Thal, y' said y'd not do that, y' said y'd forget."

Utha tried to comfort her mother as Iethen ran to them from the forge. "Stop it, Dad, Mam's cryin'!" wailed the girl, but her father, revelling in his wrath, had his wild eyes fixed on Bardcha. Utha whirled round and faced her Grandfather. "It's your fault!" she cried shrilly through her tears. "Y're always doin' it! I hate y'!" And she turned her back on him to embrace her mother.

Bardcha stiffened and seemed, for a moment, truly pained. He stared, bewildered, at the weeping woman, then, with a glance at Thaljhaz, mastered himself.

"Right, then," he grated, breathing hard. "Y' stay for the feast. Earned it, didn't y'? Made y' family right happy. We'll just have to forget what y' said, though it does spoil things, y' know." Bardcha backed away to the inn and leaned against the wall. His breath came in gasps. He thrust his lowered head forward like an exhausted, cornered animal. "I'll just sit near the fire and make the best of it," he went on. "Me other daughter chose an innkeeper, so I'll sit and watch them enjoy themselves out of harm's way." He faltered, looking at the ground in a calculating manner. "Just glad it weren't *me* as brought that up. Don't know as I'd show me face if I had."

And with that, Thaljhaz saw his folly. He, not Bardcha, had dragged before the common gaze the old, carefully buried sorrow. Bardcha had merely been his usual sullen self, but he, Thaljhaz, had broken the horrified silence of the years. Half the town had heard, and the rest soon would. Yes, he must miss the feast. He was too proud and angry to face them or admit his guilt. He stopped, snatched up a discarded pack and strode away towards the path that led to the road. Verdje and Utha stumbled desperately after him, weeping and calling. Bardcha sank onto his bench and turned his back.

Tyrmar looked between him and the road for a moment, then picked up the staff and went across to the bench. He threw the staff on the ground, gripped Bardcha's shoulder, and forced the old man to face him. "Don't think I can't see through y'," he said fiercely. "Y're twisted, y' are. Y're rotten." He turned the bitter old face away again and went with Iethen in pursuit of Thaljhaz and Verdje.

As they hurried down to the road, Iethen said, "They was always at odds, but I never saw the likes of that afore. There's badness in the air today." She pulled her shawl about her and began to run.

~

As DUSK CREPT UP on the town, the ox was being turned slowly over a fire. The aroma of cooking meat mixed with that of freshly baked bread and new-made puddings coiled in the air over the tables. Eorthas announced the players were ready to perform Shivara and the Black Emperor, and everyone assembled before the wagon once more, keenly expectant, but Thaljhaz, determined to prove himself, had not returned, and his wife and daughter had shut themselves in the inn. Some of the townsfolk had seen the play before and of those who hadn't, many had heard of it. It was a serious piece, full of drama and high deeds from the ancient past and the exotic land of Dhar.

Ilissos, of course, could barely contain himself, but still managed to pester Azhur about the Scrolls in the Shrine's Archives.

"Yes, yes, of course," Azhur assured him under pressure. "I'll tell you all I can remember. No, you can't read them. No, quite impossible, I'll do what I can—"

"What's this play about?" asked Tyr, just to complicate the situation.

"What? The play? I've never seen it. But, well...," Azhur took on a learned, solemn manner. "Lord Shivara will come to the North one day, Tyr. You know that?"

"Everybody does. Y' say, 'We'll be here till Shivara comes', and things like that."

"Yes. Then you know he was Arna's archpriest many generations ago in Dhar, in the south?"

"No, I never. I thought he were a northman, like us."

"Ah, well, his parents were northerners, from Fyrhal, but Shivara was born in Dhar's High City near the great desert."

"Ey!" exclaimed Tyr suddenly. "Got to ask y' somethin'."

"Of course," replied Azhur, with scholarly grace.

"Me mam used to tell me Shivara'd bring me presents on me birthday, what's that about?"

Azhur opened his mouth but experienced the numbing realisation that his erudition had nowhere to go. While he groped for a suitable reply, there was a sudden blare of instruments and a pounding drum and he was utterly forgotten. He wisely accepted his fate and turned his attention to the play.

After many beats on the drum and a brazen noise that was apparently meant to be a fanfare, the curtains were slowly tugged aside, and a figure emerged from the interior of the wagon where hidden lamps burned with a sudden brightness. He was garbed and painted in the character of the all-knowing sages that people believed were at every street corner in ancient times. His robes were white and gold, his beard long and silver and behind him was a painted city with a bright southern sky. The sage came forward with measured, stately strides to the rhythm of the drum. At the edge of the platform where more lamps were placed, he stopped and raised his hands. The drum ceased and in the silence he began.

Soft now! List to the song-shaper.
Words are his workings, he speaks and a spell makes.
Around him a shining, wrester of words ringed
By shades of moon-silver, and star's softness.
Hard was the making, hard the hewing
Of the speech-timbers 'til a shape seized them.
Sound, strong, they went forth singing,
Like a ship well-timbered on seas toiling.

"Ah, this is from Ceor!" exclaimed Ilissos loudly. "In Syrga we know their songs." He was roundly shushed. The sage glared fiercely at him and continued.

Listen!
In southern land was the story spoken.
All in the earth have owned it strangest.
A suzerain slain in a shrine's shatt'ring
Dark is his doom at his evil's ending,
Wrack is his reign, but another's rising:
Woe there is, weal, in the one working!

Fullness of days for the faithful priest,
Son of the North, to North returning.

And at that mention of Shivara, something moved in Tyr's mind, and it seemed to him that the story acted out on Eorthas' wagon-stage began to grow and take place beyond itself. The fanciful backcloths, gaudy costumes, studied gestures, and time-worn words in over-dramatised voices became mixed up with something else, another reality that corresponded to them and was unfolding alongside them. It was as though the years had raced ahead of their times to Tyr's own day. What he was seeing, he knew, was not really there, but neither was it his imagination. What he was experiencing within was different but no less real.

In this strange awareness, he watched the events of the ancient days, when there was no empire and no rule in the Northland. A time when Djur-chemish, the Golden Lord, ruled Dhar's vast dominions from his dazzling city at Amou Hra'im, and only thought of the North, if he did at all, as a stretch of stones and marshes he cared not to conquer. In those days came Shivara's parents to the emperor's city, taken as slaves by a raiding vessel that had ventured far along the western coast. They were brought over the Great Desert for sale to the capital's nobility and were bought quickly for the novelty of their light skin and the woman's yellow hair, and the hardness and rugged attractiveness of Ceorthas' people. A priest of Arna's great temple in the city took them to his home, and they served him for many years.

In that home, beneath the temple walls, Shivara was born. The parents had turned to Arna's rites and, as Tyr watched, the boy was trained for the temple's service, rising through the ranks of the priesthood until he stood by the Emperor's side as Archpriest. His powers of mind and hand and eye would have made Shivara feared had he not been revered for his goodness. Djur-chemish's mind and heart were open to him, and many viewed him as second in the empire. Thus, he earned the jealousy of Djur-ch'herakh, the emperor's second son. Moody and vain, Djur-ch'herakh burned for power. After his older brother's death, he would have taken up the reins of the empire if his father had permitted him to. But the old man, who had given the rule into the hands of his eldest son when his own health began to fail, again took up the exercise of his power, with Shivara at his side.

"Thus I will do," he said to Djur-ch'herakh, "for had thou but a tenth of thy brother's spirit, thou couldst rule Dhar from my throne—aye, and the whole world. But I will not suffer thee to lay thine hands upon my realm while I live, for all thy ways spring from a proud heart that lusteth after dominion and hath no desire for wisdom or understanding of what is good in the governance of men. Thou art a pampered boy, and though thou art of years for kingship, I will not give over what my fathers builded, with the rule of many nations, into feeble hands. And know thou that the Lord Shivara is of one mind with me in this." So Djur-ch'herakh's anger burned the hotter and his hate for Shivara grew.

There came a time when a rebellion arose in one of the eastern provinces. Against all advice, the Emperor rode out himself to quell it. The rebels were weakened, though not put down, and Djur-chemish returned to Amou Hra'im wounded and weak. He resolved to offer gifts at the temple to thank Arna for the victory and to beg for recovery. As he approached the temple, stones fell from a mason's scaffold and struck him. He fell, and Djur-ch'herakh, walking a distance behind his chariot, saw his father's crown roll past all obstacles and come to rest before his feet. In those days it was the custom to place the crown of a new Emperor at his feet, so he could raise it to his head himself. When the prince ran to his father, the Staff of Dominion that signified the rule of Dhar over the many lands of the Empire, fell from the place where it had been fixed on the chariot and struck Djur-ch'herakh on the shoulder. Many saw these things as signs, and when Djur-ch'herakh led his father's forces against the rebels and utterly routed them, many, with an eye to favour, began to say that Arna wished the rule to pass from Djur-chemish to his son. But Shivara declared, "If a man be not fit to rule, then he is not fit, no matter what signs may seem to come. And besides, the Golden Lord still lives." But when the old emperor died after the prince's campaign, Djur-ch'herakh was crowned on his triumphant return to Amou Hra'im no matter what Shivara could say against it. From that time, the Archpriest gave no more counsel to the emperor, for Djur-ch'herakh was wise in his own eyes and would listen to nothing Shivara said. Indeed, the emperor would have deposed him if he could, had the person and office of the Archpriest not been sacred and inviolable.

Time showed that Djur-ch'herakh could not rule alone but he would take no advice. Soon his dominions were torn by strife among his commanders, and rebellion and famine among his subjects. Worse, he developed a painful sickness that often left him weak and melancholy. His belief in his own rightness grew to the point where he proclaimed himself ruler by right whether Arna willed it or not.

Shivara had investigated the death of the emperor's older brother and deduced Djur-ch'herakh had been party to it. He also had suspicions Djur-ch'herakh had caused the deaths of several in power to make his succession certain. But without proof, nothing could be done but watch the monarch toil under the weight of his own guilt. As he sank deeper into sickness and, some said, madness, he began to fear death. He sought out sorcerers who taught him unlawful secrets. These sorcerers were powerful and evil men, who twisted his mind even as they failed to heal his body. They whispered counsel to Djur-ch'herakh, encouraging him to lead with cruelty. People feared him and behind his back called him the Black Emperor. Djur-ch'herakh went deeper into the unclean arts, his sickness continuing to gnaw at him.

In a desperate bid to live on forever, Djur-ch'herakh declared he was a god who must be worshipped. He saw himself as greater than any of the ancient kings who had been called divine. So it was that on a high and sacred day, Djur-ch'herakh entered the temple with his sorcerers and swordsmen around him and faced Shivara before all the people at the great altar by the doors of the inner shrine. "I have come to proclaim to Dhar my divinity and immortal power," he said, for the increase of his evil had made him bold, "and I will not suffer let or hindrance from thee." So saying, he broke the doors of the inner place and brought forth a sacred scroll bearing powerful words given to the first parents of men. The scroll contained a plea for life that he meant to utter as a spell to join the holy power to his own vile energies. In his foolishness he thought he could force the high ones to bow to his desires and make him immortal. Such was the fear and madness of Djur-ch'herakh.

The emperor's swordsmen kept the priests and the people at bay as he moved towards the altar. When Shivara perceived the horrifying sacri-lege that was intended, he placed himself between the Emperor and the sacred altar. All his powers burned within him so that the sorcerers shrank back in terror and the people cried out, not knowing what would happen.

"Wilt thou now assault the holy realm?" Shivara cried. "Dost nothing affright thee? Dost thou fancy that these glorious ones of the higher world will suffer this affront? Wilt thou stand in the room of God and tremble not?"

But Djur-ch'herakh was mad, or the spirit of him was dead, or both, and he said, "Aye, for I have more power than any on earth and I may do even as it pleases me. Men have bowed down before kings, but have I not set my foot upon the necks of many kings? Power of decree is mine and power of will also. I will be a god and live forever, as is my right."

Shivara stretched out his hands and a holy fire burned about the altar to protect it. "These are the counsels of ancient days, before light shone on us," he said, and his voice was terrible. "It is the counsel of the ignorant, that know not what is true, and it is the counsel of the wicked and the proud, who hate all that is higher and purer than themselves. Leave this path, I beseech thee, and thou wilt receive the blessing thou hadst deemed shut up from thee forever. Turn aside, I say. Take now my hand and we will be reconciled. Do not do this thing, and together we will seek mercy. 'Tis true that thou wilt die; but yet thou mayest die in peace."

Such was the power about Shivara, and such was Djur-ch'herakh's trembling, that many believed the Emperor would repent of his madness. But with a sudden great cry, Djur-ch'herakh strode through the fire and cast the holy words upon the altar. Shivara seized him and would have dragged him away, but the madman, snatching up an iron from the burning braziers that stood there, thrust it against the Arch-priest's heart, pressing down with all his strength. Then, as Shivara lay on the steps of the altar and horror kept the people where they stood, Djur-ch'herakh joined his spells with the chants of his sorcerers and unbound the strongest of his tainted powers as he read the life-words to draw them into his vile enchantment. But by some power, Shivara gathered his strength and, pulling himself up to the altar, seized Djur-ch'herakh's hand, trying to prevent the sacrilege. But the emperor, calling a word that made the people stop their ears, was too strong and threw Shivara upon the altar, tearing the blessed scroll and dividing the blessed words upon it.

And who will say what took place in that moment? A brightness blazed around the emperor and Shivara. Lightning came burning down upon the altar, so that its stones split. There were flames and terrifying sounds and the noise of great voices. The earth beneath the altar moved so that the pillars at the door of the inner shrine tottered and one fell, bringing the lintel with it. The sorcerers were screaming in terror. All their evil tools, amulets, staffs, and parchments had dissolved in fire, and about them moved mighty powers they had never dreamed of. Some fell into a madness and slew themselves, others fled to the doors with the people. Many priests tried to stay to see the outcome, but it was not possible. None living could remain within the temple. When the last of the people were through, the brazen doors swung to and the gate-towers fell inward, sealing them in with stone. From that day the gates have never been opened, nor will any approach them.

None saw the fate of Shivara, but the cruel reign of Djur-ch'herakh was ended. The city mourned its Archpriest for many days, and as the people gathered in the square of the city to grieve, the priest Marvhishta fell into an ecstasy and cried out that he saw the years march towards him and that behind them walked Shivara. Once more he would stand in Amou Hra'im, once more the Archpriest from the North would serve the temple.

"When?" the people cried. "When will this be? Does Shivara live?"

"Surely," said Marvhishta, "and Djur-ch'herakh has perished through his folly or the vision is false, but when we shall see Lord Shivara I do not know." And he wept, and all the people with him.

Thus it was said that Arna had shielded his Archpriest by the power of the Holy Plea and by the true intent of the sacred words and that endless life had been given, not to Djur-ch'herakh, but to Shivara. And so, blessing and a great wonder had been wrought even out of awful evil and madness.

When the years had marched a great way, Dhar proved false and her empire dwindled and fell away. It was seen that Arna had deserted her and had prepared the kingdom of the Northland in honour of his servant, the northman Shivara. So it is that when the Day of the Powers shall come and Shivara shall again be seen amongst men, it is in the north that he shall stand, for there alone is the worship of Arna truly preserved. Of all the realms on the world's face, the Northland alone was created and sustained by the will and power of Arna.

Tyr shook himself. It was over. The townspeople were clapping and cheering and the players were taking their final bows.

"Crackin'!" roared Tyrmar. "That's earned y' supper!" The actors laughed in anticipation and disappeared behind the wagon to discard the bright costumes and clean their faces. The audience moved away, intent on the final details of the feast. "Somebody keep the ox turnin'!" called Tyrmar. "Ey, what do y' think of that, Verrik? Crackin', weren't it?"

"Seen better," said rat-faced Verrik. "There's a company comes to Lukar does that play twice as good."

"Y' miserable sod, y've no soul," Tyrmar told him heartily. "Y' can turn the ox for that!" Verrik shrugged and grasped the handle of the spit.

"Tyrmar, Verdje's not here," said Iethen suddenly, "nor Utha. Bardcha's not about either."

"Well, let's be glad about that—Bardcha, that is—wish we had him on the spit."

"Well, I don't blame them, mind. That were a right embarrassin' business earlier on. I think I'll just have a look," said Iethen, and ran to the inn.

Tyrmar stamped away and found Azhur resisting another of Ilissos' attempts to discuss the Scrolls. An intervention seemed called for and so the headman whacked the young man on the shoulder. "Right, assistant novice, whatever y' are. How's about y' blessin' our feast for us?" Azhur steadied himself, "Why, well, yes, if you wish. Yes, I'd be honoured, but shouldn't Anthu Jher-val—?"

"He's not blessin' nothin'. He'd turn the ale sour."

"Oh, I know—that is, ah, I see your point, but he's my superior and of course I'm not—"

"Bugger that. I want y' doin' it. Most folks'd agree. What about it?"

Azhur wound his fingers together.

"Ey, go on," said Tyr, who had sidled up to lean on his father's shoulder. It was a welcome support as he tried to work out what had just happened. "That priest feller's cleared off anyhow," he said, doggedly attempting normality. "I saw him."

Azhur's face broke into a wide grin. It seemed to be something a little unusual for him but with a warm fire-lit tint it was an appealing sight. "All right," he said. "It's an honour." This earned him another whack on the shoulder. "But, master Tyrmar, if you don't mind, they don't seem quite ready and I'd very much like to look in on Yauva before things start. Could I manage that, do you think?"

"I'll go and all," said Tyr suddenly. "I'm feelin' all right now."

"Y're not wantin' a lie down afore the feast?"

"Nah, that's borin', and he'll get lost if I don't show him the way. I mean, *he's not really a priest, you know.*" This last was spoken in such a good imitation of Azhur's educated tones that the novice could not help but laugh at himself.

"Well, get on up there," said Tyrmar when he had stopped guffawing. "Tell Wyrdha, if he wants to come down, I'll send folk up to sit with the lad. We're celebratin' him not gettin' done in as well, tell him." Only one difficulty remained: the matter of detaching Ilissos from his new-found source of mystical wisdom, but Tyrmar managed it. "Right, master Ilissos. Give us a song from Syrga till our priest gets back and y' can have him to y'self all day tomorrow."

Ilissos accepted at once. Azhur seemed less happy about it, but Tyr dragged him away before he could negotiate better terms.

CHAPTER 4

The Dancer at the Feast

Tyr and Azhur walked towards the north end of the square, the one opposite the players' wagon, where a narrow little street led off towards the wooded hillside path that went up through the trees to the healer's home. Near to the street and lowering over the square was a gnarled, solitary hill crowned by a group of spindly, mournful trees that seemed to keep watch over a shabby, rundown house squatting on the hill's crest.

"Something special about that?" asked Azhur. He pointed to the rocky hill.

"Oh," said Tyr. "That's Gizzard's house. Y' don't want to be goin' up there."

"Gizzard?"

"We call him that. Some of us do, anyroad. Not to his face, mind, or he'd go wild. Is right name's Gizhurthra. He's our vraakhin."

"I see," said Azhur, a little stiffly.

"Oh, forgot priests don't like vraakhin."

"I don't know if I'd go so far as to—"

"Y' won't like him. He's a loony who gives everybody the willies. He's a snob and all, so he lives up there by himself. Can't get on with folk, thinks he's somebody, thinks he's Shivara or somethin'. Oh, ey, do y' think—no, never mind."

"What is it? Do you need to rest?"

"No, no, I was…" How could he say it? Azhur, I got taken back in time and I saw Shivara fight Djur-ch'herakh in the temple as it was happening. Azhur, what does it mean? What happened to me? It struck him that he should perhaps be feeling very disturbed after an experience like that, but after the initial amazement, he realised he was just slipping back into the process of life in Falakhoth. He remembered that he had enjoyed the vision. The bewilderment had only turned up afterwards and was already beginning to fade into a host of rationalisations and maybes. Still, he was none the worse and, quite simply, there were things to be done. Azhur would still be here later.

"Tyr?"

"Ahh, thinkin'. I were—I am goin' to ask y' somethin' later on, though, or we'll make Wyrdha late."

"All right, then. Is, ah—is your vraakhin down here watching the play?"

"Down here? Him? Never. There's work bein' done. Y'll not catch him liftin' a finger."

They left the fuss and turbulence of the square and entered the narrow street beneath the little hill. On their left, a path struck upwards through tangled grasses towards the lonely house. At the street's end, another path wandered away towards the place where a stream passed behind the houses before clambering through trees and bushes to Wyrdha's house near the valley's rim.

"It's not far," said Tyr as they crossed the small bridge over the stream. "I'll keep y' right." And then he stopped, staring at the path and the shadows under the trees.

"What is it, Tyr?"

Azhur's voice seemed far away, muffled under an unreasoning surge of fear. Tyr had realised that the Harrak brigands must have travelled this very path on their way to kill or enslave him. Not only was it was the quickest route from the town, it was also hidden, leading straight to the place where they had lain in wait. He closed his eyes, seeing again the bright blade skim across the house-wall, felt again the thrust of Wyrdha's arm and the impact of his fall. The scarred face and the hateful

70

eyes behind the crossbow rose anew. To take this path so soon would be like bringing those ruined lives back into his own existence, letting them blight the vision and the joy promised by the feast. Tyr had already been brought trembling down to the town by this route, but the memories had not found a space in his shocked mind. Now here they were, clawing at his thoughts. He could go the long way round by the head of the valley and avoid the fear, but that way fear would win. For a moment he hesitated, fists clenched, lips tight. Then he drew in his breath, lifted his head and ran headlong against the threat, leaping and bounding up the path with all the energy in him.

A little below the level of the house, the track curved around a rock before its final ascent and here Tyr stopped, breathless and laughing. He had disarmed his enemy. Azhur's shouts came up to him muffled by trees. Well, he would have to catch up. The victor would run now, not because he had to, but as himself, for the free pleasure of it. He gathered his strength, then leapt forward and around the rock. He smacked into a sudden shape and went thudding off the rock onto the ground. A heavy black shape struggled and scrambled and pressed on his arm, fur brushed his face. Tyr writhed and flailed and wriggled free in panic, rolling back down the path, gasping.

"*Kh'aar!* Filth!" Someone lurched to their feet, clutching the rock. "Filth!" he repeated. "Peasant filth!"

"Never saw y'!" wheezed Tyr, grabbing at air, relieved he hadn't run into a wild beast. A stream of savage words flew at him in reply. The thin green light under the trees showed a dusky-skinned man. He was a southerner, but his features were too swarthy and sharp to be a Syrgan. The fellow clutched his left shoulder and snarled at Tyr, his grimacing face plain against the leaves: narrow eyes, high cheeks, sharp nose over wide thin lips. "Did y' hurt yourself?" stammered Tyr.

The fierce head whipped round, falcon eyes fixed on him. Gold glinted under a hood and on long fingers amidst black robes.

Feet came scuffing up behind him and a breathless Azhur appeared. "What happened? You shouted!"

"That is your whelp?" said the southerner. The rasping voice numbed the young novice and Azhur stared back dumbly.

71

Tyr was in no temper to drop back into dread. "Ey! Y're too quick with your mouth, y' are!

The southerner almost choked on his own rage. "You dare? Child of dirt! What do you not deserve, lowborn! *Hē sh'khriarghim!*"

Tyr was silenced by sheer, breathless outrage.

"Oh! No! That will not do!" Azhur was suddenly between Tyr and the stranger, even though Try could feel him shaking. "That's... that's out of all proportion, you must withdraw that. We don't... we don't say that word here."

A hideous silence followed. A disbelieving fury paralysed the hawk-man. He did not know how to destroy the upstart.

Azhur's nerve began to fail. "What exactly is, is wrong, sir? Have you fallen? Stumbled?" The man let the silence continue, watching Azhur with a real, if feral, interest. "I can see you hail from, ah, foreign parts. I'm sure you're unaware, but we never call a person that in this realm. Possibly you do at home, but here, it's... it's the law."

The hawk's head inclined a little. "The law?" he said in a low, rasping voice.

"Oh, yes," said Azhur, trembling. "Allow me to explain. You will understand, I'm sure. You see, Ar-ven, the great Archpriest of our god, declared that it is a dreadful impiety to think of any human being as—" The stranger came at him. Azhur threw out his arms to shield Tyr causing his black coat to open and reveal the bronze sun on his chest. The southerner stopped dead.

"A little priest resists me," he said in a ghastly whisper. "Well, shrine-beetle, you and your boy will suffer my judgement." He advanced, speaking in some rasping tongue and pointing at the novice as though declaring a decree of execution.

"Wait! Stop it! Stop!" Azhur stumbled backwards into Tyr, but spoke out loudly, "*Tha sh'herakh tha ai'vel!*"

And the man halted. He drew himself up, as though about to strike, but no more came. He drew over to the far side of the path and stepped quickly past them. At the bend his head turned. His falcon eyes held them for a moment as if they wished to remember. Then he was gone, down towards the town.

Azhur was badly shaken, but Tyr was too angry and too victorious to be worried. "Miserable bugger, I only knocked him down. Treats us like dirt cos he's got rings on and then goes on like some mad dog. Well, he'll know how it feels, not that I'm bothered nor nothin'."

Azhur put his hands over his face for a moment, then shook himself. "I've *never* seen anyone so angry," he said. "Over nothing! It's frightening."

"Sod him," declared Tyr. "Ey! I bet that's somebody Gizhurthra's took up with. There's all sorts go up to his house—every one's queerer than the other."

"You mean other vraakhin?"

"Dunno what they are. Suppose so. We keep well away. Never seen them done up with jewellery, though." Tyr gasped, clapped his hand to his head. "Ey! He must have come down from Wyrdha's!" And he went racing up towards the healer's house.

Tyr burst out from the path into the midst of a heated discussion. He waited, ignored, in the deepening shadow of the trees. The Harrak could have waited there—a shudder—but he threw the thought away and watched the healer listening, with no great patience, to a thin, shabby man with long, greasy hair and an elongated, unshaven face. The fellow was gripping the leash of a small white dog and winding the leather round his fists as his anger mounted. He was evidently anxious to enter the house and Wyrdha, equally evidently, was not going to let him.

"Gizhurthra," moaned Tyr. "Knew it." Azhur, who had come up behind him, was still trembling from his encounter with the vicious stranger. He was struggling to recover his breath. "What's that word y' can't say?" asked Tyr suddenly. "Queer law, that."

"It's—it's *Shumár*: the old language the priests use."

"Aye, but what's it mean? Tell us what he called me?"

"Later."

Wyrdha raised his voice, "Absolutely not, Gizhurthra, not if you brought a hundred of your vraakhin friends to see him. He is asleep and asleep he will remain." The healer folded his arms to signal an impassable barrier.

Gizhurthra's long head went back, the leash wound tighter in his hands. "Well," he said, "if the *master healer* won't even let me help a sick man...." He looked distractedly about him as if he was unable to concentrate on Wyrdha, "Vraakhin have powers, y' know. Knowledge and powers. Ancient words, and *medical* things *you've* never heard of. That was no wandering quack I brought you, you know. If only you knew *half* of what he can do." Gizhurthra snorted and assumed an expression of uncomprehending disgust. "I associate with... *great* people... you don't know the half... Well, I see you despise vraakhin more than I thought. Your *true colours*, hah? Does that youth have to die to show how jealous you are? Does he? Hah? You think I've got stronger potions than you? Might spoil your reputation, eh?" The strange man was speaking in a forced, desperate kind of voice, almost a whine. His lip was tugging down at one side showing his teeth, and his bony shoulders were hunched and tense. His head moved as he spoke, repeatedly jerking back as though someone was pushing his chin to annoy him. The leash wound tighter causing the dog to look up and give a little yap. Gizhurthra forgot the healer at once. He stooped down, vigorously rubbing the dog's side, pressing its body against his leg. "There, friend," he said soothingly. "There. Was it too tight? There now, is that better? Stay by me, now. Stay, friend." The dog looked up at him and whined. Gizhurthra's brows creased. "A good friend to me, a good friend," he murmured earnestly to no-one in particular.

"It's the only friend he's got," whispered Tyr, but it was too loud. Gizhurthra's head turned, and he straightened up. "Oh, I'm watched now? Spies, Wyrdha?"

"Don't be absurd," said Wyrdha brusquely. Tyr and Azhur emerged from the trees, Gizhurthra regarding them sourly.

"The *priest*," he said. "*He'll* get in."

"Yes, he will. He is already my guest," Wyrdha replied. "Gizhurthra, this is the Baranthu Azhur va-Kherzir," he said. "A novice-priest of the Shrine, as you can see."

"The boys in black," remarked Gizhurthra, with a lift of his head. Azhur nodded defensively and let a brief, little smile twitch across his face. "And Tyr-shan. Don't you greet your elders, Tyr-shan? Ha?"

"Not always," said Tyr curtly. "Hello, though," he said to the dog. It stretched its head out to sniff Tyr's hand and was jerked back.

"Sullen boy," mumbled Gizhurthra. "Headman's son, and sullen." He looked uneasily about, then suddenly turned to Azhur. "Have you any influence with him? Does he listen to priests?"

"I'm not really a priest," said Azhur shakily. "And I only met Tyr today." He had not recovered from the encounter with the southerner.

"Oh, not the boy!" said Gizhurthra derisively. "I mean him, the healer. Talk some sense into him. He's keeping me away from a sick man. What's the use of having power if...?" The man rubbed his unshaven chin and drifted within himself for a moment. "He stood in my way ever since I came here, you know, but you can tell him..." He leaned forward to peer at Azhur through the gathering twilight. The novice had no idea what to say to this strange, shabby man, and Gizhurthra drew what to him was the obvious conclusion. "You don't know me. I'm Gizhurthra. Have you heard that name in the cities? I studied in Lukar, they knew me there, as did some in Valderthaan." But Azhur gave him no answer. Nor, it appeared, would he. Gizhurthra become annoyed. He drew himself up and his voice developed an angry, disbelieving whine. The leash wound and unwound. "Look," he said, "I know the words, I know spells against the black flesh. Don't you play around with herbs and oils, feeble stuff—"

And here Wyrdha attempted to end the bizarre conversation. "Very well, Gizhurthra. I was a little harsh, I admit it, but if you will excuse—"

Now the fellow was staring at Azhur as if he had just unmasked a criminal. "You people, you priests and your prayers. What's the good, eh?"

"Gizhurthra, please."

"I'm sorry?" faltered Azhur.

"Well, you might be. You stand there and you look down on us, but you're another one that's afraid." He shook his head, then suddenly lurched forward. "You've all got something to lose. You're all afraid of us. What good's your chants? Where's the power? What can you do? Well, you won't smile. There's a day coming, a day coming! People like you—" And he punched Azhur on the shoulder.

Tyr grabbed his arm. "Leave him, y' loony!" he cried. The dog jumped

75

"What good's your chants? Where's the power? What can you do?"

up, barking. Gizhurthra pulled his arm away and Tyr jumped in front of Azhur, fists clenched.

"Enough!" Wyrdha's deep voice smote Gizhurthra with a sudden authority that was too much for him. His bubble of words instantly burst and he fell back into himself. Head bowed, he seemed to shrivel into his shapeless coat. His eyes darted about like a hunted thing as he backed away.

"I'll go to my house," he mumbled desperately. "I'm not wanted. Nothing I can do, no point." He went abruptly towards the trees and the path to the town. Throwing one fearful glance behind him he plunged into the shadows.

With a great sigh, Azhur buried his face in his hands again.

"Oh, that man," said Wyrdha. "I'm sorry, Azhur. Sick people attract Gizhurthra like a moth to a flame. He sees them as a chance to prove himself, and he really does believe he has some kind of power. I must say I've yet to see it."

"Did he have some foreign git up here?" asked Tyr.

"Oh, the worst yet. Where does he find them? I refused to let them try their hocus-pocus on Yauva and the fellow went off in a rage. Take it you met him?"

"Ran into him. Azhur stopped him goin' for me." Tyr grinned at his hero.

"One for the Shrine! How did you do it?"

"No idea," said Azhur, very weary. "He came at us and I shouted, *Tha sh'herakh, tha ai'vel*—you know how one does—and he, well, he just left."

"What's that mean?" asked Tyr.

"Oh, it's old *Shumár* again: *The shining, the presence.* Priests say it, it's in the rituals." Tyr had more to ask, but all at once something warm came over him, something to do with the words, and he felt he didn't need to know just yet.

~

"GOT Y' FIREWOOD." Tyr's boot smashed Wyrdha's door open and against the wall.

77

"Leave me the door, Tyr," said the healer evenly. "I use it to keep the rain out." Wyrdha sat in the shadowed recess at the end of the single room, perched on the side of the bed as he carefully wound long bandages around the waist and thigh of the trembling young man lying on the pelts. On the floor was a pile of discarded crimson dressings.

"Sorry," said Tyr insincerely. "How's he doin'?"

"As well as you can after being shot. The bleeding's stopped, I think. This is the third dressing and I've put some meat on the wound."

"Meat? What for?"

"Fresh meat on a fresh wound, Tyr, stops infection. Had it slipped your mind that I taught you that last month? Aspiring healers have to learn their trade, you know."

"Oh, aye, so y' did. Well, I'll get the hang of it, don't worry." He dumped the firewood beside Wyrdha's hearth and crouched in front of the fire.

"I hope you do. You don't want to be racking your brains when someone's bleeding to death at your feet."

"Bleedin' to death?" gasped the man on the bed, unexpectedly awake.

"Not you, Yauva," said Wyrdha quickly, and patted the sweating shoulder. "Just an example to motivate my friend here—he has aspirations to be a healer one day. So sorry."

"I'm not dyin' am I?"

"Not even slightly. Now, the sooner you relax and recover, the sooner you can get home. Do you think you can do that for me?"

"I'll try," quavered Yauva, but his breath was shallow and rapid like a hunted rabbit. He drifted into sleep as Wyrdha finished his dressings and went to sit by the fireside with his friends.

"I'd like to know more about him," said Azhur. "It's unsettling, just watching him lying there."

"Doubtless he'll tell us tomorrow when he wakes up," replied Wyrdha languidly. "Meanwhile, Captain Tharval, bless his heart, will take a message to his family at the *Golden Carp*."

The healer sat down in his fireside chair, the one with carved arms and the old woven rug across it. He kicked his boots off and stared into the fire with his head resting on one hand, a furrow between his heavy brows. Tyr's mind, he thought, was decidedly elsewhere. Certainly, he was keeping an eye on Yauva, but his thoughts were filled by something else, and that something had entered since he had last been in the healer's house.

Tyr, when not distracted, was still amazed by the sense of participation in the drama of Shivara that had come to him through the play. The vision was over, but there was still the strange though not unpleasant feeling of moving somewhere between the reality that had been the ancient days and his own life unfolding under Wyrdha's roof. There were even moments that felt for an instant like living in both times at once. The boy rubbed his eyes and tried to be more aware of the earthen floor against the sole of his boots and the hard stone hearth where he was seated, but there were many shadows in many places and the moving firelight easily shaped them into the scenes of Shivara's day. A sudden anxious thought tugged him into the present moment. "He'll wake up all right, won't he?"

"Of course. It's only his hip."

"Aye, but black flesh—"

"I shouldn't worry, Tyr, it's a clean wound. Just throw on a fresh log will you, Azhur? Thank you. I see there's still some humility at the Shrine. All respect to your calling, of course, but I haven't met many priests who would risk dirtying their robes lifting firewood." The healer clasped his hands behind his head and stretched his limbs.

Azhur dusted his hands and settled back into the second chair where he discovered the need to examine his fingers. "You were tired," he said.

"Oh, forgive me, I've embarrassed you." Wyrdha smiled. "I don't mean all priests are a bad lot. Your master, now—"

"Wyrdha?" said Tyr.

"In a moment, Tyr. Your master, the senior Loremaster, now he's a very fine person. A humble man and wonderfully learned."

"Lord Galdtchav? Why yes, highly respected."

"Wyrdha?"

"So I believe. What is it, Tyr?"

"Yauva. He's restless."

"Only to be expected. Don't hold the lamp over his face or you'll make him worse. Come back and sit down."

"That chest," said Azhur suddenly. "It's for scrolls, isn't it? Do you read?"

"When I can, and then voraciously."

"Oh." Azhur leaned forward, elbows on knees and hands clasped. "You're drawn to learning, then?"

"Well, yes," said Wyrdha. He sat up a little. "I studied, you know, when I was younger."

"Did you? Where?"

"Oh, I knew some people in the cities, and I travelled. Just a personal interest, of course."

"I thought so. You don't speak like someone from the valleys."

"Ah, you've found me out. Yes, I decided to escape from city life—well, there are healers aplenty there and fewer in the valleys, and I wanted a little quietness. So here I am, with my skills and some books and my quiet life."

"What do you read?"

"Oh, various things. Texts on healing, of course, but I have some histories, some poetry. A collection of prayers and ritual, a *very* old copy of *Discourses and Sayings of Na-Ba'audrak*—ah, you know that one! My copy's rather a scribble, I'm afraid."

"I'm amazed you have one at all!" exclaimed Azhur, eyes bright. "I thought the only copies were in the Archives at the Shrine!"

"Ah, ways and means, master priest," said the healer mysteriously, "ways and means."

Azhur was now completely absorbed in the talk. "Lord Galdtchav will be astonished to hear about this," he breathed, shaking his head in delighted wonderment.

"No doubt, but I confess I am rather proud of an *Account of the Emperors of Dhar*, and I'll venture to guess mine is the only copy in the Northlands—no, I'll be surprised if there's even one in the Shrine Archives. It's astonishing what you can get from travellers and the corners of markets."

"Wyrdha!"

"Keep the lamp away from him, Tyr. You may shake your head, master priest, but it's so. Picked it up in a market in Lachir."

"Lachir! What were you doing in Lachir?"

"Picking up my scroll. I did say I travelled. But enough of that. The fellow swore the original was written during Rachtu's reign and kept up to date. It certainly doesn't mention anyone after Rachtu's great-grand-son—"

And here Yauva gave a yell that had Wyrdha by the bed in an instant. The youth was bolt upright, terrified, waving his arms. "Say the words," he howled. "Get it away, say the words!"

Wyrdha seized him and forced him down. "There's nothing there, Yauva. Lie still. You'll open the wound."

But Yauva struggled wildly, gasping like an exhausted stag in a hunt, "Comin' down, comin' down! Storm comin' down on me!"

"What words?" asked Azhur. "What words, Yauva?"

"Priests' words! Rites!"

"Priests' words? You mean the rituals?"

"Aye, say it, say it, get it away!"

"Yauva, I'm not really—"

"Shut up and say somethin'!" snapped Tyr.

"Just say the Daily Rite, master priest, before he bursts his stitches, and make sure he can hear. Tyr, lie on him, don't let him move!"

Azhur leaned over the bed and put his hands on Yauva's shoulders. He looked utterly at a loss, but he did the only thing he could and that was to repeat the ritual of the Shrine. Loudly, firmly, desperately he said it. "Not really supposed to," he mumbled after he had finished, but Yauva closed his eyes peacefully.

"It's gone," he murmured.

"Ah, good," faltered Azhur. "Has it?"

"What's gone?" asked Wyrdha. He peered under the covering. "No bleeding. Yauva, what has gone?"

Yauva slowly wiped the sweat from his face. "The black thing," he whispered. "It's all right, though." He sighed deeply and began to sleep.

Wyrdha leaned over his patient, frowned and shook his head. "See, Tyr? The even breathing, the relaxed limbs and features. This is a deeper rest than my sleeping-draught gave him."

Tyr, still gripping Yauva's legs, peered close. "What'd y' give him?" asked the lad, thinking he had better sound knowledgeable.

Wyrdha drew in his breath. "Three measures."

Tyr straightened up. "*Three?*"

"Three."

"He shouldn't have woke up till tomorrow with that in him!"

Wyrdha nodded. "Precisely, Tyr, you're learning." He slapped his hands on his thighs as if to dispel the mystery and rose from the bed. "Neither would I expect him to sink suddenly into a deeper and more natural rest." He returned to his chair and closed his eyes. "I think, master Azhur, you must be able to speak that rite as no-one else can."

A pause, and Azhur said awkwardly, "A priest's duty is to speak the words. Assuming I *was* a priest."

"Of course, good practice for you."

But Azhur was embarrassed by his own success. "Zhir-sharrak said that he who does not speak when he is beseeched is—"

"—like one who hoards his bread in famine. Yes, certainly."

"The words are holy , influential in their own right, so Zhir-sharrak said."

"Certainly, and so majestic in the Old Speech. You said—what was it? —earlier, when you met the foreigner?"

"You mean *Tha sh'herakh, tha ai'vel?*"

"Ah, yes. *The shining, the presence,* isn't it? Also in the ritual? I thought so. Well, you had to speak. A double triumph, apparently."

All this had been lost on Tyr, who had been sitting on the bed, scuffing his feet on the floor as he waited to go down to the feast. He got up, slouched to the door and leaned against it with his hand on the latch, then said, "Wyrdha speaks prayers, y'know."

"Oh, really, do you?" said Azhur, immediately relieved and at home. "Which ones? The Common Supplications?"

"Oh, you wouldn't know mine."

"I used to think it were just for priests," went on Tyr, oblivious of Wyrdha's embarrassment. The ancient days of Dhar had quite gone for the moment. "I mean I don't bother, except I ask the Lady for things sometimes."

"Ah me," murmured Wyrdha. "Tyr..."

"I bet y' was saying that one y' always say when the Harrak was comin' at y'!"

"Well, yes," said Wyrdha resignedly. "Yes, I was."

"Might have made them go funny! Mind how they was shoutin' y'd put the eye on them?"

"Well, look, the truth is, I learned it from a weaver's family in Ceorthas. They often repeated it, and they taught it to me. They said it always helped them, or almost always, but not... well, not necessarily in a way they could describe to me."

"Really?" said Azhur. "Unprescribed ways?"

Tyr thought his friend had developed an odd expression as though he had realised he was about to learn something he might not care for.

"I suppose you could say that," said Wyrdha. "But you'll be late."

"It's only short," put in Tyr.

The healer found himself trapped. "All right," he said, laughing a little. "The words are these." He was silent for a few moments, so that the sounds of the burning logs came into hearing. When Wyrdha spoke, his deep voice was slow and quiet, filled with the flame's warmth and the dark, enclosing comfort of the shadows. It brought a feeling more of safety, stability, and of strength encircling weakness. A message that came with the words but did not depend on them, and spoken not in the priests' old sacred language but in people's ordinary words:

> *Thou whom I know not, remember me.*
> *Thou whom I hear not, speak to me.*
> *Thou whom I seek, find me.*
>
> *When I am strong, protect me.*
> *When I know my way, distract me.*
> *When I am content, trouble me.*
>
> *Though I follow thee not, lead me.*
> *Though I love thee not, care for me.*
> *Though I be far from thee, stand beside me.*
>
> *O thou whom I seek, find me.*

The healer fell silent. His eyes were closed. Yauva sighed and moved in his sleep. Tyr smiled. A quietness had settled on him. What cared he now for knives or brigands or angry foreigners? All these memories had drifted from his shoulders. He looked over at Azhur. The young man was staring at the wall as if his deepest secret and greatest hope had just been exposed and he now had to do something about it. Wyrdha opened his eyes and watched him, but refused to be the first to speak.

"What, ah, what god was the weaver seeking?" said Azhur lightly in a strange, high voice.

"He didn't know," said Wyrdha. "He only used the words. As I do," he added.

"I don't think I've studied anything like this," said Azhur, intensely casual.

Wyrdha nodded. "Well, Anthu Galdtchav's scroll archives serve The Northlands," he said heartily. "These words only serve me, I think." He laughed in his deep way, trying to help the young novice skirt the awkward questions the Unprescribed Words had raised. "Now then, enough of this. You have a feast to bless. Your cloak, master priest."

"Oh, you shouldn't call me that, I'm not a priest."

"You're enough of a priest for me." The healer spread the cloak round Azhur, but his hands remained on the young man's shoulders. He seemed to consider whether to speak. "I don't challenge your studies at the Shrine," he said suddenly. "It's only that—well, many things and many, many people have passed through my life, perhaps more than through yours. Some were very different, I dare say, from those you know. Some I wouldn't have chosen, some were heavy blows, but all of them made me think, and often they made me think valuable things I didn't care for at first. But valuable they were, and they couldn't have come to me any other way, or so it seems." Wyrdha paused, then slapped Azhur on the shoulder. "Oh, but what does that have to do with anything? I read too much, my head's too full. Don't let the weaver's words bother you. Be happy at the Shrine, you might never have odd ideas like me!"

"And would it be a good thing or a bad thing if I did?" said Azhur in an odd, grey voice. He fastened his cloak, still avoiding looking directly at Wyrdha.

"That would depend, I suppose," said the healer. He watched Azhur intently, measuring the moment. "It would depend," he continued carefully, "on what the thoughts were and what put them in your mind." Azhur's lips tightened. "And it would depend most of all on what you did with them. And what you let them do to you."

Azhur looked around the room. There was something a little desperate in his eyes. "Something to mull over," he mumbled.

Wyrdha nodded, thinking he must say no more. He pointed at the hearth. "Do you see, Azhur? Your log. It was once a living tree, strong and firm. No storm could move it and nothing could change it but the force of its own life. But now, it is old and dry and placed in the fire, it will be slowly consumed. It is that way with many people's certainty when they find themselves in the fire. I envy you yours. Guard it well. It may shield you from many sorrows." Seeing Azhur both bewildered and heartened, he laughed a little. "And that is positively the last homily from me! Now, it's already dark, and the feast awaits you. I will keep friend Yauva company. His level of conversation is exactly what I need at the moment."

~

BLACK BRANCHES CLOSED OVER the pair. "Fire's well on," said Tyr. The light of the bonfire flashed through the trees like rubies on velvet. Faint sounds of music and voices drifted up to them. "Ey, they're startin'!" He grabbed Azhur's arm, and they descended through the darkness.

'Careful!" gasped the priest, suddenly less thoughtful. "I'm used to civilised streets, you know!"

"Y'll have to learn, then, won't y'? Look, there's the fire."

"Was that his own story?" said Azhur suddenly.

"Who?"

"Wyrdha. Seems some... harrowing things happened to him. Quite changed his outlook, if I understand him."

Tyr had not been listening to Wyrdha's discourse on certainty, and in any case didn't know what harrowing meant. "Dunno," he said.

They trotted from the edge of the red-tinted trees as the path left the slope and, once over the stream, became the level street that ran towards the square. Beyond squat black walls a huge bonfire spread out its light and made the villagers look like marionettes at a hearth-side. Long shadows slid out to welcome Tyr and Azhur as they hurried towards the blaze. Despite not really being one, Azhur was feeling every inch a priest, carrying his blessing to the feast like a suitor carrying a gift to his beloved. Tyr ruined the moment when he hauled him into a doorway and clapped a hand over his mouth. A heated voice reached them.

"That's a brotherhood, is it? Promises and then off? And why? Eh?"

Gizhurthra. Tyr groaned faintly and huddled back into the shadows as the vraakhin stepped into view from the path that came down from his house. After him came the shadow-swathed figure of the southerner. They were black gaps in the firelight, the long head with its high fur cap facing the hooded hawk-features.

"Well?" demanded Gizhurthra angrily. "You look down on me too, do you, like that priest? Well, I've got powers—*they* know, ask them!" He waved his hand towards the fire. "My power's my own, I was born with it! You think I'm tied to herbs and amulets?"

"Enough! What you know of my powers has made kings bow before me, but *you!*" Something horrid shuddered through the air on the rasping voice. Tyr and Azhur pressed back against the house door. "Kh'aar! You are full of peasant pride. You cannot receive the great secrets. What could you do with the southern magic? Weave enchantments for pigs? I told you he was the one, but you could not even enter the house. I allowed you force enough to send a shadow, but it could not find its way. You failed even in that. The others I tested were fools and you are no better. We will move without you." The man strode away, but Gizhurthra darted after him and snatched at his sleeve. The southerner whipped round, tore his arm away. "You dare!" And then he opened his mouth and hissed, a repulsive, chafing sound that had a thousand serpents in it.

Gizhurthra staggered away and stood shuddering. He tried to speak, but all his self-importance was silenced. Slowly, he sank to his knees, withered like the leaves in the fire, and, bending forward, pressed his forehead on the ground. He had become a limp, pathetic thing in the foreigner's shadow. "I bow," he croaked. "You are right. Please, I beg you, tell me your secrets."

The southerner said nothing for some moments, feasting on Gizhurthra's humiliation. "I will return. You will learn the secrets and you will understand our brotherhood. Watch the wounded peasant, as I told you, and be silent." He turned with a sweep of his black robes and a glint of gold, strode to the corner of the street and was gone.

Gizhurthra remained crumpled on the ground for several minutes. Tyr and Azhur were almost on the point of emerging when he rose, slowly and painfully, like a man testing himself after an illness. Once on his feet, the vraakhin stood swaying, hands over his face, then stumbled to a house-wall and leaned on it with arms straight and palms against the wall, breathing heavily. Suddenly he cursed and kicked out. There was the sound of something breaking. Now full of furious energy, Gizhurthra stamped about the street, lashing at things and snarling at the vanished southerner. "Secrets! I'll learn your secrets! *Then* you'll see! You first, then the rest, then that priest! My power's my own, you'll know it!" He stopped his pacing and stamped into the square, still muttering, head down like an angry bull.

"That's him in his place," said Tyr. They stepped out of hiding as Gizhurthra's dog appeared, scuttling down from the house. It stopped, yapped at them and went off after its master.

"Well!" breathed Azhur, astonished. "I think they're quite determined to give their herbs to Yauva. You'd better tell Wyrdha."

"And Dad. Gizhurthra's a big enough loony without that other one hangin' about. Come on, we'll go round by our house so he don't think we've come down this way."

They entered the glowing square and edged along the houses, slipping through long shadows as if through forest trees till they stood by the forge door.

"What's that word?" said Tyr suddenly

"Hm?"

"The one that's against the law."

"Oh. Well, I didn't think anybody knew that word now."

"Well, *he* did, didn't he?"

"Yes, he did. It used to be an insult in Dhar. You were absolutely nothing if someone called you that."

"*What?* Tell us!"

"Ar-ven forbade the term."

"*What?*"

"Dung-beetle." Tyr's eyes became wide and round. Azhur could see his face searching for an expression as he tried to decide whether to be angry or amused. In the end, Tyr settled for an explosive little gasp and the matter was ended.

"Right," Tyr said, and ambled across to where his father enjoying beer and jokes at a long table. Azhur followed awkwardly as a cheer went up. He glanced to the side where Gizhurthra's narrow, wrinkled eyes were glaring at him over the rim of a mug.

"Ha! Right then, me lad!" roared Tyrmar. "Oh, hang on, is it Anthu or what is it? No, y're not really... right, anyroads, up y'get, and bless us!" He heaved Azhur onto a wooden cask where he wobbled alarmingly. "Watch y'self! No point escapin' Harrak and landin' in the fire!" Laughter and another cheer went up.

Tyr looked around, enjoying the happy, red-lit faces, except for Gizhurthra's. The man's bitter features looked cold, even in the firelight, but his eyes were smouldering coals fixed on Azhur. Tyr saw rather than heard the word in the movement of his lips: Priest.

With Tyrmar clutching his ankles, Azhur shakily offered his thanks for the townspeople's welcome. "Um, well, so *happy* to join you. Real warmth, and not just the fire. The, ah, desperate events have given rise to a wonderful occasion. Loved ones safe, new friends, a true welcome. A lesson there: good things may be on the other side of... of distress... if we can go through it. But a time like this is so special, I think. Yes, yes, I think so. Very few occasions like this in Valderthaan." Azhur seemed to have difficulty finding his next words. The townsfolk were respectfully quiet even as the fire cracked loudly. "Now, the priests in the south used to bless fire, and the people gathered round it, because it was Arna's sign, you see, and they made words that honoured Arna's reflection in the flames. They asked him to send the Hra'imakhir—the nine spirits of fire

88

and light—so I think these would be good words to say. Of course, to be quite honest with you, you know I'm only—"

"Don't you dare!" shrieked Iethen. That did it. Azhur spread out his palms over the people to begin. At once, wild yelping: Gizhurthra's dog, straining on its leash, yapping at the air. All heads turned.

"Shut that thing up!" bawled Tyrmar. "Go and tie it up and y'self as well if y' can't keep it quiet!" Gizhurthra looked at Azhur with eyes of ice and wound the dog's leash round his hand. He rose from his bench and slouched away into the dark shadows. "Sorry, lad," said the headman, patting Azhur's boots. "Thing's a pest, go on."

"Please don't worry, these things happen. Now then." And he began to speak the blessing.

Things changed for Tyr. The square, the people, and the very fire were lit by a light purer and brighter than the flames. Tyr felt something freed inside, something begun that shone and waited. The light came with the words, falling into them, flowing through them. It took up their very sounds, poor human things, and made them great, clear songs, bright voices calling into the world, and the light itself was speaking. There was no telling how long this went on, but eventually Azhur finished. Nobody seemed to know what to do. Tyr felt his breath enter and leave his body stealthily, like a thief, for fear something wonderfully poised should topple, some harmony break. He could hear Azhur's voice, sounding strange in the solid world. *I'll speak some more words, the most important ones... I thank you again, of course, my personal thanks... your welcome, your hospitality... home and family, quite wonderful, master Tyrmar... a wonderful night, so kind... wonderful, here by the fire... by the fire...*

"Talks, that one," said a girl behind Tyr.

He wanted to tell her to be quiet that was a priest, but it didn't really matter, didn't matter, and she was so far away, too far to touch this time, too far to spoil it, this closed-in safe time, this time by the fire. Azhur was raising his hands and there were more words, old, ancient words, far before knowing, words from the beginning, coming out of the very first lives on the world's hide. Ah, but he must have changed them, for they all understood. Tyr did anyway. These were words for calling out, everyday words, words for people, words to talk with. Good, no mystery.

89

They all heard it. Tyr heard.

You made them, the lesser lights, to serve you, but you remembered us, so that they delight in us and guard and serve us. You who made the lesser fires, burn among us, burn up sadness, burn up what we dream we are, you who forged us for ourselves…

And the air moved, and the fire rose, and something came to the square, slow and sweeping, flowing, drifting, stately-stepping, bright-moving, slow and rich like honey pouring, light and deep, still and golden, precious, wordless like a lovers' meeting. It went eagerly over the rose-lit ground and the flame-light carried it among the people, like wood-smoke and the scent of herb-clusters on the warm breeze of a summer's night. No-one knew when it was among them, for they felt it had always been there. Then, as the music and dances began, the unfelt, glowing breeze quickened and swirled, whipped into mirth, crackled in fire, flowed with the beer. It moved the dancers' hearts and feet. It was in the breath of the songs and the children's eyes. With one hand it grasped the music, with the other your heart, then brought them together and lifted them up till you knew what sound was made for and, almost, a door edged open for another music, older and stronger, that had always played, always been ringing in who knew what voices. The best music people made, the strongest, wildest, most powerful in the heart, was all that it was only because the harmonies of that old, far music sounded for a time on the edge of hearing. So weariness fell back, and no quarrel was easily remembered, for in the glowing space between the houses moved not sounds upon the air, but a living being.

And oh, the joy of the feast, the gladness after the storm and danger: the life, the wild life of it, limbs and bodies alive in dancing, leaping feet on the firm earth stamping. Bread, drink, the roast, the voices, warm closeness, embraces, and laughter, and everyone the spring and mirror of joy.

Tyr walked through the midst. He felt his heart contained a fire that burned without pain and blazed without reek, a pure flame whose heat was unimagined joy. And as this fire burned it did not consume but gave and gave until life, plain life, was overtaken and renewed. Eyes full of wonder, the lad beheld the fire round which the people danced. Brighter and higher it burned, then up he looked and from the summit of the flames there sprang a figure, arms wide like a dancer in a great leap. Down to the people it came and whether it danced above them or among them Tyr could not tell, but it gathered all their movement up into its own whirling joyfulness, one with their delight from within a wild strange life of its own. The figure seemed to be a thing of fire itself, all glancing light and movement, never still. It leaped and whirled and turned, bowed, arched, crouched, kicked, span and fell and rolled about the ground, then up again in stupendous arcs. Tyr watched it with astonished joy. He knew it danced as it did for joy, sheer joy. It was abandoned to its own delight, more released in it than Tyr could ever have imagined, spinning in its exhilarating energy, a crackling, lashing, white-hot whip from his father's forge, pointless, useless, never a purpose save letting out joy and drawing joy in. And Tyr began laughing, there was nothing else for it. He dropped on a bench and yelled with mirth, howled with it, shrieked with it, sprawled on the bench, fell on the ground limp and weeping, utterly overtaken by laughter. Nothing was funny, no joke could have done it. Tyr's uncontainable joy fell from the fire-spirit, and as long as he looked at the fiery dancer there was nothing to do but laugh.

Then the joy flew up to a new height, a trembling, eager, bow-string delight. The laughter had only been the threshold. His body had only done what it could to make way for the joy in his spirit. He raised himself on one arm—it was more like being lifted—and gazed up. The glorious spirit was high over the town, arms spread out, motionless. It glowed and blazed as if lightning had been caught and held in place in the sky, then its fires dimmed. The bonfire glare became a broad, clear light like a sharp, determined dawn, and the spirit brought its hands together and stretched them out, palms down. Its head and shoulders dipped in a movement like a bow and then, head raised, it thrust its hands towards the west. For a second, Tyr thought of how Azhur stretched his hands out when he spoke blessings, and somehow that was right. He felt, rather than saw, the spirit's fires concentrated in its hands. Its joy had not gone, but here was purpose too.

Four times the bright hands reached out. Westwards, to the mountains,

From the summit of the flames there sprang a figure,
arms wide like a dancer in a great leap.

to Ceorthas, ancient watcher of the seaways and the road to the Great Sea and holy Fyrieg, the Fire-island. Southward to the windings of the river, the valleys and lowlands, the pastures and the fields that Tyr's people had worked for centuries before Dhar reached up to make the kings. East the spirit turned, to the great plain within its mountain walls, to the tents and herds of the wandering tribes, the stone cities and the hard shores of the Lesser Sea. Then to the north, to far Harrokaan that sent tribute from the whale-ways by the White Fields, ever-wintered, to the eagle-haunted crags of the Long Water, to Valderthaan, where the Valgraavs had built their towers and where Jarthastra, fourteenth of the high blood since great Na-veshtrazhdak, sat plenipotentiary on the lion-graven throne. And so all the Northland was blessed under an awesome purpose that none on the world's face knew of save Tyr, the village boy. As for its meaning, he could not even wonder. After the blessing—faster than speed, instant, sudden as dream—the Fire-spirit stood before him. He was somehow on his feet, reeling under the awe of it, washed by lavish roiling waves of heat, refreshed by incandescence, and looking up—oh, wonder, the glowing palms were over his head, lowering, lowering, narrowing the Northlands' blessing down, down, to Arcorath, to Falakhoth. If these hands should touch him, could he bear it? Down, down, to the square, to the people… The hands stopped, hovered above him, never resting, never touching. There was no need. Tyr stood and gazed, and whether the sight itself was mercy to his body, or whether sleep was part of the blessing, Tyr never knew, but with one glance into that wonderful face he was sent into rest and for him the feast and the dance were over.

CHAPTER 5

The First Shining

"THIS IS YOUR FAVOURITE HILL?" asked Azhur.

"Dunno. They're all me favourites for different reasons, or I've got different favourites on different days. Y' know what I mean?"

"I think so. It'll be a fine view when we're clear of the trees. The sun's only just rising."

"No, don't look then! Wait till y're right at the top and then y'll see. It's much better that way."

They kept climbing, and the trees gave way to bracken and heather with isolated pines scattered among the rocks. Generations of climbers, following the easiest way up the irregular hill, had worn a track that now led Tyr and Azhur round the farther side as they approached the summit. A few minutes more and they faced the last stretch: a short, easy slope with many footholds. Glancing up, they could see only the pale swathe of the morning sky behind the dark, rocky crown of the hill. A dozen steps took them to the top.

"Now," said Tyr.

They stepped out above the world.

Below and around, the land was spread out for their pleasure. The great green hills lay basking in the young sun, their crests awash with pale gold, while the traceries of the early mist hung on their sides and sidled through their valleys. The magnificent silver-work of the river glinted and twisted in its emerald setting, a pendant to the sapphire lake. Behind them, the countryside rose to the broad, brown mass of the Bhaniran, snow-flecked and brooding.

Tyr drew in a breath. The waiting air rushed into his body to claim it. And in that high place on such a morning, it was as if the air and light had joined in one new substance that surrounded and filled him and buoyed him up, so that to swim would be to fly as a new, exultant bird in the great heaven that had held the spirit of the fire.

He could feel it now, the power of that dazzling benediction. Was its life still shimmering in the very air? He looked down again at the scattered fields, the distant ribbons of road and river, the blue line of hill and mountain that ringed his sight and remembered with a shock that this—*this*—was the land he had seen blessed, blessed fourfold, soil and stone, tree and people. And no-one knew; no-one but—

"I don't know how you're awake so early," said Azhur, shifting about in search of a comfortable space on the rock. He rubbed his eyes.

Tyr struggled to be ordinary, "Oh, I sort of nodded off early last night, I think."

"It must've been all the excitement. Your father said he found you asleep near the fire and couldn't even wake you when he carried you to bed."

"That's who it was?"

"It was a wonderful time. I've never seen people so happy. But I don't blame you for falling asleep, not after what you'd been through." He peered into the distance, narrow-eyed. "I went back to Wyrdha's myself before they'd finished. Can you see his house from here?"

Wyrdha's house? thought Tyr. *I'm in the one place in the world where I had to be on this morning! I don't want to talk about Wyrdha's house!*

"Um, no. But there're the fields where we was yesterday when the storm came." The storm. The fury, the power, the moving shadow. In the morning, darkness and death; in the evening, fire and life. The lad needed to ask what it meant.

"And where's the house?"

Azhur, never mind the house! You know all this stuff, help me! "It's below

95

the edge of the field where the trees are. Y' can't see it from here."

"So the village is lower still. Oh yes, I can see the rooftops."

Azhur! Oh, will he say I'm just seeing things?

The novice pulled up his knees and hugged them. He stared out towards the valley and frowned. "What is it?" said Tyr.

"Yauva. He's very ill. Wyrdha and I had a look at him every hour through the night, but he didn't wake and just kept muttering all the time, even when you came creeping in at dawn to drag me up here. But Wyrdha says the sleep's good for him. He's still thanking the powers that your vraakhin, that Gizhurthra, didn't get in and put goodness knows what onto the wound."

Suddenly, Tyr felt normal again. "Y' better watch out. Gizhurthra's got it in for you."

"For me? What have I done?"

"Everythin' he wants to do, sayin' y' thing over Yauva and blessing the feast when he'd have been sayin' his stupid spells and wavin' charms about. I think he wanted to be a priest. He's jealous."

"I only did as I was asked!"

"Well, he was looking at y' last night like a cat after a bird, like he were wishing he could put the eye on y'." Azhur looked around, alarmed. "It's all right, he can't do it, but I'll tell y', y' know that dog he's got? Remember it started barking when y' was talkin'? Well, he kicked it."

"Deliberately? During the words?" Azhur was shocked. "I've never heard of such a thing!"

"Well, he did, just so he could spoil y' thing. He's like that, but he'll likely stay away if y' don't bother him. He can't do nothin'."

Hatred like Gizhurthra's seemed be a new experience for Azhur. Since Falakhoth usually gave little thought to priestly matters, Tyr failed to understand the deeper shock his friend had felt. The reality of someone who cared nothing whatever for his impending priesthood, could even insult it, was foreign to him. And to be Azhur was to be, ultimately, a priest.

The young man desperately drew in his breath and hugged his knees more tightly. Gizhurthra was wrong, that was all, just wrong. He wished Tyr would say something.

96

Unwittingly, Tyr obliged. He lounged back on the rocks, looking out into the swelling light, and said, "Arna's supposed to have made Northland, isn't he?"

Azhur instantly became a scholar again, "Yes. This is Lord Arna's land: he made this kingdom." But he could not know what lay behind Tyr's question.

"That were when King Rachty come up from South, wasn't it?"

"The emperor Rachtu, yes. From Dhar."

"Do y' know about that?" Perhaps this would lead into the mystery of a land blessed fourfold.

"Well, of course. Priests have to know the history. Don't you?"

"Well, bits. We've got stories, and folk does plays about old time, but y' know it better, don't y'? I mean, it's in them scrolls, isn't it?"

Azhur laughed, "Yes, it is, and I have to know about *them*." Ah, how unimportant Gizhurthra was now.

"You mean y' read them? All of them?" Tyr was really astonished.

Azhur laughed again, very pleased at the way the morning was going, "I might have read about a third, but there are thousands. I mean to read them all someday."

Tyr could only gape at this. After a silence he said, "Well, y' know how they say Arna made Northland? I never got the hang of that. Do y' know them ones?"

"Oh yes, very important. That's in the Scrolls of the Founding."

"The what?"

"The Founding—when the Northlands were made into a kingdom."

The Northlands, *Ke'vald-na*, blessed fourfold beneath the fiery hands, secret of the village boy—

"Tyr, you're dreaming. What is it?"

"Nothin'. Go on about the Founding."

"Well, that is the great time in history. That was when the kingdom was made, when we first learned of Arna, and when the old gods took second place. That was when Ar-ven began to worship Arna and became his first Archpriest in the North."

"And did them prayers on our mountain? Did he?"

"The stories say so. The cave's still there."

"I've been in it!"

"Of course, and the Founding was also the time when Na-veshtrazh-dak became—"

"Who?"

"Na-veshtrazhdak. King Nav." This was a great concession, but it had to be made.

"Oh, him. Right."

"Good. Well, he became First King of the Northlands. Now, the important thing is, all these things happened because Arna made them happen. The Founding was the time when Arna first shone in the North—"

"Shone?"

"Ah, yes. You remember what I said yesterday? Arna's sign is the sun, you see, and he's associated—connected—with it. He rises in it, puts his presence in it, if you follow me, and that's how he moves over the world. That's why he made it. The sun. So, if Arna, er, does something, is, well, involved with someone, we say he, ah, *shines*. As if he were the sun, or like the sun—he isn't the sun, of course. It's a metaphor. Sorry, a figure of speech, a comparison." The task of conceptual translation was very tiring, Azhur had never had to do it before. "Are you—do you—are you with me?"

Tyr twirled his long, dark hair in his fingers and squinted at his friend, "Dunno. Think so."

Azhur breathed deeply, twisted his fingers together and forged ahead. "So, we knew nothing about Arna before that, for they only honoured him in the South, in Dhar, where Rachtu Bhanir ruled. These early days were called *Va Sh'herakh*, the First Shining—that's *Shumár*, the old language—because Arna shone here for the first time. And to this day, priests at the Shrine in Valderthaan welcome the sun every morning."

"Welcome it?"

"They sing the Morning Song, thanking Arna for sending the sun and his presence, so that life can continue, crops can grow, and mankind can be joyful."

"How's it go?"

"Well, I'm no singer. Anyway, only priests sing it, and I'm—"

"Aye, we know! Get on with it."

"Well, it begins with *Ai va sh'herakh a threma shi*. Which means: It is the first shining of the day. The new dawn, you see, as there was a new dawn for the North so many years ago."

"Right. Was it a long time?"

"About four hundred years. And four hundred years before that, Dhar was at its most glorious and powerful. You saw that time in the play. That was when Djur-Chemish was the Golden Lord and his son became the Black Emperor. Shivara was the Archpriest in the South, beyond the desert."

The south. Shivara. Oh Azhur, I've seen him. He's got two spots under his right eye and these creases round his mouth. And grey eyes and funny long fingers. Is it in a Scroll how I saw that? I'm going to ask you now, in just a minute. I am. "King Rachty's country?" said Tyr by way of wistful preparation. "Is it still there?"

"Well, Dhar shrank and fell, its enemies made it powerless. It's still there, what's left of it, but it's hardly worth talking about—we administer most of the area and the desert's supposed to cover the rest. The power passed to the North and the line of Na-veshtrazhdak—that's *our* kings, our Valgraavs—who made a northern empire greater than anything Dhar ever had in the South."

"They always say that, though, don't they?"

"Say what?"

"We're better at it than that other crowd. Everybody in charge says that. So my dad says, anyroad."

Azhur was a little shocked at the suggestion that any acclamation of the glorious and divinely-constituted Northlands might simply be conventional boasting. "Well, ah, I don't know that you should say that, Tyr. I mean, the fact is that Lord Arna abandoned Dhar and chose the North instead." This assertion of unassailable fact restored the young novice's confidence. "You should be proud to live here, Tyr-shan. Lord Arna set aside the lords of Dhar in order to create your country. Shivara will come here, not to the South." Azhur gave a tight smile and a sharp little nod.

"Don't y' start," said Tyr.

"Excuse me? Start what?"

"*Tyr-shan*. That's what Wyrdha says when he's rattled. I like Tyr better."

"Oh," said Azhur, unsure how to respond now that the glory of the Northland had failed to outdo in importance Tyr's favoured form of address. "Well, sorry, I just think it's, you know..." He trailed off into a perplexed silence.

Tyr looked out over his valley again. He felt different about it now. When Azhur spoke, it didn't sound like the stories and legends he was used to hearing on winter evenings. But then Azhur had read the Scrolls. That was almost like being there, unless you'd had a vision.

"Tell us more," he said.

Azhur smiled, edged closer and sat cross-legged. "The thing is," he said, "there are a hundred versions of the old histories going around. Every village seems to make up its own and every story-teller has to have more in his version than the man he got it from. But the *truth*—" he raised a hand, "—the *facts* are in the Scrolls of the Founding, which are *very* long and written on both sides. Now, the first scroll, which we call *Kh'her Ai Thrematu a Va Sh'herakhshi*—"

"Eh?"

"Sorry: *Concerning the Days of Va Sh'herakh*. Now, that scroll was written, or at least begun, by Zhir-Sharrak the Wise, and *he* was among the Priests of the Sun who came to the North to bring it the rites and cult of Arna."

"I know him! My dad says he came up and met Ar-ven when King Rachty came up with his dragons!"

"Well, he came a little after that, but the Emperor wasn't with him... and I don't think there were any dragons."

"But Dad.... Well, who was it then?"

"Your father's half right: the Emperor came much later when the Shrine was built."

"Who brought the dragons then?"

"Well, let's start at the beginning. Rachtu was the Emperor's name and his land was Dhar. Now, Rachtu Bhanir—what? Bhanir? It means *lord* or *master*. Only very great people were called that. Now, Rachtu had enormous power, more than any man in the world, and a huge empire that his fathers had built. He was a good man and didn't want to expand his territory by spilling blood, so when he learned the Northlands were fertile, with rich cities, he sent his emissaries—messengers—to Lukar, and offered the rulers of the North trade and help if they would put their lands under his rule."

"I thought there were just one king. The first one, King Nav."

"Na-Veshtrazhdak, Tyr. He was first Valgraav in the north, but that was later. When Rachtu sent his messenger, each city in the North— they were very small back then—had its own king, and their territory only covered so many miles around the city walls. In those days, the greatest of the cities was Lukar—"

"What, smelly Lukar? Did it stink of fish then as well?"

"I don't know. Things were very different then, but it probably did. Lukar was the greatest city, and in the valleys south and west of the Long Water there was craft, learning, and wealth in the courts of these city-kings."

"We've not got wealth or learnin' in our valley. Where'd it go?"

"I, ah, don't know."

"Try and find out, eh?"

"I'll try. Now, there was little peace between the city-kingdoms. One powerful family would be against another—and the tribes of the Harrak, whose lands were mostly on the Plain, are still like that. They wanted to seize the wealth of the valleys—"

"Were they as bad then?"

"Worse. Practically savages. Not many of them had settled and most of them went about in their long caravans. That was why they often raided the valleys. They were impatient and tired of trading and probably hadn't the wit to make decent settlements and husband their land properly—the Plain's a barren place to this day. Anyway, they made a serious mistake. The Harrak often tried to march against Lukar and the other cities to take their wealth and destroy their learning. The kings of the valleys weren't united enough to stand up to them and the Harrak knew that, so they intentionally sought to keep the feuds going. Their blunder was that they were stupid enough to think they could crush the cities *and* the forces that the emperor's emissary had brought with him

101

from Dhar. Rachtu Bhanir, you see, had sent many armed men with his delegation, for it was a long, dangerous journey from the South and they expected the Harrak to attack them too. Harrak saw them as friends of the cities and they thought they could destroy them by sheer numbers.

"Now, the Emperor's emissary was named Jerchara, and he was very shrewd. When he realised the Harrak were a threat, he offered to help the city-kings against them should they ever attack in force. He had no fear of their numbers. He knew a rabble like that was no match for the skill of his forces. And he did something the Harrak could never have dreamed of."

"Wait!" cried Tyr. "I know! It was him!"

"Yes! Jerchara brought the dragons. And he threw them into the fray at the moment when the Harrak were most hard-pressed and disordered. And of course, that settled it."

"There was dragons! Ey!"

Azhur gave the quiet smile of the sage who, sadly but dutifully, destroys his pupil's illusions. "Not exactly dragons. The word in Zhirsharrak's scrolls for the animals Jerchara used is *rashta*, and that's not a dragon."

"What was they, then?"

"I don't know. Some beast from the South, I suppose. *Rashta* is the word in the Scrolls, and it's a hard one to get into northern speech. People must have thought they looked like dragons—and of course, they wouldn't have seen much of them, for they were gone soon afterwards. Imagination worked where memory failed, I'd say."

"Ey, bet the Harrak got a good look!"

"They did, and their descendants still tell stories about it." Azhur suddenly pointed down into the valley, the familiar, ordinary valley. "That's how they came up, Jerchara and his men, along by the river. The *Rashtakh*—that's the plural—came up there too when Jerchara sent for them. There was no road then, but following the river has always been the easiest way up from the South."

Tyr stared down at the familiar road with new eyes, almost with reverence. The huge events of the past were suddenly, perilously near, as if the Rashtakh had passed his house in the night unseen. It gave him a feeling in his stomach that was partly frightening, partly very pleasurable, and entirely strange. Too strange to concentrate on for long. He lay back on the rock, hands behind his head, and stared at the morning sky. The sky, where Arna had set his sign to bless the land; the sky, where the bright spirit had hovered. *Shall I tell him now? Oh, how?*

He decided to put it off a bit, get round to it. "Well, tell us about Ar-ven, then."

Azhur warmed to the task at once. "Ah, that you should know." He looked intently at the boy. "But you know something already, surely? Ar-ven, after all...."

"Oh, aye, a bit. I mean, we've got that cave up on Master's Mount where he did rituals and things, and we pick up things from folk as come to see it. He were a king afore he got holy though, weren't he?"

"Yes, Ar-ven was lord of Ceor, over to the west, and his territory was very much revered in those days. Ceor, you see, is almost by the coast, and the city nearest to Fyrieg, the Fire-island."

"Ey, Fyrieg's special, isn't it? There's loads of stories."

"Very holy, Tyr. It faces into the Western ocean, where the Deep Fire burns. On certain nights if you stand on the spot where Ar-ven spoke with Shivara—"

"Eh? He met him!?" Tyr sat bolt upright.

"Yes, thought you knew that. There are lots of stories about people seeing Shivara."

"Er—aye, aye, suppose there is—forgot that. But he really saw Shivara, y' mean?" *Ar-ven saw Shivara: him and me both!*

"Of course. Shivara didn't die, remember."

"Aye, but how do y' meet him? I mean, where does he come from? Where is he?"

"Oh, that's another story for later."

Of course, the old stories you don't bother to believe. Here and there through history, people who saw Shivara. Was it the way I did? "All right, then."

"You're worse than Ilissos, at least he's asleep. Now what was I saying? Yes, if you stand where Ar-ven met Shivara and learned great secrets, you may yet see the glimmer of the World-fire moving beneath the waves."

Shivara. He seemed so close now. On a thrilling impulse Tyr stood up and strained his eyes out westward across his sudden-sacred land to the line of mountains, far and faint, that marched to the great ocean and the holy island. A wind came out of the west and stroked his cheek, ran its cool fingers through his hair. Was it born above those miraculous waves? Did it carry some unknown potency from the sacred depths? "Can y' see it from here?" Tyr blurted out the question, then felt ridiculous.

Azhur laughed, "No, it's a few hundred miles to Ceor, and more to the sea. Thought you'd know that."

"Aye, well, I did. Just forgot."

"Look though, the mountain-chain from Naldor to Archor is clear— see where it breaks at Amouchel and forms the gateway to the Seaward lands that slope down to the Ocean. They say Bachras Fire-hand, the great healer of the Old Times, lived there. He built his hall by the old road that ran through the mountain-gap because he wanted always to be able to go quickly to the Fire-island if his art failed. And there, look, there are the Five Sisters, the Vargaraan, that stand guardians to the west. The peaks are still white, must have been a bitter winter there. Yes, Ar-ven was Lord of Ceor and all the land of the three rivers, and when his beard was white and his sons were ready to succeed him, he took ship to Fyrieg. He was Ai-varrath's priest, and his hope was that at his days end, the god would meet him and lead him to the Deep Fire."

"I thought he built the Shrine and that."

"Yes, yes, or rather he inspired it. Na-veshtrazhdak saw to the building." Azhur was now positively excited. "Nobody knew all that happened on Fyrieg, nor could Ar-ven himself describe it, but when he returned, he wouldn't even set foot in his palace but set out at once for the Long Water and the Lake. He lived there alone on the island where Valderthaan is now. He used to go back and forth in a little coracle. They say that one of the wonders of those days was that the coracle never sank, but it carried Ar-ven to the shore and back a thousand times. It was Na-veshtrazhdak's barge, of course, that took Jerchara and the Archpriest of Dhar across to him."

"He met Shivara, though?" Tyr persisted.

"Yes, and he eventually wrote about that and other things when he lived on Valderthaan's island. That's lost now, I fear, and perhaps it's just as well."

"How do y' mean?"

"Well, Ar-ven's tale had a sad ending: he became insane."

"Get away!"

"I'm afraid he did. He was very old, after all. Na-veshtrazhdak saw to it that he was cared for, but he could never appear in public. There are hints in certain Scrolls that he said and wrote dreadful things that he would never have dreamed of in earlier days. So the First King, in his kindness, saw to it that nothing of that sort saw the light of day. It would have been a terrible and unfair slight on a very great man."

"Oh," said Tyr. "Poor old bugger."

"Tyr!"

"What?"

"That! You don't say that about Ar-ven!"

"Why not, I'm sorry for him."

"But—it's just—well, you don't, you just don't."

"What do y' say, then?"

"Tyr, it's Ar-ven! He was the greatest—some things can't—you just don't."

But Tyr was utterly disconnected from Azhur's shocked perception of irreverence. He stared back blankly, conscience clear.

"Um, sorry," said Azhur. "It's just me, never mind." He lay back on the rock.

"All right, then," said Tyr evenly, but his mind was whirling. *Lots of people saw Shivara; I'm part of a company. Did anybody else see the Fire-spirit? Did Ar-ven see it? Would he know what it is? Got to know, got to know...*

"Azhur?"

"Now what? I'd almost dozed off."

"Sorry, I were wondering, did Ar-ven... did he, sort of... see things? Visions, like. Gods or spirits or... things?"

"What on earth put that in your head?"

"Oh, just, y'know, I've heard some of them holy fellers do that. Don't they?"

"Oh, yes, some of them. Jhista of Zirribh saw a gigantic horse with stars for eyes rising from the sea." Azhur shook his head and slapped himself on the face. "Oh, what am I talking about? Never mind that. Oh, Tyr, you've asked such an interesting question I've had to wake up."

"Have y'? Well, let's have it!" *Ah, the answer, the answer!*

"There are very striking stories about all sorts of people," said Azhur, levering himself up. "Several about Zhir-sharrak, for example, even one or two about our First King." He yawned hugely, rubbed his eyes. "Oh, look, I think if I went back and had a sleep, I could—"

"No! Get on with it."

"Oh my, such zeal for knowledge at this hour of the morning. All right. Ah... striking stories. Oh, yes, well, you should like this one. Apparently—it's disputed—when Ar-ven came down here to the Bhaniran, long before Falakhoth existed probably, he was following the river—oh, whatever's this?"

"What? What y' lookin' at?"

Azhur pointed down to the valley floor. Tiny figures were visible on the road, a column on horseback. The early sun glinted on helmets and spear-tips.

"That's soldiers!" yelled Tyr. He sprang up and gaped at the distant road as though Jerchara and his Rashtakh were coming north once more. "Ey! They're goin' up to the town! C'mon!" And he went leaping down the hill like a stag.

Azhur forced himself up. There would be no rest this morning.

CHAPTER 6

Sickness and Death

TYR RACED OVER THE high pasture-land. He cleared the fence above Wyrdha's house as he had done the previous morning and disappeared below the ridge. Azhur followed at his own pace, hand on his ribs where a pain was beginning. "Azhur!" Tyr was back at the fence, waving. "Azhur, there's priests! Priests and soldiers from Valderthaan!"

Azhur reached the fence, gasping. "Valderthaan? Why?"

Tyr helped him over. "Dunno, they're in the square with horses and everything. Wyrdha's gone down."

"What about Yauva?" said Azhur.

"Utha's watchin' him, come on."

The novice was dragged stumbling amongst the trees and round the corner of the healer's house. There was the plump, red-faced girl by the door, grinning in awkward but evident appreciation.

Azhur remembered a yellow-haired vision handing him ale mugs the previous night. "Oh," he said. "Ah, Arna shine on you, mistress Utha."

The girl smirked at the formality and curtsied. "You and all, master," she said. "It's all happening today, isn't it?"

"Yes. Thank you. Ah, your father, is he...?"

"Dad's not back yet." The smile slipped, then tightened courageously into place. "But that don't matter. He's a right good hunter, and them

107

things takes days sometimes. Probably sat with his feet up at the inn at Braldhach." She looked about her, not really believing her last statement. "Good feast though, wasn't it?"

"Yes, excellent. Where's master Wyrdha?"

"Master Wyrdha says he's sorry he's not here," answered the girl carefully as her eyes went back and forth between Azhur and the ground. "But he's only down at the square. There's somebody not well, so he's havin' a look at him. And he says if y' fancy somethin' hot to drink after bein' up the hill, fire's on and y' know where the wine is, and you can give some to that feller, whasisname?"

"Yauva. Is he awake?"

"Yauva," she repeated, apparently liking the sound of the word. "Aye, wide awake, if it please y'. And master Wyrdha says if y' happen to be givin' him the drink when he gets back, he wouldn't mind some himself."

Azhur went hastily into the house. Yauva lay among the pelts, wide eyes gazing at the shuttered window. His head turned slightly at the sound of the door and his tongue slid over his dry lips, but that was all. Azhur crossed to the bed and crouched beside it. Yauva's expression filled him with a desperate compassion, for he did not know what he could offer him beyond ancient words and reassurance.

"How are you feeling?"

Yauva moistened his lips again, "Baranthu," he said weakly, as if Azhur had just returned from a distant country. "My leg hurts."

"I'm not surprised. Remember what happened to it?"

Yauva grimaced and closed his eyes, "Oh, aye. Aye, I remember." Suddenly, "He said they was gone, the other feller."

"Who?"

"With the beard; he lives here."

"Master Wyrdha? Yes, the Harrak have gone. The soldiers took them away yesterday. You've been asleep a long time."

Yauva gave a long sigh, "That the healer, is it? Gave me something, made me sleep."

The latch rattled and Utha's shadow appeared on the wall in a sunlit frame. "Beggin' y' pardon, master, but Tyr says are y' comin'?"

"Yes, Utha. Tell him I won't be long."

The girl stayed where she was, leaning on the door and letting it swing her gently from side to side.

Azhur leaned over Yauva, thus taking the chance to turn his back on Utha's relentless appreciation. "I'm going down to the town for a while. Utha here's going to look after you, I think."

Yauva looked alarmed, "You comin' back?"

"Of course I am. Take your rest, now. You'll be in good hands." Azhur stood, nodded at Utha with polite restraint and edged past her.

Utha tittered to herself then sat on the side of the bed. She smiled down at Yauva and brushed his hair from his forehead with her hand. "All right then, are y'?"

"Don't know," ventured Yauva.

"Course y' are. Tell y' what, I'll get the water on and y' can have some of that hot wine master Wyrdha says is good for y'. I'll have some meself and keep y' company. Would y' like that?" A nod. "Oh, good. I wouldn't mind a bit of company today. We'll just have a nice time together and y'll be up and about in no time. Y'll be up and down them hills afore the week's out. She patted her patient on the cheek and crossed the room to put a pan on the fire.

Yauva turned his head to watch her and smiled faintly.

~

AZHUR AND TYR STOOD outside Tyrmar's forge in Falakhoth's square. The ruins of the bonfire were still sending up drifts of smoke that coiled together and hung over the town. Leftovers from the ox were in a heap on the ground, and someone had stuck its well-cleaned skull on the spit as a grisly ornament. Dish-laden benches and tables stood in disarray, and under one of them Brajhar the woodworker was still obstinately asleep. Tyr remembered the Fire-spirit with a little gasp and glanced up in case it was somehow visible amidst the coiling smoke. Did that really happen here, in this cluttered patch of trodden earth? The fire was gone, the feast was gone, nobody was dancing. It was now all so grey and flat.

The townsfolk, those who were awake, huddled around the splendid carriage drawn up in the middle of the square where it put the players'

109

ramshackle wagon to shame. The people craned their necks for a good view but kept a respectful distance from the horsemen, whose hands were resting on their sword hilts in a relaxed but meaningful manner. The carriage door remained closed and the window curtains drawn. It was as almost as entertaining a mystery as Eorthas' concealed stage. Around the ornate carriage was a little circular space, ringed by people as though they expected Eorthas to step out and give them another show.

"Party?" said a soldier unnecessarily. Tyr looked up at him and nodded. There was too much happening and too much *not* happening. He sighed and rubbed his eyes. The soldiers were guardsmen attached to the Shrine at Valderthaan. Like Tharval's men, they were instantly recognisable from their deep red uniforms. More of them were standing on the sloping street, waiting for instructions. Whoever occupied the carriage certainly required a considerable military escort.

While the people waited for the visitors' entrance—or rather exit— three lesser players occupied people's attention. Tyrmar, Wyrdha, and a tall, leather-faced man in a captain's uniform were all engaged in earnest discussion. Tyrmar, as befitted the headman, delivered an occasional line, but the conversation seemed somewhat above him. Shouldering through the people, Tyr caught snatches of the conversation.

"Well, he wouldn't go another inch. Thought we'd check anyway, that smoke hanging over the place…"

"Best get him inside, too cramped in there…"

"He won't be steady. You couldn't go in?"

"Pointless, captain. Easier if he can lie down and relax."

"She won't like it, she won't like it at all."

"She'll have to, captain, she'll have to."

"Who's the soldier?" asked Tyr, tugging Azhur's sleeve.

"Githraan. I see him every day," said Azhur. "That means it's a special detachment. Wyrdha will have to get his approval, whatever he's doing."

Tyr glanced at the Captain's forearms, thought of knotted willow-roots and decided Wyrdha had no mean task. Azhur pushed past him and out into the space in front of the carriage. The crowd began to murmur. The young Baranthu had evidently brought his influence to

110

bear on the situation. Tyr craned his neck and could see Githraan's happy astonishment at Azhur's appearance. There followed a brief conversation, with Azhur indicating Wyrdha approvingly and nodding politely at Tyrmar's interjections. Githraan seemed reassured about the healer's intentions, for he opened the carriage door and leaned in to speak to someone inside. He looked as though he was addressing a god in his shrine. Excitement swelled. The soldier's head reappeared. He spoke to Wyrdha, jerked his thumb towards the carriage and climbed inside. Wyrdha followed. The door closed.

Tantalised by this brief interlude, the townspeople broke into even louder talk, enjoying their own frustration. More people, newly woken, joined the group. Tyrmar paced up and down, Azhur wound his fingers together, and Tyr tried to relieve his excitement by taking in the details. All at once he was aware of a sound. It seemed as if it had always been going on, an undercurrent or accompaniment to all other sounds, and had only now seeped into his consciousness. The sound was high and toneless with a merciless, deadening rhythm, an unhappy echo from far away. Then Tyr realised it was a woman's voice, and it came from the carriage. Was it the woman who was sick? Hardly, she would never have had the energy to talk like that if she was. No, someone was not only ill but enduring that cataract of speech. Multitudes of possibilities gathered in Tyr's mind. Ilissos, he knew, would have no difficulty in weaving a story round all this. The Syrgan, alas, had enjoyed the feast to the very dregs and was not at hand to hear.

The door opened, and the townspeople's hubbub died. Githraan appeared, his back to the crowd, and stepped carefully down. Holding his outstretched hands was a pale, sweating man whose shallow, laboured breathing marked him at once as the patient. The people resumed their murmuring, but he gave them not the slightest acknowledgement as he planned each unsteady step. He was well past his fiftieth summer, and each one of them showed in his wide, disgusted mouth, in the lines gathered around his little peering eyes, and on the creased forehead above his arching brows. His clothing was expensive: wide fur collar, embroidered tunic, soft leather boots, high velvet cap. Draped on his thin, trembling frame was the deep red coat that, together with the

golden amulet at his neck, marked him as Arna's priest. He shakily negotiated the carriage steps and stood clinging to Githraan's arm as he
placed one hand on his stomach and twisted his narrow lips in the
manner of one who is desperately trying not to vomit. And the voice
flowed from the open door.

"Step at a time, husband, step at a time. I wish you'd listened to me
last night. I said the chicken didn't smell right—oh, do be careful, you
shouldn't be sick in front of commoners."

Wyrdha appeared, following the sickly priest, "Your pardon, Anthei.
Excuse me, please."

"But what are you going to *do*? I mean, you will cure him, won't you?
You will look after him? I don't want anything to happen to him. Only
we'd hoped to get to Valderthaan tomorrow if not tonight, but he was so
ill and I told him he couldn't go any further, not like that, and for once
he agreed...."

"Anthei, I assure you this is easily treated, despite appearances, but he
must have rest."

"But he can't rest in a carriage?"

"Indeed not, Anthei, and so the headman of this community has
offered him a bed in his own home, and yourself with him should you
desire it."

"I'm not sure about that."

Wyrdha scratched his head and frowned most expressively. He joined
Githraan as a support for the ailing priest and together they steered him
towards the forge. Tyrmar edged around them offering his awkward and
entirely unheeded greetings. His guest made his way into the house like
an oarless galley, carried forward by his own momentum. Wyrdha
assumed a role at the tiller, guiding him by tugs on his sleeves and instructions to Githraan. Iethen, standing bewildered by the door, also
received the gift of disinterestedness. The priest tottered to the bed in
the corner of the single large room. They carefully turned him round, sat
him on the bed, and let him fall back on the coverings. Iethen closed the
shutters and the door as Tyr slipped in from the square. The plaintive
voice was at last silenced.

"I'll not have the whole town starin' at the poor man when he's not well," Iethen said. "It's not seemly."

"Notice that, Tyr" said Wyrdha, catching sight of his apprentice. "Kindness is wisdom in the healer's art. Never make people into a peepshow, for it doesn't help them. Iethen, would you heat some water?" Iethen, already pleased by her compliment, went at once to obey. "Now then, Tyr, come and stand at a respectful distance and see what the Anthu here can teach you."

"What's wrong with him?"

"Well, I'm not completely sure yet, but you'll probably have to go up for the red jar in the chest. Now then." He approached the bed, where Githraan was attempting a whispered conversation with the sick man who regarded the healer apprehensively from under creased, half-closed lids.

Githraan straightened, "Afternoon, sir," he said efficiently. "I'm commanding the detachment detailed as escort. This is the Anthu Bal-jarrak, third priest of the Second Circle, legal advisor to the Archpriest, Keeper of the Fires and other titles."

"Master of Antiquities, Archivist of the Fourth Level, Overseer of Lake Revenues, Master of the Holy Substance and Precincts," continued Wyrdha. "I could go on but suffice to say at least some of us in the villages keep ourselves informed. Lord Bal-jarrak is well known, to me at least, as is Lord Galdtchav out in the carriage. Let me guess, Anthu, you have both been presiding at the Regional Overseers' gathering at Arcorath, have you not? If memory serves, it is that time of the year, a little before Renewal?"

Bal-jarrak peered at him with an intriguing mixture of pride, suspicion, and nausea. "Very well informed," he slurred. "You're not a village man."

"Not originally, Anthu. My family were in administrative circles and I have links with the academy at Ceor, though village life suits me. A permanent retreat, as it were."

Bal-jarrak grunted and swallowed. "Get the woman to fetch a basin," he said to Githraan. To Wyrdha, "You're highly recommended. Young novice fellow outside thinks a lot of you."

Wyrdha bowed slightly. "Mutual, my Lord. He is a gifted and com-

113

passionate scholar."

Bal-jarrak made no response to this. "We had news at the gathering yesterday about this place. Heard about those Harrak rats. I'd burn their tents if they'd let me." He drew in a great breath, grimacing. "Well, come on then, do what you're going to do to me." Wyrdha did so, politely moving Githraan from the bedside. Tyrmar had been reduced to pacing up and down the room.

"Pains in your head, Anthu?" asked Wyrdha. "Yes? And your limbs? Hm. And dizzy? Hard to stand, yes? As if you had taken a little too much wine?"

"That's it, that's it."

Wyrdha smiled. "Have you eaten today? No? And if our headman's lady prepared her most delicate dish for you?"

"Ach! No!"

"I see. My Lord's bowels have moved?"

"Moved? They leapt like stallions!"

Somehow, Wyrdha allowed himself only the politest of smiles. "My Lord retains his humour."

Tyr quickly turned his head away. He bit hard on his knuckle to keep himself from laughing as the priest groaned and complained through Wyrdha's investigation of his spindly body. The healer's fingers sank into his abdomen and he gave a great, choking moan that seemed to compound all the world's disgust into one long whine. Tyr snorted with hilarity and tried to make it sound like a cough. Wyrdha regarded him with a sidelong glance as he replaced the priestly shirt.

"Thank you, Anthu," Wyrdha said automatically.

"Finished?"

"Yes, Anthu."

The patient gave a sigh like a fall of stones, "And you thank me. Are you always grateful for torturing people?"

"I regret adding to your discomfort, my Lord." said Wyrdha stiffly, "but I must make a careful examination to determine the nature of your malady."

"Yes, I know. Are you going to bleed me?"

Wyrdha folded his arms thoughtfully, "I don't think so. I have certain herbs and preparations which should ease you. This sort of thing should clear up quite unaided after a few days."

"Some healers would bleed you if you cut your finger."

"And some if you were well. Myself, I think there's limited value in blood-letting." Wyrdha said and moved over to Tyr. "If you've finished sniggering," he hissed in his ear, "go and fetch the red jar and the bundle beside it!"

"Ey, Wyrdha, he's *funny!*"

"Never mind, discretion becomes a healer. Just go."

"What's the whispering about?"

"Practicalities, Anthu. I'm telling my apprentice what to fetch in order to treat you."

"Your apprentice?" said Githraan suddenly. "Send him here."

Alarmed, Tyr looked to Wyrdha for help, but the healer propelled him mercilessly toward the bed. "Tyr-shan, our headman's son."

Githraan curled a muscled hand round Tyr's arm and pulled him towards him, like a bear bending a sapling for a honeycomb. Terrified, the boy felt the soldier's breath on his cheek and gaped into his eyes like a transfixed rabbit.

"Good show was it?" rumbled the captain.

"Eh?"

"Had a good laugh?"

"Laugh?"

"Here. Come closer." The rumble sank to a crackle of breath aimed at Tyr's ear. "You look a fit young fellow. Can you run?"

"I can that."

"Good. Then I'll tell you something. If I was feeling meself, I could have disarmed all your Harrak and spitted them on a lance without breakin' sweat. But I'm a bit tired today, so I could only manage it with you, and if you don't run double quick and get what the master healer wants, I'll tear this arm off and throw it outside for me dogs." Horrified, Tyr almost believed it and turned white as a bone, then he saw, at the corner of the deep-set eyes, the beginnings of a smile. Warily, he smiled back. Githraan let go and slapped him on the shoulder. "Clear off," he said. "Fetch the stuff and put the Anthu out of his misery."

Tyr backed to the door. Tyrmar let out a bellow of a laugh. Githraan was leaning against the wall, shaking his head and sniggering quietly as his solid shoulders shook. He obviously made a habit of this kind of thing. Tyr grinned and bolted.

The townspeople clustered by the door in hope of news.

"What's it all about, then?" said little Verrik.

"Discretion becomes a healer," declared Tyr. He'd ask what it meant later.

He elbowed through the crowd and emerged at the carriage, the townspeople unsure whether to be interested in it any longer. Peering from the window was an elderly man in a red robe. A soldier was leaning inside and the woman's voice was clear. "You get Githraan out here, I want to know what's wrong. What are they doing?"

No time for more. Along the street, up the wooded path, never pausing at the stone midway, and then out from the trees to Wyrdha's house. Tyr stopped. Not to gather breath or call a greeting. A white dog was tied outside the house. Gizhurthra. He remembered the previous night and faltered. Well, Gizhurthra could have his tantrums, he was going for the medicine. He ran to the house as the dog barked and kicked open the door. Or tried to. His foot only made the door clatter in its frame. Wyrdha's door, on which he never knocked and which had never been barred to him till now. He knew the heavy wooden bolt was in place, something unheard of in daylight. He kicked again and hammered with his fist.

"Utha! It's Tyr! Y' all right?" No answer. The dog kept barking, dodging away when Tyr tried to calm it. More hammering, louder shouting. He darted to the shuttered window and battered on it with his palm. "Let us in, Utha! Wyrdha wants somethin'!"

Then he thought he heard a voice. One word, like a command. A few seconds and then the scraping of the wooden bolt. Utha peered out, running a hand through her yellow hair.

"Utha, what the hell y'—"

"Oh, it's y'." She bent down to the dog. "Quiet, y' daft thing, it's only Tyr." The dog stopped barking but kept away from her hand. "Please y'self," said Utha, and straightened up. "Comin' in, then?"

Tyr took her arm to keep her outside. "What'd y' bolt the door for? Is Gizzard in there?" The girl stared at him with her round eyes. A little too round, he thought.

"Gizzard? Aye, he's... he's...," She looked away as if she had forgotten what she meant to say, then shook her head and put her hand to her brow. "Tyr, it's y'! Tyr, I—what's been goin' on?"

"What do y' mean?"

"Well, he says to me—Gizzard, I mean—he says to me, bolt the door in case..., in case, I forget what, and he says to sit on the far side of the fire. Then he sits on the bed and talks to poor Yauva for ages. Must've worn him out."

"What's he want the door shut for? What's he scared of?"

"That's what I thought, but I just... well, I just did it."

"What'd he say to Yauva?"

"Don't know, couldn't hear. Daft spells, I suppose, like he usually does. Is somethin' wrong?"

Tyr did not answer, for he did not know. He had never liked Gizhurthra—interrupting Azhur's words was no more than you'd expect—but now, after the southerner and the bolted door, he suspected him. But of what?

"Y' comin' in, then?" Utha went back inside and began tidying vigorously and anxiously.

Tyr ducked his head under the eaves and slowly stepped down into the house. The fire was low and the daylight weak, so that at first the room seemed unnaturally dark. Somewhere in the darkness was the one he feared, the vraakhin.

"That's a nice greeting, but no worse than usual." Gizhurthra emerged from the gloom like a ship's figurehead drifting from a mist. "Bursting in on a sick man's not much like a healer either."

"Well, I'm *meant* to be here," snapped Tyr, not inclined to apologise.

"And I'm not, am I?" Gizhurthra raised his head and pulled the lines of his face into an expression intended to convey wounded dignity, but all he managed was hurt pride. "That priest's been talking about me, hasn't he?" he said, narrow-eyed. "Shrine priests don't like vraakhin. No, no. Don't know what they're afraid of. You shouldn't listen. They'll tell you things about me, not true, not true, and I've got more power than the whole lot, and you went at that door as if I'd come to kill him."

"I've to get medicine for Wyrdha," said Tyr, and made for the chest. He knew from the lift in Gizhurthra's voice that he was about to break into the speech. Most Falakhoth people had developed the instinct. Leave, challenge, or change the subject. If you didn't, he could trap you for an hour. Tyr could feel the vraakhin's eyes in his back as he bent over the chest. He found the jar and the bundle and straightened up. Gizhurthra was still watching, with an air of pained bewilderment. The silence made Tyr feel vaguely guilty. "There's priests from Valderthaan here and one of them's sick," he said. "Wyrdha needs this for him."

"A priest?" exclaimed Gizhurthra, as if priests had no right to be sick. "Ah. Better see him." He paused, looking as though he was wondering what he meant, then turned his long head and peered at the sleeping Yauva. "He's resting," he said vacantly. The head swivelled on its scrawny neck and the eyes once more regarded Tyr. This time there was something fierce in them. "I said words over him. He'll be better for it. Didn't work, did it? I got in. Everything as planned."

The man stood fingering the edge of his grubby coat as if he was waiting for an explanation of his own actions. Tyr recognised another indication that it was time to move. When Gizhurthra slipped into his befuddled frame of mind, people knew he needed them to do something, but since nobody ever knew what, and Gizhurthra never told them, they usually left him to come out of it himself.

"I'm goin'," said Tyr, troubled and angry. He backed to the door, clutching the jar and the bundle. Utha was not even pretending to tidy. "I'll tell Wyrdha y've been."

The name did it. Gizhurthra suddenly straightened and raised his hand. "I'll see the priest soon. A vraakhin ought to." He looked around. "I've done all I need to here. I'll walk in the High Fields for a while." With never a glance at Tyr or Utha, he left the house.

Utha ran to the bed and bent over Yauva. Tyr gave Gizhurthra time to untie his dog and get on his way and then flew down to the town. The anger in him thudded through his feet into the ground. Gizzard! Stupid man. A feast, a vision, excitement, new friends, and that *loony* had to

118

stick his nose in and give everybody the creeps. Past the stone. It was *his* fault, bringing these headcases into the town. Loony, stinking *loony*, ought to be *normal*.

There was a commotion in the square. The soldiers were clearing a space. Bal-jarrak's lady, a pale, chinless woman, and the Lord Galdtchav were both standing on the carriage steps. The players had woken and were climbing onto their wagon-roof.

Githraan was in charge and shouting. "Back now, get back, they're coming up, let them through!"

Two more horsemen appeared, coming up from the highway, looking weary and grim. Tyr wasn't going to miss this. He put down his bundle and jar by a house wall, jumped at its low eaves and swung himself up. From the roof it was all clear. He saw a soldier bring Tyrmar and Wyrdha from the forge. Iethen followed and went quickly behind the crowd. Githraan took Wyrdha and ran down the sloping street to the road. Tyrmar joined in making the people move back, then strode away and down to the highway. Wyrdha reappeared and stood by one of the horses as if waiting, then Githraan came up, striding in an odd way, easy and sad, with his head down. A horse decked in the red livery appeared, led by its master as Tyrmar walked beside. Tyr had never seen his father look so angry and helpless. The horse was dragging a litter roughly made of branches and rope. Tied to the litter was a bundle, a large bundle wrapped in a blanket and a soldier's cape. The horse stopped in the square and there was a silence as the litter was untied and lowered and the horse led away. Tyrmar knelt down and put a hand on the wrappings. Wyrdha's eyes were closed. Githraan scuffed his boots on the ground and looked away. Tyr watched and knew and refused to know.

A scream, wild and mad. Verdje raced from the inn, plunging through the crowd. Iethen came running behind her, but Verdje broke into the open space and flew at the litter. Tyrmar caught her, pulled her away. She twisted free, flung herself down, tore away the blanket.

Thaljhaz. Bloody hair, scored white face, terrible torn neck.

A great moan, and silence again. Verdje recoiled, rigid, hands pulled back, mouth wide with the scream she could not utter. Iethen dropped beside her, held her, shook her, spoke her name. Nothing. She pulled her away, shook her again, then with all her force struck her on the face. And Verdje screamed with a long, high wail that lasted till her lungs were empty and her arms shook with the effort.

"Again, love!" called Iethen. "Do it again!" And the new-made widow gathered her breath and shrieked her grief to the hills.

No, thought Tyr, *Utha'll hear it. Utha, keep the door shut.*

Tyrmar had quickly replaced the blanket. Now he beckoned three other men to lift the litter with him. Tyr recognised the man who had tried to talk Thaljhaz out of his expedition. There were so many emotions on his wet face it was better to just not look. They took the litter into a storehouse as Iethen led Verdje home. More sobs were rising as the crowd broke up and people drifted to their homes. A group of women made for the inn. After a moment, Iethen appeared, joining Tyrmar at the storehouse. Together they headed towards the path that led to Wyrdha's house. Tyr called them as they passed below him.

"Y' goin' up for Utha?" Iethen nodded. "She's not right well," said Tyr. "Gizzard's been in and done something. She's been half asleep and feelin' queer."

At the mention of Gizhurthra, Tyrmar's brows came down like thunderclouds. "Is he still there?"

"No, he's gone up to the High Fields."

"Right." He put an arm round his wife and jerked his head towards the storehouse where Thaljhaz's body lay. "Saw him, did y'?"

"Aye."

"Y' all right?"

"Aye. Y'd better get up."

Tyrmar nodded, "Y're a good lad," he said, and went along the street.

Tyr smiled at that. It helped. He sat for a moment, listening to the weeping that drifted from the inn door. Ilissos appeared and sat awkwardly on the bench outside for a minute, before moving off among the houses. Tyr climbed slowly to the ground and picked up Wyrdha's medicines. It felt strange to be doing something so ordinary at a time like this, but he could think of nothing else. As he crossed the square, the players' wagon looked suddenly wrong, an intrusion. He noticed that nobody had yet cleared up after the feast.

CHAPTER 7

Meetings and Farewells

THE FUNERAL CAME ON the second morning. The sun had barely risen when the whole town trudged down to the little burial place above the river. Four men carried Thaljhaz's body on the same litter that had brought it home, Tyrmar bearing the third corner and Azhur the fourth. Verdje stumbled behind it supported by Utha and Iethen. Lord Galdtchav had ordered horsemen to ride alongside and ahead of the litter as a guard of honour and insisted on coming himself despite every protest that there was no need. Bal-jarrak, sadly, remained indisposed.

The company, about two hundred in all, moved without a word along the highway. There was weeping and the coarse morning cry of rooks and the hard sounds of feet and horses' hooves. Mist was still trailing along the river, and dew glinted on the fields and trees in the thin gold wash that spread from the new sun. It was, somehow, a *good* morning. There was a certain unobtrusive beauty, a stillness, a respect. Nothing to weigh on a heart that already had too great a burden.

A flight of birds sailed over the fields, their quick, dipping sweeps good to see. The determined soaring reminded Tyr of the Fire-spirit's dance, its hands reaching out in blessing as clear as the day was still. That memory helped, it helped very much. He still supposed he should tell somebody, but it no longer felt so urgent. Telling somebody, even Azhur, might even spoil his memories. Tyr didn't know whether the spirit's presence was still with them, but he sensed that somehow even this event and Thal's terrible death were encircled, hemmed in, by something very great. It was a strange and confusing feeling, but the appearance of the Fire-spirit seemed to him to suggest that the world, or what was behind the world, really was as people wanted it to be despite appearances.

Tyr trotted on, supposing he should feel worse than he did, but he felt what he felt and that was all about it. Though he was grateful the glimpse of Thaljhaz's torn face had been over a good distance. A good man, the innkeeper. Tyr had known him most of his life. Perhaps he shouldn't be noticing the goodness of the morning, not just now. Probably he'd feel bad later. He glanced towards the river. A heron stalked with the light gleaming on its back, while tree branches threw their intricate, dark traceries on the clear sky. Thal would've liked it.

At the burial ground, the men leaning on their spades backed away, and the villagers grouped themselves around the new grave. They placed the litter beside it and Tyr thought how strange death was. The shape under the clean, patched sheet had nothing to do with the man who'd lived across the square. It was something different, something to be respected and laid in the earth, but it really didn't feel as though they were burying Thal.

Verdje was barely on her feet and her eyes were like wet, red bruises. Iethen and the other women were holding her up and trying to comfort mother and daughter. Wyrdha spoke briefly to them. Utha gave a brief, desperate smile and nodded, Verdje responded with only a gasp. Wyrdha took her face in his hands and pressed his cheek against hers for a moment. He did the same to Utha, then stepped to the side. Odd how loud his boots sounded on the stones.

Tyrmar mumbled some awkward words, gripped Verdje's hand and gave Utha a clumsy hug. They held on to him for a little while before he went to join Wyrdha. There he stood, shuffling and scanning the crowd. He was looking like a hawk, Tyr knew, for Gizhurthra, whose offer of conducting the burial had been met with the headman's assurance that if he so much as opened his mouth he would put him in the next grave himself. He had even asked Githraan to station one of his guards by the inn, to block any attempts by Gizhurthra to make a visit of condolence. There was no sign of the vraakhin, so he was probably sulking in his house. Even Yauva would be safe from his attentions, for Githraan, this time at Azhur's request, had detailed two men to attend to his needs. The captain now stayed discreetly at the rear while his guardsmen formed two lines by the edge of the burial ground.

It was soon over. The litter was lowered down, flowers and amulets were tossed on top of the body. Verdje twisted in her hand a bronze amulet of the moon on leather straps. Everyone knew it had been Thal's and that, as customary, Verdje would throw it into the grave. She needed to, for, by letting go of something so personal, she might be helped to let go of Thal. It was a good custom.

Now Tyrmar spoke a brief, gruff appreciation of Thal. He hated this sort of thing but the people were grateful, knowing that anything their Headman said he meant. "Anybody else?" he asked, when he had finished. A few friends and relatives spoke, then Wyrdha, brief and sympathetic as always.

And then, unexpectedly, the scholarly voice of Galdtchav. "I, ah… I've often felt I'd like to be nearer to people—the *ordinary* people, if you follow me—the plain citizens of the Northlands. But that's not always easy in my position. So, I wanted to join you today, especially because I was here when, ah… when things happened. I didn't know your Thaljhaz, of course, but everyone tells me he was a decent man, a good friend, and honest. I set a great deal of store by that. I'd have more like him in the kingdom. I'm so very sorry he met his end the way he did and hope you'll accept my sympathy." He paused and drew a breath. "And, though it is doubtless small comfort to you now, I've requested captain Githraan to do everything in his power to hunt down the beast. Then at least this tragedy will not be repeated. Arna shine on you all." An appreciative murmuring. "Ah… one more thing. Dear lady Verdje, with your daughter, I hope I do not intrude on your grief, but allow me, as a representative of our Valgraav and our Shrine, to give you this expression of sympathy." Galdtchav opened his hand to reveal a small amulet with fine thongs of woven leather. "This is very old. A number of Loremasters before myself have worn it, but since Court and priesthood so rarely meet our people face to face I should like you to have it in memory of a fine husband and father."

This time the murmuring was much louder as Verdje slowly reached out to accept the amulet. Galdtchav pressed it into her hand and closed her fingers over it. She nodded her thanks as she and Utha examined the gift, the Loremaster stepping back to gaze thoughtfully at the ground.

Now Azhur repeated the correct passages from the rituals of the Shrine: Ar-ven's words at the burial of Zhir-Sharrak, a reminder of the glory of having lived and died a citizen of Arna's empire and the ancient admonition to the guide of the dead, Ardhruthak, to treat such a person with due respect. Some of it was in the old *Shumár*, but Tyr knew he could ask about it later. And it was all very fine he supposed. But he kept thinking about the outstretched hands of the Fire-spirit and wondering if its blessing had somehow missed Thal because he wasn't there. Or perhaps he'd been dead by that time, anyroad. It was very puzzling.

It was time to replace the earth. Verdje gripped the thongs of the amulet till they almost cut her.

"Go on, love," whispered Iethen.

Verdje stared straight ahead. "I can't," she gasped. "Not yet." Everyone understood. Iethen glanced at her husband and he nodded to the diggers. "Hang on," said Verdje suddenly. She exchanged whispers with her daughter. The girl nodded. "I'll use this one for now, if y' don't object, sir." She held out the amulet Galdtchav had given her.

"I would be honoured," he said.

Verdje and Utha held the amulet out over the grave, both of them holding the leather straps.

"Here y' are, Thal. Nobody in Falakhoth's ever had a thing like this. This is for you."

"Bye-bye, dad," choked Utha.

She and her mother let go of the amulet together. It fell from their hands onto the sheet that covered Thaljhaz, landing where his hands were folded on his chest. His wife and daughter, having looked at its place of rest for a while, moved away and allowed the diggers to continue.

Everyone waited while the earth was patted flat, then Tyrmar stepped forward with a live chicken fluttering in his grip. Kneeling down, he held it over the grave, killed it with a quick cut of his knife, then left it to bleed. The killing was for Ardhruthak—no-one was quite sure why—but it was an ancient practice, used long before Arna's cult arrived in the north. The Shrine was, officially, supposed to discourage it, but there had been no warning. Azhur twisted his fingers desperately, while Lord Galdtchav had suddenly taken an interest in the birds over the river.

As one, the crowd trudged slowly back, silent as they had come. The horsemen rode ahead to escort them into the square. The fire was re-kindled, and the tables were set again for a funeral meal. People arranged themselves on seats and benches, and Wyrdha went quietly towards the inn to see how Bardcha was doing. Apparently, he'd been too unwell to attend his son-in-law's funeral.

~

LIGHT GREW THIN AND the dusk of a damp evening hovered in the sky. A solitary man shrouded in a sweeping, threadbare cloak picked his way up from the causeway by which he had forded the swirling river beneath the Braldhach falls. He steadied himself on a staff etched with signs and markings, before striking out through grass and bracken towards the wood west of the river. His head was lowered as though he had been this way before and did not need to attend to his surroundings. His eyes, when they did look up from the ground, glowed dully but intently. His lips moved soundlessly and the fingers of his free hand flickered in the air, tracing symbols with a determined purpose. He entered the tree-belt, passing through like a dark wood-wraith. The crowding trunks did not hinder him, twigs and branches did not so much as snag his cloak or slow his stride. There was a stillness around him. Not quietness or calm but the poised, frozen feeling of an empty space where things have simply stopped and will resume with something sudden and dreadful: a storm, an assault, a killer's lunge.

The staff-bearer stepped into a clearing. There were no stumps or signs of uprooting. Trees had not been felled, they simply did not grow.

125

In the centre of the space, a jumble of rock and boulders rose to form a mound. Partly obscured by stunted bushes and shrivelled plants was what seemed to be a cave gouged from the side of the mound. At its entrance were ancient symbols scraped in the rock and now almost smoothed away. Stone steps, ravaged and split by years, descended into the black opening that gaped as though the knoll itself was straining to be fed. The cloaked man passed over the coarse, grey grass and climbed the rocky mass, hoisting himself up by a few exposed, dead roots. He stood on the crest, breathing hard, and leaning on his staff. Beside him was a massive slab of stone that, from the ground below, seemed a natural part of the rock but, seen close by, had clearly been hewn by hand. Although a large section at the corner had split off to give the slab an irregular shape, it had once been a stone table mounted upon four thick supports. One support, like the broken corner, was missing, and the others had sunk or shifted so that the flat surface had fallen at an angle. Whatever had caused this might have happened a thousand lifetimes ago. The symbols around the slab had been blasted endlessly by ice and sun till they were almost worn flat. There were still traces of channels and runnels, grooves and hollows, but they were like a landscape under snow, blanketed by time.

A straining silence pressed in around the staff-bearer. His large, shadow-ringed eyes surveyed the bleak clearing. There were no birds, no animals. Here was a place bypassed by life. Nonetheless, the man tilted his head and appeared to be listening. He raised the staff aloft and held it perpendicular, gripping with both hands. Eyes closed, he focussed his thought. A faint and sickly glow appeared around the staff's tip. The air trembled. Some shrivelled leaves fell from the silent trees.

After a while the ragged bushes parted and into the clearing came a living thing, a huge and powerful wolf that padded back and forth before the cave-mouth, then stood staring up at the staff-bearer with round, yellow eyes. Some minutes later another joined it, a great, bristling brute that circled nervously, glancing up at the dark-cloaked man, who still stood with eyes closed. Another came, and another, until the space before the cave-mouth was filled with the milling, jostling beasts, snarling and slavering, snapping at each other. Each one was bowstring-tense like dogs that sense predator or prey, and all of them kept well clear of the steps to the cave.

The staff was lowered at last as its bearer opened his eyes. Out of the ever-moving sea of beasts there rose a man. He was naked, with long, lithe limbs whose powerful muscles stood out in taut relief. Long, gripping fingers flexed, the ridged, supple spine stretched and curved. The head of red, coarse hair was down, the large-toothed mouth open. Deep, deep eyes, round and bright, glowered up at the man by the slab.

"You should dress yourself, Kharhalkhar," said the man disdainfully. "It cannot be so hard to manage."

The feral man began to wade forward through the heaving, bristling sea. "I likes the freedom," he said in a deep, hollow voice. "Air on y' skin, y' know? That's how y' got us into it. Taste of the feeling, eh?"

"And what have you brought to me?"

Kharhalkhar began to climb the mound. "Couldn't get it," he said warily, not looking up.

The other did not move. "Couldn't get it," he repeated, with no hint of feeling. "An entire pack and you couldn't get it."

"They turned off the road," said Kharhalkhar, still climbing. "We was goin' to get them where it twists round the hill at Marjhaz, but the other one got sick or somethin', so they turned off at Falakhoth. They're still there."

"A village has never held you back before. I repeat, an entire pack."

Kharhalkhar stepped onto the mound's crest. His long, supple frame seemed to flow rather than move.

"You should clean yourself also."

The red-haired man ran his hands over the dark, crimson smears about his mouth and chest. "Another bit of feelin' free, isn't it?" he said, daring a touch of anger. "Y' just go for it, don't y'? Y' don't think about cleanin' up or lookin' nice." He lowered his head, showed his teeth. "There ain't no bathrooms nor perfume shops in these woods."

"You would not appear before Gehrava like this," said the man flatly. Something flickered in his colourless eyes causing Kharhalkhar to grimace. The naked man spat on his hands and wiped them around his mouth. The wolves below snapped and snarled. "Who was it?"

127

"Got one of them buggers down by the falls. He saw."

"Sport, then. You will not try an honest hunt."

"No, I'm not an animal."

"As you say, but why did you not pursue to Falakhoth?"

Kharhalkhar was silent, his eyes darting about the space as if there was a door to escape by. "Couldn't," he said at last. "We went up last night, but—well, we couldn't. There's somethin' wrong, somethin's happened. We couldn't go in, we couldn't have found it."

"You feared the town?"

"Not exactly. Senses went all wrong. They'd brought that feller back there, the one we got at the falls. I could smell him. Don't like that." He crouched down and raked his nails through the dirt.

"Well, no matter," said the staff-bearer dispassionately. "We do not need it for the assault. We know who has it, we will take it at their Shrine. I must go to Falakhoth tonight. They have a vraakhin, so-called, who may be our eyes in their district, and I will hold counsel with V'karra. Meanwhile, you must continue to administer our… retribution in the valleys. Be swift, be savage, be unpredictable. Anxiety is our ally. Extend the work on the Plain and into the west. Go as near to the island as you can, but concentrate on the valleys. Mere hours remain till Vardresh and Valderthaan's time. I will tell you when. Is Braugheer ready?"

"He's ready, all right. Been round the Shrine court, got the layout. He can hardly wait."

"Good. Continue your work, be patient and faithful. Remember Gehrava's rewards, and his punishments."

"That's not hard," growled Kharhalkhar, looking at the ground.

"Come now, think what shall be yours. That is worth endurance." The naked man did not reply and the staff-bearer began to descend the mound. "I will see this village that you could not enter," he said as he went. "I take it, since you are here, there will be veneration?"

Kharhalkhar started. "Go downstairs, you mean? I'm not stupid. This is as far as we go. Don't know why y' met us here, anyway."

"Why not? It is most fitting. Will your… patron not appreciate it?"

"Watch y'self!" hissed Kharhalkhar, alarmed. "Mind where y' are.

Aren't y' scared of him?"

"No," said the staff-bearer flatly. "They shall all fall." He reached the foot of the mound. The wolves snapped and growled deep in their throats, but made a way for him as he strode towards the trees, planting the staff in the earth with each step.

~

As THE DAY SETTLED into the last of dusk, Ilissos the Syrgan left the nameless inn and stepped into Falakhoth's square. With no news of Baljarrak or Galdtchav available, the townspeople, taking the last of the mugs and benches with them, had left the square nearly empty to return to their houses where the flicker of cooking-fires now showed at their windows. The feast and the funeral meal were both slipping into memory.

A few visitors called at the inn where friends attended to the soldiers who were lodging. Some would be sleeping on the wooden floor that was Verdje's pride. Ilissos now shared his own narrow booth with one of the soldiers. This was no great hardship, for the man had bought one of his scented oils for the inevitable lady in the city who might deserve even more gifts. And if one soldier had a lady, a whole troop might be very lucrative.

Stars cautiously came to life in the sky. Watching them, the Syrgan caught the faint rattle of wheels as a carriage arrived down at the highway. Soon, a woman appeared at the head of the sloping street. She carried a bag, her head was down, and she held a heavy shawl around her as though she were hiding in it. Her pace was unnecessarily urgent, like someone who had reason to be indoors and out of sight as quickly as possible. Ilissos had listened to enough gossip to know who she was. He had learned she managed a dye works in the city, that there was now no man by her side, and that she had a son. He had even heard her name: Antha, Bardcha's 'other' daughter, who had so spectacularly outraged the countryside by falling into the arms of a nobleman from the city. A message had gone to Lukar with one of the soldiers and now, here she was, come to comfort her sister, her niece and, if he would allow it, her father.

She paused to answer a question from watchful guardsmen, then went rapidly across the square and into the inn, vanishing in a square of fire-light.

Githraan was lodging at the forge with Bal-jarrak, the Lady Vareina having deemed she was needed back in the city. The soldiers he had posted at the door and at the head of the sloping street were starting the fires that would see them and their successors through the night. Ilissos' southern smile flashed through the twilight at them. He waved. They would be relaxed, and a little bored later, ready to chat about their homes and possible presents for their wives. He touched the amulet of Cynathé on his wrist and brushed the sun-disc that hung from his neck. They must be in agreement, the foreign sun-god and the Lady of the hills. The Northmen's god had honoured the Syrgan's guardian and allowed her to protect her worshipper outside his own land. Wearing the bronze sun pleased him. It had been a wise decision. Ilissos clasped his goddess' amulet again and smiled broadly. Cynathé had done well to bring him here. Not only a town full of soldiers in a potentially receptive mood, but a vraakhin and a healer. Both used herbs and oils and must welcome a supply on their doorstep. At least, the healer would. He had left a message for him saying he had items to offer.

Ilissos wasn't clear about what vraakhin actually did. Depending where you were, a vraakhin was something like a healer or something like a priest or the person who knew all the tales and customs of the area or the person who gave guidance or someone who seemed to embody the local legal system or a combination of any or all of them. The name, Ilissos learned, was an ancient word that had come up from the south, from the speech of Dhar, and lodged in the language of the North. He remembered a sunny old man in the town by the forest he had travelled through. He was 'vraakhin', though he never saw him do more than play with the children and hand out shrewd advice. But he had bought some oil for his feet. And there was the mountain village where he'd met a swarthy man with eyes like frozen lakes and an eagle's skull at the belt of his wolf-skin robe. The villagers had called him vraakhin, mostly at his own command, but Ilissos had decided not to offer him any oils. Still, vraakhin usually indicated somebody who, if not a healer, tended to be asked about remedies for this or that, so Ilissos would try Falakhoth's version and then loiter pleasantly in the square until the healer appeared after his visit to Bardcha. He patted the bundle of goods under his arm, clutching it with something like affection, and left the square, making his way to the green hill and the lonely house.

The evening crept from the shadow of the valley's western hills, so that Gizhurthra's home was a featureless outline against the pallid sky. Ilissos took the path that rose on his left towards the huddled trees. A woman hurried past, and he caught a question in her eyes, but she turned her face away and moved quickly on. As Ilissos climbed, he saw no light at the house or any sign of a fire. The hill seemed to be a dark island rising from a sea speckled with lights and flames. Directly below him was the watch fire of the soldiers, and all around them were the yellow squares where light seeped out from doors and windows. Farther below was another blaze where men had been posted at the entrance to the town near the north road. Herdsmen's fires dotted the fields across the river. No more brigands would come without a challenge. Drifting up with the smoke and sparks were voices, the laughter and shouts of soldiers off-duty, a call, a snatch of song. Though Verdje and Utha grieved at the inn, light and life were around the town while Ilissos climbed into the silent dark.

As he approached the house, Ilissos found himself treading on things under his feet that snapped or made him stumble. He peered down to find well-gnawed bones. Of course, the white dog. But there was no barking as there was no light. Bushes and briars grew thickly around the house as if to support it in their grasping stems. Trees stood guard, drooping their clustered branches into a shield against the darts of starlight that were now glinting from the sky. Ilissos clutched his amulet again and approached the door. It was open, swinging a little on its hinges. The wooden shutters were all wide open on the windows, so he peered inside and made out bowls and pots, even the odd garment, lying with the bones in the long grass that came up to the house-wall. He wondered if he was at the wrong house. Did someone really live here among every sign of neglect and abandonment? Ilissos had seen the vraakhin go in—the door was just visible from the square—but perhaps

131

he lived elsewhere. He paused and looked around. It was unnaturally quiet and there was an odd feeling of being *enclosed*. The trees, no doubt, leaning over him. Well, there was just enough light that he could look inside to discover if this was a home or a shell. If it was the latter, he would have to ask for the vraakhin elsewhere. Ilissos reached out and cautiously tapped the door. Nothing. Maybe the woman had been wondering why he was climbing to an empty house. The door hinges grated faintly and a wave of song rose from the square below, deepening the feeling of silence around the house and the watching trees. Ah, but it was a drab place. Ilissos knocked again.

"Master varcchin? You are there?"

Nothing. Without thinking, he pushed the door further open. "Master varcchin?" He stepped down into the house. "Your pardon, Master. You are asleep?" Ilissos took a step or two into the chilly gloom. The last wan light showed he was alone, but the house was not abandoned. Moving carefully around, he made out a hearth with perhaps the morning's ashes heaped in it. Wooden bowls, some with food, were scattered across the earthen floor. Jars and bottles clustered on a bench against the wall. More bones splintered underfoot. Vague shapes hung from the rafters. Ilissos put out a hand and found dried meat and bunches of herbs and vegetables. A confusion of straw and shabby pelts on a low wooden frame indicated a bed. Other furniture loomed in the shadows: a table of sorts with more bowls and a dead lamp, a bench, thick logs for seats, something like a parchment pinned to a wall, a cluster of objects, and myriad scraps of things. And there was a smell or rather many smells, herbs and oils, spices and unguents, sweet familiar odours and sharp, strange tangs. Ilissos relaxed with a long sigh, listening with pleasure to the soldier's faint song. Surely his bundle would be well received here. His hands moved gratefully in a sign of thanks.

"*Sirtha tha vei, Cynathé,*" he murmured. "*Aigentha tha rei.*"

He heard voices, louder than the sounds from the square, and approaching quickly. A bone crunched. Ilissos gripped the amulet and made for the door to meet the vraakhin. Being found alone in a darkened house would do him no good, but the owner of the second voice might be interested in buying....

Suddenly he was afraid. Intensely afraid. He felt the weight of it thrown over him like a blanket. He could not—should not—face the men outside. His body was shaking and his mind was clouded. *Hide.* The instinct somehow escaped his fear. Ilissos staggered in the near-darkness, frantic for a hiding place. The only thing large enough to hide behind was the bed. He scrabbled wildly into the narrow black space between bed and wall, tugging a pelt over him as he did so. There he lay, his mind reeling from its blows, fighting to control his breathing, straining to understand why he was hiding.

The light from the doorway parted for a black shape that slid across the floor, the shadow of a cloaked man who stepped into the room a moment later. From his refuge, Ilissos stared along the floor in a terrified, needle-sharp awareness. He could make out the fur edging of the man's cloak, and the supple leather and glinting buckle of his heavy travelling boots.

"He will come," said a rasping voice. "I bade him, he will come."

Another wave of fear hammered at Ilissos. His juddering fingers fumbled for the amulet as his stomach shuddered. Could someone's mere presence do this?

"We'll talk about the magic when he's gone?" A thin, eager voice, spoken without fear. "Oh, are you staying there? It'll get cold." A dog snuffled in reply, "Stay with your bones then. Tell us when he comes." A second pair of feet with shabby, cracked boots stepped down into the house. If the bones belonged to this man's dog, then Ilissos assumed Gizhurthra had just entered his house.

"The beast will not come in," said the harsh voice. "There is a power about me. It is fear to him."

"I'm not afraid," said Gizhurthra.

"That is because I shield you. As I will shield the other when he comes. But at the hour I open the southern magic to you there will be no shield. Unless you raise one within."

"Yes. I'll get more power then, won't I?"

"Power?" The word sloughed out on a grating breath, Ilissos spasmed with horror at the sound. "What power do you want? Will you command the lice from the beds? *Kh'aar!* You think the energies are toys.

You think what you call magic will make you a great one among these hovels. You will only be a dog among gutter-rats." The man's harsh accent made it clear he was someone from the distant south. The easy sneer of the voice, utterly at home in arrogance, scoured across Ilissos' mind like sand.

"I told you before," whined Gizhurthra, "my power's my own. I didn't get it from wizards or anything. If you tell me about the magic now—"

There was a long hiss, "Your power is your own? Ha! So the great ones say, so they spoke in the high ages. Listen, this thing is wild and strong. It is an ancient beast seeking prey. Can you tame it? It is the strength of those who break the Earth. It is the chaos of the Dark Sea. If it is opened to you, are you able to bear it?"

"Yes, I am. I know what's inside me! They're not just words, you know, the spells I say." There was a scuffling noise and a sudden movement of the shadows. The thin voice of Gizhurthra broke off.

When the cloaked man answered it was in a low, harsh breath as if he had pulled Gizhurthra's face close to his. "Yesterday, I cast from your mind the memory of our meeting with a word, and today I restored it with another. Can you do this? You cannot approach it. A small feat, nothing among the brotherhood, yet it can only be learned in pain." A pause, and the man walked to the doorway. He seemed to be surveying the town. "I was not afraid," he said at last. "I learned many things because I trampled on my fear. Can you do this?" There was silence, and Ilissos, lying in the grip of his own fear, could hear the slow breathing of the man who was its centre. "Give us light," rasped the voice at last. Ilissos heard a fumbling and clattering that indicated a frightened hand.

"I... I can't find the flints," said Gizhurthra at last.

"Hold out the lamp."

Ilissos did not know the next word the man spoke, but it was like a knife in the stomach. He closed his eyes, and when he opened them again, he realised the earthen floor—all that was visible to him—was washed in a yellow glow of flame. Squinting round the pelt, towards his feet, he saw the same light flickering on the walls and ceiling.

"What's that word?" gasped Gizhurthra. "Teach it to me!"

"No! Already you know more than you should use."

"But you said I could—"

"Enough! Close the door and the shutters. He is not far, we will wait."

Gizhurthra obeyed and Ilissos saw the bottom of the door swing out of sight, then heard it close and make a prison for him. He pressed himself desperately against the floor, fighting his terror, forcing back the rapid breathing that might betray him, searching his mind for some escape. Unless Gizhurthra and the stranger left, his only alternatives were to reveal himself or remain behind the bed. But how could he explain why he had hidden at all? And he had heard about southern magic. Not that he understood a word, but if a man whose very presence tore at him learned that he knew his secret... Thus Ilissos lay, mind racing, and the terror swept away every reasoned thought of emerging. He heard the shutters close, watching Gizhurthra's boots as they scuffed about the room, from the door to the furthest window, to the window by the door and—horror!—toward the bed. The boots became black growing shapes against the lamplight, filling his vision, treading across his senses. Fear wound in his stomach like a snake, sweat stung his eyes. Should he bolt for the door as the pelt was pulled aside or spring up now and gain an advantage?

One foot disappeared, then the other, a creaking above him as Gizhurthra knelt on the bed, leaning across it... If he looked down he would see Ilissos. Should he reveal himself first?

"What are you doing? That shutter is closed."

"You have to wedge it. The wind blows it open."

Ilissos almost wept with relief as he listened to Gizhurthra ram a piece of wood under the shutter. A window above him, and he had missed it in the gloom. The lamp was small enough and far enough away to leave a dark trench of shadow behind the bed that had left him hidden. His lips moved as he silently gave thanks. Sirtha tha vei, Cynathé—

"What was that?"

"Didn't hear anything," said Gizhurthra, climbing off the bed.

"Someone is near. Someone unbidden."

"The dog would bark."

"My spirit hears, they may not be close."

135

A tense silence, with Gizhurthra wondering what to do.

"Well, we will wait. Give us fire."

Gizhurthra made a sound as near to laughter as he dared, "Isn't there a word to kindle fire? You can tell me that, surely?"

"Enough!" It was like a blade. "You have flame, why do you seek a word? Make a fire, then wait." Gizhurthra must have protested, for there came a dreadful throaty hiss. "*Kh'aar!* Do not speak! Your thoughts soil my spirit. Make the fire and wait."

Another silence. Ilissos did not doubt Gizhurthra would obey. He listened to logs thudding into the hearth and watched the vraakhin's shuffling feet. At length there was a crackle and the smell of burning as flame added to the light. Ilissos moved his head as much as he dared, but he could not see the fire. Gizhurthra seemed to be crouching on the hearthstone, leaning back against the wall with his feet drawn in. Ilissos thought he could make out his hands as he leaned anxiously on his knees.

No-one spoke or moved, watchfulness tensed the air like a bowstring. It displaced the fear somewhat, but Ilissos knew he must stay where he was. He could make out a swathe of darkness near the fire that did not move with the shadows. It was the robe of one who, with gloom gathered round him and within him, sat and waited.

~

"AND WHERE IS THIS SYRGAN?" asked Wyrdha. "He should have stayed if he's so much in need of me."

"He don't need y'," replied Bardcha. "He's got herbs and things, stuff you use. Wants to sell them to y'."

"I see. Well, tell him where my house is. These travellers are very useful sometimes. He didn't leave anything, did he?"

"No, gone up to Gizzard's. Wants to sell him some."

"Then if Gizhurthra's going to waste it, I'll buy it all. But you mustn't waste this. Ask Antha to heat water in an hour or so and mix this in it." He shook a little powder into a wooden mug.

"What's that?"

"It'll give you a good sleep. Verdje has some too."

"No point. Y' just wake up to it all again."

Wyrdha wanted to say something very sharp to Bardcha. Instead, he told him, "Things are better with sleep, both of you need it. Rest as I told you, and in a few days speak with Verdje."

"No point. I can't help what the fool did. Not to speak ill of the dead, master Wyrdha, but he took it into his head he would go after that thing. Never forced him, did I?"

You did, thought Wyrdha, *and you didn't*. "He made his decision," he said aloud. *Which is true, and I know you only wanted to hurt him, admit that at least*. "Come and lie down. I'll help you."

"No, I'll sit here for a bit. Watch the fire." Bardcha nodded towards the farther end of the inn's large common-room. "Now there's *her*," he said, peering at dark-haired Antha sitting with Verdje in the shadows. "I know what they're sayin', but they'll not listen. Mind's made up, she'll not look the road I'm on."

"Give her some time," said Wyrdha. "And perhaps… draw her in," he added without much hope, then rose resignedly. "I'll see you tomorrow." He placed a hand on the old man's shoulder, nodded to the two women and left the inn. Once outside, the healer let the sadness of the house fall from him. Glancing up at the hill, he saw yellow, fire-lit squares appear at the door and windows of Gizhurthra's lonely house. There was a brief, dark movement of a figure as Gizhurthra closed himself in and the house was a black eyeless shape once more. It struck Wyrdha that there was something very fitting about it.

He waved a greeting to the soldiers on watch by the forge and made his way to the path that threaded up to his home. As he climbed, he found himself wearied. The boughs were a little darker overhead tonight, the path underfoot a little rougher and steeper. He was glad when he emerged from the trees near his house and saw the lamplight on the grass. It surprised him to find that he was stooping.

Warmth moved round him as the door swung in. Yauva was asleep, and by the fire was Azhur and, no surprise, Tyr. Across the hearth, quietly smiling, sat Iethen. Tyrmar stood awkwardly behind her. Sitting beside Iethen was a dignified, elderly man whose long silver hair lay about the collar of his deep red robe. He rose and smiled at Wyrdha with eyes full of kindly knowledge.

"Good evening to you, master healer. We met briefly at the forge. Loremaster Galdtchav of Valderthaan, at your service. Your young friend invited me here for an important meeting."

"Wyrdha," said Tyr, "I've somethin' to tell y'."

CHAPTER 8

The Visit to the Hill

No-one moved in the house on the dark hill. One had not the will, another dared not, and another sat rock-still in an intensity of watchfulness. The mindless fear had left Ilissos for a while, leaving the ordinary anxiety of a man terrified to reveal himself to strangers, one of them probably dangerous and certainly powerful. Just how powerful he did not know, neither did he wish to.

Time edged on. It seemed that it could only be measured by the worsening cramp in the Syrgan's arm and leg. As he tried with tiny movements to ease the pain, he realised that in any other room he would have been discovered already, traced by the scent of the herbs in his bundle. Here the air was heavy with such smells. A few more would not be noticed, except by their freshness. In the respite from terror, Ilissos clutched at Cynathé's amulet. She must be able to deliver him, she and the god of the North, if they were in agreement. He mouthed silent promises, costly offerings at the goddess' altar in Agoras and at the sun-god's shrine. For the first time in his life, his broad white smile was no use to him. But if the gods would not give him kindness for the asking, perhaps he could buy it.

Movement. A long, inward breath. "He is by the hill," said the rasping voice of Gizhurthra's guest. "Stand, we will greet him."

139

The two men rose. Ilissos could see from their feet that they turned to face the door. Gizhurthra's frightened breathing filled the silence. All at once, footsteps outside. A low growl, cut short. A pause, as if the waiting had resumed. Gizhurthra twitched and scuffed his feet.

A slow, cold lance entered Ilissos's mind as the awful voice spoke into the void to the person outside. "Come you by sun or moon? Light they your way in the earth?"

The answer was another chill stab; it pierced through the door, pulling the night in with it. "In the strength of the Dark Sun I am here. I need not flame nor shining, and my power is my own."

"Enter and make the eighth sign. A power has been here."

Ilissos could not tell what it meant, but the feel of it was terrible.

Gizhurthra darted forward, lifted the bolt and laid it on the floor, then moved aside.

The door swung open with a slow squeal and the cold air wound in. Ilissos saw the cautious feet that stepped over the threshold, the frayed hem of a long robe, a heavy, sweeping cloak. A thick staff was planted on the floor, the sound of it hard and final. Then there was the voice, soft and flat as though words were not worth utterance, and in it was a horrid melancholy. "The dog sleeps."

Gizhurthra started, then shuffled behind the man. He closed and bolted the door, then stayed leaning on the door-frame.

"I felt... influences, my Bhanir," said the staff-bearing newcomer. Ilissos was not familiar with the word *Bhanir*, but he easily recognised the deference in the man's voice. The man whose fearful presence had caused Ilissos to irrationally hide behind the bed, was this new man's master. The sad voice continued, "Pressures near at hand. Something lingers. I am concerned."

"Their feast was visited. I sensed it." The master's voice sent a wave of hatred crashing across the tiny room, causing Ilissos to involuntarily clutch at his stomach as his muscles knotted. "But my spells divert our enemies' eyes, they do not see us."

"As you say," replied the staff-bearer flatly. "I drew a shadow round myself at Archraad's gate. Another at the Tor. But you should know that Kharhalkhar's pack could not enter the village, they could not take it."

"Could not? Why?"

"They do not know. Their will failed them. But I assure you once more, Bhanir, we do not need it for the assault or the Dark Sun's rising. There will be many opportunities to wrest it from the old Loremaster."

"Then no matter, we will throw the old Scroll-leech to Kharhalkhar and his brothers," said his master.

The staff-bearer's cloak swirled as he moved to face Gizhurthra. "And this is the one?"

"Welcome, master, welcome," blurted Gizhurthra. 'My house... modest, modest, they don't give me—"

"I was to come myself for this?" said the staff-bearer. "*Mei'h shu h'avra ne'krenu?* Not that I question you, Bhanir."

"You were to come. Braldhar is not equal to it."

"Something to eat?" whined Gizhurthra desperately. He was trying to enjoy his role as the confidante of great men, but he was mortally afraid of them. "You must be starving, cold up on those moors this time of night. There's bread and some meat from yesterday—honoured, master, great honour, don't know how to...." His thoughts wandered a second, then returned, gleaming with confidence. "I've waited for this for years. They haven't a clue round here, but we're drawn together, people like us, people that *know*, eh? Not the common herd, eh? Brotherhood, a cut above. I've heard about *you*, sir, of course."

"And I of you." The sad, soft voice of the staff-bearer cut like a blunt knife. A pause. Ilissos could hear Gizhurthra's quick, excited breathing and saw how his feet shifted about. He was aware, too, of the shimmer of a lie. "Come now, you who dwell apart," said the voice. "You wish to be vraakhin?"

Gizhurthra stopped his fidgeting, "I *am* vraakhin."

"Truly?"

"Yes," said Gizhurthra edgily.

"I mistake my summons." The robe trailed round as the man turned to his master. "Forgive me, Bhanir, but at least I have found you. Where is the one we must admit to the brotherhood?"

"Before you, it is no mistake."

The newcomer turned back to Gizhurthra. A moment vibrant with scrutiny; the lie pulsed, gained strength. "Yes, yes. Bhanir, your pardon. Your eyes read deeper than mine as always. Yes, the marks are there, I see them. Ah, you did not tell me one third part of what is in this one. I would have left the preparations—"

"What marks?" Gizhurthra almost shouted. He was shaking with excitement.

"Those that I may see. My power is my own."

"What?"

"There are such in the world. My power was born with me, and out of it—"

"I'm like that! It's my own, I didn't get it with spells."

"Therefore, we meet. Peace, I will speak. People are told the great ones that were on the earth in the far days came to an end and now there is no-one whose power is part of them, like their blood and their breath. More, we are told that there are few powers in these days and those so feeble men need not trouble with them."

"That's right, that's what they say at the Shrine," broke in Gizhurthra. "I asked a priest once and he—"

"We do not listen to priests," said the unnamed staff-bearer. "They lie, they are ignorant, they serve themselves." Ilissos' muscles quivered like lute strings. "I see it," continued the sad voice. "You asked if the power you knew was in you could truly be there and he gathered his red robe around him and told you he had read in his scrolls that the powers were no more."

"Well, yes, more or less, or... no, you're right, that's what happened."

"And you saw how much he despised you." Silence. "How stupid you were, how confused and deceived. He thrust you away."

"Not thrust, exactly." Gizhurthra's voice faltered a little, sounding fainter.

"I mean, in his heart. How small you felt. Many people have made you feel like this, wretched, small, and dirty. How twisted and broken you thought you were."

"Yes," said Gizhurthra weakly.

"How guilty and confused you felt as you left the priest. It has often been like that."

"Yes." Now there was a hint of a sob.

"How painful, how useless. Arrogance and ignorance."

"Ignorant."

"Ignorant, and so wrong."

"Wrong?"

"Why, yes. Wrong to deny the truth and wrong to spurn one who truly has power."

Now Gizhurthra was weeping. "I have? You really think I have?"

"I do, for I have the skill to see within. All the marks are there."

"What... what are they?"

"You ask a difficult thing. When you have grown in the power I will teach you, not now, but will you trust me?"

Silence for a moment. Gizhurthra sniffed, swallowed hard, and wiped his nose on his sleeve. "Yes," he whispered. "Yes. Nobody ever—I mean, sometimes I didn't believe it myself—" He broke into sobbing, and for a while it was the only sound. The others were silent, Ilissos felt the air tighten. At last Gizhurthra moaned and spoke as best he could. "Nobody ever... well, mother, when I was a boy... and somebody in Lukar I knew—well, he didn't, not really—I get angry a lot and it's hard. People are hard. But not since mother, nobody ever—"

"How well we know," murmured the staff-bearer, his voice sliding into the midst of Gizhurthra's incoherence. It was soft, soothing, and laden with understanding and sweet grief. Ilissos felt a greater tension. "How well we know. They are afraid. Those who lie in the trough of ignorance always strike at those above."

"Above?"

"Indeed, and your heart knows it. You see where you have made your home."

"My home?" It seemed to be a difficult word for Gizhurthra.

"Your heart drives you to live in accordance with what it knows. Come now, why do you dwell apart on your lonely hill save that you know you are *above* these... others?"

It was absurd. Ilissos would have known that yesterday, walking in a field under a morning sun, he would have laughed at this morose logic. But here, lying in the dark with the pressure of the spell in the taut, thick air, it was more sensible than sense, the only way to see things.

He heard Gizhurthra draw in a long breath of amazed relief, "Yes, yes, I see. That's how it works, eh? Never thought, never thought, but now you say it…."

"I say it. And now, will you submit to us? There are still those on the earth whose power is their own—I and my Bhanir, my master, are among them, though we have not said so till now. Once we were as you, but now our power is quickened and active and we seek out the mighty ones, those of the high and ancient race who do not know themselves. There is a brotherhood, a welcoming circle, a safe place. Submit to us and we will open the gates of your power."

"This is beyond you," said the Bhanir. "Your thoughts will hinder us. See to your dog."

Gizhurthra tried once more, "But if you're going to talk about the magic—"

"If you are to be the brotherhood's eyes and ears in this place, you must not hinder what we do. It is your first test. Submit or no."

The passionless statement was enough. Gizhurthra perceived a choice had to be made if power was to be gained. He scuffed his way to the door and out into the night.

The staff-bearer was the first to speak. "Well," he sighed, "little in *that* one."

"Still, it is good. When he is fully ours, the energies will find more room in him. Meanwhile, he plays his part."

"The aura?"

"Certainly. The spirits will withdraw from it, he will think he has chased them away."

"You spoke of the assault?"

"No, we must wait for that," said the master. "The Moon priest we found—I sense him near. He still carries all the words and influences we placed on him when we spoke with him in the market. His malady grows, I can feel it. He will go straight to the healer's house and meet the one from Lukar tonight."

"Is the one from Lukar ready?"

"He is. Your Harrak played their part and their marksman shot true.

He has his wound."

"They did not meet me at Braldhach," said the staff-bearer.

"They will not. They tried to take a child and drew the Shrine guard down on themselves. I warned them, I set my fear on them. Now they are captive or dead."

"The Harrak fear you indeed, Bhanir. They call you V'karra, the terrible wizard."

"Then I shall be more terrible. But no matter, they did their work before the guard struck them. Our little vraakhin with his dog has gone to the one from Lukar, and spoken the words I taught him."

"Better if you had spoken them, Bhanir."

"He refused me entry, that healer. One day I will settle with him. Still, I was wise, I chose not to break him. I will not punish so openly with our move so near."

Ilissos, somehow, felt in his own trembling mind a stir of uncertainty in this V'karra's thoughts. He had been unable to force his way into the healer's home. This had frightened him, but he was hiding it. How Ilissos knew this he could not tell. He felt the angry mind shake itself free of the memory.

The staff-bearer broke the momentary silence. "A hunter came for Kharhalkhar from the town here, but he did not live."

"Then we are repaid. And Kharhalkhar?"

"Returned to Vel Charig. He starts to gather his kin and will come to us again at Lukar."

"There is word from Lord Gehrava?"

"A message came to Archraad. He will join us there for the rising."

There was a silence, and Ilissos could feel the breathing of the man who was the centre of his fear. His next word was low, eager, charged with desire, brim-full of waiting, "Vardresh?"

In a soft, fierce whisper, the staff-bearer replied, "Ready, Bhanir. The tribes have every sword ready. They wait only for our word. I have traded thought with our brother in Vardresh and he is fully prepared. He will unleash his arts with his fullest strength."

V'karra made a long, deep sound in his throat like a satisfied tiger. "Hatred is a wondrous thing, to live so long and grow such strength.

On Renewal Night, the North will begin to die. I am glad we chose that day; they will feel it more."

~

EVERYONE SAT STARING AT TYR. At length, Iethen was the one to break the trembling silence. She eased herself slowly and happily over to her son, hugged him and swayed him back and forth. "Oh, love," she crooned. "Oh, love, love, love."

Tyr hugged her back, his chin on her shoulder and his eyes closed. A little tear escaped and dampened the side of his nose. He sighed, deeply and happily.

"And it was there, at the feast?" asked Wyrdha quietly. The boy nodded, still in his hug.

Old Galdtchav leaned forward, "The greatest respect laddie, but I have to ask. Is it possible, even a bit, that you'd dozed off? What I mean is, might you have dreamed it?"

Tyr didn't even need to think about that, "Oh, no. Not in the middle of the square, not with folk dancin' round me. I weren't tired anyhow."

"But your father found you asleep."

"Oh aye, but that were after. It were the... the thing got me to sleep." Then he glanced at Azhur and burst into a laugh, "What a face! Y' want to see y'self."

The young novice started, suddenly aware of the astounded mask his features had become. He opened his mouth once or twice, gasped, then managed his own question. "A human figure, Tyr? Very vigorous and lithe, like... like a dancer? An athlete?"

"Aye. All bright and shinin', like it were made of fire. But I never saw anybody dance like that thing. Right quick it were, like birds and squirrels and that. There's nobody moves that way."

"And the face? The face was special?"

A little silence. "Oh," said Tyr softly. His eyes became unfocussed, and he turned his face against his mother's head. It was answer enough.

Galdtchav touched the mystified and thunderstruck Tyrmar on the arm, "Let's ask your father, Tyr. He knows you best after all."

"Him *and* me," said Iethen.

"Of course. Master headman, have you any notion of what this could be about?"

Tyrmar slowly shook his great head, "Not a damn clue. Brilliant, though, isn't it?"

Galdtchav nodded slowly, "It is indeed, master Tyrmar. It is indeed." The old priest turned suddenly to Azhur. His eyes were wide, intent, and his lips were tight and serious. "The Eighth Scroll, I think," he breathed urgently.

Azhur sat up. "Yes," he said. "Oh, yes. And I think the twelfth and fourteenth. And the index to the three hundred and twelfth."

"Three hundred and twelfth?" queried Galdtchav.

"For the histories, Anthu."

"Ah, yes. Yes, of course. Bless me, what that laddie knows."

"Ey!" said Tyrmar suddenly.

Iethen looked out from her embrace with Tyr, "Are y' havin' another idea, love?"

"Aye, I am."

"Not another feast?"

"No, no, I thought somethin' different, somethin' right special after Tyr seein' that... whatever it is."

"But y' don't know what it is."

"I know, Ieth, but it's *special*," insisted the headman. "I mean, the Anthu here very near fell off his seat when Tyr told us!"

"I wouldn't care to commit myself *just* at this point," said Galdtchav.

"Aye, but I reckon y've got a fair idea. Somethin' from Arna, isn't it?"

"We'd have to consult the Scrolls," put in Azhur quickly.

"Well, you just do that, my lad, but *meanwhile....*" Tyrmar paused and glanced around, chewing his lower lip for effect. "Meanwhile, seein' as Renewal Night's comin' up and that, and seein' as we've got the Anthu here with us, and y'self, Azhur, and... what's name...?"

"The Lord Bal-jarrak."

"Aye, him, shame his missus couldn't stay."

"Oh, I don't know," said Galdtchav absently.

"Eh?"

"Nothing, nothing. Do go on.'"

"Well, seein' as we've got more and better priests in our village than we've had for fifty years, apart from that miserable sod as insulted Azhur yesterday—savin' y' presence, Anthu—and seein' as all them things happened to my boy here, I thought, well, could y' do a ritual for us? Afore y' go home, like? We never gets the chance to see them things, not proper, like. Folk'd appreciate that, they would. Will y'? Will y' do that?"

Azhur gasped aloud, then became excited and stared eagerly across at Galdtchav.

The old priest thoughtfully extended his lower lip, then smiled a slow, broad smile. "I would be honoured indeed, master Tyrmar. May I suggest we celebrate the ritual of the Coming Forth? It is the traditional prelude to the Renewal: the birth of Lord Arna followed by the rebirth of the dynasty of the Northland."

Tyrmar slapped his knee. "That's crackin'!" He laughed, leaned over to Tyr and ruffled his hair, then said, "We'll enjoy that. Oh, aye. Just… what is it, if y' don't mind me askin'?"

Azhur pounced on the chance to apply his knowledge. "The Coming Forth? That's the ritual that celebrates the birth of Arna. He was born from the Deep Fire, as you know."

"Aye," said Tyrmar. "Well, I've heard somethin' like that. Haven't y' heard that, Ieth?"

"I have that, love. Very important, they say."

Now Tyr was interested, "Deep Fire," he said. "Under the sea, right out west?"

Azhur nodded keenly, "The fire of creation," he said impressively. "The world-fire. It was there before everything, and everything goes back to it and comes from it. Even Lord Arna."

"Does he? I thought he made everything."

"Yes, he made the whole universe, but he was in the Flame when he did."

A long silence. Wyrdha laughed deeply, "I can hear the wheels, Tyr."

"Shut up, shut up, I'm thinkin'."

"You don't need to tell me, I know the signs well."

Tyr bit his lip, stared fixedly at the dark, and waved his hands with his fingers in an odd spasmed position. "Ah!"

"Y're for it now, lad," Tyrmar looked at Azhur as he spoke.

"Right, right. So Arna were in the Flame, and...," said Tyr with more waving motions. "Right. How'd he get in the Flame, then?"

Azhur's head went oddly to one side, "How...?"

"Well, he made the Flame, didn't he?"

"Ah..."

"C'mon, thought y' knew all that."

And here the young priest's fingers leapt at each other and began to grapple, "I, I don't remember reading that exactly, anywhere."

"Well, he must've, because he made everything, so he must've made the Flame too, so there must've been just him and no Flame, so he must've made the Flame and then went in it and then did everythin' else."

"Ah... no, no. The life of the Flame is in everything, and Arna's life was the life of the Flame."

"Don't *quote* it, laddie, *explain* it," said Galdtchav, greatly amused.

"Ah... he was the Flame's life, because he was in it—within it. That's the hundred and fifty-third scroll. His life was one with the life of the Flame, so... so, he would *depend* on the Flame."

"What scroll's that in, then?"

"It's not actually *in* a scroll, not one that I've *read*."

"Ohh, y're makin' it up, then," yelled Tyr in triumph. "Y' don't know, do y'?"

Galdtchav swayed chuckling in his seat and slapped his knee. "I think your learned friend would say he's just thinking aloud, laddie."

"Eh?"

"It's what Loremasters say when they, ah..."

"When they don't know!" said Wyrdha suddenly. He was enjoying the whole thing immensely.

They all burst out laughing, covering Azhur's embarrassment and letting Iethen and Tyrmar enjoy seeing their son get the better of a not-quite-priest. True, the issues involved were less than clear to them, but had they known there was such a thing as a theological argument, and that they had just witnessed one, they would have been even happier.

"Allow me to assist my assistant," begged Galdtchav. "Let me trump him just this once. The official statement regarding Lord Arna and the Deep Fire is that the Fire is an... extension of Arna's being... part of him that stretches out around him, if you follow me, and so he and the Fire are one and the same. Now, that's not in the Scrolls in so many words, but long ago some wizened old Loremasters like myself put together various statements from the Scrolls and the result was—well, what I've just said. So, you see, us priests aren't completely at a loss. Is that even the slightest help, Tyr?"

"Think so," said Tyr cautiously. "What's the right word for it? Y've got sort of proper words for things, haven't y'?"

"Proper words? Oh, I see. If a thing isn't fraught with religious complexity it can't be true. Well, the *proper* term is the doctrine of Inherently Simultaneous Coexistence in the Extension of Reciprocal Being, but I shouldn't let that worry you in the slightest."

"Bloody hell!"

"Tyr!" scolded Iethen.

"Please don't worry, good lady," said Galdtchav. "My own sentiments on first encountering that term could well have been expressed in similar terms."

Wyrdha suddenly leaned forward, "But what you do know, my Lord Loremaster," he said, "is that you will return to the Shrine and make straight for the Archives to test what Tyr has told us." He and Galdtchav locked eyes. Wyrdha's voice became an eager whisper, "You will, I would guess, go to the Addenda to the Scrolls of the Founding, to Ar-ven's account of Fyrieg."

And here Galdtchav sat up in his chair as though struck, "But they're disputed; the Addenda are disputed. Unread for decades—"

"Disputed by some," said the healer firmly.

Galdtchav drew a hand over his face and gazed into memory as the ancient writings passed before his inner eye. "But surely you don't think...?" He said no more.

Nor did he have the chance. A moaning began behind them on the far side of the room. Yauva was shifting uneasily, weakly waving his arms in front of him. Wyrdha went to him and sat on the side of the bed. The young man's eyes were staring, his honest, open face ran with sweat that reflected the little lamp beside him. He raked his fingers through his yellow hair, then pawed at Wyrdha's sleeve, alternately grasping and stroking. "Got to go home," he managed through shallow breaths. "Got to go home."

"Did we wake y', love?" asked Iethen as she joined the healer. "We was a bit noisy, wasn't we? I'm ever so sorry." She stroked the tangled hair and Yauva seized her wrist.

"I can't stay here! I've got to get away!"

"No, lovey, y've hurt y' leg. Y'll just make it worse if y' get up."

"No, no, that black thing's come back, it's coming down, look."

"You're dreaming about the storm cloud again," Wyrdha told his patient. "Wake up properly and it'll all be gone."

Iethen took a wet cloth from a bowl by the bed and wiped Yauva's face. "Such a nice lad," she murmured. "Right shame, it is." Yauva relaxed a little, swallowed and looked around. This time he met their eyes. "There now, lovey. No more clouds, eh?"

"No. No more clouds." He drew his hand across his face. "But somethin's comin', I can feel it. There's somethin' comin'."

And three loud knocks rattled the healer's door.

Wyrdha was at his front step in moments, staring down at the round little man who occupied it. Leaning on a staff, hood up against the rain, the traveller gripped his stomach and gazed up with large, bleary eyes.

"Are you—are you the healer?" he asked faintly, in a voice rippling with nausea.

"I am he," said Wyrdha cautiously. "And you, I think, are in need of me, yes? Come in, while your legs permit." The man tottered into the house, tugging a sodden travelling-bag after him. Wyrdha lost no time. "Let me see your eyes. Look up. Hm. Sweating and fever, yes. Dizzy, sickly, can't eat? Yes. Pain and trembling in the limbs, no doubt. Quite so." He stepped back. "You haven't been speaking to someone called Baljarrak, have you?"

"Bal...?"

"Never mind. Throw your cloak over there—Tyr, would you mind? Now, tell us your name and join the company."

The little man shuffled into the group around the fire. "Brilt'thig Na-kh'hakhaloth," he wheezed, with no small difficulty. "I've just come down from Lukar. Thank you so much, master healer, the Lady love you. They said I'd find you here."

"Really? Who said?"

"Oh, people I met in a market a few miles away. This came on me quite suddenly while I was talking to them, and they said I should go to you if it got any worse. Gave me directions. Recommended you highly. There was a very nice fellow from the east, very polite, and his friend, a kind of swarthy chap, foreigner, didn't say much."

"Wyrdha…"

"I know, Tyr. Do go on, sir."

Brilt'thig took the cup of warm wine that Iethen handed him, sipped and settled into his seat. He scratched at the sparse beard that clung beneath his lip. "Well, that's it, really. Just as I shook hands with them, I felt this coming on—very sudden too—I must have looked dreadful. They said, 'What's wrong?' and when I told them they said, 'Ah, You ought to see the healer at Falakhoth because he had special herbs for this kind of thing, or so they'd heard.' Then they gave me directions and here I am. Been thanking the Lady ever since for my good fortune. Could've missed those chaps completely, after all."

The mention of the goddess' goodness got Tyrmar animated. "She's been good to us an all," he said with enthusiasm. "We honours her round here, of course." Then he stared at Brilt'thig, brow furrowed. "Y'know, if y' don't mind me sayin' so, y' look a bit like a priest."

The little man sniffed, choked, and laughed as best he could. "Don't apologise, sir. It's not a disease, you know." He swept a hand down his deep blue robe, then pointed to the amulet of the Moon on his wrist. "Priest of Iathena, fourth order, serving at the Towers in Lukar. I've come down here to visit—oh!" He pressed Wyrdha's bunched-up handkerchief against his mouth, for he had realised that there before him was a senior priest of Arna. Frozen in embarrassment, he still could not stop the barking little cough that began to punctuate the silence and send regular quivers across his ample second chin.

Tyr sniggered audibly in anticipation of some fine entertainment.

"Baranthu," intoned Wyrdha soothingly, "may I present the Anthu Galdtchav na-Vajhavhru, Senior Loremaster of the Shrine?" The old priest nodded serenely and Brilt'thig struggled to his feet.

"The Moon salutes the Sun," he gasped, swaying. "The servant of the handmaid bows before the hand of the master."

"Charmed," said Galdtchav. "But don't fall over, laddie. Take your seat, you're a sick man."

His blue-robed salutant flopped down. "Thank you," he gasped, "thank you." He peered round the circle. "I have to do that, you know. My duty. Iathena's priests must honour Arna's priests."

"Very proper, very proper," remarked Wyrdha. "Allow me to complete the introduction of our circle." And he went round each person by name. When he came to Azhur, Brilt'thig began to rise.

"I don't think you have to do it again," said Azhur. "I'm actually still a novice."

"Ahh," breathed Brilt'thig, and re-applied the handkerchief. Then he pointed beyond the fireside group. "And... er... is your other friend asleep?"

"Hopefully, replied the healer. "A young fellow from Lukar, injured the other day. I don't suppose you ever take a refreshment at the *Golden Carp?*"

Brilt'thig sat up at once. "*Golden Carp?*" He quickly shuffled over to the bed and peered down at the patient. "Good gracious me," he remarked.

Wyrdha glanced at Galdtchav and folded his arms. "I think, master Brilt'thig, you're about to tell me something quite unexpected. Aren't you?"

The priest continued to gape down at the bed, dabbing his nose the while. "Well, it's just that—well, bless me, it's young Yauva, mistress Yenl's lad. His uncle's my Archpriest."

Wyrdha looked up at the shadows moving on his low wooden ceiling. "Something is... *happening* here," he murmured to no-one in particular.

~

THE AIR, IT SEEMED, grew thicker in the vraakhin's hut. Heavier, more oily-foetid, a force in itself, and reluctant to crawl into Ilissos' lungs. He tried to breathe cautiously, knowing that the deep, rapid gasps he ached for would surely betray him. He fought to control his body that trembled more each minute. Gizhurthra was still outside, anxiously stroking his sleeping dog in the chill night, while the two sorcerers talked calmly of appalling things and laid dreadful plans against the north. Every so often some phase or word would judder through the cloying air to stab at Ilissos' nerves and stomach. Especially painful, with a horrid sense of foreboding, was any mention of "the Rising," though he could not understand what they meant. He also heard them speak of something they called the Dark Sun, a name that made no sense at all, but each syllable was like gravel rubbed in a sore, a sharp, mad meaninglessness that scoured the very nerves. Tears burned his eyes and sweat seeped through his clothes. The light-hearted traveller who had, not so long before, come jauntily up the hill and entered Gizhurthra's house, was beaten down by the tension of hiding. His happy spirit nurtured in the green southern hills had fallen into some deep rift within until the threat should pass.

Eventually, the onslaught died down, and Ilissos needed to endure nothing more than a tremor in his limbs as he recovered some strength and sanity in the hope the sorcerers would eventually think of other business and leave. Then he could crawl painfully down the hill, get far away from this place, and try to find himself again. They talked in low voices about many things, but nothing affected Ilissos.

Once Gizhurthra tapped on the door and nervously called, "Masters? Finished, masters?" but they ignored him.

At last, with almost unimaginable relief, the Syrgan heard V'Karra say, "It is enough. We will go. Make the tenth sign. Give me your hand and we will speak the words."

Chairs scraped and shadows moved as the men moved towards each other. A weak blue light began to flicker about the floor and a low, stately sounding chant commenced in earnest.

Deep in Ilissos' bones a fire grew. It baked the marrow, seared the joints, ran burning along the nerves. Now, with mind and body seemingly cracked and blistered, the glowing destroyer swirled and swept away, out through his feet, and there arose in his ashen self a miasma of disgust. It seemed that twisting, filthy things writhed and smeared themselves among his innards. There was a loathsome wriggling beneath his skin, vile pulpy movement under his tongue. His soul was sickened, utterly revolted, and his whole impulse was to flee to air and bright water and smiling faces and scream for love to clean him. But he dared not, for he could not say what would come at him if he were discovered. In a distant corner of his mind he knew that, still, he had his life. Thus far.

The horror and the loathing continued to increase, and deepened till he was hung, seemingly undefended, like a naked spirit in the dark, over an abyss a million miles below where light was swallowed. He must not fall, it would be the end of him, the utter end. There was no choice now, for a greater fear had come. Discovered or not, he must wake from the destroying vision or be lost. And so, in hideous panic, he writhed and dragged a cry together in his mind, drew it to his lips and, howling to the gods or whoever listened, vomited out his agony. And he was in his body again, hammering his hands on the floor, howling, howling, but though the voice was his, the thought was another's and words came that he had never learned:

A Bhanir! A rhukh'halva! Yevu sh'hima, Yevu ra'shem n'achani! Krenu va Yevu!

An awful shriek, a rush of light, a wave of energy flung Ilissos about and sent the bed whirling across the room. He found himself scrabbling at the feet of the man who held the staff. From its tip came a searing blue-white blaze like an immovable lightning. Every corner of the hut was exposed, the Syrgan most of all.

Near him, V'Karra struggled among the tumbled chairs. He got to his feet, but fell again, hampered by his wide black robe. He grasped the table, lurched up, and forced himself to turn and face Ilissos. His limbs were shaking and his body shuddered with violent gasps of panic. There was a hawk's face within a scarlet turban. It was horribly twisted in a deathly glare, eyes bulging in terror.

"Not here!" V'Karra choked. "You may not send him here, not now! I am too strong!" He thrust out a palm. "I forbid it! I forbid it!"

"Who are you?" the staff-bearer shouted at Ilissos. He glared horribly

Every corner of the hut was exposed, the Syrgan most of all.

through black-orbed eyes laced with reflected awful light, and Ilissos felt a scrutiny claw at his mind.

Even in that mad moment, he knew somehow, despite his debilitating terror, that the sorcerers were mortally afraid of him. He could not understand it, but it fed him a grain of hope, "I... I am Ilissos of Syrga," he babbled, "a story-teller, a traveller. I visited the varcchin, but I was afraid, I hid—"

"You *heard!*" hissed the staff-bearer.

"I will forget, I did not understand."

"You will forget," spat the hawk-faced V'Karra. "You will forget forever. I will burn your mind." He stretched out a hand, and Ilissos could feel the force that twined around his fingers.

"Master, no! Mercy!" He flung himself forward, grabbing at the master's black robe. V'Karra roared and brought his hand down. Suddenly that other voice was on the Syrgan's tongue again:

A Bhanir! A Yevu!

V'Karra screamed. The evil force aimed at Ilissos, went wide and impotent. The man was battered back against the wall and fell. He struggled and squirmed like an upturned beetle, shrieking like a dying beast through spurts of bloody foam, before he twisted round on spasmed limbs and went animal-like on knees and elbows across the floor. V'Karra clawed at the door, fell out upon the ground, and struggled away. His screams receded faintly down the hill.

There was an awful quiet as the staff-bearer gazed at Ilissos intently, great, sad eyes showing a mixture of fascination and fear, filled with the bleaching light. He walked round him a little as if he were circling a coiled snake. "And what is this?" he breathed. "A little peasant from the Green Jewel who is not content with Cynathé's chants! How is it you call like the Great Angel with the ancient prayers?" He stopped pacing and leaned forwards. "Do you know what you have said?"

Ilissos found that he could meet the man's eyes, "I think I called on Cynathé and... and was it Arna? The Northmen's god? But, no." He shook his head. "I did not know these words. But they are a terror to him." He motioned towards the door. "What do they say?"

"I will not speak of that, my charge is a different one." The man was breathing slowly and deeply, his eyes wide and staring. Ilissos saw the intent that formed in them, but he was too worn out for fear. "There are laws, old laws, that say you cannot touch... him and live. You snatched at him as if he were like—other men. Like you. There is a penalty." He raised his staff, then pointed it forwards.

Ilissos buried his face in his hands, sobbing afresh, "No, master, no. I meant no harm, I was afraid." Then a force entered his body and he could speak no more. He tried to stretch out his hands towards the vraakhin but he fell forward into darkness, away from the body that sprawled, the wreck of a man, at the staff-bearer's feet.

CHAPTER 9

The Ritual and the Tor

As a cold but pleasant spring afternoon wore on, Oiechē, the miller's daughter from Tarnesh, was starting to tire of watching dragonflies by the riverbank below the Braldhach falls. Next to her sat the gangling figure of Rurhdt, a local farm hand. The things Oiechē imagined doing with him were going to require a little more privacy than they were likely to find by the much-frequented river.

"Look!" he said, breaking into her thoughts. "There's a dragonfly the colour of your eyes."

"Oh, y're sweet," Oiechē told him. "Y' really does cheer folks up, y' know."

"Does I?" exclaimed her swain. "I never thought of it. How does I do that, then?"

"Well," said the girl tantalisingly, "Y're sort of daft—"

"Daft?"

"Oh, in a nice sort of way. Y' funny, like. Y' makes folk laugh. That's how I started fancyin' y'."

"Y' really fancies me? Really?"

"I do," said the girl, laughing and putting her head to one side in a way that had *exactly* the right effect.

"Oh, Oiechē! Well… I does too."

159

"What, fancy y'self?"

"No, I fancies you! Oh, Oiechē, me love, do y' think y' dad'll let us get wed?"

"Y'd have to come and work for him. Y' fancy bein' a miller?"

"I'd turn the mill meself if it'd get y' for me, I would. Oh, Oiechē, let's ask him."

"Ooh! Well, my love, I reckon we oughta talk about this. Just our two selves, like."

"Oh. Oh, aye. Where'll we go, then? There's always folks up and down the river this time of year."

"Let's go to the woods," she suggested. "Nobody goes there."

This muted Rurhdt's passion considerably, "Dunno 'bout that, Oiechē. Y' know what they say—"

"Rurhdt! Give over! Y're not a feared of the Tor, are y'?"

"Well, I... I.... Well, there's been stories about that place time out of mind!"

"Aye, well, I feels like bein' a bit wild today."

"Oh, I... I fancies bein' wild today and all, Oiechē. I fancies bein' wild with y'."

"All right, then. Course, if y're a feared of the Tor..."

Rurhdt found himself suddenly possessed of both ardour and courage. He wondered briefly why he always did what Oiechē said whether he wanted to or not, but he decided it must be the effect of love and gallantry, that kind of thing. "Right y' are then," he said. Once among the trees, his courage proven, Rurhdt's ardour flared afresh. "Oh, Oiechē," he gasped. "Oh, y're that lovely y' is. All sweet and dumpy and smellin' of hay!"

"Y' *what?*"

"Oh, fresh hay, me love. Which is very sweet and pleasant and invigoratin' and—oh, give's a snog!"

Oiechē let herself be reminiscent of the new-mown hay, which did indeed invigorate Rurhdt considerably. Several minutes later, she halted his rapturous inhalation of the harvest.

"What?" he gasped.

"There's people over there. Pickin' mushrooms or somethin'."

"Don't care, come here!"

"Well, I care! I likes me privacy! We'll go to the Tor, Rurhdt, there's definitely nobody there."

"The Tor? The Hill in the Wood? Oh, Oiechē, now listen—"

"Rurhdt, I do believe I'm braver than y' are! Perhaps I ought to just go on home."

"Oh, don't do that! Oh, Oiechē, I'm brave for you, I am!" Oiechē giggled and grabbed Rurhdt's hand. Together they plunged into the deep wood. Motionless and calm, the clearing received the pair. The cave mouth yawned silently at them, the barren mound lying there like a dead thing.

"Strewth, it's quiet here," muttered Rurhdt. "Gives me the willies."

"What, y' never been here afore?" said Oiechē.

"Bleedin' right I ain't. Don't tell me y' have."

"I have! Used to come here with Revkha, and Gerzhet used—"

"Oiechē! Y' mean I'm not the first!"

"Rurhdt! D' y' know what age I am?"

"Oh. Aye, well, I just—"

"I know, but y're the first that's, y'know, *real*, like. Like I really, really means it."

"Y'do? Oh, I don't—oh, bloody hell!"

"Oh, what is it now, Rurhdt?"

"Look at that! That's a wolf turd, that is! In the grass, look!"

Oiechē stooped to examine the alarming object, "That could be anythin'. How do y' know it's a wolf?"

"I just does! I works on a farm, y' know! Y' got to know if there's been wolves about. I'm tellin' y' a wolf did that!"

"Well, what if it was a wolf? It's not here now."

"That don't look too old to me. Bugger, there's another there! I think we ought to just go back, y' know. It's goin' to rain anyhow."

"Oh, well, if y're scared of a bit of dog muck..."

"Now don't y' start that scared thing, Oiechē. Y'... y're tryin' to get y' own way, y' know. Y' always does it."

The girl's lip trembled, "Rurhdt," she quavered. "Oh, Rurhdt, I thought y' loved me."

"I does, stop it!"

"Well, y' called me selfish, and y' said.... Y' said—" A sob heaved itself out. "Oh, Rurhdt, I'm that unhappy! Comfort me, Rurhdt. Don't hurt me, comfort me!" Sobbing began in earnest, but comfort, Rurhdt found, was easily combined with savouring the scent of new-mown hay. "Oh, Rurhdt," crooned his love, "that's really comfortin', that is. Oh, y're that strong."

"I does a lot of heavy liftin'," admitted Rurhdt, grinning modestly.

"Say y' sorry, then."

"Eh?"

"For what y' said. Say y' sorry."

This seemed to Rurhdt to make less than complete sense. The issue, he suspected, was not completely resolved despite what Oiechē said, but her demand for an apology was so emphatic it gave her a definite, if elusive, air of correctness. And besides, gallantry.... "Sorry," he said, inevitably.

Oiechē brightened at once, "All right then, I accepts y' apology. We'll not mention it again."

Rurhdt struggled with a strange sense there was something not right with this. Even if that were true, he thought, it would be very difficult to discover exactly what. "Oh. Right," he said. "Can I have a snog then?"

"Course y' can. Come here!"

They found a mossy niche behind a rock at the foot of the little hill and allowed their restored relationship to develop for quite some time.

After a while they sagged back on the moss and relaxed in each other's arms.

"Gettin' dull," observed Rurhdt. "Hope it don't rain."

"Colder and all," said Oiechē, and nestled closer.

"Bloody cold," Rurhdt agreed. "It's like winter here. Hang on!"

"What, me love? Should have brought me shawl."

"I hopes me eyes aren't goin' funny."

"What's wrong with them? Look all right to me. A nice brown colour, like our sow."

"Well, is it me, or is it darker over there than anywhere else? Hope I don't need them seein'-glass things. I heard they costs a fortune."

Oieché peered along the foot of the Tor where the slope of the hill met the flat ground. She could make out a side view of the steps leading down into the dark cave. "Do y' know," she said, "I think y' might be right, me love. It's sort of foggy or misty or somethin' along there."

"Not smoke is it? Fire in the cave?"

"Can't smell smoke, and it ain't driftin'. Ooh!" Oieché plunged back behind their rock, stifling giggles. "There's somebody come out that cave!" she whispered. "Am I respectable? Oh, me hair!"

Rurhdt tried not to laugh, "Shush, will y'! Don't give us away!"

"Why not? We're not doin' nothin' wrong!"

"I know, but—who's that raggy old feller? Its not y' dad, is it?" They both snorted with hilarity.

"My dad! What a cheek! Look at him: skinny old scarecrow."

They watched as the figure, shrouded in robes with a swathe of wrappings around the head and face, turned to face the cave mouth. The person spread out their hands, then walked backwards a little way, stooped in a reverent bow.

"Come forth if it please you, great one," he said in a low, crackling voice. The couple behind the stone found themselves rubbing at their hands and faces as a chafing sensation of barren dryness crept over them. Rurhdt found himself thinking of shed snakeskin, shrivelled by summer heat. "Come," repeated the voice. "Look for a while on the place where you will rule. How I anticipate that day."

"What the hell's this?" whispered Rurhdt.

"Reckon it's some old lad full of scrumpy," said Oieché hopefully.

"I don't think so, my love. He ain't drunk."

They watched, anxious and fascinated, but nothing further happened.

"Do y' know, I feel like I'm makin' an arse of meself sat here worryin'," said Rurhdt at last. "I let this place get to me, I did. I'm just goin' to say hello to that feller and his friend and we'll be on our way."

"Rurhdt!"

"Well, y' wanted privacy and y' ain't goin' to get none with him about now are y'? Which is a bit annoyin' I do say, but there y' are. So, come on, my—oh hell! Oh, bloody hell! Oh Arna, Iathena!"

"What is it, lovey, what?"

"Look at it, look—"

Together they stared horrified at the cloud of shadow by the cave-mouth. Long guttural, rattling breaths could be heard from the opening, along with a scraping sound as if something huge was dragging itself up a stairway. Out of the cave, over the mouldering steps, came the questing snout of some grotesque beast. A black shape with obscene slits that dilated in the murky air and a longer split that opened to emit the ragged breaths. The elongated, tapering mass of sinew looked as though a horse's head had been seized and stretched in a deforming torture.

The robed man was still backing away, bowing and moving his out-spread arms in what looked like welcome. "You have been confined under the earth too long, great G'chraada," said the dreadful, wheezing voice. "Though your highways honeycomb the world below, come and see the sphere above where you shall be worshipped here long. Shield yourself with your glorious shadow, defy the sun, be proud in the sphere he thinks is his. All of us shall welcome you when your time comes. Not many days and the first stroke shall fall. Your servant at your great temple on the Plain is prepared. Come forth now and savour the upper air."

With more grunting and heaving, a gigantic clawed hand clamped down on the steps and a huge head emerged. Grotesque, horned, slavering. The air around it seemed filthy; tiny shapes flickered from it like bloated flies disturbed on carrion. It was the centre of the shadow, the counterpoint to anything that sought to live. The shoulders of the beast remained in the opening of the cave while the great head moved slowly from side to side as though taking in the view of the clearing. The man before it stood and waited. At last there was a rushing, guttural sound as the thing drew in a deep breath. Its long mouth opened to reveal jagged brown teeth, and with a sound that felt like the very voice of the under-world, far below any depth or pit, the thing said, *Mine.*

"Yours indeed, great one," grated the swathed man. "By right of strength, by right of length of days, by right of just revenge, by right of recompense. For did not this world invade that blessed darkness where you and your brothers ruled? Did not the upstart drive back your bound-aries, and should you not take this place and be repaid?"

"Come forth now and savour the upper air."

The horned head tilted up to regard the sky. *Good*, said the beast. *Soon*.

The man bowed deeply, and as he did so there came a scuffling and snarling and, running from the shadow under the trees, a host of wolves entered the clearing. They gathered behind the man, fur rising on their backs, yellow eyes staring up at the creature.

You see me, it said. *Bow*.

Insanely, the wolves bent their forepaws under and lowered their heads to the ground before the monster.

Good, repeated the beast. *Good*.

Rurhdt and Oiechē, numb with horror, stared and stared at this unnatural obeisance.

And then they saw the wolves transform.

The pair wrenched their eyes from the mad tableau to look at each other. In silent agreement they went, by tiny movements and praying to any god that could bear that sight. They kept the rock between them and the horrors as they edged over the ground, hardly breathing, till they reached the edge of the trees. Then they picked their way, step by little silent step, till they emerged to the sound of Braldhach falls in the distance. They fled like the wind to Tarnesh with never a word spoken and threw themselves into the miller's house. Oiechē's mother shrieked, scattered her baking. Oiechē flung herself on her, shaking, mouth open in the scream she could not utter.

"What's this, girl? What y' done now?"

"The door, the door!" gabbled Oiechē. "Rurhdt, the door!"

Hardly able to move for terror, Rurhdt moved back towards the door as Oiechē's father, Gern the miller, appeared in the doorway.

"What the hell's this?"

Without thinking, the lad seized the miller, dragging him inside, before slamming the door shut and the solid beam into place. Oiechē's hands shook as she pulled the bolts to and moved around locking the window shutters.

"I said what the hell's this?" bellowed Gern.

"Oh, dad! We been up Braldhach Tor—"

At once Gern hammered his fist into Rurhdt's face. "What'd I tell y'? Y're *never* to take my daughter up there!" He strode over to Oiechē and

166

slapped her hard with each hand. "And that's for y' to teach y' some sense! What was y' doin' up there? Tell me!"

"Oh, dad," whimpered the girl. "Don't hit me! There's a horrible thing. We saw it, this horrible thing...."

"Talk sense! What horrible thing?" There was a blow to the door. "Bugger off and mind y' manners!" roared Gern. "We're on family business here!"

Silence.

"Don't let it in," stammered Rurhdt as he cowered on the floor. "Don't let it in, sir, don't open the door!"

"I'm not openin' that door till I get some sense out of you pair!" said Gern. "I don't care who it is."

A blow of monstrous force fell, that tore door and frame from the wall and ripped away the iron bolt and the brackets of the splintered beam. Gern and his daughter fell under a barrage of wood. The women shrieked, Rurhdt howled.

A man stepped into the room. He was filthy, bloodstained, and naked. His lean body was a mass of sinew. "We want them," he said. "They saw."

"Y' dirty bugger!" yelped Gern's wife. "Cover y'self up!"

"I likes the freedom," replied Kharhalkhar, and they saw the long, black, cruel nails on his fingers. Others like him entered the room, and they began to fulfil their errand.

~

BAL-JARRAK SAT HUNCHED in a heavy wooden seat and glowered morosely at the people of Falakhoth. He had not enjoyed their company and watching them assemble for the ritual did nothing to dispel the sourness that had been seeping out of him since his arrival. There had been the embarrassing moment when he had asked to be taken to his room and had been awkwardly told he was already in *the* room. His disgust, he felt, had probably been obvious despite Githraan's guffaw. He did not care. At that moment, he was full of hate for the headman's house, the village, and fate for striking him down near such a dismal place.

167

After wondering whether it was possible to resent Arna, he decided that Arna had nothing to do with it. Even the inner workings of a priest of the Second Circle, such as himself, were too trivial for the imperial deity to be aware of. The same went for the boy. Visions round the bonfire, no less, and some kind of mental trip to Shivara's days. Why Galdtchav took it so seriously, he could not fathom, but that was Loremasters for you. Too much time closeted with parchment gave them ideas. The lanky, cocksure, rude, definitely rude, ignorant boy—though admittedly he could read—was a pitiful candidate for such high experiences. In any case, he had the usual rough-and-ready attachment to 'the Lady,' as the rustics referred to Iathena, Arna's consort. Her makeshift cult had been there in the valleys long before Arna transferred his favour to the north, and it had survived embarrassingly well, even when Iathena had been absorbed into the sun-god's cult to be the one by his side. However, the lady was most definitely not even a close second within the pantheon. She was very subordinate in the scheme of things, despite her honoured position. Those who felt they needed her would not be receiving any visions from Lord Arna, especially peasants. The god would live up to his reputation.

Thus ran the thoughts of the Anthu Bal-jarrak, Keeper of the Fires. He was waiting to begin the ceremonies that celebrated the birth of Lord Arna from the Deep Fire. It had fallen to him to take the place the Archpriest would have occupied beneath the golden dome of the Shrine. He remembered the myriad candles, the burnished images of kings and holy men, and the gold that gleamed around the tomb of Ar-ven. The Coming Forth, as it was officially known, was an ancient ritual meticulous and beautiful in every word and gesture. Arna was indeed honoured when his birth was celebrated—celebrated properly—with imperial dignity and splendour. But in Falakhoth it was cold and damp and the sky slid over them like slabs of slate. At least they'd had the sense to put a canopy over him in case it rained again.

Bal-jarrak tugged his heavy robe around himself feeling outraged and glaring with detestation at Galdtchav for suggesting this farce. Where was the awestruck veneration and the sense of sacred history? Where was the understanding of the mysteries of the god and all the ancient meaning that lay behind the ceremony? There they were, the villagers, shuffling into the muddy square, gawking at him as if he were a sideshow. He felt that precious, august things were being prostituted to the ignorance and curiosity of these peasants. Their knowledge of the Scrolls put together would hardly run to two columns. No-one had even bothered to wear anything special for the occasion—not even the headman who should have known better—and there was no gold but that on Bal-jarrak's fingers.

Voices sounded behind him: the Assistant Loremaster and Captain Githraan, coming down from the home of the local healer. Bal-jarrak surveyed the square once more. Everyone must be here by now, including the soldiers of the priests' escort, who continued to guard their charges. Those on watch had been posted on ridges on the hillside where they could look down into the square and even those who guarded the street leading to the North Road were at the top, rather than below, at the junction.

The priest cast an irritated glance at a wooden figure of Iathena. It really should not be there, not now. It intruded on this celebration of Arna. Those so inclined could even see it as representing an equal, even an alternative, and he knew there were not a few of those in the realm. In front of his wooden seat and just under his cheap canopy stood a metal basin full of water. It was balanced on a stand over a smoking fire. To Bal-jarrak, it was a pathetic contrivance in comparison to the Shrine's great glass laver, supported at its outer rim by the stone mountain-lions of the house of Na-veshtrazhdak. From where the Archpriest would sit, he could look down through water and glass to where great fires burned far below, mirrors casting back their light through the waters to leap and shimmer on the gilded walls. It was the perfect representation of the primal fire, the great burning beneath the waves of the Western Sea, from which sprang Lord Arna on the first morning of the world.

Admittedly, there was a scroll which permitted Falakhoth's basin and guttering fire since they fulfilled the basic content of the symbol: fire beneath water. The scroll had evidently been written in a day when the ceremony was not confined to the Shrine and might be performed in all sorts of situations. The writer had even been aware that fire might be unobtainable, for after stating how fire beneath water was the only essential, he had continued: *If it be that flame may not be kindled owing to some lack or danger, or if needs be the festival must be kept in some place where nothing that will burn may be found, then the semblance of fire is permissible, such as a golden ring or gem or coloured glass. Look not at the trappings of that which you do, but at the intent to figure the birth of the Lord Arna, which alone makes your ceremony acceptable.* There was a great deal more on the same lines, at the end of which the writer admitted that if the worst came to the worst the ceremony could be performed with no symbol at all and still be acceptable. Bal-jarrak, frankly, would have preferred this. He was offended by the ramshackle basin, but they had insisted on having something and he had agreed, if only to stop amateur Loremaster Azhur quoting the whole Scroll at him. The lad knew his stuff so at the very least there would be the proper words and lore, spoken decently and reverently. Even that had been achieved with a struggle since the town's pet wizard or whatever he was had insisted on taking part in the ritual as if he had some kind of authority. Eventually, he had been flatly told that with two high-ranking priests and an expert in lore present he wasn't required. He had begun to shout and make claims for himself until the headman, overhearing, had picked him up by one arm and taken him to the farther end of the square, where, apparently, he had said some very stern things to him. Bal-jarrak could see the man now, sitting on a ridge overlooking the houses and talking to two soldiers who were attempting to get a fire of their own going.

And now here was the wonder boy himself, chatting with Lord Galdtchav and Githraan as if he was their equal, and Galdtchav looking the boy up and down all the time as if he expected a Fire-spirit to leap out of his pocket. If imagination made you Senior Loremaster, then every gullible priest in his dotage would be eligible. *Look at him!* Letting the boy introduce him to a relative without even a pretence of dignity. Galdtchav was unaware of how the square of people viewed him as venerable and dignified as anyone they were ever likely to meet. The Loremaster never gave it a thought but his courtesy, his age, his relaxed, lively manner, and his sweeping, silver hair gave him a dignity as natural as the

170

air. Bal-Jarrak, did not see the stiff, jerky postures which he himself sub-stituted for dignity.

"Have a talk with Wyrdha, Anthu," Tyr was saying. "He's knew me since I were a little sprog. He'll tell y' if there's owt different."

Wyrdha laughed at this, "Well, Tyr, I know you don't think you've been affected by it all, but I'd certainly like to speak with the Anthu later, if it pleases him."

"Most respectfully put, master healer. Yes, it would please me indeed, but first—" The old man clapped his hands together and said loudly, "Good people, I think we should start! Everyone must be here. Lord Bal-Jarrak is waiting most patiently, and without a cushion. Azhur! Ready, Assistant Loremaster?" The priests took up their positions near the guttering fire.

"What about Yauva?" asked Tyr. "Is he on his own?"

"No," said Wyrdha, "Utha's with him, as if you need ask. He's far more interesting than the birth of Arna. Brilt'thig's there too. When Yauva's fever passed, he wanted to come down to the ceremony, but quite im-possible. He won't be moving for a long time yet."

"What if he tries?"

"Utha would stop him. In any case that leg wouldn't support him. Now, hush! Our priestly friend wishes to begin!"

Bal-Jarrak was glowering in the direction of their conversation, his sharp nose pointing at the offending voices like a finger. When silence was complete, he stood up. The people of Falakhoth stared, gaped, squinted, and peered at him. Several coughed and somewhere near his feet a child wiped its nose loudly on its sleeve. Bal-Jarrak closed his eyes for an instant: what a charade. Still, it had to be done. Bracing himself, he spread out his arms and addressed the people.

"The Lord Arna shine upon you," he intoned with an almost aggress-ive apathy. "May he who rises in the sun send the Nine among us, they who are fire and light, to dispel the darkness of your ignorance and warm the coldness of your spirits."

It was an ancient blessing, not a prayer, and thus not spoken in the Old Tongue. Galdtchav looked round the square and saw confused frowns. He sighed. The blessing, he knew, wished its hearers a deepened insight into the ways of Arna and warm contentment in the knowledge of these ways. The Archpriest could speak those words in a way that would transform any gathering, but Bal-jarrak's curt tones had made them sound like an accusation. The Loremaster resolved to speak to the Archpriest about the phrasing of the blessing. A small difference would remove any ambiguity when someone with Bal-jarrak's tone of voice spoke these venerated words. A little imagination…

"This is the rite of the Coming Forth," Bal-jarrak informed the townspeople. "It is a significant ceremony within the cult of Arna, who, as you know, made this kingdom of which you are citizens."

Galdtchav sighed again and bowed his head as Bal-jarrak spoke.

"Although this is Arna's land, he graciously permits our Valgraav, through whom he rules, to recognise and allow the worship of Lord Arna's consort and—"

"Arna's what?" said a woman rather too loudly.

"Aye, what were that?" responded a number of voices.

"Never knew he had one."

"Lord Arna's consort!" repeated Bal-jarrak with furious authority, but every face remained blank.

"His, ah, companion, his wife," said Azhur helpfully.

"Ohh."

"Well, why didn't he say so?"

"Was Arna married, then?"

"Suppose so, that's what he said."

Bal-jarrak glared at Azhur as if to obliterate him. "To continue," he snapped. "The worship and cult of Iathena—whom you call 'the Lady'— is recognised, but you must understand that it is not an equivalent, in law or in reality, of the cult of Arna, the observance of which is the highest and most significant activity of which humankind is capable. The ritual we enact today is of primal and cosmic significance. It is a concession, a gift. It is part of a cult that is far above any god's permitted rite, ritual, or devotion normally practiced here or elsewhere in the realm. Listen to this with gratitude, try to understand, and be aware of your privilege." There, he'd said it. He could see they hadn't a clue what he meant, but he'd said it. He didn't have to, but, oh, how he'd wanted to. He squared his narrow shoulders and aimed his distinctive nose at his audience. "We will begin the rite."

~

GIZHURTHRA, SEETHING, WATCHED THE townspeople assemble. Tyrmar had ordered him out of the square with dire threats of punishment should he cause any 'trouble.' He persuaded an area of his face to twist in a kind of smile and gave a brief, bitter laugh. Trouble! What trouble could he cause if he had a mind to? And could they punish one who, not long before, had been initiated into the mysteries of the southern magic? He had told them he had power, and he had been arrogantly brushed aside, as so often in his life. Very well, let them disbelieve him. He had suffered ridicule often enough before when he had stood up for the truth about himself. If that was how they treated a person's integrity, let them flounder through the ceremony on their own. He would watch from this ridge, knowing the help they had refused. The white dog looked up at Gizhurthra and yapped. He sat beside it on a dry stone and ruffled the smooth fur.

"There, friend," he said softly. "Sit by me." The dog whined and put its forepaws on his lap, nuzzling into his coat. Gizhurthra smiled, quietly and genuinely this time, and stroked the dog's head. "Friend," he repeated.

"Trouble with the priests, then?"

Gizhurthra's frown returned. He turned his long head to the speaker, a soldier who leaned on his spear while his companion busied himself trying to light a fire.

"Come over here," said the man. "It'll be better when we've got a fire going." Gizhurthra and his dog joined the two soldiers. "D'you always have such miserable springs down here?" Gizhurthra was about to say that he never paid attention to the weather, when the man broke in with, "Hang on, they've started."

Bal-Jarrak was on his feet, giving the ambiguous blessing.

"Look at that, will y'?" muttered the second soldier. "Ferret's standin' in for the Archpriest! I thought this was a celebration."

"Ferret?" said Gizhurthra.

"We call him that at the Shrine," said the first soldier. "On account of his nose: long and sharp and sniffs out trouble."

"You want to watch out if you're havin' bother with him," continued the second. "That's one feller you don't want t' cross."

"I offered to help with their ceremony. The headman dragged me away." He looked down at the dog. "But I do not fear *him*, do I, friend?" The dog whined in agreement.

"You a priest, then?"

"No...." Gizhurthra hesitated. "I am... vraakhin." He looked out defensively from under his creased lids and saw he had unsettled the men.

"Vraakhin, eh? You're, er, you're not from the Plain?"

"I'm no savage. There's my house, on the hill behind your Ferret."

"Well, no offence, master. It's just, well, we've been told t' look out for anybody from the Plain as calls themselves that."

"Calls themselves what?"

"Vraakhin. Some as does are Harrak, you know, and that worries them at the Shrine. No offence though, Baranthu."

Gizhurthra did not answer for a moment, then he indulged in the rare and luxurious experience of smiling broadly. "No, don't worry. I am not offended." He turned to watch the ceremony, still smiling. Baranthu. They called him *Baranthu*. A warm shudder of joy went through his body. *They* had seen, these common men, unblinkered by pride and ritual. *They* had felt what was in him. Of course, it must be obvious to anyone with eyes to see. He had always had power—hadn't he felt it all his life?—and now he was an initiate, one who had learned deep secrets from the south. Why, it must shine from his very eyes. Did those powerful words he had been so carefully taught not move vibrant in his mind? Gizhurthra, Baranthu. And one day it would be *Anthu*. Of course. He patted the dog vigorously.

They watched the ceremony for a while. Azhur did most of the speaking, reciting the lore and translating the prayers, which were spoken in the Old Tongue. The afternoon became very grey, and the sky hung over them like the ceiling of a cave.

"Wish I could see this in the Shrine," said the soldier who had been

174

working at lighting the fire. "Beautiful, that is."

"You'd get fire in the Shrine, all right," said the other. "It's freezing up here. Have you given up?"

"Yes I have. Wood's too damp. Do it yourself if you're that cold."

"Right, I will then." The man laid down his spear and set to with the tinder-box.

His companion carried on talking to Gizhurthra, "Saw this last year—in the Shrine, I mean. There's a brilliant bit comin' up in about ten minutes when Lord Arna gets born. Been in the Shrine, have you?" Gizhurthra nodded. "Well, you've seen that great thing like a basin with the lions round it? Well, the bottom's made of glass and down below it they've got these fires goin' so the light comes up through the water. Supposed to be that Deep Fire business, whatever that's about, and when the Archpriest says, 'He is born, he rises in the sun,' they throw somethin' on the fire, and it flares up and they bring mirrors all round it, and y' get this fantastic light shootin' up through the water! Lights the whole place up, it does. Wish I could see it again." He turned round to the heap of wood with its sad wisps of smoke. "We could do with some of that stuff and chuck it on this fire. Ain't that goin' yet?"

"Doin' me best."

Suddenly the frustrated soldier turned eagerly to Gizhurthra. "What about you, Baranthu? I bet you know spells and things. I bet you know words that'll get a fire going."

"Of course," murmured Gizhurthra edgily. "That's a small trick."

"Oh, right. Well, go on then. I know there's people can do that. Never saw it meself, mind, but my old mum used t' tell me, 'Son,' she said, 'there's more t' this life than meets the eye,' and I believed her. So, let's be havin' you Baranthu, show me my mum was a truthful woman." It was the great moment of crisis in his understanding of reality, and he sat back on the grass, imploring Gizhurthra not to fail him.

"Of course," said Gizhurthra. "Of course." But his mind was racing, trying to remember the word the southerner had taught him. The same word that had lit his lamp when he could not find his flints. He fumbled in his memory, seized a sound, and turned to the smoking wood. He waved his hand at it and spoke. Nothing. He cleared his throat and repeated word and gesture. Still nothing. He glanced at the two soldiers. The beginnings of disbelief were showing on their faces. Gizhurthra punished them with a glare, but he was desperately wondering what had gone wrong. It was the right word, he was sure of it. Had he said it wrongly? He recalled the southerner's rasping voice. Yes, he had pronounced it differently. Perhaps it was not simply a matter of a foreigner's accent. Speak it as he did and see. "I wasn't concentrating very hard," he said defiantly. "Usually you don't have to for a little thing like that. Your wood must be *very* damp."

The soldiers said nothing, unsure whether to believe him or not.

Suddenly Gizhurthra was intensely angry. Dismissed yet again as a fraud? Betrayed even by his own power? *Never!* He thrust his hand towards the wood and spat the fire-word through his teeth. There was a brief, soft sound, and a flame burst out of the heart of the pile of wood, scattering twigs and sending a gust of heat into their faces. In about a minute, there was a good blaze, large enough to challenge the damp chill. The soldiers gaped, amazed and afraid.

Gizhurthra himself felt a kind of fear, mixed with the thrill of seeing his own power in operation. He had known what was in him, but to see it before his eyes at last was frightening. His world had shifted. It was as if he had dreamed that he held the leash of some wild, strong beast and then woken to find it true. But that was part of the thrill. Knowing there was a unique power at his disposal but unsure of all that it could or would do, that was a heady draught. But whatever it could do, whatever it was, he was the bearer, the one to use it, direct it, contain it. The knowledge tasted to him like wine, rich and sweet, dissolving his insignificance, and releasing new, intoxicating thoughts.

He rose slowly to his feet to make his way down to the square.

CHAPTER 10

The Coming Forth

THE LORD BAL-JARRAK frequently leaned over to peer out at the sky from under his canopy. Rain threatened, but Azhur reasoned the ritual really should have kept his attention. It had shocked the intellectually fastidious young novice that Bal-jarrak was, in fact, consoling himself over a perceived degradation of the ceremony. Instead of the customary splendour and great magnificence he was used to under the gilded roof of the Shrine, Bal-jarrak was under a threadbare blanket listening to an Assistant Loremaster reeling off the Two hundred and fourteenth Scroll to the peasants of Falakhoth.

Tyr sat on the stonework of the town's well, listening to his friend. He had no time for Bal-jarrak. He had seen how his distinguished nose had wrinkled when its owner had recovered sufficiently to take in the sight of his parent's home, and Tyr had written him off. The Anthu's manner and behaviour since had given him no reason to change his opinion. When he first spoke, Bal-jarrak's voice and posturing made it clear his first concern was his own dignity and he had small interest in the gift of the Rite to Falakhoth. Now, whenever the priest rose to say what was required of him, Tyr glowered and kicked on the well until Azhur spoke again. In contrast, Galdtchav's brief contributions were a pleasure. Tyr had taken to the venerable old man at once, delighted that Galdtchav took him seriously enough to reel off long, careful explanations of everything the lad's awakening intelligence wanted to know. And besides, he had been nice to his mother.

Azhur was being very meticulous, leaving out no part of the lengthy ceremony, even though he knew that much of it would be unfamiliar. He had tactfully explained this at an early stage, saying that people could ask him afterwards about anything they didn't understand. Prayers, he warned them, must be said in the old language of *Shumár*—it being the preference of Arna to be addressed in that holy tongue—but Azhur would translate for them at appropriate intervals. He had told them the Scrolls allowed this, provided he began the translation with, 'I have spoken thus to the Lord Arna.' This ensured the translation itself did not come over as a prayer.

The words of the vigorous, ancient tongue thrilled Tyr by their very sound. *Was that how they spoke in Dhar?* he wondered. *Did Shivara talk like that?* He clutched at the memory of the vision he'd had during the play, attempting to pull it back into his thoughts as Azhur's voice told the story from the world's natal days.

"Listen now, and I will speak of the coming forth of Arna." Azhur was now wholly immersed in the ancient ceremony, making himself a channel for those words worn smooth by time as though he was the first to utter them. It was the Lore of Beginnings, received and proclaimed in the days of Va Sh'herakh, when Arna first let himself be recognised by humankind and was venerated as Hra'im by the men of the burning southern desert before they had risen to be rulers of their world or had appointed the kings of the north. As Azhur spoke, Tyr heard the million voices that had proclaimed the Lore before rising from shrines and temples, ornate palaces and the crudest of stone altars, from tents and city gates, mountain caves and desert oases. Now, here, the people of Falakhoth huddling under their slate sky and waiting in the damp, green chill of a northern spring for the burning truths of the words from the desert.

Azhur knew he would soon forget himself. He would not be the person who anxiously drew to himself more and more knowledge, exploring the minutiae beneath the dust and fearing all the while to let his mind run free. He knew the uncertainty and furtive lostness would fall from him as the great words lifted him up to become both priest and Loremaster: one who held understanding of the gods and the knowledge of the centuries. He stepped forward a little.

"It is said that before the world was made, the Deep Fire already burned. The spirit of the Fire was Arna, and he dwelt there. In that time his name was Ver'rauthtar, He Who Walks in Flame.

"Now the Deep Fire did not consume, for its life is its own and its burning makes nothing perish; rather, it will give of its life and power and not diminish. So Ver'rauthtar fashioned Iathena from the living flame, and the power of Ver'rauthtar and the life of the flame gave her being and she dwelt in joy with Ver'rauthtar for years unnumbered. From their union sprang the lesser of the gods, and those gods brought forth those who are lower than themselves, and they in their turn brought forth the lesser fires, the spirits; but the life of the Flame was in them all, according to the order of their being. And all dwelt within the Deep Fire. Beyond the Fire was the ancient gloom where evil is. The spirits of the dark hated Ver'rauthtar and the gods, for they lived within the life of the Flame; but these spirits of shadow were outside its life, and so lived always in wrath and envy."

Tyr realised with embarrassment that he was hardly listening. He began to feel sleepy and rubbed his eyes. When he opened them, he gasped and almost fell into the well. In front of Azhur was a heavy wooden table and seated at it was an old man. His beard lay in his lap, and his long white hair hung about his shoulders even though the crown of his head was bald. He was bent over the table, writing on a parchment scroll and glancing up quickly as he dipped his pen in a stone ink-jar. Amazed, Tyr realised with a shock that he was working by candlelight, despite the broad daylight of the square; in fact, the yellow, moving light seemed to be the only kind that fell on the man and his table, making deep shadows behind and beneath. Everyone else stood in the flat, cold light of a spring afternoon, where there were hardly any shadows. The old man finished his work, rolled up the scroll, placed something inside it, then bound it with some red material and wrote on the outside. He sealed the binding with wax melted in a candle-flame and pressed into the wax something bound to his right hand like an amulet. All the while, Azhur continued speaking and no-one paid the old scribe the slightest attention. The sage looked up as though interrupted and suddenly he vanished. There was not so much as the mark of a table-leg in the mud or the slightest pause in the flow of Azhur's speech.

"There came a day when Ver'rauthtar looked beyond the Flame to the great shadow that lay outside it and he said in his heart, 'This is not good; for the life of the flame is given only to those within it and beyond itself it is despised.' So he took a hundredth part of the Flame (and for all that it was not diminished) and cast it beyond the Fire into the darkness outside, saying, 'Be thou a world, be thou heavens and earth, sky, mountains, and growing things; and let the Flame be your life, to uphold you and sustain you.'"

Tyr had given up trying to listen to Azhur, for he saw that his friend stood on a wide stone platform intricately carved and shining as if it were white, molten gold. Then he realised that, like the Scribe, it was not illuminated by the same light that fell on the square. He had only seen such light at noon on the hottest Summer days when the earth of the square cracked and shimmered. These stones must be under some fierce sun in another land unless the northern summer had come forward by several months. He looked quickly around. No-one so much as glanced at the sunlit stones. One or two people were tugging their coats around themselves, obviously cold. Tyr even glanced at the sky, for it seemed inevitable that there would be some break in the clouds through which the strange sunlight poured, but there was only moving grey above him. It was no spring sunshine.

"And so the world was made in the darkness around the Fire, and the flame that Ver'rauthtar had cast out drove back the darkness. Its life entered the world even as Ver'rauthtar's power created the world from the Flame. Now the darkness had drawn away from that part of the Deep Fire that Arna had sent into it, but its hatred for the Fire was more bitter than before; for since the world came from the Light and was a work of light and partook of its life, the darkness and the spirits that were in it could not understand the world and feared it. Then the mightiest among them said, 'Our realm is invaded: we will not suffer this affront. Let us take forms and go into this thing that has been made. Perhaps we will comprehend it and have the mastery of it; and if not, we may destroy it.' So the shadow-spirits came to the world that Ver'rauthtar had made, worming into it under its hide, like maggots in bread, among the caverns and deep places within; and their very coming made blight and pestilence so that growing things sickened and died, and the world was stained by their presence. But they could not understand the work of Ver'rauthtar, for anything not from darkness was folly to them, and they sought to destroy it. Two of the strongest, R'thammak and G'chraada, led them and they would have broken the very earth had they been able."

"Are you all right, Tyr?" murmured Wyrdha in his ear.

"Eh? Oh, aye. Why?"

"Well, I would have thought none would be more interested in this lore than yourself, especially with friend Azhur reciting it, but you're obviously not listening—almost as if I were trying to teach you about healing."

Tyr shook his head and rubbed his eyes, "I'm all right."

"Frankly, I doubt it. You look as if you'd just met a bear. No, two bears." Wyrdha paused a moment, then laid his hand on the boy's shoulder and stooping close, murmured, "Tyr, is something happening?" Tyr could not resist this appeal and nodded. Wyrdha saw the anxiety in his face. "Tell us afterwards?" Another nod. The healer patted the boy's shoulder, and he tried to attend to Azhur.

"Ver'rauthtar was wroth, for he loved the world he had made and was jealous for it; and he said, 'I will not suffer this evil. I will arise, and the gods with me, and we will shine within the world and heal the work of my hands. It will not be left unguarded, for the dark to do as it wills. I will walk in fire no longer, for the Flame has been but a womb and a beginning. I will come forth from my mother the Fire, and it shall be as a birth, but in power and splendour. Ver'rauthtar I shall be no longer, but Arna Zhivhaltaur, Light of Heaven and Earth.'"

It was no good. Azhur was still standing on the sunlit stones and by his side was a stone construction with a broad, flat surface like a table, carved with many letters and symbols inlaid with bronze and gold. It was badly broken. Fire burned before it in a round brazier. Tyr looked away again, wanting it all to stop. He saw the stones had now gone and Azhur stood once more on the muddy ground by the guttering fire, but Azhur's tunic and shirt were open and a terrible wound was gouged across his chest. Blood was running down his clothes and onto the ground as he spoke. Azhur seemed completely unaware of this. Tyr remembered hearing how soldiers in battle could sustain serious injuries and still fight on as if nothing had happened. Maybe that was it, he thought wildly, maybe somebody threw a knife or something, but nobody else in the square had noticed. From sheer instinct, Tyr began to get down from the well so he could look for something to staunch the wound. He felt a hand on his arm. Beside him was a slim young woman he didn't know. She was dark-haired, with swarthy-looking skin, brown like nuts or berries, and she had funny eyes.

The woman put a long, thin finger to her lips and whispered, "No, don't. He doesn't know, and don't tell him, don't tell anybody. It's not time, and you'd only make it worse."

"Look at the state of him, though," said Tyr.

"I know, but he doesn't know how bad it is. He'll feel it, really feel it, but not for a while yet. It's infected, but he doesn't know. It only bothers him sometimes and he thinks he can manage."

"He'll be all right though?"

"Oh, you can do something about it, but it takes a while, and it has to be the right time. Don't you worry though."

"All right then." Tyr said. He tried to listen again.

"So Ver'rauthtar drew into himself the life of the Flame and he became glorious and terrible, so that the other gods hid their faces, even Iathena the Beautiful. And Ver'rauthtar took of the Flame of the Deep Fire and fashioned a great orb that burned and shone, and he set a portion of his own power within it so that the life of the Flame and the power of the god were mingled. Then Ver'rauthtar said, 'This shall be my sign and in it I shall rise over the world: thus will I bring power and healing, life and light to both heaven and earth.' And he clothed himself with the burning orb and rose from the Deep Fire, and all the gods and spirits with him, singing, 'Rise, Arna, Light of the heavens; rise, life of the earth. By your glory banish darkness; by your presence, heal the world.'"

Tyr realised Azhur's wound was gone. Not a drop of blood remained on the ground and Azhur seemed in perfect health. He turned to speak to the odd young woman, but she had moved away. He noticed her moving behind the people towards the street down to the road. Funny sort. He'd seen people like that at fairs, but she seemed to know what she was talking about. Perhaps she was a healer like Wyrdha. But where was the wound?

"Thus Arna entered the world he had made, and when the spirits of the darkness saw the beauty of his glory in light they were dismayed and in great terror, for they could not comprehend it. Arna smote the strongest in a terrible war that changed the world's very face, so that they fled howling to Arahoth and into the emptiness under the earth; and he made stars of the Flame and set them in the heavens as a boundary, knowing that no foul thing would dare to pass their light, for the life of the Flame was in them."

Azhur paused as he heard a murmur from the crowd, someone was pushing his way to the front. Tyr saw his father shoot a fearsome glance towards the disturbance, then he recognised the tall fur cap of Gizhur-thra. The vraakhin reached the front of the crowd and stood with arms folded and head back, ignoring the protests of those behind whose view he was spoiling. Tyrmar lowered his head, glowering at him. Uneasy now, Azhur continued the Lore, remembering Tyr's warning about Gizhurthra and wondering what had brought him so close. A white muzzle poked silently between the defiant man's ankles.

"The orb Arna set in the heavens, to shed the light and life of the Deep Fire on the world; and he decreed that the orb should pass also under the earth, to weaken the darkness that was there. It was at this time that Arna brought forth the oceans around the Fire, and so it burned in the heart of the great seas that are in the West of the world. But the orb that Arna had made from the Fire he bade move in a great circle across the limits of the heavens and it was renewed by the Deep Fire as it passed ever and again to the West to journey beneath the earth and rise in victory over the darkness. Thus the Lord Arna came forth into the world, born of the Flame into his greater glory. Thus did the days and years begin and thus was the world healed. This is the Lore of Beginnings."

The recital finished, Azhur stepped back to a position facing Galdtchav across the fire. Bal-jarrak, remembering his cue, rose to his feet and spread out his hands.

"The Lord Arna is born," he said sourly to no-one in particular. "Let us celebrate his coming forth."

"He rises in the sun," chanted Azhur.

"And his power is in the heavens," responded Galdtchav.

A weary supplication in the ancient language from Bal-jarrak followed. He glanced at Azhur who translated for him, "I have spoken thus to the Lord Arna: Accept our thanks, O Arna, Creator of the world and the Kingdom of the North. As faithful priests we offer you this worship on behalf of all in this Kingdom you have made and humbly beg you to shine on us evermore."

"He smites R'thammak."

"And the darkness is scattered."

"He sets forth his sign."

"And heals the world."

Bal-jarrak took a pace towards the fire, "Seeing his likeness in the fire, let us worship him. He bears the life of the Deep Fire: let us worship him." He spread out his hands over the people in the sign of blessing. "The Lord Arna shine on you. He has made the world of men, he has come forth from his Mother the Fire to reign over them. This day he comes forth: he ascends, he is born, he rises in the sun—"

A shout and a roar of flame. The fire surged into an immense blaze. Bal-jarrak flew back against the wooden chair as the canopy dissolved in flames over his head. The rite became an uproar, the square in chaos. Those at the rear thought the fire was part of the ceremony, people near the blaze were pushing back, terrified, to escape the heat. There was shouting and arguing and panic as people reacted to a danger they did not know by trying to force their way out of the crowd.

Above the hubbub Tyrmar was shouting, "Nothing's wrong, nothing's wrong, keep calm!" And then, "Githraan, there! Grab him!"

Gizhurthra was standing motionless, staring fixedly at the blaze he had created, and offered no resistance when Githraan and a soldier seized him by his limp arms.

Bal-jarrak scrabbled on all fours, having rolled away from the burning canopy with his back hurt by its impact on the chair. Azhur was trying to help him up, but he was unable to rise.

Wyrdha ran and knelt beside him, "His hands are burned. The salve, Tyr, and some bandages. Quickly!"

"Go on," said Azhur. "I'm all right."

Tyr began to sprint out of the square, then froze. Yauva's image was walking towards him with Yauva himself lying in pain. It was too much. He had had enough visions for today. He turned back, desperate. "Wyrdha?"

But Wyrdha was staring past him and Azhur had forgotten Bal-jarrak, and they and Galdtchav were stock still, gaping at the entrance to the square.

Did they see it too? What was happening?

A shrill voice broke the spell.

"I'm that sorry, master Wyrdha, honest I am, but he would come. I told him he couldn't walk with his leg like that, but he—"

"Don't go on, Utha. I'm not pained." Against all evidence, in defiance of torn flesh and splintered bone, Yauva was walking towards him. He limped a little, but he was walking.

The square calmed down as people realised who the newcomer was and whispered it through the crowd. In a few seconds, the only sound was the crackle of the fire. Yauva rubbed his eyes as though he had just woken up, then recognised Tyr. He laughed and came up to him, limping sturdily on the impossible leg.

"Well, what do you think of this? Not bad for a little prayer, eh?"

"Eh?" repeated Tyr.

"What prayer?" breathed Galdtchav.

"Oh, that were little fat Brilt'thig. He did healin' words over me and now look!" He laughed aloud. "Oh, here he is." And trotting into the square came the portly, blue-robed figure of Iathena's little priest.

"I do hope it's all right," he gasped, breathless and still dabbing with

Wyrdha's handkerchief. "Only he was so unwell and truly beseeched me—"

But Yauva flung his arms around him and smothered him against his chest, "He done it," he shouted. "He's cured me, him and his words!" He slapped Brilt'thig's back, held him at arm's length and looked him up and down like a proud father. "Oh, I'm that happy! Dunno when I was last as happy! I could dance."

"Don't you dare!" called Wyrdha.

"Oh well, perhaps not. Think I need a bit of practice." Still hanging on to Brilt'thig as if he were a comforting pillow, Yauva caught sight of the astounded faces that surrounded him, especially that of Azhur, who had both hands over his mouth as if to stop himself crying out. "Oh, no offence to your prayin', master. It's just Brilt'thig here said the words and, er, it happened."

"What happened?" Bal-jarrak's sharp tones cut through Yauva's happiness like a scythe. "Magic, is that what you're saying? Are you claiming magic, priest?"

"Oh, no, no, no, no." cried Brilt'thig, waving his hands. "Not at all. I wouldn't—I couldn't. Wouldn't contradict the Scrolls, oh, no, no, no."

Bal-jarrak lurched painfully to his feet, grasping at Azhur's arm. "You'll have to claim something," he snapped. "*He's* claimed plenty for you already. You'd better not be a magician on the quiet. Heavy fines for *that*: ten columns in the twenty-fifth scroll."

"Here!" burst out Yauva. "Don't you shout at him. Who are you, anyway?"

"Ooh, Yauva, don't!" squeaked Utha.

Yauva ignored her, watching Bal-jarrak with a heady mixture of anger, puzzlement, and happiness.

"I think," ventured Galdtchav, seeing what was coming, "I think, in the circumstances—"

"Who am I?" Bal-jarrak drew himself up and stuck out his velvet-covered, unimpressive chest. "You ask, who am I? I am the Lord Bal-jarrak, priest of the Second Circle of the Shrine and Keeper of the Fires. I may wear the sign of the Lion and I carry authority from the Archpriest. Who are *you*?"

This display cowed Yauva for a moment and he looked at the ground. "Well, I'm sorry, master," he mumbled. "I don't mean to offend nobody, but, well, I've been at death's door, or so they tell me, and now I'm well I think you might be pleased for me instead of worrying about magic. It were a prayer, an honest prayer to the Lady. Nobody's been doin' no magic."

"Nobody can! Nobody has the power!" The high, wild voice came from the other side of the fire, through the flames.

Bal-jarrak whirled, then yelped and clutched his back. "What? Who said that?"

"Nobody but I may do this! Me! Nobody! I have the power, and I was not given it. My power is my own!" Gizhurthra looked a limp, crumpled thing, gripped as he was by two soldiers, but his eyes were wide and bright, and his voice shook with destiny. "Haven't you got eyes? Can't you see the fire?"

"Oh, that was you, was it? Master headman, how long has Falakhoth harboured magicians who disrupt sacred ritual?"

A great *Ohhh* went up from the villagers. A ritual, a spell, and a miracle made for marvellous entertainment, far better than the players, but now it was getting a little nasty. Their headman was in an awkward spot.

But Githraan, well-used to Bal-jarrak's little ways, stepped into the breach. "Never saw this rat before, Anthu," he said curtly, "but I'll take care of him for you. To the inn with him, lads. Keep an eye on him, we don't want no more tricks." Gizhurthra made to protest. "And one sound from you and I'll have your head rollin' down to the river!"

The vraakhin was silent, but looked over his shoulder in utter disdain as soldiers dragged him away.

"How did he do it?" asked Bal-jarrak in a quieter voice. "Did you see? Did he throw something on the fire?"

"Didn't notice, Anthu," said Githraan brusquely. "Sorry." And he began to clear the square of people as best he could.

"Is that it?" said a woman to Bal-jarrak. "Is it finished?"

"There should have been a little more," snapped the priest, "but yes: it is finished!" He grimaced and put a hand to his back.

"Bothered with y' back, are y'? Me too, got to watch out." She turned to Azhur and patted his arm. "Thought it were lovely. I'd never heard all that about orbs afore. Y've got a nice voice, though."

Bal-jarrak watched her go with the appalled disbelief of which only a true aesthete is capable.

Iethen attempted to fuss round Bal-jarrak, holding her skirts above the mud. "Shouldn't y' perhaps lie down, Anthu? Y' rose too soon anyhow, I said—"

"I shall be quite well, madam. The ritual required *me*, you understand. Very sacred, can't have just *anyone*—"

"Young lady here's lost her mam," bellowed Tyrmar, holding a sobbing child high in the air. "Y' name's Aelwen, isn't it, darlin'? Y'know, when I couldn't find our Tyr when he were little, I'd shout his name as loud as I could and he'd come runnin'. Will we shout for y' mam?"

"Yes," said Aelwen tearfully, and joined her shrill voice with Tyrmar's thunder.

"Aelwen's mam! Come on then, ma, where are y'?"

"Here!" cried a woman's voice. "Where y' been, Ael?"

Bal-jarrak felt a madness had descended on the square, an insane chaos. The august occasion was in tatters, majesty trampled in the mud. He himself had been insulted, spoken to by a *peasant*—a peasant *woman*—as though she were his equal, and practically attacked. Why Galdtchav had agreed to all this was beyond him. Everyone knew people like this could never grasp what the rituals were about. That was why they had priests; that was why they had the Shrine. At least he could make sure nobody talked about it. He had been ill after all. An error of judgement. Then it occurred to him he could still maintain the high dignity of his calling by shouting at Brilt'thig. He turned, predator-like, but the little priest was gone, and Yauva and Utha were heading back into the street that led from the square to Wyrdha's house.

"You!" he roared after them. "Where's that priest?"

"Dunno," called Yauva, without stopping.

"Where do you think you're going?" demanded Bal-jarrak.

This time Yauva halted and turned round. "If you want to know, I'm goin' for a pee. Happy now, are you?" And he stamped away, Utha

188

hanging on his arm.

It was a moment of numbing unreality for Bal-jarrak, something in utter contradiction to the direction of his entire life to that point. So great was this unprecedented conflict he could scarcely move or speak. His whole identity tottered: he needed a target. Fortunately, one walked up to him.

"Anthu," said Azhur tentatively, "I wondered if, ah—"

"Where's your friend? Where's your miracle boy?"

Azhur's fingers locked together at once, "The healer's house, I think, Anthu. He went to speak with—"

"With his limping friend? Planning new embellishments for their hoax? Eh?"

Azhur found himself feeling strangely guilty. He began to stammer. "Oh, no. There's no hoax, Anthu."

Bal-jarrak was feeling much better. "No hoax? Really? Well, I'll get to the bottom of this. I don't know what's going on, but I'll expose it, do you hear me?" A small voice somewhere in his thoughts informed him he was about to become utterly irrational, but he could not stop himself. Nor did he wish to. "I mean, really, Assistant Loremaster, is this what you bring us to? Insults, magicians, impiety? Fun for your yokel friends, of course."

Azhur was overwhelmed, but Galdtchav hastily intervened, "Bal-jarrak, please! Lower your voice, we are guests here."

Bal-jarrak adjusted his screech to a snarl, "The Rite of the Coming Forth conducted over a tin basin!" he spat. "I despise that. It's my *duty* to despise that!"

"Externals, Bal-jarrak, externals. Look not at the trappings of that which you do, but at the intent to honour the Lord Arna."

"Precisely, Galdtchav! How is Arna honoured in this shamble? We *squandered* the Rite on these oafs. I shall put it to the Archpriest that the Rites of Festivals be forbidden out with the Shrine."

"But Anthu—" Azhur raised a hand to his mouth, but the words were out.

Bal-jarrak turned on him. "And what does the *Assistant* Loremaster say?" There was a horrid emphasis on assistant.

"Only..., only that the Scrolls could not, ah, permit it, Anthu," gasped the young man desperately.

"What?"

"The Fourteenth Scroll, Anthu. It assumes the Festival may take place anywhere."

"Are you telling me what the Scrolls say? Your business is lore, not interpretation! What's your Circle? The Second? The Third? You're not even fully a priest, boy!" He strode to Azhur and stabbed at his chest with a bony finger as he spoke. "You're. Only. A. *Novice*."

Azhur stumbled back. He could think of no answer, nor dared he.

Galdtchav saw the pain of Azhur's humiliation. "That will do, Bal-jarrak!" he said.

An astounded, wide-eyed hiatus: Bal-jarrak literally could not speak. At last he managed a high-pitched sputter from his constricted throat, "Galdtchav, he spoke back to me! I am the Keeper of the Fires!"

"Then you should know the word of the Scrolls when you hear it! Azhur has said no more than that!" Galdtchav saw the incandescent spite in Bal-jarrak's face and wished he had restrained himself, but gratitude shone like a dawn in Azhur's eyes and he regretted not a syllable.

Bal-jarrak knew there was nothing he could say. Paralysed with rage, he stood like a bear wondering who to attack next. Dark clouds slid over them and plunged the dim afternoon into gloom, the first of many heavy raindrops fell. Bal-jarrak laughed, a slow, ugly sound. "There's a sign for you, Galdtchav: the celebration of the sun's creation ends in a rainstorm. There's meaning for you if you care to see it! Might even put the fire out." He limped to the door of the forge as the rain grew heavier. Thunder growled overhead and the last of the people fled to their houses. "You think the wonder boy's seen signs? Well, there's a sign: the very sun's hiding. Open your eyes, Galdtchav! Your boy's a freak, a circus act, or he's sick in the head. He's a peasant and the peasants never understood Arna. Arna's ours, he's for people that can rule. 'Stone beneath the Sun, wood beneath the Moon'? So be it! I know what I'll tell the Archpriest!" He went quickly into the forge and flung the door into its frame behind him.

Galdtchav sighed a deep sigh and clapped Azhur on the shoulder, "I think we should shelter with master Wyrdha," he said. "The forge is perhaps not the most amenable place at the moment." And at that, Tyr emerged from the house with a blanket over his head.

"I thought you'd gone to Wyrdha's," said Azhur, glad of another friend.

"I'm goin' now," replied Tyr. "I'm not stoppin' here with that miserable sod."

Galdtchav laughed, extended his bottom lip and said, "Tyr, I have reached a decision. How would you like to visit Valderthaan?"

~

"Now THEN, RAT, let's hear you squeak," said Githraan with all his considerable menace. Gizhurthra glowered up at him but did not raise his face. This was an attitude that made him look unusually sullen and did nothing for the captain's temper. "Don't play games with me. What did you do to the fire? Don't you know that's sacred, what they were doin'?"

Gizhurthra looked away, "Yes, I know. I know about all these things." He lurched to his feet from the corner of the inn's common-room where he had squatted by the hearth since his capture. Spears rose, but he ignored them. "And don't *you* know that's when they feed the fires beneath the Laver in the Shrine and light and flame rush up?" He flung out his arms and swept them upwards. 'He is born, he rises in the sun!' There's *meant* to be flame, you stupid man! Why do you treat me like this for making it?"

"Well, you sort of overdid it a bit. You nearly roasted Anthu Bal-jar-rak."

Gizhurthra looked away again. "Ferret?" he said quietly.

One of the soldiers laughed, then checked himself as Githraan turned a burning eye on him. "We'll have respect from *you*," he roared. He let the man wither under his glare for a second or two, then went back to Gizhurthra. "Look, the priests said they had it all in hand, and the headman told you to keep well away. From what I can make out, you won't do a hand's turn of honest work for this town. You just sit on that hill as if you were the Archpriest on holiday."

"No work? They daren't lose me! I'm their vraakhin."

"I don't care if you're the Valgraav's auntie. In this province, people work and make a contribution to life, or they live somewhere else. You follow me?"

"Contribution?" said Gizhurthra, sounding greatly hurt. "I know spells and prayers, I've got charms against the spirits, I've got my power—"

"It doesn't get the harvests in. People can't trade it or spend it."

"Are you calling me a cheat?"

"I'm calling you nothing, I'm just telling you what a contribution means. You be a vraakhin if you like, but do it in your spare time. As of now, you can roll your sleeves up, get your back into it, and keep out of trouble or I'll see to it you're out. Clear?"

Gizhurthra stood immobilised for a moment, apparently gripped by some inner argument. When he spoke it was in a thin, laboured, desperate voice, "None of you understand, nobody ever does. You can't waste power, you have to… direct it, use it for its proper purpose. I can't—it mustn't… If I work—digging, carrying—it… it escapes, my body uses it, and it gets wasted, it all gets drained away." He pulled his thoughts together and thrust his head back defiantly, finally true to himself. "I can't do that to my power. I can't treat myself like that. It would be wrong!"

Githraan was silent, frowning down at the shabby man who seemed to be many men: arrogant, pleading, sneering, angry, sincere. "Where'd you get all that, then?" he asked, a little more gently.

"I had a master in Lukar. He showed me what was in me and how to guard my gift." He really believed it, and he was pleading earnestly with Githraan to allow him to protect his power. Well, the captain might take him seriously, that far at least.

Githraan leaned forward, "So, let me get this right. You're saying your whatever-it-is, your power, is so strong it can do that to a plain little fire?"

"You saw it."

"Yes, but on the other hand it's so weak it'll run off the ends of your fingers if you so much as stick a spade in the ground. I don't follow that."

Now the defiant version of Gizhurthra raised his head again, "You think I'm telling riddles?"

"Well, it's a riddle to me, so you'd better explain it." The hint of a growl in Githraan's voice unsettled his captive once more, and he collapsed into his plaintive self.

"It isn't weak, the power isn't weak, it's bound up with me—it's *in* me. So I've got to *decide* I'm a vraakhin, live like a vraakhin, think, speak as vraakhin. And the power, you see, the power, if it's inside somebody whose spirit's like that, goes *with* their spirit and their mind. It works beside them, lets them use it. That's the great thing, can't you see, the amazing thing and... and the danger."

"The danger?"

"Yes, the danger of... of changing it. The danger's in me, in my spirit, for if I say, 'I'm no vraakhin, I'm a worker. I'll dig fields, I'll work in metal,' then I direct my mind, my spirit, to these things. But I'd have bent them towards lower things and away from higher things. Away from knowledge and spells and words the power can ride on, away from... *those* things..."

"Those things?" said Githraan. This strange fellow had somehow drawn him in.

Gizhurthra put his hands on the captain's shoulders and gently pulled him down towards him till their faces were close. "Yes," he whispered. "Things you can't see. Things you can't touch." His features tensed and his voice took on a deadly seriousness. "I carry this power in my spirit. If I bend my spirit to ordinary things, I make the power ordinary. It becomes just human energy, mere human skill and strength. It changes, it lessens, it turns into something else. That's why ordinary work's below me. It's not because I'm proud; it's below the greatness of the power. I won't diminish it."

Githraan gritted his teeth and peered into the vraakhin's eyes, but they were transparent. Arna help us, he wasn't bluffing: he really did believe it. "Deep," he said. "Now you just stay there while I make my report. Watch him, lads." And he made a hasty and relieved exit.

"I think he's mad," Githraan told Tyrmar once he was back at the forge.

193

"Should we lock him up, then?" asked Iethen.

"Put him to work, that might cure him. I told him to mend his ideas or move on. You might have an easier time with him now."

"But where'd he go, poor love?"

"Dunno. Said he learned all his vraakhin stuff from somebody in Lukar. You could send him back there."

"Absolutely not," snapped Bal-jarrak. He stretched out his burned hands for Wyrdha's bandages. "There'll be an inquest, I'll see to it."

"From personal observation, Anthu, I should say he's a poor, harmless soul," said Wyrdha. "The trick with the fire can no doubt be explained. His skill in relationships is, I'm afraid, greatly impaired, but perhaps some discipline—"

"I'd send him back to Lukar all right," said Tyrmar darkly. "I've had about enough of him."

"What's that?" said Iethen.

"What, Ieth?"

"That shoutin'. Here, that's our Tyr's voice!"

The door to the forge flew open and Tyr was there, wet and breathless. "Dad, come quick, the inn's on fire!" He dashed across the square to the well.

"Bloody hell!" said Tyrmar and plunged after him.

Flames were streaming from the roof of the inn and smoke surging from its doorway. Verdje was screaming for help as she ran desperately to the well and back. A bucket chain was forming and men were crawling on the roof, trying to douse the flames or soak the wood that was not yet burning. Tyrmar saw that the soldiers had hauled Gizhur-thra outside and had him pinned against a house wall, spear-points against his stomach. He stood limply, detached from the commotion, and not even looking at the burning inn.

Tyrmar gripped one of the soldiers. "What happened?"

The soldier was terrified. "It was him, master headman. Dunno what he did. He just points at the hearth and says somethin' and up it goes. Just got out in time, we did."

"Tryin' to escape?"

The soldier shook his head.

"No? Why the fire, then?"

The soldier turned pale. "He was just... just showin' us he could do it."

"Y' *knew* he could do it, y' bloody fools. What did y' say to him?"

"I says... I says, 'Where's y' magic now, then?' and Vachthav here, he says, 'He's not got no magic, he just threw somethin' on the fire,' so I says, "Come on, then, let's see y' magic," and he points at the fire—"

Tyrmar pushed the soldier aside and bore down on Gizhurthra. The vraakhin did not flinch. His eyes were glazed, and he hardly seemed aware of the headman when he grasped his coat.

"Couldn't resist it, could y'?" Tyrmar was trembling with fury.

The long head tilted slowly back and the pained, languid eyes fixed on him. "He questioned the power," said Gizhurthra faintly. "He demanded a proof."

"Proof?" Tyrmar shook him till it seemed the bony frame would come apart in those hammer-trained hands. "Y'd burn a widow's house down for *proof*?"

But Gizhurthra did not respond or could not.

"What's the matter with y'? Are y' sick? Are y' sick, rat?" Tyrmar heard a woman's frightened shriek: more sorrow for Verdje.

"Dad? Where's Dad? He's not here! Did anybody see him come out?"

Githraan ran up to her. "Where will he be?"

"At the back: he sleeps in the afternoon."

The soldier darted into the smoke-filled inn, his cloak over his face.

"The very back," cried Verdje after him. "On the left!"

In less than a minute, though the wait was agony, Githraan was back hauling Bardcha after him. He pulled the unconscious old man clear of the smoke, then dropped to his knees coughing.

Wyrdha was beside Bardcha at once. "Not too late. He'll be all right, but it wouldn't have been much longer."

Verdje sank down beside her father in tears. Wyrdha went to attend to Githraan.

The headman turned back to Gizhurthra. "Not too late," Tyrmar repeated through his teeth. "Nearly, though. He nearly died, just so y' could show off y' tricks!" And then the resentment of years spilled over and he brought his great fist hard against Gizhurthra's face. The vraakhin

195

battered back against the house wall and crumpled into the mud. Tyrmar stooped, hauled him to his feet. "Damn y' powers!" he spat, and threw him against the wall again. "If y've got any!"

Gizhurthra stared in a stupefied terror, trying to keep his feet as the blood ran from his mouth.

"I've decided what do with the rat!" roared the headman. "Listen, rat: here's me judgement! Y're leavin'. Y're gettin' right away from these parts. Go on back where y' come from if y' like, I don't care, but if I find y' round here again, y'll know what to expect. Now, get up to y' house, pack y' things, and get out. Go on." And he seized Gizhurthra's arm and heaved him across the square.

The vraakhin stumbled, fell once to his knees, then lurched erect and staggered away through the rain, never looking behind him. Busy with the fire, few saw him go.

~

WHEN GIZHURTHRA COLLAPSED AT his house door, the white dog was there to meet him. It whined and licked his bloody face.

"Friend," he said weakly as he began to sob. He clutched the dog to him, rocking back and forth and repeating, "Friend, friend," until the white coat was marked with tears and blood. When his weeping ended, he dragged himself into the house and fell onto his bed. As more tears formed in his eyes, he slept.

He awoke in darkness. The door was open, and it was cold. Below him, he could hear horses and carriage wheels leaving the town. But no matter, the threat remained and his spirit was broken for the present. He got up, found water and bathed his face, wincing at the pain. He took a candle and lit it with his flints for the hearth was cold. In its light, he put a few possessions and some food into a bag. From a box he took a ring. It was of bronze, with designs etched on it. He looked at it for a long time until his eyes grew soft and tears filled them again. He put the ring on a finger and closed the bag. There was nothing else dear to him in the house. No gift, no keepsake, no warm memory.

Gizhurthra found the dog's leather leash and stuffed it into his pocket. "You'll need that on the roads, friend, there's too many horses there." Abruptly, he crouched down and hugged the dog. "We liked it here, didn't we? The hills and the river, and you liked to swim in the lake." His throat tightened. "I was glad you were with me up here. It gets very cold and I feel... I feel very—" He checked himself and wiped his eyes. "Come now, we have to travel again."

He stood. The dog gazed up at him, head on one side. It looked eager to begin. Gizhurthra smiled at it. "And you've forgiven me for kicking you. I'm sorry, but he made me angry, that priest." The dog whined. "Yes, I know, we should have got to know people, but, well...." He sighed and took a walking-staff from a corner. "Some things are hard. I don't know why." He slung the bag over his shoulder and went to the door. "Come and look, friend. You will not see these hills again, nor drink from that river, but at least I will have you with me." He half-turned, meaning to blow out the candle but stopped. He looked round the shabby house. Leaning heavily on his staff, he bowed his head. After a moment, he took a breath and went quickly into the night. The candle still burned.

As Gizhurthra entered the square, he found a group of people waiting for him.

"Just here to make sure y' go," said a man. There was a heavy stick in his hand.

"Go on then, afore y' really do kill somebody," shrilled a woman's voice.

Gizhurthra could not look at them. He went quickly past the buildings and descended to the highway, then gasped as a rock thudded into his back.

"That'll help y' move quicker!" There was a peal of laughter.

"Not so mighty now, is he?" More laughter and triumphant yells.

Gizhurthra half ran from the townspeople. A stick flew past his head and clattered on the street.

"Find another hole, rat!"

"Try the city, there's sewers there!"

He reached the highway, breathless with fear, but no-one had followed him. He heard the voices grow quieter as they went to their homes. The dog nuzzled his leg.

"Shall we go to the city, friend?" he asked. "Come, then." He took a few steps, then halted. He looked behind him, up at the dark hill where a faint light showed from the window of what had been his home, and his face twisted in fresh grief. He had tried. He had fought with himself, straining to go out to them, but he had been afraid so often, always glad to be back in that house away from the terrifying eyes of people who feared him or made his insignificance burst into anger. Now the whole long, sad episode of fearful loneliness and failure was ending.

Very well. Let there be an end. He dropped staff and bundle, weeping afresh at the pain of leaving even that lonely house. Arms raised trembling, he threw back his head and howled the fire-word into the night, thrusting his hands towards the house on the hill where the lonely candle danced. The window filled with fire, and flame rushed from the open door. In seconds, the house was blazing, with flame snatching at the trees that stood guard around it.

Gizhurthra took up his staff and bag and, as fresh shouting broke out in the town, he left the road and struck out westwards towards the river and the hills, the dog bounding ahead of him.

Soon there would be the cities.

CHAPTER 11

Archraad

ILISSOS JOLTED INTO AWARENESS as a heavy blow to the side of his head sent streaks of fire behind his eyes. He could not concentrate on what was happening or determine whether it was some brutal dream. Another blow knocked him further into wakefulness, then a series of violent cuffs stung his face until he opened his eyes. He was half lying on a hard, cold floor, his limp body supported by a hand gripping one arm. The swirling room was no village hut but some spacious place with many shadows. He could not take it in. His head drooped, his eyes closed. Someone pulled his head back by the hair and forced a cup against his lips. Oily, stinging fluid went scouring down his throat and lay smouldering in his stomach. The heat of it rippled through his body. His mind and vision cleared, and he found he could support himself with one arm as he sat on the stone floor, despite the pains that still hammered in his bones.

"You wake up," said a harsh voice. "Talk to master." Another blow to the face.

He looked about him and took in his surroundings. He was at one end of a wide, lofty room whose vaulted ceiling was supported by rows of pillars. At the farther end was an arched doorway and a high, shuttered window. Torchlight fell on a haphazard collection of seats and benches, crumbling ornamentation and, near the centre of the room, a

199

deep, sunken area surrounded by cracked and faded tiles as if it had once been a bath or an ornamental pool. Ilissos and the man who held him were on a raised area that ran the width of the hall, much like a low stage where musicians would have played for masques in happier days. The whole place had the feel of brokenness and neglect and of inevitable decay. A mustiness of fading, damp decline drifted in the feeble air, unpleasant on the tongue and stale within the lungs. It produced a sense that nothing could stay bright or wholesome in this place for long. A tomb long prepared and waiting only for a death.

Ilissos abruptly realised someone was watching him. His burning eyes focussed with difficulty upon a huge wooden chair with a high, elaborately carved backrest. Part of the carving on the backrest had been hacked away and the ornamentation on the ends of the two armrests had been similarly hewn off. This had been a splendid piece of furniture when it had emerged from the workshop, but it now bore the same air of faded ruination that permeated the rest of the hall. Seated in it, staff across his body, was the man, the embodiment of melancholy, who had arrived in Gizhurthra's hut to induct Falakhoth's vraakhin into the mysterious brotherhood. He sat like a motionless spider who had been there forever, elbows on the arm-rests, shoulders hunched, and his head drooping forward. From beneath his fur-edged cap, long, lank hair trailed down over his chest. His dark beard was straggling and sparse, scarcely any burden to the wide, full mouth in the narrow, pallid face. Under straight brows sat huge eyes set deep in the skull and ringed with colours that emphasised their melancholy: violets, ailing blues, and tones of dark earth bound together with a grey that seeped down into the shadows of the face. The eyes themselves were of no colour. Dead lanterns placed in hollow caves. Ilissos looked into them and found himself thinking of caverns and wells and pools with invisible depths.

"*Sa qanir. Va bhanir ai-sa, lukh? Ayim sa shachti?*" The drear voice of the man seemed to come from a chest bound with bands of iron. The Syrgan began to feel that something was whirling around inside his head as he groped for some answer. "*Ai krenakha shri qanirakh?*" The eyes were a cold fire, but they could not burn a response out of him. "You know this speech? You know what it says?"

Ilissos shook his head desperately. A massive hand smashed into his temple. Ilissos gasped as the trails of fire went across his vision.

"You speak to Master," snarled the coarse voice of the man that guarded him.

"No, no. I do not know this."

"It is the same tongue you spoke in the villager's house. What did you say then?"

"I... I cannot...."

"Do you remember it?"

"Yes, but I do not know what I said."

"You lie to Master!"

"Gurdjatt, no! I will hear him. Tell me, Syrgan, did you call to the little spirit of the Green Hills? You know her name."

"To... to Cynathé? I do not know. I called to her before, when I hid, when you did not hear me, but I do not know what I said that frightened the black one, the one who ran—"

"No more!" Something writhed within Ilissos' abdomen. He gasped and was silent. "Is there a power in you? Is there a power that is your own? Speak true or I will know."

"A power like people in the stories? I have no powers, nothing. I sing, I make songs and stories, I tell tales, I can do nothing that a tale cannot do."

The colourless eyes did not blink, "Do you believe you serve a god?"

"I... I serve Cynathé: she is goddess in Syrga."

"How do you serve her?"

Ilissos became confused. "How? As everyone does. I... I wear her sign, I take the little cakes and grain and honey and put them beside her image, I listen to her rites sometimes. Perhaps I sing a chant that her priest has made. This is what everyone does in Syrga."

"Why?"

Now Ilissos was truly at a loss. "Because... because... I do not know. We have always done it this way, so that is what we do." He was very frightened. This drear, dark man seemed determined to get answers he could not possibly give.

"Why were you in the house? Why did you hide?"

He could answer this. Ilissos described how he had brought merchandise for Gizhurthra and how a terrible, unreasoning fear had fallen on him at the sound of V'karra's voice. This seemed important, for the man rose from the chair and, carrying his staff, strode forward, the swish of his robe on the stone eerily loud in the empty hall. He came up to Ilissos, stooped, and placed his hand on his captive's brow, gripping the front of his head. Close up, the large, wan eyes seemed to pull the Syrgan's thoughts into them, and he felt the sorcerer march through the house of his mind, flinging open doors, searching forgotten rooms and sealed-off cellars, tearing aside curtains, and peering into places narrow and spacious, open and inviting, closed and shadowed. His very thoughts were shifted, upturned, and rearranged for this man's curiosity. "So," he said at last with his hand still on Ilissos' forehead, "Why were you in Falakhoth?"

"Travelling, master," said Ilissos, trembling, for he felt the thoughts behind the words lifted and examined as he spoke. "Travelling, going home. I came down from the moors and men from Falakhoth met me."

"Why were you on the moors? What happened there? Why not the road?"

"I chose the moors for quiet and beauty. I sheltered from the great storm, I met soldiers going north, I..., I...."

"What? What happened?"

"I stopped to look at the mountains and... something happened. I do not know what to call it." The grip on his forehead tightened. A stinging sensation was creeping into his skull.

"Remember it! Describe it, I will see."

"I saw the mountains, and the earth, how beautiful it is, and a great beauty came from another place, from behind the beauty that I saw... I... I cannot tell.... A wonder."

At that the man pulled in his breath and bared his teeth in an agonised hiss as though Ilissos' head had become hot metal. His arm shook, his face reddened, and sweat ran down into his bulging eyes, but still he kept his hand in place, breathing hard. The stinging was deep inside now as Ilissos felt the man probe his thoughts for truth.

"You came to the town," said the sorcerer through his teeth. He spoke with great difficulty.

"I did, master," gasped his terrified prisoner.

"What did you do there?" The man was shaking violently.

"I lodged at the inn, I took food with the headman, I... I met his son."

"I see him: tall, dark. He sits beside a fire."

"Tyr-shan. Yes, master, you see true."

"Go on."

"Then... then there is nothing. We did as people do."

"Tell me!" roared the sorcerer in pain, yet struggling to endure whatever was happening. "Everything!" His face was crimson, the sweat seeping through his coat.

"We... we ate, we talked. There were two priests. I asked them to tell me the meaning of...."

"What? The meaning of what?"

"I cannot name it! The beauty I felt on the moors."

The sorcerer cried out. His arm seemed to be burning inside but still he held on. "What did they say? What was it?"

"They did not know! One said it was nothing. The other said it may be in the Scrolls of his Shrine."

"Then?" The man's arm was shaking furiously.

"The headman argued with one of the priests, then players came. We saw a play, there was a feast, I slept."

"Nothing more?"

"Nothing, master. Well, the next day was sad. A wolf had killed the innkeeper, and I later came to the house on the hill."

"That is all?"

"Yes, yes." Ilissos paused. He felt strangely compelled to continue talking. "Well, one thing more, but it was nothing. A thing about the feast."

"Tell me! Recall it. I will see the memory!"

"Only that... well, I was by the fire and I... I looked up to the reach of the flames, to the top of the blaze and I... I do not know what it was, but I felt there was something. I did not see it, but there was a great wave of the happiness—the same beauty I felt on the moors—something was there, I think."

The sorcerer howled and pulled his hand away. He reeled back, dropping his staff, and putting a hand over his eyes as if to shut out a terrible sight. His legs buckled, and he lay scrabbling on the floor, desperate to get away from something Ilissos could not see. Blood streamed down the man's nose. The hand that had held Ilissos seemed unusable. The whole arm shuddered and spasmed uncontrollably, and the Syrgan could see that the palm and fingers were a deep, ugly red as if the fire from the feast had scorched them itself.

"Away! Get him away!"

Gurdjatt seized Ilissos' arm, hauled him down the few steps from the platform and through a side door. They marched through shadowy passages and up a narrow stair, Ilissos scarcely on his feet, knocking flaking plaster from the walls as he went. His guide stopped at a torch-lit door and slammed his charge against the wall.

"You hurt master!" he said savagely. "Nobody hurts master, nobody able! What do you do?" He was both terrified and furious.

"I do not know, I do not know! I answer what he asks. I do not know what happened!

The man glared in astonished outrage. Ilissos shrunk into himself, fearing another beating, but his guide kicked the door open and flung him inside. Gurdjatt gave Ilissos a final enraged stare, before backing out and slamming the door. There came the sound of heavy bolts and retreating feet.

The room that caged Ilissos was roughly square. It was empty of furnishings except for a filthy mattress on the wooden floor. Beside the mattress was a bowl of food and some water. A bucket sat in the corner. A small, barred window, impossible to climb up to, was at the very top of one of the high walls. Through it filtered a little light from the night outside. There were no other windows and no lamp. It was a perfect prison for mind and body.

Ilissos realised he was ravenous and ate whatever was in the bowl, thinking perhaps the lack of light was a blessing. He drank, then squatted on the mattress, trying to think about what was happening. He had no clue where he was or even who had trapped him. Everything was an immense and frightening mystery. He thought of the beauty he had felt on the moors and tried to catch it again, but it was impossible. Why, he wondered, had it so frightened the sorcerer? Why had simply hearing about it caused him such distress? But there was no answer and the wondering simply added to the pain of his bewilderment. He did the only thing he could and keeled over on the mattress exhausted beyond measure.

Morning light was seeping through the high window when the door scraping open woke Ilissos. He opened his eyes and found even the thin early morning sunlight painful. Gurdjatt was bending over him, his broad bearded face still suspicious.

"Master want you," he growled. "You eat that." He set water and another dish of food on the floor, then leaned against the door to see his order was carried out. "You know Archraad?"

Ilissos shook his head.

Gurdjatt frowned and, as if making a huge concession, said, "It is a city in the Plain. You are there. Quick. Master waits."

Ilissos forced his body round into a sitting position despite the agonies that still ran through his limbs. He took the water and food and then, as though he could not quite remember how to move, got clumsily to his feet. It was necessary to lean on the wall while the pulsing in his head died down. When he was able, he stooped for the jug, almost falling on his face, and threw the last of the water over his head, hoping it would clear his mind. He scuffed over to the corner without lifting his feet from the floor and made liberal use of the bucket. This done, he gave Gurdjatt a brief, pained grimace of a smile from sheer habit, then drew in a long breath and let it out again.

Ilissos was taken once more through the mouldering corridors to meet the sorcerer. A whack from Gurdjatt's hand sent him staggering the final few paces into the spacious hall which had hosted his interrogation from the night before. The shutters on the tall window were still closed, but they were broken and dilapidated, so lines of sunlight pierced through to warm the dreary place a little. The light somehow made things feel safer, even more wholesome, but it cruelly revealed the broken plaster and rubble that littered the floor, and the debris lying in the sunken, dried-up pool. Even that much honest sunlight was a concession, an unavoidable and resented intrusion.

As Gurdjatt guided him towards the steps to the platform, Ilissos made out the sounds of a city's day filtering through the shutters. There seemed to be a busy place outside, evidenced by the noise of horses, traders' cries, and many voices. A glance toward the high-backed chair showed that this could not compare with the frenzied busyness in the mind of the sorcerer. The colourless eyes were sunken amidst even darker circles. Here was a man who had not slept. The whirl of the man's thoughts was aimed at Ilissos like a spear point. Gurdjatt shoved him towards a low, wooden stool. Ilissos sat down, wondering anxiously what was coming. He gave his captors uneasy glances while the sorcerer's eyes bored into his mind like a drill.

Suddenly, the sorcerer rose and brought his staff down hard on the floor. The noise went ringing round the doleful hall. "I have the measure of you now!" he cried. "You think I am some sad mortal you may play with! The old arrogance as from the beginning! Well, I am not your toy. None of us are." The man stood furiously straight-backed, head up, chest out, trembling with passion. "You think you have found a way to hurt us, to come among us. You think you will spy on us and cripple us from within."

The Syrgan had no idea what to say to this, he could only stare. The sorcerer began to pace up and down.

"I have communed in thought with Lord Gehrava—no, you need not search, you cannot find him. He is under the earth and you know not where. But he has shown me how you have played this trick before! You found a way into the temple complex through Virzhith of Burdtha. Ar-kharhova agreed to let you use his servant, and he became your eyes among the dog-priests. Ur-thromath gave you the insane old warrior to be your doorway to Vel Shirriva, and he died in that great desert when you had used him up. The tales are many and they prove your limitation. You cannot act, you are too feeble, you must find some pitiable slave to be your channel if you are to frighten those you fear! We see your strategy! We despise it and you!"

He aimed all this at Ilissos in a ferocious snarl as though he were guilty of all the sorcerer had said. The Syrgan, however, was utterly at a loss. The strange names meant nothing to him.

The staff thudded on the floor as the man strode up to him, stooped down, and glared into his eyes as before, though this time he did not touch him. "Ha!" he cried. "I see it! He has no memory, no knowledge! You have blocked his thoughts, he does not know what you are doing with him! Well, are you seeking to be cleverer with us?"

The sorcerer stalked back to his chair and leaned on it. He had an air of frightened triumph. Ilissos concluded that he was both powerful and mad. He resolved to go carefully and remained silent. Apparently the man was not addressing him at all, but someone he thought was secretly using him.

"Well, you have called the little hill-sprite away from warbling in her green playground. Is that the best you could bring to Uerathel? The strongest, the greatest?"

Ilissos realised with an outraged shock that the fellow was speaking of Cynathé.

"She has given you one of her admirers to try in your game. Will you attack us through this… *storyteller*? I shield myself easily." He moved his staff and the surrounding air shimmered and moved as over a fire. "Have you not rather given us a trophy? Hurt me, then, if you can." He stepped up to Ilissos. "I defy you: you cannot harm me." And with the manner of one who spreads out his arms before a crossbow, knowing there is no arrow in it, the sorcerer planted the end of his staff against Ilissos' chest as if he were going to run him through with it. He kept it there until the fear he was trying to conceal faded and a breathless, rhythmic laugh of triumph began. "You see. Nothing! You cannot reach to me! But I will send my energies into him. I will search you out!" He began to tremble and sweat, still with the grotesque smile of victory. He seemed to be performing some huge, immensely dangerous task he knew might destroy him, elated and hardly daring to believe he was managing it.

Sitting on his stool with a length of wood on his chest and listening to the man rave at someone who was not there, Ilissos was doubly convinced the fellow was mad. Then the stinging, prickling sensation began under the place where the staff was pressing on his chest. It intensified and spread inwards.

"Ha!" yelled the sorcerer again. "You are undone! What shall I learn? What shall I see?"

And then Ilissos felt a breath of freshness and sweet fragrance sweep around him, rushing into his lungs and revitalising body and thought. With it there was an entry, an arrival, a reaching through that seemed to slant in from a divergent place, an actuality at an angle to his. This influx, this reality that had found a way in was so authentic, so genuine, its presence made his own world feel like the one that was angled and askew. Astounded, suddenly hopeful, he caught a snatch of the glorious beauty he had felt on the moors and above the fire at Falakhoth. The beauty carried with it new perceptions. A series of images unfolded in his mind, so vivid as to be almost sight:

A woman, seated, spinning wool. She seemed very large. A little hand reaches up and taps her arm, but she shakes it away without looking, engrossed in her spinning.

The same woman, busy with food, appearing immensely tall. The small hands again, holding up a little figure roughly made of sticks and bits of cloth. The woman, irritated at the interruption, takes the figure and throws it on a shelf without looking at it. A feeling of confusion arises, a sense that something that should have arrived was absent.

The woman with a man. They do not seem quite so large. The man tries to speak with her, but she shows little interest and so they look in different directions. There seems to be an invisible, threatening barrier around the woman. The confusion thickens into bewilderment. Ilissos has the feeling that he is talking to the man but receives little response and the man will not look at him. A sense of absence appears.

The shrine of some god or goddess, dull and musty, the man and woman nearby. A sense of resentment, of having been forced here. Ilissos feels himself restless, the woman, full of rage, grips his arm painfully to control him.

The woman's face, angry, curling her lips to show her teeth, incensed eyes bulging. The feeling, almost the sound, of an incessant series of blows, but not to the body, a hammering within, a wearing down. The sense of resentment deepening into outrage.

A dim, red perilous place. The woman very close to him, sometimes appearing very large, sometimes his own size. The man is absent. In the woman's eyes is the knowledge that she is very wrong, but she curls her lip at the knowledge and thrusts it away. He is telling her that her inner voice is right, but she scorns him, not meeting his eyes. Her unseen barrier seems very dangerous. The feeling of confusion is profound. A sense of threat is growing as he notices a strong yearning for protection and looks for the man but cannot find him. The woman's nearness is intensely frightening, but he cannot understand why. The way she wears her dress is unfamiliar, and that too is very frightening. Now the awareness of confusion and disorder is all there is and when it passes he finds a dislike of himself has appeared. There seems to be something wrong with his body. It is no longer a good thing to live in. He is angry at the woman and this feels right and good. But the eyes, the curling lips and the teeth are hammering at him and his feelings seem to turn grey. He wants the man to help, but he looks at other things and cannot defend him. There is the sense of becoming small, of his body splintering and bending. Realising he must be his own protector, he pulls a heavy door between himself and the man and woman.

Last of all, he is suddenly in a great round space, an immense building. There are screams and wailing. People are lying on the floor or running in terror as smoke billows in the air. A man stands before him, confronting him, there is a sense of triumph, exaltation, power, and attention at last. He feels himself speaking words that terrify, uttering threats, praising his greatness. He is aware of the staff in his hand and he raises it, about to do something terrible, but there is a blast of light and authority from some high place. The power of his threat is swept away, and he is terrified and furious, feeling small and frustrated again.

The images swirled away. A glance at the sorcerer's horrified, astounded face showed Ilissos that he had seen them too.

"Is this all you show me? You try to hurt me with this?" He forced out a yell, baring his teeth with the effort. "You do not know how strong I am now? How far I have travelled? Pitiable weapons!"

The wonderful fragrance still sweetened the air. Ilissos knew somehow that a power or energy was moving away from his chest along the staff to the sorcerer who held it.

"No!" howled the man. "You will not burn me up! You will not poison my thoughts with this stench!" He drew in his breath and gathered himself for a mighty effort. "Hear me! I take your servant from you for my own! I tear him from you and bind him to myself! You have lost him!" He wailed other incomprehensible words.

There was a rush of energy, a burst of light and darkness and a sudden violent crack. Ilissos felt himself thrown away across the floor and after a fierce, blurred moment was lying against the opposite wall, Gurdjatt lay beside him, stunned. The sorcerer was sprawled in his chair, body twisted grotesquely over an armrest. His head lolled at an ugly angle and, until his chest moved, Ilissos thought he was dead. On the floor scattered between them lay the charred and splintered fragments of the staff. Over them hung a dirty yellow smoke. Ilissos suddenly sat up, mind clear, the wonderful fragrance around him.

You are known, Val-zajjhak, Ilissos said, astonishing himself. *We will not give up.*

The sorcerer stared for a moment, apparently shocked, then marshalled a sneer. "More threats," he hissed. "That is all you know." He waved his hand again as he tried to sit up. "Away! I have done! Away until Vardresh!"

~

AFTER A LONG TIME huddled on his mattress, his back against the wall, thoughts whirling, Ilissos slumped into an exhausted sleep. Gurdjatt woke him again by clattering another dish of food on the floor. As he sat up, he saw the man staring at him with a mixture of fear and awe.

"I do not know anything," said Ilissos, knowing what was coming. "Do not ask me, please."

"You know master's name," said Gurdjatt nonetheless.

"No. Was that his name? I do not know."

"I smelt it," replied Gurdjatt. "The beautiful smell. Better than the very precious perfumes. No woman has a perfume like that. What is happening?"

"Truly I do not know. You do not understand, I do not understand. I am sorry."

"Both of us have a puzzle. I think Master does also."

Ilissos felt it best not to comment and instead said, "Can you tell me what Vardresh is?"

"A town, that way. Bel-ghirá is governor." But even this seemed evasive.

"Ah. Does something happen there?"

"Yes, tonight, you will see." This time Gurdjatt seemed to think very hard. He glanced outside the room then closed the door behind him. "Something is happening with you and Master. Because of that and because of the beauty I will say something."

Ilissos sat up intently as the other man crouched at the foot of the mattress.

"You have been in the sleep many days," Gurdjatt said in a low voice. "I brought you from Falakhoth with Master. Tonight in Valderthaan is what they call Renewal Night."

"Renewal? I have heard the name. It is a festival?"

"Yes. They say Arna makes the line of their king, their Valgraav, new again so that there will always be Valgraavs. They say Arna makes himself new again, and he does something so that the Valgraav's kingdom will always be here." He scowled and looked at the floor. "Harrak hate the Valgraav. He should not be here."

"I have heard this," said Ilissos, feeling encouragement was called for.

"My tribe is Jurghūn, but tonight we ride with warriors of the Vorish. When Renewal is happening in their Shrine, we will strike at Vardresh. It is the first blow. Soon there will be no Valgraav." He stood abruptly. Clearly, he had said more than he should. "Harrak will be free again," he added, going to the door. As he stepped out of the room he paused. "I will always think of the beauty," he said, then closed the door quietly.

After his meal and another visit to the bucket, Ilissos again propped himself against the wall, his lively but frustrated mind in a whirl. A little had been learned, but not enough. The sorcerer's name was Val-zajjhak. He apparently had influence with the tribes of the Harrak and he, the Harrak, the foreigner V'karra, and no doubt others were about to begin a campaign against the rule of the Valgraav. Gizhurthra, he remembered,

211

had apparently been inducted into their scheme as some kind of lookout in the Falakhoth area.

But why had the images that had flowed through Ilissos' mind so alarmed Val-zajjhak? And why had the Syrgan said what he did? Who did his captor believe he was speaking to when hissing at him? Whoever it was, he was furious at them. And what could explain the burst of energy that had destroyed the staff and nearly Val-zajjhak himself? His last questions were happy ones: What was the astonishing fragrance? And why had it come with a glimpse of the beauty above the moors?

Once more Ilissos made the mistake of trying to relive that experience and stay in it, but all he could manage were some pale reminiscences that brought nothing like the comfort he wanted. He stood, despite his pains, and shuffled about the room from sheer frustration. The place had very few details, and he knew them all. There was nothing that could be of any help to him.

He considered Val-zajjhak and his allies, especially the fearsome V'karra. The man was not simply bad, but evil. He must be, to be surrounded by such an aura of fear and hatred. Whatever he was planning, any design saturated in that much hate must be wrong. And they all despised Cynathé. From his childhood, Ilissos had looked to her as the kindly Mother of his land and all the richness of the earth. Her name brought together all the sensations that had ever come to him from tree or river or field. She was the green shade of the cypress groves, the restless gold of nodding corn, the stream leaping from the crags, the swelling vine, the rich loam. She was goodness, life, and endless giving. And these sorcerers hated her, belittled her, as if they had forgotten her image in their own mothers. Ilissos realised with a shock that their dark minds must be blind to every green thing, must scorn the feel of grass underfoot or the rain-bearing wind, must despise the very smell of bread. Whatever might be amiss in the Valgraav's lands, whatever grudge Val-zajjhak and the southerner, V'karra held against him, this could not be right.

The Syrgan thought of the town Vardresh. He knew nothing about it, but towns had people and even if a despot ruled, there would still be mothers, fathers, children, ordinary people who were not part of it and under the Valgraav's rule. There were good people in the north, he had met many, they must not fall prey to V'karra. He must get away from these men to send a warning. He looked desperately round the room. The door was useless; the window was barred, and too high, well above even his strongest leap. He tried it anyway. No good. His grasping fingers came well short of the windowsill each time. But he could see that the bars were part of a metal square that was set into the window aperture. He might, just might, be able to haul it out. Desperately, he gave the room another pointless survey: mattress, dish, jug. Nothing to stand on, nothing to climb. Could he lever up a wooden floor board and use it to clamber to the window? The thought left his head as soon as it entered. He could see the beams beneath him were massive and firm, wedged together by age and skill. They would yield to nothing less than iron bars and the strength of oxen.

Suddenly, Ilissos was furious. He bared his teeth at the expanse of mouldering plaster beneath the tiny square of sky. Freedom might be ten feet above his head, but he was helpless. At any other time, he would have snatched at his amulet and uttered a prayer. Instead, he yelled and kicked savagely at the wall. His foot scattered chunks of plaster and left a deep score. It did him no good, but there was some satisfaction in causing such damage. He glared at the gouge in the wall and something stirred in his mind. A memory of a boy who climbed the rocks among the Syrgan hills, hand over hand, fingers and toes grasping the clefts in the stone, pulling himself up. He looked again. If that scrape were deeper, it would be such a cleft.... And if there were several....

He snatched up the dish. Yes, it was an ill-made thing of some soft metal. He brought it down on his knee, bending it, then forced it against the floor with his foot until it buckled over. He stamped on it so it became a half-circle of double thickness, strong and pointed, a tool to gouge at the plaster wall.

Dusk was falling by the time he had hacked out the holes. The highest was at the limit of his reach. Carefully, he wedged the toe of his left boot on the lowest. With the bent plate held in his teeth, he gave a jump, so that his left foot and right hand met the first and sixth crevices. He was trying not to rest too much weight on any one spot, unsure of the old plaster's strength. It held. Spider-like, he clung to the wall and with his left hand reached up and scraped out a seventh hole, trying always to strike downwards, lest the force of his thrusts push down too hard on the supports already made. He returned the plate to his mouth, placed his fingertips in the hole, and slowly brought his left foot up to the third support. With his right hand, he scraped out the next support. He was climbing.

How long this went on, Ilissos did not know. He worked in fear and pain, knowing that at any moment the noise of his scraping and the clatter of the falling plaster might bring someone to investigate. His fingertips shook agonisingly as they bore the weight of his body, his splayed-out limbs aching to keep him unnaturally flat against the wall, his head swam with the effort, and sweat stung his eyes. Perhaps he should not have tried. Perhaps he was still too weak after his days in blackness.

Suddenly, where the next handhold was to be, one was ready for him: the window ledge. His whole hand could grasp it, his whole arm. Ilissos' head cleared at once. He grabbed the ledge. Keeping his toes in the notches in the wall, he pulled himself up and took hold of the bars with one hand. Here was the final barrier, the moment of success or failure. He tugged. Nothing. He shook the bars. The frame edged a little in its mounting but stayed in place. The frustration was almost unbearable. Ilissos could see the quiet evening sky and the vast plain laid out like a blanket underneath it. The sun was leaving and soon he'd be too late to warn Vardresh. It was too much for him. Fury rose within him. He drew strength from his pain, threw it along his arm to his bleeding hand, and roared with potent rage. Ancient rust and plaster yielded to a massive, furious wrench. The grille flew across the room. Ilissos let his body swing free and heaved himself up onto his elbows. Yelling in triumph, his scrabbling feet sent down a rain of plaster fragments as he hauled his body on to the windowsill.

He gasped in the clear evening air like the very breath of life. The early stars seemed like beacons lit for his escape. Far away, the last red tint in the western sky withdrew behind the mountains of the Long Water, its dying light briefly revealing to Ilissos the great grey Plain and its white roads. The mountain shadows merged with the night that fell over that vast place and all detail disappeared. Near his prison he could make out the dark silhouettes of streets and houses. Just behind them stood a wall protecting the city, with two great towers that must flank a gate, undoubtedly already shut for the night. Watch-fires were being lit on this encircling wall, and in the great darkness beyond the lights of towns and campfires appeared.

Bracing himself on his elbows, Ilissos looked down. His arms were trembling and his head hurt, but peering into the dimness he thought he could make out a mass of thick foliage. He judged he was directly above a large veranda that had once been cultivated as a small garden from which to overlook the city. Val-zajjhak seemed to have taken the same care with this as with the rest of his house, and all seemed to be a tangle of tree, shrub, and creeper, left to grow and choke each other as they pleased. Vines and ivies had begun the ascent of the wall as if their aim was to smother the house entirely. Ilissos listened for a moment to the caressing murmur of the leaves. It was natural, fresh, a call to freedom. He glanced to his right and hope leapt up afresh. Some sturdy vine had scaled the wall almost to the roof and passed his window on the way. It looked strong, but should he try it? The only other option was a direct drop to the ground below hoping some bush would break his fall. It was an easy decision. He leaned out, dangerously far, grasped for the vine and tugged. It held. He paused for a agonising second, then brought his other hand round to snatch the vine, leaving only one knee braced on the ledge. He let go.

For an instant he swung in space. His wrists twisted, confusing his grasp. The vine shuddered and rustled, but he did not fall. Instead, he hung in disbelieving gratitude, gasping prayers to Cynathé and whatever god watched over night in the North. He clambered down the gnarled stem and into the overgrown chaos that had once been a garden.

The Syrgan paused, crouching in the darkness behind the thickest bushes. It struck him suddenly how empty the city was. The streets were desolate and hardly any windows seemed to be lit. There was a strange sense of waiting. Motionless in shadow, Ilissos realised he was conscious of something on the edge of the silence: a confused, collective swell of hundreds of tiny sounds. Dull stamping and pawing, soft snorts, little rattles of harness. He strained to hear, before realising he was listening to a great crowd of horses ready for swift passage but being kept unnaturally still. Given the faintness of their sounds, Ilissos reasoned they were stationed somewhere just outside the town's walls. Inside the walls the tension was so palpable that Ilissos imagined the walls themselves would have fallen outwards had the city gate not swung open.

Running feet stopped somewhere near him. He drew in his breath. He was not alone on the veranda. Framed by branch and leaf, and black against the torch-lit walls, the stooping figure of Val-zajjhak was unmistakable. The sorcerer leaned over a crumbling parapet, looking down into the street. He was gripping, as usual, a staff, apparently a replacement for the one that had shattered earlier in the great hall. The man himself seemed to be restored, his calm deadness in place again.

A voice came from below: "All ready, master! Gate open, horses eager! Not long to Vardresh!" It was Gurdjatt.

Val-zajjhak called down to him, "The full force is there?"

"All! I join my kinsmen of the Jurghūn. We ride with the warriors of the Vorish!"

"It is good. What do the watchmen see?"

"Fires, master. The best-sighted say it's too much for campfires."

Val-zajjhak straightened, breathed deeply, and in a voice horribly flat and toneless said, "Vardresh is burning. It is time. Ride swiftly."

There was a wild, rough laugh, "My boy has his gift, master?"

"He does, Gurdjatt. You may take it for him yourself, I hope. May it be joy to him!"

"Which one? Ha?"

Val-zajjhak himself laughed, a brief, coarse sound, like a crow finding mirth in carrion. "Why, the one that wears the most rings!" Another laugh from the street, then running feet as Gurdjatt made for the gate to join the men of his tribe. Val-zajjhak stood like a statue, head bowed, as though the thoughts of all the city were open to him, and perhaps they were, but he did not so much as move when a great voice rose outside the walls. It was as if the great Plain itself had found a tongue to cry a challenge to the mountains.

Bergund-ja, Harrak! Grir, r'kamma! Harrak, va! Harrak, reycha! Ai!

There came an immense roar of many voices: *Harrak! Ai!*

The unseen company shook the ground as they swept towards Bel-ghirá's burning city, dust rising with them like a pale, vengeful thundercloud. Val-zajjhak waited, motionless, till the last drumming of the hooves had gone, then abruptly turned and swept back into the house.

Ilissos had no idea how long it took to plunder a city, but he assumed that at the very least he had three or four hours to make his escape. If the gates were still open, it should be easy to get outside the walls. Once outside, he would make his way west at the southernmost edge of the Plain, to Valderthaan, keeping well clear of the roads. In the city of the Valgraav, he would tell what he had discovered. He hoped that Bel-ghirá and his people had had some kind of warning and were able to make a good defence. Perhaps, despite the burning, they had even escaped ahead of time. The governor, after all, was a servant of the Sun-god who had helped Ilissos.

The street was twelve feet or so below the balcony, an easy drop. Ilissos quickly made the descent and stood poised in the shadow of a column as he made sure of his bearings. He was in an open space where several streets intersected in front of the large, sepulchral building that was Val-zajjhak's dilapidated home. The watchtowers of the city gate were still visible above the houses. The street to the left, he surmised, must lead to the broader way that normally ran through a city from its entrance. When he reached Valderthaan, he would give thanks at the golden Shrine. He began, keeping to the shadows. The streets were empty apart from the occasional dark shape moving hurriedly along them. None of the people on their anxious errands so much as glanced at the Syrgan. This seemed to be a night when no-one wished to be outside for long. But then, if the people who lived here were aware of the sorcerer, they might fear the open street after dark.

The gate-towers were near, looming over him. He glanced back to his former prison. There was neither light nor movement—thankfully, the window he had escaped by was dark—and beneath the balcony the heavy door that led onto the street was closed. No-one had noticed he was missing.

He kept on moving. Around this building and the gate should be....
No, he was mistaken. Here was a closed courtyard, but thankfully one
with an archway that led directly towards the gate. He ran through it and
found himself almost at the very base of the gate-towers. The end of this
street would hopefully open onto the main thoroughfare. He ran the few
yards to the turning, avoiding the dim lantern at a larger archway, and
stopped in another straight, dark street that joined the first at an unexpected angle. He glanced up at the nearest tower, surely it was only yards
away. Ah, an alley between two squat buildings. Its farther end was dark,
but it went straight towards the gate. Ilissos plunged into it at once,
freedom drawing him on. A projecting wall made him turn, and another
turned him once more. He emerged panting in a square bordered by
large houses. A street led off it into the city's heart, in the direction
Ilissos had, he imagined, put behind him. He glanced to his left. The
towers seemed no nearer than before, another alley leading straight
towards them. He headed towards it, but something felt wrong. Even
though he was judging distances in the dark, he knew those towers
should be nearer than they were. This square should have been at the
base of those towers. Ilissos realised there should not have been room
enough between street and tower for the previous alley to be as long as
it appeared, and no way was there space for that alley and the one ahead
of him. The horrible realisation of what was happening stole over him.
Despair drew cold fingers over his shoulders, sapping his body of its
strength.

The brief, dry laugh came as no surprise. He had heard it not long
since, the voice of the carrion-crow in the mouth of a man. With a
terrible weariness, he turned. Not far away a chariot stood, a lithe grey
horse between the shafts. Swathed in shade, a thin, stooped figure leaned
on the rail. In its hand was a staff.

"Do you think I have no power beyond my own house?" said the
voice. It was without anger or triumph or any feeling. "Did you not know
I felt your mind beside me among the leaves and followed it through the
streets? Could you not perceive my craft in the confusion of the ways?"
There was silence. Under the invasive scrutiny of the other's mind, Ilissos'
hope and determination wilted into an anguished bleakness. "This is the

hour of death for Vardresh, the first wound in the Valgraav's hide. May its poison never be purged." Now an uncharacteristic vibrancy came into the voice, "I must go now to Lukar and Vardresh, and so shall you, my trophy, whether you will or no. Come, servant of the gods." Val-zajjhak pointed the staff forwards and Ilissos felt among his thoughts the notion that he could never again leave the sorcerer without permission. "It is natural that you try to escape. We will not speak of it again. Tonight sees the first spark of a great fire. Shall we look on it?" He beckoned and Ilissos went slowly into the chariot.

"There are no reins," Ilissos said weakly.

"No need," said Val-zajjhak. He spoke a word, and the horse took them from the square. Far away in the darkness, the fires of Vardresh glowed. Val-zajjhak trembled with a terrible vitality. Ilissos, horrified, caught that energy in his mind's eye as pictures of the pursuing lion, the swift spider, and the merciless mantis. Val-zajjhak's eyes flashed with deadly intent. No longer did they appear colourless but full of glints and gleams of every hue, bright as rubies, cold as sapphire.

"They will be in the city," he hissed, like the scrape of a blade leaving the scabbard. "Perhaps even in the governor's palace. Gurdjatt's lad will see his tenth year tomorrow, he will have his present soon. I must fetch it for him."

"His present?" breathed Ilissos, fearing the answer.

"Yes," said the sorcerer, staring ahead. "I have promised him the hand of Bel-ghirá." He glanced round at Ilissos. "One of his hands, that is. The rings on it will provide for the boy for many years."

Sickened, Ilissos realised that Val-zajjhak was serious. The hideous gift was to be no crude gesture of triumph but deliberately, logically practical. He could not contain his horror. "Why do you do this?" he gasped, almost sobbing. "Do you not fear the gods?"

"*Fear the gods?*" It was an animal snarl, not a human cry, and for a second Ilissos saw the twisted face of a beast, blood in its open mouth and burning cities in the soulless deeps of its eyes. "Fear the gods? Savage! What do they dream of in the Green Hills? *The gods will fall!*"

The staff flashed out its deathly light, and the horse leapt into the dark, towards the burning. Like the winter wind they drove, like the storm-cloud bearing its own blue lightning, sweeping towards the growing ring of fire that was Vardresh. Ilissos clung terrified to the chariot rail, but the sorcerer stood erect: one hand on the rail, the other on his blazing staff, his hair and robe streaming out in the gale, his features fixed in a spasm of hatred.

They rode through timeless darkness towards the fire until they could see the flames fly up and hear the shouts of men and the wails of women and the maimed. Behind a spur of rock, the chariot stopped in the shadows.

"I will not look on this first," said Val-zajjhak suddenly. "It pleases me that you, the servant of the gods shall see it first, and let your masters view their folly."

Ilissos looked into the face of Val-zajjhak. What he saw there he could never describe.

"Go and look, storyteller, and later you shall make the tale of our fame."

The staff's blue glare became an unendurable white. Ilissos staggered from the chariot. He climbed the spur of rock that momentarily shielded him from the horrors. Up the black mound he went, limbs resisting every step. Smoke billowed over the top, the sky blossoming with roses of flame oddly beautiful amidst the darkness, and the howling agony of the rape of Vardresh became louder. He came to the top of the rise and crouched down in terror of seeing. He glanced back down at Val-zajjhak in the pool of evil light and saw him staring up, mad and wild. Powerful unseen hands seemed to force him to his feet and turn his eyes to what was before him. Against his will, Ilissos stared at the horror. Unable to turn away, reality slipped away from him. He came swiftly and mercifully to the edge of his endurance: his mind could hold no more, his eyes could not bear to see again. He swayed and fell, leaving the horror behind him as he tumbled down the rocky slope into blackness.

CHAPTER 12

Valderthaan

"WHERE ARE WE?" said Tyr, looking around from his horse. "I dunno these hills."

"We're not lost," Azhur told him. "The King's Road is over that hill there, to the West: it would take you up to Lukar."

"King's Road goes right up by the river from Lachresh bridge. Y' get straight to Valderthaan that way."

"Yes, that's quicker, and you can see Valderthaan from Lukar, but I want you to see it in the first real sunlight. You'll never forget it if you do. I don't know why you've never been this way before."

"What for? I live in Falakhoth. I could be in me scratcher at Lachresh, instead of bein' sat here in the dark."

"Oh, Tyr, really! I think you're loving this, you know."

"I've not woke up yet."

"Shake yourself, Tyr. What will you do when you meet the Valgraav?"

"Wet meself, probably. I'm not meetin' *him*, am I?"

"Oh, no, no, just a chat with Lord Galdtchav. Probably with me and one or two other priests. You are very interesting, you know."

"That's all right, then. Well, move y'self, the birds've started." Tyr kicked his horse's sides and set off at a gallop.

Tyr breathed deeply in the last tang of departing night as they rode quickly along the valley floor. His eyes went wide with the beauty of the world that rushed by them. Rising backs of half visible hills, the black skeletons of dew-damp trees, birds drinking in a glinting stream, and the strength of the green matted earth braced to catch each flying hoof. It was wonderful, he thought, wonderful and natural. No vision, dream, or inward sight, just the common beauty of the great earth drawing him into its life as it was part of his. Could stone towers and beaten gold compare with it in the least?

He *was* eager to see Valderthaan's first appearance on the horizon. Already, the eastern sky was the grey of a gull's wing, and the greens and browns of the landscape were forming out of the departing shadows. They moved swiftly on, riding into the still birthplace of the dawn. The hills on their left rose and swelled into crags and cliffs and slopes of scree, and soon they passed dark pines that clustered around a gnarled mass of a mountain.

"That mountain is called the Mardhoran," Azhur cried over the hoof-beats. "We'll go round it to the valley that carries the road from the Plain to the Lake where Valderthaan is. You'll see Mardokhal in a moment, where I used to live."

They came at last round the mountain-spur and the ground fell away before them in a long slope scattered with pines and rocks. In the pale light of the newborn day, Tyr looked down into the wide valley where the mists curled. The great road passed to the east and Mardokhal within its walls sent up the smoke of its first fires. He made out a cluster of fields, tiny animals, and houses huddling against the town's wall.

Tyr turned to Azhur, "When was y' last there, then?"

"About six years ago."

"Did y' like it?"

"Suppose so, yes."

"Was y' a priest there? Novice, I mean."

"No. Family was there."

"Oh, right. What were y'? Merchants?"

"Administration."

"Are y' folk still there? Can we get a bit of breakfast?"

"No."

"Mine of information, y' are."

"Keep moving! We need to be at a certain place when the sun shows himself." Azhur turned his horse westwards, towards a thick pelt of pines.

When Tyr followed, he found himself on a well-ridden path flanked by tall, dense trees that hid everything but the pale sky. "Where's this go?" breathed Tyr, delighted by the stately green corridor.

"Along the side of the Mardhoran. There used to be watch-places here. Faster!"

They travelled for what seemed several miles. Mist trailed down the mountainside and dampened their hair as they rode through. The sky grew clearer. Twice they passed stone arches that marked a kind of long platform into the trees on their right, but Azhur ignored them and hurried on. At the third, he stopped and dismounted.

"Here," he said.

They left the horses and went beneath the arch. Tyr found himself on a long, stone floor with parapets on each side like a jetty running out from the mountainside. The light was green and thick, and the sharp fingers of the pines bobbed and snatched at them. They strode across the jetty into a circular turret with floor and walls of stone, built for watching the mountain-path. There were two high windows and light seeped past their shutters into the room.

"Ey!" cried Tyr. "This is brilliant!" His voice echoed and sang round the walls. "Can y' see it from here?"

Azhur smiled, "Yes, but not just yet. You've got to see it at its best." There was a little silence as he looked at Tyr. "I, ah, I'd like you to see it at its best," he added, then, as if he had surprised himself, he coughed and quickly crossed the room to a wooden shutter and opened it slightly to peer through. "A few minutes," he said.

"Oh, never mind! Let's see!" Tyr ran to the window, but his friend pushed the shutter closed. "Azhur!"

The young novice laughed. The curving wall catching the happy sound and throwing it from side to side in the chamber. "About two minutes, Tyr! You'll be glad I made you wait."

"If it's not worth it, I'll have y'! Ey, is that a waterfall?"

"There's a stream by the side of the tower. You'll see that too, if you're patient."

Tyr tried to wait, stamping and fidgeting and watching Azhur grinning, but it was no good. He grabbed his own hair, bent up and down, stamped round the perimeter of the room, and ended with a kind of mad, drumming dance. He began laughing furiously at his own frustration. "Bugger this! I'm goin' off me head here!"

"Nearly there," said Azhur tantalisingly. He opened the shutter a crack and peered out again. A shaft of soft, strong morning light slid into the dim chamber.

Tyr tried looking round him. "Get out of it!"

"Oh no you don't!" Azhur grabbed him, slamming the wooden panel shut and forcing him back against it, facing inwards.

"Y' rotten sod!" yelled Tyr, loving the struggle. Azhur got the shutter open for one more discreet glance, then grinned.

Tyr stopped thrashing and simply looked. His new friend had, he thought, woken up. He was animated, laughing, with a spark in his eyes. For once feelings had overtaken his constant thinking, and he seemed to be experiencing his own small sunrise.

"Right, then," said Tyr. "Y' happy? Can I see it now?"

Azhur grinned wider, "I think so. Close your eyes."

Tyr gave him a look of exasperation before obeying. He heard the hinges of the shutter move and felt warm light seeping through the widening gap. There was a cold breeze on his face and the silent chamber had become filled with the sounds of falling water, birdsong, and the restless movement of branches in the wind.

Azhur guided Tyr's hands to a sill, and his soft, deep voice said quietly in his ear, "*Ai va sh'herakh, a threma shi. It is the first shining of the day.* Open your eyes."

Tyr opened his eyes on light and grandeur. Valderthaan. A great radiance had descended. It rested upon the shimmering lake and the building-encrusted isle at its centre. For a moment, it seemed the sun itself had settled among the stupendous buildings. The massive golden dome gripping the rock of the island at its highest point drenched the city island with the reflected blessing of the one who rises in the sun. It was the great Shrine of the North, where fire burned always and where Ar-ven slept forever in his holy tomb. The vast claw of foundations and buttresses had fastened there for four centuries and the tenacity of the red stone sinews had not lessened upon this central glory.

Behind and around the Shrine stood towers, their ancient faces turned to the morning to become glorious columns of light. They seemed innumerable, springing up from all parts of the city like young trees in a forest, saplings intricate and beautiful. The towers were built of many hues of stone and crowned with iron, bronze, copper, silver, or gold, and decked with swirling banners and pennants of every colour. But five towers dominated the city. They were the great oaks, the ancient trunks, the first to grow. Their bark was the crimson stone, scarred and pitted by the rain and ice of the northern skies. Gold and bronze and silver were their leaves, and their dazzling fruit the myriad of scarlet and azure and bright yellow banners, the colours of the three great divisions of the Kingdom. Drifting from a high pinnacle was a vast banner of deep red that bore in gold the sign of the royal house: the mountain-lion of Na-veshtrazhdak. Tyr gazed at the foremost of these towers. From its seat behind the Shrine where its foundations seemed to embrace the golden dome and its buildings, the vast structure climbed into the morning sky. It had the appearance of many buildings welded into one, with turrets, pillars, flashing windows of great halls, verandahs, stairways, straining buttresses, and leaping arches crowded together in an impossible mass which rushed upwards through the sunlight, like stone flames bursting from an unimaginable furnace.

"What's the big tower?"

"The King's Tower," said Azhur reverently. "Na-veshtrazhdak built it to be his palace and his tomb. And to honour Lord Arna, of course. Look, near the dome."

Tyr narrowed his eyes and realised what he had taken for a gilded piece of ornamentation was actually a human figure of gold, sparkling and brimming with light. Though it looked small from his perspective, it must be massive up close, the height of three houses or more. It seemed to hover above the city on huge wings, watching and protecting from a cloud of reflected light.

"That's the image of Lord Arna," said Azhur quietly. "Na-veshtrazh-dak placed it there in the tenth year of his reign, after he completed the tower. He declared that while the likeness of Arna was over the city it would endure, for it would have his blessing."

Tyr remembered the hovering Fire-spirit and thought, *all the land must endure. It is blessed fourfold.*

"Come on," said Azhur as the sun drifted upward, "We'll go down. Your parents will be leaving Lachresh and we must be at the Valderthaan bridge to meet them." He led Tyr from the watchtower to the horses that waited under the pines on the mountain path. It seemed like a green twilight after the glorious blaze of the waking city. "Well, was that worth getting up early for?"

Tyr merely nodded. He had no words for the experience.

Azhur laid a hand on his shoulder. "You've seen the heart of the Northlands, Tyr, the city that lord Arna commanded to be built."

Tyr saw how the light of the city lingered in his friend's eyes. He was amazed. Why had no-one told him all this before? In truth, he had never been interested before.

They mounted and set off along the corridor of trees. The path descended quietly, like a brown brook flowing in a deep, green channel until at length the trees thinned and the riders found themselves among the rocks and scrub at the feet of the Mardhoran. Tyr's excitement mounted, expecting to see the city again, but all that faced him were hills and wild fields, speckled with houses and cattle. Among the fields was the familiar broad river and below, where the ground rose to the mountain-side, was a wide, straight road bearing the first carts and travellers of the day.

"Where's this?" he demanded.

"Where we ought to be. The path winds round the mountain and brings you out facing south. That's the North Road, and Valderthaan and Lukar are behind you. When we get past the last of the trees turn around and you'll see."

Soon the path doubled back on itself and took them quickly down to the road. Another turn and they were on the lowest slopes. The trees were gone, and the descent was nearly complete. Tyr twisted round in his saddle and saw the land spreading away from him. Miles away, Valderthaan gleamed and beckoned, framed now by the crags of the Long Water. It seemed all the brighter against the dark masses of rock towering behind it. Not far away, smoke drifted wearily upwards from the cluster of buildings that clung to the lake's southern shore. Lukar. Grey and flat, Lukar shone with neither gold nor sunlight, for its ungilded stones still lay within the shadow of the hills on its eastern side. He traced the road ahead with his eyes until it divided, one branch curving through the fields to Lukar, the other following the lakeside and making straight for the great bridge that would see them over the lake to Valderthaan. To Tyr, it looked as if it would take them ages to reach that divide and to at last turn north toward the bridge.

A man and a woman stepped out from the bushes at the roadside, shouting and waving. Tyr was startled, but Azhur leaned over to reassure him. "Don't worry, I know this pair."

Tyr could see the couple was nothing like the robbers he'd feared. They were elderly, walking with staffs and smiling as they waved. Tyr relaxed and waited.

"Ho, don't pass us, Baranthu! Give us a blessin', for the Sun's love," called the old man. He came up to Azhur's horse, put a hand on its shoulder and gave the young novice a scrubbed, pink, wrinkled grin. "Thought it were y'." He turned to the woman. "It's him right enough, Naida me dearest! What did I say?"

The old lady's face became a million joyful lines, "Well, Azhur! Isn't that a wonder! Us comin' out this lovely morning to Dragonstone and you turnin' up! Aren't the powers good? Aren't they good, Vesh?" She caught Tyr's eye. "Who're you then, lovey? This your friend, Azhur?"

Tyr smiled and introduced himself. "Azhur's takin' me up to Valderthaan," he said, avoiding his real reasons. "I've not seen it afore."

The old woman wagged her finger at him. "Well, don't you go gettin' into bad ways in that city, my lovey."

"Don't mind her, son," cackled Veshren. "Azhur here'll look out for y'."

"Now, Vesh, there's them in that place as don't *want* lookin' out for. They'd have to mend their evil ways, they would."

"Tyr," said Azhur quickly, "let me introduce Master Veshren and his goodwife, Mistress Naida. Veshren used to work for my father at Mardokhal when I was a boy."

"Store master, I was. Best one he ever had and all."

"Me dad's headman at Falakhoth," said Tyr. "He's a smith. Famous all round, he is. What's Azhur's dad do in Mardokhal?"

Veshren paused, then scratched his head and smiled vaguely. "Oh, I haven't worked for him for years. Nice to see our lad here doin' so well, though."

Azhur swung off his horse. "Shall I give you that blessing? I, er, can only do certain ones, being a novice."

"Can y'? Oh well, whatever y' can, son."

"Don't call him son, Vesh. He's Baranthu now."

Veshren waved a hand, "Give over, me dearest, he's son to me." The old man caught himself, looked at everything and nothing.

There was an odd, detached moment of time. Tyr dismounted slowly, seeing how Azhur looked at the ground seeming both pleased and sad.

"Well," said Naida, "fancy all these years since—I mean, since—you remember Squirrel runnin' round that storeroom? All them years, fancy."

"All right, is she?" asked Veshren. "Won't be long now, eh?"

"Ah, well, I hope not," said Azhur. He glanced uneasily at Tyr, who he could tell was making a mental note to harass him later over Squirrel.

"What about you young Tyr?" chirped Naida. "You goin' up to be a priest as well, then?"

Tyr found himself unexpectedly silent, looking into her bright eyes brimming with years. The sun crept up over the Mardhoran and flung its first beams into his eyes so the haloed faces of the old couple seemed to shine with golden light like the image of Arna on the great Tower. Could it ever, he wondered shockingly, in any wild possibility, lead to that? A priest's life in the gilded city? Could the village-boy ever want to leave his hills and rivers for stone houses and ornate towers? The question tingled through him as he stood in the spring grass with the river glinting near him and a sharp wind in his face. He realised how he had never thought where his strange experiences might take him and that frightened him. Not the experiences themselves but their unguessable consequences. Things had happened over the past few days he would never have dreamed of, and yet here he was at this very moment, travelling to the city of the Valgraav and the holiest place in the world. Could it all possibly mean Arna wanted him for a priest? Should he give his life to learning and ritual, bowing before fire, and living amongst the stones? Did he want that?

He looked up at the sun-crowned mountain and wondered if what he wanted mattered at all.

"All right, son?"

Tyr noticed the people within the light again. Whose voice had asked the question?

"Tyr?" Azhur's head and shoulders came between him and the piercing sun.

Tyr felt his friend's hand on his arm. "Oh, sorry, dreamin'. I..., I'm just on a visit, missus. Azhur's showin' me the Shrine and all that."

"Have you somewhere to stay?"

"Azhur's sortin' that."

"Could've stayed with us with pleasure," said Naida. "Some other time, eh?"

"Aye. I'll come another time."

Tyr could tell Naida was about to ask more and he searched desperately for a change of subject. "What's a Dragonstone?"

"You what, love?"

"Y' said y'd come out to the Dragonstone. I've not heard of that."

"Never heard of it? Well, that's a wonder! Isn't that a wonder, Vesh?"

"It is, my dearest. The Dragonstone, young Tyr—listen, now—the Dragonstone's the place where King Rachty stopped when he saved Lukar from them heathen Harrak. And he had his dragons with him, his, er—what's the right word, Azhur?"

"Rashtakh."

"Aye, them. Anyroad, he brought them up from south when he came up here to make the kingdom. That were hundreds of years ago, mind, and y' don't see dragons these days, but they was here then, they were. Oh, aye, great fierce things they was, and they kept them out here, out of the way of things, till they was wanted. Those Harrak took one look and ran, I'll bet. Anyroad, there's a big rock just by the road up ahead of y'—

229

of course, there weren't a proper road then—and folk called it Dragon-stone, cos of it bein' where they kept the dragons. Folk have spoke prayers there time out of mind. Some folk says it looks like a dragon, but I dunno. Never seen one, so I can't tell!" And here he burst into a long, wheezing laugh. "Ha! I used to know a grand song about them. There were this big one seemingly, all blue scales like armour, and he goes straight for the Harrak chief—"

"Vesh, lovey, never mind that song. It's far too long and Azhur and Tyr haven't time. You always forgets the end as well."

"Yes, we must go," said Azhur quickly and, Tyr thought, with real regret. "We have to meet someone at the Bridge."

Veshren immediately abandoned his story. "Oh well, bless us then, Azhur—Baranthu, I mean—and us'll see y' at our house afore long. And bring Tyr, mind."

"I promise," said Azhur. As the old couple bowed their heads, he stretched out his arms in the sign of blessing. Standing before his friends, facing North with arms spread out, he made a black mirror image of the golden form of Arna that faced them across the miles, holding out its own massive arms to bless the city and the land. The earnest novice spoke slowly and deliberately in the ancient speech.

Tyr did not understand what Azhur was saying, but he caught *Hra'im*—that was Arna, he had learned—and *Sh'herakh*, which was Shining, or something like it. The sound, however, ah, the very sound was itself a message. A meaning alongside the words. Tyr gave a little shiver. Imagine having to learn that tongue for *yourself*.

After the blessing and a brief farewell, Azhur and Tyr continued along by the river watching the first barges going up to Lukar and letting the morning grow as they rode. In time they reached the Dragonstone, a not very convincing slab of rock with a furrow in it that only a person with a lot of imagination could think looked like a dragon's open jaws. That person though had painted ragged teeth round it and daubed on vivid red gums and an eye. It failed to persuade Tyr. The stone was fes-tooned with trinkets and prayers on scraps of wood and paper. Placed in front of the stone were bowls and dishes full of ashes. One still smouldered, presumably having been recently lit by Veshren or Naida.

"They've been offering fire," said Azhur. "They shouldn't really without a priest. You can get fined." He glanced at Tyr and smiled. "You were very mysterious with Naida."

Tyr made a noise between a laugh and a snort. "Aye, well: 'What y' doin' in Valderthaan, lovey?' 'Oh, not much, I've just been seein' visions and things as aren't there, so the priests are wondering what the hell's goin' on.' 'Ooh, are they, lovey? Well, have a nice time.'"

"I thought you were thinking that," said Azhur.

"What're they like?"

"Who?"

"The priests as are goin' to be lookin' at me." His head whipped round. "Y' sure I'll not have to see the Valgraav?"

This gave Azhur a fine laugh. "Oh dear, no! He doesn't attend to this sort of thing. A little scrap of paper with a note saying they had seen you might reach him someday, and he'll probably be at dinner when it did. No, no, don't you worry."

Tyr almost fell off his horse with relief. "Thank the Lady for that," he gasped. "Who'll do it, then?"

"Well, as I said, I expect Lord Galdtchav will get a few junior Loremasters together, then have you and your parents sit round a table with them for an hour or so. They *might* ask me, seeing I know you."

"Oh. That's all right, then."

"Just think of it as a holiday in the city."

"Right, I will, then."

There followed a few more minutes of thoughtful riding before Tyr spoke up again. "Y' was a bit mysterious y'self. Who's Squirrel?"

"What?"

"Squirrel. Her as ran about y' Dad's storeroom."

"Oh." Azhur's fingers tangled in the reins and in between each other, as Tyr was not slow to notice. "Oh, ah, she was a little girl in the town. Squirrel was her pet name. She was very quick, darting here and there, you know, and she had these big, dark eyes. Eyes like, like a squirrel, I mean."

"Ah," said Tyr, suspicious. "What's her right name?"

"Aienna." And the young man breathed that name with such blatant,

231

soft affection there was no disguising how he felt about the woman.

Tyr grinned broadly. "That y' girlfriend?"

"No! No, not at all, hardly see her in fact. Just a—just a friend." But the ascending sun shed its pitiless light on his face and revealed his crimson, burning cheeks.

Tyr gave out a long, derisive yell. "Girl-friend! Girl-friend! Caught y'! Y' kept that quiet!"

"Well, we're... we're... friends. I've known her since I was a boy. A good friendship, and not until recently—the last year or two—that is, I—"

"—started fancyin' her!"

"I wouldn't say that exactly..."

"Did she fancy y' back?"

Azhur stared fixedly ahead, gaped, then placed a hand over his scarlet face and released a smile of astonishing width. "She, ah... was not unre-sponsive."

Tyr cackled, slapped his thigh, and rolled about in his saddle convuls-ively, delighted by the mortification he had inflicted.

"Oh dear," murmured his victim. "Oh dear, oh dear. Tyr-shan, you are without mercy."

"Brilliant!" exclaimed Tyr who thought that the finest criticism he had received. "Y' gettin' wed, then?"

"Oh, we're nowhere near that. Aienna's father hasn't even given me permission to court her."

"Do y' think he will?"

"Well, yes I do, actually. We get on well and I impressed him when I became Lord Galdtchav's assistant. He's a priest himself, serves in the Shrine precincts, and they have a very fine house on Third Level, near Shrinegate."

Tyr made an elaborate flourish. "La-di-dah, eh? Go on, it's just her money y're after." He barely managed to dodge the swipe Azhur made at his head.

The road veered away from the river, clinging to the hills. Westwards, away to their left, the smoke of the early fires wandered up to join the pall that hung over grey Lukar. The city's fishing boats huddled in their harbours where the buildings gripped the lakeside around the river mouth. There were only a few unremarkable towers. Azhur pointed out the two largest, black with age, which stood close together.

"That's the Towers of the Wound, the Lady's shrine in Lukar."

"Don't look much," observed Tyr.

"Well, that's only proper. And in any case Na-veshtrazhdak, bless his memory, made a law that it mustn't be ostentatious—showy, that is. Iathena's only Arna's consort, you see."

This unsettled Tyr. His belief, such as it was, centred on the Lady of the Valleys, while giving Arna only a compulsory nod. A long discussion followed about the rights of a goddess in her own vales and what a consort was, anyway. This took some time and Tyr was never really satisfied, but at last the debate tailed off, for Valderthaan was drawing near.

The city came towards them like an immense ship. Its solid walls came down to the very shoreline of the island that carried it, making it appear it sat on the waters like a royal barge of giant kings or a mountain broken loose from the earth. The prow, the highest point on the mile-long vessel, bore the gleaming Shrine and the foundations of the many-structured tower of Na-veshtrazhdak where Arna's floating golden form, truly monstrous now, lit up the morning. The Tower gathered its stones together, compressed them, hoisted them up to a brave pinnacle challenging the hills, where one could keep watch over the whole of the north. Other towers, fine as they were, reared up from the city's higher points not as companions but as courtiers paying homage to that splendid stone monarch. All along the backbone of the island, clusters of marvellous edifices gripped the rock like immense seashore limpets. They were massive yet sweeping in form, imbued with a strong, ponderous grace that said, *the hand that built us is strong; we house the great ones of the world and we are here forever.* The arches were raised, the colonnades laid out for mighty ones to walk to secret halls where they would sit and order what was to be for the dwellers upon the earth. The windows sparkled back the swelling morn, the stone walls of crimson, golden, white, and bird-winged grey hues, were tapestries upon which light hung.

The city's prow sloped down south and carried stairways, gardens, and descending terraces of sun-swathed buildings till it reached the level of the lake where quays and jetties held the bright ships and galleys that carried the Valgraav's servants to the shores and the wider kingdom. Already, the pleasure-boats were putting out to spend the morning on the water and the scarlet-sailed diplomatic barques were speeding from the western shore. Gulls followed them all, wheeling and diving and ducking down between the piles of the long bridge that linked the city to the traffic of the western provinces between the lake and the distant ocean and holy Fyrieg. A stretching span reached out from the shore to a lesser island in the lake's centre, then changed tack and leaped a shorter distance to the city's farther, unseen side. On the nearer edge, a shorter bridge anchored Valderthaan to the eastern shore and gathered in the roads from the great Plain and the valleys to the south. From this southern road, Tyr could make out the layered structure of the city. Streets and districts were wound around the island on three main levels, following the natural contours of the hills and cliffs that had been there before them. The upper tier seemed reserved for the more imposing, larger structures and was almost a city in itself, as if built by different hands and inhabited by a different race. The central swathe had more buildings, though they were less grand, and held the foundations of some lesser towers. It lay around the wall that hung beneath the magnificent upper level and spilled down to its own wall that kept the crowded lower level at bay. For here was the domain of most of Valderthaan's denizens. Tall, narrow wooden houses crushed together, leaning and jostling along the confined ways, encroaching on the bridges, and jammed around the ancient rocks. Parapets, huts, bothies, and hovels sprouted on rooftops, swelling like a wooden fungus under arches, edging around the sides of squares, and in desperation clinging to perilous walls and throwing themselves across the slimmest streets. There were a few poor towers down there, but far from adding a little crumbling grandeur, their half-hearted cheapness was an embarrassment even among the dilapidations of the First Level.

And there were levels within levels, houses added to houses. Everywhere the city was veined with lesser streets rising and falling and linked by multitudinous rows of steps and sloping hills. A few broad stairways were the main arteries for the flows of people, cutting through the buildings and thoroughfares from city-crest to lake-level and fitting themselves around the island's natural pinnacles of rock. The most prominent came cascading from the distant, tiny gate before the Shrine and descended in jagged twists to the level of the lake-walls and the city's great gate at the farther end of the eastern bridge. Any Shrine priest living on the bottom level, thought Tyr, would be fit indeed.

His eyes followed the city wall north, but the island curved round so that it was lost from sight behind its own shoulder. Looking out beyond the remaining miles of water led to the huge, grey, mist-veiled cliffs that reared up from the flat blue. They had kept their place when, long ago, the land had buckled into the lake-bed and the valleys. According to Azhur, the Scrolls told how the northern lands had split all the way from the far White Fields to the southern valleys during the great war between the gods and the powers of night. That great gash in the earth's hide was there still. It was the Long Water, a river two hundred miles long and bounded by a chasm whose sides had never closed. That great gouge was one of the Wounds of Earth. Any ship entering by the great split in the lakeside crags would sail long days to emerge in the wide bay of Harrokaan, near the ice fields and the whale-ways of the north. When the primal conflict had passed, the great open, sunken sore of ruined rock and scattered strata formed by the underworld itself collapsing was healed and softened. At that time, it was said, Iathena bade earth, grass, and tree to cover the desolation and form the green valleys that had been her own since that day. To water the vales, she opened springs on the heights of the west so that the deepest hollow became the basin that held the great lake. Yet one great slab of rock had not sunk down and, despite all, held itself proudly as a monument to the unspoiled days before the might of darkness struck the world. The healing waters surrounded it and Iathena blessed it and made it green and full of life as a sign forever that the world had not come from the night and would not go into the night. Ages later, Ar-ven came fresh from the hidden thing that befell him in Fyrieg and made the Lady's Rock his home and sanctuary. There Lord Arna directed great Na-veshtrazhdak to build Shrine and city as the heart of the new empire of the Northlands. All this Azhur had carefully explained to Tyr over the past few miles. By the time they finally rode up to the bridge, the boy's head was spinning. He gawked at the city as though it had fallen straight from the sun.

Before them stood a massive arch with bronze gates that had swung open only a little while earlier. Carriages, wains, riders, and a great crowd on foot were already heading into the city beneath the great burnished crest of the sun and the royal mountain lion mounted on the giant gate. They were mostly the buyers and sellers of the day's markets, Azhur told him, for as yet there were no horses or carriages grand enough for priests or government servants on their errands. Most of the wealthiest citizens, apparently, would not have been awake long enough to put in a showing on the bridge at such an hour.

The broad, paved square in front of this arch was becoming noisier and busier. Mounted soldiers yelled over the hubbub or edged their horses into the advancing human streams to keep them going forward without confusion. The carts and crowds built up in a broad, moving queue. Everyone was more than a little mindful of the rows of spearmen stationed nearby. Large, crag-faced men in scored leather armour, the soldiers were emphatically not there for decoration, and their message was very plain: there will be order and safety, or suffer the consequences. Slowly, slowly, the queue moved forward. Near the gate, under the watchful eye of more soldiers, city officials examined each person's pass, stamped it, and if it was not forthcoming asked why not. Occasionally the soldiers hauled some unhappy individual from the mass and sent them back where they'd come from or hefted them to one of the large buildings nearby.

Tyr stood up in his stirrups and looked around. Away to his right rose the Mardhoran, where he had looked on the city from the watchtower. Near it to the north, was the burgeoning hill whose spurs sheltered Azhur's home town of Mardokhal. Between the two, a broad road ran from the gate past towns and woods and out onto the Great Plain in the east. Harrak country out there, he remembered with a shiver of recall. He involuntarily rubbed his neck and shook himself to put the memory out of his head. Where were his Harrak captors now? He had no idea but guessed they probably were not safely back on the Plain.

He had other business, though, and after a few minutes he spotted his parents. They were standing on the other side of the mass of people by an artless statue of some long-gone pass-issuer, clutching their newly granted passes. Tyrmar, arms folded, looked in the mood to take on the whole contingent of spearmen, while Iethen sat with her usual indestructible patience on the base of the unlovely statue with their bags anchored firmly between her feet. Tyr saw his mother was wearing her 'best' clothes from the chest beneath the window at home: the blue coat with yellow embroidery that Tyrmar had brought her from Fyrhal, and the peach and green patterned dress she had made herself from a bale of cloth a merchant had given her for her hospitality. A coloured headscarf crowned her head in tones that were strong but restrained, like herself. Her husband looked as he always did, except that, while he had pulled on the brown coat he thought of as 'best', it was simply the least worn coat he owned that didn't look too ridiculous with a sash. Beside the two stood a dark-robed, vacant-faced man whose shadowed eyes and bored, weary pose declared 'Official'. He was drumming the fingers of one hand on the back of the other, obviously wishing he was elsewhere.

Tyr punched Azhur in the arm and pointed at the group. The pair dismounted and led their horses through the throng and over the patchwork collage of wheel-tracks, mud, scattered straw, old trampled passes, squashed vegetables, and horse-droppings.

"Was it worth it?" asked Iethen as she rocked in Tyr's hug. "Are y' glad y' got up early?"

"Oh, aye!" exclaimed Tyr, and told his parents about his first view of the city. "Bet y' wish y'd come, Dad."

Tyrmar ignored Tyr's comment to complain. "Don't know what they want us for, anyroad. It's y' as seen them things."

"It's all right, Dad. It's just gonna be some old priests round a table."

"I think," said Azhur, "that Lord Galdtchav feels speaking to the people closest to Tyr might shed some light on things. No stone unturned, you know. It also wouldn't surprise me if he thought you'd enjoy a holiday in Valderthaan at the Valgraav's expense."

This brightened Tyrmar considerably, "That's different, then." He turned to the official. "Here, have they got baths? I wouldn't mind a bath."

"I'll see," said the official. "Possibly." He sighed. "It's the chamber-maids, you see. Someone is needed to heat the water." This utterance did not require him to look at Tyrmar or move in the slightest.

"Aye. Well, this feller's to take us to where they're puttin' us up. Old Galdtchav's gone up the Shrine with Ferret-face. He said Azhur should show Tyr the sights and bring him back later. Said y'd know where to drop him off."

"Ah," said Azhur as his eyes lit up. "A tour? Yes, I think I could do that." And he would have set off at once but there came yells and horses screaming from the bridge. They turned and saw a horseman thundering away from the city at an impossible speed. People on the bridge howled and scattered as best they could as he came smashing through the crowds, heedless of anyone in his way.

Folk near Tyr threw themselves aside, though one woman was not fast enough and was flung broken against a pillar as the maddened horse passed under the archway. There was a glimpse of the rider's broad, heavy, and hateful face. Harrak without doubt.

Flying in his wake though was another rider, a guardsman of the Shrine, fiercely intent on a capture. It seemed the Harrak would reach the Plain and freedom, but the guardsman suddenly reared in his saddle, drew back his arm and threw. There was a silver flicker in the air. The tribesman's limbs spasmed, and he whirled from his horse, a long dagger jutting from his neck. He fell in a bloody tangle in front of a group of women whose vegetables would not see the market that day.

A division of spearmen ran up, elbowing the women aside to examine the man. He was no possible danger, but they risked nothing. One of them shoved his spear into the Harrak's back and wound it round as if he were making a hole in his garden earth to plant potatoes. The pursuing guardsman clattered up and dismounted, delighted by the success of his inspired throw. His comrades shook him by the hand and clapped him on the back, laughing. Then he stooped, pulled his knife out of the Harrak's neck and turned to face the city. He bowed low, breathlessly, happily triumphant, and raised the glistening crimson blade to Arna's golden image on the Tower. The other soldiers clapped and saluted and one or two bowed as well. Some cheers and applause went up from the people standing near.

Tyr and his family watched it all with open mouths. They had heard of this sort of thing of course but thought it was only in stories.

"Bloody hell," said Tyrmar.

It took the horses five minutes to cross the bridge to the city gate. Azhur could not explain the incident of the fleeing Harrak. He had broken the grief-like silence only to say that no doubt they would hear in due course, before taking a great breath and lecturing Tyr on the features of the Bridge. It was a monstrous creation, built on colossal arches anchored in the lake. Between each arch, and built onto its own pier, was a guardhouse or, occasionally, what looked like a small shrine. The shrines had smoking metal basins laid out in front of them, like those Tyr had seen at the Dragonstone, and each had a sleepy priest who stood with hands raised, speaking out the intricacies of a long, melodic chant from a wide scroll. Sometimes the oratories were built above the guardrooms, the priest sending out his prayers over an elaborate balcony hung with cloths and royal emblems. Whatever the combination, the two were housed in the bases of colossal statues that faced each other in twelve pairs along the Bridge. Azhur looked up in admiration as the giants from vanished days marched by.

"You see?" he said. "Our history is sacred history. Look, Tyr, Ur-thromath the Conqueror. And Archpriest Zhareightak, who first gathered the Scrolls together. All men made great by Arna."

Tyr listened and forgot every name as soon as he heard it. It was no good, he knew, asking for a repetition, for his friend was adrift on his sea of knowledge. Azhur woke up, Tyr realised, when he could communicate from his immense store of other people's thoughts and from his catalogue of their finished lives. More at home there, Tyr wondered, than in any other life he could have had? At any rate, he was unstoppable. Until he suddenly halted his horse and gazed ahead.

They had come to the end of the Bridge and were before a great leaping arch bound in iron and set into the city wall: the gate of Valderthaan. Its iron doors were open and flanked by many guardsmen, some mounted and some on foot. But the most awesome guardians were the two gigantic figures at its sides. Lofty as oaks, one had its hands raised in the sign of blessing and the other stood with crown and sceptre as the rays of a carven sun touched its head and shoulders.

"Don't tell me," said Tyr quickly as Azhur opened his mouth. "That's Ar-ven and that one's King Nav."

Azhur smiled awkwardly. "Ah," he said. "You have me. Very good, Tyr. You're a fast learner."

"Not much choice, with y' about." It was a rebuke of sorts, but it affirmed Azhur's mastery of facts.

The young priest grinned, then raised a finger. "Wait just a moment," he said. "I have to do something." He dismounted and stood facing the gate. After a pause, he crossed his arms on his chest and bowed deeply, once to Ar-ven and once to Na-veshtrazhdak. Next, he walked to the right of the gate where a stone shelf was positioned beneath Ar-ven. Little offerings littered the shelf: flowers, coins, small waxen or wooden figures, and crudely done pictures of holy men and heroes. There were even some bowls and dishes of meat or vegetables. Blackened metal containers had little fires burning, with piles of wood and tinder and flasks of oil beside them. Azhur took some fuel, added oil, and placed the bundle in an empty container. He lit it from one of the fires and set it before a carving of the winged Arna and his sun-disc that adorned the wall above the shelf. The stone was full of chiseled sentences, written in *Shumár* Tyr assumed, since he could make nothing of it. For a few moments, Azhur stood leaning on the shelf, contemplating. He glanced up at Ar-ven's immense, down-turned palms through twisting blue smoke as though expecting some colossal benediction to plummet down on him. Apparently satisfied, he returned to his horse.

"I was offering fire," he explained to Tyr as he hoisted himself up. "Priests are supposed to when they pass the gate. Even novices. You shouldn't just stroll into Valderthaan."

In they went. Ancient, bronze-cast symbols passed overhead as the great arch swallowed them.

"Right," said Tyr, "I'll just have a guess: it's that First Shinin' thing, isn't it?"

"Of the day," finished Azhur.

Tyr found himself in the entrance-hall of Valderthaan. It was a paved square from which led the stairs and roads that sloped and climbed away into the city or round beneath the massively thick outer wall, arteries for the flow of carts and wains. Turning in the saddle, he could see the solid rampart wide enough for six men and the backs of the heads of the guardians of the gate. The square, he noticed, was not overly large. Any enemy who by some miracle got past the gate would have to fight in very cramped conditions. It could be enclosed too, for all the exits from the square were fitted with solid iron doors. An excellent situation, thought Tyr, for the deployment of boiling oil, but he could see no equipment of the sort that figured in fireside tales. He remembered the dead Harrak with the knife in his neck and the old stories became grim possibilities. Whoever had built Valderthaan had known these possibilities very well. Tyr felt he had come to a fortress, not a city. Was it one huge garrison surrounding Shrine and court, or did people *live* here, in homes of their own? Were there any *citizens*?

And then he saw the beggars. He had never imagined there could be so many in one place. Falakhoth had none unless you counted Widder Mikhlakh and her sister. The village maintained them gladly, and being well over seventy with unpredictable backs, they hardly counted as beggars. The hopefuls who hung about the fringes of Lachresh market looked like lords beside the run-down unfortunates Tyr was gaping at now. Their spectacular poverty hung on them like cobwebs. It was not their fate but their being that shocked him. They had absorbed their poverty until it was as ingrained in their souls as the grime in their skin. Diverse strata of clothing, almost all they owned, appeared bound to their very flesh by long-accumulated sweat. Sunken eyes peered out through the swathes of now-colourless fabric and tangled hair, and communicated *they knew who they were, and it is not much*. They crouched, squatted, huddled, and hunched in corners, against walls, or beside pillars. They were present in the streets for no reason but to be there for the possibility of catching a coin in blackened hands and thus maintain a body that had lost all purpose, save to provide a storehouse for a circling, undirected mind. Tyr stared horrified at the stupor of the desolate of Valderthaan.

"They have to register, you see," said Azhur. "Some of them receive a meal each day and if they beg they need a license. They get tokens for the meals and the Master of Revenues has to be satisfied they can't work." He pointed at men in long brown coats who were moving along the rows of the destitute, examining them without seeing them and scribbling on long lists. Behind each scribe, a young lad dished out paper tokens to such creaking, wheezing figures as were found worthy of the grace of the Master of Revenues. Here and there, stern women in huge aprons and sparse, drab head-cloths dealt with doubtful cases, peering with distaste into white-tongued mouths, pulling down the red-rashed lids beneath unhealthy eyes, and assessing alleged injuries. When satisfied, the women whipped erect, folded their hands and nodded sharply at one of the brown men. Pens moved, tokens were proffered. "I know the Master of Revenues," went on Azhur seriously. "He has a great responsibility. And that's one of his staff. I know him too. He's the Custodian of the Chamber of Bounty." He raised a hand to the sturdy big man whose large, ringed eyes watched the registration of the poor under broad, black brows beneath a wide, over-decorated cap. His heavy features seemed suspended from his cheeks so that his face hung down onto bulky grey jowls. The Custodian caught Azhur's greeting, nodded bleakly so that his jowls quivered and shook against his collar, then hunched himself deeper into his furred brown robe.

"Cheery feller," observed Tyr.

Azhur frowned. "Very serious responsibility," he said doggedly. "Very serious. Daily contact with such need and so forth."

"Aye," said Tyr. "Who's that?" He pointed to a statue, old and rather poorly done, that formed a crumbling centrepiece to the destitute throng.

"Ah. It's Val-Nhakh'hant'than, the first priest to study the poor. The unfortunate of Valderthaan should have special care, he said, since they suffer in the shadow of the Shrine."

"Thought it'd be somethin' like that," said Tyr. "Will we get on, then?"

"Yes, good. Well, Second Level, I think. And a walk near the Tower and the Shrine. We won't go into the Shrine, not today. There won't be time before the Renewal ceremony tonight, but you'll see it from outside, which is splendid."

"We're goin' to Renewal Night?"

Azhur smiled, revealing the plan already hatched with Galdtchav. "Of course. You don't think I'd bring my friend to Valderthaan and let him miss Renewal, do you?" He wheeled his horse round into the morning traffic, towards the broad way that rose from the square, clinging on its right to the island's exposed primal rock and guarded on its left by an ornate wall.

Tyr followed, eager for the splendours of the upper city. He cast a last fascinated glance back at the beggars but pulled his horse up short. Then he froze, half-turned as he was. Among the living bundles of rags beneath the crumbling statue, a young woman sat, her thin face bent towards the baby in her arms. She had wrapped the child in cloths as clean as she could make them and was feeding it at her own starved breast. Her clothes were the cast-offs of those only a little less poor than herself and her hair hung like withered straw from a frayed and grimy head-cloth, but to Tyr she was clothed in the stately, nurturing honour of every queen and mother since the world began. The compassion in her dark-ringed eyes for the child of her body could have shone in the face of Iathena herself.

And the Fire-spirit sat beside her.

He knew the shimmering being saw the girl in the same way he did, and he realised, without knowing why, that it felt all the grinding desolation of the beggars as its own. He watched as it placed a caressing, incandescent hand on the baby's head. The Fire-spirit looked up to meet Tyr's eyes. *Oh.* A wave of nurture coursed through him, nearly causing him to weep. He would have cried out, but with a fiery smile the spirit raised one finger to its lips and bade him be silent. Tyr gasped and wiped his eyes and felt the warmth around his heart. He looked again with longing, but the Fire-spirit had gone into the morning. The girl carried on feeding her baby. There was a light about her still, but it was the light that rests on all mothers.

For the rest of that morning Tyr's reeling senses were hammered, dazzled, pierced, stretched, and occasionally soothed as Azhur plunged him in the deepest part of the great lake of experience that was Valderthaan. They left the First Level—"nothing much to see there," said

Azhur, with unknowing irony—and followed the broad, sloping way up to the artificial platform that encircled the southern hill of the island. It rested partly on the rock, partly on constructed foundations, and was shored up and supported on its outward side by massive walls and buttresses. These supports themselves were crisscrossed and pierced by stairs or tunnels, and houses gripped them like great limpets. High towers rose at regular intervals on this outer wall, their own foundations stretching down to seize the rock. All were equipped as guard-houses, but they might also be tenements, embassies, mansions, temples, or even tombs.

"What, there could be somebody dead in there?" cried Tyr.

"Only important people," Azhur told him. "Most of the towers in the city are tombs. People paid for them before they died. A splendid, useful building, *and* a memorial."

"I wouldn't fancy all that on top of me."

"Oh, they're not buried. The actual resting-chambers near the top. There are plenty of windows, so Arna can shine on the person every day. With the sunlight, you see."

Tyr snorted and blew out his cheeks. No amount of social or spatial elevation would sanitize for him the idea of leaving somebody dead above ground at the side of a street. After a while the thought of the towers' silent residents left his mind, for there were the beggars again. They were creeping and limping from the stairs and little streets that came up from the First Level. Registration over, they were cast onto the bosom of the city to seek its compassion and bounty. Some of them scuffed quickly over to what appeared to be their appointed stances where they took up attitudes that neatly combined dejection and anticipation. They looked about them with eyes filled with gratitude for the gifts that would surely come. Tyr fingered his few coins but had no great inclination to enrich the tattered people. He remembered briefly how the Fire-spirit had been among them, but they had their chance every day, he reasoned, while this might be his only visit here in his lifetime. So they went on with Tyr gawking at buildings and investigating stairways and closes. He paused briefly at a stall to buy a trinket for his mother, a bracelet of copper wire with little enameled moons along it. He listened as a grand person in yellow robes proclaimed poetry to stringed instruments (not half as good as Eorthas' players), and drank spiced wine in what he took to be a banqueting room until Azhur assured him it was only a tavern of Second Level standard. This sent Tyr into a speculative dream about the hostelries of the third level so that Azhur had to pull him out of the reverie and into the street.

"We won't go to the north end," said the novice priest briskly. "Quite enough to see here, and it's nearer the Shrine."

Tyr glanced up, hoping to see a glimmer of the great gilded dome, but it was not visible. Still, over and behind the buildings reared the upper reaches of Na-veshtrazhdak's looming palace-tower, red and brooding and softened by the high air. It was so lofty and far away it looked like a minutely detailed model perched on the roofs of the Second Level, and that was only the upper part. He could not see the massive golden figure of Arna above the Shrine and its court.

"Are we goin' in there?" Tyr asked.

"The Tower? Oh, your parents are probably there already. There are lots of rooms for visitors. Important ones, anyway."

"Is there one for me?"

"Of course, you're the most important visitor."

Tyr's eyes became wide and vacant for a moment, "Bloody hell," he breathed.

"You're sounding like your father," chided Azhur gently.

"Aye. Well, everybody does. Don't worry, I'll not say it in front of priests."

"That's not what I meant."

"Bothered y' though."

"Well," replied Azhur cautiously, "it wouldn't help." He realised his fingers were locked in combat, then tugged his hands apart, looked for somewhere to put them and ended up giving himself a clumsy hug. "Well, we'll get on, then."

Through the varied, multi-hued flood of Valderthaan's populace they went. Often, the deep red robes of priests burned the eye and drew a respectful nod. Nobody bowed to Azhur's black. A few red figures were followed by minor priests and preceded by another in a tall mitre chanting aloud from words painted on a wooden board. As these exalted beings passed, Azhur would stop in his tracks and bend in a deep, respectful bow. Tyr would gape and snigger.

"Who's *that*?"

"Ah, these are senior Loremasters who offer fire for the provinces and city governors. The governors are *very* high priests who, well, run the city, like the Master of City Revenues and the Master of Conduits."

"What's that feller singin' for?"

"He's chanting. Well, yes, it's a sort of singing, I suppose, but the Offering Loremasters should be constantly surrounded by the Scrolls, as the saying is, so the *Kh'horish*—the one in front—is chanting the set passage and prayer for the day. So, you see, the Loremaster even hears the histories walking in the street."

"Must get fed up of that. He'll not have a minute's peace."

"No, no, he maintains serenity, as they say. He absorbs the chant at a very deep level—"

"I'm rumblin' at a very deep level. Can we have a bite?"

Azhur gave up and led his friend towards a place he called Potters' Square. "There's an inn there that'll feed you well," he explained. "The soup is particularly hearty."

On the way there they passed a procession of two dozen priests to gawk at, pacing two abreast and carrying sun-discs on long, decorated poles. In their hands were statues and paintings of various striking individuals. Some of them held elaborate iron censers with burning coals inside, and their chant was deep and impressive. This time Tyr had only to look at Azhur with wide eyes.

"Priests of the Circle of the Holy Actions," the young man told him. "Certain rituals *must* be done at certain points in the city: Presentation of Fire to the Gates, the Obeisance to the Sun, the Censing of the Stairways and Thoroughfares, and so on and so on, every day. Now, all this protects the city. The things the priests carry—"

"Right," said Tyr, and made off.

Azhur continued his commentary for some time before he realised he was alone and hurried after his charge. He found him standing with his mouth open and limp with astonishment.

"Look," Tyr whispered. "Look."

Tyr was gawping at a woman as though he had never seen one before. The whole city had become a pointless blur and that she alone remained real. Indeed, she was the most physically overwhelming person to pass before him in seventeen summers. She was stepping down from the ivory doors of a splendid palace-tower and with each measured tread she moved like a ship on silken seas. Above straight, strong shoulders and a long, perfectly balanced neck rode a head formed beyond the skill of any sculptor. Her cheeks were high ramparts under large, brown eyes, almond-fashioned, that hid their slow gaze under the black awnings of their lashes. Her brow and temples were immaculate shapes that built the peerless temple of her mind. Her black hair was pulled tightly back and held in a thick, bunched mane by silks and coloured combs. Wide, full lips were set above a curving chin that was both strong and gentle and that whole marvellous face was quite without the foolishness of paint. She had the wisdom to understand what she had been given without seeking to improve it. Gold and ivory and yellow topaz hung from her ears and around her throat, and a sweeping gown in the strong colours of all things near the sun was swathed around her lithe body and long feline limbs, with a paler gold with brown gems wound along the length of her fingers. She was surely a queen and the daughter of queens from generations. And she was proud, proud to her bones.

Tyr looked and looked, drinking in the image before him. He could only see, not describe, for he knew no words that fitted this woman. Beautiful she was, but that was a word used so often it was almost mean-ingless beside her. Lovely? That was better, but it was a homely word, domesticated, and she was fierce. To call her pretty was ridiculous, to say she was gorgeous was cheap, to call her exquisite, fine, handsome, or magnificent was the plain truth, but it suggested images of the polished, high-bred creatures that adorned the masques and feasts. No, this woman had left all words behind. She fitted no category, for she was herself and no-one else. And yet the aspect of her splendour Tyr could not take in was the most immediately obvious thing about her, for her skin was the colour of dark, polished wood, as though she wore the deep evening dusk as a garment.

"Who's that?" Tyr managed at last.

"That's the lady Aia Djtenga," Azhur told him. "Don't stare! She hates people gaping at her. She's a very great lady."

"What happened to her?"

"I don't follow."

"The, er… her…she's…" The boy waved his fingers over his own face. "Is that paint?"

"*Paint?* Oh, I see. No, no, that's what people are like in her country. They live close to the Sun, a very great honour. But of course, you've never seen one, have you?"

Tyr shook his head as he watched Aia Djtenga speak to her companions and her sharp white smile shone out. She stepped beneath a tasseled orange canopy carried on four poles and made vivid progress through the respectful crowds. It was as if the sun had gone in for shame.

Gradually, the street reasserted its presence around the dazed visitor from Falakhoth.

"She's from Murinde, a kingdom in the far, far south," said Azhur, still grinding his information mill. "Even farther south than Dhar. Her father is king and could be deposed, so she's sought sanctuary from the Valgraav to represent her father until it's safe for her to return. Formidable lady. I never know what to say to her."

"Y've *met* her?"

"Oh, yes. She visits the Shrine archives, always wanting to learn. Lord Galdtchav regularly has long talks with her about Shrine lore. I'm usually there," he added modestly. "Chip in a few words."

Tyr gasped and backed away. Lady Aia had left her canopy and was making her way towards them. Her ladies followed, frantic, but the sheer force of her presence cleared a way for her. Azhur bowed as she made her approach.

"Arna shine on you, Lady Aia."

A brilliant, wide smile opened in the Lady's features. "He is shining on you, Barun—Barnan—oh, I cannot say it!" She laughed and lightened every spirit in the street.

"Baranthu," said Azhur, grinning widely despite his delighted embarrassment.

Lady Aia raised a finger in the air and ticked off the syllables, "Bar.

"He is shining on you, Barun—Barnan—oh, I cannot say it!"

An. Thu. I will hold this. Oh, your hands are fighting! They are telling me a thing moves in you." She waved a hand over Azhur's chest. He grinned wider still and tried to look anywhere but at Lady Aia, a most difficult feat. "Oh, it is not a good thing! What is wrong, my Barnathu?"

"Baranthu. Nothing, my Lady, nothing wrong at all. It is the excitement of meeting you."

"I do not know excitement!"

"I mean, ah, I mean, I mean... it is... a very good, a very happy thing."

"Ohh, excitement is what is moving in you?"

Azhur laughed.

Lady Aia patted his chest. "Well, I will make excitement move in you again. I will go to the Renewal tonight in your Shrine. But I am asking, this is good if I go? The Renewal is for the North and I am in Murinde."

"We will be very glad if you are there, Lady Aia. It is a great honour."

"Oh, then I will watch and take everything to myself. I will see what priests do for your Valgraav and I will come to you and Lord Galdtchav after the time and you will tell me all the meaning."

Azhur gave a little bow. "That will make us... excited," he said.

Lady Aia beamed the wider, "I am glad," she said. "Now, my ladies are worrying—oh!"

After a moment, Tyr realised her astonishing almond eyes were fixed on him.

"Ohh, now," exclaimed the Lady, tilting her head. "There is one watching me. This is a servant with you, Barnathu?"

"Baranthu," said Azhur, and pulled the utterly shocked Tyr closer. "This, ah, this is Tyr-shan. He is a friend I met in the valleys and he has come to see the city. You should bow, Tyr." A hard nudge in the arm only made Tyr jerk his head in an awestruck spasm.

Lady Aia nodded, not without amusement. "I am pleased, Tyr-shan. Arna is shining on you. I think I say this?"

"Quite correct," Azhur informed her.

"I learn. But I see how your friend's mouth is open very far. In Murinde there are people who stand with their mouths open and they catch the *tsegendi* fly and they are stung. Are you stung, Tyr-shan?"

Bewildered, Tyr gaped the wider.

"Well, I will go to my ladies. Oh, there is a thing. My ladies are afraid. They have heard that a bad man was in the city this morning, a man from the Great Plain, a… Harrach?"

"Harrak, yes. I saw him… dealt with at the Bridge."

"This is good. We will be safe in your Shrine tonight?" She seemed genuinely anxious for herself and her ladies.

Azhur seized the opportunity for lore to pour forth. "You will be completely safe, Lady Aia. Safer than anywhere on the world's hide, in fact. Ar-ven himself, and the Eight sages who gathered round him, declared that, on Renewal Night, the Shrine is protected from all harm and evil. The sacredness of the time, and the utterance of the Twelve Declarations of Safety are like an armour around it: it is sealed, closed in. The Loremaster He'aivarkh'haratha said—"

But Lady Aia threw up her hands. "We are safe? I may think it?"

"You will all be quite safe."

The Lady gasped and patted her chest. "We are happy. Goodbye, Barnathu. I will greet you at the Renewal. Perhaps I will see you again, Tyr-shan."

"Aye," said Tyr. "I liked meetin' y', missus."

Azhur grimaced.

Aia put her head on one side. "Miss-is? I am miss-is? Well, I will learn this. Now I go." And Lady Aia hurried back under her canopy where she could laugh all she wished.

Tyr looked at Azhur and spread out his hands. "What did I…?"

"It's all right, don't worry."

Tyr was grateful to have escaped a lecture on etiquette. They resumed their journey to The Potters' Square.

As much to clear his mind of the southern lady's spectacular features as anything, Tyr paused to listen to a gruff old priest who stood in a niche and narrated the high points in the Northlands' history from an immeasurable memory. A group of earnest listeners stood around him.

"Our history is sacred history," Azhur reminded his friend. "We always need to hear it."

The priest reached the end of his recitation. "There now," he said through his extravagant beard. "Any questions?"

"My husband's not been over the door for two weeks," said a strained-looking woman. "Can you get Arna to make him better?"

"Mine's got the runs," said another. "Can you?"

"Fortitude, madam," grated the old priest. "Lord Arna is ordering the kingdom and directing the sun, he is constantly occupied with keeping the dark at bay. Draw on your courage. Any *other* questions?"

Here Tyr found himself gripped by a thirst for knowledge and asked why all the important people in history had such terrible names and did it matter? This silenced the grizzled historian so completely that Azhur seized the chance to move his curious charge away.

At last the friends came to a place where the native rock of the island receded, making a natural shelf. Here the city's builders had extended the wide platform supporting the Second Level to allow for substantial streets that could run behind the grander buildings of the main encircling roads. Azhur branched off the broad way and under a tree-flanked arch to a shadier, humbler street. The buildings were all tenements, high and narrow, stacked together like a giant bookshelf. There were stalls and street-level shops and a large, round well. It was a greyer, plainer place, with few trees and Tyr realised that it must spend most of its day in shadow, sitting as it did between a massive rock face and the rear of the main street's imposing buildings. Still, it was busy, with its own small fruit market and weavers' shops.

There were no towers, but over the heads of the people rose the inevitable statues of the great and the presumably good. As a flesh-and-blood counterpoint to the carven worthies, the street's appointed beggars had arrived and become near-motionless figurines themselves, silently holding out for golden opportunities to lessen the wretchedness of a kindred soul. But one figure was not silent. Standing beneath the statue of a venerable priest who raised his hand in admonition (or would have, had it not broken off), a tall, fleshy man was flinging out his arms in wide, exaggerated sweeps as he harangued his hearers, who mostly kept their minds on their own business. He was a priest rather than a beggar, judging from his red robes and crimson cap, and he was standing on an opulent-looking square of carpet beside a small black brazier in which a fire was burning. With a flourish, the man threw something into the fire and the smell of sweet incense came curling out. And there seemed to be something on offer. It was all very intriguing. Too intriguing for Tyr not to investigate. Azhur, he saw, was rummaging in a stall that boasted both fruit and pictures of ancient scholars, and so he let his feet trail over to the priest. He was a striking fellow in his way. Sallow features touched with nobility and overlaid with clustered red blotches and a dark, unshaven chin. He had a wide, flexible mouth with thick, red lips and black, arched brows with more than a hint of a frown upon them.

"You need this!" he boomed. "You need this, you know you do. Don't you know the power of a prayer offered in the Old Speech? Words like this bring rain, grow crops, banish the fattest and most voracious field mice. Bad spirits about your house? They'll run. Lost anything? You'll find it. Ha! The young master there! Do you offer prayers?"

Tyr looked behind himself, then realised the man was staring straight at him, hand out, waiting for an answer. "Not much," he blurted, then shifted around, feeling that would hardly do. "Well, if me mam's sick, or somethin', but that's it, like." He edged closer to the red-robed man. Suddenly his country brazenness flickered out. "Thought that were your job, anyroad."

The man jerked back a little. "Ah. Well, yes. Yes! Very knowledgeable for a lad from the valleys—it *is* the valleys? Thought so. Beautiful area, fine people. Yes, it is our job to offer the prayers, we of the holy priesthood, and we do it for *you*."

"For me?" said Tyr.

"Oh, yes. Come here, my friend."

Tyr stepped up to the man. Another priestly acquaintance! He must attract them. Maybe it was the Fire-spirit's influence.

"Now, young master...." A large, hairy hand slid beneath the red robe and returned with a tantalising, rolled-up parchment. "You know what this is?"

"No, what?"

"*This*, my friend, is the five hundred and tenth page of the Scroll of Benedictions."

"I thought scrolls was all one piece."

"Ah. Well, they are, normally, but this is a special dispensation, see?"

"A what?"

"That's a priest's word, don't worry about it. But basically, they cut bits off the end, like pages, so we can take them to the people. The people, you see, like you, so we can offer the prayers for them."

"Is that the prayers there, then?" asked Tyr, wondering why he was becoming so uneasy.

"That's them. Old Speech, of course. Now, if I just offer *one* of those prayers in Old Speech—no, you can't do it, you're not a priest—if I just do that for you it'll do you all sorts of good."

"Does it cost? I've not got much."

"Oh, *I* don't charge, not me personally."

"I can read a bit," tried Tyr.

"Ah, but its Old Speech. Funny letters, see?" The parchment flapped for a moment under Tyr's nose. The script was indeed funny. "Well? Prayer, then? The deepest desires of your heart sent straight up to Arna himself. Can't say no to that."

"Well, how much, then?" It did in fact sound very inviting, especially to someone whose community was used to feeling ignored by priests and Shrine from one year's end to the next.

The prayer-seller looked regretfully at the ground, "Well, I don't charge, as I said, but the *other* priests—the *Shrine* people, you know—they want something for each prayer I do. They offer fire, you see, and it pays for the charcoal."

"What, then?"

"They entreat the suppliant—that's you—to offer one city mitre."

"Eh?"

"Two bronze bits, son. What about it?"

"I've only got ten." And here Tyr and the priest simultaneously noticed Azhur strolling towards them. Tyr waved and the man suddenly seemed oddly agitated.

"One, then," he snapped. "Works the same." He shoved the holy parchment back under his robe and Tyr briefly spotted food stains and unsightly patches on his long tunic, which, not to be indelicate, was shockingly threadbare.

"Well," mused Tyr. "I dunno. I'll ask me friend there."

But this was too much, the man's pretence vanished shockingly. "What's he know? He's a bleedin' novice!"

Tyr was stung. "Good as you!"

"Look, you want a prayer or not?" All persuasion was gone.

"Not from *you!*"

"Well, why don't you bugger off, then?"

"Well, I will!" spat Tyr. "Miserable sod!" And he stamped over to Azhur.

The priest, seeing the genuine article bearing down on him, and knowing that even a novice brushed shoulders with the authorities, rolled up his carpet, seized the brazier, and went nimbly into an alley behind the statue.

Azhur was scandalised by Tyr's adventure.

"Two bits!" fumed Tyr. "I never knew priests carried on like that. Do they not pay them?"

"I know him," said Azhur, shaking his head. "He's not a priest, Tyr. He's Aljhaz Va-ghrir, and he hasn't a scruple in his body. They have banished him twice from the city for this sort of thing."

"Never!" gasped Tyr, rather thrilled at having passed unscathed through something so monstrous. "Well, I thought he were funny meself. How'd he get a bit of that Benediction thing?"

"Oh, Tyr! Ar-ven wrote that! Do you think we'd send it round the alleyways in bits?" Azhur was so shocked at the idea it forced him to laugh.

"Oh," said Tyr with an embarrassed grin. "Was it not real, then? Oh well. Can we have our soup?"

For the next few hundred yards, Azhur murmured deeply felt expressions of regret and dismay about the depths to which people could sink, even in Valderthaan, and his fingers twisted constantly. Tyr saw he was not only offended but embarrassed and disappointed too. The deceitful prayer-seller had tainted his gift of a visit to the sacred city and his regrets sounded like an admission of guilt.

"Never mind," Tyr told him. "I've met crooks afore."

"It's just so... ugly. You shouldn't have seen it, not here."

"Well, we've got Gizhurthra, and Falakhoth's still all right."

Azhur considered this, "Ah," he said, and forged ahead.

They came to a place where there was a great fold in the island's rock as though a god had reached down in its early, molten days and scooped out a great handful of soft stone, leaving a recess the depth of a town square. This had been paved, with pillars set up at the opening of the space to mark the access to a broad area edged with a horseshoe ring of low, broad buildings. Fires were glowing inside and smoke sweeping up.

"Forges!" exclaimed Tyr. "Me dad'll like this."

"Oh, no," Azhur corrected him. "Not forges. This is Potters' Square." He pointed at the two pillars. Fixed on top of each was a large, red earthenware jar, wholly unsuitable for a street ornament but an excellent announcement of the wares available inside.

The Square itself, Tyr thought as he walked in, was very unpromising for anyone anxious for soup. He saw dozens of clay vessels of all sorts surrounding the buildings, stacked in lines and slowly drying as they waited for the glowing kilns. Some workshops had open fronts like Tyrmar's forge and inside, intent, meticulous men grappled with the spinning clay. All very interesting normally, he thought, Falakhoth having no potters but not when he was so hungry. "Where's the scran?" he asked.

Azhur grinned and marched him forward. At the very rear of the square was a jumble of the high, narrow tenements, pushed back against the very rock face that rose sheer to the third level. They looked as though the city's sculptors had grown tired of the great figures of the past and decided to carve a relief of their homes instead. One tenement was lower than the rest, its narrow chimneys scarcely reaching the roofs of its neighbours. Outside it were tables with stools and benches. Over its door, a confident green and gold sign proclaimed *The Cure*. Hunched, intense men carried on vigorous conversations at the tables, nodding and stabbing fingers quite unthreatened by the vast, sheer wall of rock rearing above them. Tyr lowered himself onto a bench and bent his neck to stare upwards. He had been at the bottom of cliffs before, but this one seemed strangely unstable now that he had to eat his meal sitting at its foot. But he supposed *The Cure* might be the safest place to be should those lofty coruscations detach. He pondered this and discovered that his limbs had tensed, ready to spring into the house's open door.

"Well, who's this you've brought?"

Tyr shook himself. A slim, dark-haired woman was looking him over with intense but friendly interest.

"Tyr-shan of Falakhoth," announced Azhur rather grandly. "Visiting the city with his family."

"Oh, aye," said the woman. "Nice round there. Been past it a few times, but I've not been in." Her voice spoke from the valleys, not the hard city streets. She wiped her hands efficiently on the cloth tied round her deep red dress, replaced them on her hips, and tilted her head to the side a little. Tyr liked her; he was at ease at once with her open country manner. "Sazhura," she went on. "My dad used to be buildings inspector at Lachresh." She jerked her head towards Azhur. "How'd you get attached to him, then?"

"Oh," said Tyr, and instinctively began at the beginning. "Well, there was this storm—"

"Oh, that? You got it too? Nearly sank us here. Priests've been wettin' themselves ever since, wonderin' what it means. King Nav's statue got blown to bits with the lightning, y'know. There's still stones and roofs in the streets and I don't know what all. But anyway, there was Azhur in a storm, in Falakhoth..."

And here something stirred in Tyr's stomach, reminding him of present realities. "It's really interestin' how we met," he said desperately, "And I'll tell y', I will, but can I have some scran first?"

"I was lauding your soup," explained Azhur.

"Talk properly," Sazhura told Azhur, and grinned at Tyr. "Priests, eh? *Laudin' the soup!*" And she swept away through the aroma-wreathed door, returning shortly with plates and bowls and a feast that surpassed even Tyr's gnawing desires.

The Cure's soup was indeed laudable. Laden with unexpected vegetables and meats and suffused with sudden, secret spices, it clung to the slabs of hard white bread and drank their butter into itself as though eager to match Tyr's ravenous appetite.

"Brilliant," gasped the boy. It had taken three bowls before he felt free to speak. "How'd y' make it?"

"Takes a country girl," said Sazhura in the evasive way of those who hold the secret of a truly superior dish. As compensation, she set out cheese and pickle and the village-boy's inbred love of banter surfaced.

"Do y' get a lot of priests eating here?"

"We get all sorts. Him there, for example." She nodded towards a big, bearded man who scribbled vigorously on the mounds of parchment that surrounded his soup bowl. "He's writin' a history of the Valgraavs. Rather him than me, but he likes workin' here. Says it helps him think." Sazhura glanced up. "Must do, with King Nav's tower over his head." She began to gather up the plates and bowls.

"What cure?" asked Tyr suddenly.

"What, love?"

"Its called *The Cure* here. Cure for what?"

Sazhura straightened up with her tray full of dishes and looked at Tyr for a moment longer than she really had to before her gaze traveled past him into nothing. There was, he thought, a new set to her jaw she was perhaps unaware of. "Oh," she said, drawing out the word into a vague, sing-song note, "Ills. Y' know, troubles." She smiled tightly and was off to her kitchen.

Tyr found this mysterious, but his restless mind found untraveled paths. "Do y' sound like y' dad?" he asked the near-dozing Azhur.

His friend shook himself and raised his head. "Do I what?"

"Y' said I was soundin' like me dad, so do you sound like your dad?" Azhur looked about the table and his fingers flexed. "Well, I don't... I suppose you could say—"

"I don't mean does he say 'bloody hell' and that. I just mean, are y' like him?"

"No. No, I wouldn't say so. Not particularly."

"Does he know a lot, like y'? Is he clever?"

"In a—in his own way. We were very different. He was... less complicated."

"Was?" said Tyr, then clapped his hands over his mouth. "Oh. Sorry. Was he not well?"

"Accident," replied Azhur. He looked grimly down at his grappling fingers. "Very sudden. Like my mother. Sudden." And he took a great breath and stared pointlessly around the square. "Happier times now, though, forging ahead in the Shrine." He coughed unnecessarily. "I particularly like Mhurvas-tal's work. The blue vases, there. Do you have a preference, Tyr?"

And no more did Tyr learn about Azhur's father that day.

With the awkward conversation and the laudable soup behind them, Azhur and Tyr ascended the city streets towards the lower buildings of the King's Tower. There they would meet Iethen and Tyrmar before the Renewal ceremony. In a busy third level street they halted and stood aside when a disturbance began behind them. A hand-bell was ringing and a shrill, sharp voice was slicing through the air.

"Bread, bread for the poor! Stand aside, for the Sun's love, and let the poor come! Stand aside!"

Horses and people made a path for a group of women clad in black with the bell-ringer at the head. The bell startled some horses which made their owners shout in annoyance, but the clanging and the calling went on, regardless.

"Bread for the poor! Come for Arna's bounty! Let the poor come!"

The women passed Tyr and Azhur. There were sixteen, swathed in tall head-dresses and full-length robes as black as night. Even the boots peaking out from under the hem of their robes were black. Each wore at her throat the amulet of both the Sun and Moon, bronze and silver. Their strained features looked pale against the black cloth wound about their faces and none wore anything like a smile. They seemed to have a grim determination about what they were doing, though some looked simply unhappy and one or two had no expression at all. Each carried a large basket of bread or scraps of food, rather than censers or golden pictures. The woman who led them held only a bell. She was perhaps sixty but may have been younger. *You'd have to see her face without all that black wound round it*, thought Tyr, but she walked in the settled stance of authority born over many years, striding forward with purpose, her back straight and her head up.

"Who're they?" asked Tyr. He hoped this fresh chance to explain something would tug Azhur's mind away from his accidentally deceased father.

"They're the Daughters of the Moon," replied his friend respectfully. "They have a house at Shrinegate."

"What, lady priests?"

"No, no. They honour Arna in their service of Iathena—that's the purpose of their order." Azhur noticed Tyr's puzzled expression. "An order? Well, it's... It's something like, well, like a club. Sort of. They live together and have their own customs and they do the things the order was started for, like feeding the poor, for example." Azhur felt that this was a terrible definition of an order, but then no-one had ever asked him before.

Tyr, however, was quite satisfied. "Right. Well, let's watch them, then. I wouldn't mind a laugh." And he trotted after the women.

The Daughters of the Moon stopped where several streets converged at the open place at the top of some steps and dumped their baskets down by a large arch with obvious relief.

"The steps go down to the Second Level," Azhur explained. "And then they're near stairs from the first. Watch this."

The woman with the bell positioned herself at a parapet by the wide stairway. She swung her bell furiously and called into the street below her. It was busy and noisy, but she had no difficulty in being heard.

"It pleases Lord Arna to shine on the poor as on the rich, so that all men should praise his beneficence."

"Kindness," said Azhur, before Tyr could ask him.

Tyr clambered up on the rim of a fountain for a better view. Not that there was a crowd, for most people just walked past. There were even a few laughs and a snatch of a disrespectful-sounding song. From his vantage point, Tyr noticed how this was a place where the inner walls of the city's tiers came close together. This meant he could see the street beneath and, on its further side, a gateway and steps to the lower city. And there were the poor. A crowd was struggling up the steps from the lowest places, surging like an undulating sea of ragged backs and desperate, gaunt faces to reach the street beneath the woman with the bell. They swarmed through to the Second Level, pushing towards the steps that led to the Daughters of the Moon and blocking the street. This drew yells and curses.

"Get on, there! The city can't stop for you!"

"Move, you ragbag! Feed yourself instead of crawling up here for pickings!"

The bell gave a short, violent clang. "Who. Are. *You?*" The woman was pointing down furiously into the street. "Name yourself!" Raising her hands for silence, she turned and spoke to everyone. "Quiet! Quiet everyone and listen!" The street noise died away before that compelling voice. "Listen! Tell Valderthaan who scorns Arna's bounty!"

A pause and the sound of a man's voice saying something Tyr couldn't quite make out.

"Oh, you're not answerable to me?" said the woman. "No, but you'll answer to Arna and his Lady! Speak, if you're not a heathen. Where have you come from? G'chraada's temple?" A roaring protest from below. "Well, then, tell us who you are."

The wait was longer this time. Tyr glowed with thankfulness that her voice was not aimed at him. The man responded, speaking again too quietly for him to hear.

"Well, Shuvar the Silk-seller, this is what you will do: since you have despised Arna's bounty by the Daughters of the Moon, he will give his bounty through you. Get down from your inbred horse and give that ragbag, as you call him, a gold coin!"

A great gasp went up from the crowd and a cry of dismay from Shuvar.

"How's she get away with it?" asked Tyr. "Is she royal?"

"No," said Azhur, "she's Mother Vashira."

There was a great cheer from the lower street. Shuvar had evidently parted with his gold piece.

"Good," rang Vashira's voice. "Now the kiss of kinship."

This time Shuvar was quite audible, "Kiss *that?* If you think—"

"You are both citizens of Arna's realm! You understand that, do you not?"

"Don't you get clever with—"

"And you understand that our Mother Iathena, *Arna's consort*, is gracious to all without distinction by the *will* of Arna? Or do you wish the Chamber of Observances to explain this to you should you come to their attention? Well?"

"Got him!" laughed Tyr and clapped his hands. "It's better than the players, this is!"

"*Both* cheeks," snapped Vashira. A hubbub of cheering and clapping arose. "There," she cried. "Now Arna *may* shine on you again." She raised her bell, whirled it around her head like a battle standard and rang it furiously. "Let the poor come!"

CHAPTER 13

Renewal Night

THE DAY PASSED AND as the night welled up from the east, Tyr and his parents took their places beside Azhur outside the Shrine, in the great semi-circular court where the city was assembling for a spectacle that would outdo even Mother Vashira. They sat in the highest row of a semi-circle of tiered seats that sloped from the floor of the court to the single walkway along the ramparts of the encircling wall. Tyr leaned back contented, he would miss nothing from here. Bending his supple spine as far as he could in an exaggerated curve over the back of his seat, he could peer along the rampart of the Shrine's monstrous curving wall and out east over the city to the descending dark. A deep, black-blue night had fallen on the Plain. The torches beside each guardsman shone like great jewels set in velvet. They were too high to see anything of Valderthaan itself, but all its lights would be out anyway, waiting for renewal, the god's infusion of life.

The last of the weak evening glow was creeping away to the west behind the King's Tower, when Tyr saw a procession of priests approaching. They carried censers and jewelled statues and pictures of the man who even Tyr knew now as the First of the Blood, great Na-veshtrazh-dak, who lay not many yards from him in his gilded tomb within the Shrine. The leading priests, in ember-hued robes that glowed more richly in the torchlight, held long, decorated poles on which glittered the image of a flame. Leading them was a silver-bearded man magnificently garbed, who paced slowly forward with hands raised, speaking as he went.

Tyr stuck an elbow in Azhur's ribs, "Go on then," he said, nodding towards the bearded man.

Being on the very cusp of Renewal, Azhur was in just the mood, "Ah. Well, that gentleman is the Master of Armaments, a *very* senior priest of the Second Circle. At the moment, he's anointing the ramparts. That means this court will be completely protected during the ceremony."

"Protected from what?"

"Anything. Everything. Even time."

"Eh?"

"Oh, yes. The renewal performed by Arna takes place outside time, in the eternal reality. We're completely sealed off. No-one here will grow any older while they're inside the court. It won't show, of course, it's only for an hour or so. Not that time passes. You see how powerful things done in the Shrine can be?"

In fact, Tyr didn't. He knew he should believe his friend, but it was, well, difficult. This impasse absorbed his thoughts for some moments, and when he shook himself free from the dilemma, the venerable Master of Armaments had paused in his work of rendering the Shrine court invulnerable and was bending over him.

"Well now, Azhur," said a rich, comfortable voice. "This is he, is it?" He bent lower. "We'll be having a look at *you*, my lad, my friends and I." He was clearly amused.

"Aye," Tyr choked desperately, before throwing in, "Anthu."

Azhur intervened, "Tyr, this is the Anthu Beld'drudrastar, the Master of Armaments. Anthu, this is Tyr-shan and his honourable parents."

"Charmed," said the old man. The three villagers stared wildly at him.

"Hello," Tyr managed. "What do y' do, then?" He shut his eyes and bit his lip, but the stupid question was out.

"Ah," intoned Beld'drudrastar, raising his silver brows. "Well, sometimes I wonder, but what the Scrolls say I do is that I'm in charge of everything even remotely military in this kingdom. I can order the generals and captains about if I like, I can tell the cooks in the messes to change their menus, and I can even tell the blacksmiths down in the armouries to change the shape of the horseshoes."

"Have they got to do it?"

"Oh yes, and quickly. No arguments. Are you impressed, young sir?"

"Aye!"

"So you should be. In practice, of course, I take advice and delegate considerably. Oh, and I advise the Valgraav, but that's by the way. We'll meet again, Tyr-shan, but now it's back to work for me. May I say, madam, that gown is most charming?" And he went back to his chanting priests.

Tyr thought he murmured 'nice boy,' to Azhur as he moved away.

Tyrmar drew in a breath and opened his mouth.

"No, love," said Iethen quickly. "Not here."

As the evening deepened, Tyr and his parents sank further into the otherness of the vast space that held them. Above them, the monstrous, impossible bulk of the King's Tower seemed to be one black arm that lifted the sky. Tyr thought of the weight of these millions of stones and could not imagine how it supported itself. There were no lights in its myriad windows. Like the kingdom, the tower too was waiting for renewal. Glimmering faintly on its darkened wall was the gigantic golden figure of Arna, peering out from the gloom as though waiting for the right moment to step down to his worshippers. The court joined directly on to the tower and great, elaborate gates and doorways opened out on various levels, most obviously onto the huge, paved area before the tiers. Here, the flagstones were incised with ancient words and images, softened by millions of feet and stirring in the torchlight as hurrying shadows glanced back and forth. On the farther side of this great floor of traceries, broad stairs went up to a higher, smaller court that lay before the massive bronze doors of the Shrine itself, fast shut till the god should work his wonders. The astonishing building appeared to hoist itself into a series of circular plateaus, rearing up to be the crown of Valderthaan's island. Though it was dark, with only a trace of red, westering sky behind, the fires on the highest points of the Shrine allowed a faint shimmer of glory from the sweep of the great golden dome.

I'll see this in daylight tomorrow, thought Tyr. Surely, even the old temple beyond the desert could never equal this perfect bonding of stone and years. The leaping arches, the ranks of pillars graven with the figures of the past and all the forest of detail in carving and tracery that the fires made appear looked as though they had been shaped and positioned by time itself, so that the building had already been ancient when the first stone was laid. It was the fitting home of the highest god, a place to bow the head of any man living.

The red sunset gleam had almost sunk into the west to be lost in the sea, but the ceremony could not begin until darkness had fully come and so the court continued to fill. The visitors from Falakhoth passed the time by examining the great of Valderthaan and the north. Colourful, glinting figures drew the eye, and there was a splendid moment when a long, black procession crossed the flags like a patch of wandering night. The Daughters of the Moon knew how to make an entrance.

"Where'd they get all these folk from, then?" asked Tyrmar. "They all live here?"

"Oh, not all of them," Azhur told him. "The provincial governors are here, and the archpriests of the lesser gods. There's Tal-ver of Lukar, Ia-thena's archpriest at the Towers; and there, much against his wishes, we have the ambassador from Harrokaan." He pointed to a lean man in grey robes and ivory jewellery who maintained a grim, furious dignity, and glowered around as though he expected to be set upon. Nearby, a digni-fied, dark-haired man huddled into his heavy blue robe as the air cooled around him. Tyr took in the olive skin, the dark eyes. "The *Aurocharos* of Syrga. Escorting the tributary delegation, no doubt."

"Wonder where Ilissos went off to," remarked Tyr.

"Who?"

"Ilissos. That feller from Syrga as had his tea with you in our forge. Just cleared off. I thought we'd get a good story out of him. Left his stuff and all."

Ilissos, in fact, had Tyr but known it, was at that moment enacting the best story of his life as he scraped and hacked at the walls of his prison room in Archraad, making his agonised ascent to the high window.

"Oh yes, him," said Azhur. "Well, a sudden urge to be on the move, I expect. Storytellers are intuitive and impulsive. Now, there—"

"Bet he's not havin' as good a time as us—ey, look!" Azhur had to force his friend into his seat for there, shaming the firelight, sat the splendid Aia Djtenga. But Tyr was not to be contained. "See there, mam! Look at her, dad!"

"Blimey!" said Tyrmar moderately. "She's all right."

Iethen cooed in the unselfconscious admiration of another's beauty that many women are blessed with. "Well, I've never seen the like of her before. Isn't she lovely?"

"I'll wed her," declared Tyr.

"Don't be daft, love. Y' ought to wed Utha."

"Never, she's fat."

"She's motherly, or will be. Y' think on it."

"I have. I'm not weddin' no fatty."

"What about her over there, then, on that little platform?"

"She's skinny. Who's she anyway?"

"Well, *that*," said Azhur with a kind of scolding amusement, "is the Princess Iente, the Valgraav's daughter."

"Get away! Well, that big woman's—"

"The Graavinda, the Anthei Iera. There's her other daughter, Princess Aelwe, and the young man is Prince Arthodt."

"There y' go, then, eh? Hang about, though."

"What?"

"Where's the Valgraav? Is he late?"

Well over four thousand people now stood or sat amid the fires.

"It's my taxes as pays for them outfits," muttered Tyrmar. "They should get jobs."

"What about plain folk?" Tyr asked. "Y' know, real folk."

Iethen gave a trilling little laugh and several people turned round to frown. Tyrmar frowned back. "All of them looks real to me," said Iethen.

Azhur laughed, despite the occasion. "We know what you mean, Tyr. Look, they're letting the *real* people in now."

They saw the great iron gates pulled slowly open. Now the court received all comers. They surged in as a wave on a stone shore: the untitled, down-at-heel, plain, shabby, poor, unremarkable, ordinary folk of Valderthaan; the weavers, boatmen, fish-gutters, merchants, beggars, stable-boys, charm-sellers, and needlewomen; the dealers in food and spices, in incense and vapours of intoxication, in images and amulets and the powerful sign of the Sun; those who would pray for money and chant a spell for a meal; the curious, the idle, the wide-eyed youngsters, old folk with long-ingrained devotion, and hard-working people wanting a spectacle. People in all shades of belief, knowledge, apathy, and superstition entered the court. The wildly devout were there to see the miraculous moment in the Northlands' year and, for all they knew, an overwhelming vision of their god. The fearful dreaded Arna's wrath should they stay away, while the satisfied and confident saw their attendance as buying the smile of the god. For the great mass it was too majestic, too incomprehensible, too far out of their reach. They merely clutched at whatever god or prayer or power might dangle before them some scrap of help in life, while they prudently made room to honour the highest of the gods, even as he ignored them. Or not, as he chose.

Some two thousand or more there were, herded by the guards to the area they were to occupy on the engraved stones of the court. There were no seats for them, so they squatted or stood where they could. There were fewer fires in these places and the newcomers made a great shadow-brown mass bordered by spots of livid scarlet, where guards faced into the open space.

When the very last of the daylight had slipped away to the sea, Tyr made out footsteps behind him. His seat on the high tier was a vantage point for both directions. As the scuffing of the heavy boots mingled with low, urgent voices, Tyr strained his country ears.

"Can't be. Sure it's not a bonfire?"

"Position's right—there's the second, look!"

"Should be three."

"There, three! Tell the Captain: three beacons at the pass. It's Vardresh."

Feet went quickly along the rampart and out of hearing. Figures began moving among the fires, now black, now red, with a controlled urgency intended to avoid alarm. A soldier spoke briefly to men who looked like senior officers and they moved off with the same restrained haste. Several swordsmen followed and here and there on the walls men quietly left their positions.

Tyr made out the activity at the gate as they passed into the street. He nudged Azhur and pointed, but the priest only shrugged. Soon the sound of horses reached him from below the wall. Tyr thought they broke into a gallop just as they passed out of earshot. It was too much. The boy stood up in his seat and twisted around. Beyond the wall, night was complete. There were lights below at the gate and on the bridge, but further along the East Road, three beacons hung in the black, two in the valley and a higher one on the slopes of the Mardhoran. The hills directly behind Mardokhal that rose to the Long Water were just visible, a rough black outline. There should be no light behind them, but it was there. A dull red glow, still faint, that rose from some point on the Plain.

Iethen tugged on her son's sleeve, "Sit down, y'll miss it. What y' lookin' at?"

"Light," he said. "Azhur, somethin' on the Plain! Somethin's burnin'!"

"Bonfires," murmured the priest, tensed for the ritual.

"It's too big! There're soldiers gone off on horses."

"Well, they'll see to it. Settle now, it's starting."

Tyr saw that there was nothing he could do about strange lights or anything else and decided the soldiers could indeed see to it. He looked down and saw he was above a lake of firelight in a land of night. The great buildings were lost in the darkness. Heavy cloud cloaked the sky and even Arna's golden form was invisible, hidden and waiting.

The gates were closed with a great, iron noise. The thousands within the Court were suddenly closed off from all the world, kept amidst the fires in that vast stone womb, where the power of the god would infuse new life into the line of kings that was his creation.

For a moment, they seemed to hang in a void, silent, still, then, as if from the earth's heart, a great gong sounded. Once. Twice. From high above came an answering voice, deep and slow and strong, thrilling Tyr with a shiver. The tolling of the great bell Namau Ramá answered across time, as it had since the Kingdom was made, demanding in a deep, hard voice of power the submission of the earth to Arna and his chosen king.

Again a great gong sounded over Valderthaan, and again the bell answered. Light and sound welled out from the Shrine itself as the doors were opened and sonorous, rolling voices sang slowly, richly, in flawless harmony with the tolling above them, weaving their song round the voice of the bell. It seemed the crags themselves were singing, such was the strength of it, or that the deep places of the lake had found a voice. This was ancient music, older than the north, more distant and primal than the desert or the unbroken earth. It seemed to Tyr to catch the vibration of the cadence that expressed itself as reality and made truth what it was. He could not understand why everyone sat and listened to it so calmly.

A solitary figure stepped out into the firelight. The breeze snatched at his long, grey hair, as the fires danced over the gold on his scarlet robes and in the gems of his gilded mitre.

"Lord Shar-ra'ul, the Archpriest."

Tyr was aware of Azhur's voice, but it sounded far away, as distant as the red glow above Vardresh.

Shar-ra'ul came slowly forward to the top of the stairway from the Upper Court and stretched out his hands over the thousands below him. The bell called out again, and the singing dropped to become a background to the blessing.

"The Lord Arna shine upon you. May he who rises in the Sun send the Nine among us, they who are fire and light, to dispel the darkness of your ignorance and warm the coldness of your hearts." It was a mellow, resonant voice, kind and strong, and every person felt that Shar-ra'ul had spoken it to them alone.

Tyr remembered Bal-jarrak's curt, offensive version, "Better than Ferret," he said, and was shushed.

At the next peal of the bell the Archpriest lowered his arms. The voices swelled out again and from the Shrine came priests in slow procession singing so that they seemed to wade in a river of sound. It carried them along, poured out from the Shrine and over the throng, flooding the court till the very air was crammed with their song.

Tyr could not move. He watched the priests descend from the higher court, passing the Archpriest on either side. Shar-ra'ul remained in place, his grey head like a rock in a scarlet river. Namau Ramá was

270

fainter, but the singing did not stop. The meaning of the song had detached itself from the words and music and given itself a marvellous, burgeoning life. It rode on the singing for a while, then launched itself off to fly about the Court and soar up to the heavens, before sweeping down, low and near, as though it loved the gathered thousands and would not be parted from them.

Another priest now stood on the upper level. He sang, his voice rising above the chorus of priests and the fading bell, yet still one with them, weaving around their song, leaping from note to note in its own superb dance. As the procession continued through this wonderful unity of sound, bearing fire and gleaming images and the banners of the new-made Sun, Azhur murmured in Tyr's ear the meaning of the ancient song.

> *Hail, Greatest of all that is.*
> *You have brought Arna newly born from the Fire.*
> *We honour him, wielder of Fire*
> *We honour him, maker of Ke'vald-na*
> *We honour him, bestower of dominion*
> *We honour him, High One who chose us*
> *We honour him, renewer of blood.*
> *We sing to you, health of the earth.*
> *Holy One, you made us the Sun:*
> *Decree that the dawning rise in us all.*
> *Holy One, you are balm to the earth:*
> *We will find in you salve for the wounds of earth.*
> *Thou whom we know not, remember us.*
> *Thou whom we hear not, speak to us.*
> *Great Flame of the Fire of God,*
> *Shine from the Deep Fire,*
> *Give us the True Fire.*
> *Set us in Uerathel, flames of your burning.*

Tyr's face was wet with tears.

"Tyr," whispered Azhur, "whatever is it?"

"Dunno, dunno," he gasped. "It's lovely, it's grand, it's that grand. I never heard nothin' like it."

271

"Well, it's an old ceremony. Just listen—"

"No, but that bit. It's different."

"Keep that boy quiet," hissed a sour voice. "Or I'll tell a guard to take him out."

Tyr pulled Azhur closer to him and gasped in his ear, "It's different! *There's a bit of Wyrdha's prayer in it!*" He dropped back in his seat and tried to catch his breath.

The overwhelming beauty of the harmony spread out over the Shrine court like a canopy of protective warmth. He felt its excitement, the vastness of its strength, the store of meaning it carried, the wonder of its happiness in being with the sons and daughters of humankind. Joyful waves of heat rolled over him and he knew without doubt what had caused it. There was nothing to see, nothing at all, but he could sense the Fire-spirit stretching out his burning hands over the court and looking on with joy. He did not need or wish to understand it. This wonderful being could only be understood if it remained a mystery.

The priests ended their march in positions around the dais and on the steps. Some remained in the Upper Court, standing to the left of the Archpriest. The sound of the bell faded quickly until, in the midst of a long last note in the singing, it gave a last quiet peal and was gone. There was an immense silence. Breath itself seemed deferred. Nothing moved but the flames.

The strong voice of Shar-ra'ul spoke into the stillness: "The Lord Arna summons the mountain-lion. Zhivhaltaur calls for the blood that was chosen. From the Seas to the Gate of the Sunrise, there shall be no king but he. Come forth, Lord of the North: your throne is empty and your strength is waiting. Lord Arna calls you: come now and secure the endless rule. Step forth." The last words rang round the court with utter authority. Shar-ra'ul turned to face the Shrine.

From the vast doors stepped a solitary man. He stood motionless for a second looking east into the darkness, before walking slowly, almost cautiously, towards the Archpriest. His robe looked black, with golden thread and embroidery glinting in the light. The collar and sleeves were edged with the thick pelt of the black bear and dark, grey-touched hair swept from his bare head to mingle with the fur. Tyr wished he could make out his face properly, for he knew he was looking at the Anthu Jarthastra, the Valgraav.

"The Lord of the North is here," said the Valgraav. His voice too was strong enough to be heard, but it carried an unexpected edge to it. "Fire have I offered and in the resting-chamber of the First of the Blood a flame is set." The embodiment of kingship, Jarthastra descended the stairs and stood in the open court. "I come now to the Lord of Fires, who has risen in the Sun. The rule is his: he must renew it to me. The blood is his: he must bless me and my seed. In me is the life of his chosen line. By Arna's will, I bear in my body the Lords of the North to all generations. Life cries for life, strength for strength, the rule for rule. Zhivhaltaur holds them for the House of the Lion."

Shar-ra'ul took the Valgraav's right hand and led him forward among the fires, and there were many prayers and much singing and long recitals of the histories of the Kings and the Lore of the Founding, the account of Arna's creation of his dynasty. Then at last, the Valgraav stood before a silver-rimmed glass laver nesting in the paws of four bronze mountain-lions that held it over a flame. Jarthastra opened his black robe and, swinging his arms wide, let it fall behind him. He wore only a scarlet sash tied like a loincloth, and on his breast was the emblem of a golden sun.

The Archpriest, raising his arms over him, said, "Unless the Lord Arna shine on the land and on you, your line is without strength and has not the right or power of Kings and you are a lamp whose flame has perished, your Kingdom is as the ashes when the fire is dead and the rule in the North is but cold and darkness. Call then on him whose sign is the Sun, whose image is in the flames." Now the old man scooped up water from the laver between the two of them and with each phrase poured it over Jarthastra's head and body. "I wash from you all taint of night, the contagion under the earth, from the scent of the black lion. I lave you from all weakness of your blood, from all spoliation and curse of your seed and line. I cleanse you with fire as Arna refines you in the crucible." He passed a torch's yellow flame over Jarthastra's chest and limbs. "The Lord Arna shine on you. Let him now renew you and the Blood forever. *A rukhadzhir vei ai rema vei Yeva, ve krenu. Ve lema, sh'her na vecha ye h'yarrim. A Bhanir, valdhur se lemarche. A Hra'im, Me'iaathra!"*

And at the call of *Me'iaathra*, the priests gave forth a vast burst of sound and from the darkness above leapt the blazing figure of the god, poised above the Court on vast, burning wings: Arna, Zhivhaltaur, Light of Heaven and Earth, the life of the North and the House of the Mountain-Lion.

A great gasp came through the singing as the golden image shimmered and seemed to move in the glare of the fires that had suddenly ignited in a trough at its feet. The tower itself was dark and so the astonishing figure appeared to float, hovering over the Shrine and city. The priests' song deepened, strident and triumphant, as Shar-ra'ul came bearing the tiered crown of the North, fashioned as ascending tongues of flame and bordered with the pelt of the dread wolf of Archran that great Ur-thromath had slain in the terrible realm in distant days. The archpriest placed the crown, flashing and glittering, upon the bowed head of Jarthastra, Thirty-fourth of the Blood by the will of Arna. Over them both the golden hands were lifted. And above them all, Tyr knew, were the hands of fire. He sighed and sank back against his seat and let himself return to something like ordinary life. He felt comfortable, glad to be Tyr-shan, a village boy enjoying himself.

"You are renewed; you are the purest gold; you reflect the sun."

Priests brought splendid garments of scarlet and robed the Valgraav as a sign of his replenished life. Jarthastra remained standing as Shar-ra'ul left the dais and without a glance at any of the crowd made his way between the fires to the gates. They ground open just enough to allow him to pass though, out into the city.

"Where's he off to?" said Tyr. This seemed no time to leave.

Azhur shushed him. "He must leave," he hissed to forestall any more irreverence. "The Archpriest goes straight from Renewal to seek for Shivara. He'll travel west for three days."

"What, to the Sea?"

"Yes, close to the Deep Fire. Now, *shush.*"

The priests' song had quietened as Shar-ra'ul left the Court, but now it grew into a regal chant. Everyone got to their feet as the Anthu Jarthastra walked with deliberate poise to a great stone chair carved on either side with roaring mountain-lions. It was the ancient Lion Throne made for Na-veshtrazhdak. Jarthastra lowered himself onto the seat, rested his hands on the heads of the lions, regal, powerful, the Lord of the North. He turned once towards Arna's image, touched the amulet of the Sun at his breast. He bowed his head and closed his eyes. There was silence: the rite was ended. Lord Arna had renewed his rule through his chosen line. The song was over.

For almost a full minute there was no movement. The fires beneath the image sank and died. Arna's form returned to the darkness. The Valgraav sat like a statue in a garden of flame. Then, once, came the voice of the gong and a slow, muffled peal of the great bell began. The priests commenced a slow, quiet chant, gradually beginning to file back to the Shrine. Jarthastra would follow them with his guard. The throng resumed their seats. The guards relaxed a little.

"Where's the old feller?" asked Tyr. "Might just have needed a pee."

"Tyr, please! He's in a boat by now, crossing to—"

A woman's shriek silenced Azhur. Murmur of talk died to a new, horrid silence. The shocked woman lay on the ground beside the man who had flung her aside as he stepped into the open space. Her companion seized him by the shoulder, but he too went down with a savage force that battered his face on the stones. Two guards ran up, but the intruder broke them like reeds with terrible swinging blows to their necks. There was shouting and a flash of swords. People were trying to tug the gates open and struggling to get out. Guards ran between the fires, bows raised, spears lifted. The terrifying man paced to the foot of the stairs to the upper court and stood, tall and regal, utterly in command as he surveyed those around him with a palpable, wrathful contempt. Slowly, he raised his arms a little above shoulder height, palms open, and trembling fingers spread like jewelled claws. Robes, black and red, billowed and swept around him. On his chest hung a golden collar and on the scarlet turban around his head sat a gleaming crown. He was the counterpoint to the rejuvenated Valgraav. He wore command like another skin. And like a challenger in the lists he roared out a dreadful word into the trembling air, causing people to clutch their ears and writhe away. In reply came a violent roar as braziers nearby flared out incandescent white and vomited their flame in huge gouts of fire. The crowd scattered terrified in the glare. The falling, fiery darts finding them and setting their garments to burn and their flesh to sear. Hundreds fought and kicked to reach the stairs or the tiers where there were no fires. The priests were scrabbling up to the Shrine.

And through the terror, the evil king strode heedless of fire or weapon, fear a shield around him as he deliberately retraced Jarthastra's approach to the archpriest. He came to the laver and paused, standing in the pool of water that had cleansed the Lord of the North. A movement of his hands and the air buckled. The laver went spinning in a spray of water, shattering when it hit the stone. He stood, arms still out, staring at Jarthastra. Confusion had fallen upon the court and none could move or resist him. He lowered his arms and around him twisted slow, white vapours. With a shock those close enough realised it was steam. Even the cleansing water could not stand this man's terrible presence. The flagstones dried and with a whip-like crack, they split across, cancelling its ancient carving with a long, sharp fissure that glowed red within. The man raised his head, breathed in the stink of heat, and leapt towards Jarthastra. To the very Lion Throne he came and stood for a moment leaning over the astounded Valgraav, before sending a stunning blow into the side of Jarthastra's head that sent the Crown of the North bouncing over the ground.

Still no-one could master their senses to move against him. There were only cries of horror as his hand fastened like a jewelled claw on the Valgraav's neck and dragged him from the throne. For a hideous instant, Jarthastra was held aloft by one unbending arm, then flung away with a terrible force against the tiered seats like an unwanted toy. The victor now raised both arms, fists clenched, and with head back cried out a word, a terrible word, so that horror raked at every mind and every flame flared with triple strength. The arms came down like executioners' blades. White light blazed and the ancient stone of the seat shattered. The man looked briefly at the broken throne, ignoring the screams of thousands blundering through fear and smoke, and the whining, snapping arrows that could not reach him. Suddenly, he raced to the steps and in a moment had mounted the tiers and stood on the ramparts. There, the

Confusion had fallen upon the court and none could move or resist him.

terrible king paused and surveyed his desolation.

There was awful recognition as his eyes fell on the group from Falakhoth.

Tyr was half out of his seat with Azhur clutching his arm to hold him back. He gaped at the apparition in his exotic robes and golden trappings, horrified and fascinated. He could not take in the immensity of hatred in the sharpened features or the violence in the crease-ringed eyes. When the man turned his head, Tyr caught sight of the jagged profile, the hawk's features, and he knew. There in the firelight was the southerner who had collided with him under the trees at Falakhoth. He saw in the man's beast-wild eyes the same realisation. The dark king knew who they were. He raised a hand. Tyr recoiling from the spell that would crush them.

"I stay you! By the power of these anointed ramparts—"

Old Beld'drudrastar, strode forward at last with outstretched hand and clutching his holy censer. The black king saw he had only seconds. He leapt forward and gripped Tyr and Azhur by their shoulders.

"Your punishment will come," he hissed in their faces. "You are marked. I will find you." Then he whirled to face Beld'drudrastar and howled his unsustainable word. A hammering force of fire flared out from the censer and all were thrown away like scorched straws.

Tyr's senses returned. Both the dark king and the priest were gone. He lurched along the blackened ramparts and thrust his head over the parapet. There was no sign of the southerner, but in the street below was the smoking body of the Master of Armaments.

CHAPTER 14

Conclave

IN A DREAM OF RITUAL and red-robed priests, a hand seized Azhur's arm. Around him, singing ceased and the whole Shrine fell away. All at once he was awake, with a hand on his arm and a figure crouching by his bunk.

"Come on, Loremaster. Get yourself together."

Azhur recognised the voice and let the fright drain out of him. It was Sher-tal, one of the senior executive secretaries. Though not a priest, he ran the errands of the Archpriest and his higher colleagues.

"What's this? What time is it?"

"Never mind. Up you get, Loremaster." He slapped Azhur on the shoulder.

Azhur hoisted himself from his mattress and reached for his clothes. But Sher-tal pulled the black robe out of his hands.

"No. Your things are over there." He indicated garments lying folded on a bench.

"Sher, what's this?" groaned Azhur blearily. "I'm the Loremaster's *assistant*."

"Are you?" said Sher-tal, then stooped for the dim lantern.

"Yes, I am. Now, what's going on? I'm on first for the Histories in the morning, you know." He reached automatically for his bronze sun-disc, but his visitor snatched it away.

"Never mind that. Bring this instead. Don't open it." He handed Azhur a small leather pouch, then went to the curtain that pulled across the recess. "Sorry about this, but... well, meet me in the corridor. Don't use a light. Five minutes please, less if you can." With a whisper of the curtain he was gone.

Bewildered, Azhur examined the new clothes by the light of his small window. They were red: priest's robes. Why was he donning them in the middle of the night?

Everything was there: an embroidered undershirt, leggings, boots of soft brown leather, the calf-length coat with the appropriate designs—he couldn't see what—and the bronze clasp of the Sun and the Lion. Azhur clambered into it all as best he could in the dark, wound the broad red sash round his middle—he was bound to have it wrong—and pulled on the wide outer robe. Tying the cords at the wrists of his shirt proved impossible for sheer nerves. He gave it up and stuffed the shirt-sleeves into the cuffs of his coat. After several deep breaths, he patted himself over the heart, grasped the leather pouch, and stepped into the novices' sleeping-hall. For the thousandth time in his life, he drew the curtain to close off his recess. He paused. That simple act had seemed significant. Which bewildered him all the more.

Sher-tal was waiting, none too patiently, under the statue of the revered and utterly forgotten Novice-master Meldjuthauthtar. "Not bad," he remarked. "Straighten your sash." And he set off along the corridor at speed, Azhur following and struggling with the sash.

They went quickly through the winding ways of the Shrine, heading by unusual routes, Azhur thought, in the direction of the senior priests' chambers.

"Sher," he attempted, "you're really too mysterious. Don't you think you—"

"Reasons, reasons," he said, hurrying on.

Eventually Azhur found himself pacing along grand stairways and corridors he had never seen before.

"I won't dwell on the points of interest," was Sher-tal's single dry remark. "A proper tour later, eh?"

A good many guards watched them pass without challenge. Azhur spotted several faces he knew, all of them confused by the sight of him hurrying about the Tower in priestly robes. There was activity everywhere—too much for the hour. People passed in twos and threes, hasty and grim-looking. Those who were alone were almost running. Torches were burning, too many torches.

Suddenly Sher-tal halted. They were by an inconspicuous arch that could not boast so much as a small inscription. It was set in a broad space where several passageways met. Azhur thought the guards here looked bigger. His guide reached behind a hanging and tugged at something. The action reminded Azhur of a bell-pull.

"Was that—?"

"Wait," said Sher-tal.

They waited.

Sher-tal set his lamp down and drummed the fingers of his folded hands. He looked silently down at the pattern the light etched among the ancient flags and his lips made tiny movements as though he were counting under his breath. "Right," he said at last, and steered Azhur though the arch. Five brisk paces, then without pausing Sher-tal pushed on a narrow square of panelling, thrust it inwards and tugged his companion through. "Anthu," he said. "Azhur va-Kherzir."

They had stopped at last in a small, many-shadowed chamber scarcely twelve feet square. It was plain and empty, with a stone ledge set in the wall as a bench. A lamp hung from an iron hook beside a door in the opposite corner of the chamber and in its steady light Azhur saw who waited for him in this secret place.

Quiet and patient as the stone, the tall, spare figure of the Archpriest was standing in the room's corner. Behind him was a strong, dark door that might lead anywhere.

Shar-ra'ul lost no time. "Azhur, we are in haste. I ask you to forgive such a meeting, but it must be so."

Azhur was silent with the shock of seeing the Archpriest back already.

"I left to watch at Fyrieg, but I abandoned the search. I have been here scarce an hour."

"Abandoned?" repeated Azhur. "Does Shivara come?"

Shar-ra'ul's deep eyes became grave, "No, though each day I seek Shivara, and I will set out again next year. But peace. You know that I may return early at need." He paused and sighed deeply. "I fear there is such need, so I am the first Archpriest for a century to cut short his quest. Messengers told me what happened at the Shrine and in the city tonight."

"The city, Anthu?"

"You will hear. Now. The conclave has gathered. That is why you are here."

Azhur searched his mind and uttered only what he knew, "Anthu, a novice cannot enter Conclave," he said weakly. "Only priests—"

"—of the Fourth Circle and above. Yes, that is the ancient law." The Archpriest leaned forward, stern and calm. "But the Chosen's Council will admit a Loremaster of the Second Circle and that is what I shall make you."

Azhur stared—very stupidly, he thought later—at the Archpriest. He attempted desperately to think of something correct, something fitting, and then found he could hardly think at all. Instead, he silently moved his lips in an attempt to form a question. Sher-tal was steadying him and the Archpriest's voice sounded from the bottom of a well.

"The Conclave needs your knowledge, Azhur. Things are happening that we desperately need to understand, but we simply do not have the knowledge. The Loremasters are essential. We feel this may be a unique crisis and although Lord Galdtchav is there, he requires the help of another mind."

"Then... then surely the Master of Novitiate study—"

"I asked, but he will not hear of it. Anyway, Lord Galdtchav wishes you, and only you, beside him. Your understanding is almost miraculously wide. You know obscure things, ancient detail. You memorise scrolls that others never glance at. And you have the turn of mind for interpretation. No-one in Conclave would even pretend to equal you. We need your mind tonight, Azhur. But the law will not be broken, a Loremaster will sit in Conclave."

Azhur made one final attempt. "I have read in the seven hundred and

282

tenth scroll, Anthu, that the Valgraav and his Archpriest are deemed sufficient in their knowledge—"

Shar-ra'ul laid a firm hand on his shoulder. "On one interpretation. But now we speak of *practice*. Learn tonight that even the minds of the great need other minds." He smiled. "And Lord Galdtchav is very proud of his assistant. Are you ready?"

Dazed, Azhur let himself be led rapidly through a reduced version of the ritual that raised him to the priesthood: time-honoured words and statements, Shar-ra'ul's own decree, and that rich, strong voice speaking the rite with an authority that lost nothing to urgency. The new priest bowed his head as the Archpriest took from the leather pouch the Loremaster's sign of wisdom and knowledge, the eagle of the crags in flight across the sun's disc, and placed it about his neck to rest upon his breast. For his finger there was the golden ring of the priesthood, set with a single ruby, and bound about the wrist and fingers of his left hand was the sign of the Deep Fire. Then, in the midst of an astounding dream, Shar-ra'ul let himself be so ordinary and fatherly as to slap him on the shoulder.

"Now," he said, pushing open the door behind him, "we will go directly to Conclave. Will you come, Loremaster?"

Azhur entered a passage, following the Archpriest's lamp. A door had opened in the wall of his very life so that he could step out from all he had been thus far. Within seconds Shar-ra'ul was opening another door, another life, and spoke into a world that was still being made.

"My Lord Jarthastra, my Lords of the Four Circles, I present to you the Anthu Azhur va-Kherzir, Loremaster of the Second Circle."

Confused, Azhur looked about in his dream. On his right were many figures terraced in red. The priests and officials of the four ranks of Conclave sat in rising banks of curved seats, obscured by the light and shade of the torches. Ahead of him, Bal-jarrak stood behind a wooden table. Above him on his left, a huge bronze sun that bore in its centre the mountain-lion of the royal house, and below it a carved wooden seat with the heads of roaring lions carved on the armrests. He froze. There sat Jarthastra, resting his arms on the heads of the lions and leaning back against a crimson cushion. The new Loremaster began to sweat and his mind whirled, but there was the calming presence of Galdtchav at another table, beaming all over his face and clasping his hands in what looked like triumph.

The Archpriest made his way to a seat at the Valgraav's right hand. All the priests rose and gave a slight bow, first to Shar-ra'ul, then to Azhur.

"We greet you, Loremaster," said a strong, tired voice. "I give my blessing on your entrance to the fuller service of Lord Arna."

Earnestly, deeply, Azhur wanted to faint. The Valgraav—*the Valgraav!*—had spoken to him. He held his breath, bowed deeply to Jarthastra, then to the priests, then looked helplessly for something else to do. As if to restore reality as sharply and as quickly as possible, Bal-jarrak cleared his throat. Azhur stared at that sour face and felt himself back in the square at Falakhoth with the sharp finger prodding his chest and the thin, sneering voice reminding him you're only a novice! The narrowing of his little eyes told him Bal-jarrak remembered too. How would he react now Azhur had left the novitiate utterly, spectacularly, behind him?

Azhur knew it was the traditional duty of the Keeper of the Fires to welcome new priests to their red-robed status, so he waited. There was a pause and a look from Bal-jarrak that said *I am doing this only because I have to.* With his voice in bizarre contradiction to his face, he said, "We welcome you to the sacred priesthood, to the Brotherhood of the Sun, to the circles that surround the Chosen." He rattled it off in his stiffest, most formal tone. "Azhur va-Kherzir, Loremaster of the Second Circle, may the Lord Arna shine on all your service for him and the kingdom he has made." Having done the hateful deed, Bal-jarrak visibly relaxed. "Now, if you will take your place by the Lord Galdtchav, Conclave will *resume.*"

Someone coughed a little abruptly.

"Anthu," Bal-jarrak added.

This subtle snub from Bal-jarrak lowered Azhur's spirits, but with another bow and with *Anthu* ringing in his ears he made his way to the table where Galdtchav sat with a number of important scrolls. The old Loremaster gripped his hand tightly, smiling in the restrained and vigorous way that was his, before rising to his feet. It was an interruption both sudden and stately and only Galdtchav could have managed it.

"The Keeper of the Fires will forgive me," Galdtchav said briskly, regarding the table-top in careful humility.

Bal-jarrak's mouth, open for its next sentence, shut like a trap.

"Forgive me," repeated Galdtchav, "but I of all people should not let this moment pass without a word." He glanced towards Jarthastra, who nodded. "I will be brief, fear not."

Bal-jarrak writhed with impatience.

Briskly, Galdtchav continued. "I need not repeat Lord Bal-jarrak's most excellent welcome to the priesthood. I am simply grateful for the gifted young man Arna has today added to our ranks. *The praise of ability is the honour of the One on High,* as Ar-ven told us. Therefore, I extol what I have observed, namely the abilities of the assistant whose learning most likely outstrips my own, and who I regard as my equal."

Azhur burned crimson.

"It is, I am convinced, a sign of Arna's favour that Lord Azhur's priesthood should first be exercised in such a company." Here Galdtchav bowed deeply to the Valgraav and took his seat to a ripple of approval.

"Very proper," said Jarthastra quietly. "Very proper."

Azhur leaned closer to Galdtchav, "Your *equal?*" he whispered.

"Of course. You don't think I'd let Ferret get away with a miserable effort like that?"

At a movement of the Valgraav's hand, Bal-jarrak stood. "Lord Galdtchav has spoken fittingly," he said, gathering his thoughts and his papers, "in combining appreciation with *brevity.*"

"Oh, nasty," murmured Galdtchav.

Bal-jarrak drew himself up in what he believed was an impressive manner. "If it please you, Lord Jarthastra," he said, "the Council will resume."

Jarthastra nodded.

As Bal-jarrak took up some papers, Azhur noticed the tension that came over the Conclave. His appearance had evidently been a welcome interlude, but now they were getting back to serious business they frowned at the burden they shouldered. Several priests were even in ordinary clothes. One had simply thrown a robe around his nightshirt and pulled on his boots. It all had the air of secrecy and speed.

Azhur tried to get his breath. He had only been a priest for minutes and yet so much seemed to have been said and done, so much praise bestowed and enmity recalled. And why were they all here?

Bal-jarrak laid down his papers and leaned forward, fingertips pressing on the table. His face had ceased to be sour and was for that moment just afraid.

Shar-ra'ul rose to his feet. There was silence as the Conclave waited for the Archpriest to speak. "Tonight," he said, and the word was like a dagger striking wood. A numbing chill descended and his dignified face tightened. The moment passed, and the priest mastered himself again, but much of his poise had fallen away. "Tonight, I remind you, there have taken place events so dire, so unprecedented, and so threatening that I have found it needful to abandon my sacred journey to Fyrieg. My lords, things have been seen and heard that demand explanation." He stared down at the floor. "Interpretation."

Azhur leaned forward.

"If we cannot reassure the city," Shar-ra'ul went on firmly, "there may well be panic."

At this, Bal-jarrak raised his head and Azhur saw in his darting eyes that the Keeper of the Fires himself longed for reassurance. The priests shot covert glances at Jarthastra, but he was stroking the bruise at his throat and looking straight ahead.

With a catch in his voice, the Archpriest continued. "The night's events mean that the task of this council is to decide not *whether* we must act, but *how*. The Lord Shedrathra is gathering reports and eyewitness accounts. By now—"

A pattern of knocks sounded. All heads turned.

"Enter," called Jarthastra, scarcely moving.

A grim-faced priest with a thick iron-grey beard and heavy, level brows entered the chamber, bowed to the Valgraav and went quickly to a place by Bal-jarrak's table. There was a wad of papers in his hand. The Archpriest took his seat: this clearly could not wait.

"My Lord Shedrathra," said Jarthastra, not looking up. "Proceed, if you will."

The priest began at once, "I have collected reports from the watch while you gathered, my Lords, and spoken to as many witnesses as I could. I included many of the injured." He paused and seemed unable to look at his papers. "May I never need to repeat this task."

And at that, Azhur felt afraid. Shedrathra glanced across to the Master Physician.

"We will lose more," said the priest.

Shedrathra dipped his burdened head.

"Amends shall be made," said Jarthastra suddenly. Still, he had not moved, and his voice was strange.

Azhur felt Galdtchav touch his arm. He looked up to follow his gaze. With a tiny gasp, he saw how wide Jarthastra's eyes were.

"Have you the reports, my Lord?" Shar-ra'ul asked loudly.

Shedrathra lifted his papers and began to read. As he did so Azhur wished he was hearing him in a garden, or by a river, or anywhere under the blue sky and sunlight. If they had even waited and gone to the Audience Hall and opened its great triple doors onto the bright terraces and morning light. Here the night hemmed them in and fear coiled in the shadows. He saw how hands tightened on the arms of chairs, how the torchlight melted faces into masks of dismay, how bodies stooped and hunched under the weight of the words that none thought they would ever hear.

In the middle night, the reports told, with the moon near her zenith, there had been lights in the sky over Lukar. The watch had seen them descend flickering around the Towers of the Wound. There had been sounds that might have been wailing or might have been like singing— no-one was able to say. Terrified, the Captain of the Watch had sent a despatch to Valderthaan. The rider arrived shaking with terror and crying, "Did you see it? Where is it?"

Valderthaan had also seen lights. Shapeless, bright patches had moved in the streets, but people said that no matter where the lights moved, it remained dark. There were dozens of reports of terrified people battering on guardhouse doors for no reason that they knew, save that, alone in an empty street, they had suddenly felt themselves surrounded, stifled, and afraid.

Worse followed. Guardsmen had been attacked at their posts by a large, clawed creature, almost certainly a wolf. Four were dead and six more badly mauled. The watch at the Bridge Gate had heard a horse canter along the bridge and up to the gate. They heard the voice of that night's commander and opened the postern: a wolf sprang through, almost killing a man before racing away towards the Second Level. This tallied with the report from the watch station at the Bridge's eastern approach of a wolf-like beast that had reached their parapet in a single leap, scrabbled over, and gone flying towards the city. The Watch had fared badly. By the city's southern gate, at the quay that served the traffic on the lake, a contingent of the guard stood sentinel under statues of Arven and Na-veshtrazhdak. Beacons, watch-fires, and the lamps on ships and by the statues had rushed up in huge fires. Five dead, a dozen injured, four vessels gutted or sunk, and the revenue buildings still burning. The ferocity of the heat had blackened both statues, that of the First King had split, with one side shattered away. After an hour, the same story at the northern gate of the Third Level. The guard-tower was still smouldering, the gate itself merely charred wood on twisted hinges. A despatch from the watchtower on the Mardhoran, brought by boat because no-one would use the Bridge, reported many lights on the north of the Plain, away from the cities and the usual Harrak camps. Another, from Mardokhal, gave word of travellers pounding on the gates saying they had seen bands of armed men, or huge wolf-packs, or they knew not what.

And here Shedrathra paused.

Shar-ra'ul leaned forward, "Is there more?"

Shedrathra put down his papers, then placed his hands on them, leaning on the table like the weary man he was. They saw he carried words in him he did not wish to utter. "There is more, Anthu," he murmured, then drew in his breath. "The watch by Shrinegate saw... an animal. It came up towards them from the Second Level."

The priests waited, and through the silence came Jarthastra's breathing: slow, deep, and laboured, like the broken bellows of a cooling forge. His eyes were closed and his fingertips pressed on his temples.

"They say they saw a lion," Shedrathra said, watching Jarthastra. "A black lion."

An ancient fear stole into the horrid quiet. The Conclave became one with every child frightened by old legends, every shepherd huddling closer to his watch-fire in fear of something worse than wolves, every night-traveller in the mountain passes clutching an amulet and whispering fearful prayers. The figure of the black lion—a dread reversal of the golden beast of the royal house—was woven into the mind of the North even before Rachtu Bhanir knew of it and was ancient when first he sent the priests of the Sun. It was the sign of disaster, malice, and sudden death. It was the embodiment of evil itself, the enemy of Arna, the would-be destroyer of his chosen line and realm.

Horrified, Azhur held the sign of the Deep Fire to his heart and all at once an energy stirred in his breast and he found he was speaking.

> *In brightness, the darkness is nothing:*
> *In darkness, the light cannot die.*
> *No blackness may cover its burning:*
> *In the shining, the shadow must fly.*

The room was still. The priests stared. Jarthastra raised his head.

"Where did you get that?" gasped Galdtchav. "What scroll, laddie?"

Azhur opened his eyes and shook his head. He felt warm and limp, unexpectedly rested. Not knowing what else to do, he slowly took his seat. Raising his head, he met Jarthastra's eyes. They were clear, keen, full of vigour.

"Arna's favour is indeed upon our new Loremaster," said the Valgraav. "We thank you, my Lord Azhur."

Azhur half-stood and bowed. The room had changed. The ancient fear had been beaten back, but no-one could say how.

Shar-ra'ul gazed at the new Loremaster with a wondering intensity. "We will speak of this, my lord," he said quietly.

Azhur gave a bemused nod.

Bal-jarrak slowly rose to resume. He looked quietly bewildered, but the glance he threw at Azhur was still not entirely free of hostility.

More knocking. This time it was Sher-tal, who delivered his message in a whisper to Bal-jarrak. The Keeper of the Fires gave a long, slow sigh.

"More wolf attacks," he said flatly. "And a despatch from Lukar: the Dragonstone is destroyed." He listened to the groan that went round the chamber and stared unfocussed at the end of his fingers pressing on the table as his wide, thin lips became thinner still. "Right," he said to Sher-tal, without looking at him. "I have to know everything. Bring the peasants."

Azhur wondered for a moment what he meant, then suddenly sat up, stung by the priest's disrespect. "Anthu, this may not be the best time," said Azhur tersely. He luxuriated in being able at last to use such a tone to Bal-jarrak.

"It won't wait," remarked Bal-jarrak, eyes still on his fingernails. "They're waiting outside, we have to examine them *now*. Whatever's been happening in that boy's head might be... relevant."

Azhur noticed the resentment with which Bal-jarrak made the concession and found himself thinking punitive thoughts. "Tyr-shan—the boy—can be excitable and being brought suddenly into this assembly at this hour will alarm him. He may not recall—"

"I've *found*," said Bal-jarrak in a voice like nails on a blackboard, "that if you can get these rural types when they're unsettled they often say more than they intend." A pause. "Anthu," he appended, with a vicious little inclination of the head.

Azhur tensed and held his breath.

Bal-jarrak continued, "If you would listen carefully, my Lords, and try to recall passages of the Scrolls that may be relevant, the council will be in your debt. We must know what's going on."

"We will set their testimony beside the Scrolls," said Jarthastra's strong voice suddenly.

"A high and holy guidance, Anthu," Galdtchav pronounced gravely. "Another memorable feature of this night."

The pattern of knocks came again and Sher-tal half-shoved, half-ushered the three terrified villagers into the chamber.

Tyrmar, barely awake, could not believe what was happening to him, staring and staring at the august lords as if to deaden the assault on his senses by sheer shock. His wife stood trembling and on the edge of tears, all too aware, clutching a shawl and raking her fingers through hair she had not been given time to comb. Tyr stood rigid, eyes riveted on the Valgraav like a rabbit in a snare.

Azhur suddenly felt desperately sorry for the village family. Having shared their life for a little while, he realised that being thrust into such an assembly, in such a room, must be little short of traumatic for them. He wondered how Tyr would fare, and whether his country directness would survive the presence of the Valgraav and the hostility of Bal-jar-rak.

"This Conclave greets you and your family, Master Tyrmar," said Jarthastra gravely. "May Arna shine on you."

Tyrmar froze for some seconds, mouth wide open. "Yes sir," he managed. "Thank y', sir."

These pleasantries over, Bal-jarrak felt the need to reassert his presence. He tugged at the folds of his heavy robe, specially chosen to lend bulk to his thin-limbed frame, and towered unimpressively over his table. "You saw the futile and... *impotent* gesture at Renewal not many hours ago," he informed the villagers. "There have been several... smaller incidents since then. We are not greatly perturbed, but we do not wish to delay in deciding what to do, so we want your stories *now*. Do you understand?" Tyr and his mother nodded, so, leaving Tyrmar in his stupor, the Keeper of the Fires turned his deadly little eyes on the boy. "Tell us what you know, young fellow. Tell us all you said to Anthu Galdtchav na-Vajhavhru and to Bar—to the Anthu va-Kherzir. Don't leave anything out. Am I clear?"

"Aye," quavered Tyr, and nodded violently with the ghastly feeling that his insides were about to dissolve. He suddenly realised he was taller than the odious man, which helped, as did the name 'Ferret' that crept into his mind. A liberating little smirk appeared at the corner of his mouth.

Bal-jarrak flinched. "What're you smiling at?" he demanded.

"It's an itch," said Tyr, and rubbed his nose vigorously. "Sorry."

"Well, get on with it," snapped the priest. He folded his hands and fastened what he imagined was a penetrating gaze on the boy before him.

Azhur saw with relief how his friend had unexpectedly relaxed and was glad for him. Without knowing the reason for Tyr's smirk, it was easy to think it involved Bal-jarrak. That happy thought gave Azhur his own smile.

Tyr took a breath, held it, then let it out slowly with his eyes closed.

"What's this?" asked Bal-jarrak. "Is that a spell?"

"Relaxing, so's I can concentrate, like."

"Concentrate quickly, then. We don't have all night."

And so Tyr rehearsed all that had happened at Falakhoth: the visions of the Fire-spirit at the feast and the old scribe at the Coming Forth, his mental sojourn in the days of Shivara, as well as Yauva's astonishing healing. He almost mentioned the wound he had seen in Azhur's chest, but remembered the odd young woman's warning and kept it to himself.

"This Yauva? Who is he?"

"Dunno, he just turned up in the storm. Lives in Lukar."

"And why was the Lukar priest there?"

"Wasn't well. Come to see our healer."

"Did he use spells for the cure?"

"Dunno. Wasn't there."

"The fellow who made the blaze at the Coming Forth, what do you know about him?"

"That was our vraakhin. He's a daft bug—he's a bit of a loony, him."

"Loony?"

"Well, he says he knows spells and that, but I think he makes them up. Everybody thinks he's a pain in the bum."

"Has he ever done anything like what he did to the fire before?"

"Oh, no. Never does nothing."

Bal-jarrak changed tack, "Do you serve Arna?"

"Aye. Suppose so."

"You *suppose* so?"

"Well, y' do, don't y'? I mean, y' got to."

And so on. Tyr mentioned the sight of the Fire-spirit among the beggars and the words of Wyrdha's prayer. When Gizhurthra became the focus of attention once more, he said all he could about him, this helpfulness being a good opportunity to vent some of his backlog of spite towards the vraakhin. Mention of Gizhurthra's various odd associates caused great interest, especially the account of the vicious southerner.

"And who do you think *he* was?"

"Dunno. Just some feller he'd met, I suppose." Tyr jerked to a halt. "Oh, bugger."

"Remember where you are!" hissed Bal-jarrak, rearing up in righteous affront.

"Sorry. I... I saw him. Up at the Shrine." The boy stared terrified at Jarthastra. "That was him as hit y', sir. I forgot, sorry, I weren't right awake. Sorry, sir."

A great, solid silence seized them. Tyr feared he had done something horribly wrong and watched terrified as Jarthastra leaned forward into the light. He saw his long, sad face, the wide, tight mouth over the strong jaw. Large, deep eyes held him, but they could not hide from him the dreadful bruises at the Valgraav's brow and throat. The inward strength of the man was immense. His powerful mind had brought him to this Conclave in the depths of night only a few hours after a vicious assault and yet his thoughts were poised, absolutely in command. Conclave had witnessed that mind wander, to the consternation of the priests, not long before, but to Tyr, at this moment, it was the single strongest force in the world.

"You saw him?" said the measured voice.

"Aye," Tyr managed.

"Tell us. You need not fear."

Trembling, Tyr told the man a god had made, of the hawk-faced southerner who hated priests and described again his dispute with Gizhurthra over his mysterious brotherhood. He told how the man had tried to kill him on the ramparts of the Shrine. He told of the waves of crushing force that came from him and the fire that swept around him. He described the evil features, the scarlet robes, the long black hair like snakes, the shining gold trappings. And then he realised that he had not had time to be afraid or feel his shock and he shook as tears rolled from his eyes.

Azhur, alarmed, wondered if things would finally prove too much. Tyrmar clapped his firm hands on his son's shoulders, and then the Valgraav himself came to the rescue.

293

"It is enough," said Jarthastra quietly. "Go to your chamber, Tyr-shan."

"There's nothing else?" asked Bal-jarrak with a faint suggestion of empathy.

"No, sir," choked Tyr and backed away.

"Off you go then. Sher-tal?" Bal-jarrak stooped to his papers.

Tyrmar touched his forelock to a series of spasmodic bows, "Thank y', sir. Thank y' very much, sir."

"Please don't leave us just yet, Tyr-shan." Galdtchav was rising to his feet. With your permission, Anthu—thank you. Ah, we have a little test which I have devised—don't worry, it won't take a moment. Tyr, would you step forward? Good lad. Now, let me show you something." The Loremaster opened the wooden box that had been resting mysteriously beside him and took out an object wrapped in thick fabric. He carried the bundle to Tyr and placed it carefully in his hands, then stepped back. The Conclave leaned forward intently as one, wondering what Galdtchav could be doing.

"Heavy," said Tyr, feeling the bundle's bulk. "What is it?"

Galdtchav beamed, "That is for you to tell us, laddie."

Tyr gaped. "How am I goin' to know?"

"We shall see. Just unwrap it and tell us what it is."

"Is that it? The test?"

"That's all. Tell us what it is and then you can go back to bed." Tyr looked from the Loremaster to the bundle to Azhur, but there was no help forthcoming.

Azhur spread his hands, showing he too was mystified.

Tyr unwrapped the hidden object. It was well protected, the ample coverings taking some time to remove. When he was done, the lad held a bronze sculpture of a man's head.

Galdtchav smiled and nodded, Jarthastra watched wide-eyed, Azhur put a hand over his mouth.

"Nothin' else in it?" asked Tyr.

Galdtchav smiled again. "Not a thing, Tyr-shan."

Tyr examined the bronze. He took it over to a cluster of candles and held it close to the flames. A moment of scrutiny. "Oh, it's him!"

Galdtchav's intake of breath did not reach him.

"Aye, it's him. That's Shivara, him as I saw in me vision."

"You're quite sure?" said Galdtchav as evenly as he could.

"Oh, aye. It's obvious, isn't it? I mean, I saw him. Would recognise him anywhere." To Tyr, it was all blindingly obvious.

Tyrmar gave his son a hearty clap on the back while Galdtchav simply smiled.

A gentle quietness fell, a witness to the joining of mystery and clarity. The priests of Conclave eased once more into the caressing silence that had followed Azhur's unexpected verse.

Jarthastra unexpectedly spoke. "Your eyes are wide, Tyr-shan. They explore. What do they search for?"

Tyr started, "I was just lookin' about, kind of thing."

"Why?"

Tyr shifted awkwardly. "I thought—just a funny thing—I thought..., well, I wondered if it were maybe in here."

Jarthastra leaned forward. "What may be here? Tell us, Tyr-shan."

Tyr took a breath then gazed up at the ceiling, beyond the candle-light. "Y' know, him that come from the fire: the dancer."

The silence grew thicker, more palpable.

Quietly and evenly, Jarthastra said, "You think the spirit of fire is with us now?"

Tyr let his eyes range through the comfortable dark that hovered above. "Dunno," he said. "Dunno, it just felt—well, for a minute, it just, well... it were lovely."

Everyone relaxed. There was nothing more to say.

Jarthastra sat back in his chair. "We have heard all we need, I think. Master Tyrmar, will you take your family to their chambers?"

Tyrmar jolted to attention. "Yes, sir. Yes, I will, Anthu. Great honour, great honour. Right. Tyr, give the Anthu that thing back. Ieth, give the gentlemen a curtsey."

Iethen did not move. She stood twisting her shawl as if she would throttle it. "Beggin' y' pardon, sir."

Up came Bal-jarrak's long nose like a ploughshare from the earth, "Yes?"

"There was somethin' else, if it please y' sir."

Time stopped. Tyr gaped at his mother. Tyrmar appeared to imagine his wife had just determined their executions. The priests leaned forward. Azhur sat open-mouthed. The keeper of the Fires narrowed his little eyes again.

"Something else has happened?"

"Yes, sir."

"Why didn't you tell us before?"

"Well, it's only just happened, sir, just afore the gentleman come to fetch us." Tears started to fall down her cheeks, and Tyrmar and his son each slipped an arm around her.

Bal-jarrak sighed, an impatient gust, but Jarthastra spoke before he could. "Come now, goodwife," he said. "You are safe. Tell us your news and—who can say?—you may save many." And then he placed a hand on the arm of his massive chair and pushed himself to his feet. Taking the cup of wine that was beside him, he crossed the room to stand before Iethen with the cup in his right hand and supported on the palm of his left. In the stunning quiet, the sound of his heavy robes were like the wind among trees. "We have driven back the black lion this night," he said. "Take this and be warmed. Speak and do not fear." Iethen took the cup and sipped. Jarthastra laid a hand on her head for a moment, then returned to his seat and waited for her to speak.

With a trembling breath and gripping Tyrmar's left hand, she began, "Well sir, I couldn't sleep, not proper like, not after what happened. And I was tossin' and a turnin', must've kept my husband awake—"

"What happened?" hissed Bal-jarrak.

"Sorry, sir. Well, suddenly I woke up proper. Wide awake like I'd not been sleepin' at all and... and it was like my head was fillin' up with things."

"Like water filling a bucket?" said Galdtchav suddenly.

"Well, yes."

"You could feel the level rising?"

"Aye. Aye, that's just what it was like. Up and up. How'd y' know that?"

"A lucky guess," said Galdtchav, and waved a hand. "Do go on."

Azhur leaned close to the Loremaster, "Scroll of Manifestations?" he murmured. "Column nine?"

"The same," whispered Galdtchav. "Excuse us, Mistress Iethen. Please continue."

"Well, like I said, my mind filled up and then I was thinkin' of things. Only I couldn't help it. It was like I hadn't decided to think about them, but they was in my head whether I would or no."

"Of course," remarked Galdtchav absently.

Azhur leaned across his table, "What did you think about, Mistress Iethen?"

"Me gran, Azhur."

"Your... grandmother?

"That's right. Great-gran, as it happens. Old Matha as lives in the hill country up by Terchas."

"And what about this woman?" Bal-jarrak asked, more as a threat than a question.

"Well, when Tyr was born we took him to see her."

"Tyr-shan? This boy here?" Bal-jarrak drummed his fingers.

"Yes, sir. Well, when we got there, she takes him in her arms and looked at him a long time. She has the sight, y' see—"

"Why are you telling us this?"

Iethen started and took a gulp from the wine-cup she still held. "Well, this is what happened, sir."

Bal-jarrak tightened his hands into fists. "It happened over seventeen years ago. Why are you bringing it up now?"

"Ah, well, that's it, sir. Y' see, I forgot it all."

"You forgot it?"

"Yes, sir. Till I woke up this night."

"So you remembered all this about your great-grandmother just before Baranthu Sher-tal came to summon you? My lords, I cannot see what value—"

"We will hear this goodwife," said Jarthastra suddenly. There was the sound of millstones in his deep, even voice.

Bal-jarrak opened and closed his mouth ineffectively. "Your pleasure, Anthu," he managed before attempting to salvage his dignity, as he thought, with a sharp "Proceed" to Iethen, who gave a little curtsey and did indeed proceed.

"Well sir, Matha looks at Tyr and says, 'I've got a song for y', my lovey,' and then she sings. Like this." And Iethen, in a sweet, soft, innocent voice, charmed that venerable chamber with the song that had come to her in the night.

> *Maker's mind and maker's heart*
> *Set thee for his own apart.*
>
> *Here the love that quickens thee:*
> *Heart of thy heart beats above.*
> *Sea and mountain, babe and tree,*
> *Came to be from naught but love.*
>
> *Love for thee for all thy hours,*
> *Love for weal and woe and tomb.*
> *For the power above the powers*
> *Nestled by thee in the womb.*
>
> *Maker's mind and maker's heart*
> *Set thee for his own apart.*

Iethen stopped singing and stood in a soft silence. She sipped again from the cup. "After the song, she gives Tyr back to me and says, 'He's special, sure as I've got the sight. Bit too special, really, so y'll forget all this till the time's right.' And I say, 'How am I goin' to know when that is?' and she says, "That's the point, lovey. Y' won't know, cos y'll forget. But don't worry, it'll all come back.' And it has."

The strong, gentle quiet continued.

Tyr stood staring at his mother. "Was that about me?" he breathed.

"Yes, lovey," she said, eyes wide with love. "And maybe somebody else. I've got this feelin'."

"But what—I mean, who?"

"Don't know, love."

Tyr huffed out a great sigh, "Blimey."

Tyrmar and his family quite forgot where they were and hugged each other with a passion. Sher-tal had the presence of mind to take the wine-cup.

After a little while, the Conclave seemed to have received some kind of permission to make noise again, for there was shuffling and the sound of stiffened bodies moving in their seats. Azhur continued to sit still, one hand pressed against his lips and his brow twisted in an effort of recall. Galdtchav glanced at him slyly, but said nothing.

"You bring honour to Falakhoth," said Jarthastra, with a new resonance in his voice. "I am glad you dwell in the North. I thank you."

"Thank y', sir," said Iethen. Tyrmar made a grunting noise that conveyed the same. Tyr gave a jerky nod and looked about him; he awkwardly handed the statue back to Galdtchav. Sher-tal saw his cue and creaked the door open.

"Oh," said Iethen suddenly. "Hang on."

"We will not hang on," replied Bal-jarrak. "This is an extremely serious—"

"No, beggin' y' pardon, sir, but it's not finished."

"Your part in it is. You will leave us."

"No, I mean there's another bit, sir. The song, sir."

Bal-jarrak leaned forward aggressively, his teeth showing. "This is not a concert. You are disrespectful, woman—"

"She is not, my Lord."

Bal-jarrak whipped round at the sound of Jarthastra's voice. "Anthu, I... I merely meant—"

"This goodwife perceives her duty. Lady, is this another song about your son?"

Iethen curtsied, "No, sir, no. It's about Azhur."

A buzz of surprise, and more than one laugh. The new Loremaster seemed immobilised.

"I've just remembered this as well, sir, so I thought I ought to tell y'. It's just a verse, won't take long, not if y' want to hear it."

"You are willing, my Lord Azhur?" asked Jarthastra.

The freshly minted Loremaster could not decide whether he was willing or not.

"Anthu," said Galdtchav, "I believe my colleague will concur."

Jarthastra smiled, "Then we will hear this, lady. Sing it to us."

Iethen curtsied again, gave a little cough and sang:

> *Never seek, but still be found:*
> *One is near when you are far.*
> *When you see the whole world round,*
> *Love will tell you who you are.*

"That's all, sir."

Jarthastra inclined his head, "Lady, I thank you. Take your rest."

Azhur was suddenly on his feet, "Mistress Iethen—ah, forgive me, Anthu—Mistress Iethen, if you will. A small thing, but may I ask do you know... ah, that is, are you aware of something called the *Compilations of Berushta?*"

Iethen gave Azhur a sleepy laugh, "Oh no, Azhur, lovey. Dunno what a compilay-thing is, even."

"Well—"

"Is it a scroll? Because I couldn't read it if it was. What about that song though? What'd y' think?"

Azhur hesitated, at a loss of what to say. "It was... very nice," he said. "Thank you."

"Are you answered, my Lord?" asked Jarthastra.

"I am, Anthu." Azhur seated himself abruptly.

Jarthastra steepled his fingers, "Then may these good people sleep soundly."

"Thank y', sir," said Iethen. "Goodnight, sir. Goodnight, Azhur."

Sher-tal ushered the villagers from the chamber without further incident. The heavy door closed and everyone waited.

"Well, my lords," said Galdtchav at last. He held up the bronze sculpture. "You know what this is. We were all shown it when we were novices. The likeness of Lord Shivara, modelled *from the life* by Curathir of Dhar and sent here when Rachtu Bhanir made the Northern kingdom. Since the day it was made, it has been the most devoutly guarded, most highly revered object in the world, other than the Vhaltaur." The Loremaster paused, the enormity of his own words overcoming him for a moment. He gave a little grin. "As regards the means by which it comes to be in this room... well, I have my little ways."

As an amused murmur ran round the Conclave, Azhur leaned his chin on his hands and thought, *Oh, clever! The one infallible way to prove Tyr's vision and only Galdtchav had the mind to think of it and the nerve to do it.* He leaned back and folded his arms, feeling oddly rebuked. *It's a statue, not a scroll, so I forgot It. A fine start to a Loremaster's career.*

Galdtchav, meanwhile was holding forth. "And yet, as you know, there was always a shade of doubt. Could something so small pass through many centuries and not be lost? Could not the chances of the world have substituted a copy, a mistake, so that the True Likeness was lost? Tyr-shan has never seen this, has never even heard of it, but you witnessed his instant recognition of Lord Shivara. I suggest that there is no more doubt that this is what we have always believed it was, and that there is also no doubt that Tyr-shan has received a true vision and has indeed, somehow, seen our sacred past. We must now seek for meaning. What message or warning has been set before us?" Galdtchav lowered his head beneath the weight of his own words, then bowed to the Valgraav and returned to his table.

"Loremasters?" said Jarthastra at last.

"I believe I can find resonances in the Scrolls, Anthu," replied Galdtchav. "Azhur, have you anything...?"

"There's something... but I must reflect. Forgive me, Anthu..."

"Of course," said Jarthastra. "You will inform us." He closed his eyes and leaned back in his chair. "My lords," he said quietly. "Has Tyr-shan seen the gods?"

There was a great murmuring in the chamber. Jarthastra's question had taken the priests unawares.

"Can one see the gods?" asked Shar-ra'ul. His voice was a mixture of hope, doubt, and fear.

"In my days?" said Jarthastra unexpectedly with eyes still shut.

Galdtchav hesitated. "There are accounts from ancient times before Dhar fell. Kh'erukh Bhanir walked with a high one by Kherem's walls; the priests of Vel Shirriva received proclamations by the Lords and Ladies of the Desert; and Gaienal of Ceorthas, it is said, met often with the Lady and heard the songs of Uerathel, where she was led. But for this realm, no-one since the Founding has told such things. Perhaps they have been written and kept secret or perhaps they have been

301

remembered within families or tribes. But there has been no recorded tale like that of Tyr-shan."

"They're peasants," said a voice that scraped across the calm: Bal-jarrak. "We're not dealing with the great and mighty here. The gods have *standards*."

"We require quiet," said Jarthastra, deep and composed.

Bal-jarrak shrivelled into himself. Soft whispering began.

During the pause, Galdtchav leaned close to Azhur, "Leave this aside for a moment," he murmured. "I think things took a rather personal turn for you."

Azhur watched his knuckles closely. "Did they?"

"The songs, laddie. There was something for you there—I feel it. No hints? No resonances? No... help for you? Your heart needs it."

"There are Scrolls—trivial Scrolls, probably apocryphal," whispered Azhur stiffly, now looking straight ahead. "But she can't possibly—I mean, she can't read, anyway!"

"She's certainly got to you. Hm?"

"No, no, I'm just taken aback. An astonishing coincidence..."

"Allow me to guess, they're the sort of Scrolls only you would bother reading. This *Compilations of Berushta* thing for example."

"Well, yes, probably. I'll look at it."

"Iethen's song ruffled your feathers, my dear friend."

"Not at all. Why should it?"

"Well, we both know the answer to that." Galdtchav patted the young man's arm as his fingers locked furiously together. He felt the tension that seized the new Loremaster's body and read in his face the thoughts that were as clear as if he had spoken them. *I will not admit this. I will not show the terrible memories. I can still be strong.*

"I think that possibly—just perhaps—this is not the time to speak of my father," said Azhur tightly. "Thoughts elsewhere, that sort of thing."

"Yes, sorry," whispered Galdtchav. "Not wishing to revisit that now, but do think on all those verses. I thought they sounded... hopeful for you. You need that."

But Azhur was inaccessible, lips tight, eyes glaring ahead.

"Loremasters," said Jarthastra suddenly, still without opening his eyes. "The spirit of fire. It is the most astounding thing in all that we have heard. The spirit and all it brings with it. There is a wholesome joy about it; a life, an energy that I would have spread about this realm and in my heart. What think you, my lords? Does this bring us hope?"

"I pray it does, Anthu," said Galdtchav. "We will search earnestly for its meaning."

Jarthastra opened his eyes. "It is almost dawn, my lords, and we must rest. The Morning Song will soon be heard, and I propose we adjourn to the Shrine court to listen. My Lord Bal-jarrak, need we consider any other matter at this time?"

The Keeper of the Fires stepped readily into the circle of importance once again. "If it please you, Anthu, there is one small but significant thing: the council will be aware that the Lord Bel-ghirá has returned from Vardresh and must be honoured for its defence." He glanced at a conspicuously empty seat. "I suggest that this Conclave bestow upon him the title, responsibilities, and privileges of Master of Armaments."

At once, there was a murmur of assent.

"So be it," said Jarthastra. "Let it be entered in the Scroll of the Third Circle for this year. And now, my lords, the Morning Song."

The Conclave rose and bowed as Jarthastra left the chamber, then the priests came down from their tiered seats and followed him out.

~

BAL-JARRAK, HAVING METICULOUSLY tidied his papers, was last to leave. As he closed the chamber door behind him, a man stood forward from the shadow under an arch and spoke. "You have done as I told you: I commend you. Now wait for your next instruction. Remember, if you continue in this way, there will be great honour for you." The speaker withdrew into the dark and was gone.

Bal-jarrak blinked, shook his head a little, and looked about vacantly as if he did not know what had happened. He shifted the documents in his arms to bunch them neatly together and hurried off after Jarthastra and the Conclave. He didn't want to be late.

CHAPTER 15

The Morning Song

JARTHASTRA'S PARTY WENT THROUGH many secret ways, passing high windows that betrayed the rising dawn. At length, they emerged from an inconspicuous porch that opened beneath the Shrine's great bronze doors above the court that had seen the atrocities of the night before. Behind them was Na-veshtrazhdak's tower and near them the curving mass of the Shrine reared up. Its vast, golden dome was set against withdrawing night and was showing a pale reflection of the dim, grey morning. Across from it, Arna's golden image picked up the first trails of light. It was the time that was no time, neither night nor day, and the court below lay in an unnatural, unreal stillness. A chill breeze made the unnecessary torches dance, and the priests tugged their robes around them. Despite the hour, the court was busy. Kneeling figures were scouring away the scorches from the paving-stones and the empty tiers. The buckled braziers were being replaced and sweating men were edging into place a replica of the Lion Throne, carved through the night by teams of masons. All would soon be as before.

The guard on duty snapped into extra watchfulness at the sight of the Valgraav. The captain ran up and bowed low.

"Arna shine on you, captain," said Jarthastra. "We are here for the Morning Song. How went the night?"

"In this court, nothing, Anthu," the soldier told him. "But terrible things in the city. A giant wolf, apparitions—"

"The Conclave has heard. What of the fallen?"

"Readying for burial, Anthu."

"How many?"

"Forty-seven, Anthu. And over a hundred burned or injured. Couldn't get out."

Jarthastra stared grimly at the scarred courtyard and out over the walls to where a shroud of smoke still hung over the Plain. He slowly pointed down. "Do not remove the burns before the Lion Throne. We should remember."

The captain bowed and went about his duties and the group of priests moved on. Jarthastra halted them again at the spot where he had stood at the head of the stairs from the court the night before. The broad steps continued up to the looming doors of the Shrine itself and there, under the huge arch, two figures waited against the dull bronze that as yet needed the dawn to colour it.

"My Lord Bel-ghirá," called Jarthastra. "You do not rest? You cannot be long arrived from Vardresh."

"Vardresh burns, Anthu," said a high, dispassionate voice that echoed oddly in the stinging air. "But the defence was for Arna's glory."

"Indeed," replied Jarthastra, "and we will hear his song. Will you join the lords of the Conclave, you and your companion?"

"If it please you, Anthu," said the odd voice of Bel-ghirá. "We too are here for the Morning Song." The two figures descended. One of them moved hesitantly, taking a step at a time: Bel-ghirá's companion, it appeared, was elderly. The two men came up to Jarthastra and Bel-ghirá bowed. His aged friend seemed unsure of what was expected of him.

The Valgraav leaned out from the group of priests. He had heard often of the governor of Vardresh but had never met him. Now, here he was, and he was very... strange. To begin with, he was extremely short, not even up to Jarthastra's shoulder, and he was round and tubby, a little sack of grain in a red robe. There were many rich rings on his short, thick fingers, and on the narrow, fleshy shoulders sat a perfectly round head, bald as a stone and polished like ivory. Not one hair marred that im-

305

"We too are are here for the Morning Song."

maculate pate or face, no trace of a beard on lip or chin, not even brows or lashes. Jarthastra stared at the eyes. Round and blue they were, like huge glass orbs straining to escape their liquid setting and hooded above and below with long, thick lids. And yet, for all their impressive form, there was no hint of depth or emotion. Below them was a little knob of a nose and an absurdly wide mouth with long, rounded lips. The impression was of a giant fish that some children had dressed up for a joke.

Behind the Valgraav, most of the priests accompanying him were not really attempting to conceal how they found the diminutive Master of Vardresh an embarrassment. Jarthastra, nonetheless, tried to impart some of his own unassailable dignity to Bel-ghirá. "The city rejoices that you have returned, my lord," he said.

"Yes, Anthu," replied Bel-ghirá flatly, "I and my Guard of the Sun."

"Guard of the Sun?" enquired Jarthastra.

"My elite, Anthu. My personal choice of great warriors brought from many nations to serve Arna."

"Indeed?" Jarthastra tried to appear affirming without being overly impressed. This sort of thing was a little vanity not unknown among governors and those climbing the ladder of authority. It was when personal forces showed signs of becoming miniature armies that they required watching. "And your companion, my lord?" he asked as he attempted to avoid a condescending stoop. Bel-ghirá looked up, all at once alert, and Jarthastra was reminded of the little, flat-faced dogs he had sometimes seen on the princesses' laps.

"Anthu," said the toneless voice, "I present the holy and venerable Mauzhrevhar of Elchorath. He was the priest serving my person at Vardresh. He daily read to me the Histories and rites and offered fire. With me, he has survived the assault and wishes to remain in my service. I am honoured to retain him by the will of Arna."

"Then we welcome you to Valderthaan, Baranthu Mauzhrevhar," said Jarthastra. "May Arna shine on you."

Mauzhrevhar made what appeared to be a noise of assent and raised his wandering eyes so they almost, but not quite, came to the level of the Valgraav's face. He smiled vaguely and made a little bow.

"Well, then," said Jarthastra. "Will you walk with us?"

The priests moved on again, but once more Jarthastra halted them. A small round object came rolling from behind a statue's plinth. It curved, wobbled, changed direction and came to rest at the Valgraav's feet. Jarthastra looked down and found himself confronted by a homely bread roll.

"Bugger," said a familiar village voice.

"Tyr," said another recognisable voice, "don't say that in here. It's not proper."

"Not losin' me breakfast, Mam." And Tyr appeared, in pursuit of the roll.

"We greet you again, Tyr-shan," said Jarthastra, a laugh hidden deep within his even tones. "You enjoy Arna's hospitality, I think."

With his hand almost on the roll, Tyr froze, horrified, staring up like a rabbit in a lynx's paw.

Iethen's head appeared from behind the plinth. "Tyr, it'll be all mucky, leave it—"

Tyrmar appeared next. It was now his turn to be overcome with shock.

Iethen found her voice first, "We're sorry, sir, excuse us, sir, only we were that hungry, and we passed this kitchen, and this cook or somethin' said why not have this and have our breakfast out here, she said—"

"It's not proper, I says," Tyrmar began. "Shouldn't have picnics in here, I says. We're right sorry, sir. Anthu, sir."

Jarthastra smiled wearily and the bruises on his throat moved in the growing light. "And are you sorry, Tyr-shan?" he asked.

"Well," Tyr said lightly, "don't know if I am, Anthu." There was an audible gasp from some priests. He stuffed the grubby bread roll in his pocket. "I mean, don't suppose Arna'd mind us havin' our scran in here." His voice of sweet reason faltered as he saw the priests' eyes widen at this irreverence. "I mean, he wouldn't. Would he?"

"All things for Arna's glory—" began Bel-ghirá, but Jarthastra raised a hand.

"Let me answer for these lords, Tyr-shan. Dreadful deeds have been done here but a few hours ago. I think the sight of innocent folk eating their bread must now gladden the Lord Arna." He glanced at Iethen. "I

308

only regret, goodwife, that I have no more wine to offer you."

"That's all right," said Iethen before she could think, "we've got some milk in a jug here."

Jarthastra laughed outright, "Arna shine on you, lady. Will you leave your meal and hear the Morning Song with us?"

"The—well, I don't—"

"They sing it every day, Mam," Tyr informed her. "It's a prayer or somethin'."

"Oh. Then thank y' sir, I think we will. Will we, Tyrmar?"

"Aye," said Tyrmar. "Oh, aye."

"Then walk with us," said Jarthastra. "We will listen from the parapet above the gate. The singer's turret is clear from there."

The space before the Shrine doors gave access to the parapet that ran around the entire court, so it directly connected them to the spot on the ramparts behind the highest tier where Tyr and his family had been sitting the previous night. A little past that place was a small ornamented turret built into the wall. It had glazed windows and a narrow wooden door and there, the priest who was to sing the Morning Song would be sitting, waiting for the sun to show itself above the crags on the eastern side of the lake. When the time came, the man would ascend the few stairs within the turret and sing from a roof ringed by golden emblems of suns and lions. Tyr was hugely thrilled by this, and it showed. Jarthastra too relished the moment after so many hours of grim deliberation. The boy's excitement was thawing him. His tense, bruised limbs moved less stiffly, and he went so far as to clap the astounded lad on the back.

"The first shining of the day, Tyr-shan. Perhaps you will return to Valderthaan and hear this song again. My guard always seeks strong men to lead it."

"Aye," said Tyr, thunderstruck and not daring to believe that the hand that moved kingdoms was gripping his shoulder.

The unlikely party reached the parapet above the great double gates that led from the Shrine court out into the city. Here they could look along the street that sloped down to meet the steps from the second level. Beyond, the eye flew out and over the great bridge to the hills that bordered on the Plain. Tyr realised that he was looking directly across to the watchtower on the Mardhoran where he had had his first view of the city the previous morning. He glanced down. Outside the massive wall was a wide, paved area edged with impressive buildings and the usual statues. Even at that hour, there was a considerable busyness with a great many guards about, some of them mounted, and among them the efficient, black shapes of the Daughters of the Moon carrying food and drink to the hungry men. This, then, must be Shrinegate and the big, graceful building nearby must be the Daughters' house, to judge by the cluster of black around it and the coming and going at its door. Tyr peered hard. Yes, standing under a torch like a monument to night was Mother Vashira. She occupied a watchful position to the right of the house's door which was surmounted by the bronze symbol of the moon. On the left was an elaborate marble figure of Iathena. At her feet swirled green, polished waves, indicating that she had created the lake around the city, and her hands were stretched in blessing towards the house of her servants, the Daughters. Her head was turned to let her gaze adoringly towards the King's Tower and the golden form of her consort, Arna. All very fitting, as Azhur would no doubt say.

"Tyr-shan of Falakhoth, destined no doubt to be one of our greatest generals." Tyr realised with a shock that Jarthastra was introducing him to the captain on duty and gave a jerky little bow.

"Honoured," said the captain, enjoying the game. Then, seeing how the boy's embarrassed excitement lifted the Valgraav's spirits, he decided to make his own contribution. Drawing his sword, he presented it to Tyr in the elaborate traditional manner, holding the blade in his right hand with the pommel resting on his left forearm. "Baranthu Tyr-shan," he said grinning, "accept this battle-tried blade for your future service. It's killed a hundred Harrak and ten dragons, but that's nothing compared to what you'll do with it."

Jarthastra laughed and clapped his hands. The priests saw their cue and followed suit.

"Get it back in a minute," whispered the captain. He bowed to the Valgraav and went off to see to his men.

"Well," said Jarthastra, "if the warrior Tyr-shan will consent to guard

310

me, I will hear the Morning Song. Let us await the singer."

Tyr glanced at his parents. If literally bursting with pride was ever truly a possibility, now was the moment. He grinned and hefted the sword. It was far too heavy for him, but the balance was good and he gave a few swipes to show off.

"Take care, Tyr-shan," said Jarthastra. "Do not assassinate me."

Everyone but Bel-ghirá and old Mauzhrevhar laughed, glad to be light-hearted at last. Then they all stood quietly and waited for the singer to appear above his turret.

Tyr felt every inch a warrior and gripped what was to him a magnificent blade of the Imperial Guard. His back straightened, his chin lifted, and he planted his feet firmly apart, ready to act.

Jarthastra's eyes were closed, and the breeze moved his long greying hair like gentle curtains around a face that had become almost serene. They waited and Mauzhrevhar felt the need to shuffle to a seat. "My Lord Shar-ra'ul," said Jarthastra at last, eyes still shut, "has the time for the song been altered? The sun shows himself, I think, and I hear nothing."

"I made no change, Anthu," replied the Archpriest. "It is not unknown for the singer's attention to wander, however, causing him to miss the first rays."

"Ah," said Jarthastra.

"In extreme cases, of course, the singer has been known to *sleep*, but that is extremely rare."

And they waited.

"The singer is *there*, I take it," said Jarthastra at last.

"He is, Anthu. I can make him out through the windows."

By now Tyr was smirking broadly, warrior or no. Things were getting comical.

"Then I fear our singer has succumbed. Will you send someone to knock on the door, my Lord?"

"Certainly, Anthu. I am most—ah! I believe the door is opening."

Jarthastra opened his eyes. "The door? Does he not sing from the roof?"

They peered towards the turret. The heavy door swung slowly out, battered on the rampart wall, and swung idly back and forth. Inside, the singer appeared to be sitting with his back to the doorway and making no attempt to move. Shar-ra'ul was about to dispatch a guard, when he saw the priest slump to the side against the doorframe.

"Asleep," he murmured. "And today! Anthu, I—"

But the man was not sleeping. Slowly, horribly, he slid back against the wood and fell through the doorway onto the parapet. His robes were ripped open and his throat and chest were one bloody mass. Blood welled out and went running down the tiers.

It was a terrible moment. The horrors of the night before came flooding back. No-one could move or take it in. Tyr went white and almost dropped his sword. Jarthastra gripped his shoulders, ready to move him behind him. And as they watched aghast, a great, grim shape came stepping from the turret door. It pressed its clawed feet on the dead priest's chest and bent its dreadful head, sniffing and peering. A long, vile, swollen tongue moved across the torn throat. The thing took the man's neck in razor teeth and shook it a little, as if to wake him for his song, and the head bobbed grotesquely. Here was the wolf that had terrorised the city and slain so many of the guard through the night. How it knew to hide in the turret they could not guess, but there it was to deliver a final insult and blight the moment that welcomed the fresh day.

Slowly, unconcernedly, the awful thing paced out and along the parapet, looking calmly around as if in a forest clearing. There were powerful wolves in the dense forests of the hill country—they had all seen them—but this was a monster. Bigger than a man, muscled like a horse, it stalked on stretching iron sinew. Tufts of filthy, brown-grey hair stood up along a knobbled spine, the pelt oozed and ran at bright, bare patches of leprous mange. The pointed, questing head swung back and forth, mad eyes burning beneath the knife-blade ears.

Tyr had been close to wolves before and he knew they feared people and would avoid them, preferring their own business. They would not attack for the sake of it. Not even a threat to their cubs would necessarily provoke them. The thing to do was to leave them alone or, if it came to it, you could drive them away with stones. But *this* creature was different, Tyr's country instincts felt it. It had a black intelligence. It had *purpose*.

What a thing like this would do, no-one could say.

The workers in the court below had not seen it and the guardsmen were busy with their captain. Jarthastra and his priests were exposed, with nothing but the length of the parapet between themselves and the beast. They all stayed motionless and silent, not daring to call for the guards. Perhaps some spearmen or archers would see it and intervene.

The wolf padded quietly along at the top of the tiers and the singer's blood continued to trickle down.

Old Mauzhrevhar sneezed.

The head of the beast came up. Its muscles locked ready to spring and its eyes ranged around.

It saw Jarthastra.

The wolf's jaws opened in a roar that voiced all the rage and wildness on earth. It broke into a sweeping race along the parapet. In seconds it was rounding the corner that gave it a straight run at the group above the gate. There was yelling and screaming now and shrieking for the guards, but there was no time and the speed of the thing had it in the air filling the world. Tyr saw the great maw bearing down, the curve of the leap that seemed so slow. He felt the length of metal in his hand, and did the only thing he could and swung it with all the strength humming in his bone and sinew. A juddering crunch went down his arm jarring his joints. A massive weight slammed onto him and there was a flash of light and dark confusion and his mother was crying and pulling at him and something rough and stinking was lying on his arm.

He writhed away and lurched over to the rampart, fighting the blinding spears of pain in his head. There was more shouting and screaming below him. He looked over. In a ring of howling women, Mother Vashira held her shaking arms above her head and shrieked and shrieked. On her face and shoulders was a great smear of blood, and at her feet, streaming gore and horror, was the head of the wolf.

~

SOLDIERS RUSHED TO PULL Jarthastra out from under the gore-drenched carcass of the wolf that had landed on top of him. With a huddle of

313

priests and soldiers surrounding him, he was borne swiftly into the King's Tower and taken by little-known passageways to the room where he dressed and bathed. There he was laid on a couch.

"Get those off him," said someone, and the blood-sodden robes were peeled away.

An alarmed attendant was already filling a bath with the hot water that was always ready. "Arna's wings!" he said. "What happened?"

"You needn't know, Thjurrik," replied Sher-tal. "Just clean him up. Syrgan Lilies, I think."

"We have a jar, yes...." Thjurrik was the Honoured Master of the Anointing Unguents, an old and venerable title given to the servant who assisted the Valgraav at his bath and with his robes. The honour came from how the Master was one of the few permitted to touch the Valgraav. This Thjurrik began to do, helping his hurt and unsteady ruler ease himself into the hot bath where the perfumed water began to wash the Wolf-blood off the Valgraav's body.

Jarthastra laid his head on a cushion and gratefully closed his eyes

The Master Physician ran a practised eye over his battered ruler while Thjurrik added an aromatic something to the water and the other priests in the room clustered at a respectful distance. They were all less anxious now and relished the rare opportunity of inhaling the scent of Syrgan Lilies.

"The Anthu is most tense," said Thjurrik, as he began kneading Jarthastra's neck and shoulders.

"You're not his wet-nurse," hissed Bal-jarrak. "Get on with it."

"My lord, I am the Honoured Master," said Thjurrik, offended. "This is my duty and calling. If something—"

"It doesn't matter," snapped Bal-jarrak.

"Doing a fine job, Thjurrik," said Sher-tal, soothingly. "Carry on."

"Should I be here and not another, my lords?" Jarthastra asked suddenly.

"Oh, not that again," muttered Bal-jarrak, a little too loudly.

Archpriest Shar-ra'ul leaned over the bath, "Anthu, these doubts rise in your mind when you are weary or sick or have some great sadness, and when those times pass you know yourself the Chosen. You have been viciously assaulted, have missed your rest, and now a frightful beast has almost slain you. Old anxieties cannot but show themselves. They are phantoms to put aside, I pray you."

"But all this took place at the Renewal that was to establish me," said Jarthastra. "Might Lord Arna be showing us my father's choice was wrong?"

"I believe not, Anthu," declared Galdtchav. "Yes, he chose you to succeed him and not your older brother, but the Scrolls declare his right to do so. As Ar-ven told us: *The Highest of the Blood shall order the kingdom as his heart perceives.* The world knows you are among the finest to sit on the Lion Throne."

Jarthastra stared anxiously at the ceiling. "But the precedent of appointing the eldest son...."

"Ah, but what is precedent beside Ar-ven's written words, Anthu? Calm yourself, I pray. Be confident."

Thjurrik oiled his fingers and rubbed Jarthastra's temples. This elicited a long, groaning sigh from the Valgraav.

Bal-jarrak sighed noisily, "This will take forever, as usual. I'll see to the peasants."

"Things to do myself," said Sher-tal. Together they left the chamber.

~

"You'll say nothing about it, do you hear me?" said Bal-jarrak. "Keep it quiet, keep it to yourself!" He leaned over the bunk where the shaking Tyr lay, making Iethen jump back. "A guardsman did it!" he hissed in the boy's ear. "You didn't do it, it wasn't you!"

"It was," whimpered Tyr.

"We can't say that. We can't say it happened at all, so keep your mouth shut. If this got out—"

"Beggin' y' pardon, sir, but the Anthu nearly got it," said Iethen with the boldness of a mother's outrage. "I think y' might be grateful."

"Grateful for a panic? Grateful for morale destroyed? You do not understand these things, believe me." Bal-jarrak stamped around the corner of the guardroom where Tyr had been hastily carried after the attack.

315

Azhur stood in a corner hugging himself and occasionally chewing his nails. Tyrmar sat hunched and speechless on the farther side of the bunk.

With a flurry of efficiency, Sher-tal arrived, "Anthu, I was told—"

"Yes, yes."

"Your orders?"

Bal-jarrak pressed clasped hands tightly against his mouth so that his long nose rested on the knuckles. "We can't let any gossip about a Black Lion get about. Get the wolf carcass, dye it black, show it to the guards that saw the lion. Mistake in the dark, tell them. Say the carcass was found in the city. Ask who killed it, offer a reward. Burn the head."

"People saw it in the Shrine."

"All right, say a hunting dog got out, one of those big wolfhound things."

"The singer?"

"Seizure, anything. Where is he?"

"Mortuary, sealed coffin."

"Good. Funeral with full honours. And clean the—"

"It's done. And I've seen to the captain too. He'll keep quiet."

"Then go to the Archpriest. Plan the ceremony for this afternoon: full guard, dress regalia, all available dignitaries. Full deployment on the Bridge and through the city, but make it look like a holiday."

"Vardresh?"

"Not a word. Well, be vague: great victory, rebuilding, gathering details. Go."

Sher-tal melted away with practiced haste.

Bal-jarrak bore down on Tyr's parents. "Now, listen to me. The physician says your son be all right, so you have to take him home. There'll be a carriage in an hour. And *listen*, not a word. If you say *anything* about what happened this morning, it will be denied and you will be under suspicion of conspiring against the realm. Do you understand me?"

Tyrmar and his wife were too shocked to speak, Azhur put his hands over his face.

"We never done nothin'," stammered Tyrmar. "And our Tyr—"

"Don't think we do understand y', sir," said Iethen. She had dispensed

316

with awe and saw only an inexplicable enemy. "How's it conspirin' if we says our boy saved the Anthu? How'd y' like it if that thing ate him? That's not sense!"

Bal-jarrak flared up. "Don't you speak to me like that! You understand who I am? I could have your village dispersed with a word!"

This was too much for Tyrmar. "Would y'?" He was breathing hard, too angry to be afraid. "Would y' do that? Is that what priests do?"

Bal-jarrak became a white, tight-faced statue, immobilised by his own rage. "You get out of here," he breathed. "Get out now, or you and your brat will be in the prisons."

Then they were afraid again, but strong too.

Azhur seized his chance, "Lord Bal-jarrak is worried about the effect on the city and the realm. If people know what happened, you see—well, it could be rather bad, especially after last night—so if everybody kept it to themselves, me included...."

"Well, that were a terrible thing he said!"

"Oh, everybody's so grateful to Tyr, Mistress Iethen. Don't cry, don't cry. Imagine the Graavinda and her daughters, and the prince... I'm sure there'll be some recognition—a gift, or... or something. It could have been so much worse."

They recalled Jarthastra sprawled on the parapet with the great, dead thing lying across him, blood gushing out of the severed neck onto the Valgraav's face.

"Well, when y' say it like that, Azhur, I see what y' mean," said Tyrmar. "But *conspirin'*? I'm right offended, I am."

"Ah. Well, Lord Bal-jarrak has tremendous responsibilities at a time like this, you see. Very hard to be objective, very stressful, so if he, er, *overstates* things—"

"*What?* Overstates?"

Azhur closed his eyes and wound his fingers together. He had forgotten that Bal-jarrak's dignity, the dearest thing in the world to him, had been rendered tattered and inflamed. Without it, he was nothing, and no cost was too great for its rescue. "Forgive me, Anthu, I did not intend—"

"I do not overstate!"

"Y' do," burst out Tyrmar, now that he had Azhur's support. "Breakin'

317

up Falakhoth cos Tyr saved the Anthu! That's bloody stupid!"

"Anthu, Master Tyrmar misunderstands!"

But Bal-jarrak had become still, frozen in a viper-calm, and his whisper hissed with venom, "We'll make him understand. The questioners for you, master blacksmith. Impeding measures for the safety of the realm and defying the authority of a senior priest. You'll be lucky if you see Falakhoth in a year."

"Y' can't!" cried Iethen.

"I can, little woman. No one more than me."

Horrified and desperate, Tyrmar and his wife looked at Azhur and the young man found his courage, "My Lord, you cannot!"

Astounded, Bal-jarrak stared. "*I* cannot? And why not?"

Azhur crossed his hands, palms out in a ritual gesture. His voice shook. "I ban."

In amazed hatred, Bal-jarrak did not speak for some time. "You... *ban?* How do *you* ban, *boy?*"

Azhur had to push the words out, "I am a Loremaster of the Second Circle. Therefore, I may speak the ban on your sentence, and you know, my lord, that Lord Galdtchav will join in this."

"I challenge," breathed the Keeper of the Fires.

"You may not, my lord. My ban has precedence. I assert the force of relational knowledge and the status of personal association. It is set down in the two hundred and first scroll, in the ninth column on the statutes, the pronouncement of Arvrakhul the Just. Your sentence falls: it may not be restated, it is void for ever." For a moment Azhur wondered what he had done and what would happen next, but then he saw the gratitude in Iethen's eyes and regretted not one syllable.

Bal-jarrak's head went down. For a horrifying moment he looked a little like the wolf whose carcass even now lay stinking in a basement. The air trembled.

Some merciful providence intervened. Sher-tal entered the guard-room again, striding briskly up to the Keeper of the Fires to present him with a broad leather wallet. "Communication from the Lord Jarthastra, Anthu," he said, flipping open the wallet and holding out a document with a red seal in front of Bal-jarrak.

Azhur wondered how the paper did not kindle under Bal-jarrak's glare.

"In essence," continued Sher-tal, "he requires you to see Tyr-shan and his parents are escorted to the ceremony this afternoon and cared for until they return home. There are one or two other private things for you at the bottom too."

Bal-jarrak looked at the secretary with an unreadable expression, then turned and leaned towards Azhur. "I'll break you," he said quietly, almost gently, so only Azhur could hear. He snatched the document from Sher-tal and walked away.

"Well," said Sher-tal, mystified. He gave a tight little smile. "Lots to do. Azhur will look after you, I'm sure." And off he went too.

The friends could not decide whether to laugh or collapse.

"What ceremony's this, then?" asked Tyrmar.

"Um, well, my ceremony. They're going to do the consecration rite, the whole thing, for me becoming a priest. And Bel-ghirá's being installed as Master of Armaments. Morale-booster after last night, I expect."

"What y' all yappin' on about?" The drowsy Tyr had fallen asleep on his bunk during the whole drama.

"They're goin' to make y' Valgraav," said his mother.

"I killed that wolf," said Tyr. "I did."

"Course y' did, lovey. And they're goin' to give y' a treat this afternoon."

~

TIME WORE ON. Tyr let himself sprawl limply on the guardroom bunk where he felt the shock of the wolf attack and the stress of the previous night's questioning drain out of him. His holiday in the city had turned into a severe test of his fortitude. Events had abundantly shown that the thing that made you able to live in Falakhoth was alive and well. Now all he wanted was to sleep and be looked after.

His time in Arna's city had been an eventful one, even before the awful events of last night and at dawn. There had been the Harrak rider he'd seen killed at the approach to the Bridge, then the pleasant but overwhelming encounter with Aia Djtenga. Tyr remembered her entrancing laughter and smiled. She had been there when the fires went up and the panic began; he wondered whether she'd got out of the way or escaped by a side door or something. He wished he could see her again, tell her he'd been worried. He recalled the chanting of the priests in the Shrine Court and that wonderful presence over and around them. He had taken it to be the Fire-spirit's presence. He was sure of it. He gasped. He had forgotten to tell the Conclave that part. He opened his eyes, frowning. Would it matter? He couldn't re-convene the Conclave and he didn't care to make a fool of himself by insisting he see the Valgraav. For a moment he imagined Bal-jarrak's sneering face. *You forgot what, village boy?* But it might matter. It might matter in ways he didn't know about.

"Get a hold of y'self. They're not bothered about y'," Tyr told himself.

"Y' what, lovey?" asked his mother, sitting nearby.

"Nothin', Mam," said Tyr. But then he saw it.

Just beyond where Iethen was sitting, an old fresco clung to the wall, spears and armour stacked beside it. It had been a vivid piece when first painted, but its original freshness had long ago faded. Tyr didn't care about the lack of colour, for he was staring at an obvious depiction of the Shrine. The stylised dome and court, with a roughly drawn figure of Arna on the King's Tower, made it clear as day. Red figures of chanting priests stood in a ring, in the middle of which was a Valgraav, robed and crowned as Jarthastra had been on Renewal Night. Above the Valgraav was a hovering figure which was surely a depiction of the Fire-spirit. If this was a coincidence, it was the biggest in the world.

"Right, then," said Tyr.

"Eh?" said his mother.

"Nothin'. Ey, mister! Can y' come here a minute?"

Thus summoned, the ubiquitous Sher-tal disengaged himself from a discussion and approached Tyr's bunk, "Master Tyr-shan. How may I serve the hero of the hour?"

"Have y' got a pen? And a bit of paper?"

"I think those could be found," said Sher-tal cautiously. "Why might you require them?"

"I want to write a letter."

"Who to, lovey?" asked Iethen. "We're goin' home soon."

"It's all right, Mam."

Sher-tal bent closer, "I did wonder myself. Who would you—"

"The Valgraav. Got to tell him somethin'."

Sher-tal stood straight and puffed out his cheeks, "I see. Well, I think I'd better find that paper." He leaned down towards Tyr again. "You wouldn't like to say what it's about, would you?"

Tyr hoisted himself on one elbow and murmured into Sher-tal's ear, "Y' remember what I was goin' on about at the Con-thing—the meetin'?"

"The Conclave?"

"Aye. I said about this spirit, like a feller made of fire?"

"Ah, yes. I remember that well."

"Well, I forgot to say—it's right daft, I'm embarrassed."

"That's all right, go on."

"Well, when the priests was singin' just afore the Valgraav come in, I felt this amazin' thing. Like there was somebody there, only more there than anythin' else. Like somethin' that came down and sort of pressed on y', and I knew it were him as was made of fire."

"You saw the figure then too?" asked Sher-tal. He was becoming very serious.

"No, not saw him. Didn't need to. Just knew it was him there."

"And what was that like?"

Tyr gazed silently into his memory. "Lovely," he said at last. "It were just lovely. And safe and good and a lot of things." He gave a little laugh. "I actually forgot. Can't believe it. I wasn't goin' to say about it, but then I saw that picture on the wall, I thought I'd better, in case the Valgraav wanted to know."

Sher-tal nodded, "I think it would go well with the other things you told us. Where did you see the picture?"

Tyr gestured, "There, on the wall."

"Beside your mother?"

"Aye, that's it."

"Oh, yes. And what was it in the picture that made you decide to tell

321

the Valgraav?"

"Oh, it's in the Shrine and that big court place where we was sittin'—look, see the dome and that gold Arna on the tower and the priests round in a circle? Well, that's a Valgraav in the middle, all done up like ours was at Renewal."

"Yes, indeed."

"And there's him, the Fire-Spirit. There."

"Where?"

"There! Just over the Valgraav. So, I thought, that's it all right, I'm goin' to let them know."

"Quite right, Tyr. I think that will please the Valgraav very much." said Sher-tal.

"What do y' call that? A picture done on a wall?"

"That's called a fresco."

Tyr examined the wall, "Do y' know, I feel good when I look at him."

"Of course," said Sher-tal. "I'll just go and hunt out some paper for you."

~

JARTHASTRA WAS STILL SOAKING in healing unguents when Sher-tal returned to him some time later. The hot water had been replenished several times by the attentive Thjurrik. The Valgraav's body was limp, his face creased by doubt. A number of the senior priests sat nearby, bored but watchful, and guardsmen stood by the door. The secretary approached the bath and bowed.

"If it please you, Anthu, I have seen to the morning's necessities within the city."

"The Singer?" asked Jarthastra.

"He will be fittingly laid to rest."

"Good. Send a commendation from my hand." The Valgraav frowned. "Is Tyr-shan well? No wounds?"

"Very well, Anthu. Somewhat shocked, but he is resting in a guard-room."

"Still in the city then. He too must have a commendation, and a gift.

I may receive him personally."

Sher-tal bowed again, "I shall be pleased to see to all these things, Anthu, but now I must present this letter."

"You cannot deal with it?"

"I am sure you will wish to see it yourself, Anthu." Sher-tal gave the Valgraav a smile but not a business-like one as usual. Intrigued, Jarthastra let Thjurrik dry his hands.

"And who is this from, Sher-tal?"

"Tyr-shan, Anthu."

Jarthastra stared for a moment, then took the paper. "From the sword to the pen in one morning! I did not think he could write."

"Lord Azhur informs me that someone in the village taught him, Anthu. He certainly brings many surprises."

"Then let us see the latest one," said Jarthastra before reading Tyr's letter.

TYR-SHAN OF FALAKHOTH TO THE VALGRAV GREETIN

Im right sorry Anthu bcos I forgot to tell you somethin at the meetin last night and I thought it might be important so this is it I was sittin in the shrin listnin to the priests singin at renewal and they was at the bit where you was standin in front of that old lad the head priest and the singin was amazin to me I never heard nothin like it ever that was when I knew as the Fire-Spirit I said about were there. I call him the Dancer sometimes bcos that's what he was like movin like a beutiful dancer. I didn see him but I could feel this great wonderfull feelin and I knew it were him and he were over the bit where you was standin over evrythin really and I was that happy and I thought it be all right now but it wasnt Im right sory about that and I hope yor better anyway I just forgot to say to you about it so I hope that's all right don't know how I forgot sory.

"You have a mention, Lord Shar-ra'ul," declared Jarthastra.

The Archpriest sat up, "How so, Anthu?"

"You have impressed Tyr-shan, he has remembered you." Jarthastra became quietly serious. "He believes the Fire-spirit he saw was over us at Renewal. He was aware of it."

All the priests stared intently.

"First a peasant merrymaking, then the Shrine itself," said Shar-ra'ul.

"And Conclave," added Galdtchav. "If Tyr-shan was right."

"But what does he mean by this? What is the boy saying?"

"I do not think he means to say anything, my Lord," said Jarthastra. "He simply tells us what he believes he knows."

"So does his mother," remarked Galdtchav with a smile.

"But the father is silent," mused the Archpriest.

"Ah," replied the Loremaster. "A well-run household you see."

There was laughter.

"And the royal household? What of that, my Lords?" Jarthastra said as his fears broke out once more. "Well-run? Did not the old man at its head make a terrible mistake?"

The Archpriest came and knelt beside Jarthastra's bath, "Anthu, be at peace. Your injury speaks."

The Valgraav looked wildly around as if accused. "I fear Lord Arna speaks, my Lord. Why would he allow my attackers into his very Shrine?"

Galdtchav hurried over. Leaning close to Thjurrik, he said, "More Syrgan Lilies, if you please. That always helps." The Honoured Master poured a liberal dose of the soothing unguent. "Now, Anthu, your father made the right choice, directly after his great and sacred journey. This you know well."

"Fyrieg," said Jarthastra distantly.

"Where he went to seek Shivara. What greater counsel could he possibly have regarding the kingdom?"

"Tyr-shan saw him."

Galdtchav nodded, "So it would appear. Rest in that."

Jarthastra said nothing. He sat clutching the sides of the bath and breathing heavily. Lank, wet hair hung down like curtains. No one could read his face.

Galdtchav tried once more, "Something to help you contemplate your security, I think. If it please you, I shall order some spiced wine." He nodded to Thjurrik.

Jarthastra raised his head, "I thank you, my lord."

The Loremaster smiled, then frowned at the sight of the Valgraav's eyes.

"I thank you," said the Valgraav's intense whisper. "It will ease my decision."

Galdtchav leant forward. "What must you decide, Anthu?"

Jarthastra took the old man's hand in his water-wrinkled grasp. He slowly turned his head and fixed his deep, helpless eyes on the wise, lined face. "I must have peace, dear friend. I cannot carry this conflict. I must cede the rule of these lands to my brother. Then harmony shall come."

The priests rose, shocked and disbelieving.

Galdtchav clutched his ruler's hand, "Anthu, there is no need."

"Every need," whispered Jarthastra. "Every need. The gods are absent."

Galdtchav could not find words, but then Sher-tal saw his chance.

The secretary stooped and took Tyr's letter from the floor where it had fallen. With an insistent brightness, he held the paper out to Jarthastra. "Anthu, you may wish to finish Tyr-shan's letter." The priests gaped at this stunning irrelevance but Sher-tal held firm. "It would mean a great deal to him. See, he has even drawn on it for you."

Jarthastra regarded the proffered document as if bewildered by what Sher-tal had done. Slowly and without a word, he took the paper in the hand that did not clasp Galdtchav's and read:

> *I ver nerly didnt send you this lettr to tell you because I thought you and the conclav wouldn't be botherd and when I was thinkin about what I seen at the shrin and wasn't sure wat to do I looked up and there was this pictre on the wall bside where my mam was sittin. Shertal says its calld a fresgo and it was a pictre of the shrin and the priests singin and there was this fella done up like you was at renewal night and there was the Fire-spirit over him like he was blesin him so I thinks ey I bettr do that lettr*

that cant be a coinsidens so here it is like it looked on the
fresgo I hope its all right so now you know can you. plees
tell the priests and that about it if it mattrs.

Yor servant Tyr-shan of Falakhoth

Jarthastra turned the paper and examined Tyr's scribbled sketch of the Renewal ceremony as copied from the painted wall.

"All is here my lords," he said. "And the Fire-spirit over me." He stared hard at the sketch, then looked at Galdtchav for a moment as if for counsel. "Thjurrik, my day robes. I will see this fresco. Though it is a strange adornment for a guardroom." He released Galdtchav and made to rise, but Sher-tal raised a hand.

"Anthu, this I must tell you: I spoke with Tyr-shan and observed him. He pointed out to me the space on the wall where he saw the fresco. He showed me where the lines and figures were and described to me what he was seeing."

Jarthastra was still. "And why do you tell me this, Sher-tal?"

The secretary took a breath, "Because Tyr-shan was pointing to a blank wall, Anthu. There was no fresco."

The moment froze in silence. An affirming quiet seemed to run through Jarthastra. He drew in his breath fully and slowly. "My lords, I am heartened. I will wear my father's mantle yet a while." He slowly shook his head. "We must keep what this boy has brought to us. We must not let it go and lose its meaning." His newly burning eyes turned on Sher-tal. "You have been wise. Now bring me pen and paper, I must write to the Lord Bal-jarrak."

CHAPTER 16

The Women from the Plain

TYR FIGURED THERE WAS just enough time to wish Azhur well before his consecration. He was well used to creeping up on animals through trees and bushes and used all his skill to move stealthily along the stairs and corridors where he knew he should not be. Dodging guards, melting into invisibility behind pillars, hangings, and statues, he made his way to the room he knew Azhur now used. Once outside the heavy door, he paused to decide between knocking or bursting in. The latter would certainly be more startling—and thus satisfying—but he realised he had no idea who might be with his friend. The Archpriest or anybody could be there and he had no wish to startle Azhur *and* make a fool of himself. Aienna could be in there and if she was, well, you just didn't know what might be *happening*. He decided to knock, but as he raised his hand, he heard two voices and one of them wasn't Aienna's. With a little concentration, Tyr made out Galdtchav's venerable tones.

"Can't they wait, laddie? You're going to be consecrated in an hour."

"I brought them specially, my lord. This is so remarkable I didn't want to wait."

"Oh, I see! These are the scrolls that—"

"—nobody but I would want to read, yes. I was searching for the one I mentioned at Conclave last night."

"*Compilations of Berushta?* Ah, well, that's different. Not that Tyr's mother would be scrabbling around the Archives looking for Inspiration. Let's have it then."

"Well, these aren't the actual *Compilations*. You recall everything we've learned?"

"How could I not?"

"Quite. Now, let me show you these, my lord. Scrolls so obscure they're not even numbered."

"They're not from *Disputable Miscellanies*, are they?"

"The little attic gallery? I'm afraid they are."

"Then no wonder you've read them! You go for these odd things like a moth to a flame."

"But I have not been burned. Now, two Scrolls, which together hold the title *The Doubtful and Unverifiable Antiquities of Ar-vrakh'heratakh the Obscure.*"

Listening at the door, Tyr winced at one of the worst names yet. How could Azhur just read them off without practicing?

"Bless me," exclaimed Galdtchav. "I heard that mentioned in hushed tones when I was a novice. You don't mean to say you've read the things?"

"I have, my lord."

"And they are what, exactly?"

"Traditions, legends—possibly some actual history—and some sayings, all interspersed with absolute nonsense. They were handed on by word of mouth for centuries, perhaps millennia, until Ar-vrakh'heratakh collected them on his travels and wrote them down."

"Ah, yes. Now, his dates were, ah…."

"At least two centuries before the Founding. Ar-vrakh'heratakh travelled in southern Sarvien and crossed several times to Dhar. He might have spent a year in Zirribh."

"Yes, yes, it's coming back. I knew a fellow in the Novitiate who went to a couple of lectures on this and said he found it extremely interesting. We worried about him."

"Well you might, my lord, but the thing is, the material Ar-vrakh'heratakh recorded could have been circulating in these southern lands since Shivara's time or before."

Ah, thought Tyr, *Shivara*.

"Really? Then why isn't it in the Histories?"

"It fails all the tests: compiled by a credulous eccentric who might be half-legendary himself; has sources that are probably the end result of centuries of embellishment; its facts, if there are any, are almost impossible to distinguish; only one copy and no-one's taken that seriously for five hundred years—"

"But it is among the Scrolls, is it not? In our archives."

"Yes, my lord. Hence our conversation."

Galdtchav sighed audibly. The scrape of a chair told Tyr he was settling himself down in an attempt at receptivity. "Well now, let me guess: somebody said something, and that set off all the usual little bells in your head? Thought so. All right, let's have the bit the bells told you about."

Tyr rolled his eyes. This was getting boring. Scrolls, scholars, and old legends were all Azhur's specialities. His friend could make it interesting when he tried, like the time he'd told him about the First Shining on the hill above the lake, but now it just wasn't working. He couldn't think what this had to do with anything or why it was so important, especially with the Consecration about to start, but that was priests for you. The lad wondered whether to walk in now, but he could hear he was too late. A rattling sound signalled a Scroll being unwound and Azhur quickly launched into explaining what he'd discovered.

"Look at this," Azhur said. "This is the main part."

"Glad to hear it," said Galdtchav. "Swift and to the point, laddie."

"Of course. Well, this was written—"

"Do just read it. They want to consecrate you today."

"Well, all right. Here we are."

Tyr tensed and put his ear closer to the door. This might be where it got interesting.

Azhur coughed and began reading with a strange, urgent feel to his voice. *"There came a day when Marvhishta the priest of the fifth order, they that tend to the cisterns in the higher court, came to the Lord Shivara by the figure that looks upon that awesome room by the broad court of the altar stairs, where one may—"*

"Azhur, I am extremely conscious of the time of day."

Tyr sniggered softly. This had all the makings of an utterly dreary wander through ancient trivia, just the kind of thing that fascinated his friend.

"Ah. Yes, sorry. Well, I suppose the crux of it is this," said Azhur, and he read out a later portion of the scroll.

> Marvhishta asked, "My lord, what is the meaning of your service and of your person? Why is it you are in the world?"
>
> "My brother," said Shivara, "I cannot give you the proper answer, for indeed I cannot give it to myself. My part in the life of Dhar is open for any man to see that will, but when the tale of the whole world is told, what my full part in it will be I do not know. But I know that the One on High has shown me this: my story is broader than that of Dhar."
>
> "But you have never left Dhar," said Marvhishta, "and its chronicle has grown through centuries: how can your tale be more than this?"
>
> "When all things are made well I shall know," said Shivara, "and perhaps not until then. But this I am told: my kinsman shall see me, though I do not see him, and it shall be the sign that Shivara has more to do upon the earth than the realm of Dhar has given him. The great power will take up my kinsman into its kindly ways and has resolved in mind and heart to put him in a place that no other can occupy or dream of: I will enter his story and he will enter mine, and we shall see what will become of that."

"Ey!" murmured Tyr to himself as the reading came to a merciful end. He could almost feel the numbness creeping over his head. What could Azhur not dig up? Pity the Loremaster that had to wade through such stuff for a living.

"I see, I see," came Galdtchav's voice. "It's… compelling, I suppose.

This kinsman is… suggestive; but the significance of all this is what, exactly?"

"Well, ah, we don't yet know, of course. Haven't done the study yet."

"Azhur, please. Just give me your immediate impressions, eh? There's a good fellow."

Tyr could almost hear Azhur's knuckles cracking through the door.

"Ah. Yes, well, *those*…," said his friend, "those are quite startling. What we have here, my lord, is in effect a cache of *new material about Shivara!*"

A long silence echoed through the door.

"New?" said Galdtchav at last. "How…?"

"No-one has read these scrolls for centuries. They may as well never have been written. But look, my lord, new to us is a statement that Shivara's story is not confined to Dhar, and that there is more for him in the world. And has he not figured remarkably in all that we have heard?"

A brief, gasping sound came through the door. "*But*, Azhur! *Disputable Miscellanies…!*"

"These scrolls are part of the Archives, my lord, and thus they have authority." Silence. "I have a note prepared for the Chosen. Shall I…?"

"*Prepared?* Oh yes, yes. Better do it now."

Tyr started back as Azhur's feet approached the door.

"Oh, I meant to say," said Galdtchav suddenly. "Did you think any further about the song? The one apparently for you?"

"No, my lord," replied Azhur, rather tersely. "Frankly, it irritates me. I cannot identify with it. I ask you, what… what should I, of all people, make of that last line? *Love will tell you who you are.* It is, well…."

"I see. Yes, I understand. Well, off you go, my almost Loremaster. Not much time."

Tyr jumped away as the sound of Azhur's boots came up to the door again. As the latch lifted, he sped sprightly along the corridor back towards to the guardroom where his parents were waiting. He went nimbly and secretly along the endless stone ways. *Waste of time that was,* he thought. *Doesn't like Mam's songs either. Should've just gone in and let Galdtchav off all that rubbish. Is that what priests do all day?* Nonetheless, he found himself wondering who they'd been talking about.

~

AZHUR WAS FORMALLY AND publicly declared a priest and Loremaster that afternoon. The immense figure of Arna gleamed in the bright daylight as Shar-ra'ul's voice sent the words of the consecration rite ringing round the Shrine Court. The Valgraav, his court, and the highest priests stood on the lower steps of the stairway that swept the eye upwards to the Shrine's grand doors of cast bronze. History seemed to live upon these doors. A thousand figures from the four centuries of the kingdom's life danced, fought, and offered fire in the clear brightness of the spring morning. Here were the battles, the holy men, the building of the city and the Shrine; here were Rachtu Bhanir and Jerchara and the indomitable men of Dhar; here were Ar-ven, Zhir-Sharrak and the priests whose vast labour created the scrolls' great store of history and piety; here were Na-veshtrazhdak and all the rulers of the house of the lion. There were no Harrak, except a few shown kneeling in abject defeat. Above them all was the huge golden disk of the sun, hanging over the centuries, powerful, untouchable. These were the Ke'nūl Talá, the Doors of the North, that opened into the heart of the shrine. Others named them the Talachraadin, the Doors of the Numberless, from the myriad figures that stepped out from the bronze. Through these doors the Valgraav, his family, and his priests had come with Azhur and Bel-ghirá taking up the rear.

A movement caught Tyr's eye, and he looked along the front row of people. A slim, lovely girl with corn-yellow hair was waving frantically at Azhur. He smiled broadly and waved back nervously, painfully aware of his new dignity. Aienna at last, and she was worth the wait. The new Loremaster glanced at Tyr and the boy grinned, jerked his thumb in the girl's direction and made a vigorous and meaningful gesture with one fist. Azhur shone crimson in full view of Valderthaan, and his friend threw himself into violent spasms of laughter.

The splendid party stood facing a crowd of people. Many who had endured the horror of the previous night had naturally not returned, but thousands had still chosen to brave their fears in a determination to be reassured and to throw off, for a while, their shock. This time, there was no preferential seating. The audience, mostly of ordinary people, sat or stood where they could find room, with a most generous and visible presence of the Guard standing in and around them.

Tyr and his family, to Bal-jarrak's disgust, were at the front of those who were standing in the wide space ringed by the tiered seats, with an attendant and two guardsmen of their own nearby. They marvelled at the finery ranged before them on the steps and stared at the well-muscled men who held the chains of four superb mountain-lions, startlingly eloquent symbols of the royal house. The creatures wore their leather collars and sun-amulets with a fierce docility that made them look like little feral kings. Tearing his eyes from the regal beasts, Tyr recognised the Lady Iera and the Princess Iente. The Graavinda was solemn and striking. The gold on her forehead and at her throat intensified the deep strong colours of her heavy gown, purples and greens with slashed scarlet sleeves. Or was it she who had the strength and simply loaned it to the hues she wore? Princess Iente held herself like a statue whose limbs, carved daringly thin, might easily shatter. She held up her head in trembling pride and her huge, round eyes gazed unblinkingly at her father.

Beside Princess Iente was her sister Aelwe, who looked surprisingly unremarkable and as bored as Iente was excited. On the far side of the Graavinda, a little apart from the women, a young man stood with his arms folded. Tyr had never seen him before, but figured this must be Prince Arthodt. Not only did his golden sword hilt and splendid clothes give him away, but he had his mother's square jaw and his father's deep frowning eyes set above high cheeks. Long, thick hair of no particular colour or style hung about his face and he affected not one but two large jewelled earrings. Jarthastra's thought and intelligence did not appear on his features and the Prince's wide, slanted mouth had no sign of Lady Iera's strength. He had seen around twenty-five summers, Tyr thought, but he did not know if he liked him or not. He looked at the moment like no particular sort of person. Thankfully, there was more folk to look at than the jaded prince. There were Governors, higher on the steps and decked out in their finery; the Syrgan noble from Renewal Night, thickly clad and looking no warmer; the thick-set figure of Harrokaan's

333

Ambassador, clad in ceremonial mail and flanked by a personal guard as though he expected to be set upon. Tyr searched for the splendid form of Aia Djtenga but could not see her.

All at once there was a commotion. Everyone gasped and tensed, wondering if this was some new violence. Pushing through the crowd from the gates was a disordered group of a hundred large men. They shouted and buffeted people aside as they tramped towards the steps. When they reached the front, the rabble paused and bowed clumsily to Bel-ghirá, making fist-salutes and yelling coarse acclamations. The Guard of the Sun had arrived. They were massive, over-muscled fellows bred to fight, with massive hands and shoulders like battlements. Broken noses, shattered teeth, scarred faces, and deep, dull eyes. It was impossible to imagine them wearing anything other than their irregular and outlandish armour and weapons. The men moved with a shared devotion to conflict, violence, and winning. The question *what is right?* never formed beneath their bulky brows, they asked only *what do we want?* All of them bore the rayed, golden sun fixed somewhere about them that declared them to be servants of Lord Arna. If they understood that much. Amulets, engravings, and tattoos to other gods suggested their allegiance to Arna was based on something other than faith.

Bel-ghirá turned his head a little, indicating Jarthastra. Apparently, the Guard had been told he would be there, for they turned awkwardly and—most of them—bowed clumsily and half-heartedly in the Valgraav's direction, arms crossed gawkily on their chests. Some of them thought this a fine game and were laughing. Jarthastra acknowledged them with his most severely formal nod.

"Where did he find those apes?" he asked the Archpriest beside him. "I was not informed. Lachiran mercenaries, and some from Zirribh, I think."

"Well," remarked the Archpriest, "thankfully they're on our side."

"Should we be thankful?" asked Jarthastra.

The unconvincing obeisance over, the Guard of the Sun were herded off to the right onto a low balcony that overlooked the steps and the front of the crowd. There, they would be on display as a trimming for the ceremony honouring their master Bel-ghirá. The Shrine Guard were posted throughout the square and especially by the steps. They clearly found the foreigners a crude intrusion and ignored them as best they could. Elsewhere, amid the coloured silks and cloth-of-gold, stood the rigid figure of Mother Vashira and the inky swathe of the Daughters of the Moon. The Guard of the Sun's balcony placed them somewhat above the Daughters, which amused the men tremendously. The women twittered anxiously as little bits of stone were dropped on them and were called things in guttural languages the Daughters did not care to enquire about.

Still, they held their ground, persecution notwithstanding, amulets glinting like uncertain stars in a wandering patch of night, and took courage from their leader. One glance at Vashira's straight back and the way she held up her head with shining eyes showed that she who had been struck with a severed wolf's head cared nothing for the taunts of thugs. Hands clasped in front of her, she gazed up at the shimmering sun-disc over the doors of the Ke'nūl Talá.

Even so, Tyr was trying not to laugh at her, and having small success. Every glance at the black cluster made him think of the rooks that nested in the trees above Falakhoth.

"What y' laughin' at, young Tyr?" asked his father. "It's a serious business, this."

Tyr explained about the rooks and Tyrmar had to avoid looking at Vashira for some time.

But Vashira was looking at them. Tyr noticed her staring in their direction almost as intently as at the gleaming sun. Suddenly, she gave a start and put her hand over her mouth as though shocked. *Now what?* thought the boy as the woman left the huddled Daughters and came quickly across the square. She negotiated the narrow space at the foot of the steps, sometimes walking sideways because of the press of bodies, and bore down on the village family like a hawk after prey. She stopped in front of Tyr, ignoring his parents. Her large, powerful eyes bored into his face.

He looked back uneasily at the tense features, pale within their black swathing: thin, arching brows that peaked in the middle, grey shadows round the eyes, tight bowstring mouth, flesh that in a year or two would begin to sag, and the many premature lines told their own story of a woman who had suffered. Without that black thing and with a little paint, Tyr thought, Vashira might look, not beautiful exactly, but perhaps not bad. But this was probably not the moment to say so. He peered anxiously at the little snaking blue vein pulsing on her forehead and wondered what was coming. At last her exalted thoughts escaped.

"I saw," she said. "I glanced up. I saw the beast leap, I saw your sword swing and save the Chosen. You sent me the glory, the head. I did not wash the blood away for hours. It was a trophy from Arna for his Lady, our Beautiful Mother."

"Sorry," stammered Tyr, "I didn't know y' was there."

"I survived the fires last night. They came within feet of me. Then I was selected for glory. What does it mean?" She gave a little cry and her head jerked round. Sher-tal was beside her, tapping on her shoulder.

"Lord Bal-jarrak's compliments," said the secretary, "and could you possibly take your place with your order so we can begin?"

"Shortly," said Vashira fiercely. "I am engaged."

"Lord Bal-jarrak also wishes to underline the content of this morn-ing's communication to the Daughters of the Moon—"

"I am aware of it."

"—and to enquire if the twelfth of this month would be convenient to undertake the review of this year's grant to your order."

Vashira opened her mouth, but closed it again like a trap.

"Should that be appropriate," added Sher-tal, straight-faced.

Vashira glared destruction at Sher-tal, but to Tyr, she said, "I will not forget. I will watch you." Then she whirled away and returned to her black brood.

Sher-tal smiled vaguely at the villagers and went about his business.

~

THE OCCASION HAD BEEN well calculated to boost Valderthaan's flagging spirits. Not that it was superficial—there were the many deceased awaiting burial, after all—but grief was eased a little by generous and heartfelt grants to the bereaved and by an edict from the Archpriest declaring that, after their magnificent funerals, those who had died in such circumstances would go straight to happiness in the company of Arna without the usual drear prospect of journey and struggle. The inclusion of such martyrs (as the edict daringly called them) in their ranks meant a permanent rise in the social status of the deceased's families.

There had been no further incidents after the night of horror when Azhur had been privately consecrated. Very few had seen the wolf, but it had transformed into an escaped hunting dog that may or may not have been killed. The wolf attacks at the gate and in the city were undeniable, but the reward offered to the non-existent slayers in the unspecified street brought so many applicants it practically made it a certainty that the animals had been dispatched nowhere near the Shrine. Much of the night's anxiety was drifting away in the sunshine and already explanations and diminutions were being skilfully circulated by priests and secretaries who had honed vagueness to an art. True, there could have been a longer wait before the ceremony, but Jarthastra had judged it best to attempt to lift the city's mood as quickly as possible and so, here was spectacle and splendour, a chance for people to crowd together beneath the bright banners to see their indestructible Valgraav and the new Loremaster receive the honour they deserved. There was also Bel-ghirá, of course, but that wouldn't take too long.

At last, Jarthastra stepped forward and raised his hands for silence. Even that movement sent a tiny spasm across his features, for he had refused all but the mildest medicines in order to keep his head clear.

"Arna shine on him," crooned a woman behind Tyr. "Don't he look grand!"

Jarthastra did look grand. He stood firm with the breeze stirring the golden traceries of his splendid robes. His calm, carefully maintained smile seemed to catch and hold the morning light. There was no sign of his bruises, only a few knew they were painted over. Arna had clearly restored him to his people. Now he spoke to them and his voice was strong.

"*Ai va sh'herakh, a threma shi!*" A deep sigh welled up from the crowd. "It is the first shining of the day. So it was of old and so it is now. Evil showed itself, but it is banished. Indeed, darkness is inevitable, permissible, so we may see the light. Our dead journey to Arna and he sends his sign once more through the heavens. He rises over the world and the kingdom he has made. The darkness is over. We will rejoice in the light."

Immediately, thousands of voices cried out in relief and thundering above them came the rolling peal of the great bell.

"Namau Ramá!" called Jarthastra. "Hear him! While his voice sounds over Valderthaan it will never fall and no evil power will fasten on it. That is Ar-ven's word."

Shouting and cheering broke out afresh. Scarves, hands, and banners waved. Soldiers clashed spear on shield. Mothers lifted their infants above their heads to let them bask in the sunlight that flashed down from the golden sun above the Talachraadin, as Arna shone upon the people of his kingdom. The deep-throated bell seemed to speak with the very voice of the god, declaring his power, reclaiming his land from the contaminating violence that had touched it. Thus, amid noise and light and in the presence of the Chosen, the people of the North revelled in the security of their realm and the protection of their god and bellowed away their fear and anger.

At long last, Shar-ra'ul came forward, Azhur with him, and spoke of the sacred priesthood and the sacredness of minds steeped in the Scrolls. He presented the new Loremaster to the people, telling how he had been consecrated secretly, at need, for the help of the High Conclave in countering the malevolence in the city. He told of Azhur's learning, more than that of any novice, and of the acceptance he had won in all levels of the Shrine. But it was right, said the Archpriest, that a priest's consecration should be seen to be publicly performed, despite a lawful secrecy. So he spoke the ancient, powerful words that change a man so he may offer the fire that others may not touch and serve the god without fear of sacred things, shielded by his consecration and by the fragment of the Sun's light that Arna caused to burn in his mind. When the priest descended the dark slope, stern Ardhruthak, perceiving that holy flame, would guide him swiftly and easily to Arna's throne. Such a man Azhur had become. Tyr watched it all with his mouth open, glad this had happened to his friend.

Then it was Bel-ghirá's turn. With no trace of excitement, pride, or gratitude disturbing that fish-mask of a face, the little priest stood in the ceremonial armour of the Master of Armaments. The burnished breastplate would hardly have turned a fruit-knife but with the crested helm and scarlet robes, it made regalia in the ancient style that allowed almost anyone to look honourable and splendid. Bel-ghirá, however, looked somewhat absurd.

Jarthastra stepped forward, next to Bel-ghirá. This was the most difficult part of the ceremony. It was not yet entirely clear to the city what had happened at Vardresh. A Harrak attack, the city burning, and a dark stain left hanging in the sky to the west were the main details known. The main military concerns were the policing of the area, establishing order, and deploying forces against a further assault. A sizeable contingent was watching Archraad, where the commander had been granted emergency powers as temporary governor for the area. The mood of the crowd had cooled. The soldiers stood stiffly, several them were looking away. Attention within Valderthaan had focussed on the night's events, with matters on the Plain left in the hands of military commanders. It would be those men and their soldiers who had the real information. Guardsmen were always sworn to secrecy at a time like this, but Jarthastra was not so foolish as to believe they would stick to it. Soon information and gossip would seep through the populace. He glanced at the governors. Some of them were looking elsewhere. What had they been told? He wondered if Bel-ghirá's reward should have come later, and less publicly.

Too late.

Jarthastra knew there was no particular reason for any ordinary citizen to know even the name of the governor of a small city on the Plain, far less any details about him. He therefore spoke briefly and vaguely, mentioning Bel-ghirá's defence of his town almost in passing, as one achievement among many. He repeated his words about the defeat of the dark, then conferred on Bel-ghirá the responsibilities and privileges of the Master of Armaments. The little priest crossed his arms on his chest and bowed deeply. The mood of celebration had lingered long enough for this to merit a muted cheer, but Jarthastra noted that the soldiers did not join in, except for a vigorous performance by the Guard of the Sun. What did the soldiers know, he wondered, that had not reached him?

The cheering faded and Namau Ramá, the great bell, called a single deep note. Now there would be a long, stirring chant from the priests gathered by the great door and the Archpriest would offer fire from the bronze brazier at the side of the steps. The people quietened.

As if from the underworld, a shrill cry tore through the moment.

"*Ai!* The gods hear me and do not slay me! I will speak! We all speak or sorrow will not be healed!"

She was pushing her way to the front, a Harrak woman with a young boy, and behind her, a group of about thirty other Harrak women, some with children beside them, some carrying infants, and a few white-haired and leaning on staffs or their companions' arms. The marks of smoke and flame marked their clothes and burns covered their faces and hands. Somehow, no-one had thought to close the gates after the invasive entrance of the Guard of the Sun. As the women struggled inward, the one who had cried out began a long, wailing song, a dirge that could not be kept in her heart. The other women took it up, sending the sound of their grief through the whole court. It shadowed the bright afternoon and cut away all that had gone before.

Guards clattered down, but Jarthastra waved them back. The silence flooded in again and made the tiered court a vast crucible to hold the tortured song. The women reached the steps yards from the Valgraav and the priests. There they stood, arms held out helplessly, as they wept and sang the terrible depth of their grief. Everyone knew they had come from Vardresh and why they mourned. No-one dared move or speak in the presence of such suffering. No-one offered comfort for it could not have been received. And though some were shaken, many felt a kindred grief as though these women had taken the pain and loss, the ache of Valderthaan's heart, and mirrored it within their own sorrow. Few understood the words of the song, but never had mourning for a soul's dear love been plainer.

Tyr had never seen grief like this. Verdje's weeping at Thaljhaz' grave seemed almost to be a different thing. These songs of pain were a mourning so fierce it frightened him. Nonetheless, he watched the women closely to see why they had come. In fact, he had heard almost nothing about Vardresh, but now he wondered what could have happened to these women that made them bring their desolation to the feet of Arna's Chosen, beneath the image of the god.

Then he saw the boy.

He was standing beside the woman who had called out, not weeping or singing but staring ahead at nothing as if he had lost even the will to cry. He looked limp, leaning against his mother with his arms by his side and making no attempt to hang on to her. Her arm around his body was all that supported him. Tyr started when he saw that the boy's clothes were badly scorched and that his hands and arms were gashed and bruised. Suddenly the boy became agitated, tugging at the loose shirt that seemed to be irritating him. He struggled for a moment, then pulled the shirt open and off his shoulders. Dark-stained pads, makeshift dressings, dropped at his feet, and Tyr saw the weals and bruises, the livid, weeping burns that covered half his chest and stomach. He could not have been more than eight years old.

The woman knelt by her son, pressing her wet cheek against his, trying to replace the dressings and hug him without touching his wounds. Tyr looked away, afraid of what he might see if he kept his eyes on that awful group of mourners. He wiped his eyes and saw the Valgraav gazing horrified at the women. Azhur stood, bewildered and numb, the joy of his consecration forgotten in the display of such public grief. Bel-ghirá's face remained blank. If anything, it looked colder than before, reminding Tyr of bloodless stone. The very ability to react to these broken women seemed to be draining out of Bel-ghirá.

The Harrak women stood silent. Their grief spent for the moment. Children began to moan, but the women were exhausted by their sorrow.

"Women, is it to me you come?" said Jarthastra slowly. "How may I ease your grief? At this time, your families—"

"They go down to the dark way." The interruption was not insolent, merely blunt.

Jarthastra hesitated. "Will you tell us who you are? And why you are before me?"

The woman continued to gaze dully at the steps. At length she said,

"Yes, I speak to you, Chosen King, or to him who was master at Vardresh."

A great murmur swelled up at once, then quietened as the woman continued.

She spoke slowly, for her native speech was the old dialect of the Arta. Sobs and children's whimpers made an undercurrent to her words. "I am Varrinil," she said. "My tribe is Arta. Gurdjatt, Ruldtag's son, was my husband." She waved a hand to the women behind her. "Other tribes: Rikhatha, Nerth'ten."

"Have your chieftains sent you?" asked Jarthastra. Some response from the tribes to events at Vardresh was expected, but he was determined not to be drawn into a public confrontation. Resolving to speak to the women privately, he searched for words that would end this episode quickly but not coldly.

"Chieftains?" repeated Varrinil. "No, Chosen. My sisters and I, we stay together to share, to pass our grief to each other. This was in the night, for there was no sleep. We cared for those living, but some died. We are Harrak. This was our duty. We say those who may die are *rhuga*—sacred, your priests say. The hurts, the cold, no sleep. Maybe the cold took some to the dark."

"The cold?" said Jarthastra. "Had you no fires?"

Varrinil met his eyes.

"We will not light fires," she said.

At a stroke, she brought back the terror of Renewal Night. Everyone who had seen the inferno at the Shrine understood.

"Why did you come to me?" Jarthastra asked.

"Forgive, Anthu," said Varrinil wearily. "We seek judgement. We need you to help after..." She stopped, mouth still open. The words would not come out. She paused, took a deep breath, placed her hand briefly over her eyes and continued. "We are Harrak. We have ways that are ours, things we have done from days when there was no king in the North." She closed her eyes as she spoke. "Our way is to seek out the one who does evil or one who understands what has happened. We do this when we do not know whose hand did the wrong or why he acted so. We wish a right path. When we have our answers, we know what to do, for our

342

wise people tell us it is a wrong when a man is punished too much or suffers for evil when he wanted good. And if even a bad man or an enemy fall, that too is an evil, a sadness. So, we want the truth of things before we punish. It may be that someone did what seemed right to him and did not know what would happen. But we must know. We must have the right path because of the gods. And because... because it is *right*."

Here Varrinil opened her eyes and raised her head.

Jarthastra, looking into the eyes that now held his, saw she did not truly believe there could be an excuse for what she and her people had suffered. Yet, she was proud. She demanded the truth of things for the sake of her people and their ancient sense of justice. The Arta would do what they had always seen was right.

There was a noise. A little, trivial cough that hardly anyone heard but which was all the more horrid for it. Tyr, standing near the steps, caught the sound. Bal-jarrak's hand was at his mouth. Satisfied, the priest patted himself on the chest and looked vaguely at the ground, drumming the fingers of one hand against the back of the other. He was actually bored. His utter disinterest in what Varrinil was saying could not have been more obvious. To him, these women were Harrak. Nothing they said or did could matter.

The same expression of weary detachment was on the faces of several priests and courtiers. They were simply waiting for the woman to finish because their duty demanded they had to. They didn't care for the women but were impatient for Jarthastra to tidy them away quickly and move on.

Tyr gasped at this observation. He had learned something about Valderthaan, but he had also learnt something about himself. He remembered how Harrak had almost killed him outside Wyrdha's house, not many days before. He had thought then that the Harrak were all monsters, more or less the same, but *these* women took that view and ground it to dust.

Mercifully unaware of any priestly boredom, Varrinil continued her plea to Jarthastra.

"When the dawn came after the sorrow, my sisters said, 'How can we bear this? The lord of Vardresh is in the great city. We should seek him out. He must know why this evil happened in his town.' We had heard that the same evil fire had sent many to the darkness in this place. This was some balm to us, a little comfort, to know our grief was in other hearts. Perhaps, we thought, the people of the great city will sit with us to share grief, but when we came today and found rejoicing we did not know how to seek those who mourn. My own pain would have taken me to the darkness if I had not let it cry out. It is so with my sisters or we would not have sung the lament. There was no choice for us. Arna must know this or your priests must tell him. We did not choose. We must speak and the gods must hear. Let Arna hold back his anger."

Jarthastra genuinely wanted to do something for them, but felt it prudent to get them out of the square before any potential trouble could start. He decided to tell the women he would meet with them privately after his physicians had attended to their wounds. He caught Sher-tal's eye and paused to word his reply carefully. These women must not feel hastily dismissed.

And in that brief silence, Bel-ghirá found a way in. "*What* gods?" he said.

"All the gods, Lord. Arna and his Lady and Vaurjhaz and Thumarrat who looks on us from the mountains and more beside. We ask the gods to listen to what we discover—"

"*All* the gods?" grated Bel-ghirá. He spoke as if he were being throttled. "All the gods? Then you call on G'chraada?"

"No, lord. Only the grey clans of the Vorish bow to the one under the earth."

"And you say that defending Vardresh against the Vorish is an evil? You call to Arna against those who fight the dark for him?"

At this, a murmuring began and ran through the square.

Confused, Varrinil was unable to answer.

Jarthastra glared furiously at his priest. He saw the eyes of glass, the marble face, and realised the man was utterly incapable of a compassionate response to the situation before him. Bel-ghirá spoke from a dream to a dream and there was no knowing what he might say.

This had gone far enough. Jarthastra made to raise his hand to silence

344

Bel-ghirá and then found he could not. A burning pain ran through the concealed bruise at his neck. Words and thoughts suddenly fled. Confusion fell on him like a leaping beast. He could not think, could not speak. Fear and pain struck him and darkness came before his eyes. He swayed and grasped Shar-ra'ul's arm.

Varrinil's voice came shrill: "Evil in the land! Flame and sword when we sat in quiet!"

"That is the way of Harrak!" snapped Bel-ghirá.

"The way of some, yes—Grey Vorish or the wild men of no tribe—but there is a dark thing on the Plain. It draws good men to madness and blood, it makes hate. I was wife of one who listened to the sorcerer of Archraad and his foul promises. Now he is dead and his body hewn."

Jarthastra still fought to regain his mind, but a weight like a heavy claw lay on it. He could end this in moments, if he could but speak.

Varrinil, unaware of Jarthastra's struggle, was pouring out her story to Bel-ghirá.

"Terrible promises, Lord—oh, do not be angry. The sorcerer wished your death. He said he would cut your hand from your body for my husband. Ah, wicked, wicked! If the burning had been at Archraad's gates we would have known, we would have understood. But at the place of rest and sleep that should be guarded! And my husband with the Vorish!"

The other women began wailing again. The angry crowd around them was shouting. The glorious day was sinking into chaos.

Jarthastra watched in agony. He knew no-one would move without his command, but a huge invisible wall had risen around him. He could not reach the situation.

"Attack a priest! Attack Lord Arna! Your husband could not escape. How will Ardhruthak guide *him?*"

A cry of pain from Varrinil, as Bel-ghirá continued his assault.

"Do you think we were ignorant of Archraad's promises? A gift to your son on his name-day: a severed hand with many rings." Bel-ghirá gloated. "Valderthaan! Hear what the vile minds of the Harrak think fit for their children!"

Varrinil shrieked again and again as she swayed on the very edge of her suffering.

The people were becoming restless, shouting and jostling, angry and confused.

Jarthastra saw the riot building. And more. Suddenly, he was looking into the eyes of a man standing a little way back from the front of the crowd. He was a still point in the sea of people, intent on the Valgraav. Raising a hand, he smiled slowly, widely, his white teeth gleaming. Absurdly, Jarthastra felt that the man's hand had seized his mind. The man made a fist and placed it against his head in the same place where the Valgraav had been struck on Renewal Night. Jarthastra saw the hawk-faced, swarthy features, felt the dreadful force that came from the man, and cried out, for he understood. He forced himself somehow to grasp Shar-ra'ul's arm and point towards Bel-ghirá and the women.

The Archpriest glanced at his monarch and at once took charge.

"Peace!" called his irresistible voice. "We will have peace here!"

With the sight of that venerable figure, arms raised for silence, Varrinil's shrieking stopped and the hubbub died down. Shar-ra'ul waited until there was something like quiet then slowly lowered his arms. He turned to Bel-ghirá, but his voice was still intended to be heard by as much of the square as possible. "This is not the place, my Lord," he said, keeping his eyes on the expressionless little priest. "These women need rest and quiet. They will be better able to speak their complaint to the Chosen at a later hour. Desist, I pray you!"

That did it. The voice of the god's Archpriest momentarily broke the shell around Bel-ghirá's mind. The little man became stiff and silent at once. He stepped back a pace and did not so much as look at the Harrak women.

Shar-ra'ul beckoned to Sher-tal and the courtiers. To Varrinil he said, "Will you and your sisters go with these men? They will take you where you may rest and bathe. I will send healers."

The women nodded agreement and came hesitantly up the steps onto a level with Shar-ra'ul and the others. They stared fearfully at the mountain-lions until Sher-tal shepherded them towards a doorway at the side of the stairs. Most of the women gave a bow as they passed Jarthastra, though some seemed unsure of who he was.

The Graavinda nodded to each of the women as they walked by, her

346

tight smile a thin line holding back her outrage. Princess Iente stared, expressionless, her sister stood cowering beside her, while Prince Arthodt simply gaped.

Jarthastra felt himself relax. His mind cleared somewhat. The ghastly episode was ending. He looked for the southerner, but he had disappeared. Had he imagined it? Still, he would have time to recover himself and think how he would deal with the women's grievance. Bel-ghirá, of course, would not be involved.

"*Ai! Thurech! Thurech! Barl'ag nu rava! Thurech!*" The women began screaming and babbling in terror.

Jarthastra shook his head, regained his senses and saw that Varrinil and her sisters had stopped dead and were staring and pointing, horrified, at the low balcony. *Thurech! Thurech!* rang in his ears.

Varrinil's voice gave translation to the foreign tongue: "The slayers! The slayers! They slew our husbands, they hewed our young men! They trampled the old and the children! Slayers! Slayers!"

The shrieks were almost a chant, a ritual accusation. The women crowded together, grasping their children and each other.

Jarthastra realised with dismay they had recognised the Guard of the Sun.

"They walked among the fires! Blood without cause, death without need! Why do they stand here? Death they deserve!"

Bel-ghirá's guard heard all this calmly, even with some amusement. Then some of them spoke to their captain and with much guffawing and shoving sent him down from the balcony. He was a great, muscle-bound monster with a broad, flat face and uneven, slanted eyes. Heavy mail swung around him as he approached the women with an easy, swinging gait, a spear on his massive shoulders. He leered at Varrinil through his sparse, black beard.

The women backed away, crying out in fear. Shouting and ripples of movement began again from the crowd. Shar-ra'ul raised his hands but this time it had no effect.

Varrinil did not retreat. She tottered and clutched at her head. Two of the women found their courage and came to support her.

"Why?" she moaned. "Why? I bring my sisters to find judgement and *he* meets me! How have I angered the gods that they send me my husband's slayer?"

Her voice had risen to a shout, and she could be heard throughout the tiered court. A deep, angry mood stirred the crowd. The Shrine soldiers gripped their weapons and stood ready, watching for a signal. Several priests and courtiers slipped away by familiar doors.

Jarthastra found himself trapped by enchantment once more. Still, he could stop this, but though he could hear and see clearly, he could not respond. The lumbering warrior gave him an excuse for a bow and turned to speak to Bel-ghirá, ignoring the women. With the man so close, Jarthastra saw how brutish he was. Were they all like that? If it came to defending them from the crowd, he wondered if his guardsmen would offer much assistance.

The loutish captain, too brave or too stupid to realise the disturbance he was creating, was bent almost double, muttering into Bel-ghirá's ear. He should have been sent to his place, but no-one would act without Jarthastra's order.

Bel-ghirá gave a vacant nod. His captain straightened and stepped toward the Harrak women. They backed away, all but Varrinil and two others. The grotesque man stood over her, glowering down and grinning like a boy who thinks he is about to do something very clever.

"You," he said. "Redbeard's woman." His coarse voice struggled with the northern speech.

Varrinil stared up in utter terror, clinging to her boy. Her courage was immense. She and her two friends held their ground. Pride forbade them to back down to this lowering beast, even if it killed them.

The man dimly realised this and lost some of his swagger. He hefted the spear into a better position and straightened to his full height. These tactics had no effect. He became angry, glancing at the restless crowd for a moment. "Your Redbeard dead. No more do work for you. No gold, no money from him. Dead." He paused to gauge the effect he was having. He knew his men were expecting to enjoy the spectacle of this woman's intimidation, yet here she was, refusing to move or weep. He was being made a fool. Furious, he decided to finish his business. "Bad man, he makes promise—hand, rings. Your Redbeard kills Lord Sun's priest, then money. Bad promise now Redbeard dead. Lord Governor, he is better. He says, give her money anyway. Boy, little, can no work. Lord Governor better than wizard. Keep his promise for him. Now you take this, thank Lord Governor. Thank Belgeera."

He thrust something into Varrinil's hands then stood back, watching her.

Slowly, she unwrapped a small cloth bundle. Those near her saw how she struggled to keep her calm, determined to hold on to her dignity as her trembling hands lifted the folds of cloth aside. Then at last Bel-ghirá's gift was revealed. For a moment, Varrinil stood like a frozen statue, then she dropped the gift with such a wail of pain the square was silent at once and every heart burned to know what she had been given.

Jarthastra saw and his mind reeled.

The soldiers saw and a cold fire came to their eyes.

Azhur stared and looked away.

Tyr looked, horrified. He never thought men would do such evil.

At Varrinil's feet lay a hand. The wrist was a mess of flesh and bone, but on the fingers a dozen gems flashed sunlight from their golden settings. She knelt and spread out her quivering hands as though she dared not touch even the air around the vile, glittering thing. When she spoke, her voice was hard like the diamonds, sapphire-cold.

"Devils," she said, and every word was slow and measured. "Devils, devils, it is his! There is the mark he had from his birth! There is the scar of his first wound! It was this hand I took when the elders made me his wife and he led me to his tent." She paused and looked about her. "I find this in Arna's city? Has such a thing been done on the Plain?" She gathered up the hand in the cloth. "I will bury this with his body," she said, "but I will not take your rings."

At this, Bel-ghirá's captain stamped his foot. "There now!" he barked. "There is money many years. You do not take it, this is bad to Lord Governor. There! You speak to him!"

Varrinil got to her feet, holding her grisly bundle. She turned to face Bel-ghirá, looking for a moment into the empty fish-eyes and, almost calmly, said, "Governor, I take your gold, and may you soon go to the darkness, you and these *thurech* who think they are men and do things that shame a beast. My sisters and I, we see where the truth is. Now we go." Then, fiercely, "I take my son his gift." Varrinil put an arm tightly round the boy, turned her back, and strode down among the people.

Even as the crowd parted for her, there was a great gasp of fright and cries of warning. Varrinil turned to see Bel-ghirá's captain, mad with rage, arm raised, his spear about to fly. A sudden sunlight-flash and the spear was released, but not at her. It clattered across the steps as a man of the Shrine Guard came to her rescue, his sword gleaming with sun and blood.

With a shock, Tyr recognised Tharval, the soldier who had rescued him from the Harrak at Falakhoth. He was poised to strike again, but shock and fury had left his grotesque enemy stupefied. He clutched his wounded arm and roared.

Tharval glanced at Varrinil. She caught the message *go quickly* in his eyes. Bowing her head in gratitude she plunged deep into the crowd. The Harrak women followed her at once, making signs of blessing towards the soldier. No broad avenue opened in the crowd this time. People defiantly gave them enough space to pass and no more, closing the gaps behind them to make the women impossible to target.

The crowd was seething and shouting, edging forward as if it might crash upon the steps at any moment. A stone flew out from the mass and cracked on the flags at Bel-ghirá's feet. The guardsmen loosened their swords, but no more. They could tell the Guard of the Sun would be the targets of the mob, not themselves or those they were sworn to protect.

Bel-ghirá's thug of a captain pulled out his sword left-handed and waved it insolently at the crowd like a flag. More stones flew and the Guard of the Sun moved down from their platform, yelling at the people with weapons drawn. The priests were in confusion, the female members of the royal family had fled, and the mountain-lions bared their teeth at their handlers.

It had gone too far. Tharval made signs to the guards to be ready to form a shield-wall across the steps. Thousands were in the square and at their backs would be the Guard of the Sun, ready for a fight. It wouldn't be ideal. He put his hand to the sun-sign at his breast and made his decision. He signalled to the Shrine Guard to hold steady, at the same

Varrinil turned to see Bel-ghirá's captain, mad with rage,
arm raised, his spear about to fly

time he caught Sher-tal's eye and jerked his head towards Bel-ghirá. Then he faced the armoured lout before him.

"You go!" he roared. "Go, you bastard! It's not children now!" He pointed to the archway that led from the Court and prayed the man would take him for someone in authority, but his wounded foe did nothing. Tharval raised his sword to the sun-disc. To the brutish Guard of the Sun he bellowed, "Lord Arna's sword! I hold the sword! I speak, you obey! I command! Go!"

And at that, the huge captain's fury melted. He lowered his sword, backed away, and suffered the ireful guardsmen to shepherd away him and his men.

But Tharval was not spent. He was shaking with fury and rushed up the steps until he was standing over Bel-ghirá. "What was it about?" he howled into the priest's face. "What the hell was it about? Why did you let them...?" But he could not finish.

The lord of Vardresh looked up at him, a slight crease of blank puzzlement on his brow. "Arna's glory," he said vacantly. "All for Arna's glory."

Tharval stared at him for a moment, then bared his teeth and roared. Flinging his sword down ringing on the stones, Tharval whirled away and fled from the Shrine.

~

A CONGRATULATORY CUP OF WINE was drunk in Azhur's rooms. It was as much an opportunity to recover as anything.

"The Fire-spirit," said Galdtchav. "During the Renewal Rite. You really believe it?"

"Tyr's sure of it." replied Azhur. "A presence, he says. Not something visible."

"Ah, well," remarked the old Loremaster. "It's a week in the Scroll of Manifestations."

"His Fire-spirit should have been there this afternoon," Bal-jarrak spat. "That boy's brought nothing but disruption and confusion. Offered nothing tangible."

"But for him, we should have no Valgraav," said Shar-ra'ul.

"Sheer good luck."

Shar-ra'ul peered into the depths of his wine-cup. "And yet more than the rest of us managed to do," he said. "The Lion Throne is occupied."

"Could easily be filled again," remarked Bal-jarrak meanly. "All we'd have to do—"

"I don't think so," said Shar-ra'ul quietly. "What charming rooms you have, Azhur. Has the Lady Aienna lent them her touch?"

The new Loremaster shook off his shock at Bal-jarrak's unfinished remark to answer the Archpriest. "Ah, yes. She has done this and that."

"And that witch Vashira is fawning round him." Bal-jarrak's focus was still Tyr. "Something brewing there. She's got too many privileges. Not safe. And who allowed that young soldier fellow on the steps?"

"Let's be glad someone did," said Galdtchav. "I wonder what he meant by *not children now?*"

"I think some children must have been injured in the melee," Shar-ra'ul observed.

"Don't worry about damaged children, my Lords," said Bal-jarrak, taking some more wine. "There are now a few less Harrak to bother us in ten years' time."

"What did happen?" asked Galdtchav. "I must say I'm not clear."

"Well, neither am I," admitted Bal-jarrak. "But it sounds like the same old thing: Harrak attacked, did some damage, and we taught them a lesson. I really wouldn't worry, my Lords."

"I, ah, tried speaking to a number of soldiers," Azhur said. "Tried to get some details, but very little forthcoming. They all looked angry."

"Don't take it personally," muttered Bal-jarrak. "They're annoyed about the extra duty they'll have for a couple of weeks, that's all. Someone sensible will write a report."

Galdtchav shook his head. "That woman in the Shrine made it sound as though something absolutely dreadful had happened."

"No, no," said Bal-jarrak through his wine. "That woman was no fool. She wanted insurance."

"How so?"

"To avoid further repercussions," Bal-jarrak said, waving his cup and pointing a finger with the same hand, by this time no small feat. "Wail and moan so you get Jarthastra's sympathy. Isn't it awful, look at my poor boy, my poor sisters weeping away—they have professional mourners, did you know that? They weep on cue, no emotion, none at all. Completely false. You know, I think Jarthastra fell for it. But they were sent, these women. Nice plan by somebody. Is that wine finished?"

"For all practical purposes," said Galdtchav, putting the wine jug behind his chair.

Shar-ra'ul leaned forward, "Are you saying then, Anthu Bal-jarrak, that Vardresh is a minor matter for the military, and not for the Shrine or the Circles around the Chosen?"

Bal-jarrak nodded. "Our Harrak lady's performance will fade into memory, as will the whole business. But still, the Harrak haven't dared anything like Vardresh for a long time. Perhaps some token executions would—"

"I really should try to follow these things more," interrupted Galdtchav, sensing a long and bitter speech brewing.

"I'd like to keep an eye on Tyr-shan," the Archpriest said, his worry about the Harrak seemingly dispelled. "There may be other signs."

"Once Tyr-shan is back in Falakhoth, things may seem very different in hindsight," said Galdtchav. "However, I think Jarthastra may well follow these matters."

"He's had more of your assistant's notes, I believe," said Bal-jarrak, running a finger over his largest rings.

"The *Anthu* Azhur has communicated, yes," said Galdtchav.

"I see. Secured some money for your peasant friend, have you?"

"There will be a gift, yes," replied Azhur. "Only fair." He leaned forward. "Ah... my Lord Bal-jarrak, the, ah, *occasion* of our disagreement in the guardroom earlier..."

"I've nothing to say," said Bal-jarrak, looking away. "Let's carry on, shall we?"

"I meant no offence or disrespect," tried Azhur. "I was tired, as we all were, and I would be sorry if there were any—"

"Others might not be," said Bal-jarrak. "Leave It."

"My Lord Archpriest, how fares Jarthastra?" said Galdtchav.

Shar-ra'ul sighed. "Quiet, I believe. I shall wait on him myself when he wakes up."

"*If* he wakes up," said the Keeper of the Fires sourly. "He barely managed to leave the square. There's something wrong with him."

"Really?" said Galdtchav. "Whatever gave you that idea?"

Azhur shifted uneasily in his chair. "I spoke to the Master Physician. He, ah, thinks the blow to the head last night—"

A pattern of knocks and Sher-tal glided into the chamber. He murmured in Bal-jarrak's ear.

The priest sighed and rose.

"Called away, my Lord?" asked Galdtchav innocently. "We'll miss your insight."

"You'll get by, I'm sure," said Bal-jarrak, with a hateful glance at Azhur. "I'm wanted in the basements, apparently. Something about the wolf."

"Now that *was* a token execution," remarked Galdtchav.

~

IN A CHILLED SUBTERRANEAN CHAMBER, Bal-jarrak was received by the Master of Diversities, a ubiquitous and utterly indispensable priest whose function nobody knew.

"You have to see this," he said.

"I've seen it," Bal-jarrak told him. "And smelled it. What else do you have for me?"

"Just wait," said the Master, and led him by lantern across the dank windowless room. On a large wooden table lay a shape huddled under a dirty blanket. At one end a pair of animal paws protruded and at the other someone had thoughtfully placed a basin beneath the severed neck where gore still dribbled out. The Master swept off the blanket and stepped back to let Bal-jarrak make his discoveries.

Repelled but curious, the Keeper of the Fires examined the carcass. The fur still stank and the mange still seeped disease. He brought his lantern round to the end where the head had been. Bal-jarrak started. The wolf's front legs stuck out over the edge of the table so that the paws hung on either side of the bloody basin.

But they were no longer paws.

Where the foot should have terminated in a wolf's padded toes, the clawed pads themselves extended out into long, jointed digits covered with dark, stretching skin. At their tip were thick vicious nails, black and curved.

"What's this?" asked Bal-jarrak.

"You tell me," said the Master.

Bal-jarrak looked again. The back of the foot appeared somewhat too long, somewhat too broad. The taut sinews made it look very like…, "I didn't notice this before," he said.

"It wasn't there before," replied the Master. "When I brought the thing down here, it had paws."

"Are you saying…? But that's an abomination! Something like that couldn't get into Valderthaan, not while Namau Ramá—"

"You can't hear him down here."

"But look, it can't have changed. These can't be hands."

"You see what I see. Look at the toe on the side. That's a thumb or very nearly."

"What are you saying?"

"Nothing at all, my Lord. I'm just showing you."

Bal-jarrak stared, seeing but not believing. He strode to the other end of the table and peered at the rear paws. The toes had not stretched out but had bunched together a little, and the pad behind them had elongated. Before the joint of the ankle the bone had rounded and swollen out. There was more: the haunches were a little too thick, a little too long; there was hardly any tail left; the proportions of the rib-cage were not right; and the spine was incorrect for a loping predator. He was suddenly terrified.

"Nobody sees this," he whispered, staring at the dreadful thing as though, if he let it out of his sight, it would escape. "Nobody at all, do you hear me?"

"Very clearly, my Lord," said the Master of Diversities.

A familiar pattern of knocks sounded on the chamber door. The priest flung the blanket over the carcass an instant before Sher-tal materialised.

"How did you know I was here?" hissed Bal-jarrak.

"My job, my Lord," Sher-tal said. "And I told you to come."

"Well, what is it?"

"Communication from the Lord Jarthastra. The boy Tyr-shan will return home in the morning. These are the instructions to carry out prior to his departure."

Bal-jarrak snatched the document and read. His eyes became very wide. "It's an error," he said. "Some scribe—"

"I received it from the Lord Jarthastra myself," said the secretary. "I watched him write it as he bathed."

Bal-jarrak scanned the paper again, then once more. "No," he said. "No, I won't. I won't."

~

THE LAST GREAT EXCITEMENT for Tyr before leaving Valderthaan was to meet Aienna. Following scribbled directions, he rushed along labyrinthine corridors, found the imposing door and, because it was Azhur's room, barged straight in. There was his friend, decked in splendid shades of scarlet, and beside him Aienna shamed the sun in a robe of yellow and fresh green, and a head-cloth of purest white linen with embroidered ribbons of emerald and gold. She had obviously been well prepared for the moment.

"Oh," said Tyr, gaping as usual. He was coming across women for whom village courtesies, such as they were, were just not adequate. Aienna laughed, and he noticed that her eyes too were green.

"Tyr-shan of Falakhoth," she said in a voice like nightingales by a mountain stream. "Welcome to the chamber of the Anthu Azhur va-Kherzir of the Second Circle." And she came forward and kissed Tyr on the cheek.

Tyr smiled and gasped as a surge of something not entirely unfamiliar but suddenly very focussed rose from his stomach to his throat. Azhur was grinning in sympathy. The boy swallowed and tried a greeting. "Mornin'," he said. "How's y'self, Squirrel?"

Aienna gasped and stared. "Squirrel?" she said. "Azhur, you told him!"

"Tyr! You really—"

"It weren't him, it were that old feller Veshren," said Tyr, grinning hugely and relishing Azhur's alarmed embarrassment.

Aienna broke into a laugh, took Tyr's hands and held them.

"Y' don't look much like a squirrel to me," he told her.

"Oh! Oh well, that's quite all right then! I still like you. Mind you, though," she continued in a different tone, "you're much more handsome than Azhur let on. I don't know if I'll let him court me after all."

"Oh, just a moment!" exclaimed the Loremaster. "Tyr, would you please leave, I'm feeling terribly threatened."

"Eh?" blurted Tyr. For a moment he thought Azhur meant it, but his friend broke into a long, relaxed laugh at Tyr's expense. Relieved, Tyr joined him. "Daft bugger," he said. "Ey, y' look grand in them robes."

"Oh. They're a bit heavy."

"He was born to them," said Aienna, and smoothed Azhur's long, black hair over his chest, where the sun-disc hung. "Now, I want to get to know you, Tyr-shan. Azhur was telling me how much he enjoyed his new friend. I think you're good for him."

"Yes, well," blustered the new Loremaster, "I thought that—if you've time—we could go down to one of the terraces and get a late breakfast."

Before Tyr could reply, someone strode through the open door behind him. He whirled round and found Bal-jarrak standing there like a black cloud on a bright day. Tyr glowered at the man who would have locked up his father on a trumped-up charge.

"And Arna shine on *you*," said the priest. "Don't trouble to smile, we understand each other." He stepped forward and handed Tyr a small scroll. "From your admirer. He's authorised me to do this, though I can say it gives me no pleasure at all."

And then Bal-jarrak, with a face that would curdle milk, offered Tyr a place in the novitiate of the Priests of the Sun.

CHAPTER 17

Lukar

THE GROUND SWAYED AS Ilissos was dragged, stumbling from the carriage. His knees and feet scraping and thudding over sharp stone edges. The stink of fish smeared queerly across the whirling dark, before he left the street behind and passed through a doorway. A floor and wall came up and jarred his bones. Voices and firelight, shouting, crashing, sickly surges, then a long darkness and someone holding his head and feeding him. He eased his eyes open.

He was in a high, round, fire-lit room, with stairs up to a door. He could make out three people and their looming shadows: Val-zajjhak, seated and sullen; an old woman huddled on a mattress; and a man who came lurching towards him, dragging a foot.

"Well now, well now, your chum's woken up, Crow."

"Do not use that name."

"Why not? Fits." A rasping laugh. The voice was odd and thick, like speaking through a mouthful of food. The face that accompanied the voice came unpleasantly close to Ilissos'. It had tangled hair and beard, wild eyes above a clump of a nose. "Welcome t' Lukar, son. Honoured t' have you in the humble home of the Skull-man, Gaur-van the vraakhin." He laughed in a kind of mock fanfare and waggled his hands. "You got a bit knocked up at Vardresh, son," continued the oddly amused voice, "so lie quiet now, cos we've got work t' do, me and Crow. Head back, now, that's it. On that pillow. There you go."

Ilissos thought someone was patting his head. As his thoughts floated away, he heard: "On your feet, Crow. Get your powers stoked up, we're going t' be busy."

A long swathe of swirling dreams later, and Ilissos shook himself, rubbed his eyes, and tried to form a coherent set of thoughts. Sensations swam and reeled as the last of Val-zajjhak's enchantment sloughed off him. At length he saw the large, circular room filled with shadow-shapes and fluttering fiery light. It smelled of damp and smoke and greasy food. He jolted up to a sitting position and the room slowly came into focus.

He found himself huddled against the wall on a pile of pelts and blankets. To his left, further along the wall, a long, low plinth was partly set into a shallow recess, and on it a meagre fire burned with two buckled, blackened pots amid the flames. Shadows shuddered and bucked, tethered to the sticks of furniture and to the people in the room. Leaning on the flaking plaster nearby was the long, melancholy swathe that was Val-zajjhak. His dull eyes refused to hold even the glimmer of the cooking-flame but angled down on Ilissos with a heavy-lidded, dispassionate watchfulness born of the sorcerer's own languid fire.

A rasping little laugh and there was the man who had been feeding Ilissos earlier. A crumpled old fellow in a long, cracked, leathery coat leaned hard on a wooden crutch whose grimy support was jammed under one arm. He held his head on one side, studying his guest with an amused, strangely paternal curiosity. Round eyes under brows like bear-pelts and an ungainly, swollen nose were framed by a rough fur hat and a thick, chaotic beard that might once have been red. His tongue ran constantly over his thick, wet lips that stretched in an endless grin of ambiguity, and for no clear reason he would occasionally give a series of rasping little chuckles.

On the opposite side of the room an old woman sat hunched in weary unease, mixing something in a bowl and looking anxiously around like a squirrel in a wolf-pack.

"Back again, are you?" rasped the old man, fierce and jovial, "Missed a lot, you have, son. Missed all the fun."

"There is no *fun*."

With that blade of a voice, something cold and dire fingered Ilissos' spine and slid around his belly. Opposite the fire-slab, the slope of stairs curved up the wall to a little balcony at a heavy wooden door. By the door, on the balcony, there seemed to be a coalescence of shadows. Ilissos had not noticed it before, but now it moved and stretched, as a hawk's-head of a face leaned into the firelight and glared over as if the mass would spread inky wings and sweep down. Ilissos started back, horrified, as he recognised V'karra, the southerner whose deadly presence had carried the paralysing fear to Gizhurthra's hut at Falakhoth. His heart thundered as he waited again for the maiming terror to fasten on him again and rend the levels of his mind. But it didn't come. Whatever enchantment or evil had caused that fear, it held no potency in this place. He only felt the insidious touch of the man's malice, which was horrid enough.

"Fun," repeated the crushing voice, as if the word did not come easily to it. "You should be serious. We handle the world."

The old man tilted his head to one side again, oddly reminding Ilissos of the little birds that looked for pickings in the gardens at Agoras. The man made a rough little sound and something glowed in his eyes.

"Yes, course we do," he said. "And no disrespect, but you got t' admit it's sort of entertaining. Bit of a game, know what I mean?"

"No game," said Val-zajjhak. "This time has ripened for generations."

"Yeah, course, but we got *him* now. Bit of a turn-up, eh?" He flashed a wide leer meaningfully at Ilissos, but the Syrgan could not think what it meant and shuddered at the fearsome possibilities that rose in his mind.

Val-zajjhak clasped his hands and glowered at the floor. "He is no prize," he said. "They are dreams. He is not yet their servant."

"Oh," said the old man, with guttural mock-surprise, "So *you* think. Got t' say that though, don't you, Crow?"

"Do not use that name, Gaur-van."

"Oh, excuse *me*, Baranthu Crow. Perhaps we got one up on your old boss. You worried about that?"

Ilissos felt a deadly tremor shudder in the air and prickle his skin. He realised dimly and strangely that it was connected with the hatred burning in Val-zajjhak's eyes.

Gaur-van laughed raucously. "Don't you know who this is, eh?" he asked Ilissos. "You ain't got caught by just anybody, son. It's one of Arna's Shrine boys that nabbed you." He hopped towards the Syrgan and leaned over as if to impart some secret knowledge. "Old Crow here's a *priest*." And he savoured the final word in a long, thick, lisping sound that wound off his swollen tongue. He straightened up and grinned at Val-zajjhak. "Or was, till him and Arna fell out."

Val-zajjhak convulsed with unfamiliar energy, "You have no right!" He was white and livid, and again Ilissos felt the extension of it, uninvited, in his own mind. "I do not feed on fables! It is renounced!"

"Have it you own way," said Gaur-van. Then, slyly, "Don't know why you keep this servant of the gods in tow, though."

"I am commanded, but life under the gods is not my choice. My power is my own. I walk in that."

"Good for you, son," replied Gaur-van with jovial venom. "You stick t' that. We'll look after you."

This time Val-zajjhak's wrath thudded like a pulse in Ilissos' thoughts.

"You go too far," he said in a bile-choked voice. "Expect nothing from me. Look only for my enmity." He moved his bony hand in front of him and a red, ireful glow spread out and hung in the air.

Gaur-van quickly raised his own hand, and though it made nothing visible a juddering began in the air and moved out from him. It seemed a terrible danger was beginning, but his fixed grin remained and his eyes gleamed with the thrill of the fight.

Objects moved away from the two men, and Ilissos felt himself pressed gasping against the wall, with a force on his body that threatened to bend his ribs. Mouldered plaster flaked and fluttered down as cracks criss-crossed above his head. The old woman squealed and scrabbled behind the fire-slab. Tension grew and strained till it seemed the air would break.

Then there came a lance of energy that drained the contesting powers. V'karra had become bored of spectating from the little balcony. His hand was now raised, black and potent, glowing over them like a thunderhead.

"Hold back your fires," he said, authority deep in his chest. "We will not be divided against ourselves. That is planned for those we conquer."

Val-zajjhak lowered his hand. "I obey, Lord. But he will have no love from me."

"I do not command you to love," replied V'karra. "It would not serve us. But I command oneness. I command that our powers be joined." He unhurriedly made his way down the curving stair, flexing his talon-fingers where the gold flickered and gleamed. He came to a stop in front of the ruby firelight, ominous and strong. "Hear me," he said, narrow-eyed. "Oneness or wrath."

Val-zajjhak, cowed, made a bow. "I obey, lord," he repeated.

Gaur-van made his brief, rattling laugh, but V'karra seemed satisfied. If anything truly satisfied him.

"We will dine," V'karra said to the terrified woman, the issue resolved.

The woman pushed herself to her feet and feverishly made busy with bowls and cups. It seemed to Ilissos that *dine* was a grand word in the circumstances, but he decided that nothing could feel normal in the insane circle of this room. He lay limply against the wall, drew up his knees, hugged them, and waited to see what would happen. He seemed quite forgotten, and he preferred it like that.

V'karra paced about the narrow room. Each stride, it seemed, traversed a kingdom. The long, ornamented fingers clenched and spread and grasped, and the imperious black robes swept and swirled as his words, the overspill of his hateful mind, grated against the peeling walls. He was born to authority, Ilissos could see that. A man who would be followed, not from love perhaps, but not wholly from fear either. Even his bitterest of enemies would still hold an admiration for him, maybe even a trace of awe too. Great he was, for though his aim was to flood the world with woe, such calamity still required a towering stature to be its channel. It was absurd that he should even be in this wreckage of a room.

"There have been many victories," he said, though to what invisible audience Ilissos did not know. "Often we have contended and often we

363

have had the mastery. Many conquests, many secret triumphs. Zirribh could not stand; the Suzerain could not match me." He stopped, breathing heavily as he stared at some memory of strife. His lips tightened and his even, ravenous teeth showed in the firelight. Then his head went back and, thrusting his arms out, he cried out from his rapacious soul to the high, shadowed ceiling, "*Vei krenu! Meí keruch'tha nūvaajh, Hra'im! Va krenu vei va krahir shi!*"

The vraakhin stood for a moment, outside himself in far-off fiery thought, then brought his hands together and clasped them in a ferocity of passion that forced the gleaming rings into his flesh. Two little rivulets of blood ran down and V'karra bowed his hawk's head till the brow rested on his knuckles. He murmured a deep, vigorous chant that made Ilissos shiver, then looked up, abruptly calm.

"We have struck the first great blow against the gods," he said, quiet and passionate. "All thus far has been building and shaping. A preparation." He held his head as though listening. "They travel now. They come to me. I hear their footfalls in my spirit. Calaros is weary and Shishak drags a sprained foot. Ra'ug stumbles on the rocks—he is unsure and leans hard on his staff. Vorthas strides easy in the forest, treading eagerly upon pine-needles. Nalach'huk tramps the ice no longer for he nears the Plain. Kharhalkhar runs to us with the moon tonight." V'karra's eyes shifted like a beast in a thicket. "There is another. Someone bends his spirit here, but I have not called him."

"What of Lord Gehrava?" asked Val-zajjhak in a whisper. "Do you sense him?"

V'karra closed his eyes, creased his brow. "He is under the earth. He will reach Varcath Gate this night." His eyes opened, and he peered into hidden distances. "The powers will join at Archraad. The dark sun will rise and the gods will tremble."

"And in the meantime," said old Gaur-van with his dark glee, "we've got their chum, eh?" He leered at Ilissos with a long, throaty laugh. "You the only one, son? They got more like you?"

The Syrgan was frozen dumb. He had no shred of an idea what all this could mean, but he was terrified to say anything at all, lest he made things worse. V'karra turned his vulture stare on him, so that a cold, sharp tingling went along Ilissos' arms and hands.

"He is the only one," said the southerner, and watched his prize with a piercing fascination. "The force that was around him when I discovered him at Falakhoth marks him out. A god stepped between us. They are cunning. They seek to twist the laws of the High Combat, so I withdrew to order my powers. I would not waste them in unlawful struggle."

Val-zajjhak raised his head at this, but he said nothing. Ilissos noted this, feeling a strange sensation of conflict brewing.

V'karra maintained his serpent stare. "The gods have not taken up one like this for eight centuries. He is the first such since the Burned One. All their other servants are overshadowed. They were foolish and hasty to reveal this at Falakhoth. This is their chosen servant, and he is our prize. I know the lore of this, and Lord Gehrava too. There is no doubt."

"And they ain't lifted a finger, eh?" cackled Gaur-van.

"They cannot. The sum of our powers makes a shield, and when the powers are fused at Archraad, their sway over the earth will wane. All is ready. The Northland waits for my word." V'karra held up a tense, triumphant fist. "With this hand I struck their Valgraav, the one they say their god has chosen! I smote the Mountain-lion in the heart of his realm! In the court of his Shrine I smote him, and he shall not know wholeness again. The North is crippled by my hand."

Gaur-van leered and cackled and clapped his gnarled hands together. "That's the stuff, that's the stuff!" His eye glinted. "Pity about Braugheer though, wasn't it?"

Something cold and sharp rippled across the room.

"Why do you say this?" asked the southerner quietly, like a blade sliding slowly from its sheath.

Gaur-van flapped his arms out and shrugged. "Just... just stating a fact. It's a pity, just a pity. A terrible shame. We'd have been rid of old Jarthastra if that village kid hadn't done that lucky swing with the sword. So, it's a pity. That's what I mean." He put his head on one side and smirked the wider.

"There was no *luck*," said V'karra dangerously. "There is no... *providence* that mars what we do."

And here Val-zajjhak made a servile bow and said, "It may be, Lord, that the powers about Jarthastra are such that only you may smite him. Braugheer was, I think, deficient."

The southerner's face broadened into a slow, wicked smile. "A strange word from one who says there are no gods," he replied. "But a good one. I put the harm-mark on Braugheer and spoke futility for him. He could not know it or escape it. Thus, he provoked the forces, and they took the sword and struck back at him. The energies of intention cannot mix. You speak true. I have bested the Valgraav's god in this contest."

Gaur-van gave a long, rattling cackle that ran into a wheeze. "That's it, that's it! Wish I'd seen his head a-flying, though! Look on his face!" And the grotesque old man made a grimace that could well have been seen on an astonished, if severed, wolf's-head that finds itself suddenly in flight.

"Braugheer would have challenged you, Lord," said Val-zajjhak suddenly, with an unexpected emotion that lifted his voice from its prison in his chest. "He yearned for your place. He would have deposed you if he could. I saw the image in his mind before he crossed the Bridge to Valderthaan. I felt his thoughts as I watched from Archraad."

V'karra pondered this, narrow-eyed. "He hated me," he said at last, sounding strangely puzzled. "I felt it as we went up to the city. That is why I gave him the harm-mark. There was no loyalty in him, he was not like you."

Val-zajjhak bowed again.

This was the nearest V'karra had come to anything like a display of comradeship—and it was not very near—but the unspoken suggestion of what might happen should he deem Val-zajjhak's loyalty to be deficient, still nestled under his words. If Val-zajjhak realised this, he gave no sign.

"Lord, Braugheer deserved your judgement," he intoned.

"Stupid sod," confirmed Gaur-van. "Should have known better. Here, though! They got his body! What if it shifts?"

"No matter," V'karra told him. "They deny such things. If they see the change, the fear will numb them."

"They can have no plans for it," added Val-zajjhak. "There is nothing in their Scrolls about those like Braugheer."

Gaur-van perked up, "Well, you'd know about that, eh, Crow?"

Val-zajjhak's head lowered and his eyes shone like cold moons under the threatening clouds of his brow. "Do not speak of that," he said.

Gaur-van leered and laughed, and it seemed the forces of their hatred would rise again, but V'karra raised a hand.

"Oneness," he said in a voice that sent a tremor through the room. The tension broke. The southerner turned to the old woman stirring the contents of her pans in terror. "Serve us now. We will celebrate Braugheer's fall."

V'karra seated himself on a broken chair, feet well apart, leaning forward like a lord presiding at a feast, one hand turned inward on his knee. His ramshackle chair boasted a padded, threadbare backrest and a well-compressed cushion, but Gaur-van, who had most need, had to limp to a hard stool where he could lean back against the fire-slab. Val-zajjhak lowered himself impassively onto a bench. They had suddenly been transformed into guests at the court of V'karra.

The old woman scuffed back and forth serving some kind of stew with trembling hands. The southerner would not take the bowl, but waited until his pressed hostess set it on the arm of the chair and backed away, patting her chest and gasping with fear. She served the other vraakhin, then brought a bowl to Ilissos. As he took it, she quickly cupped her hands round his, squeezed them and whispered, "I'm sorry, love." It was all she dared, and in the next moment she was pattering back to her mattress to feed herself with whatever remained.

Ilissos scooped up stew-soaked bread, chewed, then stopped, for he realised the woman had been speaking in Syrgan. He stared across the room at her. She squatted on the mattress, hunched over her own bowl. As she spooned the food to her mouth, she looked up and their eyes locked. Her glance silently told him she was trapped too.

There was a hammering on the door.

V'karra was on his feet, taut as sinews. "Make the eighth sign!" He wove a pattern in the air with his long fingers.

Gaur-van dragged himself to his feet. "Who's that?" he roared. "We're busy here!"

"You know me," came a voice.

"What's your business?"

"To see you again, master."

"Don't know you," barked the old man. "Sod off."

A long silence, and then the latch lifted and the door hesitantly edged inwards.

"Oi!" called Gaur-van. "This here's a private dwelling. Sling your hook!"

Val-zajjhak had finger-tips pressed to his temples. "He has a shade over his mind," he said anxiously. "I cannot see him."

The door swung in and back till it struck the wall. A swirl of air, and a thin, shabby figure was on the balcony. A travelling-bag flopped down and an animal muzzle poked into view.

"Don't you know me, master?" said a plaintive voice. "They threw me out. They didn't understand me, so I came here. Where else could I go?"

Gizhurthra.

The white dog whined. Gizhurthra rubbed its back and clutched it to him in his arms as though he would absorb it. "They turned on me," he said, close to tears. "Master Gaur-van, I told them. Everything you taught me. I said I'd lose the power if I worked. I tried to give them your teaching. I told them all about you, how you trained me to be vraakhin, but nobody cared."

Here, Val-zajjhak made a small derisive sound in his throat.

Gizhurthra didn't hear him. "When I used the fire-word, the headman made me leave."

"Ah," said Gaur-van vaguely.

"He *hit* me! They threw stones at me!"

"Ah," repeated the old vraakhin. "Scared. Tiny minds, you see."

"Oh, I know. None more than I. Years I took. I tried to teach them. I offered them cures and prayers and lore and words against the spirits. No thanks, no thanks at all."

"Hard world, son, cruel hard. Folks like us ain't always welcome. Told you that, didn't I?"

"As with the priests, so with the people," said V'karra unexpectedly.

"Eh?" said Gizhurthra, his lament spoiled.

"The priests despised you, you told us. They would not believe your power is your own."

"I hate them," growled Gizhurthra into the fire.

"Well, you may. They have poisoned all the north. How many more are like you?"

"A *lot*."

"One day you will find them and raise them up," said V'karra. He moved his hand, causing the air to thicken. "Know that the village curs are thralls of their goddess. She bends them to the earth, she makes their minds heavy. Your powers guarded you."

Gizhurthra stared. "What? Against the Lady?"

"You think the gods are so strong? Hear me, she is a petty spirit. She would not let her earth-grubbing slaves see what is plain to the wise: that you are vraakhin, that she has a jealous fear of you. Why else would you suffer at Falakhoth?"

Gizhurthra's head swam. Here was a new sunrise in the black sky of his frustration. "You mean... you mean, I'm so powerful that—but she's a goddess."

"They tell you the gods can move worlds, but the ancient knowledge speaks differently. It comes down from the fathers of men who knew these spirits and who knew they were not so different from themselves. It was the old kings that called them gods. They worshipped them as mighty beings so they could feed their pride and keep nations subject through fear of what the imagined gods of their masters would visit on them if they disobeyed."

And here Ilissos felt not words but understanding echo in his awareness and he realised a silent communication between the minds of V'karra and Val-zajjhak was spilling over into his own thoughts.

Lord, why do you tell him this?

To win him, why else?

We tried to win him for a mere village-watcher at Falakhoth. He is empty.

No, there is a change, something has woken. Perhaps something great.

Yes, there, very deep. This covered his thoughts when he approached.

It did. But I will draw it out. I will offer him knowledge, he will admit me.

369

V'karra leaned toward Gizhurthra, closer this time, so that the dumb-struck man could feel his breath on his face. "You are a man of power," he murmured. "One day all the gods may fear you."

"Eh?" gasped his prey, head swimming. "What do you mean? How?"

"Our brotherhood strives in a great conflict," said the irresistible voice of V'karra. "The age of the gods is ending. Soon they must lose their grip on the earth and let us hold sway. Few know this save our brothers, and we alone are ready."

Gizhurthra's features leapt from one expression to another as he tried to make sense of this. At last, with utter perplexity on his face and after his mouth had worked soundlessly for a while, he said, "You... you talked about... you said you'd open the southern magic to me. At Falakhoth. Will you?"

V'karra seemed to look within for a moment and Ilissos was aware of the communication rippling out from his mind to the other vraakhin. He saw each of them make tiny, careful movements with their hands before the southerner spoke again in his deep, enchanted voice.

"Much of the power of the south lies in *knowledge*."

The word rolled forward like a wave, laden with enchantment and a sweet promise of significance, a gift to make one count at last. It seeped easily into Gizhurthra's eager, undefended mind and meshed with his barren, yearning heart.

"Our brotherhood has... understanding," V'karra went on. "We are those who know, and thus we are set apart. We have looked into the secret things. We have power to move the ancient energies. We are hidden, but we are the great ones of the earth. Will you join us?" Start-lingly, the vraakhin reached out and laid his gilded hand on Gizhurthra's bony, shabby shoulder. His voice became strangely warm, with a fatherly gentleness. "I tested you at Falakhoth," he said, as a shadow of grief appeared on his brow. "It was necessary. Forgive me."

Gizhurthra's eyes were moist. "No, no, nothing to forgive, no, no."

"I fear there is," murmured V'karra. "But understand these things cannot be settled quickly or without trial. We must be sure. This is why I seemed harsh, but I saw what is in you: your power is your own."

Gizhurthra brought his hands up to his mouth as if to hold something in. His tears brimmed over. "He hit me," he repeated unbelievingly. "Father used to—" He stopped, breathing heavily. "That headman hit me."

"He shall pay," said V'karra quietly.

"I can use the fire-word now. I don't know what you did, but I can. I'm powerful—more than I thought. Knew it was true all this time. I set their inn on fire and they had the Coming Forth with those priests and that novice from the Shrine—"

V'karra raised a hand. "The dark-haired youth? Bearded?"

"Oh, you wouldn't know him. Do you?"

"He insulted me."

"You? No! I can't—well! They've no idea, have they? He doesn't think much of me either. Didn't you, er, strike him down? Something?"

"All things in their time, he too shall pay," V'karra informed him.

"The boys in black, eh? And the rats in red. Upstarts, arrogant, too high-minded to let me in, wind the villages round their fingers." Gizhur-thra had gone on one of his customary wanderings. "But a day's coming, they'll see—*he'll* see, him and that headman's son that's tagged on to him. That whole town—"

But V'karra stopped him again. "The boy: seventeen summers, tall?"

"Yes, yes, and his hair everywhere. Yes, that'll be him. A more insolent—"

"He slew one of our brotherhood."

Gizhurthra jolted back. "Tyr-shan! He couldn't! How?"

"In arrogance, like his father, to defend their little king. But we will collect his dues. Since he pretends to mete out Arna's wrath, he will feel the weight of ours."

"How? When? What'll you do to him?" Gizhurthra's eyes glowed and he could not hold back the hint of a most unsavoury smile.

~

YAUVA HAD RETURNED TO LUKAR on the day following Tyr's first depar-ture for Valderthaan and now, as letters sped back and forth between Falakhoth and the Shrine, and between the Shrine and the kingdom's leading Loremasters, he eased back into the normal life of the *Golden Carp*. True, it was not quite normal. His story of danger and miraculous escape now embellished his mundane, rather insignificant days. The limp was a badge of honour, drawing both sympathy and admiration, and ensured people believed him. Not overly bright, not overly noticed, Yauva was now the centre of attention daily and talked about throughout Lukar, at least for now.

His mother, Yenl, basked in his reflected glory and relished the chance to pour forth maternal distress over her only child. It frustrated her that Yauva no longer felt he needed her to look after him, an activity Yenl normally plunged into whenever she could. Whereas his stepfather, Volthar, drew on all the resources of his dour personality to cover the jealousy he felt. He considered Yauva would not tolerate his limp so well when he had outlived his own popularity, but when those who came to hear his story also bought ale, Volthar at last allowed himself some pleasure in the new confidence of his stepson, and in the *Golden Carp's* increased income.

As Yauva limped about the inn and the Fish-quay, there was something different in the wider world. The air was full of stories. Fishermen, priests, stall-holders, and fishwives all knew a terrible thing had happened at Vardresh and that Renewal Night had been disrupted with some dreadful accidents. There had also been a wolf, or a mad dog, or both, padding around Valderthaan of all places and some Harrak had disrupted a gathering at the Shrine.

Everyone had a story and no-one agreed. Everyone's story was better than the one it was based on. Nobody was entirely clear what had happened anywhere.

And so it was meant to be. The machinery of disinformation and confusion had begun to grind almost before Jarthastra had been lifted from the flagstones of the Shrine Court on Renewal Night. Notices, proclamations, heralds, and personal interviews had insinuated a powerful vagueness into the minds of everyone who heard an account of events. Even those who had seen things with their own eyes became willing to consider that, in the fire-lit confusion of the moment, they had not quite grasped what was happening and now misremembered.

Thus, it was bad, but not *that* bad. The Vorish had attacked Vardresh, but they raided often and you could expect no more from them. This inexplicably rendered the attack nothing to be concerned about. And, inevitably, the refrain ran, this was Arna's kingdom, Arna's kingdom, so do not worry, do not worry, all will be, all is well.

Vagueness, however, stilled few fears and created an insatiable appetite for some facts. When a tall, lean figure in a guardsman's uniform ambled through the sunlight at the door of the *Carp* he was made welcome.

"Ha!" cried old Garfin. "Come and have a jar, lad, and tell us y' news!"

Captain Tharval looked down blankly at the long shadow that spilled away from his feet and turned the fur-edged helmet in his hands. He had no sword. "Aye," he mumbled, and joined the group of patrons at the long table. He leaned forward, elbows on the wood, looking at no-one.

"So," said Verjhan the street-sweeper, "what do y' know, then?"

"Y' was goin' for a spell of duty at Vardresh, last time we saw y'," added Garfin eagerly. "We've heard so many daft things about it we don't know what to think. So tell us, lad, what's been happening up there?"

Tharval fingered the handle of the ale-mug that had appeared before him. "Can't," he said distantly.

"Can't? How can't?"

A pause, a breath, a twist of Tharval's lip. Lines appeared at the corners of his eyes and an angry little cloud drifted into their vacancy. "They don't want it getting out," he said.

A rock-wall of silence. Everyone knew by this he had decided to tell them something he could not bear to carry alone. The soldier filled himself with breath and straightened his back, still looking down at the table, not ready to meet the eyes of his friends. Waiting till he could break free of his memory and drink the comfort of their gathered souls.

"I've come here," he began. He closed his eyes, shook his head a little, rubbed a finger over his brow. "I've come here, back to Lukar, because I'm finished."

They waited, wondering.

"I'm done with the guard."

A low *ohhh* rose from the men and hung over them like a pall. Tharval's secret had begun to leave him and his head and shoulders sagged a little.

He looked up and his eyes moved over the company. "I'm done with the guard, and I'm done with the Shrine, and I'm done with Arna's bloody kingdom."

"Why, lad?" whispered Garfin into the deep well of shock. "Why?"

Tharval took a long drink. "Well," he said, "I'll tell you. But here's something else first." And he told them the facts about the awful scene in the Shrine Court, when the captain of the Guard of the Sun had tried to murder Varrinil and he had beaten him back.

"No, no," crooned Yenl. "Wicked!"

Tharval gave a strange, ugly smile at this and his eyes lit up for a moment. "Aye, wicked it was, mistress Yenl. Shall I tell you why I was so wild? Wasn't just that, you see. Shall I tell you?"

And so they huddled round, rapt and ravenous in the heavy silence, and Volthar pulled the inn door closed as Tharval, like a priest speaking mysteries, told them the truth about Vardresh.

He carefully set the scene. He and his men had been doing routine policing of the broad area between Vardresh and Archraad, where the road from Valderthaan branched off to both cities through the hamlets and little townships clustered by their fields.

"Sun was just going down when we headed west to Vardresh. They asked us to look in, because the Arta were camping round their walls. Sometimes the tribes don't settle down in the Plain like they usually do or they're on the way to another patch, taking their herds for new grazing. They use the city wells and all. Anyroad, we wasn't worried, because you never gets no bother from the Arta. They just want to live and let live. When we come up near the gates, we could see two or three hundred of them, shelters going up and the cooking-fires starting. They were just getting their sheep penned up for the night and the old ones was sitting round jawing and the kids was running around daft." Tharval paused in his recollections. "You know that way when it's getting late but it's still daylight, and the sun's all low and red and the shadows is all stretched out and the light goes all strong and red like rust."

His listeners nodded, thinking of the peaceful scene.

"Nice," said Garfin.

Tharval clasped his hands like vices and bent forward, elbows on the table. "We headed up to the gate so we could check in with the Vardresh garrison. Suddenly, a dozen men come through the gate blocking our way. The lead one holds his hand up. So we pull up and wait.

"*Stop*, he says. *You stop.*

"*We have*, I says, *or didn't you notice?*

"I didn't like the look of him so I felt like being cheeky. Great big feller. Don't know where they got him from. Anyway, he gives out his name like it meant something—I don't remember what it was.

"*Lord Belgeera's first man*, he says. *Great in Vaddish.*

"Couldn't even say the name of the place—three goes and still got it wrong—but I could see he was a captain or something, so I talk like I think maybe he understands.

"*You're not in the guard*, I says. *No red. Not wear the red. Bring the first man that wears the red.*

"Well, it was useless.

"*I am first man*, he says again.

"I tell him, *I'm first man from the city. Big king's first man, bigger than you. Big king angry you play silly buggers with his first man. Bring first man with red coat.*

"Well, he got that and looked worried.

"*Lord Sun's big king*, he says and does this bow and they all goes off through the gate.

"I got the garrison commander after that. The big louts were the *Guard of the Sun*, some big personal bodyguard the priest Bel-ghirá's put together from all the lands. All allowed by Valderthaan. The commander told me Bel-ghirá was practically letting them run Vardresh, leaving the garrison wondering what they were there for. But anyroad, we do the formalities and deploys for the night and that was it. We thought."

Tharval paused again. His listeners saw how the corners of his mouth tugged down and how his expression resembled something like grief. Still staring forward, he made little beckoning motions with his hands.

"Come in a bit," he said with a child's voice. "Come in a bit closer."

They all drew closer still, till Tharval was held by a press of bodies.

Yenl stretched across and took his hands. "Go on, love," she said.

Tharval met her eyes briefly, then looked away and continued. "We did the rounds, checked the guard posts, watched the road, then went into shifts for sleeping. They closed the gates, and the Arta settled down. A Nerthen band had joined the Arta by then, so there must have been three or four hundred round the walls plus the sheep and cattle and all. Bit unusual, so near Archraad—the Vorish don't like them, y' see—but I think they probably wasn't worried with us and the garrison there. Anyhow, they'd set up them little wooden figures they carry around and said night prayers and they were all in the tents or stretched out on mats round the fires—those that wander turn in early. They had all the little kids in one big tent..."

Tharval gripped Yenl's hand so tight she gasped and bit her lip, but she held on.

"That's how they do it. All together." A pause, a breath. "All together." He filled his lungs, swallowed, and hurried on. "It was well dark. We was all bored and hating it. It was Renewal Night, and we knew there'd be celebrations in Valderthaan after the Shrine ceremony.

"*Bugger this for a Renewal,* I says to my Number Two. *Arna must not like us.*

"*Aye,* he says, *they'll just be starting in the Shrine now.* Then he says, *Here, what's that?*

"*What?* I says.

"*Is that horses?* he says. We listened, and there was this noise getting louder and louder.

"*That's horses!* I says. *Must be hundreds! It's an attack!*

"Well, we moved like scalded rats. We had time to sound battle stations and get in position when we saw the first wave coming around a hill about half a mile down the road. They was Vorish—didn't even try to hide it. They was riding like mad things. They wanted Vardresh that night.

"We formed ranks. The gates opened, and the garrison sent out units to back us up. Our force must've been about a hundred horse, plus two hundred foot and archers on the walls. Our unit priest was yelling the battle prayers and some of us was singing best we could. The Vorish was hurtling down on us and we could hear them chanting the name of that damn god of theirs: *G'chraada, G'chraada!* We went cold hearing it. When they was less than a hundred yards away the archers fired and we turned them. The wave behind came over the dead horses at us and we pulled them up short with more arrows. They drew back to regroup. We must've killed about a hundred of theirs already. The Vorish lined up and their chieftains went riding up and down in front of them yelling things—big fierce buggers they was, all painted up with that braided hair and the headdresses they wear.

"No sign of the Guard of the Sun, though.

"I called the alert, and the archers and the spearmen got ready again. We was going to send the horse in if they came again, and then the foot, and shoot arrows over them. I had me hand up to give the signal and then there was a noise, a terrible roar behind us. I looked round and there was this great gush of fire going up inside Vardresh. Then there was another one and another and suddenly there was about a dozen buildings burning *inside* the walls. The Vorish yelled and pulled back—they was as surprised as we were.

"*Hold firm, lads,* I shouts. I rides like hell to find out what was happening. I get through the gates and everything on Vardresh's main street's burning. There was bodies all over. People running and screaming. Right in the middle of it there's this feller in a robe with his arms up, shouting the same thing over and over."

"What was it," asked Yenl. "Tell us, love."

"You'll not believe it," said Tharval.

"Tell us anyway," Yenl said.

"Well, it was—I thought I'd not heard it right—but it was: *Ai va sh'herakh, a threma shi.* Over and over. He was loving it."

"What the priests say," Yenl whispered in shock. "At the first shinin' of the day,"

"Aye. He was a priest. He had the robe and all the trimmings. Even walked like one and held his arms the way they do."

"Did you tell them at Valderthaan?" asked Garfin.

"A hundred times. They didn't want to hear it."

"But who was it? Bel-ghirá?"

"No, I'd know that little sod a mile off. I never saw this feller's face. I'll tell you the worst, though."

Yenl tightened her grip on Tharval's hands. His listeners scarcely breathed.

"He had magic."

"No! I thought priests weren't—"

"They're not. But magic it was. Some filthy force—I never thought I'd—well, there was this bunch of men who came out of a side street to try to grab him. They runs under this lamp on a wall and the priest points at the lamp and shouts a word... and... and this *thing* comes out from him. Everything shook like it does when you look through heat and this force slams into me. It knocks me on the ground, and I felt filthy and sick. The lamp went up in this great blast like when you burst a wineskin, only it was fire. The fellers running underneath got all burned up. And then he did it again to another street lamp, and it went up too. All those people rolling about screaming and burning.... There was women running with babies and—oh gods, no!—and he kept shouting a word...."

"What was it?" asked the horrified Garfin.

"Don't know, don't know. Gods grant I never do. It pulls your body about and it makes you feel you're all full of rottenness and dirt. And your mind—your mind—"Tharval waved his hands in a helpless gesture. He could not speak of what the fire-word did to his mind.

After a moment the story went on. Screams and howls and burning men. Searing, bursting fireballs and great columns of fire surging up from swaying buildings as the monstrous priest roared the terrible, crushing word through a dying Vardresh. The fire consumed the gates, and he strode through. Outside the city walls he pointed and bellowed at every flame he saw. The Arta cooking-fires blew up and blazing waves engulfed the people around them. Tribespeople cowered on the ground, caught between Vorish and fire. Tharval's men raced between the bright, deadly blossoms, trying to find a safe escape for the Arta even as they battled the Vorish on foot and horse. Then the ground shuddered with the newest menace: round the shoulder of a reddened hill came a fresh contingent of the Vorish horsemen. Three hundred there must have been, and two hundred foot with packs of maddened dogs with sharpened teeth and steel barbs on their racing paws. They had held the force back until the madness had reached its peak and now they rushed in to seal Vardresh's fate. As the great wedge of man and beast bore to break the brave red lines of soldiers, they pulled up a short distance away.

"We wondered what stopped them. They had the advantage, it made no sense." said Tharval. "I looked behind me and there was the Guard of the Sun clustered outside the city gates. They was laughing and holding torches. Brutes and savages all. The Vorish was trying to keep their horses steady. They was all ready to fight, but they was holding back. Many beckoned towards the Guard of the Sun, before patting their chests. When the Guard didn't move, the Vorish began yelling and waving their spears at them. Then it hit me. The Vorish was expecting the Guard of the Sun to fight with them. The Vorish leader jumped off his horse he was that angry. He was a big lad with a red beard, the look of betrayal across his face, if ever I saw it. He approached our ranks screaming past us at the Guard, waving at them with wild arms to quit stalling and join with them. Redbeard glared at the Guard. No-one moved. Not the guard, not us stuck in the middle, not even the Vorish. Time stood still, all except for one of the Guard. I caught him out the corner of me eye too late. He'd flanked us and was running fast across our front line in the Vorish leader's blind spot. We'd all been so focussed on the leader, everyone had missed him. Redbeard still had his arm out waving at the Guard. Before he or the other Vorish could react, the ape swung his sword through it. The arm's spraying blood over our front line. Next thing I know, the sword's into Redbeard's chest.

"The ape grabs Redbeard's hand, swinging it round his head, singing *Promise kept, promise kept, Belgeera safe!* I didn't know what he meant." Tharval stopped, exhausted by his memories. Everyone kept still, respecting his endurance. "I've a damn good idea now, though."

The terrible story continued. The magic-priest appeared at the head of the Guard of the Sun, thrust his hands upwards and, at his shout, the Guard flung their torches high over the city guardsmen and the garrison. Those who chanced to look saw the swift, bright points in the air, arcing over them towards the Harrak mass. The Vorish warriors stared horror-struck as the priest howled his fire-word and the flickering, descending swarm poured down upon them in an incandescent, implacable blaze. It flowed under armour like a killing fluid, consumed the hounds and the soldiers' very horses beneath them, poured in their shrieking mouths like a fatal wine so they staggered and convulsed, drunk with pain and death, till they fell in a chaos of blackened limbs, staring with astounded, sizzling eyes.

"Well, we was glad about that," said Tharval. "But we still didn't know whose side that priest was on. He'd burned the Vorish, but he'd burned the town as well. Them apes in the Guard of the Sun then comes wading in. They was swinging and hacking, and I don't think they knew who they was hitting or who the enemy was supposed to be. They knew we was on our side, so they ignored us, but anybody else—men, women, Vorish, Arta—they didn't care. Just swung at them with them great swords of theirs. Slice a horse in two they could. Our lads tried to protect the Arta, but when we did they went for us too. All the time that priest was striding about yelling, *Arna's glory! Arna's glory!* Some other priests had joined him and they was holding holy pictures and banners and things like they do in processions. Then they come to the big tent...."

"Tent?" asked Garfin. "What tent?"

"Where they had all the kids," faltered Tharval. "Must've been well over a hundred kiddies."

It seemed the silence would snap and lash them. No-one wished to be the one who asked the terrible question.

"One of the Sun Guard ripped the flap open and there was all these little kids, crying and hanging onto each other. Some of them was too young to fear the big feller. They must've thought he was somebody dressed up. The mothers and old grannies with them didn't dare move.

"Then the big captain turns and shouts, *What are these? What will we do for Lord Sun?*

"The priest says, *When they grow up they will be his enemies. Bring him glory! You know how!*

About a dozen Sun Guard walk into the tent swinging their swords like scythes at a harvest. I saw an arm... just an arm..." Tharval traced an arc through the air with a shaking finger. A solitary tear rolled down his

380

cheek. "I heard them..." he faltered. "All them little voices..."

Just as it seemed the flood of Tharval's grief would pour out, he became horribly calm and his moist eyes glazed over. His listeners waited.

"Well," he said, and stood up. "There you go." He fumbled for a coin and dropped it on the table without looking to see what it was, then edged sideways through the knot of people. "There you go. Better stop there. Better get home." He moved stiffly to the door in the self-conscious manner of someone attempting to hide that they were in fact fleeing and stepped out to the Fish-quay.

Behind him, the patrons of the inn sat in horrified silence.

CHAPTER 18

The High Fields

WHEN TYR TOLD HIS PARENTS he was going to the high fields, they knew exactly what he meant.

"I know him," said Tyrmar. "He'll have his mind made up by the time he gets back. Best have his tea on."

Iethen leaned her head on her husband's shoulder and gazed over Falakhoth's rooftops through the smoke haze towards the pastures where she knew her son was walking. "Aye," she said. "Mind, he's probably made it up already. He's just gone to the fields to see what he's decided." She sighed. "*Maker's mind and maker's heart set thee for his own apart.* Don't know as that means stayin' in Falakhoth, my love."

"Well, why not?" asked Tyrmar. "We've been smiths five generations. I don't like it stoppin' with me."

"Well, think on it, lovey," said Iethen. "All them visions and all, and the Anthu and the priests takin' an interest. Whatever that's for, it wouldn't work out in a back of beyond place like this, now would it? Can't see how, anyroad."

"Well, Azhur could visit him or he could send them a letter if he has a vision, somethin' like that. He ought to have a trade, I say."

Iethen patted her husband's chest and kissed his cheek. "Think on it," she repeated. "I'm for a walk down the river. Just meself, like. Y' understand, love?"

"Aye," said Tyrmar. "Off y' go." He watched his wife stroll down the street to the King's Road. At times like this he realised there were parts of her he could not understand. Perhaps they were things that went with being a woman, but it made him feel powerless when they appeared. He loved those parts of her for their enticing mystery, but he himself had simpler methods of seeing himself through difficult spells. He turned and slouched back to the forge, mindful of the keg of beer that had been so faithful to him in just such times.

~

TYR SAT ON HIS usual rock and tried to order his jumbled thoughts. In the distance sat the hunched backs of the Western hills in their pelt of pine and heather. They looked out across the river to the high ledge where Tyr and Azhur had talked together above the mists in a dawn that seemed to belong to a distant year. Behind the hills stood the sweeping rise of the Bhaniran, the retreating mountain snows making way for the familiar newness of spring.

If he had been used to probing his own mind, Tyr would have recognised sooner that the sensation sweeping over him in the high fields was a recognition of change. The world about him hadn't changed, even though he'd now seen more of it. Instead, change was happening inside of him and he did not yet grasp how.

Tyr left his stone and wandered over the pastures. He thought of Valderthaan, the Shrine, and Azhur—*Loremaster* Azhur, he reminded himself. Would Loremaster Azhur have gone climbing with a village-boy at sunrise? He felt a flurry of anxiety. If he went to the Shrine, could he count on Azhur's company? When there were no more visions or danger to talk about, other duties would no doubt consume his friend.

He stopped and stared hard at the green hills and the distant blue of the mountains. He wanted their permanence, their strength and safety, for his mind had suddenly filled with memories of fear and destruction. In such a short time away from these quiet hillsides he had seen violent death, terrible suffering, and the cold brutality of power's darker face.

383

Now he knew *he* was different.

Tyr realised he was hugging himself. Wildly, painfully, he looked about him for some kind of help to appear, but none arrived. The faces of the Arta woman and her child burned in his mind and the hills answered only *understand, decide*.

He recognised these experiences had become part of him. He was not a person who could bury such things and carry on with life unchanged. He knew he would never forget the works of darkness he had seen. Suddenly, understanding flowed. He had seen evil, but it had not laid hold of him. Something else had done that. In the holy song of Renewal Night, in fire-lit gold and the Shrine's great gloom, in the presence of the Chosen, and through the strangeness of his experience something unimaginable and vast had come near. Something at the heart of the Kingdom and, for all he knew, the world. It uttered itself through the chants, lay waiting in the ancient lore, came alongside the Valgraav's presence, and leapt up within the fires. It could be seen in all the privilege and responsibility of the priests, in both the wisdom and the dust, in the ink of crackling parchment, in the sweep of robes black and red, in the boots upon stone, and in the incense and the shadows under the great dome. It could be seen in the lives of all who lived in Valderthaan and beyond that great city in all who lived in the North. And yet it was none of these things and more than these things. It was beyond them and through them and contained them all and made each touch its own deep mystery. For a moment he remembered Ilissos' description of what had happened on the moors, but then turned back to what he knew. The unimaginable something had come to him through his own visions and the wash of joy that signalled the Fire-spirit's presence.

Did the wonderful being hover unseen above the fields, waiting to know his decision, helping in a way he did not perceive? He hoped so, glancing upward. But not today. The decision must be his, and the response must come from his heart alone.

That, he somehow knew, was the law of things.

~

IETHEN TRAILED HER HAND along the river grass and rushes. The water's steady flow seemed to her like the movement of their lives. Endless motion, a million currents, an easy surface over deep, deep places they might never see. Even in a place as quiet as Falakhoth, life flowed and was never at rest, despite appearances. The short time since the storm had been like turbulent rapids. How might their courses change, their banks overflow? She would have to wait.

Suddenly she was not alone. A little way ahead of her a woman sat at the river's edge. She was engaged in a game with a group of otters, fighting a gentle battle as she softly buffeted them, knocking them off their feet and keeping her fingers just out of their reach as they wriggled up again. A gown of green and white, like the newest ivy on cottage walls, hung about her, and over her shoulders swept a mantle of the deep, dark, shining green of ivy found on the homes of lords or wound around great forest trees. Her hair was a vivid, glowing red like the warmest autumn leaves and flowed about her in a rich, uncombable tangle. The woman wore no ornament—it would have been a foolishness to distract from her natural beauty—and the green dress was splendid, despite its clever simplicity.

Here, thought Iethen, was a great lady from the cities.

A long, noble face with skin like rose petals and wide, full lips tinted with berry-hues turned towards her. "Good day, Mistress Iethen." The woman smiled, natural as a breeze over a corn-field. This was no court lady, surely. There was not a trace of refinement or mannered pose about her, yet she was so stately, so *regal*.

"Good day to y', lady," said Iethen, strangely unsurprised at the sound of her name. She felt at ease in the woman's presence.

"Will you sit by me?" asked the lady. She spoke a soft word to the otters, and they threw themselves happily into the water.

Iethen settled by the woman, taking care not to sit on her moss-like gown. "Well, this is nice," she said. "Are y' from Valderthaan? Only, it's like I know y'. I never met y' there, did I?"

The woman smiled again. "I saw you," she said, "but we didn't speak." She looked carefully at Iethen. "What do you think Tyr will decide?"

Oddly, the mention of Tyr's name did not surprise Iethen either.

Word must have got about, she supposed, so she felt no need to ask. "Well, I think it's shapin' up for him to go to the city. I said to Tyrmar as how it wouldn't make sense if he didn't, after everythin' that's been happenin'. Tyr's like that too—thinkin' what things mean, like. He'll ask, *What's happened?* and he'll try to get a clue about what it means for him."

"What would you like him to do?" The woman sat poised, listening.

Iethen sighed, "Well, I want him to stay with us. I'm his mam after all, but...." In the silence, the lady patiently waited for her to continue. Iethen began again, "Y're a mother, I'd say. Y've got that look about y'. So, y' know how when they're little and they're on y' apron strings and never away from y'?"

"I do," said the lady.

"Well, it's lovely, havin' them close all the time, but then they want to move away from y' and explore and that, and not be tied to y' all the time."

"What was it like when Tyr did that?"

"Well, that's what I was goin' to say. Honestly, it hurt, and I wanted to pull him back and keep him with me. Tried it for a bit and we both had tempers about it. Then, one day Tyrmar says, 'Give over, Ieth. Let him be a boy.'"

"Did you?" asked the lady.

Iethen smiled at the memory. "Aye, I did. I didn't want no little puppet as does what his mam wants all his life, like that soppy wet butcher's lad at Lachresh—oh, he's a sad sight, he is—I've got to let my Tyr live and be his own wee self. I've not to be selfish. So, I've always tried to be like that with Tyr."

"Are you glad you've been like that?" asked the lady, smiling broadly.

"Oh, aye. I think we're all happier for it."

"I think you are. So now, what do you want him to do?"

Iethen laughed a little. "I want him to do what he really knows he ought to do. I hope he sees where he's supposed to go. He'd not be happy doin' anythin' else. Wouldn't be right." She dabbed at her eyes with her head-cloth. The lady took her hand.

"Have you no advice for him? Will you try to guide him?"

"Oh, no. It would all go round in his head and he might do the wrong thing. We've given him advice before, like y' do when they're growin', but all this is somethin' that's just to do with him, y' see. It's just happenin' to him, and what could we tell him?"

"Mistress Iethen, you are wise, loving and brave," the lady told her.

"Am I all that?"

"Oh, yes, they go together."

The two women embraced and rocked back and forth for a while.

"Oh, thank y'," said Iethen at last. "I do feel better. Mind y'...."

"Yes?"

"Well, I hope I won't worry. I mean, there's been such goin's-on up there, and this horrible priest with a long nose—"

"I'll look after Tyr," said the lady. "My husband will too."

"Oh, would y'?" said Iethen. "Oh, that's grand. I'll not worry now."

The lady rose and stepped away from the water.

"Are y' off, then?"

"I must meet my husband," the woman said.

Iethen saw she was barefoot. "I'll get your shoes, shall I?"

"My shoes are perfect," said the lady, and walked away lightly over the grass. The otters made a splash and turned Iethen's head. When she looked back towards the lady, she was alone.

~

TYR THOUGHT HE UNDERSTOOD, at least a little. The hills and the pastures were different because he was no longer seeing them as things he had come back to live with but as things he had already left. Valderthaan had birthed something in him. Alongside the awe and fear, a longing had been kindled for something beyond the vast mystery of joy that had moved over him like an unreachable cloud, parting at points to show a shining heart. It reminded him of the vast, dark storm cloud that had stooped over Falakhoth the day the brigands came for him, saving him by concealing Tharval's soldiers in the tempest's noise. He remembered his joy in its magnificence and terror, his longing for it, yet not for storm or cloud. He had yearned instead for the majesty shown through its stately progress over the sky. Not for the storm, but for the strength in it. To be a witness to something uncontrollable and immense, that could not be gainsaid, that was unimaginably higher than him and at the same time reached down to him.

Had the storm first awakened this longing? The storm that had given birth to his desire was but a symbol of the deep, unknown, compelling reality he now desired. Its existence spoke to him: *seek, seek, go deeper, go forward, enter.* It told him what he knew already: that he must not stand still.

For a moment, Tyr stood between two choices, two lives, two worlds. If he was to move towards the source of the longing, his way lay through the Shrine and the priesthood and his gift of vision. If he took no steps towards the mystery, he would dam up a river in his heart and might never feel that yearning again. With a clarity that made him shudder, to chase the beauty that reached out for his heart, even if the depth of his longing went unsatisfied, would be a life of joy and enrichment. Living the opposite would be less happy than if he had never known it at all.

Raising his eyes, he caught the glare of the western sun, scarlet and weary in the golden sky. It sank low, as the far mountains burned red and cooled to black. It looked as if it would settle like a diadem upon the topmost peak. It reminded him of the dazzling dawn sun at the crest of the Mardhoran and Naida's aged but joyful voice: *You goin' up to be a priest as well, then?*

Goin' up to be a priest?

~

Tyrmar awoke from a most consoling beer to find someone leaning through his doorway and looking at him across the room. The person continued the knocking that had roused him.

"Nodded off," slurred the headman. "Sorry." The visitor stood in the doorway with sharp spring sunshine behind him, so that all Tyrmar could make out was a dark outline. "Come in, come in." He heaved himself to his feet. "What can I do for y'?" The smith peered blearily at a man who he felt at once was his equal: tall, broad-shouldered, with a deep chest, and long, athletic limbs.

388

"Master Tyrmar?" he asked. "The headman?" He placed his right hand on his chest and gave a formal bow.

Tyrmar saw that, despite his obvious physical strength, his movements were controlled, even a little stately. A swordsman, perhaps, or a soldier of rank. The man straightened and his long brown coat swirled around him, exposing a lengthy embroidered tunic and elaborate belt from which hung an eloquently impressive decorated knife. The coat was edged with fur and he wore a fur-lined hat in the eastern style with long side flaps turned up and fastened over the crown. His crinkled, copper-brown hair was long, in the northern fashion, half-hiding an earring of enamelled bronze.

"Well now, Master," mumbled Tyrmar, trying to wake up. "What is it? Y' want y' horse shoe'd? Want a sword?"

"Well, no," said the man. "I saw you in Valderthaan, and you remember the players? I was in the area and here I am." He paused and smiled and the scar on his right cheek moved. Tyrmar noticed it was a tribal mark such as they used in the far north-west, a curve that went into a sharp diagonal surmounted by a smaller flourish. Not only was it a symbol of tribe membership, it was also a badge of a worshipper's allegiance to the tribe's god. The cheeks bore slight scarring, a legacy of some infection in youth, the worst of it partly hidden by a brown beard cut short with a cluster of golden hairs appearing on the chin. Intent, dark eyes were set beneath broad, expressive brows in a tanned, weathered face. "You knew Nauthrar the miller," continued the visitor.

Tyrmar was unsure whether it was a statement or a question, but he brightened at once. "Y' knew old Nauth?" The man smiled again, but did not answer. "Well, I'll be! Have a seat, Master, have a seat." He settled his guest onto the chair with three cushions and poured beer. "Ah, a fine feller Nauth was, a fine feller. How'd y' know him, then?"

The man took a deep swig. "A shame about his leg," he said.

"Oh, aye. Aye, terrible accident that were. Mind, he wouldn't watch out for them millwheels. *Nauth*, I says, *y'll get too close to them things one day and there'll be an accident, sure's fate.* And was I right? I was that. Daft bugger—beggin' y' pardon, but he was. Never walked right again."

"No, no," replied the man regretfully. He took more beer. "But he kept

389

that great spirit of his. It was greater than ever after the accident. It saw him through. You admired him very much."

Tyrmar reached for his mug. He was about to drink, but raised the mug aloft. "Aye, we all thought the world of Nauth. Here's to his memory." The headman took a long drink.

"Never gave up," said the man. "Always the adventurer."

"Aye, he'd come and do his bit with the harvest, bad leg or no. Even used to ride a horse till his back went."

"There was a story about a mountain..."

This got Tyrmar in full flow. "That's it, the mountain! Mad bugger climbed Master's Mount! By himself and all. Wouldn't have nobody helpin' him."

"The Bhaniran."

"As ever was. Of course, we all told him he was cracked, and he'd kill himself, but he says no. The whole town'd been up there that year but him and he had to go. He'd let himself down if he didn't."

"And he managed."

"He did. Took him a week there and back, with food and a blanket for sleepin'. When he got back y'd think he'd been to the sun. Kept sayin', I had to do it, I had to do it."

The stranger drained the last of his beer. He leaned back in the chair and crossed his legs. "So, your lad's going to be a priest."

There it was again: statement or question? "Well, don't rightly know. Word got round then, has it?"

"Oh, my wife and I know about lots of things at the city," said the weathered man. "We don't miss much."

"Is that so?" replied Tyrmar. "Well, I don't mind tellin' y' I'm worried about our Tyr and this priest business. Tyr's a country boy. I don't know if he's the sort for the Shrine and that. I mean, he's clever. He can do the learnin' and all, but it'll be hard for him if he goes. Not that I suppose it worries him."

Tyrmar's guest gave a smile, "He must have something of Nauthrar in him; the something you admired."

The headman stared at his visitor for some time.

"Do y' know, I reckon y' hit the nail on the head," he said at last.

"That's Tyr all over. He's never turned down a challenge. Thrived on them, in fact." He thought for a while. "Y' know, when Nauth come back down from Master's Mount, he says to me, *Tyrmar, it was like bein' right up in the heavens. I wasn't stuck in the valleys no more and everythin' looked different. Y' see it proper when y' get up high.* Never forgot that. Made me think."

"I wonder if there's something Tyr needs to see." The bearded man's remark seemed to hang with the dust-motes in the sunlit air.

Tyrmar leaned forward, elbows on knees, staring into the course of his son's life. "Well, he's always been one for seein' an' understandin' and thinkin'," he said quietly. "Doesn't get that from me, that's from his mam's side. But if there was somethin' needin' found out, somethin' that mattered for him, well, he'd be after it."

"Even if it was very difficult? Even a little risky?"

"Oh, aye. That'd draw him."

"You'd admire him for that. As you did Nauthrar."

Tyrmar looked up into the man's eyes, "Aye, I would. I brought him up to face things."

"And if he didn't face this? Would you think well of that?"

"No," said Tyrmar softly, "I wouldn't. If he turned his back, I'd be sorry." Silence surrounded them in a great well of pride and heart's feeling.

"Great light shine upon you, Tyrmar," said the strange man. "Your fatherhood is named from the One on High."

"Thank y' sir," said Tyrmar, a catch in his throat. "After seventeen years, it's good to hear that."

The man stood, "Well," he said, "I must meet my wife by the river." He went slowly to the door, then paused. "We'll be near Tyr in the city, so you needn't fear for anything."

"I'll not, then," Tyrmar told him. "Thank y' sir." The man stepped out into the sunshine and the headman stood thinking. Then he realised he did not even know who his visitor was and shook himself. He hurried to the door and stood leaning out, but the man was nowhere to be seen.

Only Verdje was walking across the square.

~

WANDERING IN THE GREEN PASTURE, throwing his thoughts at the northern sky for inspiration, Tyr decided a good meal was in order, and then some discussion with his parents. He wanted to eat at Wyrdha's house as was his norm, but the house was empty, as Tyr had seen on the way up to the fields. The healer was away near Braldhach on a kind of tour. He had various sufferers to look in on, a bone to set, and a birth that might prove very difficult. The hearty meal that Tyr would usually cadge from him would not be forthcoming. No matter, Wyrdha's finest fare was never a match for his mam's cooking. He could almost smell one of her stews.

He turned to stroll down the sloping field and halted.

Creeping up towards him were four huge wolves. They were going slowly, bodies near the ground, ready to spring. Yellow eyes stared wildly, black lips strained back from armouries of fangs. He saw each muscle tensing tight, taut before the leap, once would be enough.

With no idea why, Tyr snapped, "Sod off! This is nowt to do with you! Go on!" And for good measure he threw in *"Aiva sherrik!* Gerroff!"

The wolves jerked back and almost leapt in the air. They stood trembling for a moment, like dogs smacked on the muzzle, then flew off as if for their lives. They gave Tyr a wide berth and went racing up towards higher land and the moors. And that was that. The potential novice, whose career had almost been cut short before it had begun, stood blinking and bewildered. He supposed he should shake or gasp, but he felt not the slightest scrap of shock. He was more irritated than surprised because he'd said *Ai va sh'herakh* wrongly.

He grinned. "That's it, then," he said out loud. "I'll be a priest."

He took a deep breath and planted his hands on his hips. He turned to face Falakhoth and ran over the glowing fields towards the town. Wondering whether to tell his parents about the wolves, he decided not to. It was over and nothing had happened, so why give them something to worry about? There were more important things just now. He had to tell them how he must let his longing take him to Valderthaan.

He jumped the wall by Wyrdha's empty house and slowed to a stop.

The door was open with claw marks on the wood and things were scattered around outside. Tyr put his head inside to see ripped bedding and the healer's belongings everywhere. Bloody wolves. Ah, but they'd sort it all out before Wyrdha got back. He slammed the door and ran down the path to the town, elated, for he knew he was letting himself be drawn into something great and utterly mysterious.

Not once had he thought, *Arna wants me for a priest, I'll have to go.*

He was not answering, but seeking.

~

VERDJE SAT ON THE EDGE of the three-cushioned chair. "I've just come to tell y'," she said, head down. "Oh, Tyrmar, it's hard."

"Thal was a good feller," said Tyrmar. "We'll all miss him."

"Aye, I know, but that's not what I meant. There's somethin' I've got to do."

Iethen walked in peacefully through the door. "I met this lovely woman," she said. "Oh, hello, Verdje. What's up, love?"

"I'm leavin'," said Verdje, emboldened by female support. "Me and Utha. We're goin' to Lukar."

"Lukar? What, to live with Antha?"

"Aye. I can't stay here anymore, not without Thal. I must start again."

"Oh, wait a little while, love."

"No. It won't work, I know it." She took a breath and met Iethen's eyes. "I can't live here, just meself, seein' him every day."

"Y' dad?"

"Aye. If he hadn't said that to Thal...." Verdje's face reddened. Iethen took her hands, and she gripped them. "He knows he shouldn't have said it, but he won't admit it. And he won't look at me. He turns his head with that sour face he puts on as if it were my fault or Thal's fault—"

"Is that what he says?"

"He doesn't say nothin', but I can't stand it no more. I have these dreams, horrible dreams."

"Dreams, love? What dreams?"

"I, I keep seein' Thal sittin' on his grave holdin' the amulet that old

priest gave us, and he's sayin': *I'm not goin', I'm not goin'!* It's horrible!"
Verdje broke down as Iethen put her arms round her.

"Oh, Verdje. I think perhaps y' should go to Antha's."

"Bloody hell, aye," said Tyrmar. "Havin' dreams like that then livin'
with that old sod every day—beggin' y' pardon. Y' can't put up with that,
father or no father!"

Verdje nodded, gasping, and wiping her face. "I'm that glad y' said
that! Y're right, if I don't get away I'll... I don't know what I'll do."

"Bardcha's stoppin' here, then?" asked Tyrmar.

"He can stop where he likes," said Verdje. "Long's as it's not with me."

"Well, who'll run the inn, then? He's not up to it."

"I'm sellin' it."

"Oh, Verdje," sighed Iethen. "Are y' sure?"

"I am. There's this feller at Lachresh who was at Thal for years wantin'
to buy it off him, but y' know Thal—dug his heels in. So, just the other
day I sent a letter sayin' he could have it now if he still wanted it, and that
same evenin' he's at the door with a notary and a contract all ready for
me to sign. Didn't think twice."

"But what about y' dad?" asked Iethen.

"New feller's lettin' him stay on—I gave him a reduction. Dad can
keep his little room and he'll get fed and sit by the fire at night, long's he
makes himself useful."

"And is he happy with that?"

Verdje shrugged, no longer sacrificing herself to her father's bitter-
ness. "Don't know, he didn't say nothin'. Suppose so."

A silence. There was really nothing to say.

"Well, I hope y' got a good price," said Tyrmar at last.

Verdje gave a little smile. "Trust y', Tyrmar. Yes, I did as a matter of
fact. I might even give y' a few free ales before I go."

The door was suddenly booted open and Tyr walked in, his chest
heaving and his hair all over his reddened face.

"Y' all right, Tyr?" asked Verdje.

"Aye," said Tyr, taken aback. "Are y'?"

"Yes, I am," said Verdje. "Or I will be. Y' Mam and Dad will tell y' all
about it. Well, I can see y've got news, or somethin', so I'll leave y' to it.

Bye-bye, all." She left the house, her back straight at last.

Tyr stood staring at his parents as if braced for a fight. He truly did not know what to do. Iethen hugged herself and bit her lip, while Tyrmar clung to an empty beer mug, waiting. Tyr continued to pant after his long run, his moist eyes wide, lips trembling but not opening, mouth filled with words he could not speak. They all stood poised in silence on this pivotal point of their lives.

Tyr heaved a great breath into himself and said, "I'll miss y'."

And even as he moved towards his parents, arms out, there came shouting and the sound of a horse racing into the square. A villager threw himself into the house and staggered to a seat, trying to reclaim his breath.

"Ahrl," cried Iethen, "what's up!"

Ahrl drew his fingers over his face and through his hair.

"I've just come up from Braldhach," he managed, hands still gripping his skull. "Wyrdha's dead!"

CHAPTER 19

A Novice in the Dark

WYRDHA WAS LAID IN the earth not far from Thaljhaz. It was grimly fitting, for they had come there by the same means, a wolf attack at almost the same place, the area near the trees at Braldhach Falls where a predator could easily creep up. It was possibly even the same beast, to judge by the bites. Or so they had been told. The body had arrived at Falakhoth firmly sewn up and readied for burial by the people who had found him.

"Y' really don't want to look," they had said. "So, we thought we'd get him ready ourselves and spare y', like." The kindly people had known Wyrdha well and were well known in Falakhoth. They mentioned a birthmark and produced clothes and belongings that everybody knew belonged to the healer. It was enough. No-one was prepared to endure the sight of what the merciful cloth contained.

Everyone at the funeral stood shocked, as the body, formless within a sewn-up cloth, was lowered into the damp ground. It jolted as if to remind them how dreadfully real it all was. Tyr shuddered as the pallet came to rest and the round shape at the top shook a little as only a man's head can. It was a cruel reminder that there was no undefined shape under the cloth but a person, his friend.

For Tyr, there was extra pain, for he had never told his friend what he had decided about the priesthood. A few days before he had gone to the High Fields to seek his mind, Wyrdha had started off for Braldhach with his medicines and they had walked for a while beside the river.

"You haven't asked me," the healer had asked.

"Asked y'?" said Tyr absently. He was enjoying the brushing sensation as his long legs swung through the tall riverbank grasses.

"For my opinion or for my advice. You usually seek my guidance so eagerly."

"Aye," said Tyr, and filled the awkward moment by slashing at ferns with the stick he usually carried on walks like this. He had suddenly realised how much older he had become. "Well, the sort of thing it is, means I thought it's got to be me as decides. Just me."

Wyrdha continued to stare at the path, listening.

"There's that many thoughts in me head, see, and it's just me that knows what they mean. I've got this feelin' it's just me who can sort them out." Tyr paused. His friend's silence made him continue, "It's not y'—I mean, it's not like I thought y'd tell me somethin' wrong, like—it's just got to come out of my head and nobody else's. Y' know, just me." He glanced at Wyrdha. "Is that all right?"

Wyrdha turned, looked deeply and lovingly at Tyr, and smiled. "Thank goodness for that," he had said. And that was all. Tyr had gone home with his thoughts and Wyrdha had gone on to Braldhach.

And now he would never know.

A few days after the funeral, a messenger from the Shrine arrived to ask Tyr what he had decided. Tyr declared his acceptance of a place in the novitiate without showing much excitement. The messenger, an intense junior priest, was taken aback, and lectured Tyr on how most lads his age would leap at the chance to go to the Shrine. Tyr heard none of it. The messenger gave up and got him to write his name and his father's name on some parchments, then he put a seal over the names. He handed Tyr a small pile of parchments that told him the when, where, who, and how of what would happen next.

Later, Tyr read out the parchments to his parents—who listened as if they were hearing a recital of the Scrolls—and later to anyone who was interested, which was most of the town. Heads shook and benedictions were offered, with a hundred variations on "Our Tyr, eh? Who'd have thought?"

The exception, inevitably, was Bardcha. Tyr went to tell him his news out of a sense of obligation more than anything and felt a flash of pity at the sight of the visibly ageing figure hunched at the door of the inn. Bardcha seemed to wither daily, sinking into himself as, one by one, he brought down his bridges to the world around.

"Shrine, eh?" he said from somewhere far within his chest. An eye flicked up but failed to connect with Tyr. "Wish y' well of it. It'll be better than here." The eye dropped to the ground again and Bardcha's response to the revolution in Tyr's life was over.

Less than encouraged, the budding novice took his parchments into the inn where he found a more enthusiastic welcome.

"Shrine? Fancy! Well, we'll be at Lukar," said Utha, glowing with anticipation. "Y' can come down and see us!"

"Oh aye," said Tyr guardedly.

"That's if she's got time for y'," remarked Verdje.

"Mam! Stop it!"

"Time?" repeated Tyr, fearing the worst.

"Aye, she'll be *busy*, y' know?"

Tyr didn't know. Whatever it was, Verdje found it highly amusing and Utha did not. Utha left briskly to some task away from her mam.

Verdje handed Tyr some bread and cheese and seated herself by the fireside log-pile.

"Mistress Verdje, I'll not be weddin' Utha." Tyr blurted, deciding this might be a good time to unburden himself. "I mean, there's nothin' wrong with her, I just—"

Verdje laughed. She leaned forward conspiratorially, glancing about to make sure her daughter was definitely out of earshot. "Tyr-shan," she said, mock-serious, "eat y' bread. As one that knows, let me tell y', y'll have no worries on that score."

Tyr gaped for a moment. "Oh," he said. "Well, that's all right then."

Turning serious, Verdje asked quietly, "How are y' managin' without Wyrdha?"

Tyr gripped his wooden plate and his lips tightened. "It were a shock, but—well, I'd have been goin', anyroad."

"Not the same though, is it?"

Tyr shook his head.

"Y're never ready, not really. Same with Thal."

Tyr wiped his eye. He bit deeply into the bread and cheese for something to do, then found he could not swallow. "He was always showin' me things. Taught me to read." A cough, another bite. Another recollection would burst the dam.

"Y'll be keepin' on with the healin' though?" asked Verdje.

"Aye, aye. He wanted me to have his healin' things. He left them for me in his will."

"What, that great big bag he took about?"

"Aye. Other stuff as well, special stuff."

"Well! We'll call on y' if we're poorly. Y' could earn a bit in Lukar."

Tyr didn't know what to say to that, so he quickly finished his bread and cheese, thanked Verdje, then ran across the square to the forge. There, he found a space to cry in peace.

After a while, Tyr wiped his eyes, blew his nose, and went to the corner where he had laid his few possessions out ready to go into his saddlebags. He took up a large leather satchel and stared at it red-eyed. Two new tears ran down his face. He squatted by the pallet that was his bed and took from the satchel several objects he set out on the blanket. Blades, bottles, various tools, a mortar and pestle, a set of brass scales, and long-handled spoons with carefully graded bowls. There was something for almost any disaster. Here were the saws for removing hopelessly shattered limbs or other bony parts that had to go. Tyr had seen Wyrdha do this twice, rasping the metal business-like through a thigh. He hoped he would never have to do it himself. Here were the various tweezers for removing splinters of metal or bone from a wound or wherever they should not be and here were other tweezers that held the wound open while you worked. Here were the gossamer-sharp blades that pared off torn flesh or opened the way to deeper troubles. Here were the magnifying lenses, the dressings, the cauterising lamp, the probes, drills, funnels, syringes, tubes, and pinchers that extended the reach and skill of able fingers. Wyrdha had availed himself of everything new, everything proven, hopeful, and ingenious to serve mankind, and now he had passed his bag and his mission to Tyr.

The next day, the future Baranthu Tyr-shan, priest and healer, sat on the horse the junior priest had brought with him from Valderthaan. Strapped to one side of his saddle were Wyrdha's bag and some scrolls his friend had left for him, and balancing the weight on the other side was a bundle of his clothes and some parting gifts.

The whole town, down to the smallest child, huddled together on the King's Road. The two horses were ready to go. Tyr twisted in the saddle and surveyed the people who had nurtured his life, shaped his soul, and been his world. He looked at the fields, at the roofs of the houses visible over the trees, and up at the hill where Wyrdha's empty home could just be seen, then back down at his friends—even grumpy Bardcha was there—and lastly at his parents proudly weeping.

Tyr braced himself for the final terrible wrench of leaving. Almost everything within him wanted to get off the horse, tell everybody he'd changed his mind and climb up to the forge for a bowl of stew. Almost everything. *I hope I'm doing the right thing.* He gave one more wave, through a deep, empowering breath.

He faced the road, kicked the horse, and moved off.

During the long ride to the city, the junior priest took it upon himself to pump Tyr full of instruction and information. Far from being helpful, this constant barrage was only effective in creating a sense of foreboding. He wondered if someone had specifically chosen this officious escort to bewilder him and lessen his confidence. This seemed a strange idea, so he dismissed it and tried to remember as much of what the priest was saying as he could. He thought he'd managed fairly well—for him, at least—but his attention lasted only as far as Lukar. When he caught sight of the dark fingers of the Towers of the Wound, his concentration found itself worn so smooth by the endless verbal millstone it could no longer find any purchase on his companion's declamation. His mind rippled away to more interesting things, which meant, in this situation, almost anything. By the time he passed between the monstrous statues on Valderthaan's Bridge for the second time, his thoughts were absorbed in such deep matters as the quality of food at the Shrine and whether they had baths. He continued pondering these as his companion dismounted at the great gate and offered fire at the little altar, as Azhur had done a world ago.

Tyr breathed in a warm anticipation at the thought of seeing his friend again. He had sent him news of Wyrdha's death, and Azhur had replied with a beautifully crafted letter of sympathy for Tyr and the whole village, complete with meticulously chosen sayings from someone nobody had ever heard of. Still, they were comforting and Tyr had felt a glow of friendship from the parchment that had eased those bleak days.

The priest finished his offering, mounted, and they moved on towards the gate. Soon they were through and in Valderthaan's first level. Tyr stared around the broad open space where he had seen the beggars gather and witnessed the Fire-spirit's blessing over the poverty-ridden young mother. He was at once alert. Perhaps, he thought, he would see the incandescent form again. Perhaps the fiery spirit *lived* here. What a start to his novitiate if he received the burning benediction again. He looked around, hoping and afraid, in case the wonderful figure should step through into the mouldering grey reality of the first level, but there was nothing. Not even the beggars. At this hour, they were all deployed at their appointed stations or huddling in whatever space served them for a home. Only Val-Nhakh'hant'than's crumbling, artless statue was there to welcome Tyr to Valderthaan. He supposed it was better than nothing and rode on.

The horses laboured up the multitudinous ramps, paths, streets, hills, and ascending ways until Tyr found himself once more in the paved area before Shrinegate. He craned his neck up towards the parapet over the gate, to the spot where his wild sword-swing had saved Jarthastra from the jaws of the springing wolf. He felt again the judder down his arms as the blade hacked into the beast's neck. The lower vantage-point helped him imagine Vashira's ghastly experience that dawn, his eyes following an imaginary wolf's-head soaring down from the parapet, streaming gore as it flew, and then landing on you. Had it knocked her over? He had never found out. He hoped wickedly that it had, if only to give him a spectacle to relish in his thoughts. True, he would have missed it, but it would have been almost as good to know that it had happened.

He glanced over to the house of the Daughters of the Moon and wondered what they did all day, besides feeding the poor. Whatever it was, he couldn't imagine it was very interesting.

The afternoon slipped by and a grey wind swirled about Shrinegate. The beggars stationed nearby abandoned any hope of enrichment from the moon-women and scuffed away. Tyr's priest had been engaged in an intense exchange with two red-robed figures by the gate and now returned.

"Right," he said, then mounted and took them on a westerly course along a street that curved around the wall of the Shrine Court and below the vast, impassive bulk of the Shrine itself. Lights appeared among its stones, and far above the incalculable mass of Na-veshtrazhdak's tower challenged the sky with the confidence of centuries. He could just see Arna's golden image, glowing weakly in the dusk.

The curving street ended in a small square with a few shops built onto the wall, a high block of houses opposite, and a dignified stairway down to the second level. Ahead of Tyr and his guide was a heavy door overlaid with elaborate iron patterns and flanked, inevitably, by two impressive statues. Tyr didn't bother to ask who they were. He would undoubtedly hear it from Azhur soon enough. Door and statuary took up most of the distance between wall and steps. A parapet that hemmed the street beside the stairs prevented a rapid plunge to the doorsteps of the houses that were built against the sheer rock. Over the broad door was something that could have been a battlement or balcony with an elaborate, gloomy arch recessed into the wall behind it. Above, the wall rose stone by stone, gripping the windows, parapets, and carven figures until it joined the climbing, layered immensity of the Shrine and its cluster of attendant buildings.

They took the horses up to the door, halting by the feet of an imposingly disinterested image. The priest leaned out from his saddle and hauled on a massively elaborate bell-pull. A brazen clang sounded in some distant place and after a while a little panel opened in the solid door and someone in a dark robe leaned out.

"Oh," said a youthful voice. "Is that him?"

"It is, master Authran," said the priest. "Do your duty and I'll be off."

"Oh," said a youthful voice. "Is that him?"

"Sure?" asked Authran. "It's stew."

"All the more reason," was the flat reply, and the priest wheeled his horse and made off back towards Shrinegate.

"Silly minion," remarked Authran. "Tyr-shan, wasn't it?"

"Aye," said the new arrival. "I like Tyr better."

Authran tilted his head mock-rudely on one side. "Do you, though? Well, good. A bit more pally, eh? I'm Authran, Archpriest in the making. I'm to look after you. Hang on." He withdrew and closed the panel.

There came a great noise of bolts and the snapping, springing working of hidden devices and half the high door inched slowly inward to the sound of agonised noises from Authran as he heaved. An aperture established, he came around and shoved mightily with his shoulder until there was space enough for the horse and its jutting baggage.

Authran sagged against the door and made a breathless hooting noise, then held up a hand. "No, that's all right," he said. "Don't worry, I'll manage. Takes two or three fellows usually, but all's well. Come on."

Tyr urged his horse through the narrow opening and into the pool of light flung out by Authran's lantern. His baggage bumped and scraped on the door's edge but, with care, he got through and found himself in a long, ornate corridor whose dimensions matched that of the door. He realised with amusement he was automatically looking around to see where the statues were and found them lining the corridor. The lantern could not reach that far, so the figures were mostly only shadowy shapes, strengthening the feeling of being watched. The corridor's farther end was open and appeared to lead into one more court, cloistered this time.

"Give a hand, will you?" gasped Authran, applying himself to the inside of the door. "These hinges stick."

Tyr got down and rammed his shoulder onto the wood beside Authran and with the strength he had brought from Falakhoth the great stubborn thing grated, whined, and began to move. The two lads shared their strength against their massive, creaking, iron-bound foe. With their muscles straining, an elated Authran grinned at Tyr, and the newcomer laughed the coarse, genuine laugh of a village festival.

"Come on, y' bugger!" Tyr shouted. "Shut!"

Authran yelled with delight and they both renewed their effort against their wooden enemy. The lads glanced at each other, realising a bond of friendship was naturally and mysteriously forming, unplanned but inevitable because of who they were.

Creaking and groaning, the door gave ground, then moaned defeat with a final dying boom. Authran dragged on metal rings and bolts, and levers leapt to secure the defeated foe. The lads gave victory yells and slapped each other's palms.

"So much for the *bugger!*" proclaimed Authran, relishing the exaggerated emphasis. The shocking, wicked forbiddenness of the word wonderfully liberating to the novice priest.

"Aye," gasped Tyr, breathless. All at once he felt the weariness of his long ride. "What about this stew then? What about me stuff?"

"Oh," said his lifelong friend of thirty seconds. "Oh, yes. You've got the bunk under me, so that's good. Now, take your horse down there, where our porter will see to him. Very good job you came on a Wednesday."

"Is it?" said Tyr, expecting to hear how Arna especially blessed that day. "Why?"

"The stew! It's always stew on a Wednesday, Arna shine on it." Authran grinned massively in a way that Tyr already felt was a sacrament of their friendship. It was so easily summoned—and so many teeth. Authran whacked his charge solidly on the shoulder. "Bags to the dorm, then down to the Wait."

"What's the Wait?"

"For the stew," declared Authran with astonished earnestness, as one addressing a benighted foreigner. "You have the stew in the Wait." He took the horse's reins and started off. "Come on Tyr-shan, you're a novice now, enjoy it."

And with such high pomp and ceremony, Tyr-shan of Falakhoth entered the Tower of the Novitiate by the Gate of the Evening Stair. Its heavy door had closed upon his life hitherto. It was a small feature of the Tower's subsequent history that its door was known to the city's novices as the Bugger from this point on.

The Wait, as Tyr discovered, was the huge, vaulted hall where the black-clad novices gorged their stew, wallowed in a hubbub of clutter, indulged their disrespect for their tutors, threw bread rolls at one another, and if they could get away with it enjoyed the occasional fight. It was a haven of camaraderie and relative freedom where the youths who would grow into those who maintained cult and empire for Lord Arna forgot their awesome calling and reverted to the people they believed or truly wished they were.

"The Refectory of the Wait For Dawn," said Authran grandly. "Take your seat, Tyr-shan."

Tyr stepped down through the high-arched entrance to the hall. He felt horribly conspicuous as the only lad without a black coat. There seemed to be a blaring trumpet that announced his shameful newness, the insolent arrival of an outsider. Eyes burned into him, talk turned to his demerits, and he was utterly resented. Or so he felt. Edging along to a space on the bench at the nearest of the long tables, he wondered what mysterious understandings filled the heads bent over their bowls, what ancient knowledge was brimming in their brains. Had these fellows also felt the pull that came through the Shrine, the enchanted mystery that had drawn him in? He supposed so, but then he remembered some priests he had met and doubted if they had felt the same as he. But no matter. He, Tyr-shan, was here and a priest he would be.

The two novices sat backwards on a bench, then swivelled their feet over it and under the table. Long-limbed Tyr bumped his knees.

"Dignity," said Authran, mock-serious. "Show a bit of dignity."

Tyr slumped forwards, village-style, with his elbows on the table and looked around the trembling light-pools of the lantern-lit hall. Above him, on the high ceiling carved with shapes and shadows, dangled the broad metal hoops that carried the host of candles. Hangings were softly alive in the yellowed light that fastened on the amber pages of scrolls and papers and half-written treatises that their owners had flung on the seats and benches around the walls while they attended to their meal. At one end of the hall was a great, broad fireplace that looked to Tyr like a small room. The logs heaped within it were crackling. To its left was a wide arch billowing smells and steam from a kitchen. Servants moved constantly, refilling the cauldrons on a big oak table and hefting huge bowls of steaming vegetables. All this reassured Tyr. He took food seriously.

"What's that wait for dawn thing about?" he asked Authran.

"Ah. The Refectory of the Wait For Dawn. Well, you're sitting in it."

"Oh," said Tyr, still not entirely illumined. "The Wait?"

"The very same. You see, we all wear black? Well, when you're consecrated, when you're a full priest, you wear red and get the gold sun to wear—"

"Aye, I know that," Tyr broke in. "Me friend's a priest. His name's va-Kherzir, I've seen his ring and the sun and all—"

Suddenly Authran sat up. "va-Kherzir? Is he serving here?"

"Oh aye, he's Loremaster, Second Circle."

Authran's mouth flapped open. "*Azhur?* Well! Azhur! Oh, all the gods! Oh, Arna's wings! Azhur made history! He ate in this hall only weeks ago! Oh, Ar-ven's beard!" He held his face in his hands, still in shock, then slapped himself about the brows to restore some measure of calm. But it was too much. He could not contain the news and swung round to shout at the older lads sitting nearby. "Look, here's Wringer's chum! New fellow knows Wringer!"

Heads whipped round, their stares burning into Tyr.

"Shut up," he hissed. "I want me tea!"

Authran clapped him on the shoulder. "Oh. Now! We don't have a personal friend of an Anthu very often. Wringer! Well! How'd you meet him?"

"He was in our village, got caught in the rain." The memory of his first meeting with Azhur stabbed at him, for it had been at Wyrdha's house. Wyrdha, side by cold side with Thaljhaz, far away in the earth at Falakhoth. A horrid empty pain welled up in Tyr's chest and gripped at his throat. To shake it away he swallowed and asked, "What do y' call him Wringer for?"

"Oh, you know, that thing he does with his hands when he's nervous." And Authran gave a very passable imitation of an agitated Azhur twisting his fingers together.

Tyr had to laugh. "Aye, that's him. Go on about that wait thing, though."

"Oh, yes. Well, when you're a full priest, you wear the red and gold. It's a manifest representation—"

407

"Y' what?"

"Representation? Oh, you'll do all that, it's a symbol, sort of. They say Arna's risen upon you, sort of like the sun, when you're consecrated, so that's what red and gold stand for. They're sun-colours."

"Well, what do y' wait for?" said Tyr, lost.

Authran held up didactic fingers. "When does the sun come up?"

"Er... dawn?"

"So, dawn is sunrise, the red and gold. What do you have before sunrise?"

"Ey, I'm not daft," said Tyr, who had milked cows and tended sheep at all hours, and was feeling like a child being taught to count.

"I know," said Authran, determined about his precise explanation, "but what's before?"

"Nothin', it's dark!"

"Precisely, yes. And what do we wear?"

Tyr sagged in relief with the end in sight. "Oh. Right. Black." He slumped over the table with his head on his folded arms and his eyes closed. "Aye right. Y're a novice and y're waitin' to be a priest, so y've got black on and y' have y' tea in the Refectory for waitin'. Right, got it. Bloody hell."

"Yes, I know it sounds complicated," said Authran with a hint of apology. "Bit of a bugger, I think you'd say, but you can't just talk normally in the priesthood, oh no. You have to dress it up a bit."

"Daft idea, that."

"It enhances and makes manifest the transcendent numinous that permeates the religion and cult of Arna both in the whole and in the multitude of its parts and facets."

Tyr stared. "Y' never thought that up y'self."

"Well, no. Zhirakhrat'thar the Analytical said it. It's handy for remembering things, but you'll—"

"—do all that. Will I have to?"

"Of course you will. You'll love it."

And with that disputable statement, Tyr felt a prodding sensation in an unexpected region and turned to find himself looking up at a mountainous woman whose canopy of an apron bore an absorbed and absorbing display of that week's menus. Her broad red face glowed with effort and she was puffing from the side of her mouth, trying to reposition the strand of brownish-yellow hair that flopped down from beneath the broad, greasy kitchen cap. One hefty hand and arm held a massive tankard, the other a large steaming bowl. The stew had arrived.

"You're the new un," stated the woman. "Here's yer tea." She thumped tankard and bowl onto the table.

"Greitha, this is Master Tyr-shan," offered Authran. "Tyr, meet Greitha. As sweet and succulent as the stew she bears to us."

"Less lip, yer cheeky bleeder." Greitha swung a hand at Authran, missed, then ambled off to her kitchen lair.

"She likes it really," said Authran. "But she can't let on. We all love her to bits."

Tyr began on the stew and was impressed. The bowl was pewter for a start, and the stew itself had less meat than he wanted but more than he expected. There was a generous presence of vegetables, many creative little herbal flurries, and huge slabs of bread in a dish on the table. He remembered the startlingly superb soup at *The Cure*, the inn at the Potters' Square where Azhur had taken him on his first day in the city. And where was his friend, come to think of it? He had expected a welcome in person but, well, Loremasters must be busy, especially Second Circle ones. Wringer, though! He'd embarrass him with that. He might be with Aienna, right enough...

Tyr stopped tearing up his bread, realising he was jealous. His brow creased, and he grimaced. Didn't he like Aienna? Wasn't it lovely to see Azhur and her together? Wasn't he glad to see his friend come alive when she looked at him? Yes, yes, and yes.

But he was jealous anyway.

He plunged his bread into the stew then chewed on it as if to exact revenge. Dark, new thoughts swarmed behind his eyes.

"Now then, Tyr, here's someone I want you to meet," intruded Authran's voice.

Tyr looked up, chewing. Across the table, an older lad stood looking down on him with a vague smile of curious amusement.

"Friend of Wringer's, I believe," he said, sizing Tyr up with dreamy eyes. "Well, well."

"This is La'auchrad," began Authran, showing more than a little deference to the elegant youth, who cleared his throat and smoothed his neat auburn hair. "So sorry, *Baranthu* La'auchrad."

"I thought only priests was Baranthu," said Tyr a little curtly.

"Oh, they are," La'auchrad informed him, "but we call seniors of the novitiate, final year men like myself, Baranthu. If the Masters believe they merit it, that is." He cast his eye over the jewelled amulet bound to his left hand, where it offset the perfect fingernails. "Wringer got through. I expect you know that."

"Not the time, Lauch," attempted Authran.

"Aye," said Tyr, head lowering.

La'auchrad scanned the nails of his right hand and rubbed at the monstrously stunning rings. "Well, Arna shine on you. I always like to meet the new boys. Are you here for three years or five?"

"Dunno. They haven't said."

"I see. Well, I'm a five-year man. Year in the Shrine next, then probably end up in provincial administration. Possibly ambassadorial work. I think I'd like that. What about yourself?"

"Hadn't thought. Just see, I suppose," replied Tyr evenly, with the feeling that La'auchrad didn't think he was there. He was detesting this fellow heartily. He reminded him of a youthful edition of Bal-jarrak. Even the nose...

"Where did you say you were from?" asked La'auchrad, drifting on to another tack. "Only, I can't place the accent. It's certainly not Ceorthas."

Tyr opened his mouth, but Authran leapt in with, "Tyr's from Falakhoth."

"Falakhoth," murmured La'auchrad as though he had learned of an obscure disease. "Falakhoth? No, there you have me."

"Arcorath," said Authran hurriedly. "By Bhaniran, I think."

"Oh, the valleys? Oh, got it now. Farming community, isn't it?"

"Aye, it is," said Tyr with growing menace. "Me dad's the headman."

La'auchrad forced his features into a suitably impressed expression that eloquently expressed his utter disdain. "Really? Well, I'm sure your father's very excited at the honour. You've done your community proud.

Not every day—"

"I got invited," snapped Tyr, mentally drawing an unseen sword. "They *asked* me up here. Weren't my idea."

A few lads got up and moved away. Authran had reached out a restraining hand to Tyr.

La'auchrad, all unaware, continued to stoke the fire he had kindled. "Invited?" he said with a little lopsided smile. "Well, of *course* you were; that's *very* nice for you. But I suppose you *would* be invited, you'd have to be, really. Normally it's just assumed—well, you know—people from the cities, certain strata—"

"I like the valleys," Tyr told him from deep in his throat. The unperceived sword threw sparks from an invisible whetstone.

"Oh, don't misunderstand me, I'm sure you'll do well. There's lots of little jobs you can do as a priest. I'm not denigrating the villages—I wouldn't. I've known lots of very capable peasant lads just like yourself. With just a little help and effort—"

The bowl of stew flew into La'auchrad's face and Tyr was over the table like a hungry lion. The Baranthu slammed on the floor with the weight of a hard-worked, well-fed son of Falakhoth on him and a forearm used to pinning down sheep firm across his throat.

"Y' snotty bugger!" spat the capable peasant.

An admiring roar of *wohhhhh* went up from the novices and a rhythmic clapping and stamping began.

La'auchrad fought back, furious, not courageous, striking and clawing as best he could, but Tyr made his defence with a single swing of his forge-trained fist. A crack, a howl, and all the fight went straight out of his foe.

Tyr sat astride him, both hands forced down on his shoulders. "Take it back!" he roared. "Take it back or I'll give y' another! Say y' sorry! Say it!" La'auchrad forced an apology through his teeth, but Tyr shook him. "Again! Say it like y' mean it!"

Stronger hands grabbed onto Tyr's shoulders and hauled him away, up and on to his feet. The clapping and stamping faded to a trembling hush and Tyr writhed in the grip of two guardsmen.

"Hold still son," whispered one. "Make it easy."

411

But Tyr showed his teeth and struggled harder, so angry was he.

"I see you've met my nephew," said a voice he hated. The Keeper of the Fires himself, the Anthu Bal-jarrak of the Second Circle.

Tyr froze in horror for a moment, but he glanced at the arrogant La'auchrad struggling off the floor and remembered Bal-jarrak's vile treatment of Azhur and himself, and his anger blossomed again. Fortified, he stood proud against the hateful priest.

"You've arrived," said Bal-jarrak unnecessarily, drawing himself up in his impressive and utterly ineffective way.

"He hit me," sputtered La'auchrad, face grimed with stew and blood.

"We will leave that matter for the moment," replied his uncle meaningfully. "Is it broken?"

La'auchrad was fingering the elegant but bloody family nose. "Don't think so," he said. "Only just here, uncle, he's no right."

"Indeed, he has not," said Bal-jarrak, serpent-like. "Go to the Master of Physick, then come to me later."

La'auchrad wiped his bloodied hand on a young novice's coat and savagely elbowed away through the black-clad crowd. Tyr received a look of surpassingly malevolent contempt over his shoulder, another family trait.

Bal-jarrak's lizard head swivelled round until he fastened a similar stare on Tyr. "To be brief," he said, "I am here *on behalf* of our Lord Valgraav to bid you welcome to the Novitiate of the Sun." The words slid out of him like an ice-floe; they were indeed not his own. "Also," the priest continued, almost with a strange hint of warmth, "I am to inform you, you shall have an attendant, a guard, who will *watch* over you." The emphasis was very much on *watch*. "And here he is, the Baranthu Maurdjil va-Khradh'hir."

A man behind him stepped forward, much as a hunting lion would step into a clearing where a terrified goat strains at its tether: relaxed, slow, but watchful and ready. He wore a deep red version of a priest's coat with flames and a lion head embroidered flamboyantly across the chest and on the cuffs where his hands were crossed in front of him. Two large, melancholy eyes welled out of his heavy, sallow face. Set among many deep grey circles, they floated under two broad, dark brows. Shadows clustered at the corners of the heavy lids and across the man's wide, silent mouth. His chin and neck were of the kind that can never quite be fully shaved, so that a weighty shade seemed to cling about the lower edge of his features and drag them down. He did not make a bow but merely inclined his head without taking his eyes from Tyr. A long, deep scar at the side of his face came into relief as he moved. Here was a man who clearly knew his business.

"The Baranthu will visit you later," announced Bal-jarrak, and Maurdjil stepped back again. For a moment Tyr thought Bal-jarrak was leaving, but suddenly the priest moved forward, thrust his head close to Tyr's ear and, low and passionate, hissed, "Listen, wonder boy, you've seen nothing any peasant drunk on his filthy beer couldn't see. You farm-hands never understood Arna. You're an insult to this Shrine. If you weren't Jarthastra's pet I'd have you scrubbing latrines. Don't expect an easy ride." He straightened up and squared his narrow shoulders like a blood-spattered conqueror after a desperate trial of courage, then curled one corner of his lips, raised one eyebrow. "Well, study hard. May you realise all your potential." The priest smiled in a twisted little way that altered the shape of one nostril, thus, he felt, subtly expressing his belief that Tyr's potential was tiny. Then he swivelled on his heel and swept away, a motion that failed entirely to create the intended impression of grandeur, except in his own mind.

The guardsmen released Tyr. One patted his back, the other grinned and vigorously held up one thumb before they followed the departing priest. Maurdjil stared intently and expressionlessly before he left too, languid and stately.

Tyr rubbed his pinched arms and looked around for support. The novices were standing round-eyed, slack-jawed, still paralysed by de-lighted, reverential shock. Greitha was there, astounded and rocklike, one hand over most of her bloodless face, the other clasping a leather tankard to the battlements of her bosom as if to protect it. Their hero glanced down and considered the cold, greasy splatter on the floor.

"Er, sorry." he said with a grimace. "Anybody got a mop?"

Nobody moved.

Then, hesitantly, someone on the far side of the hall started a slow stamp. Authran took it up and added a vigorous, rhythmic handclap. More joined and the Wait quickly filled with an unbridled thunder to honour the victorious son of Falakhoth. Tyr gaped round at his inky swathe of worshippers, laughed and scratched his head. He threw out his arms to the acclaim as Authran hugged him and pounded his back.

When something like order returned, Tyr noticed Greitha. She was still staring at him, but her cheeks were joyful scarlet, she had dropped the tankard and both hands were clasped on that protective bosom, battlements no longer but hills that rose and fell in the earthquake of her admiration.

"Er," said Tyr again. He coughed, wiped his nose, and rubbed his stomach. "Can I have more stew?"

~

"You DID WHAT?" gasped Azhur.

"Smashed his stupid long nose," exulted Tyr. "And then his miserable uncle comes in, Bal... Bal... him! Anyway, hates me, he does. Do y' have to do y' lore with him?"

"No, no," said Azhur, grimacing. "But do be careful. Bal-jarrak's in the Second circle too and I... well, I have to get on with him."

"He hates you too," Aienna told him. "Why should you?"

"It helps. It's easier. Tyr, please don't hit that lad again."

"Hit who I like," Tyr affirmed. "He'll get what for from me if he talks about our folk like that."

"You can't hit a senior priest's nephew."

"Bugger that. He's not sayin' that in front of me. What's it to you anyway, Twister?"

Azhur gaped and Aienna trilled her tinkling laugh, rocking with mirth. She pointed, and the Loremaster knew he had locked his fingers in another round of their endless combat. His hands whipped apart and searched for pens to hold or pockets to hide in. Finding none, they set to hugging his middle and scratching his beard.

"Who told—they shouldn't have!"

But Tyr was convulsing hilariously on the Loremaster's couch, gripping his stomach. Trapped by this pincher movement of mirth, Azhur could do nothing but join in.

At last, Tyr wiped his eyes, sat up and said, "Are y' comin' to see me dormitory?"

"Well, no. I can't."

"Ey! Why not?"

"Well, for one thing, I saw it every day for years. I had one of the big alcoves with the curtains, at the far end."

"Oh, right. But y' can show me how to get in and out."

"Use the door, Tyr."

"No, I mean when it's late and y've been out. Is there a window they leave open or a little door they forget about, that kind of thing?"

"Oh, I don't know..."

"Ah, guilt by association?" asked Aienna knowingly. She ambled across the room to Azhur and leaned lazily against him, arms about his waist. She rubbed her forehead against his chin and looked up. "Come on, Wringer," she crooned. "You're getting too serious. Don't do that to me."

The Loremaster placed his red-robed arms around his lady and grinned haplessly in a delighted, molten embarrassment. Tyr saw it and smiled. Aienna was turning Azhur like a gem against the light so he could see new, bright-lit facets of his friend. It was a happy discovery. And then the little jealous dragon twisted in his chest with a reminder that Azhur *could* be spending those minutes installing him in the dormitory. It spoiled the moment. Tyr sighed and twisted his mouth. He was feeling many contradictory things all at once and didn't know if his heart had the room.

"What about it, then?" he asked, deliberately pulling Azhur's attention back to himself and feeling shamed.

His friend raised his brows and opened his mouth. Aienna put her head on one side in gently amused coercion. "Well," began Azhur and grinned, back in his own early novitiate. "All right. You go down the little stairways behind the embroidered curtain..."

"At the basins?"

"Yes, then there's a corridor to a little postern..."

415

Azhur warmed to his task until Tyr had a good half-dozen escapes and entrances and propitious times for their use. Authran, Azhur assured him, would learn a few things.

"Brilliant!" declared the fledgling novice. "Come and I'll show y' me bunk, then."

"Ah… no, I can't—Aienna, you're pouting. Really, I can't Tyr, sorry. I have to meet with Lord Galdtchav and do some work on your visions."

"Y're not still on about that?"

"We are, and there's also your mother's song."

"What song?"

"The one she sang at the Conclave. 'Maker's mind and Maker's heart.'"

"Oh, aye. Are y' doin' that one she did about y'?"

"No."

"That were Conclave as well."

"Irrelevant, nothing to do with it. It doesn't… relate—I don't relate—to the song."

"Don't get y' knickers in a twist. I thought it were a nice one."

"Yes, very pleasing, but fond as I am of your mother… well, I think she made a mistake. She would have been extremely tired."

"She were doin' her best for y'. Bloody hell, Azhur."

"It's not a criticism, Tyr, it's just an observation. It happens. A major rule of interpretation is that anything offered to or about a person must resonate with them."

"What's that mean?"

"It must, ah, chime in with them, ring a bell, make sense to them."

"Me mam always makes sense!"

"Yes, calm down."

"Y' calm down. What y' all worked up about that song for?"

"I'm not! Sorry, I mean…." Azhur took a deep breath. "I don't relate to what she sang. And we have to do more on the material about you. We have to follow all references through the Scrolls, compare one scroll with another. In context. That sort of thing. It's a very extended proced-ure."

Tyr sat up, agitated. "Do y' soddin' procedure later, I've not seen y' for

416

ages. And now Wyrdha's gone—" His own emotion silenced him and he turned his eyes away.

Azhur sighed heavily and Aienna rested her head sadly on his chest. The Loremaster's status was closing in on him. "We won't finish till late," he tried, "and then Jarthastra must have a record of the investigation and interpretations before him in the morning and *then* it's preparation for the Shrine ritual tomorrow. That's your great day, your initiation," he added lamely, looking at the floor in grief and guilt. His fingers began to twitch and he released Aienna. "Oh Tyr, I know you miss Wyrdha. I do too. He was a remarkable man. He affected me very profoundly in the short time I knew him. Look, I'll come up to the dorms later, and say goodnight. Then we'll make time another day. Really we will."

Tyr forced a half-smile. It was better than nothing. "Aye," he said. "All right, then."

~

As part of his providential governance of the universe and all-sufficient ordering of his kingdom of the Northlands, Lord Arna had provided Tyr with a cupboard and some shelves in which to store his possessions. Or so it said on the cupboard door above the new novice's freshly painted name. The awesome declaration was in *Shumár*, the old sacred speech, so Authran had to translate.

"Ey!" said Tyr on hearing it. "It's a bit much, isn't it?"

"They say that about everything," Authran told him. "Arna's glory, all that stuff. But I suppose everything goes back to Arna in the end, if you think about it."

"Is that in a scroll?"

"Loads of scrolls, you'll see. *Really* interesting actually."

"Hope so," said Tyr, unconvinced.

"Oh yes, really," insisted his friend. "For instance, there's a superb bit in a Ve-Haldthraad scroll, a few lines down from the picture. It's sort of a naughty bit—lots of the priests don't like it. It really gets you thinking. If you want to think, that is."

Tyr wondered despite himself. "Well, what is it then?"

"Well, you know where Arna came from?"

"Deep Fire," stated Tyr with an intellectual glow. "That's Lore of Beginnin's that is, I heard Azhur sayin' it."

"Yes, very good. Well, Arna rose from the Deep Fire and made the world, yes?"

"Aye."

"So, everything in the world goes back to Arna?"

"Aye, I suppose so."

"But Arna lived in the Deep Fire before that. Arna Zhivhaltaur, he was called."

"Him as walks in fire," said Tyr proudly and not quite correctly.

"Near enough. So who made the Fire?"

Tyr looked at the ceiling and screwed his face up. "Arna?"

"Maybe. It doesn't say so."

Tyr pulled out his shirts from his luggage. This was getting technical, but he remembered the joy of the theological disucsstion in Wyrdha's house and decided that no novice, no matter how keen, was going to get the better of him. "What about Inherently Simultaneous Coexistence?" he asked casually, amazed he could even recall the ridiculous sounding title. He had quite forgotten what it meant, but if Loremaster Galdtchav had said it, it must be true.

Authran fell silent, apparently in shock. "How...?" he said. "We don't do Inherently Simultaneous Coexistence in the Extension of Reciprocal Being until third year."

"Ah, well," said Tyr. "It's all about who you know."

Not to be outdone, Authran swung close to him, hanging on the upper bunk, and dropped into a low, relishing, conspiratorial tone. "That old scroll," he said, as though he were about to divulge the most secret of secret plots, "that old scroll wonders if *somebody else* made the Fire. Another god maybe. A god older than Arna."

"Oh, right," said Tyr, "Who's that, then?"

Authran rose to this at once. "I can't say. Nowhere is it written, but some people wonder if that god made Arna."

"Right," repeated Tyr, trying to sound impressed. He knew all of this was apparently astounding or world-shaking, but he couldn't completely grasp why. He knew about so many gods already that one more didn't seem a great cause for excitement. Life at Falakhoth was severely practical, and he wasn't given to undue speculation. "Well, there y' go, then," he tried. "Deep, isn't it? Give us up me bag will y'?"

"You'll do all that, of course," said Authran proudly and inevitably. "You even get to handle scrolls that Ar-ven wrote. *Actually* wrote, I mean. With his *actual* hand."

"Ey!" remarked Tyr and paused in his unpacking. He was, in fact, somewhat impressed and would have been more so had he remembered more about who Ar-ven was. Would he, he wondered, become as obsessive about scrolls, or ritual, or something else as Authran was? He gave a little laugh and shook his head. You had to take friends along with their obsessions. "All right then," he said, "tell us more about y' scroll."

Authran lit up immediately. "Yes!" He gave a little jump and pummelled the air. "Thank you, Tyr. I know I go on, but most people don't want to listen so I don't get the chance. And it matters! Hang on." Authran feverishly raised the mattress on his own upper bunk and reached under it. He pulled out two large flat boards and set them with trembling care on Tyr's bed. He explained, "I'm doing a treatise on that scroll. It's called *The Scroll of the Circle Hand*—really, really unusual."

"And darin'?"

"Oh yes, definitely daring. I drew a picture of it—look!" And he removed the upper board to reveal a meticulously drawn picture brilliant with coloured inks.

"Y' can draw." said Tyr. "That's good."

"Yes, I'm not bad. Now look, that's an illustration of Arna in the Deep Fire, and there's that blue circle round them both."

"What's it for?"

"That's sort of the universe. All that is, that sort of thing."

"All that is what?"

"All that *exists*. The circle stands for, er... everything. The whole of reality. You'll do all that in Representations Class."

"What for?"

"So you can understand the representations, the holy images."

"Them pictures the priests carry about?"

"Exactly. Anyway, there's the Circle of Existence, the universe, and there's a hand coming from *outside* of it. And there are those rays of blue light coming from the hand onto Lord Arna."

"Oh aye," remarked Tyr again. "It's nice, that. Me mam would love that on our wall at home."

Authran started. "That *was* a joke?"

Tyr clenched his fist on one his shirts and held it up like a shield. "I just meant…."

"She'd offer fire in front of it?"

"Oh, aye, she might." He gave a loud and unnecessary cough. "Blue, eh?" And he went back to the shirts. He was struggling with the new experience of folding them, and only because he had promised his mother he would. The result approximated folding, but was more of an organised crumpling. Tyr, however, was satisfied and crammed the garments into his cupboard. His interest in the Scroll of the Circle Hand was waning. "Blue?" he repeated vaguely.

"Blue rays are for power, especially for conferring authority or creating."

"Oh aye," said Tyr again. Having run out of shirts to fold, he was labouring to find some enthusiasm for the discussion.

Authran, however, was at the summit of his tale. "Well, these Ve-Haldthraad priests said it looked as if this meant someone from right outside the universe had reached into the Circle *and created Arna*. Now that could only be a god or gods, but there's only one hand. A Locus of Disputation, they call it, but you—"

"I know." Tyr was thinking hard. He supposed you only got excited about stuff like this after you'd been learning for a while. "Oh well," he said at last, "there's a lot of gods. I suppose *somebody* made Arna."

But Authran jolted away dramatically and clung to the bunk. "Oh, Tyr-shan," he said in a low, grieving voice of wonder. "Oh, so green! Oh no! Oh, wings of Arna! Oh, Lady's kirtle! Oh no, no, no. Nobody *makes* Arna."

"But Arna made all them other gods."

"Not the point. He made them from the Fire, and he was already *in* the Fire and always had been."

420

"Aye, but if he made—"

"No, don't think it."

"Well, who *put* him in the Fire?"

"Nobody! It's who he is. Was. The One Who Walks In Fire, his retrospective modality, his—"

"*What?*"

"Sorry, sorry, too technical. Er, his being prior to emergence—at the Coming Forth, I mean—or his temporally unconditioned existence."

Tyr was starred at Authran with something bordering on horror.

"Oh, never mind, you'll do—"

"*No!* I don't want to!" Tyr cried. "Is that what they do here? Make y' so nobody can understand y'?"

"No! No, no. Oh, it's the ideas, Tyr. The thoughts and the concepts. We love them, we play with them. We love all these terrible words and the awful names. They make sparks in our minds and we shiver when we think with them." Authran paused and looked a little vacant. "Well, some of us do—the ones that think there's more to life than being a Provincial Secretary or something." He brightened again, features all alert. "Oh, but thinking's so beautiful, Tyr! You see things under words, and what the great people might have meant that nobody's seen yet. You get to look in the corner of people's minds, and your own mind gets bigger and bigger, but there's always room for one more thing, something else new and true, always another room you can go into, and the new room's got a dozen doors in it so you can explore and explore and explore and never get out of your chair. You can join up dozens of facts and make a thought nobody ever had before. You can take a beautiful glittering idea, all made with shining, burning *facts*, true things you saw how to join up into something new and sharp, and you can go up to somebody with their back breaking under layers and layers of heavy, rusty, laboursome, hampering errors, dragging iron mistakes, and the weighty things that got attached to the mistakes, and you can swing your shimmering, shining thought-sword and slice all that rubbish away. Then the person's free! All because *you thought*! Because *you had ideas*."

Tyr had never seen or heard anything like it. Authran was smiling and alight, literally breathless. Tyr smiled. It was all he could manage. "Will

I get like that?"

"Hope so. You never know."

Tyr contemplated this, *thought* about it. "Are they all like that?" he asked wonderingly. "All the priests?"

"I wouldn't say that *exactly*."

"Most, then? If they've done the studyin' and all."

Authran sagged somewhat and let out a brief sigh, a lament for priests who were not like him. "The fact is that many people like to learn stuff that's a version of what they think already, or at least something based on it. Every time these people meet an idea they want it to say to them, *You're right!* This makes them feel clever and in control and safe—especially safe. They like life to be simple and if you say there's more to it than that they can become frightened."

"I don't think I've met nobody like that."

"Oh, you have, you just don't know it until you challenge them."

"Challenge?"

"Show them an idea that's bigger and better than any of the ones they've had."

Suddenly, Tyr understood perfectly. He had seen this thing happen under his own roof when the priest Jher-val so crassly and insultingly failed to understand Ilissos the Syrgan's vision of transcendent beauty on the moors above Falakhoth. He made a little sound, somewhere between laughter and disgust at the memory of the odious man's arrogant fury when Azhur had pointed out—from the Scrolls, no less—that the priest could be mistaken.

"Vile!" said Authran, when he heard the story. He rolled his eyes and sighed. "It *would* be a priest. I'm afraid people like that are really quite excellent at keeping the kingdom running. But Azhur, he's a thinker. Gives you hope. He's the sort that brings the real changes."

"I think y' are and all," said Tyr. He was feeling rather in awe of his new friend.

"Hmmm," said Authran, in a sing-song tone. "Well, you never know." He looked straight at Tyr, suddenly serious. "I'm not daft, you know. I go on, and it's fun, but I'm not."

"I know that," said Tyr, wondering what this was about.

"It's just that, back home, being a… well, I'm just going to say it: being a smart-arse was so disgustingly important it was the only thing about me people latched on to. To my parents it was our son the scholar; to the other lads it was look how clever he thinks he is. I was worshipped or reviled, but people didn't notice *me*, just this thing they loved or hated. It was only one part of me, not *me*. You follow?"

"I'll not revile y'," said Tyr, relieved that he knew what his friend meant.

"No, but… you are looking impressed. Please don't be, Tyr. Please, please. Enjoy my thoughts, but be my friend first and always. There's a *me* sitting here in front of you."

Tyr found himself more moved than he could understand. His throat tightened as he realised what Authran was asking of him. "Hello, *me*," he said and gave Authran a long, inevitable hug.

"You've still got to listen when I rabbit on, though," said Authran.

"Aye," said Tyr, and smiled. "Oh, aye. I might like this study lark."

"The joy of knowing and finding out, the pleasures in the box."

"What box?"

"Sorry, it's a metaphor. By box, I mean head: enjoying having ideas in your head."

"The pleasures in the box," Tyr tried it out. "That's good. I'll have a brilliant time in my box. Darin', my box will be."

Authran laughed wildly. "Brilliant! That is indeed utterly and thoroughly the spirit, Tyr-shan of Falakhoth! This Tower will not know what's hit it! You start tomorrow! All you have to do is…."

"What, what?"

"Do your Initiation. Before breakfast."

"Before scran? What do I have to do?"

"I can't tell you." Authran raised his open hands in frenzied assurance. "But you'll love it, trust me. You'll love it. Honest."

~

IN A REMOTE REGION of the Tower of the Novitiate, the drab light of a single invisible window seeped down a long shaft into a musty, unfurnished hall. Here, Tyr and Authran stood by a venerable wooden door set in an arch round which snaked an elaborate, rippling design.

"Have I got to do all this?" asked Tyr

"Yes. Just get it done and then we can have breakfast."

"I'm hungry now."

"Well, never mind. This has to be the first thing you do today, then you can go down to the Wait wearing the black as one of us. The new novices get a great breakfast—loads of bacon."

"It's stupid, this. Why can't I just put the black stuff on?"

"Absolutely not. We've all done it, you know. You're not getting out of it."

Tyr grumbled some more but stopped himself when a priest in a Novice Master's robe came into the chamber. He was rubbing his eyes and trying to keep hold of an elaborate wooden scroll casing.

"Morning, my lads," he said, not overly brightly but trying nonetheless. "Ready for breakfast, I expect?" He ambled over and beamed blearily at Tyr. "Well, you'll be the new one, eh? Obvious really, dressed like that."

Authran gave a little bow. "Anthu, this is Tyr-shan va-Tyrmar of Falakhoth. He comes to us by the urging of Lord Jarthastra."

The priest nodded, drew a hand through his disordered hair, and looked intently at Tyr. He made a long sound of realisation through his slight, permanent smile. "It's true then. I'd heard things, vague, you never know. What can you think? Yes, it's you." He shook himself as if to frighten off whatever thoughts had settled on his mind. "Well, I'm Jerh'herakhan va-Ralh'hanthan, Third Rank of Novice Masters. You'll get me for *Shumár* and Histories and, ah, well, plenty of things, really."

"Oh aye?" said Tyr, liking the man. "That sounds grand."

Authran coughed.

"Anthu," Tyr added quickly.

"Well, you wait till you hear me. Now, Authran, if you'll assist me, my fine fellow. Just stand yourself there in front of the door. Good. Now, put your hands out, please, and hold this case." The novice positioned himself and the Master dumped the bulky casing in his arms, across his chest. "Done this hundreds of times, but I still have to look at the words.

You're not supposed to, really, but I'd never remember it if I read it till Shivara comes." He clicked open the brass fastenings and raised the hinged upper half of the case to reveal a parchment scroll nestled in the cloth-lined interior. The master took the wooden rod attached along the scroll's exposed edge, then raised two wooden slats from the upper edge of the lid. He pulled on the rod and the scroll unwound like a blind. The rod attached to the tops of the extended slats so that the whole of the inner side of the parchment stretched out and could be easily read. "Handy, isn't it?" remarked Jerh'herakhan. "Only a short one, you couldn't do this with the big scrolls. Now then, we won't be long."

"How important is it?" asked Tyr. He had decided he might as well gather knowledge from the start.

"Absolutely essential," the Master told him as Authran rolled his eyes. "If I don't do this, your initiation's invalid. Now, cross your arms on your chest and bow your head a little. No, no, fingers straight... that's it. Now."

Jerh'herakhan raised his hands and held them over Tyr, turning his head to the right as he read from the page stretched out under Authran's chin. The document was a beautiful work, every letter a painstaking masterpiece of form and proportion. Some words were picked out in gold or crimson and a riot of images surrounded the whole text: people, vines, fabulous beasts, and the sign of the sun. The letters of the first line were especially large and intricate with strange coloured animals twisting among them like creatures running in a forest. It looked as though the first letter of all had taken weeks to create. It was worked around an illustration of someone entering the novitiate, as Tyr was doing. He deduced this from the two figures standing by a blue circle he thought must represent the great Laver in the Shrine. One figure was holding out a black robe to the other, as Authran would soon do for Tyr. He noticed that intruding into the picture was a blue hand and a ray of light, the same hand, apparently, that he had seen the night before in Authran's drawing of the controversial scroll.

"What's that there?" he asked.

Authran glared at him over the top of the parchment.

Jerh'herakhan stopped reading. "Eh? Oh, it's supposed to be someone taking the black, as you are. Now—"

"No, the hand. What's that for?"

"Oh, Arna's feathers!" said Authran, sighing mightily. "*Told* you all that last night!"

"Aye, but what's it *there* for in *this* scroll? Do y' know, Anthu?"

Jerh'herakhan was by now quite off track. Luckily, he was the kind of Master with whom his novices could take all kinds of trustful liberties and whom, as a result, they genuinely loved. "Oh, well, whatever Authran told you, that'll be what it is. He's terribly good at that sort of thing."

"There weren't nobody takin' the black on the thing he had though."

"I see. This scroll is a copy of a copy of a copy and so on, right back to the first one—which by the way was drawn up by Ar-ven himself—and Zhir-sharrak the Wise illuminated it."

"He what?"

"He did the pictures," said Authran.

"As for the hand," went on Jerh'herakhan, "that's, um—well, to be honest, we're not sure. They used that symbol in the Southland, in old Dhar where Zhir-sharrak came from, but you'll do all that soon enough."

"Didn't say a thing," said Authran.

"What's it mean though?" asked Tyr determinedly. He wondered why this mattered to him.

"Oh, dear me," said Jerh'herakhan and laughed wearily. "You are a dog with a bone this morning, but it is nice, I must say, to find such a hunger for knowledge among one's novices. And I'm sorry I can't say more. The hand is probably meant to stand for Arna pointing out the new novice. Or something. Ask the Master of Representations. Now, with your permission, Tyr-shan of Falakhoth, I shall speak the Rite of Initiation over you and we shall be one step nearer to breakfast. Have we your permission to do that?"

"Aye," said Tyr. "Thanks very much. Anthu."

Jerh'herakhan lifted his hands over Tyr once more and read from the beautiful scroll the words that propelled a young man on his way to Arna's priesthood. The lad remembered that thousands of others had gone through this before him, even Bal-jarrak he thought unpleasantly, and Azhur which was a much happier thought. He sighed, for he would have liked his friend to be with him, but he was busy in that new, responsible way, and, well, bugger it, he could have found ten minutes just to stand here. It couldn't be that hard. Or maybe he was having breakfast with Aienna. *No*, he told himself, *stop it. She's nothing to do with it, and you like her, you know you do.* He wrenched his thoughts guiltily back to the words of the Rite. He resolved to ask Authran what the sacred *Shumár* meant, although understanding it didn't seem all that important. As long as he stood here and heard it and did what he was supposed to do, that was it. It was a strange beginning. Nobody at Falakhoth went ahead with things they didn't understand, not if they were important, but things were apparently not so simple at the Shrine.

The words ended. Jerh'herakhan crossed his hands, muttered something of his own and rolled up the scroll. Tyr felt nothing, not even flat. Ah, well.

"Why do y' do it this way for?" he asked, for the sake of something to say.

Master Jerh'herakhan closed the scroll case and fastened the clasps. "We have to. It's a very ancient tradition."

"You can't just make things up," Authran told him.

"Aye, but there's nobody here. Nobody's lit a candle, even. I just thought there'd be somethin' y' know... Are they not bothered?"

The Master looked sideways at the floor. "Yes, I see what you mean. Lots of lads have asked me that."

"Not surprised. If me mam and dad ask me what happened, I'll just have to say nowt."

"*Nowt*," repeated Jerh'herakhan. "Haven't heard that one before. Yes, well put. Well, it's all very sparse and undramatic, I admit, but it's time-honoured and hallowed by tradition. Ar-ven established all this and Zhir-sharrak advised him, so they probably did this in Dhar." He paused and looked into ancient distances. "Maybe Shivara began his novitiate like this. Can't be sure, but it's possible. Anyway, this is what's in the Scrolls, so we can't change it. Not even for Tyr-shan of Falakhoth."

"Tell you all about it," announced Authran.

"Thought y' would," said Tyr.

427

Authran curled a lip defiantly.

Jerh'herakhan smiled. With his scholar's ramble over, he hefted the wooden case in his arms. "Well, I'll leave you to it. Enjoy breakfast when it comes." He made for the door, then stopped. "Baranthu, how unexpected. What may I do for you?"

Standing in front of the closed doors was Tyr's 'attendant,' the priest Maurdjil who Bal-jarrak had inflicted upon him. He was poised in a vigilance that seemed to rise from his being, hands crossed in front of him, watching with eyes that could scan the sun.

"Thank you, Anthu," he said in a voice impossibly rich and deep, so that the words rolled like boulders round the barren chamber. "I need nothing. I am here to witness the opening of the Rite for our unique novice. As I should."

A shaft of meaning passed between the two men. Jerh'herakhan became disinclined to question further. "Ah," he said. "Ah yes. Well, I'm just off. All's well, you see."

Maurdjil inclined his head, "I am glad," he said, and was gone like an echo.

The Novice Master shuffled after, then closed the double doors with a strange air of finality. There came the heavy sound of a bolt falling into place.

Tyr gasped.

"It's all right," Authran reassured him, "that's all part of it." He turned the handle of the door under the archway and pushed it open, revealing a short, strangely unadorned corridor where two lamps on iron hooks shed their steady yellow light. "One each," he said, lifting the lamps down. He was whispering without it being clear why. He seemed more in awe of the occasion than Tyr was.

They walked down the corridor, lights aloft, and entered a passage that curved off into the dark both right and left. Tyr let his friend steer him to the right, and they carried their ring of brightness for what seemed a very long way. The passage was oddly narrow, so that their shoulders bumped together as they went side by side.

"Why's it curved?" asked Tyr when he could stand it no longer.

"It goes round the Shrine," Authran told him. "Shush."

The passage unwound before them. Its walls and arched ceiling had a strange nakedness. There were none of the statues and inscriptions that elsewhere were constant reminders of the Northlands' sacred history. Perhaps, thought Tyr, the passageway was only for novices and so they hadn't bothered.

Up ahead was a little door. It was wooden and plain, without a lock, bolt, or handle, and set in an unadorned arch. New varnish shimmered faintly in the lamplight.

"Well," said Authran, "here I leave you. You know what to do now?"

"Aye," said Tyr, half-amused. "I'll get on with it then." Now came the part he thought was daft. He was to remove his clothes, all of them, then go through the little door and ascend to the Shrine where he would find himself by the edge of the great Laver. He was to swim across and Authran would meet him on the farther side with the black robes he would wear for several years. Alas, he had no idea why he couldn't have some kind of ceremony and put on the robes himself.

Even Authran, who'd done it before him, had only said, "It's what Arven said, the reasons why might be lost in some scroll."

Thus, Tyr now stood on the edge of his novitiate ready to walk, or swim, through a mystery. But it had to be done. He hauled off the comfortably humble garb he had stretched and shaped at Falakhoth, even the shirt that his mother had made for this occasion, and threw it over Authran's arm. "Boots an' all?" he asked.

"Of course boots and all. You can't swim with those on."

"I could leave them at the edge. Don't want to scrape me feet."

"Off! It was all smooth when I did it."

Defeated, Tyr stood on the heels of his boots and levered them off. There he stood, clad only in himself. He felt an unexpected sense of freedom. Then Authran blew out one of the lamps.

"Now what y' doin'?"

"This is part of it. I take the other lamp and go to the other side of the Laver—the passageway goes right round. When you can't see my light, count a hundred and go through the door."

"Y' never told me that bit."

"I forgot, sorry. Now, are you ready?"

All at once, Tyr was glad there was no elaborate ceremony. Friendship in the shared circle of the light seemed to hold all the meaning the rite needed to give it power. He gave a little happy laugh and his friend laughed back.

"Arna shine on you, Tyr," said Authran warmly and quietly as he took Tyr's boots and the remaining lantern.

"Y' and all."

"Don't swim too fast. Give me time to get round." Off Authran went, and the light with him. Tyr briefly saw his friend as a black, receding marionette following a moving, shifting glow, the sound of his feet hitting off the walls. The light disappeared round the curve of the passageway, then danced as a phantom of itself in Tyr's newly darkened eyes.

When he was sure it really had gone, he began to count his hundred, then yelped as a long, ghastly howl came back through the dark. "Y're very funny!" he yelled, then laughed at his own delicious fright. There was a distant hoot of mirth followed by the sound of his friend's tread, then even that had gone, and all the world with it.

Tyr leaned back against the cool stone. The cold shock of it sent a sting of refreshment through his mind and body. He felt very awake, very present, and at peace. He tapped his fingers against the wall behind him: one, two, three…. With his surroundings invisible in the black, he felt free and unconfined. Moving away from the wall, he imagined this is what it might feel like to be flying, floating, suspended outwith everything. Apart from the feel of the floor pushing up on his bare feet, there were no bounds, no limitations, almost no points of reference save himself. He found himself intensely aware of his body, his own physical reality that housed his thoughts and his heart and his spirit. He had an acute awareness of his own self, his own being, someone truly existing and real. With shocked delight he saw that self for what it was: a marvellous gift, something to dwell in, something to be, something to touch the world with. He, Tyr-shan, had been given to himself forever, a blessing to the earth. Let no-one come against him.

He returned, as it were, to the passageway, thoughts dazzled by invisible light, no longer simply waiting, but in a state where waiting was being and everything he did was his existence. His person was one, his mind and spirit were fused with his body. He had entire ownership of himself. Surprised, he found his fingers were now tapping on his thigh and he was oddly aware of the number he had reached: ninety-eight, ninety-nine, one hundred.

Tyr blinked in the darkness, shook free the vision of his existence and wondered what had happened. He rubbed his eyes, then laughed, thinking that doing that in the pitch black was almost as daft as the ritual itself. It was time to go through the door.

The doorway was narrow and also very low, forcing Tyr to edge through sideways in a stooped position. There was no latch or even handle and the plain wooden panel swung in easily, allowing him to move forward into yet more blackness. He reached out and at once felt his hand on a wall. A sweep to the right and another wall rushed up. He waved an arm through the left-hand dark and felt nothing. Left it was, then. Fearful of tripping or walking into something, Tyr waved both of his hands in front of him and gingerly took each step through the utter darkness. The passage he was in started off only as broad as himself, as though it had been built for him and for this day, before the walls disappeared. Not even his groping hands could feel a wall to the left or right of him. Disorientated by the loss of cold stone next to his skin, he stopped.

Now, he noticed how silent it was. Voices, wagon-wheel, sweep of garment, every human sound was gone, along with the whispering trees, bird-call, and the running-song of water. All the voices of the world were dumb and Tyr was his own world there under the earth, blundering he knew not where, hearing nothing save his own breath and his own heartbeat. He was the whole of humankind, a race of one, with no possibility of hand to grasp or voice to hear, no chance of breath on his cheek or thoughts to touch his mind. Down here in the womb of the earth, this secret place, there was no sharing or companionship, no-one to be a person with, no other soul to make him human. His hand trembled for another hand to hold, his body felt the pain of not being embraced, his mind grieved for the voice of another's thoughts, and his heart ached to forget itself in love of another, even should that be a rich, happy suffering.

Above him, he knew, was the monstrous weight of the Shrine and Na-veshtrazhdak's Tower, and it bent him down with a crushing loneliness as if it would lose him under its immensity. The great buildings became a symbol, not of exalted power, but of the dread doom of isolation, the tangible press of lostness in the dark, of burial in a pit of meaninglessness, knowing that the nature of the world was after all not relationship but sheer force and fate forever. This grim vision drew unwanted thoughts with it: the ancient terror of abandonment; the claustrophobic closing of a grave; the old fears of Ghalta, the spiteful spirit, who sought to harry and confuse souls journeying after death. Perhaps he, Tyr-shan, had been led astray even now. Perhaps he should go back. It would not be too difficult to do. Maybe he could end up accepting that he would never know if that resonating inner call and aspiration were to something that truly existed. People did that all the time, retreating and failing. He would not be so different.

No. He would not be the one to make his own dream fail. He did not want to live knowing he had perhaps missed the answer to the question that was his life, because he had been too afraid to carry on to see if it was there. The voice of his own inner authority had called to him on the High Fields and bade him seek the dark mystery of joy he had sensed in Valderthaan. He would answer it. He dared not live his life never knowing if it had spoken true or if it would have led him to something real. Yes, he had not known he would have to make this journey under the earth and feel this chilling grind of isolation, but that was not the point, he understood that. All that was before him now, palpable in the dark, was a challenge to face. Will you follow the path you know lies through Shrine and priesthood? Will you still seek what you thought you saw?

And then there came an earthy thought that felt entirely out of place: if he had the gumption to crack the obnoxious La'auchrad on the nose surely he had the gumption to walk down a passage. He smiled in the darkness at the absurdity of this interruption.

And so he blundered on naked in the dark, his hands acting as his eyes as he reached through the darkness for the route ahead. The passage turned, doubled back, broadened, narrowed, slid down slopes, and went up steps. He paused only when the floor under his feet suddenly stopped being flat and became scored with curving patterns. He felt them with his toe and discovered regular, flowing lines like waves. He remembered the stylised blue lines that represented the water of the Laver on the Initiation Scroll. Was he near?

He padded on, more confident, expecting his release. The passage turned another corner, still with the Laver-lines underfoot, and Tyr stopped again. Was there the faintest of draughts playing on his skin? His straining eyes bored through the dark. Hanging in the black before him was the vague, misty outline of a door, faint as a breath, but there nonetheless. Tyr trotted forward over the scored floor, exhilarated at nearing his escape into the world again. Breakfast would be a joy, a triumph, and he'd hit Authran for not telling him about the twists and turns. He tripped the hidden spring that was waiting for him and a broad, glass window opened above, while a solid wooden panel swung down and blocked the way. Tyr skidded and staggered but battered into the panel, scraping a shoulder as he tried to avoid the impact.

"Bugger!" he said, inevitably. Yet more daftness from Ar-ven. He stepped back, rubbing the shoulder, glaring at the panel. It seemed to blaze with light after his time in the dark, but he soon realised it was ordinary daylight slipping down from the glazed square in the ceiling. It shone on two words carved deep into the wood before him: Consider. Remember.

Well, he certainly wouldn't forget all this in a hurry, but he hadn't thought about considering it. What was there to consider? He felt whatever it was could be best achieved after breakfast, when Authran would be at hand to explain.

The panel spanned the whole passage. Why did it come down just before you got out? It was daft. He'd hit Authran for not warning him about that as well. The panel turned out to be hinged, so Tyr lifted it up and crawled under. He was only halfway through when it got away from his fingers as his hands twisted, and it scraped his back as it fell back into place. It was only a few yards to the door, now dimly clear to his adjusting eyes. It was another low, narrow affair with no handle and Tyr stepped through easily. He looked up a flight of steps to what seemed to be windows high above. Thin, cold morning light eased down on him. Here at last was his return to the visible world: it felt like a birth. He was almost at the top of the stairs when he pulled himself up short. He realised he was about to appear for the first time in Arna's Shrine, the vast, sacred centre of the Northlands. He had no idea what lofty personages would be about and he, the humble almost-novice, would be highly visible. Not to mention naked.

Tyr had never entered that great echoing circle before, or aspired to do so, but he knew it could hold hundreds. What if the entire Third Level felt the need to offer fire that morning? Had the Novice Masters thought of that? Had they made arrangements? He couldn't stand on this stair forever, and he'd been told that every priest and novice had done this, even Azhur, so he supposed it must be all right. They could laugh about it later. Nice if Azhur had been there, though.

With an odd tingle of perilous adventure, Tyr poked his head just above the level of the opening and looked around. This reminded him of the toads that surfaced, eyes only, in the Falakhoth pools, an absurdity that helped. He was peering out of a square space cut in the wooden floor of a small platform. Next to it, he knew, would be the Laver, but its encircling rim was below the level of his vision. In fact, most of the Shrine at floor level was invisible and would be until Tyr stood on the platform. He carefully emerged into the visible world.

The embryonic novice stood within the huge, encompassing space of the Shrine. Had he noticed, he would have seen he was at its very centre. The vast half-sphere of the dome hung like another sky that rested on a spinning, aerial colonnade of windows, impossibly high above him. In the vague light of early morning, all was grey and pearl and soft white, obscured by contrasting shadow and shifting haze from the smoke of fire-offering and candle. Behind the haze wheeled the great, turning ceiling of lapis lazuli, where the light flowed and hung and rippled through an artifice of billowed stars and the sweeping, shimmering, circling lines that traced in gold the paths that stars and planets, moon and sun took through heaven. At the very apex of the dome, hovering and spinning straight above the head of Tyr far below, was the broad, round window edged in brass and filled with the sign of the Sun in vivid, tinted glass through which Arna burned down from the highest reach of his sky-journey at the summer solstice. Today, the light was weak and flat and all the splendours of the Shrine were humbled in a drab shade. Which suited Tyr-shan of Falakhoth very well.

He looked cautiously about him for signs of life. There were in fact several red-robed figures scattered about the vast, dull space. They were going about unexciting routines, conversing, pottering, or just sitting. All of them were fairly distant and none of them appeared in the least interested in Tyr. He listened to their remote voices and the wandering echo of their footsteps and wondered if they knew he was there. Perhaps he could get this over with before they realised.

Having established who was about and where, Tyr focussed on the Laver. It lay before him like a great round womb inviting him to enter and be born. Its waters wavered at his feet where a few steps went down to a stone jetty almost level with the surface. Thirty feet across, the immense glass basin held in its depths a mirror-image of the sky-dome above. It was a flawless witness to the Deep Fire, the great Flame beneath the western sea, the eternal burning where Arna had dwelt from infinite time and from which he had fashioned the gods and all things in the universe. The giant bowl had been crafted from a single swirl of glass thick enough to support the tons of water and shot through with the finest colour-work: clear, living greens, yellows, and rich, pulsing reds to represent the new-made world around the Flame; and figures of crimson, piercing blue, and hot ochre to show the gods and bright spirits that soared and wheeled around the burning ere they went into the world. But the lowest part of the basin was clear and so he would soon see the unceasing fire that had been tended hour by hour since Naveshtrazhdak built the Shrine four centuries before. He himself had lit the blaze and Ar-ven and Zhir-sharrak had blessed the waters and opened the conduits that released them into the Laver above. Since then, thousands of men had spent their lives in the great, low chambers hollowed out of the rock, often passing from father to son the honour of endlessly carrying away ash, bringing in more fuel, and brushing away the soot from the gleaming glass belly hanging over them. All in order that the firelight might pass through the waters and tell the Northland of the Flame at the heart of the world.

All at once, Tyr felt a gust of cold air on his back. He whipped around. Guardsmen were hauling open the massive double doors that faced onto Shrinegate. The day's activity had begun and Tyr gaped in dismay at the first few devotees, led by a bent old lady with a stick, shuffling in to pay their yawning respects to Arna. Tyr tried frantically to position his hands appropriately and swung back round to face the Laver.

A strange calm came upon him. He stood straight, feeling quite at peace, all at once disinclined to be modest. He was supposed to be here, like this. Tyr stood quiet with proper pride, enjoying being there, then he plunged into the fire-lit waters of the Laver. His dark hair swirled about his head like sea-fronds as he swam to the depths and put his hands against the clear part of the glass. The Flame burned far below him. He could feel its heat warming the water as if he were sitting beside a fireplace. He imagined the embers glowing in his heart. He thought of taking the coals in his hand and tasting them like an incandescent fruit, squeezing the gleaming juices into his mouth, swallowing its molten nourishment and feeling the white blaze sear along his throat, before roaring forever in his belly, the purest lava spreading out through his veins. Surely, that was life. He wanted it more than his own existence.

The Flame shifted into a face and Tyr looked through the water and glass at the Fire-spirit. All his senses were taken up with the burning spirit before him. And the strangest thought came to him: the spirit was made of love. The Fire-spirit smiled at Tyr, thrilled this link had been made.

There was no feeling of movement or change, but Tyr found himself floating on his back between the fire and the wheeling sky. He stared upwards, understanding how this first morning as a novice wasn't just some daft initiation ritual. The dark, the isolation, the nakedness all reminded you that you were only and ever yourself. With everything else gone—clothes, company, and sight—you knew it and felt it. Nobody could do it for you. No society, rite, scroll, cult, community, or priest could create this experience and bear it for you. It began from some-where right outside all that and met itself in its other beginning within your real self. It could only be contained and carried and known by what was truly you, only you. Everything else was lost for a time so you could see that, and that loss was worth it.

Tyr turned over and with a lazy kick swam towards the jetty on the farther side. There stood Authran, grinning down at him with black novice robes and a towel over one arm. He bent down, took Tyr's hand, and hauled him up out of the water, hugging his friend in the same motion and getting rather wet himself.

"Arna's wings, eh? Welcome to the black, Baranthu Tyr-shan." He laughed and made a courtly flourish with his hand.

Tyr laughed back, elated, wringing his hair and not minding who might be about the Shrine. "Is that it, then? Is that me a novice right enough now?"

"Once you've got the stuff on. Come on now, you can catch your death with the doors open."

Someone hauled Authran aside and Tyr was suddenly face to face with a dishevelled, unshaven man with wide, red eyes. He gripped Tyr's shoulders painfully and pushed his face close so the lad could hear his rapid breath.

"One of us, now!" gasped the madman. "Sent to save us!" He peered into the new novice's wide eyes. "I dreamed of you last night," he said plaintively. "Has Arna spoken? Does Shivara come? Will you keep the wolf away?" He covered his face with his hands and wept.

Tyr realised with horror who he was. Jarthastra.

There was running and calling and Azhur and old Galdtchav were on the little jetty, pulling the man away. Behind them came the impossible figure of the Lady Iera, the Graavinda, hair streaming down and a gown flung over her night-clothes. Now modesty was no option. Authran had the presence of mind to fling the towel at Tyr even as he bowed to Iera and Jarthastra. Not that anyone cared. All that mattered was the rapid removal of the Valgraav.

"You must tell me!" he howled over his shoulder as they dragged him to an open door. "Should it be me? What does Arna say?" They pulled him through.

Iera reappeared and bore down on the novices like a war galley. Tyr's reflex was to leap back in the Laver for safety, but he clutched his towel and braced himself. She swept up to them, her strength flashing out like arrows. In that moment she was the sole arbiter of reality.

"You did not see this," she said with words like axes. "This did not happen. Should I hear that one of you has let out even a breath touching this matter, it will be denied and you will never enter here again." Her flaring eyes ordered a response.

Authran bowed low. "Anthei, be it far from me. I will revere the Anthu's honour."

Iera's head snapped round to Tyr. He thought he could feel steam rise off him under the heat of her glare.

"Aye," he gasped. "Oh aye, me and all." He wished the towel was bigger.

Iera held them under her eyes for moments more, reading and warning them until satisfied. "So be it," she said, then whirled away to see to her husband.

"Oh, Arna's wings," gasped Authran and leaned on Tyr.

"Bloody hell," said Tyr. They stared at the door, then at each other.

Another figure, black and red, strode up. "Remember your promise," said a voice like turning millstones. "Much may depend on it." The alarming shadowed eyes of the priest Maurdjil turned on Tyr. "Now I have another reason to attend to you, Tyr-shan," he said. "Do not increase my cares." He left as quickly as he had appeared, by the same door that led to the mystery of Jarthastra, his eyes fixed on Tyr till the last moment.

No-one in the Shrine appeared to have noticed the frenzied little incident. Tyr shook his thoughts free. "Right. I better get this black stuff on."

CHAPTER 20

The Bearpit

DURING THE BRIGHT AFTERNOON, once the immediate distress of Tharval's story had dissipated and the narrative itself was spreading like a pestilence, Yauva swung his broom at the door of the *Carp* and covered a young woman's shoes with his sweepings.

"Well," said the bright country voice, "is that all the welcome I'm gettin'?"

Yauva looked up and gaped. Utha's broad smile shone like a sunrise in his heart. He gaped a moment more, then dropped the broom and folded his awkward arms around the laughing girl. For almost a minute he stood, swaying her from side to side with his cheek to hers, unable to make any other movement save tighten his hug. Eyes screwed shut, lips tight together, he lavished every mote of his awareness on the feel of that wonderful rounded body. A tear escaped his eye unbidden and his muscles eased into an unexpected peace. He drew back his head to look into her eyes. Full of summer they were. She laughed again, more quietly, her yellow hair all disarranged under her head-cloth.

"Y're strong," she said softly.

That pleased him, and he smiled. "What're you doin' here?" he asked, hoping she would say it was anything but a short visit.

"Well, after dad died, Mam said she couldn't stay at Falakhoth by

439

herself. So, we've come to Lukar to live with my aunt Antha."

Yauva gasped. "You're goin' to live here?"

"That we are. Mam's helpin' aunt Antha with her dye business and I thought, well...."

Yauva frowned, "You thought what?"

"I thought there might be a job for a servin' girl in that *Golden Carp* place. I heard they keeps a good house, so I thought it was worth a try, like." Utha nibbled her lip then smote him with another smile. Before he realised what was happening, she had kissed him.

Yauva was left gaping at her. He was about to kiss her when his step-father's voice interrupted him.

"What the hell you about, lad? Eh?"

Yauva dropped his arms and span round. "Hello Volthar. This is... this is Utha." He waved a hand at the girl. "She's lookin' for work. She thought we might have a position."

"Hard at work already, I'd say," Volthar grunted, voice dripping with insinuation.

Yauva rallied his courage. "She looked after me at Falakhoth when I was poorly, and now she's livin' with her mam at mistress Antha's on account of her dad died."

"And she's goin' to serve our ales!" Yenl said.

Volthar had prepared a scathing remark, but it died instantly on his lips. His wife had suddenly appeared on the stairs from the upper floor. A trim little middle-aged woman in a dark dress, a swathe of sheets over her arm.

"I was stood here listenin' and I heard it all," said Yenl. "Anybody who has done well by my Yauva, has got a place in the *Carp*, far as I'm concerned." She descended, beaming, then gathered Utha in a great embrace and planted a kiss on her cheek.

Yauva quivered with delight. "Do you think we can, Ma?"

"Yenl, we can't afford a wage," mumbled a determined Volthar.

"Now, Volthar, I look after the money, as you well know, and we had a good summer last year and a not bad winter. And so far, spring's good, so we can well afford a bit of help. Which we very much need, in my opinion."

Volthar admitted defeat by walking off to do other work.

"Well," chirped Yenl, "that's all settled, then. What was your name again, love?"

"Utha." Utha discarded her head-cloth, tied her hair back and made her fresh wide smile and cheerful manner the newest attraction for the patrons of the *Golden Carp*. The word was out within the hour. Even customers infrequent or lapsed found themselves possessed of a sudden strong desire to slake their thirst to meet her.

"Thing is," confided the elderly Garfin to Yauva, "there's nowt to see in Lukar but fish, so they've all come along to have a look."

Yauva took this as a compliment. "Aye, she brightens the place up, she does."

Yenl leaned on the bar and beamed. "Look at that, Volthar. It'll be wedded bliss for my Yauva soon. You'll be a step-granddad."

"Wedded what?" said Volthar, horrified. "We'll have to pay somebody else if he gets wed!"

"Wish the lad well, my love, and don't be so miserable. Stepfathers can take a bit of pleasure in these things too if they're so minded."

"If you're goin' to bring Yrthrad up—"

"I bring nothing up, Volthar. Yrthrad never had the chance to see him wed, rest his soul, and you have, so I think you might try to stand in the gap, if you get my meanin'."

"But he hardly knows her."

"Take your blinkers off, Volthar. He's besotted, as my mother used to say. It's only a matter of time." Having pronounced this, she swept her shawl regally about her. "Now, you look after all these customers, Volthar. And see you're nice to Utha." She cast a final satisfied eye over the inn, turned and strode away.

"Bit of a tiff, there, eh?" remarked Garfin to Yauva.

"They'll be fine," said Yauva, amused, as he collected empty mugs.

"Hasty marriage," said Garfin to anyone who could hear him. "Very sad when y' dad got caught in the nets like that, of course. *Yenl*, I says, *do without a man for a bit and get the lad brung up*, but no, she wasn't—"

"Shut it, Garfin," said several voices, in the tone of those who had heard it all before.

~

BAL-JARRAK STRODE ACROSS the cold subterranean room, looking grim and apprehensive.

"Thank you for coming, my Lord," said the Master of Diversities. "I felt you should probably see—"

"Thank me later," said Bal-jarrak. "Get on with it."

"Of course," replied the Master of Diversities. He swept the blanket from the table.

The Keeper of the Fires examined what was before him with as little expression as he could manage. "A beheaded man?" he said at last. "Who is he? A Harrak? I'd behead the lot, but why do you want me to view the body?"

"Anthu—"

"I didn't even know there'd been an execution, the courts didn't inform me, and they usually send the body back—"

"My Lord, I'm sorry, there has been no execution."

"What are you saying? This isn't... It can't be."

"It is the same, Anthu. This was the wolf body."

"That's not a wolf, that's a man!"

"It is indeed. But remember the changes to the *former* carcass you observed. After your visit I looked in a few times a day and was able to document the progression of the... conversion."

Bal-jarrak breathed hard and backed away from the table. "Abomination," he said. "You should have burned it."

"I had no instructions."

"Well, burn it now. And say absolutely *nothing*." Bal-jarrak backed off another few steps. His hand groped behind him for the door-handle. "We do not believe in things like this," he stated. His voice trembled a little, such was his conviction.

"Of course not, Anthu."

"We are intelligent, rational men. Our thought, our cult of Arna, does not allow for this kind of thing. We do not accept it, we do not accommodate it."

"By no means, Anthu."

442

Bal-jarrak felt his voice was now annoyingly high, but he continued regardless, "However, you will find out anything—do you hear me, *anything*—remotely connected with wolves, or... or... anything, and you will tell me at once."

"I most certainly will, Anthu," said the Master of Diversities. He withdrew a bulky wad of parchment from his coat. "I actually took the liberty of preparing a detailed report for you, about the inexplicable number of recent wolf attacks. In the valleys south of Lukar, in Ceorthas, and on the Plain, many wolf packs have been seen running across country. Within a twenty-mile radius of Archraad there have been many reported attacks by large wolves along main thoroughfares. Two immense packs have been sighted along the edges of the northern forests towards Harrokaan. In—"

"Yes, thank you, that will do."

"Of course." The Master of Diversities went to hand Bal-jarrak his report, but the man swept out of the chamber without taking it or even closing the heavy door behind him. The priest glanced over at the headless corpse. "Dear me," he said. "You do upset people, don't you?"

~

IN THE MIDDLE OF the afternoon, two breathless men came hurrying into the *Carp*. Yauva recognised one of them at once as Brilt'thig, the little priest who had spoken Iathena's healing-words over him at Falak-hoth. He was wearing his blue priestly robe and looking distracted.

"How's you?" said Yauva shaking his hand. "Will you have a jar on the house? You and your friend, that is?"

Brilt'thig seemed to have difficulty in replying.

"I'm still walkin' if that's what you're worried about," said Yauva brightly. "You don't look yourself, if you don't mind me sayin' so."

"Ah, yes," gasped Brilt'thig. "Ah, yes, ah, yes."

His companion stared at Yauva as though he had found an impossible treasure. His long grey hair and beard swept down from his broad hat and thin, tapering face and under his thick black brows were two pieces of glass fixed over his eyes by wires that went around his head and over

443

his ears. Yauva had seen this thing before and knew it was used by rich people in Valderthaan who couldn't see well. It was supposed to help your eyesight, but he never understood how it worked.

"The Baranthu is, ah, elated," said the man, gesturing with long, thin fingers. "He has had an *exalted* experience."

"What's that, then?" asked Yenl, overhearing.

"Ma," said Yauva, "this is Baranthu Brilt'thig, from the Towers."

"We've met. My cousin's his Archpriest, you know."

"Well, he came and said prayers when I was laid up in Falakhoth."

"Oh, that was you? Ta ever so much, Baranthu. So nice."

"But there's more!" burst out the little priest suddenly.

His companion intervened, "Allow me, Madam. I am Eirth'thog va-Haldrath, a distinguished healer, established at Arcorath. I am also a widely acclaimed student of physical anomalies and irregularities."

This brought conversation in the *Carp* to a dead halt.

"Blimey!" said someone in the silence.

Eirth'thog continued unabashed. "Now, because I take an interest in the unusual, my respected friend took me into his confidence regarding certain events—"

"It's about you, Yauva!" said Brilt'thig shrilly, finding his voice at last. "You were in a terrible state at Falakhoth. I didn't realise how bad your wound was until I spoke to Master Wyrdha later. If I'd known I might not have spoken the words at all, but when I said those prayers you were out of bed in no time."

"Aye," said Yauva, bewildered. "I just felt better. Was it bad? He might've told me."

"Well, I'd never seen the like. I thought about it all the way home. What could it mean?"

"Dunno," said Yauva.

"Tell us, then," said Yenl.

"Well, this morning, I was cleaning in the Lady's shrine—daily tasks, you know—and as I was dusting a candlestick, a vision fell upon me."

There was a tremendous gasp, and Brilt'thig swayed a little.

"What was it? What was it?" cried a dozen voices. This was far better than the new barmaid.

The priest steadied himself, then pointed straight at Yauva. "I saw *you!*" he cried. "You were standing as you are now, and then I saw a woman's hand touch you on the hip, just where you were injured. Then the vision was gone. Brief it was, but so real. Yauva, isn't it obvious?"

Not to Yauva, who answered the man with just a puzzled look.

"She cured you, Yauva. The Lady cured you, personally."

"What, when you said that prayer?" gasped Yenl. "You mean she answered it?"

"Yes. Ah, yes," breathed Brilt'thig. "My prayer. And I'd thought of going back to tailoring. The Lady forgive me."

The thunderous silence in the *Carp* was almost palpable. All the patrons knew that prayers innumerable rose daily to the host of the gods. But here was one that had had an answer. A direct, specific answer lavished on someone they had all known from his childhood. The Lady truly loved them.

Old Garfin rose. His simple soul went always to the heart of things. "I never thought I'd see the like," he said, choking a little and wiping his eye. "And I'd be proud if y'd let me shake y' hand." With tears on his face, he gripped Yauva's hand, and arm, and shoulder, as though it meant life itself. No-one had known what to do, but Garfin's example opened the floodgates and a frenzy of hand-shaking, back-slapping, and hand-clapping broke out.

Yenl and Utha gripped Yauva in simultaneous hugs and held on, Yenl in a kind of tightening ecstasy and Utha quietly weeping into his jacket. Volthar gaped for a while, then offered his stepson a quick but apparently sincere scuff along one shoulder.

After a while, Eirth'thog va-Haldrath spoke up, loud enough for everyone in the *Carp* to hear. "We believe," he said, "but let us also prove. May I, with the deepest respect, and as one whose business it is to probe the mysteries of the body, may I... *palpate* the site of your injury and cure?"

This brought a blanket silence again.

"You see, trained and experienced fingers may discover much that the eye can not."

"I think he wants to touch your hip, love," said Yenl to her gaping son.

"You know, like healers do."

"Oh. Right then," replied Yauva. "Shall we go upstairs, then?"

"Oh no," breathed Brilt'thig, "we must all be witnesses."

"Just tug your britches down a bit, love," said Yenl, ever business-like. "I'm sure it won't take a minute."

"What about decencies?" asked a horrified Yauva.

"This is clinical," intervened Eirth'thog, "purely clinical."

"There's ladies in here," retorted Yauva.

"Oh, give over," said an ample matron. "I've been a married woman these fifteen years."

"Not to me you haven't, beggin' your pardon, Mistress. I'll just ask all of you to observe the decencies, if you don't mind." And so, the patrons' wives and sweethearts and a few idle women who had drifted in brooded by the door and watched their menfolk gather in a protective crowd around Yauva. Even Utha and Yenl went to the door, the latter somewhat reluctantly.

"Get a good look, now," she snapped at Volthar. "I want a full report." She leaned close to Utha. "I'll see it later anyhow."

Eirth'thog flexed his knuckles and adjusted his pieces of glass as Yauva perched on a stool and tugged his breeches aside to expose the spot where the crossbow bolt had hammered into his hip. An answered prayer, he thought, should not be so embarrassing.

Eirth'thog peered at the spot for a long time, surrounded by a trembling, watchful silence. "But..." he stammered at last. "But this is not possible."

"Don't keep us in suspense," called a woman at the door. "What've y' found?"

"Nothing I should," replied the healer with a shaky voice. "The wound is there, the flesh is there, I can see where the arrow impaled him, but there's no scar, no joining, and no bleeding. This wound has never healed."

"Is it that bad?" asked Yauva, suddenly worried.

Eirth'thog placed his quivering fingers over Yauva's wound, gently pressing from various angles. He looked up. "Smashed," he said. "Smashed to bits. The fragments even move around. But one more test."

He carefully eased the sides of the wound apart and edged his fingers inside. To a gasp of horror from the crowd, he extracted a splinter of bone. "Does it hurt, my friend?" he whispered. "Does it hurt at all?"

Yauva shrugged and shook his head.

Eirth'thog closed his eyes. "No healing whatsoever," he said. "You should not be walking."

Yauva stood up and adjusted his breeches.

"Well, I am, so why shouldn't I? You won't credit what he did, Ma," he called, but a cry cut him short. It was Brilt'thig.

"Look, look!" he called. "The owl! The owl!"

"Where?" folk cried.

Brilt'thig pointed to Yauva and almost shrieked. "I see it! The owl, the Lady's bird! It's shining! It's flying over Yauva! It's perching on his shoulder!"

"I see it too!" howled Garfin.

"And me! And me!" called several voices.

The little priest put a hand to his eyes, staggered and fell heavily among the stools and benches. "Oh, Yauva," he whispered weakly. "Her favour, her special favour. She's chosen you for something, she must have."

"A gift!" cried a new voice. A tall, dark man nobody had noticed before was on his feet. "A gift to you all. Her magic on a son of Lukar, as it was of old, before the kings. He is yours!"

~

VAL-ZAJJHAK SAT FOR some time, seemingly with nothing better to do than idly sip his ale, but he knew his next step and only waited for the moment. The *Carp* had emptied. Carrying on normally after the revelation of the Lady's healing seemed the wrong thing to do.

Volthar edged about the room, going often to stand at the street door, as if to reassure himself, with the sight of the fish-quay, that the normal world still remained outside his inn. The vraakhin watched him and felt his fear. The miraculous and the magical had come too close. Val-zajjhak fingered the lion-teeth that hung around his neck and sat unnoticed.

"It's queer, Ma." He heard Yauva say. "It's just queer. I'm glad I can walk and all, but I just don't know what to think. What's goin' to happen now?"

"Maybe nothing, love," said Yenl. "Just enjoy walking and get on with things." She took her son's hand and looked at him a long time. "You're just like your dad," she said. "How about you just take Utha and go off somewhere? Have a think, clear your head. I know I need to."

"That's an idea, Ma. I could do with that. We'll have a walk down by the Towers and have a chat with Uncle Tal, maybe even go along the river a bit."

And now Val-zajjhak leaned forward. The right time had arrived. "The Bearpit promises a fine show today," he said. "I intended to go. I would be happy to have Yauva's company. And, of course, that of his charming lady."

Utha giggled and Yenl turned with a little squeal.

"Excuse us, Master. I didn't know you were still here," Yauva said as recognition dawned on his face. "He saw me at Falakhoth as well, Ma. Just looked in for a minute, like."

"I see a changed man," said the vraakhin. "In many ways. Will you join me?"

"Haven't been near the pit for months. Can't afford it."

"My pleasure," said the vraakhin smoothly. "Please do not concern yourself about the cost."

"Now isn't that decent?" said Yenl. "There's good folk in the world yet. Off you go then and I'll tell Volthar—he won't moan to me." She gave a little curtsey to Val-zajjhak. "Our thanks, Master. We're right grateful."

The vraakhin smiled. "My pleasure," he said.

The three left the *Golden Carp* with Utha clinging delightedly to Yauva's arm, while Val-zajjhak strode slightly ahead of the young couple with his staff measuring the way. They walked along streets that led them out of the Fish-quay and towards the marketplace at Lukar's farther side. The Bearpit was next to the market, conveniently tempting traders and drivers who had made the weary journey up to the city to spend a little of their newly earned money.

The news of Yauva's miracle was spreading fast. People stopped to look at him or gather others over to point him out. He did not know if he liked this. A new and most uncomfortable mix of pride and embarrassment at the exposure was stirring.

Their route crossed the ancient square at the feet of the Towers of the Wound, Iathena's ancient shrine. Here, at the sound of shouting and a tinny rattle, Yauva pulled Utha and Val-zajjhak to a halt. A ragged old man sat on the flagstones, propped against a wall, and sharing a scrap of matting with a display of roughly made amulets, figures of gods, and a bizarre jumble of animal skulls, teeth and claws, some carved with symbols, some strung into necklaces. Stood against the wall was a crutch, the armpiece padded with layers of dirty cloth. Hundreds of teeth hung from it threaded on cords. Tied to the armpiece was a crude metal bell and as the old man shook the crutch, the bell and his own hoarse voice easily drew the attention of the people in the square.

"C'mon then, who'll buy from the skull-man, eh? Lion's skull for the bad spirits—keeps them away! Owl skull under your pillow—makes you wise! Lion's teeth round your neck—gives you courage and scares the spirits. Come on, then! Don't think you don't need 'em!"

"There's old Gaur-van!" said Yauva. "Hang on, I want to see what he's got." He ran over to the old man and crouched down beside him.

"Well now, it's the miracle man!" cried Gaur-van. "Wonderful, it is, wonderful. Honour ter have your patronage. If you're looking, that is."

"Well, I might be," said Yauva happily, not stopping to wonder what patronage was. "Got anything with the Lady's signs on it? New, like, not somethin' I've had afore."

"Well, now, I might have, I might. Them's the things for you, I reckon, eh? Lady's signs, I mean. Not surprised that's what you want after what she done for your leg. Bet it makes you feel real special, eh?"

Yauva smiled and nodded.

"Well then! Let's see what me got." Gaur-van tipped a bag out onto the matting and rummaged through the bone and wood carvings. "Don't want no claws nor teeth, I'd say. Not t'day. We want something special for you t'day!"

Yauva pointed to a tiny shape of bone tied to a leather thong. "What's that?" he asked.

"That? Got the Lady's name on it in Old Speech, that has. Carved out of a mountain lion's tooth, it is. You tie it round your head and it protects your mind from the bad spirits. Makes you strong as well, same as the lion. Come here and try it."

Yauva leaned forward and Gaur-van held up the thong in his broken-nailed fingers. He placed his hand on the young man's forehead for a moment, holding the amulet in place. Silently, he appeared to gauge the effect.

"Nah, what's the point? Reckon if she'd do that for your leg, your head's in no danger. Leather's too short anyway and I've got no more."

"I quite like it, said Yauva. "I could get a bit of leather."

"Nah," repeated Gaur-van. His hand moved slightly.

"You're right," said Yauva. "Lady can look after my head without it. What about that one?"

"Ah, now that's different," croaked Gaur-van. "Carved that one meself. Lovely bit of oak as I come by. How do you like it?" He held up a polished wooden figure of an owl. Its eyes were inset with glass and lines of bright paint highlighted the carefully cut wing feathers.

"That one!" said Yauva at once. "I'll have that!"

"Sure, now?" said Gaur-van, watching intently. "Got some other stuff here, real nice—"

"No, give us the owl! How much?"

"Couldn't take your money!" croaked Gaur-van. "Not you, not t'day! Have it on me." And his fingers moved secretly.

"No. I want to pay for it. I want to make it special."

Gaur-van smiled, and his thick tongue ran across his lips. "Know what you mean. Makes it mean something, don't it?" He affected a deep sigh. "Well, it's two copper bits, son. Sounds a lot, eh? But I got ter make a living."

"There," said Yauva, thrusting the coins into the skull-man's grimy hand.

"Arna shine on you, son, and the Lady of course, but she has anyway, eh?"

"She has that." Yauva pocketed the owl. "Not half, she has!"

"That's right, that's right," wheezed the old man. "Well, you look after that owl, and it'll keep bad spirits miles away and do all kinds of good for you. More than usual, I suspect, being as the Lady's got a special interest in you already. Yep, keep that owl by you and I'll bet the ale at the *Carp* will taste twice as good!"

"That's not saying much," laughed Yauva, rising to his feet.

"Where you off to?" asked Gaur-van. "Going to the Towers?"

"No, the Bearpit." He grinned. "That feller there is payin', so it's all the better!"

Gaur-van leered broadly, "Nice," he said. "Well, you have a good time, son. Bear-baiting it is t'day and they've got some whopper of a bear, from what I've heard. Make mincemeat of them dogs! Mind out for pick-pockets, though. Don't want ter lose your owl!"

"Oh, it's safe," said Yauva. "You have a good time yourself. Hope you make a bit of money."

"Thanks, son. Do me best." And he began his clamour with the bell.

Heads turned and Yauva made to leave, awkwardly aware of groups of staring people. As the young man trotted across the square, Gaur-van caught Val-zajjhak's cold eye and nodded. He had felt the vraakhin's work in his customer's mind and now he had added his own.

"Old Gaur-van says there's a real big bear at the pit today," Yauva informed the vraakhin as he rejoined him. "Should be good."

"Then we must get a good place. Did you find something to your liking?"

"Aye," said Yauva. "Look at this."

Fishing in his pocket, he missed how, once more, the two vraakhin exchanged glances. Gaur-van's tongue darted over his dry lips as he stared in excitement. Val-zajjhak was as impassive as ever.

"There, look," exclaimed Yauva. He produced the owl from among the bits and pieces in his pocket.

"Ooh, that's nice," said Utha.

Val-zajjhak took the owl in his hand a moment. "Ah, yes," he breathed in finely simulated surprise. "I have seen this kind before. They are very powerful."

"You know about things like that? Are you a vraakhin?"

"I have been called that, for I have a little learning." Val-zajjhak

451

looked at the owl as he spoke, and a light seemed to flicker in his eyes. His heart quickened a little, for much of the power in the amulet was his, placed and bound there by spells and strong charms. It had been ready for Yauva for many months—or rather, for the one who would fill the part in the vraakhin's plans into which Yauva was unwittingly stepping. And it was working. Once Yauva had seen the spell-laden owl, it had been nearly impossible for him to refuse it.

They had only walked a few yards past the towers when Val-zajjhak was stopped once more.

"Hang on," said Yauva. "I'm goin' in here." He jerked his head towards the eastern tower, whose wide, weathered door opened onto the square.

"Go later," said the vraakhin hurriedly. "We should be at the ringside for the start."

"Won't be above a minute. I want to get this owl blessed. My uncle Tal-ver's archpriest here, you know. He'll speak a word over it." He dashed up the steps into the Towers, dragging Utha with him and ignoring calls and pointing fingers.

Val-zajjhak paced the cracked flags of the square for some minutes. He feared no goddess, but he was impatient and something was disturbing him. He looked up at the dark, ancient towers and recalled a younger man who had come there proud and confident in a red robe, the sign of the sun glittering in gold thread beneath his throat. Without thinking, Val-zajjhak fingered his robe beneath the collar, felt the rents of ripped-out threads, the ragged stitching of the patches. Fourteen years since. No-one would know him in that tower now, though some in Valder-thaan might.

Another simple memory came to him. He was standing in the terraced gardens below the Shrine on a summer's dawn. The Morning Song drifted down to him and sunlight flashed on lake and river. Suddenly, he had become aware of a reality outside of himself, of something greater than him, that seemed to rush from the valleys, the gardens, and all the world, calling to him through the glory of the morning. Val-zajjhak darkened his mind at once. This single, lovely thought was the enemy of all he now was. He could not permit himself to think it. His thoughts now contained a colouring of fear. If the thought of sun on the lake was to become intolerable…

He dismissed the memory as sentiment brought back merely by his presence next to this tower. He noticed Gaur-van struggling to his feet and peering at him intently, so he gripped his staff tighter and strode to meet Yauva and Utha as they came down the steps of the Towers.

"Wouldn't do it," said the young man miserably. "Took it and looked at it and said no, wouldn't do it."

"Indeed?" said Val-zajjhak, relieved. "But come, we are almost late." He propelled Yauva from the square with his free hand, making for the solid old bridge that spanned the river and led across to the markets. They hurried across as a bell struck the hour, the river itself flowing beneath it straight through Lukar like a hasty traveller. Overhead, the two Towers of the Wound reared, just as they had done all Yauva's life. The huge bronze signs of the moon in her phases had always moved him, but today he paused and looked at the buildings as if searching for something.

Val-zajjhak watched, knowing what was happening, and choosing his moment said, "You seem disturbed, my friend. Nothing is wrong, I hope."

"Don't know, don't know," muttered Yauva. "Somethin's up, but I don't know—oh! There! It's them! Them suns! They shouldn't be there." He pointed at the Towers' main doors. Above them were the inevitable reminders that this was Arna's land: two gold suns and the sign of the mountain-lion.

"What's wrong with them, lovey?" asked Utha.

"I do not understand," said Val-zajjhak in long-rehearsed puzzlement. "Surely this is Arna's kingdom?"

"We had them Towers afore we had Arna! Someone built them for the Lady. Lukar was *her* city. Arna's lady she might be, but this place is hers."

Val-zajjhak seized the moment. "I understand you," he murmured. "Such a state of affairs distresses many. But you know this, and perhaps a day will come when you can speak for them." He moved a hand stealthily. "And who better, eh?" He slapped Yauva on the back. "Well now! Shall we go?"

453

"Never used to bother me, them things," mumbled Yauva, now very confused. His companion moved his hand.

"You must think other thoughts today," Val-zajjhak smiled broadly, pleased with what he had seen surface in Yauva's mind. "Come now, the bears will not wait for us."

In its earliest days, the Bearpit had been just that: a dug-out pit where the men of Lukar could watch bear-baiting or professional fighters. Before the time of the kings, one of the city's rulers had enlarged the pit, lined its sides with stone, and built terraces for the viewers. He erected a covered seat for himself or any of the city nobility who fancied an hour's diversion. Many years later, another leader built a wall to encircle the entire arena, so that anyone wishing to see the entertainment could not avoid paying on entry. The fighters and animal owners had welcomed each development, but did not care for the percentage of takings that went into the city coffers for the privilege of using the improved Bearpit. Like most of Lukar's old buildings, the pit was now an example of good work ravaged by decay and inadequate repair.

Yauva and Utha ran up behind a group of people still filing in. Val-zajjhak strode up behind, preoccupied with his thoughts.

"You've just made it," said the man ahead of them. "We're nearly full. Shrevar's got the place today."

Another man in the queue turned, leering. "Goin' t' be a good show." He said and tightened his grip on the waist of the woman beside him. "Promised y' that, didn't I, darlin'?"

"It's not messy, is it?" she asked, trembling somewhat. "I heard there's blood and all sorts."

"Just have another drink, me love. Nothin' t' worry about."

"Better not be." She took her paramour's near-empty wineskin and helped herself. Then she noticed Yauva and stared at him with a puzzled expression as if she was trying to remember his face. Suddenly her eyes went wide, and she talked excitedly to her man. Obviously, she had heard about his miraculous healing and soon the queue was buzzing.

Utha laughed. "You're famous, love."

"Aye," said Yauva, "I know."

They found seats against a wall, but they were well back from the pit itself with only a partial view. The couple who had been in front of them had found seats directly opposite at the edge of the pit where spectators could take the risk of leaning over the wooden railing attached to the partition that ran round the entire circumference.

"Well, we'll make the best of it," sighed Yauva. In truth, he was glad to be away from the centre of attention. The couple had quickly spread the news that the Miracle Man of Lukar was present. Most people did not know what had happened in the *Golden Carp*, but this was hardly a problem. The woman offered her own freely embellished version of whatever had been reported to her and others passed it on. By the time Yauva was seated, a dozen variations, vague but sensational, were circulating. Worse, the couple were scanning the tiers, searching for their hero.

Val-zajjhak was leaning forward in his seat, eyes fixed on the audience opposite. His hands, white-knuckled, gripped his staff. His eyes narrowed and still staring ahead, he gave a sharp nod.

"There, look! There he is! Told y' it were him!" The man was on his feet, brandishing his wineskin as his woman screeched and waved her scarf. "That's him," he cried. "That's him she cured!" He faced Yauva and made a drunken gesture somewhere between a bow and a salute. "The Shinin's been on y' right enough, mister! Beautiful, and lovely, and it's wonderful. Anybody as cares about the Lady thinks it's wonderful!"

Yauva waved back, embarrassed and hating the exposure. Longing for the show to start, he glanced round at Val-zajjhak and shrugged.

The vraakhin leaned close to his ear and murmured, "You mean so much to them." And with those enchanted words, Yauva's eyes widened, and he gave a gasp of amazement. He saw it now. He was part of Iathena's religion, part of the way of belief and life that had been old before the kings came. She had cured him, had she not, and brought her old rule of the valleys into the present moment. Now he was a focus for the beliefs of almost everyone there—almost, in fact, the whole of the North. It *must* be true. Magic wasn't dead. The Lady must have chosen him to prove it.

Over the noise of the crowd came the irresistible voice of Val-zajjhak. "Masters, men of the valleys and the hills, this is a great day for all of us who honour Iathena, our Beautiful Mother. We dedicate this spectacle to her honour, for *the man she chose*—" he lingered on the phrase as Yauva squirmed, "—is among you. *But...* will you only stare? Will no-one give this privileged man a seat where his view will be the best? My brothers, it is only fitting."

A silence tensed for a few seconds, then came a shout. "Aye, I will! Come round here, master! Have my place and welcome." The drunken man was pushing his way round the seats, pulling his woman after him. She went without protest, wide-eyed, clutching what now looked to be an empty wineskin.

Yauva would have refused the offer, but Val-zajjhak whispered, "Go on, do not disappoint them." And so he obeyed, tugging the giggling Utha as they shuffled crab-like along the row.

Val-zajjhak remained where he was.

When they reached the place at the rail on the pit's farther side, Yauva felt as if he had been slapped on the shoulders and grasped by the hand a hundred times. Oddly, there were people who simply wanted to touch him, as if that would do something for them. Queer, thought Yauva, but still, it was a nice feeling.

Once settled, they waited for the show to begin. The wait was a long one. Everyone was growing impatient, but nothing was happening. Suddenly massive iron grilles crashed down in the doorways at each end of the pit. This was confusing. Something should be coming out, not being kept in. An incensed roaring and bellowing filtered through from unseen passageways.

"Listen to that, will you?" said the man next to Yauva. "What size of thing'd make a noise like that?"

Yauva gripped the wooden rail in excitement. "It's a big one, right enough!" he said. "Hope the pit's deep enough."

"Don't you fear," said the man. "I've seen giants of bears in here and none of them could reach nobody. Not for want of tryin' though. They'd pull you down and eat you, soon as look at you, some of them things."

"What're they waiting for?" asked Yauva. "Supposed to be a bear-baitin' and I can't hear no dogs. Must've got somethin' else lined up."

A horn sounded from the box that had held the seat of the lords of

Lukar. There, lowering the horn from his lips, stood a figure instantly recognisable. Va-Shrevar the showman. He was dressed impressively in a grey wolf-skin hat and an embroidered deep blue coat, over which his long grey hair and beard flowed. A silver earring glittered as he grinned all over his broad, scarred face, looking every inch the ex-fighter he was. He raised his arms, brandishing the horn.

"Good people," he called in his deep, coarse voice. "My patrons! My friends!" Applause and laughter. Va-Shrevar waited for silence. "Friends," he continued, "this is a unique day, absolutely unique. Our spectacle has become—what should I say?—a celebration!"

Murmurs and scattered applause as the showman executed a reverent bow toward Yauva, who groaned and folded his arms tightly, trying to become as small as he could.

Va-Shrevar was a good performer. He knew exactly how to manipulate the heady excitement of his audience, caught up as they were in the miracle of their goddess. "Friends, this spectacle has become the Lady's. Your enjoyment will mean her honour."

Applause and stamping met this.

"I said there would be a bear...." He broke off purely for effect. He looked around the lines of expectant faces. "And there *is*—one of the biggest I've had the uneasy privilege of owning. Straight from the western forests. How my trappers are still in one piece I'll never know! Perhaps the Lady kept the beast quiet for this afternoon."

Cheers accompanied the stamping this time.

"But where are the dogs, you may be thinking?" He savoured the silence this produced. That was precisely what many of them had been thinking. "For a *day* like *today*, a bear against dogs would not be appropriate. We need something bigger!"

The crowd shouted out in agreement.

"We need something *grander*." More cheers. The crowd was now at the edge of hysteria, right where Va-Shrevar wanted them. "Let it be, bear..." He paused with a grin on his face, "*Against* Bear!"

A great howl of acclaim went up.

Va-Shrevar put the horn to his lips and blew two long notes. The grilles went clattering up and the two dark doorways confronted each other across the pit. The shouting died down as a hideous roaring and bellowing erupted from the doors as if they were two black mouths screaming hatred. Nearer came the roars, vicious and full of fury. Everyone leaned forward, holding their breath. Women clung to their men or made ready to cover their eyes. Nobody knew what was coming.

Then the first beast appeared, men behind it forcing it into the pit with torches and long goads. It lurched bewildered into the daylight to gasps and delighted screams. Standing almost directly under Yauva, it reared up and sniffed the air.

Yauva yelled and recoiled. "The size of it! Look at the size of it! Look at them claws!"

Va-Shrevar saw his fright and called across, "Don't worry, master! Those walls are far too high for him! And the Lady will keep you safe!"

Despite this, the bear made some trial swipes. His great claws scraped the side of the pit not too far below the feet of the front row. They shrieked and jumped back.

The second bear appeared. Not so huge as the first, but a terrifying beast nonetheless. Red eyes, black pelt, claws like scythes, and shaking with fury. It flung itself at once on the other animal and brought a rending blow against its head. Blood spattered out as the bears grappled, tearing and biting.

Odds were called and wagers taken. People began to shout for the smaller black bear. Yauva put a few coins on it. What it lacked in bulk, it made up for in strength and sheer ferocity. Its reckless attack so resembled human courage the spectators sided with it at once.

Hunger, confinement, and the powder Va-Shrevar reputedly put in the bear's last feed before the fight had made the creatures frighteningly wild. Now hundreds of shouting people maddened them even further into a frenzy. Wounds went unheeded as they gouged and clawed at each other. Around they circled, lashing out in what seemed an endless contest.

The sand was reddening and the larger brown bear was now dragging a limb. It was more easily beaten down and the crowd's support for the smaller black bear got even louder as they sensed victory was near. The brown beast pulled itself up against the wall, roaring, spitting blood, and striking sluggishly. The great black head of the smaller bear lunged past the haphazard attacks and fastened onto the throat of its larger rival. The full strength of its terrible jaw drove through pelt, flesh, and sinew as the black bear gripped and shook, clawing all the while at the body beneath it.

At last, the movements of the heavy brown limbs grew weaker, slower, then stopped altogether. Even then, the black bear waited for a while, jaw still clamped shut on its opponent's neck, as if to be sure its prey was truly dead. It placed a hind paw on the dead body, wrenched its own head back and tore out the throat. The creature slowly looked around the cheering audience, chewing its mouthful of flesh, then dropped on all fours to feed in earnest.

Yauva shouted in delight. The black bear had won. It had won his wager for him. He leaned out and yelled at it. "Go on, Blackie, have a good feed! I'd stand you one at the *Carp*, but it don't look as if you'll need it!"

Laughter and applause, the bear ignoring him. No-one saw Val-za-jjhak's hands make a brief movement, drawing together then suddenly apart.

Yauva was making the most of the occasion. "Let us know when you're ready, Blackie, and I'll get you a jug of ale to wash that down! Cellar's best!"

The wooden rail split. Yauva lurched into space. There was a collective gasp of horror as he swayed, missed the grasping hands of those around him, and fell headlong into the pit.

The impact winded him and he could hear Utha screaming from far away. The bear turned its head. Dazed, Yauva pushed himself up and spat sand out of his mouth. The bear stared at him, then opened its blood-filled mouth and roared as it realised a new enemy had arrived. Yauva was jolted back to his senses. He scrabbled to his feet and tried to scale the wall, jumping at the hands straining down but to no avail. They built the wall to keep even the tallest bears in the pit. He ran wildly to the nearest passage but the iron grilles were still down to cut off the bears' escape. Yauva screamed down the passage, but no-one came.

The cries of the crowd drifted down to him as if from far away. *Let something down! Where's the handlers? Why don't the handlers come? Is there a spear?* But confusion or shock or an enchantment had fallen upon the place and no aid came.

He turned to face the bear—oh, Iathena! The size of it! The black bear may have looked the smaller from his seat, but from a dozen feet away in the pit it was the largest living creature he'd ever seen with claws as big as daggers. It reared up on to its hind legs and roared.

Yauva sank down, numb. He had no will to run. What could he possibly do? The bear dropped to all fours, baring its teeth at him. Those teeth! Yauva found he couldn't take his eyes off the bear's teeth. Oh, may it be quick, not too much pain. His hand moved with the habit of years to his pocket and drew out one of the amulets he kept there. It was his new one, the owl. Then he screamed, for the bear came at him, lumbering at speed over the bloody sand. Yauva curled up at once, hands over his head, eyes squeezed tightly shut. The screams of the crowd and the grunts of the bear filled the air as he waited for the bear's talons and teeth to rip him apart.

Nothing happened.

Silence descended in the pit. All he could hear was the deep breathing of the bear.

What was this? Why was nothing happening? He shook with fear. The thing was right there, but by Iathena, he had to look. It almost stopped his heart. The bear was standing over him, watching him with its insane eyes, the claws of its hind feet hardly a foot away. Gradually, hideously, the great black mountain stooped over him, moving its face closer. Blood and slaver dripped on him and he felt the beast's hot breath on his face. The stench of it made him dizzy. A massive claw moved at the edge of vision, but he could not tear his eyes away from its jaw. Any moment, those teeth would end it all.

Without warning, the bear reared up again. It raised a forepaw, growling. Yauva, shocked, saw his owl-amulet dangling from a claw. He wasn't sure how the bear had gotten hold of it, but for a second he let himself hope there was a power in the little wooden thing that could save him. The bear let the carving drop and Yauva snatched at it. And hope fled, for the beast was stooping again and the murderous paws were stretching out. Yauva covered his face, writhing as he felt the paws close round his body. It was going to crush him, then.

Lady let me die now, before me ribs are split....

The bear picked him up.

He shook as the muzzle brushed his cheek. He felt the movement of the iron muscles against his body, the heaving of the furnace-bellow lungs. *Lady, make it quick, don't want to feel it, don't let Ma grieve, guide me on the Dark Path. Will I meet my dad, will I know him? Don't remember him well.*

But the bear was not crushing him. When he swung back to awareness, he realised that the thing was lumbering across the pit, carrying him. Was it taking him over to the dead beast to kill him there? No, it was making for the place where he had fallen into the pit. He felt himself being lifted. He forced himself to look and there, a little above him, was the broken rail with Utha's face behind it.

He hung there for a moment and heard a voice say, "Grab hold, then. You're all right, come on." Someone had found a rope and was lowering it down.

Yauva reached up, grimly grasped the rope and felt himself lifted from the bear's embrace. He was dimly aware of hands grabbing his arms and clothing, of the paws letting go and his limbs bumping on stone as he was hauled back onto the tiers of seats. He wondered about the bear and turned his head. The last thing he remembered was the sight of the great creature staggering to the centre of the pit and sitting down heavily, like a confused and weary man. Darkness came down then and through it, a voice saying, *You see this sign? The Lady must have chosen him!* Shouting and crying welled up, but faded away in the blissful blackness that overtook him.

CHAPTER 21

New Information

TWO HUNDRED NOVICES ALMOST choked on their venison when Azhur appeared in the Wait during evening meal. Not only was this the novice who had achieved the most astounding advance in the Novitiate's history, it was also a visit from a luminary who was surely the first Loremaster of the Second Circle to stroll unannounced into the private world of the novices and act as if he thought everyone there was his equal, but that was Azhur. His exalted identity was so new and unfamiliar to him he seemed to have difficulty perceiving it was there.

As he came down the steps under the arch some older lads, who knew they could get away with it, started a chant of *Wring-er! Wring-er!* and hammered on the tables till the Tower of the Novitiate trembled with the shouting and pounding. Azhur was mortified beyond measure, but nonetheless delighted by the welcome. He grinned widely and covered his crimson face with his hands. He still had the delightful presence of mind and sense of fun to cross his arms on his chest and bow deeply as if he were before the Valgraav's court. This provoked a roar that almost brought down the Tower.

Those who knew the former novice best rushed to him and added to his happy embarrassment with much backslapping, hugging, and hand-shaking, with not a few vigorously congratulatory punches. Among them was Tyr, who deliberately hung back until the melee was over in order to have his friend to himself for a while. When things died down, he grabbed Azhur by the arm, dragged him to a bench and sat him down. Last of all, he thumped a tankard on the table in front of him.

"Where y' been?" he said. The question carried more force than Tyr had intended.

"Ah," said Azhur, instantly acting out his nickname. "Being made Loremaster...."

"Takes a lot of time does it?"

"You've no idea. It never stops."

"I thought maybe it were just for that Conclave thing. So y' could help Galdtchav."

Azhur shook his head, "Oh, no. A priest is a priest, and a Loremaster is a Loremaster. You can only leave the Lore, as they say, if the Valgraav and the Archpriest agree. Same goes for leaving the Second Circle, and nothing's been said about that. In fact, they're throwing duties at me: Shrine, ritual, instruction, research, I don't know what. I'll be tucking the novices up at night at this rate."

"Suppose Galdtchav's happy."

"Oh yes. Well, he needs the help."

Tyr looked directly at his friend. "Y' see Aienna?"

Azhur's fingers became oddly still. "Ah, yes. Yes, I do."

"As much as before?"

The Loremaster set his jaw. "Well, almost, yes."

Tyr looked down at the table. He appeared slightly angry, slightly hurt, extremely awkward, slightly glad. But he said nothing.

"Um... it's, well, you know, a special thing. You know that. And... and I'll be with her all my life, I hope, and that needs time. At the moment, you understand?"

Tyr smiled. "Aye, suppose. It's not like me and Widder Grinhshin's lass behind the grain shed, is it?"

Azhur opened his mouth but found nothing to say for a few moments. "I don't imagine so."

"Mind," said Tyr with country frankness, "I wanted y' to do me initiation with me. It would have made it special."

Now it was Azhur's turn to examine the table. "It, ah, it's always special."

Tyr turned abruptly to his friend. "I thought y'd hold me towel and me blacks." It was half a declaration of sorrow, half an accusation. It escaped from him before he could stop it.

"Ah," said Azhur. "Yes. Well, I would have, if things had been, ah, as they were. But it's different now, not so easy. I can't just… you know."

Tyr heard himself mumble, "Wyrdha would have come." Awful. Tyr regretted it as soon as he said it, but it was out there now.

Azhur's hands gripped each other so tightly the knuckles cracked. He looked away, not knowing what to do.

"Well, what *were* y' doin'?" asked Tyr at last. He knew he should leave it alone, but he wanted to know.

Azhur looked around distractedly. "I'm sorry, Tyr, I just didn't, you know, fit it in."

"Havin' y' breakfast with Aienna? Were y'?"

Azhur straightened up, all his habitually concealed emotions struggling across his face. He was suddenly honest, courageous, defensive, and loyal to Aienna and himself. "No," he said tightly.

Then Tyr shocked himself, for now he thought of more things to say. Things about Azhur he could punish him with, things about their friendship he could force into his heart and twist. The wonders of his initiation were momentarily forgotten, the soul-light of the Laver flickered as if at risk of going out. He clamped his jaw shut, suddenly ashamed at how easily his resentment had turned him on his friend. Azhur was in love, and that was something he did not yet understand. He only knew it was a great gift. And he liked Aienna. He was determined to like Aienna. He swallowed, breathed hard through his nose, and made himself say, "I don't grudge it y'," said the lad. "Y' know that? I just wanted y' there."

"Ah, I know," replied Azhur with some difficulty. "Thank you. I'm so terribly sorry I wasn't there." This earned the Loremaster a hard but affectionate punch on the arm.

"Right then. Well, we'll talk about it sometime, eh?"

Azhur continued to look at the table. "Yes. Yes, of course. Some time or other, yes." He kept staring at the wet rings left by the tankard and seemed to be trying to say something. Suddenly he turned and looked at Tyr with an intensity so unlike him that the lad started back. "I *have* to do this, Tyr. I must. It's who I am, it's what I'm meant to be. If I'm to be Aienna's husband, I must be as good a priest and Loremaster as I can. I owe it to her—I promised her. It's for myself and for her I'll be the best Loremaster possible. My elevation was meant, don't you see? Fated. I must be a priest for the woman I love, and for my mother, rest her. That's who I have to be. Do you understand? Do you?"

"Aye, aye!" cried Tyr, alarmed by his friend's sudden earnestness. "What's up with y'? I've never seen y' like this. Y're like somebody else!"

"Well, it's me!" stated Azhur firmly. "My... my calling. It's what Arna made me for. It comes from him, straight from him. That's why I do it."

"Aye, but y' look right angry. Have I done somethin'?"

At this, Azhur seemed to settle, "Angry? No, no, not at all, I just—it's very important to me."

"Must be. Y' give me a right fright there."

The priestly fingers interlocked. "Sorry. Comes from a very deep—well, it's very deep. Very."

"What do y' mean?"

"Can't, ah, can't say more than that, sorry. Closely guarded—it has to be. And... and that's it." This last seemed to be said as an act of courage, a confrontation with some great threat just to utter the words. An invisible but very solid wall had risen. Azhur clearly intended to stay on his side of it.

Tyr gaped silently, stunned at the transformation he had witnessed. Yet Azhur's words sounded familiar to him. They held the same determination he'd found to complete his initiation. He had a thousand questions, but he knew must ask none of them now. The only thing to do was break the moment. He snatched his tankard, took a violent swig and, wet-shirted, said, "Right then. There y' go, eh?"

Azhur looked around, took some token sips from his own tankard and said, "Yes. There you go indeed." There was a moment of not looking at each other as Azhur recovered from his own assertiveness. The invisible wall slowly disappeared. "Ah... I came down to, ah, sort of make it

465

up to you for the initiation. I discovered since that I can actually res-chedule duties for an entire day. It turns out there're things a Loremaster can make happen if he wants to, but, ah, that's between ourselves."

Tyr sat up at once. "Aye, crackin'! What about Aienna, though?"

"Oh, she'll give me the day off too. So, it's settled? I'll fix a day and meet you at *The Cure*, the tavern in the Potter's Square, then we'll eat and make a day of it. You could bring Authran."

"Right, y're on!"

"Marvellous. Well, off I go. I have to help some archivists be boring."

"Borin'? You, bored with Scrolls? Get off!"

"Oh, so much to learn! Let me tell you, Tyr-shan, Scrolls are never boring, but archivists! Be warned!"

"I'll look out for them! Ey, talkin' of archives and stuff, I were won-derin'—"

"Not going to have time, Tyr, sorry. You might need an archivist after all."

"No, it's got to be you. I can't ask anybody else."

"All right. Quick, though."

"Well, it's nowt to do with archives, y' just put me in mind of it. Remember when I'd come out the Laver at me initiation and y' was runnin' after Jar—"

"Voice *down!*" hissed Azhur in his fiercest whisper. "Tyr, that's the biggest secret in the kingdom! Have you—"

"It's all right. Look, everybody's gone, nearly. No, I've not said nothin', neither's Ran. Lady Iera'd skin us!"

"She would, actually." Azhur put his head in his hands. "Oh, Tyr. My heart! Please don't do that again."

Tyr was bent over the table, convulsing with laughter. "Sorry," he said, whispering. "But, look, tell us this...."

"All right, but only because the shock's made me too weak to leave. What is it?"

"Well," whispered Tyr between stifled explosions of mirth, "remember when, y'know... *that feller* said, 'Is it me, is it me?'"

"Keep it down. Yes, what about it?"

"Well, I were thinkin' about it and I don't get it, neither does Ran.

So…?"

Azhur relaxed at this, though he kept whispering. "Oh. Well, that's not exactly a secret, so I suppose…."

"Go on."

"Um… All right. Well, you know that the person in a royal family who succeeds a king is always the eldest son?"

"Aye. What if he's got a lass?"

"That doesn't matter, just assume it's the oldest son. Now, when *that feller's* father died—"

"Anthu Feller, aye."

"Tyr!"

"Sorry."

"Good. Well… our—" Azhur mouthed the next word, "Valgraav—wasn't the oldest."

"Bugger!"

"*Tyr!* Please!"

"Didn't say anythin'."

"The, er, you know, thought his oldest son was… unsuitable to follow him."

"'He'd have been rubbish, y' mean?"

"Um… yes."

"Would he?"

"Yes, probably. Never mind the details. The fact is, the second son was far more gifted and capable, while his brother might well have been disastrous. So, their father decreed his second son should follow him. For everyone's sake."

"And the second one's…?"

"Our current feller, yes."

"What the other one do?"

"Oh, he was furious, but his father had to get his way. Fathers do. They shouldn't always, but they do." Azhur was silent; his face seemed grim. Perhaps he thought the old Valgraav's decision was foolish.

"Azhur?"

"What?"

"What about the other one?"

467

"Oh. Well, he rules the eastern part of the realm from Amouch Arna, on the east coast. Under his brother, of course, but he still resents it bitterly."

"Never knew all that."

"Not too many people do. It's not really a secret, but it all happened in court circles and nobody mentions it now. Most ordinary people don't know and don't care about that sort of thing. Amouch Arna's a long way away, and it's nothing to do with most of us, is it?"

"Right enough. What's it got to do with *Is it me?* though?"

"The, er, younger son—"

"What's his name again?"

"Tyr, behave. The younger son wasn't sure about the arrangement at all, and said so at court, but his father prevailed, and it was done. No public explanations of course, it just went ahead. But I think the, ah, younger fellow had to admit his brother could actually ruin the kingdom. He realised it really was for the best and went along with it, but he was a sensitive, scrupulous type, and he struggled with nagging questions: *Should I really have done it? Was it proper? Was it fair?* He worried about his brother and tried to keep the peace, but his brother was very bitter. They've hardly seen each other since. So, there you are, mystery solved. And now I really do have to go."

"Azhur, does—"

"Don't you dare! We'll have that day, I promise. Now I'm going!" And Azhur slapped Tyr's shoulder, grinned at him and made his way from the Wait, dodging the open arms of Greitha, the kitchen maid, as he went.

~

THE PROMISE OF TIME with Azhur lifted Tyr's spirits as he headed to what was still a fairly new experience for him: classes. Already, little lights of learning were being lit in the dark recesses of his mind. A sensation made sweeter by knowing how no one else from Falakhoth knew the facts his head was filling with.

Tyr raced up ancient stairs to The Fifth Hall of Learning and joined the other lads in a room hung with lists of ideas and charts showing how they connected and who had thought of them. Bulky scrolls sat heaped on shelves and tables, while daunting paintings of the kingdom's greatest thinkers peered down off the walls daring the novices to get something wrong. The newest novice threw himself on a bench, slammed a writing-board and paper on his knee, and again thanked the Lady that Wyrdha had taught him to write.

The melancholy that overcame Tyr as he thought about Wyrdha, and the restless noise of the other lads in the room both ceased abruptly as the Exalted Master of Impartation of Holy Understanding walked into the room. He was a terrifying old priest with a face like an oak tree and a name so fearsome Tyr had known at once he would never remember it. Instead, he had followed the other novices who, in honour of their teacher's face and voice, had named him Barker. The Venerable Master closed the carved oaken door with a portentous thud and ambled to the centre of the room where he stared vaguely toward the floor as though he was about to read the sentence for a capital crime.

All at once he began a fierce recitation from the Scrolls, all from memory: *"Do we not see most clearly that Arna, to further protect his kingdom, has caused a bright ray to be shed even by the side of the First of the Blood, namely he who, by learning, wisdom, and the garnering of years, is the centre of a radiance that falls even upon the hands, ears and eyes of the Chosen. Thus, the kingdom is doubly guarded, doubly guided; for there is one of the Blood and one of the Sun. But both are guardians, for he that is of the Sun finds that the light gathered by his mind is a most effective and necessary shield, fortress, and rampart for he that is of the Blood and the Sun. Indeed, who shall separate them? For as light falls upon the one, so the power of right and of the realm's ordering flows out and is quickened."*

The Venerable Master ended his declamation and acknowledged the novices for the first time as he lifted his gaze to range over his black-clad class. This act compressed his already corrugated features into patterns of even sharper menace. "Relation of Archpriest to Valgraav. Three Hundred and Twelfth Scroll of the Archpriests," he said. "Thirty-eighth column. The scroll better known *as...*?"

"Scroll of Vē-Haldthraad, Anthu," blurted a terrified lad under the Master's glaring eye.

"Correct!" snapped the master. "There is of course considerable *debate* about whether this passage should be among the Scrolls at *all*." His eyes seared the bench-loads of anxious novices, daring them to remain ignorant. "Can one among you reveal to us who *began* the debate? Who *objected?*"

The most courageous lads raised tentative hands. It had taken Tyr only a single lesson with Barker to discover that saying you knew the correct answer and then being found to be ignorant, wasn't worth the public shaming that followed.

"Come sirs, come," cawed the Master. "There are five lines—five lines, sirs!—in the Forty-third Scroll of the Chosen, which you read several days ago... or did you?" His predatory eyes fixed on a sandy-haired youth who gripped his writing-board with the hopeful tremor of a trapped ferret that thinks the hunter may yet be kind. "Uanyé of Ceor? Tell us."

"Priests of the Ma'auchran-nau order Anthu based in Ceir absorbing local traditions Anthu," gasped Uanyé in a single breath.

"Good," said the Master with a discernible trace of disappointment. "And for what *reasons?*"

Uanyé's mouth and eyes widened: the information was not there. But Barker's head had swung to the side and Uanyé breathed a sigh of relief.

The Venerable Master took a long step forward like a crane in the marshes. There was a little whispering sound as the hem of his robe hurried after him over the floor. He stood relishing his own savage patience as he waited for the novice he loomed over to notice.

Tyr's remembrance of the Forty-third Scroll of the Chosen from the previous day's lesson was worse than hazy, so he stared at his desk as hard as he could to avoid Barker's attention. A prolonged silence in the room made him look up to see which poor novice the Master was waiting upon, only to realise with a jolt it was him. "Bugger," he muttered.

Fortunately for Tyr, the Exalted Master's hearing was not the best. "So glad you could join us, Tyr-shan," he grated. "Were you traveling in thought to the temples of the White Fields? Do you explore beyond Vel Sh'hirriva? Your body is among us, but there is no indication of your *mind*. We await the reasons."

Tyr squirmed. It was hard for any sturdy son of Falakhoth not to chafe under the Master's bludgeoning display of authority, let alone one who could not list any reasons. He gawped at the Master, lost for words.

"Just as I thought," the Master grated. "We continue. Uanyé, on your feet."

~

"Before being put to their sacred use," said the Master of Representations, "the brushes, knives, and all other tools of the Artificer are passed through fire. Why do you suppose this is so, Tyr-shan?"

For the second time in two lessons, Tyr found himself put on the spot by a Master. He shrugged.

The Master gave him a frown that added yet more folds and creases to his already pleasantly undulating face. His untamed hair (once red, but now of indeterminate hue) floated around him as he looked down his nose at Tyr. "Making things. Creating. Fire, flame. Could this possibly be a clue?"

Tyr thought hard. "Oh," he said.

"Ah," uttered the Master. "Light dawns!"

Tyr found himself discomfited less by his Master's scrutiny and more by the way he fiddled with the wire that held the two bits of glass balanced on the bridge of his nose. He always winced at the thought of having something so fragile almost in your eyes. He knew they helped you see (though he couldn't think how), but it just looked plain dangerous.

"Speak, then," said the Master after further adjustments. He drew back to receive Tyr's revelation, fingering his chaotic beard in anticipation.

"Well," ventured Tyr, trying not to look at the bits of vision-glass, "is it somethin' to do with the Deep Fire and Arna makin' stuff out of it?" He chewed his lip and waited for confirmation.

The Master expelled another sigh, this time one of deep satisfaction. "A luminous intelligence," he crooned, "manifest in glorious perspicuity. Marvel, gentlemen, at this pyrotechnic correlation of ideas."

"Was I right, then?" asked Tyr. He thought he was, but the stifled

471

sniggers exploding round the classroom left space for doubt. Out of the corner of his eye he caught Authran was clutching his stomach and shaking helplessly with silent laughter. That didn't help either.

The Master of Representations, the Venerable Skh'hartch'haurh'helar (the worst name yet, thought Tyr, but the novices had reduced it to Scratchy, though only behind his back) beamed and smoothed his multi-hued beard. "Entirely right, my luminary of the valleys! Now...." He swung his arm in an elaborate arc that took in most of the room. On wooden shelving, in stone niches, on floor and window shelves, and even clinging to the walls and corners of the ceiling were hundreds of figures and pictures designed to teach Arna's novices the meaning and purpose of Sacred Representation. Every god had its own statue, even those honoured by only a few hundred people in remote crannies of the kingdom. Many of the gods had multiple statues in a variety of innovative and traditionally sanctioned poses made out of bronze, wood, ebony, marble, clay, pewter, or whatever had been at hand. Their forms were painted on parchment, wood, and paper, carved in relief, moulded, cast, scratched on stone, and liberated by chisel. In one case bits of stick stuck together with plant gum represented a god. The gem of the collection was undoubtedly a little portable shrine from Zirribh: an image of Zh'harúdin, Guardian of the Deserts, painted in the shell of a giant sand beetle captured as it tried to burrow away under the scorching rocks.

"Choose one," said Scratchy.

Tyr scanned the deities on display. "We've got a big one of that in the square at home," he said as he pointed at a wooden relief panel of a female figure.

"Yes, yes, the Lady Iathena." said Scratchy. "A very popular style of image in Arcorath and the valleys. Note the care given to the face: simple lines, the curve of the brows and lips suggesting compassion. We can use it to consider the bearing, the sway, of the Deep Fire's creative aspect on the sacred image. This is your choice?"

"Don't think so," said Tyr. He gave a little bow to the Iathena figure and moved on. "That one," he said. "I like that." He picked up a small figure of a man cast in bronze and decorated with enamel. "Who is it?"

"You have chosen the likeness of Lord Shivara," Scratchy told him.

"Have I?" said Tyr. He peered at the figure. "Nothin' like him."

"You would know?" asked Scratchy.

Tyr thought it best not to mention his vision, nor his experience at Conclave. "Um. Suppose not." He said, feeling strangely dishonest.

"Well, let us use it, nonetheless. I do believe you are absorbing the meaning of representation, Tyr-shan—as distinct from merely *learning* things, that is—so I think we will make rapid headway." He took the bronze figure from Tyr and addressed the class. "In due course, gentlemen, you will be allowed to see the most sacred representation of all. It is a likeness of the Lord Shivara, modelled from the life in ancient Dhar and sent north by the Emperor Rachtu. It will be the very pinnacle of our studies in Representations." Scratchy stared at the bronze figure for a moment, then back to Tyr, smiling as he did so. "From the life, Tyr. Imagine that, eh?"

"Oh, aye," he said. "That'll be crackin', that will. Can't wait."

~

THE REPRESENTATIONS CLASS HAD the distinction of being immediately before the afternoon break. Once the lesson finished, the students noisily gathered in the Wait where Greitha and her colleagues served heated wine. Sipping from his warm mug, Tyr was lost in thought when Authran dumped himself beside him.

"That was rotten of Barker. Are you all right?"

"Aye," said Tyr. "Don't care."

"Barker's face though when you said nothing!"

"Aye, nearly wet meself when I realised he was waiting for me. What's next?" Tyr knew something called The Illumined Adjuncts was next, but he had no idea what it was.

"Oh," said Authran brightly, "you might enjoy that. Don't usually do any for the first few months."

"What is it then?" asked Tyr. "Bet it's nowt like what they call it."

"Dear no, that wouldn't do. Basically, it's to do with Arna and the Shrine and running the kingdom."

"Knew that, y' nellie. What's an ad-yunk?"

473

"Adjunct. Well, somebody noticed there's stuff in the real world that isn't actually Arna or Shrine, etcetera, yet has something to do with them all the same. They sort of help everything along, so we have classes about them from time to time. Not too many, mind, because the main thing is Arna-Shrine-dee-dah-dee-dah and we wouldn't want the Adjuncts getting too big a sense of their own importance. One of these occasional delights will be offered to you, Tyr-shan, this very day."

Tyr tried to feel thrilled. "Right. What's it about, then?"

"Don't know. Adjuncts covers all kinds of things. You'll find out when you get there. If you ever do."

Tyr's wine mug halted in front of his face. "What do y' mean if?"

Authran raised his own mug. "I mean if you don't move, you'll miss it." He nodded at the huge brazen hour-disc that hovered above the tables of the Wait. The mechanised pointer showed it was a little past the Third Hour.

"Get away," said Tyr. "Loads of time."

Authran nonchalantly swallowed more wine. "If you say so. However, you should note that the disc is being repaired and observe the temporary hourglass beneath it. You may even want to observe that the room is empty."

Tyr looked rapidly around. "You're still sat here though!"

Authran smiled wryly, "I don't do this class. Off you go."

Residents of Falakhoth had to be capable of speeds exceeding that of a panicked sheep, and Tyr showed he had not lost the knack as he pounded up the twisting stair to the Halls of Learning. He pounded so far, in fact, that he overshot his mark and for a while wandered frantically. Mercifully, an elderly lecturer on his way to the latrines set him on the right track. At last he battered open the correct door.

"Right sorry, clock's buggered!" he gasped as he walked into The Illumined Adjuncts classroom to a ripple of sniggering.

"A son of the valleys, how nice," said Mother Vashira. "Please come in, Tyr-shan."

Tyr sought for a word through clouds of shock. "I never thought—what y' doin' here?"

Mother Vashira drew in her breath and inclined her head as more of the novices giggled. "Today I am an adjunct," she said. There was an un-expected sadness in her voice. "I am the Materfamilias of the Hallowed Sisterhood of our Supreme Mother the Great Lady Iathena. As she is consort of Lord Arna, for whose service you prepare, it is believed fitting that I speak to you of our Mother's cult and worship, and the ways of our Sisterhood." She paused to wistfully look about the class. "Not essential knowledge, it is thought, but perhaps useful. Tyr-shan, I think your legs will work now. Please sit down."

Tyr performed his usual jerky bow and edged to a bench. Mother Vashira drew herself up in preparation. The novices did the same. Adjunct or no, they felt her natural, irresistible authority. Tyr was awed as her slight frame appeared to grow in stature as she readied herself to speak of her Beautiful Mother. This would be good, he thought. It was what she was born to do.

Mother Vashira rehearsed the ancient stories of Iathena's fashioning by Arna from the Deep Fire and her governance, by Arna's side, of the other gods and the circle of the world. Next came the Sisterhood's un-derstanding of Iathena, spelled out in some detail, with descriptions of the spirits that attended and served her, complete with several references to a figure called The Beautiful Companion, who it seemed was never far from her.

"The Companion met one day with the Lady Eleiaraula of Ceor, a woman famed for compassion, gentleness, and joy, as well as her great beauty. Without these things she would have been quite ordinary. It is said she met with Ar-ven when he returned from Fyrieg and was with him towards the end of his life when he was frail and his wits, according to some accounts, were failing. It was Eleiaraula who founded our Sis-terhood, and she was its first Mother. She and some women from the valleys composed our rituals, our rule, our prayers, and our histories, all with the Companion's help."

"Is it in the Scrolls?" blurted out Tyr. He was spellbound.

"Yes, Tyr-shan, it is in the Scrolls; and the Sisterhood has its own writings."

"Ey!" said Tyr.

Vashira smiled quietly and, perhaps, a little slyly. "So very good to meet again, Tyr-shan." Then she adjusted her shifting vestments, and said mysteriously, "I have washed my mantle: I am ready for what comes." And she laughed; she actually laughed. Tyr had no idea what it was all about, but he liked it.

Then the strange, happy moment was trampled by the invasive sound of the door and there was the scar-faced priest Maurdjil whom Bal-jar-rak had detailed to keep a watch on Tyr. "That's enough for today, Mother," he rumbled. "The Lord Bal-jarrak's compliments, and I am to tell you he is ready to discuss the coming year's grant to your order. Arna shine on you and on your class." His melancholy eyes scanned the class, who understood that the blessing was in fact a dismissal and began to shuffle out.

Maurdjil approached Tyr. He leaned close. "You find your studies congenial, I hope," murmured the landslide of a voice.

"You was behind that door," hissed Tyr. "What y' barge in for?"

"I place myself where I can best serve the Lord Arna. Continue as you have begun, Tyr-shan. And remember, this tower is not the valleys." He straightened up, beckoning to Vashira as he made for the door.

"La'auchrad got his nose fixed yet?' said Tyr.

Maurdjil stopped, looking ahead and not at Tyr, then continued, Vashira behind him. He might have smiled slightly.

~

"OH, THEY'RE TERRIBLY RUDE to the Daughters," said Authran, having heard Tyr's account of Vashira's belittlement. "It's a kind of policy: make it totally clear to everybody that they and the Lady are definitely second class. Arna and the priests have the power, keep the valleys in their place, all that sort of thing. But she's absolutely splendid when she gets going, far more interesting than Barker. Did you enjoy her lesson?"

"Aye, it was crackin'," Tyr said, sprawled back on his bunk. Lessons had ended for the day and he and Authran were lounging in their dorm-itory waiting for the greatly desired evening meal. Both lads couldn't wait that long and were engaged in an impromptu feast of pilfered pies. Tyr played with his third slab of pie, his mind drifting to the conversation he'd had in the Wait with Azhur at breakfast. He threw the slab of pie at Authran, who threw his own slab back at him. Tyr sat up. "Had a chinwag with Azhur at midday about the Valgraav and his brother as don't speak to him."

Authran sat up too, pies forgotten while Tyr recounted the conversation. This led, inevitably, to his friend elaborating on Azhur's information. "This is the sort of thing that's known but not openly talked about, and *certainly* not taught."

"How do y' know, then?"

"My father's high up in the administration in Ceorthas. People at those levels are well aware."

"Do *they* talk about it?"

"Depends who's there, but why bother? There's a kingdom to run and Jarthastra is a good Valgraav, every bit as much as if he had been the eldest son. He gets upset though, they say: can't shake off his doubts. Breaking sacred precedent, that kind of thing."

Tyr lounged back on his dormitory bunk and stretched. He found himself mystified yet again by the deeds of the mighty. "I'm not gettin' this," he said. "Jarthastra's dad said he were to be Valgraav, didn't he?"

"Yes, and he got some stick for it, I can tell you. Conclave wasn't happy, nor were a lot of the governors. And of course, Tharsjhad's friends in high places kicked up a stink."

"Who?"

"Tharsjhad? That's Jarthastra's brother."

Tyr grinned to himself.

"What's funny?"

"He's got a decent name. All the high-ups here have got names that can break your jaw."

"Good point," Authran grinned too. "A Valgraav should have at least ten syllables in his name. We had an Illuminations Master once whose proper name took a full eight seconds if you didn't rush."

"We had this feller at Falakhoth once who didn't have a name at all. He drifted in and out, so we never found out what to call him. We just said, *Him*. He answered to it and all. 'Have y' seen Him today?' 'Mornin', Him, how's you?' Queer it was. Nice feller, but he didn't stay long."

"Ha, not surprised," said Authran. He looked longingly at the crumpled piece of pie lying near Tyr's bed, regretting his earlier retaliation. He rummaged in his bag for more misappropriated pies from the kitchen. "But it would certainly speed up administration: 'My lords, I present to you the Anthu Him.'" He pulled out a pie and tossed it to Tyr. "A lot of people would have got their pockets lined if Tharsjhad had been Valgraav. Probably one reason his father refused him."

"Have y' got apple? I don't fancy meat."

"I do, but I wanted it."

"Go on, y' like meat better."

"All right, by dispensation of Anthu Him." Pies crossed the room in twin arcs, apple one way and meat the other. "Yes, half the state revenue would probably have gone on little presents here and there for Tharsjhad's friends and drinking partners."

"Thanks," Tyr said as he bit into the apple pie. "Wild one, was he?" Authran chewed thoughtfully. "Well, you don't believe all you hear, but what one *does* hear—I mean, apparently they had to delay Conclave meetings while somebody got him out of bed, that kind of thing. Plus, the fellow was as thick as a brick—no, sorry, I take that back: two bricks *and* the cement. Dear old Ar-Vharalthar knew it and stuck to his guns."

"Who?"

"The old Valgraav, his father. I can just remember Ar-Vharalthar, you know. Father took me to see him when he paid a visit to Ceor. Crusty old boy. Looked the sort to get what he wanted. They *say* the Ceor visit came when he was on the way to Fyrieg looking for help to decide about the succession. He's supposed to have been hoping to meet Shivara— aim high, you know—right place, right time, desperate need, that kind of thing. It's always like that in the stories, but I don't know if you can *make* it happen."

"Did he meet Shivara then?"

"Well, it's all very vague. There's this story and that story, but I don't think anybody believes he did. They all just humoured him. It's the sort of thing a worried elderly gentleman would do."

"Wonder if Jarthastra thought he did. Course, he weren't mad then."

"Mad? Who?"

"Jarthastra. Don't think he's been right since that southern feller hit him on Renewal Night. Remember when I'd just come out the Laver and he come runnin' into the Shrine shoutin', *Is it me?* If Shivara'd told his dad to make him Valgraav he shouldn't be worried, should he?"

"Tyr-shan, you have a razor-like mind that deserves another pie: here. Yes, imagine the embarrassment if it *had* happened. You could hardly have a fresco up in the Shrine showing Shivara explaining that Prince Tharsjhad's an absolute waster."

"Funny though, isn't it?"

"Definitely."

"Bet Tharsjhad hates Shivara if it's true."

"Tyr! Don't say that! You can't hate Shivara. Arna's wings!"

"Well, y're not goin' to like the feller as stopped y' bein' king, are y'?"

"Do you know, I never thought of it like that. But you still can't hate Shivara, and that's the end of it."

"Suppose not," said Tyr. It all sounded very complicated. People at Falakhoth had names you could say in one go, and were apt to say what they thought about things without too much fuss, unless somebody like Bardcha or Gizhurthra was involved. He explained this to Authran.

"Things are a bit complex at the top," admitted Authran. "Tell a bad joke at a banquet and you've offended three provinces. Funny you mention Falakhoth though, I had a dream about it the other night."

"Get away! I didn't know y'd been to Falakhoth."

"I haven't. Never seen it in my life. I just *knew* it was Falakhoth, the way you do in dreams."

"And cos it had a gold statue of me in the square: Falakhoth's first priest."

Authran laughed. "Not exactly. You were in the dream though, though not as a statue."

"What was I doin'?"

"Not much, just running."

"Runnin'?"

"Well, there was the town, Falakhoth, and a road and a place with trees. It was incredibly vivid, as though I was there—"

"Get on with it," said Tyr. He flicked his last piece of apple pie at Authran who, astonishingly, jerked his head and caught the morsel in his mouth.

"Thank you very much. Delicious."

"That's disgustin'."

"Only if you haven't washed your hands. Anyway, I'm in this grassy place, under trees, and there's this fellow sitting on the ground, saying, *I'm not going, I'm not going.* And he points down to the road and there you are, running towards us. He was holding something."

"That's it?"

"Afraid so. Actually, I think it's a prophecy that the kingdom will be safe for a thousand years thanks to Tyr-shan, Archpriest of the Valleys." Tyr nodded sagely, "Aye, I think that's probably it."

"It was *so* vivid. I don't usually dream like that. I think I could draw it."

"Can't, folk forget dreams."

"Well, I didn't forget this one."

"Y' know what I mean."

"No, look, I could almost touch it, it was so real. I remember it as if it really happened, swear on Arna's image."

Tyr found this exasperating. "Go on, then, draw it! Draw it like y' did that Scroll!"

Authran sat up and brandished a pie in the manner of outraged authority. "Ho! You defy me, junior novice? As soon as the black's on your back, you think you're better than your elders!"

"Always was!"

"You contradicted me, and that is absolutely anathema: utterly forbidden to tall, dark-haired novices called Tyr-shan!"

"What Scroll's that in, then?"

"The one I'm going to write! Lord Galdtchav commissioned me."

"Y' daft sod, draw the bloody dream! Go on or I'll not believe y'."

Authran feigned shock, "Well! I couldn't live with that!" He put his latest pie aside and went to the cupboard that Arna's providence had placed in the novices' dormitory for him. He rummaged in its depths and pulled out a bundle of his drawings, some blank sheets, and one or two tools that Tyr found immensely impressive: wooden sticks that somehow had lengths of something like coal or soft stone running through them. If you pared away the wood at one end, the black coal-like stuff became exposed. By sharpening it to a point, you could use it to make lines and marks on paper. Authran used it to make his drawings, much in the way you could draw with a sharp, burnt stick. "Now be confounded, arch-contradictor," he said. "I draw, objectify, and actualise this dream in honour of the Anthu Him."

"Daft bugger,' said Tyr. He rolled over on his bunk to see the drawing appear, laughing warmly. His friend's verbal flights delighted him whether he understood them or not, for Authran gave constantly from his colourful store of words and ideas with no hint of feeling superior. It was all gift, and Tyr loved him for it.

Authran settled himself on the floor with his back against the bunk so that Tyr could look over his shoulder. With a wooden board on his knees to support the paper, he began to scribble with the marking-stick. "Now, there's the road, and there's a path off the road up to this flat bit—fairly flat anyway—and these are the trees all round it. Bushes here, quite a lot of flowers, and I'm pretty sure there was a statue of the Lady about there. There were a lot of things stuck in the ground like that, not sure what—"

"Could be anywhere," said Tyr.

"Yes, but it isn't. I'm *remembering* this, really I am. Now I was standing about here on the flat bit. I think there was a river—yes, there was—anyway, I was here, and I looked over and the fellow was sitting on the ground about here. That's when he turned and looked at me and said, *I'm not going.* And you were running along down here—"

"I'm not that thin!" said Tyr, amused by his hastily done representation.

"Ah," intoned Authran. "Speak not against the interpretation of a dream, lest thou besmirch the reality of which it speaks."

"Ey!" said Tyr, impressed. "Who said that?"

"Me: I've just made it up."

This being unanswerable, Tyr gave it up and changed tack. "Look, we'd better get down the Wait. Greitha says it's a good tea tonight and

I'm starvin'."

"You're bulging with apple pie, Tyr, you can't be starving."

"Well, I am. You city folks don't eat properly." He levered himself off the bunk. "Shift y'self. Y' get more if y're first."

"*And* wink at Greitha. Go on, I'll catch you up, I'm just getting into this. I want to try drawing the fellow on the ground. I see his face clear as day."

"Please y'self," Tyr told him. "I'll have ate yours if y' not quick. I'll tell Greitha y've gone off her.'

"You wouldn't dare," said Authran, quite unconcerned. "Greitha's my source: if she goes off me there won't be any illicit pies to give to you."

Tyr found himself defeated. "Ey, y're a smart one," he said and strode off to the delights simmering in the Wait.

CHAPTER 22

The Secret from the South

"HE WILL COME, I SUPPOSE," said Galdtchav, leaning back in his splendid chair.

"Oh yes, yes," said Azhur, perhaps a little too readily.

"It's just that I understand he's a little... unpredictable. Sudden decisions, roving thoughts, that kind of thing. And a little bird—forgive the cliché—a little bird that was fluttering about the refectory yesterday, saw the two of you in the midst of a very heated conversation indeed. Birds have very poor hearing of course, so it couldn't make out just what it was all about..."

Embarrassment and remorse and anger. Azhur stared straight ahead. "I, ah, I'm afraid I let Tyr down about a certain matter. He took it to heart."

"Oh, I see. No doubt you cleared the air."

"Certainly, Anthu. All well."

There was a difficult silence. The Loremaster scratched his chin. "He's very fond of you," he said suddenly. "He didn't expect to have you whisked away."

Azhur's head whipped round before he could stop it. His eyes, if not his lips, exclaimed *How did you know?*

Galdtchav drummed his fingers on the chair-arm. "I wondered a little how Tyr-shan would respond to your revelations about our Imperial line yesterday. I don't consider your explanation of Jarthastra's story or your warnings to be in any way improper, or inadequate. I entirely endorse your authority, you know."

"Thank you, Anthu."

"I am merely anxious that the instructions of a friend might go unheeded in some heated moment. You know how easily his thoughts, er, find utterance."

"I do indeed, Anthu."

Another finger-drumming pause. "He'll tell Authran, you know?"

"Oh. I never... oh dear."

"Now, now. I plan to send a few wise words in Authran's direction too, so don't worry."

"That's a relief. Thank you again, Anthu."

"Not at all; I—Azhur, I declare you will break those fingers one day."

"Sorry, Anthu."

"Don't apologise, dear boy. I, well—look, we know that your manual wrestling is a sign, hm? A pointer?"

Azhur was silent, his hands moving to his sides to become fists.

Galdtchav thought for a moment. "The wrestling has been appearing, shall we say, in excess for a while. Your mood when away from your lady, and your over-busyness, all those little things we recognise distract you, I've seen rather a lot of them. Your concentration has not been the best, there's an air of tension and so forth."

"I'm quite well, Anthu." Azhur kept a rigid composure and stared at the floor as if he would burn the rug.

"I'm sure you are, laddie. I only wondered if your thoughts were troubling you once more. Knowing how the memories... affect you, I was concerned."

"No need, Anthu, I assure you."

"Well, glad to hear you say it. Young Tyr's friendship is a great lifter of the spirits."

"Oh yes, it was."

"Was?"

"*Is*, I mean. Sorry. Oh yes, an excellent fellow. Good to have about."

484

"Quite. Do you think he'll be about soon? We do have our distinguished guest arriving after our chat with Tyr."

"He'll be here, Anthu. Most certainly. Especially since it's yourself. He conceived quite a... quite an affection for you at Falakhoth."

Galdtchav smiled broadly and thoughtfully, "Well, one must be grateful for affection in my circumstances. I do want to have a few words with him, but I didn't want him dragged here by the guards." Galdtchav regarded his own lined and delicate fingers and quietly frowned. "Did you see our Valgraav today?"

"Early this morning, Anthu. Good colour, quite calm. He read my documents quietly and intelligently."

"Good. It's not as if Jarthastra's rise to power is exactly a secret, but his appearance at the Laver certainly is. When Tyr graces us with his presence, we'll present a united front, a pincer movement as it were. We will hopefully ensure his permanent silence and my peace of mind. And I would hate to see the lad bear the weight of Lady Iera's wrath."

Azhur drew in his breath, "Oh no, Anthu. Oh dear, no."

"Indeed." A pattern of knocks sounded. "Here he is. To the work, laddie. Enter."

Galdtchav's attendant slid noiselessly into the chamber, "The novice Tyr-shan, Anthu."

"Thank you, Sharn. Show him in, please."

~

"I CAN'T TELL YOU HOW... how important this is," said Azhur as he wrung his hands violently. "Absolute silence from both you and Authran—please!"

Tyr half-sat on Galdtchav's heavy table (becoming the first novice to do so) and folded his arms. "Is he mad, then?"

"No! Arna forbid! He's... he's—"

"We had this feller at home once, he were right off his head. Used to do queer stuff with sheep muck. And anyhow he looked just like him: all wild, and his eyes—"

"Tyr! There is no comparison! Lord Jarthastra is... very..." Azhur waved a hand, failed to find a word, and threw Galdtchav a desperate glance.

The old Loremaster sighed, "The Anthu has been briefly unwell," he said sagely. His chamber at the Shrine had seen many a heated debate, but never one on this sensitive subject. "Unwell, Tyr. And these things pass. That's really all you need to know." He bestowed a penetrating stare on the remains of his late breakfast as he pushed it around the plate. "Besides, I believe the Graavinda made it abundantly clear that if you tell anyone what you saw, events will be set in motion that will mean you'll never be believed about any subject ever again." He took up a sausage, chewed meaningfully. "You can imagine, a sharp fellow like you, that it wouldn't help the stability of the North or our standing in the eyes of the Far Lands if our Valgraav were thought—I say *thought*, not *known*—to have been denied the use of his faculties. Some aspiring potentates would imagine a vacancy or opportunity for advancement existed."

"Eh?" said Tyr.

"Sorry, that was my statesman mode. Certain people would *have a go*. You do *understand* that?"

"Like Harrak?"

"Definitely Harrak, and more besides. You're with me?"

"Aye," said Tyr, with a little sad stab of sympathy. "I am, Master."

Galdtchav smiled more broadly and leaned back in his carved and cushioned chair. "Rather thought so. You'll be a good novice. Which reminds me, you've worn the black for a while now. Welcome to that happy estate." He poured some ale and pushed the flagon across to Tyr. "We did mean to hear how the Initiation went and how your first blacked days have been, but I'm afraid I've been a dreadful old slave driver and kept your friend shockingly busy among the parchments."

"Aye," murmured the lad into his flagon.

The Loremaster saw the cloud that shaded Tyr's brow. "But here you are for us to make amends. We'll bless our new novice, shall we not, Azhur?"

The younger Loremaster jolted out of his worries about the Valgraav. "Oh yes, of course. Yes, congratulations, Tyr." He clapped his friend on the shoulder. "You look very fine."

Tyr gave a little bow. "I thank y' both," he said with a valley formality, then sipped his ale and glanced slyly at Azhur. "Can't think of you runnin' about them tunnels in the nuddy."

Azhur gaped and burned; Galdtchav's shoulders shook.

"People tend to keep their initiations to themselves, laddie. It's etiquette, so you don't spoil it for the next fellow."

"Oh," said Tyr. Normally, he would have asked what that meant, but he was suddenly pierced with the thought: *Azhur wasn't there.*

Ever the diplomat, the senior Loremaster took the chance to steer things well away from the contention he could tell still lay between his younger friends. He thumped his hand down on a hefty wad of papers. "You know what this is, laddie? These are all the references, inferences, indications, allusions, confusions, and what have you that were suggested by what has happened to you and your excellent parents. We've had to index them, cross-reference them, discuss them, tabulate connections, and then chase *them* through the Scrolls so we can tell the Valgraav the significance of our new novice." He put his head on one side and stared oddly at Tyr, left eyebrow raised. "Or whether he has none at all," he added.

Tyr gaped, forgetting his jealousy. "Bloody hell," he gasped. "Did y' find all that about me?"

"Yes, and we aren't finished yet," Azhur told him. "We're working on your mother's songs now."

"She never got them out the Scrolls; she's never read any."

Azhur raised hands and eyes, amused. "Oh, no, no, no. We take what she sang and look for complementary themes in the Scrolls, similar allusions, resonating concepts. We weigh up the contexts."

"Azhur, shut up, y're worse than Authran! Talk proper!"

"What the Loremaster intends to say," said Galdtchav drily, "is that we take what your mother said or sang and see if anything in the Scrolls sounds like it. Then we take all those bits and see what they add up to."

"Is that what y've been doin'?"

"There's a little more to it, but basically yes."

There came a knocking and a junior loremaster appeared, stooping and bobbing under a weight of respect. "Your pardon, Anthu, the Lady—"

Galdtchav waved him away to whence he had come and drummed his fingers on the table. "Ah me, quite forgotten. Well, I can't send *her* away." He looked at Tyr with alert, fascinated eyes. "Much as I would *like* to, as much as I would prefer to *continue*, we *cannot*."

Tyr stamped a foot. "Who's it *now?*" He scuffed across the room and kicked at a chair leg. "I *never* get to see y'." He slumped against the wall, head down like a bull that might charge. "Is it Aienna?"

"No," said Azhur, controlling his voice. "Not Aienna. Another lady."

The junior Loremaster reappeared and announced, "The Lady Aia Djetenga."

She walked into Galdtchav's chamber with the grace of a drifting galley, the rhythm of a swaying tree, the splendour of a thousand bright banners. She was all the high majesty of the King's Tower distilled into a human form. Her gown was deepest crimson, shot through with fine silver work in the forms of fabulous birds, each one with meticulous touches of lapis lazuli on their eyes and claws. The belt that twice encircled her and hung almost to her feet was the tawny pelt of an undreamed beast, golden-red and edged with ivory. A broad collar of crimson and ivory fanned out to rest on her shoulders, and around her neck was a multitude of glass beads, each a hand-worked masterpiece strung upon woven copper wire. On her breast lay a heavy necklace, ring upon ring of golden wire linked by the forms of tiny golden beasts and edged with hanging white birds, each carved from a single pearl that seemed to shake and flutter as the wearer moved. Above the necklace hung a veil, cascading down from her eyes and heavily worked in copper thread so that her face was invisible. At her temples were the curved, carved teeth of unknown beasts, and across her forehead rows of burnished and enamelled copper scale-shapes quivered and shimmered below the high, broad swathes around her head. But where one would have met her soul, between the copper scales and the veil, a stretch of gauze closed off her eyes so she saw all but was invisible herself. Aia Djtenga was a fortress, a covered shrine to herself, an awesome and splendid mystery.

"My lady," said Galdtchav warmly. He rose, and he and Azhur bowed to the unseen majesty.

Tyr stood gaping. He knew who was under all the finery, for he had seen her in the street and on Renewal Night, but to have her so near in such opulent secrecy was overwhelming. The strength of her personality beat on him through the veils. Azhur hit him on the arm, and he managed a jerky bow. The splendid headdress turned a little towards him.

"There is a new one to teach me today?" A deep and mellow voice, rich and used to command. Aia Djtenga spoke from beyond the far deserts, from wide, flat lands scorched by huge, red suns that bore down on vast plains of red earth and yellow-white grasses. She could have sung and called the vivid birds down to her from the hot currents of the air, unimagined beasts would have loped and run, gathering to her voice.

Galdtchav's smile spread and glowed at the bronze-timbre voice. "Lady Aia, allow me to present Tyr-shan of Falakhoth, newest novice at our Shrine. It is he who saved the Anthu Jarthastra from the wolf."

The turbaned head went back so that the copper veil and its ornaments swung and glittered: the lady was clearly startled. "You swung the blade? *Mu'temba jitani!*" She slowly lowered herself onto a couch, wide unseen eyes burning through the gauze at Tyr. "It is honour to me to meet the guardian of the north."

Tyr blushed. He rather liked being called the *guardian of the north*. Nobody had suggested he was this before, but he supposed saving Jarthastra may have protected the whole realm. He now felt important, uniquely so, but his village modesty caused him to say, "I were just there. And I had a sword, so I swung it. Turned out all right." He gave an uneasy little laugh, feeling Lady Aia's eyes on him. He felt himself blush even more.

"The Lady Aia visits us here to learn of the realm and its histories," Galdtchav was saying. "She is with us on behalf of her own kingdom, an ambassador to our court, and so she wishes to understand the north. We exchange many thoughts, you see, so Tyr-shan, if you will excuse us."

"Oh," said Tyr. "Right." He crossed his arms carefully on his chest (he was learning) and made a formal little bow to Lady Aia. She stretched out a hand to him. He noticed even her hands were covered.

"Stay with me, new black-robe," she said. It was half an order, half a request, and Tyr thought it held a restrained urgency. He glanced at Galdtchav. The Loremaster smiled and nodded, but his old eyes glinted.

The three of them seated themselves around Aia Djtenga and she spoke invisibly to Tyr once more. He did not quite like this, as it was hard to know when her eyes were on him. He wondered vaguely if they were brown, then settled on them being amber, or as near to it as eyes could get. His mother had had a piece of amber as a pendant once, and he thought it would match Lady Aia's finery.

"You are the newest of the north-god's priests," she began.

"Novice," said Tyr, fascinated by her exotic presence.

"Nov-is?" asked the lady.

Azhur leaned forward, "A novice, lady. One day he will become a priest, but now he must spend years in, ah, gathering the knowledge a priest must have."

"Ah. Then your thinking is a field, Tyr-shan. Your masters have tilled it; they are sowing."

Tyr remembered Authran's delight in learning, "Aye, there'll be a harvest," he said impulsively.

Galdtchav laughed. "But for now," he said, "we only try to break up the soil and remove the stones."

This sounded ominous and Tyr grimaced.

Lady Aia smiled, or she must have smiled because her voice softened. "I saw the sun first in Southland," she continued from within her shrine. "My country is Murinde. Do you know it?"

"No," Tyr told her. "Not really." He vaguely knew there was such a place as Southland, but to him it was a feature on players' painted wagons and the elaborate maps he saw around the Tower of Novices. Everybody knew old Dhar had been somewhere down there and Shivara and the Black Emperor. He gave a little start as he remembered how his vision-thoughts had flown back to ancient Dhar as he watched Eorthas' play at Falakhoth. Had that really been a glimpse of Southland? Whatever it was, he never knew that people like Aia Djtenga lived there.

"Your heart would beat in Murinde, Tyr-shan," said Lady Aia. "There are forests and wide plains and beasts you have never seen in your dreams, not even on the borders of your scrolls. I would take you to my city far below Vel Shirriva where my family are masters. They would stare at you and laugh. They have never seen one like you. But my sisters and their daughters would look long at you, they would talk for many days about which of them would be your wives."

Tyr tried to say something to this and failed. He was painfully aware of the amusement his crimson face gave Azhur and Galdtchav. Lady Aia's shoulders shook gently; within her veils, she was laughing too. It occurred to him she would be more stunning still when she laughed, and his crimson hue deepened and spread.

"Well, new nov-is Tyr-shan, will you come to Murinde?"

Arna's newest servant shifted, coughed and ran a hand through his hair, "Aye, well, might do. Thanks very much." He tried desperately to change the subject, "How'd y' get up here, then?"

Lady Aia's turbaned head tilted to one side a little.

"Your reasons for coming to the north, lady," explained Galdtchav.

"Ohhh," said the Lady in a long, low breath. "You are at the centre, Tyr-shan. I will tell you what I try to find in your north."

She lifted one hand, finger raised, hidden away under finely worked gloves hung about with ropes of silver and embellished with carven rings of ebony and ivory. Long, agile fingers reached into a fold of her robes and brought out an object she had concealed at her side. It was a long, leather pouch fastened with thongs and brass catches. From it she produced what Tyr recognised as a scroll case like the one that had carried his initiation scroll, only shorter and less elaborate. Lady Aia eased it open, then paused, contemplating the scroll inside as she held the case up before her unseen eyes.

"I am here because one day I may rule Murinde and perhaps it will not be safe for me there, not in these days." She let this mystery hang in the air and drew in her breath. "And I am here because the thoughts of many lands and ages are gathered and sifted in the scroll-houses of Arna, and I am looking to know how the times move and what ways have been paved for Murinde and the line of the Neguenda." She carefully took the scroll from its case and said, "I am searching to find the meaning of this."

491

And things changed in front of Tyr. Without noise or disturbance, a large, solid writing desk had appeared behind and to the right of Lady Aia's chair. Azhur, a few feet away, gave it not a glance. Tyr stared at an old man scribbling on parchment. He knew him, but didn't know how. The light on the man was wrong. It was yellow and fastened to strong shadows while the room held the blue, spreading light of late morning. It was this light-out-of-place that jolted Tyr into recognising the scribe who had appeared in the muddy, grey square at Falakhoth, writing his parchment by candlelight as Azhur recited the rite of The Coming Forth. Tyr watched the pen moving with the long thick fingers, and this time, being closer, heard it scratching out the thoughts of the scribe. He could see the sage had written three columns and was finishing the fourth. Under each of the first three columns were sketches drawn in squares within larger rectangles. In one was a figure with a circle drawn over it. He couldn't make out the others as the man's arm now blocked his view. The fourth column was now complete, and the writer quickly sketched an oblong shape, made some marks on it, then drew lines to connect it with the rectangles and the column above. He dusted the parchment to dry the ink, rolled it up, and sealed it as Tyr had seen him do at Falakhoth.

A door opened, whether in the air or in the wall Tyr couldn't say, but again the light was wrong. A woman appeared in the square of yellow lamplight that washed over the old man and his desk. She looked quickly behind her and stepped across behind Lady Aia to the scribe. He raised his hand—in greeting, blessing, or warning Tyr couldn't tell—and he handed her the scroll. With a shock, Tyr saw she had the face of Aia Djetenga, but it couldn't be her. She was perhaps of her line, having the same high cheeks, the long proud neck, the regal bearing. For a second, the woman and the scribe both held the scroll. The man spoke briefly to her. She bowed and went swiftly away through the impossible door.

"I am searching to find the meaning of this," Aia Djetenga said again. As the vision cleared it left Tyr confused. "Y' what?"

"The meaning of this scroll, Tyr-shan in black. I am with a hope that your masters will find it for me in their knowledge or their... what is it? The great place that holds the writings?"

"Oh, the Archives, Lady Aia," said Azhur. "Are you all right, Tyr?"

"Aye," said Tyr, contradicting his whole demeanour. "Aye, it's all right, go on." The vision, he realised, had taken literally only seconds as far as the others were concerned.

The Loremasters stared and wondered, but Lady Aia returned to her scroll.

"It has not been opened for a hundred years, but it is as old as your kingdom. It is said that there are five columns—"

"Four," said Tyr.

"Four?" repeated Lady Aia.

"Four. And pictures underneath each one. Oh, bugger." Tyr screwed his eyes shut and thumped the heels of his hands on his temples.

Aia Djetenga stared through her veil. "Boh-gir?" she asked.

Galdtchav rose hurriedly, "Tyr-shan is... startled, Lady," he said. "Something has... *occurred* to him, I think. You will excuse us?" The Loremaster gripped Tyr and Azhur by the arms and steered them behind a rack of shelving. "Tell," he said.

Tyr shook his head, distraught. "I saw him again, Azhur. The old feller, in the square."

"What square?" asked Azhur. "What old fellow?"

"The feller with the beard as was writin' when y' was sayin' the Comin' Forth in Falakhoth."

Azhur covered his face. Galdtchav tightened his grip on Tyr. "You saw that again? Here?"

"Aye, only he took his scroll and gave it to some woman."

"What woman?"

"A woman, I dunno."

"What did she look like?"

"She were from Mu—that place where she's from." He jerked his head towards the bewildered Aia Djetenga sitting with her scroll.

"And the man at the desk, was he a northerner?"

"Oh, aye, know him anywhere."

Galdtchav let Tyr go and frowned. "I see. Well, Loremaster? Any thoughts?"

"None whatever," said Azhur, arms tightly folded, eyes shut.

His senior clasped his hands and glared at the wall. "Very well," he said decisively, then squared his shoulders, adjusted his robe, turned on his heel and walked, in his most conciliatory manner, back to face Lady Aia.

She started within her concealing swathes and quickly replaced the scroll in its case as if she feared Galdtchav might do something to it.

The Loremaster stood before the woman from the south, hands clasped as he tried to control the situation and himself. He was the man the Northlands most trusted with words and meanings, but he found that both were eluding him. Aia Djetenga waited patiently, poised within her robes. "Lady," said Galdtchav at last, "your, ah, scroll...."

"You have a new thing," said Lady Aia. "Tyr-shan has brought something to your mind."

"He has, lady."

"This is the boh-gir?"

"Indeed no, lady," replied Galdtchav, attempting not to notice Tyr's stifled snort behind him. "It does relate to your scroll, but if you will permit me, I... I have a question about its history. You have spoken of it as we discussed the history of the north and you were to break its seal today and read it to us, but you have not told us of its origins."

"Then I will tell you now," said Lady Aia. "You know it has as many years as your kingdom?"

"Indeed, but how did it come to you? What is it to Murinde?"

Lady Aia sighed and bowed her head a little. She ran her gloved fingers along the scroll case then looked up at Galdtchav.

He frowned: it was unnerving to be stared at so intently by someone with no face.

"I will tell you more than was ready," she said. "More truth, perhaps more hope." She beckoned Tyr and Azhur and they came forward, both them and Galdtchav sitting to hear the tale. "The scroll is sent to me through four centuries," began Lady Aia. "Always it is given to the first daughters of the Neguenda, the family that rules. Only once has its seal been broken."

"Why has Murinde sent it to the north?" asked Azhur. "Surely, there are many risks?"

"Murinde does not know." She spread out one hand. "Not this many know why I am in Valderthaan."

Galdtchav raised one startled eyebrow. "The Anthu Jarthastra believes you were sent to represent the Negua at his court."

"Let him, it is true, but even Madha Negua does not know my strongest thought."

"Then who has sent you?"

"Myself. I must understand the scroll."

"I see. Well, may our Archives hold what you seek, for I sense a great need in your voice. Tell us the story in your own way."

"Then the story is this," said Lady Aia. She paused, then raised her hands in a sweeping motion past her face. She turned the palms outward as if opening a door to her listeners. "*Ala ké m'djanta daladhaburuna:* they go to you, the heart-thought-gifts." She lowered her hands, composed and ready. "I walk again the journey of my ancient sister Borukini. She was first daughter of the Madha Negua when great Rachtu of Dhar reached up and made your little city-lands a kingdom. In those days Murinde was gathered into Dhar. Madha Negua served the Bhanir Rachtu, who desired that the lands he ruled be shown when your First King was crowned."

"Eh?" said Tyr.

"Representatives at Na-veshtrazhdak's coronation," murmured Azhur. "Scrolls of the Founding, Tyr."

Galdtchav waved them to silence without taking his eyes off Aia Djetenga. "Do *continue*, Lady."

Lady Aia drew in a strengthening breath. "You seek hard in your listening, Master, this is a large matter for you. Well, here is the tale of it. My ancient sister Borukini came with her brother the prince Gadchanda to see Na-veshtrazhdak crowned. They went to bow in Arna's house and listened to the histories of the north and the Lore of Beginnings. Borukini heard of the Fire under the waters of the west that you say Arna made all-thing from, and perhaps he did, I do not know, but Murinde knows of the Sea-fire. All the lands know, so my ancient sister opened a door in her thoughts to hear what the north said of it. The telling was very beautiful and Borukini felt the sea in her heart and

495

wished to understand it."

"Didn't know what the sea was?" blurted Tyr with surprise.

Galdtchav coughed, "Sorry."

"No, nor do I. How should we know? Murinde sits among other lands that are a circle round her. If one of us wished to see the great water, it would be a journey long and hard. We would carry our lives in our hands. It is easy for you to go to the sea, new black-robe, but not for us."

Tyr was still astonished. He found himself jabbing a finger at Lady Aia. "Aye, but y'—" Azhur nudged him hard.

"We know what the sea is," explained the lady patiently. "It is water, it is distance, it is sky; it is the great bowl in the earth that holds the water; it is the home prepared for things that live and must be protected from the sky, the gift of Mayuwē to the world, we say. All this we know about the sea, but we do not *understand*. We have not seen, we have not sailed, we have not journeyed on her or swum in her. We do not know the spirit of the sea, we have not felt her soul. That is why Borukini's heart moved when she heard of the holy Fire burning within this great mystery. She thought, if such a wonder as the sea is only the house that holds it, what is the Fire itself? When she thought this, Borukini re-membered that you say Arna put a part of the light of the holy Fire in a great gem."

"The Valthaur," murmured Azhur, wrapped up in the history.

"Val-tor. Well, Borukini had read that the gem housed in a place where your land greets the sea."

"Ceor," Azhur told her.

"Ke'yor. And she read that when Arna's house was growing, Val-tor was brought to Valderthaan and put in his house."

"The Gem rests in the Shrine to this day, Lady," Galdtchav said, voice soft with reverence. "It is mounted high on the western side of the Shine, where it is mirrored in the Laver below."

Aia Djetenga drew back. "Ahh. Where Borukini saw it?"

"That would be so."

But Azhur broke in. "Ah, no, actually. Your pardon, but no. You will no doubt recall that Na-veshtrazhdak built a chamber to house the

Valthaur, a special chamber of its own, on the west, because the Shrine was not yet finished."

Galdtchav raised one eyebrow.

"The, ah, fifty-third supplemental scroll to the Scrolls of the Founding," said Azhur.

The older Loremaster considered this. "Then that chamber would be what is now the Resting Chamber."

"Ah yes, and Na-veshtrazhdak had the Gem moved to where it now is. Inside the Shrine."

"Ah," remarked Galdtchav.

"You're bound to recall, Anthu, with a moment's thought, that when it was decided to bury the First King in that chamber—the Fire Chamber, they called it then—he said that he could never presume to be at rest beneath the Holy Gem and therefore had it moved."

A sigh from Galdtchav. "Well, I won't even attempt to recall all that, or all the rest you can no doubt tell me."

But Lady Aia appeared distressed. "What do I hear? Val-tor is not where my ancient sister saw him?"

"Well, no," said Azhur as though it were his fault. "She would have seen the Valthaur, the Gem, in the Fire Chamber. The Shrine—Arna's house—would have been unfinished, but that chamber was connected to it, it still is."

"This is written in your scroll-house, your... your...."

"Archives. Yes, but, ah, all that is in a *minor* scroll. A *very* minor scroll." Azhur glanced apologetically at Galdtchav. "Very easily... overlooked, I'd say, and not at all important or worth knowing. In my opinion." He looked at the floor.

"Lady," said Galdtchav steadily, placing a hand on Azhur's shoulder, "we are victims of my assistant's capacity for infinite explanation. The obscurities I did not know, or I have forgotten, are at his fingertips. I require his support as I slide into my dotage." He smiled wryly and affectionately at Azhur.

Lady Aia sat poised. She had the air of staring blankly within her veils. "What you have said to me goes past me, but I think the dark young lore-chief knows more than his master."

Azhur blushed, "Oh, I wouldn't say—"

"Quite correct, Lady," said Galdtchav. "He will succeed me."

Azhur started and gaped at him, but the old man kept his attention deliberately fixed on Lady Aia.

Tyr blew out his cheeks and muttered something inappropriate the others didn't hear.

Aia Djetenga made to return to her story, but caught herself and sat with hands clasped. She raised the gloved finger once more. "I am walking round this," she said. "I will ask you a thing: were memories written of the time when your First King was crowned? Are they in your writing-house?"

"They are," replied Galdtchav.

"Are memories written of Borukini my ancient sister or of Gadchanda?"

"Well, that would rank as an obscurity. Azhur?"

"Ah no," said Azhur at once. "There's a mention of the provinces of Dhar that were represented, including Murinde of course, but the representatives themselves aren't named. However, the entourage—"

"Second Master, I thank you. Now say this to me, your scrolls do not show how it was when Borukini saw Val-tor?"

"Oh no," said Azhur at once, "I'm sure of it. Besides, many people saw the Valthaur. There was no reason to single out one person for mention."

Aia Djetenga was silent again, tapping one hand on the other as it rested on the scroll case. Her head was bowed. "Well," she said at last. "She was indeed alone."

The Loremasters glanced at one another and at Tyr, and waited. No explanation came.

"Alone, Lady?" asked Galdtchav, eventually.

"The Shrine-house was not built, Val-tor was in the chamber where the First King now sleeps, and there is no memory that Borukini stood there, so my thoughts are true: my ancient sister was alone. It was a time for her and no other."

Galdtchav leaned forward. "Why is this important, Lady? And how can you be sure?"

"I have wondered, Masters, why did no-one tell of the glorious one of the light, of the burning? If they had seen, it would have been told in all the kingdoms."

"The… glorious one?" said Galdtchav. He was intrigued and fascinated and strangely afraid. The feeling that something of which he had no knowledge had suddenly gripped him and was introducing itself to him. The old Loremaster glanced at Azhur. The younger man was mentally leafing through hundreds of scrolls, pursuing their words in his cross-referenced mind. Tyr was looking perplexed. "Lady, we do not understand," continued Galdtchav. "Did something happen? What did Borukini see?"

Aia Djetenga's voice bore a tone of longing that her robes and veils could not filter. "I wished that you would tell me this."

"Is it not in your scroll?" asked Azhur.

"No, so I will leave scrolls and writings. I will speak to you, and I will say what Borukini told only to her sisters and her daughters, and only to them and to their daughters and to their daughters after them was it known. Always this has been heard in a living voice and never written. Not even Madha Negua has heard this, nor any sons of the Neguenda, nor any other of that blood."

"Nobody?" said Tyr.

"No servant, no counsellor or husband, no dear friend. Only the daughters of the daughters of Borukini through the four hundred years, until me. I am the last until I too bear daughters. But I will tell you, Masters, if you will promise to hold my words. Days move, the time-snake coils, and we should know where he goes. I must know who the glorious one is."

"Then I trust we may help you," Galdtchav replied, with an unusual gentle earnestness. "Your story will not leave us. You promise, Azhur? Tyr?" They both nodded. "Very good. If you will then, Lady."

"I thank you," said Lady Aia as if to an assembled court. "Well, it is this. My ancient sister stood long in the fire chamber, seeing the holy Gem and trying to open the doors of thought-palace. She hoped that what your rites say was true, and she hoped to see even a spark, a flicker like the silver-flash of the fish in a river. To see the echo of the echo of the Fire at the heart of all-thing would be a giving that no-one has thought before."

"Did she?" burst out Tyr, immersed in the tale. "Did she see it?"

"I will tell you," said Lady Aia, finger raised. "Borukini asked a priest of Arna if any people saw the Sea-fire in the Gem and he said no-one expected this, but the Scrolls said the Fire was there, so it was. Borukini thought, if something really is in the world, then a person may meet it and why not Borukini?

"*I will wait for the Fire,* she said. So, my ancient sister sat in the Fire Chamber for many hours, and it grew in her thoughts that she must not leave. She had food brought to her, and then a bed, for all her thoughts were fixed on this: she must not let her eyes stop taking in Val-tor and the holy Gem. But after a long path of time she saw nothing and thought, perhaps it is not true. Perhaps this new king has woven a story to make the lands talk of his Shrine. And she grew angry and began to hate the waiting.

"Now Borukini's heart was a fountain and not a storehouse, so she gave herself words and spoke to the Gem, saying, *Fire, I do not know if you are a god and I do not know if there are rites and customs to perform for you, but I am a first daughter of the Neguenda that rule Murinde. I must go there soon and I do not wish to go before I have seen your sign.* But there was nothing and Borukini felt alone, and she was sad like the Bauyan tree that asks too much of the sky and dies quickly in the dry time because it is too proud, too big.

"So, she changed her voice and said, *Fire, if you are a god, I am one of the many people that run on the world's hide. I am a stranger in the land that keeps you, and I wish to see your great wonder before I go to my home, so I may tell my sisters I have seen what is at the heart of all-thing.* But the gem was dark and did not shine for her.

"Borukini saw that her anger was in her speaking and that she was proud, as the first daughters of the Neguenda are taught to be, and she remembered that her pride was for the palaces and for leading kingdoms along and that it had not been given for doing what she was doing. When she thought, she saw she did not know what that was, and that she had not considered what it was she wished to see. What was at world-heart was so big a thing she could not have truly known what it meant to see it. It was bigger than any wonder she had seen on the world's hide, like a mountain higher than others or a forest with more colours than another. Perhaps it was a bigger thing than all the world. The seeing it would be a gift, but she did not know what gift she needed.

"Then Borukini felt like a little girl whose mother has not come in her time, and she said to the Fire in the Gem, *Fire, I do not know what you are, but if you are so great you have been in the heart of all-thing during all-time then you are not what I am, and what is in you is not in me. I have opened the doors of myself to the place where I am enthroned, and if I may draw in something that is in you and adorn my soul-house then that is my wish. And if not, I am content to have sat with you. But Fire, I do not know what I am asking.*

She sat a little longer. The chamber grew very still, and she felt like a *da'iya* cat that has eaten and is stretching for the sun to look at her. Borukini thought this was a very fine stillness, and she meant to take it to her chamber, but then she felt that the stillness was happy, very happy, and Borukini felt like the antelopes on the plain that leap for joy because they are on the earth. She laughed like the bright birds in the fruit trees and thought she would go up like the flamingos from the river, but she did not know why and felt foolish so she laughed more. And then there was a light in the chamber like shifting flame, though there was no fire, and it came down from the Gem and danced like a tribe after a victory. Ah, these are her words, I am close to her speaking, but oh, she did not know, she did not know."

But Tyr knew. He sat forward, leaning into Lady Aia's vivid experiencing of the ancient story, eyes bright and serious. "Aye," he said, "like a feller all made of fire, bright and shinin'. The most marvellous thing y' ever saw, dancin' and jumpin' like it couldn't keep still. And it made y' happy, it was that happy itself. Did she see that? She did, eh?"

But Aia Djetenga was on her feet, trembling. "Who has broken faith?" she cried. "Only the daughters of the Neguenda have known this! No man has known!"

"I guess the truth," said Galdtchav, rising quickly. "There is no betrayal, calm yourself."

"He has forced one of my sisters!" spat lady Aia. "How else can he know?"

Tyr stood, spread out his hands earnestly. "I saw it," he said. "I saw it meself, didn't I?"

"You cannot! Four hundred years!"

"I don't think that matters, it can't get old nor nothin'." Tyr remembered his first encounter with the Fire-spirit at the feast in Falakhoth, a strange mixture of pain and well-being spreading through him as this came to mind. "Y' dead right about jumpin' an' laughin' though, that's what it does to y'."

"I think," said Galdtchav, "a word of explanation is required."

And so the astounded Loremasters were compelled to tell Aia Djetenga of Tyr's visions of the splendid spirit and the mysterious scribe and how they had been seeking their meaning.

"Then I have made your mystery wider," said Lady Aia. "But this is a marvellous thing: the glorious one stands among the beggars in Valderthaan. I know even your Valgraav does not do that. Was your scribe there too?"

"Oh no," said Tyr, "I never seen them both together. I just seen the old feller in Falakhoth." This, he knew, was less than truthful, but he found he wanted to protect his experience, have something that was strictly his own. He had been meaning to tell Azhur and Galdtchav of his encounter with the burning spirit as he swam at the bottom of the Laver, but his resentment towards Azhur had gotten in the way, and he kept silent about it now. The one who had protected the north could keep his own counsel, surely?

Meanwhile, Lady Aia drummed her fingers and slapped the arms of her chair, overwhelmed by her discovery. "Another has seen, another has seen," she repeated, and swayed back and forth as she tried to come to terms with what she had learned. "Well, you may have something wide to say to Murinde, new black-robe. Perhaps the knowing in you is what I wish to bring into my thought-palace. Who do you say the burning one is?"

Tyr shrugged. "Dunno," he said desperately, "I just saw it. I dunno what it's about."

Lady Aia made an impatient humming noise in her throat. "Your scribe: what did he write?"

The question pulled Tyr's thoughts together. He took a breath, clenched his fists. "He were writin' y' scroll," he said, and braced himself.

"You are treating me like the simple people," said Lady Aia, low and menacing. "Take care, nov-is."

"I'm not," insisted Tyr. He dragged his eyes away from the Lady to look at the floor. Though he could not see her, he could not look at her.

"Speak true to me," she told him.

"I am. Look, it's got four columns and pictures underneath, and there's a picture of a man with marks on it, and lines joinin' it up with stuff."

A long silence. They could hear Lady Aia breathing hard as her fingers coiled and tapped on the chair-arms. "Is the boy *gujandi?*" she said to Galdtchav. "Is he sorcerer? One of your var... vraakhin?"

"Emphatically not," said Galdtchav.

Lady Aia strode across the room in a wild frustration. "Then how does he know? That is what they saw when they opened the scroll a century ago, but how does he *know?*" She threw herself back in the chair, drove her fist onto the arm. "The scribe cannot have made my scroll!" she said furiously. "I know this, because the glorious one came from the Gem and told Borukini—no words, no voice on the air, but she knew—he told her he would give her a gift for the daughters of the great Neguenda and he spoke and made the scroll out of the air for her. That is how it came to Murinde and to me, so you are wrong, nov-is!"

"Tyr?" said Azhur. He put a hand on his friend's shoulder. "Have you made a mistake? Should you put it differently?"

"No, I shouldn't," said Tyr sharply, for the question hurt. "No. Look, I know what y' doin', Lady, y've got to be sure, but I don't think that's right, what y' said. I think y're tryin' me out and I'm not blamin' y', but was it more like y' old sister goes to this room—spirit might have told her, I dunno—but she's at this room an' she's sort of nervous, like she might get caught, and there's this old lad at a desk with a candle finishin' the scroll. He rolls it up, sticks a seal on and gives it to Bor... to her, y' sister, and there's just a moment when they've both got a hold of it and he looks at her and says something to her and she's back out that door quick as she come in. Was it more like that?"

"And after this?" challenged Lady Aia.

"Dunno. She's off home like enough."

"The man: talk of him."

"What'd he look like? Well, old, right long beard, never shaved in his life, I reckon. White hair, long bits in front and tied round the back like they do in Ceorthas. What else? Gives us a minute... aye, he had this robe on, red with suns on it, and a ring like a priest. He had this right big nose, all swollen at the end. And bald on top."

Aia Djetenga made one more attempt. "And his words to Borukini, what were they?"

"Dunno. Somethin' quick though. Looked right serious. Might have been a warnin'. She was a bag of nerves already."

A long silence. Aia Djetenga's shoulders moved with the effort of containing her emotion. At last she carefully replaced the scroll case in its carrying pouch and rose to her feet. "I go to walk round what you have said," she informed them in a voice that struggled to maintain its evenness. Unable to resist, she turned towards Tyr. "If you have seen Borukini, tell me how she looked to you." The tiny movements of her copper veil showed how she was trembling.

Tyr scratched his head, cross at not being believed. "Bit like you, Lady. Dunno what else to tell y'." He thought hard, polishing the memory. "Oh, she had this cut. Scar or somethin'."

"Indeed?" said Lady Aia as casually as she could. "A scar? Across her face?"

"No, just one side. There, under her eye. Didn't look too bad." Tyr drew a line on his right cheekbone with one finger.

Lady Aia made no comment, her invisible eyes were fixed on Tyr. "Borukini looked like me? How do you know what I look like, black-coat?"

"Saw y' in the street, and y' was at the Shrine at Renewal Night. I saw y' there as well."

"The Shrine," repeated Aia Djetenga. She filled the word with feeling. "A cruel night. I am glad you escaped. But tell me nov-is, what did you think of the daughter of the Neguenda when you saw her?"

"I thought y' was lovely." He hadn't meant to say it, but it was the kind of conversation where the truth simply happened. It earned him another long, unseen stare.

The Lady inclined her head a little. "Tyr-shan, I thank you," she said, and her voice was unexpectedly rich and soft. She turned and made for the door as the Loremasters bowed and Tyr made his usual jerky lunge forward.

"Lady?" he said suddenly, "Can I ask y' somethin'?"

Lady Aia stopped, hand on the latch, and half-turned. "Ask," she said.

"Well, beggin' y' pardon, but why are y' all covered up?"

She appeared to think for a moment. "Because of my beauty," she said, and then she was gone.

"Ey!" gasped Tyr. "Hark at her! *Because of me beauty!*" Hands on hips, he delivered a mocking parody of Aia Djetenga's voice. "Ooh, me beauty," he lisped, sounding not unlike the lady at the fruit stall in Lacresh market. "Ey, it's a right big head she's got under them wrappin's."

But Azhur was affronted. "Now Tyr, that question was too personal, not fitting at all."

"Oh, give over. She said I could ask her!"

"Not the point, Tyr. Lady Aia is a royal personage. She represents Murinde at the court here. Not even Lord Galdtchav or I would speak to her as you did."

"I really think—" said Galdtchav, but the bridge had been crossed.

"Y' wouldn't, eh? Y' know why she's all wrapped up, then?"

"No, but I don't enquire. Someone in my position—"

"Oh right, high-and-bloody-mighty Loremasters don't ask questions. Too good for *that!*"

"Tyr, why are you like this?" gasped Azhur, taken aback. "I thought we were friends."

But it was too late, the underground stream of Tyr's frustration had once more found an outlet. In its torrent, the gentle vision of the Fire-spirit was swept away. "I thought so and all."

"Meaning?"

Galdtchav noticed Azhur was forgetting to entwine his fingers.

"Meanin' I never see y'. Y' never come and said hello when I got here, and I wanted—" He had to pause, for the emotion suddenly rose in his throat. "I wanted y' to do the initiation with me."

Now the priestly fingers locked together. "Ah, yes, and I've said sorry for that."

Galdtchav tried to intervene. "Lord Jarthastra will learn of your new visions, Tyr. He commands us to bring all news about you to him at once."

Tyr started, "Don't tell him this!"

"Why not, pray?"

"He's off his head already, y'll make him worse."

But this provoked Azhur. "Tyr, you're doing it again! I have to insist you show respect!"

"It's true, he's a loony! What's it to y', anyroad?"

"You don't seem to grasp that I'm a priest of the Second Circle now. That means I have a duty to make sure proper reverence is shown to the Valgraav at all times. *All* times, Tyr. I have to enforce that."

"That in some scroll, then?"

"Yes, it is. So I'm asking you to watch your language. You can't just behave as if you were in Falakhoth."

"Oh, right? Can't have them village lads shootin' their mouths off?"

"You know I didn't mean that, remember you're only—" Azhur's own words halted him. "That is.... that is... it's early days. What I *intended*—"

But the thing that made you able to live at Falakhoth had flared up in Tyr. "Say it then. Only a novice! *Village* novice! What'd y' get me up here for, Azhur? Am I showin' y' up?"

"Tyr, please," said Galdtchav desperately. "Azhur only meant—"

"I know what he *meant*, Anthu, beggin' y' pardon, so by y' leave I'll be off. I bet y' assistant's got to see his girlfriend."

Tyr gave a very formal bow to Galdtchav, but not to Azhur, and stumped noisily out of the chamber.

"Lord Galdtchav," said Azhur desperately. "I only..."

"Yes, of course, Azhur, of course." He took a breath. "Well, let us go to the Valgraav. Dear me. Oh dear, dear me."

506

CHAPTER 23

Meinze and the Sorcerer

Sun and olive groves, light glinting on river water, and a grey and toneless voice saying, *Where is the beauty? Where is the beauty I sought?* The olive-groves move, darken, and vanish. Ilissos found himself once more in the dreadful room, the old woman slapping him on the shoulder.

"Come on," she muttered. "Move yourself, move yourself." Ilissos tried to sit up. "They'll be back afore long. Crow's goin' back to Archraad tonight." She noticed Ilissos look over to the steps. "Here! Don't you go gettin' no ideas! Crow's not takin' no chances with *you*. He put an enchantment on them steps. You're special, you are," she added, and it was no compliment.

"Enchantment? What will it do?"

"Don't know, don't want to know, but it'll work all right. V'karra strengthened it after Crow went away so don't try it, please love. He said you'd regret it."

Ilissos sat up against the wall, head spinning at the realisation his captors didn't even need to be there to keep him imprisoned. Gizhurthra's white dog came scrambling onto his lap. Ilissos rubbed its back and head as it stretched up to lick his face, and he was at last able to smile.

"Nice little thing, isn't he?" said the woman. "Pity it never rubbed off on his master."

"Oh, that man's so pathetic," Ilissos said. "They're using him and he can't see it."

"No, of course not. He wants it. Makes him feel important. He was like that years ago, when Van was teaching him."

"Teaching him?"

"Well, not really. Tellin' him rubbish for money, mostly. Gizhurthra decided he was a great vraakhin, you see—it made him feel better, I suppose. Van encouraged it and took him on for a disciple. He used to come round to ours to get away from his own house. His dad was a complete animal, used to knock his mum senseless and thought Giz was a waste of space—told him so every day. I used to make him welcome, and if he had cuts and bruises he didn't care to explain, I'd clean them up. Not that he needed to explain to me. Anyway, his dad knocked his mum about so hard one day she just up and died, so Giz didn't have nothin' to stay here for. Dunno where he's been."

"I met him at Falakhoth. He was vraakhin there."

"Vraakhin? Was he? Well, I never. Never thought he could do that. He could never get on with people, you see. Just didn't know how. I always thought he could've been a nice feller if he'd sort of worked on it, but he couldn't see that. It was everybody else that was always wrong, not him."

"I don't think he got on with people at Falakhoth—oh!"

"What, love?"

"We're talking in Syrgan."

"Yes, I know, love. We used to live there. Had a little house in Paphlas."

"But... you..."

"I know, how did I get down there and why would I want to come back here? Well, I'll tell you. My name's Meinze, after me Gran. Born in Sarvien she was, so it's sort of unusual. I know you're Ilissos. Don't know his name, though." She stroked the dog and scratched him under the chin. "Anyway, I shared this little house near the Towers with some people, and I used to listen to traveller's tales in the inn each evenin'. The ones who had been to Syrga went on and on about how lovely it was. I'd

508

think about it when I was doin' me work at the Fish-quay in the mornin's. If I imagined really hard, I could nearly not smell the fish. Now, I ask you: what young girl with a bit of spirit and half a heart wants to spend her life guttin' fish once she's heard of the Green Jewel? Me mum and dad was dead, and I hadn't seen my brothers for years, so why stay? Bit like Giz, really. I packed up and got down to Syrga. Not easy, but I was lucky, and the Lady looked out for me, so I managed it. Found a little job in Paphlas and that's where I met Van."

"Gaur-van? He's not Syrgan."

"Oh, no. He'd had the same idea as me. Had some smelly job in Lachresh, got sick of it, and thought he'd try his luck in the Jewel. We was both out for a stroll one night when we met by the White Beach down from Paphlas harbour. He talked a bit funny, but not that way he does now though, like his tongue's too big for his mouth. He was really nice back then." She sighed with the memory. "Anyways, we got wed in this little grove near the Cynathé shrine by the big road from the hills. We got this old priest to do it and there was this lovely little white statue of her where he offered the honey cakes and the wine cup. I used to think she was just the Lady by another name."

"Oh no," said Ilissos. "She's Syrga's mother. Arna and Iathena gave us to her to care for. She asked them for Syrga."

"I know all that, love," said Meinze. "And I know Syrgans is proud of it, and so you should be too. Anyway, we was happy at Paphlas, Van and me. I did all sorts of jobs and he used to work in the orchards and the vineyards in that big estate outside town. Silly fool fell out of a tree once and did his leg in. It mended, but he couldn't do quite so much after that. I curse the day we met that southerner, V'karra... I don't really know who he is, and maybe it's just as well, but he pulled Van into his evil schemes."

She turned away, a hand over her face. The other hand she clenched as she trembled. Ilissos took it in his own and gradually the angry fist opened and Meinze held on tightly as she wept in silence. As her sobbing ended, she pressed the Syrgan's hand against her wet cheek.

"Bless you, love," she sniffed. "Bless you. You're the first bit of human kindness that's come in here since... since... well, I don't know."

509

Ilissos patted her shoulder, "Tell me about Syrga."

Meinze looked uncertain, then took up a bowl and pressed it into Ilissos' hands. "Get that down you," she said, "and I'll try." She settled herself, wiped her face on her shawl, and watched as Ilissos ate. "I must be quick," she said. "Don't know when they'll be back, and I wanted to warn you first you're goin' back to Archraad. There's somethin' happenin'. Lots of them are goin' to be there, far as I can make out. He wants you there. He thinks you're the servant of the gods or somethin'. Never stops goin' on about it and how strong he is for capturin' you. *Who you tryin' to convince,* I thought. Thinks I don't listen or I don't have me wits. What'd you do anyway, love? You really belong to the gods?"

Ilissos laughed, surprising himself. "I wish I knew," he said, shaking his head. He told Meinze about Gizhurthra's hut and the interrogation at Archraad. "When I said whatever I said, he howled and fled. I think I terrified him."

"What, him? V'karra?"

"Yes, and in Archraad I thought Val-zajjhak was afraid of me too. Nothing else has happened, so they must think the gods can't do anything. But I've never been... well, I was just trying every prayer I knew to get out of that hut alive."

Meinze considered this. The dog rolled over to have its stomach rubbed.

"I think V'karra wants to show you off to the gods, like, as well as to his cronies. Keep hearing him say stuff like, *I've got your precious servant* and that you're *under his thumb now.* He thinks the gods was tryin' to get at him through you—through those prayers you said—and he wants to keep you close to prove how he's beaten them. You're safe for a good while yet, lovey. You're a trophy."

Ilissos grimaced and returned to his food.

"Well," said Meinze, "Lady grant you get right away from them all, and soon."

He hoped such an opportunity would arise.

"Mind you...." Meinze was momentarily lost in thought. "I think there was somethin' else goin' on in that hut—somethin' happenin' to you that shook that Crow, Val-zajjhak. Did you know he used to be a priest?"

Ilissos nodded.

"I don't know what V'karra wanted *him* for. Mind you, he does things like that. Likes to get folk over from the other side. Spoiling a priest... I suppose that's why he went for Crow."

"Has Gaur-van been with the southerner a long time?"

Meinze's mouth tightened. She gave a slow nod.

"And he met him in Paphlas, yes?"

There was a silence so long, it seemed Meinze would say no more. When she spoke, it was a whisper. "Van sometimes worked at the dock after the harvests were in, the bit where the merchant ships come in. He used to help with loadin' and tying the ships up. Sometimes he'd do trips round the islands, helpin' out merchants. Good money, that was. Sometimes they'd sell him stuff cheap they couldn't get rid of, and I'd set a stall up in the big square, down them steps from the harbour. You know it, of course you do."

She was smiling as she and Ilissos saw together the wide river mouth and myriad craft, the beautiful hills easing out their slope towards the coastal towns, and Paphlas sitting by its deep, blue bay, where the goods, skills, and thoughts of many nations came. For a moment, everything else did not matter, for the sharp sea-air blew in their faces and they heard gulls wheeling around the mastheads, the sailors' calls, wood thudding on stone, the creak of ropes, and the slapping of the restless water between the hulls.

Meinze continued with a deep, slow sigh, "One day there was two big merchant ships put in from Lachir. Sailed from Burdaz somebody said, so we went for a look—you get some funny characters comin' off them Burdaz ships. Van wasn't workin' that day, so we was just sittin' waitin'. I remember seein' bunches of horns bein' unloaded, you know, from them big beasts they're supposed to have away East. Van told me that's what you make ivory from and I didn't believe him. We got into an argument about it—oh, if the Lady had had pity on us we'd have gone home then and never given them ships another look." She made another sigh, stronger this time, with a little whine in it, as though she was trying to gather the years of regret and strain and expel them in a breath. She looked once more at the unfolding memory. "We'd stood up and was goin' to leave, when Van suddenly says, *Hello, who's this, then?* So I looked, and there he was, standin' and lookin' about afore he stepped down from the ship. *That's no trader,* says Van. *Got ter be a King or a Lord or somethin'.* And then I saw how Van was starin' at him. Not that I was surprised. He made you stare, standin' there like a king's statue, back straight, head up, lookin' around like he owned the place. Them robes of his blew in the wind, all black an' red they was, and gold stitched throughout them, with his head wound round in some scarlet stuff, you know, like they do out East. Looked like silk, the best.

"Anyways, a lot of people was starin' by now, wonderin' if the King of Lachir had come on a visit, but he never paid them no attention. He just rested his hands on his hips—I bet so everybody could see his rings: gold and silver and every kind of jewel. There was this great knife at his belt, all curved and wicked lookin', a golden scabbard with it. And he had gold round his neck and I don't know what all. But I'll tell you, I knew he didn't enjoy it any more than if it was plain brass. Knew it from his face. Angry it was, all lines, with eyes like daggers. Now, who'd you ever see stand by the water at Paphlas on a beautiful mornin' with a face like that?"

Ilissos nodded. He too had watched the sea at Paphlas.

"Anyhow, he scared me. I didn't care who he was, I just didn't want them eyes lookin' at me, but Van was gettin' really interested. *Doesn't look the type for Burdaz,* he says. I says he might've come over from Dhar, while I try to lead him away. *Nah,* says Van, *there's nobody comes from Dhar, it's all desert.* And then he starts walkin' up to the boat. I grabbed his arm to stop him, but he wasn't havin' it. He wanted to know who it was."

"You think that was all?" asked Ilissos, remembering the power of the Vraakhin.

"Don't know," replied Meinze. "But Van wasn't one to be impressed by rings and fancy clothes. There'd be more to it than that."

Ilissos was absorbed in the story. The poet in him felt the drama, the theatre. Someone should tell these things to harp music by a fire in a banquet-hall or under the stars in Agoras' moonlight-white arena. But that was an injustice to Meinze, for she was speaking only tragedy. Every word was a tiny knife.

"Well," she went on, "he saw Van, and looked him up and down, then waved him over. Off goes Van like a little dog." Here Meinze broke off. She clenched her fists. "I see him now, wavin' at Van like he was some village idiot. Oh, I want to scream at him and shove him back in the boat and make him leave us alone. Oh, I should've, I should've'."

Ilissos took her arm, ashamed of his thoughts about songs and banquets. "You didn't know," he said softly. "How could you?"

"Well, I sort of did, but I never thought how it would go. He got Van to carry his stuff off the boat, and then they had this talk. I saw him put his hand on Van's head for a minute. He stared right into his eyes and Van give this little twitch. I thought he was bein' took poorly, but then he comes over to me and says, *This gentleman needs a place so I said he could stop with us for a while. Says he'll pay us well for it.* I tried arguin', but Van wasn't havin' it. I think he was enchanted as soon as he looked him in the eye.

"Anyhow, he—V'karra—came to our house and had our bedroom. Went out every night and hung about all day. These *people* used to come and see him at our house. They and Van would spend hours in the room with him. There was fellers from Burdaz, all robes and scars, and northerners, and I don't know what. Every one was queerer than the other. They all looked at me like I was a beetle they was goin' to step on. There was times I couldn't go near my own bedroom. It was like the air went thick and you couldn't get through to it. All the plants I had inside and outside the house was all dead in a few weeks, no matter what I tried. The food no longer tasted right, the candles burned down quicker, and the plaster flaked and the house got mould. The cats and dogs stopped comin' by for scraps, we kept gettin' maggots, and even the children stopped wavin' to us as we went down different streets. Nothin' was right.

"And Van just kept laughin' and noddin', and lappin' up power and magic and how to control people. They said he had power they'd woken up. From then on, he wanted to become a great sorcerer and help them take over the north, then Dhar, then everywhere else. V'karra would become emperor, and there'd be a golden age. How he believed that bunch could make anythin' golden I don't know. All the gold came out of our little money box, and when that was empty, Van had to work to get more for them. *Fair pay for what he was learnin'*, he told me.

"All the while his leg was gettin' worse till he needed that crutch, and it was gettin' harder and harder for him to talk proper." Meinze stopped, looking hard into the past. She sighed. "They used to bring women back and take them into the room. There'd be laughin' and singin' for a while, but not all the time. The girls was never there in the mornin'. Never saw them leave, neither. Got to say though, Van was never in that room while they had the girls over. I'm thankful for that.

"Van was that feller's disciple. When he moved, Van moved. They was all over the place, settin' up this scheme of theirs. Whatever big thing they were organisin', Van says it's now started. They've got people everywhere. There was three or four places in Syrga, then a couple of cities in Sarvien. I went too, of course, I wasn't givin' up on Van. They had us in Harrokaan a few times. That was an experience all right. Van went on a boat to Ngal once, but I wouldn't go, then round Ceorthas a bit, and we was in Ceor a little while, not long at all. Too near Fyrieg I'd say. We was a while in Archraad, as you might of guessed. That's where Van met up with Crow. Oh, it's a funny place, that is. They used to meet up with people from the Harrak tribes on the Plain. And then we come here quite a few years ago. And that's me story. To think I left here for a lovely new life in the Green Jewel... I got a new life all right, I just hope the same don't happen to you and you can get away and get home. Do you have family down there?"

And now Meinze's grief called forth Ilissos' own. "Yes," he said, a catch in his voice. "My mother still lives in Agoras. My father died about five years ago, but she stayed there to be near my sisters and myself. We had a business buying and selling wool and doing weaving. Mother's so skilled—she's almost a legend. She wove me a beautiful coat once, when she was staying at the House of Life in Labanei. She was ill, and she went there to—"Tears came, carried on the gentle memories. Terror and loss let go at last and left in great, convulsing sobs.

Meinze put her arm around him, held him, and stroked his hair like a mother with a hurting child. When at last his body was freed and quiet again, she found him a cloth for his face and sat holding his hands until he was ready to speak. Their eyes met, and they both smiled.

"You know," he said, "that coat's in my saddlebags. I couldn't bear to leave it behind." He wiped his eyes, thought and said, "Could I… well, you've given me the first touch of comfort since… since the time in the hut. So many terrible things and no help, no help at all. But you brought my home, my mother, and my family—my real life—you gave them back to me and… I feel I'm alive again."

Meinze wiped her own eyes. "You did the same, love."

"Well, I wondered… could I ask… do you have something I could remember you by? I don't know when I'll see you again, if I ever do, and if I had something…."

"That's a lovely idea," said Meinze. "Of course, love. Just wait there."

She went to a dim corner and rummaged among bags and jars, then returned and pressed something into Ilissos' hand. It was a little painted figure of a woman holding a cypress branch with her hand in an attitude of blessing. The dress, the hair, the bright colours seemed to hold the essence of the beautiful land kissed by the sea. "There she is, Cynathé herself. Bought it off a stall in Paphlas. Looked really pretty, I thought. Reminded me of all the good times. She's yours now, my love."

"Oh, thank you," whispered Ilissos, as the simple, happy thing touched his poet's soul. "But I have nothing to give you."

Meinze took his hands, so that the little figure was held within Ilissos' hands and hers. "Yes, you have. You've no idea, but you've already given me your gift."

"But all the same," he said, "I wish…." He trailed off. Looking at Meinze and feeling her warm, bony hands cradling his own, it came again, that startling knowledge of a voice from outside the world or from deep within the world, promising that all was good and had been whole and would be so again. Ilissos was washed throughout by a surge of joy far above happiness that flew up from within reality. The room, Meinze, the dog, himself, were knife-edge real and sheared into his delighted senses like a blade. He was broad awake, as though the cataracts of Cynathé's hills had rushed down on him and sliced into the very place where he existed. This was the wave of knowledge that had come to him on the moors above Falakhoth and which the leaden priest Jher-val had so crudely dismissed. But still the Syrgan did not understand it, indeed, he had forgotten it since his terror in Gizhurthra's hut. Now it had followed and found him again without him knowing how, except that Meinze's compassion had been the open door, the strong hand that had drawn aside the curtain to let him see it again…. Well, he did not know what he had seen, or rather known, but the comfort had refreshed his whole being. Grateful, he clutched his goddess' amulet on his left wrist. *Sirtha tha vei, Cynathé, Sirtha tha vei…*

Outside, a sudden roar. Sharp words followed, and they recognised Gaur-van's voice. Again, Ilissos anxiously gripped the amulet. Just beyond the door, a croaking cry. Ilissos quickly put the little figure away in a pocket.

"Lady save us!" gasped Meinze. "Now what?"

They noticed the dog. The little beast had backed away behind the ledge where the fire burned. It was cowering in a safe cranny, shaking and staring at the door.

"What's up with you?" Meinze crooned to it. "What's wrong?"

Gaur-van appeared at the top of the steps. "Evenin'," he said in his rasping way, and laughed his leering laugh.

"What's happenin' out there, Van?"

Gaur-van walked down the steps. He slapped his knees and grimaced genially at Ilissos. "How you doin', son?"

Ilissos met his eye, half defiant and half sad. "*Mai alla ta eu tha'emeron,* and I thank you that you ask, Master."

Gaur-van started, "Eh? How'd you…?"

"I told him," said Meinze.

"What for? You got no right!"

"Well, I don't know about that. Makes no difference anyhow and I got to talk to somebody while you're out ruinin' the world. Your nice friends have got him whether or not he knows."

Gaur-van glared at his wife, making angry sounds deep in his throat. At last he looked away and growled at the floor.

"Van, you got to get away," Meinze burst out. "They're never goin' to win!"

"You sure of that?" leered the old vraakhin. "What about that bear,

516

Ilissos met his eye, half defiant and half sad. "*Mai alla ta eu tha'emeron,*
and I thank you that you ask, Master."

eh? What about that feller's leg? It's working in Lukar, ain't it? All going ter plan, eh?"

"Plan!" said Meinze, trembling. "Did you plan havin' all of them people killed in Vardresh, Van? All them Arta that had nothin' to do with it. And them kiddies! Did you plan that? Did you? Get away from it, Van! Look what they done to you!"

"That went wrong," said Gaur-van looking away from his wife. "That Guard of the Sun went wild. I never knew that would happen."

"Van," said Meinze, "look at me. I got to ask you somethin' afore they comes back. Look at me, now." The old vraakhin made himself meet his wife's eyes. "Van, I'm sorry, but did you ever kill anybody? Did you ever do that for them?"

Gaur-van shook his head and seemed to relax. "No," he said, still looking at Meinze. "They never asked me." Thankfulness trembled in his voice.

"Van, if—"

"What's up with him?" asked Gaur-van, glancing edgily towards the cringing dog.

"Never mind the bleedin' dog, Van! What's up with *you*? I want me husband back!"

Gaur-van glared at the floor, the fire, everywhere but at Meinze. "Not long now," he growled. "It got a bit out of hand, but not long now. After tomorrow night it'll all be done quick." He showed his teeth in a lopsided smile. "I'll buy you that big house in Paphlas yet." He grinned awkwardly, but Meinze stood like a stone, staring at him with her mouth open.

"You'll what?" she said at last. "You dragged me about all them years and had me livin' in a bloody grave so you could buy me a house in Paphlas?"

"Now then," said Gaur-van, wagging a finger. "Now then, me girl. I mean, this is a big thing, and I've got power now. I have. He woke it up in me. I mean, look, we got the gods' own servant under our thumb—"

"If you think," cut in Meinze, firing her words like arrows. "If you *think* for one *moment* I have trailed along with you and put up with that foreign devil and his evil cronies and his schemes and watched you

turnin' into some mad monster just so I could have a house in Paphlas....
Well, I never knew you thought so little of me!"

Gaur-van lowered his head. "You're not your usual self, girl. You be nice and quiet now, like you usually are."

Meinze folded her arms, "Well, sometimes Van, you just can't be quiet. Sometimes there's things as has to be said if you're to live with yourself!" Tears were rising into her wrath. "Are you tellin' me you really don't know why I'm still here?"

"Because you ought ter be," snapped Gaur-van. "I'm your husband."

"And why ought I to be?" asked Meinze. "Where's the ought in it, eh?"

Gaur-van rounded on her. "Well, where is it then?" he rasped. "Why're you here?"

Meinze shook with rage and justice, "Because I bleedin' loves you!" she cried. "Are you that blind?"

Ilissos held his breath in the silence, as Gaur-van and Meinze stood poised on a moment of hope. The vraakhin opened his mouth but found nothing to say. His face showed a mixture of wonder and grief. He drew in a breath, stammered, then rose and took a lurching step towards his wife.

"I thought," he said, "I thought... I don't know, I never...."

There was a swirl of bitter air and Val-zajjhak was at the top of the steps.

"I will take the Syrgan to Archraad," he informed the pair dully. "Lukar is sinking. Our powers are manifest."

"Are they now?" said Gaur-van in a small, dark voice.

"Of course," replied Val-zajjhak flatly. "The youth's imagined cure and deliverance from the bear has bewitched them. The people are in thrall to their Lady's new hero and the story of Vardresh. The hatred spreads. All the North will soon turn on the House of the Lion. This was long prepared, are you uncertain now?"

"Suppose not," growled the older man. "Nah, of course not."

There was a taut, grey silence.

"Then all is as it should be," said Val-zajjhak at last. "But let Lord Gehrava reassure you."

Meinze squealed and backed into a corner.

Gaur-van stared up in shock, "He's not coming here, is he?"

"Why should he not? Is it not an honour?" Val-zajjhak turned and leaned out of the doorway. "Here, my Lord, this is the place." Val-zajjhak pressed himself against the wall to make room. Another figure appeared on the little balcony and spread its black shadow over him.

Ilissos immediately felt the immensity of Gehrava's presence. It came upon him as an intense concentration of time, a solid mass of years experienced as though all history narrowed and converged to a point and pressed its unguessable weight on this one place. The stones of the walls felt new and freshly minted, only recently molten, and Gehrava himself seemed to stand within an abyss of years wherein he had accrued an astounding power. His head turned within its wide, grey hood. The face was wound about with faded cloth, like a traveller in a sandstorm, and palpable waves of hate swept down from the barely exposed eyes. He gasped, his hand moving instinctively towards the Cynathé amulet and his lips parting to form a prayer to the goddess. At a tiny movement of Gehrava's fingers a shocking pain went through the nerves of his wrist, and a bolt of energy in his teeth numbed his mouth.

"This is he?" said a voice from the eddying dust of dry, dead wadis. "How like them, to imagine this sad thing could be a path for power. What folly will they not attempt? It will be an easy contest." The sorcerer let out a long, sighing breath, the whispering slither of hot, hard lizard-skin on stones, the rustling death of all green leaves.

"Will it please you to deal with the Syrgan here, my Lord?" asked Val-zajjhak from the shadow.

"No, no. We will bring him to Archraad. Their powerless servant will be there as the Dark Sun rises. I will wave their weakness in their faces."

"Then will it please you to travel with us?" asked Val-zajjhak.

"No," said the scraping voice. "I go my own ways. Is this V'karra's servant?"

Gaur-van realised the invisible eyes were looking at him. "Yes, that's right, me Lord," he said and bowed with an absurd flourish, leaning on the back of the chair. "Great honour, sir, great honour, ter have you in me humble home. Here, sir, me lady wife, sir."

"I allowed you to keep the female. It was my decree some years ago, my reward for your service to Lord V'karra."

"Thank you, sir. Very kind of you, sir. Meinze, step over here, me dear."

"No," said Gehrava, turning to the door. "I do not waste sight on them. The male carries the strength; the male is human." He made to step outside but a low growl came from below. Gehrava stopped, his hand on the lintel. "I am not welcome," he said, with the faintest hint of hurt feelings. "Who does not care for me?" He raised his hand and Gizhurthra's dog appeared from its hiding place as if it was being dragged by an invisible rope. "Come," whispered Gehrava, almost affectionately. "Let me see you."

"My Lord, there is a barring spell on the stairs," Val-zajjhak told him.

"I know," replied the sorcerer, "I feel it, but no matter." His hand made a clutching motion, and the dog moved towards the steps, writhing and howling. Gehrava laughed, or seemed to. "He comes after all! He braves your enchantment!"

Meinze held her hands to her face, watching in horror with the others below as the dog, convulsing in terror, was hauled up the steps. Somehow it reached Gehrava's hand, eyes bulging, teeth bared, trying to claw him. He held it close to his shrouded face.

"Gehrava has never kept a pet before," he grated. "Shall I brand him?" With the fingers of his free hand he traced a shape on the white shoulder, slowly and carefully, like a master craftsman. There was the smell of burning fur and flesh. The dog gave a howl that became the harrowing sound of animal screaming. "It is my sign," said Gehrava, as though pleased with himself. "I must declare my presence whenever I may." He held the muzzle of the shaking dog close again. "You are mine now, little one," he told it in a grotesquely crooning tone. "Go where you will: Gehrava's mark will give you passage." And he flung the dog out into the night. There was a yelping and scrabbling, then silence. "There now," said the sorcerer, with something like a sigh of satisfaction. "It was your beast?" he asked Gaur-van.

"No, me Lord. It belonged to the feller as did the fire-word."

"Our new brother. Well, I will reward him. And now I go my ways to

Archraad. We are at work here and not one of them know. Vardresh will make them hate their masters. Soon Lukar shall be taken and sealed. Take the servant of the gods. It's no matter if they see him. We will show them their impotence tomorrow when we have their black-coat village boy who serves the sun and who dishonoured my servant V'karra. Then, when the Dark Sun has risen, I will fulfil my priesthood and we will advance."

Ilissos had sat listening to Gehrava in utter bewilderment, now his confusion had made way for nausea after witnessing the torture of Gizhurthra's dog. He swallowed down bile that left his throat sore. His own emotions were suddenly swamped by the pleasured anticipation coming to him through his mental link with Val-zajjhak. Not that Val-zajjhak was happy. Rather, it was a reversal of joy or a negative image of happiness. He was finding delight, not in being raised up but in plummeting to the very depths. Ilissos had never encountered this sensation before. It was alien to his experience of humanity. He recoiled and pressed against the wall. Gehrava stared at him. *Did he realise this link existed?*

"Up," was all he said. "We taunt your masters, and for that we need you."

Ilissos got stiffly onto his knees, his world swimming. He got to his feet unsteadily, making himself slide up the wall for support. Watching the spectre above him, he unthinkingly moved a hand towards the amulet on his left wrist. Two tiny points of light, infinitely sharp and far away, flashed in the dark under Gehrava's wide hood. Something stabbed at his insides, and Ilissos quickly withdrew his hand. He sensed a leap of fear, but it was not Val-zajjhak's or his own, which was vivid enough already. Gehrava was afraid. *Why was he afraid of a prayer to Cynathë?* He could not comprehend.

The dark under the hood seemed to regard him a moment more, then the shapeless robe swirled round and away into the night.

"We will go now," said Val-zajjhak. "Come, I will lift the spell."

Knowing there was nothing else he could do but obey, Ilissos crossed the room to the steps. He paused halfway, took Meinze's hand and kissed it. "*Eianna va, se natha,*" he said simply. *Thank you, my mother.* It was a saying of deep respect and affection. Meinze held his hand to her cheek, and he knew she had understood. Gaur-van met his eyes for a moment. "*Edasta veiai*," he whispered to the old vraakhin, then went up the steps, not knowing what was ahead.

CHAPTER 24

Azhur's Story

AZHUR EASED WITH DISCOMFORT into the daily life of a Second Circle Loremaster. The position was an exalted one, he knew, the duties crucial and hallowed, yet to his dismay he was finding the reality didn't match his years of anticipation. He was elated at the beginning but now his life as a priest was quickly becoming routine. His sense of anti-climax was crushing. The immense drama of his secret and public consecrations seemed very far away, and was, he reflected, not the best introduction into the priesthood.

The next thing duty demanded found him on a horse ambling down the sloping street to Bridgegate. The evening's sunlight fell on the western side of the island-city and he could see the red-gold light touch the remoter sides of the tallest buildings and slide between them in a last attempt to warm the farther streets. As the city dimmed and cooled, Azhur found that, since the horse was more than familiar with the route, there was nothing to do for a while but think. And he was well-practised at this.

For years, Azhur's mind had been an inner shrine of thoughts and thinking. Facts were his friends, analysis his heartbeat. There were people he loved, yet he seldom ventured far outside of his head where the coals of holy knowledge burned. Now, a long slant of light spilled in from outside as the hands of Aienna gently edged open a heavy door to his interior world. This had frightened him at first, but now he longed for this intrusion, hoping for the time when this door would stay fully open. He was even beginning to help her open it in her company, for the disquiet that often clouded his mind could not live when she was with him. And then there was Tyr, whose approach was a battering-ram to his inner sanctum's defences. His new friend was forcing light in without Azhur's help, exposing confusions by its unfamiliarity and persistence. Tyr often slipped past the doorstep now. Whatever effect the people closest to him had, Azhur's stress and confusion were not long in sidling back when they were not with him. This was most acute when Aienna was not present. The absence of her light left him unsettled. When his new priesthood provided a less than suitable distraction, an invisible weight rested upon his shoulders and a heavy band felt placed around his head. Galdtchav's kindly wisdom did not always ease the feelings that had simmered for years and which now writhed at the surface of his mind. The Consecration had driven them down, but they were creeping up again, faster this time, pulling all the joy from his new role.

With a shake of his head, his thoughts returned to duty. Ahead of him the entrance-square was quiet and dull, its only patron the crumbling statue of Val-Nhakh'hant'than, priestly student of the poor of Arna's city. The daily throng of visitors and traders had long left the city, even though the yawning portal to the Bridge still stood open. The guards had even tidied away the poor from Val-Nhakh'hant'than's accepting gaze. At the far end of the square a detachment of guardsmen stood by each door of the colossal gate, ready to seal the great arch for the night. Once the gate was closed, they would keep watch through the darkness. A little group of priests and novices had arranged themselves just outside the arcs the massive doors would swing through as they closed. Before them stood a black metal brazier. Azhur reined up beside them and dismounted.

"Evening, Wringer," said a novice cheerfully. "How's life in the red?" A bald-headed priest beside the speaker gave him a hefty cuff, "Now then. Respect to the Anthu."

"Sorry, Azhur—Anthu," said the novice, rubbing the back of his head.

"Glad it's you, though. Been looking forward to it."

"Well, that's good," replied Azhur. "Ah, thank you. Thanks very much. Hope I get it right."

The novices laughed and grinned. "Come on, if you don't get it right, nobody can," one said.

The respectful priest nodded.

"Here, how about a lecture before you start?" asked another novice. "We might have to do this ourselves someday. Be good to have some tips."

"Running commentary even," chirped the first novice.

Azhur wound his fingers, the novices wisely choosing not to notice. "Ah, well—yes, I suppose that would be all right," said Azhur through a rush of stress. "Yes. You can never learn too much."

The priest smiled and nodded again, "Very good decision, Anthu."

"Oh. Thank you. Well, we begin."

A novice punched the air, "Go for it, Tw—Anthu."

The Anthu went for it: "We are here to perform the Rite of the Blessing of the Gates. I shall recite and offer fire and, ah, you will assist me. Why is this rite essential?" He paused for an extended moment while the novices plundered their memories.

"Oh!" said one suddenly. "Safety! Makes the gates safe!"

"Good. It is in fact a…"

"Rite of Protection!"

"Correct. Now, we speak these rites at all the important gates in the city, and walls, ramparts, the Shrine Court, and so on. They are also said for the Bridge by each priest stationed in the niches below the Effigies of Crossing."

"The…?"

"Oh, come on now. Effigies of Crossing? The statues along the Bridge."

"Oh, right, of course. Got it now."

"Now, the gates—especially the ones at the ah, entrance to the city standing before us—receive the Blessing daily, at appointed hours. As you should have learned by now, this renders them impassable. The Rites of Protection, suffused with the power of Lord Arna, are the means, together with the men of the Red, the city's Guard, who have their own rites, are... are..." Azhur grasped for the words that were no longer there.

"The Rites are the means," said the bald priest helpfully.

"Yes, quite. The means."

"Big sentence, there," said a witty novice. "Even for you, eh?"

Azhur ignored him, clawing for words, "We begin..."

"Are you all right, Anthu?" the priest asked.

Azhur stared at him a moment before gathering his senses. "Yes. Yes, quite all right. Now..." He turned so that the brazier was just in front of him. Looking over the fire and through the great gate, his eye could travel along the Bridge, past the statues to the Lake's eastern shore, over the buildings and green land to the long hills of the Mardhoran, where he and Tyr had revelled in the sight of Valderthaan under the early sun. And there was the gap in the hills, where nestled... where nestled... his home town of Mardokhal. Azhur felt unsteady as memories threatened to invade. There was a mounting feeling of pressure on his head. *"Bring the fire!"*

Shocked by Azhur's sudden barking of the Ritual's first words, the novices edged forward. The lad on his right muttered prescribed words over a metal container, before handing it to the Anthu, who gripped it tightly—and with something of a tremor—as he stared furiously at the spot where Mardokhal lay cradled between the hills.

Azhur seized the words of the Rite, grappled them, and sent them battering through the gate and out along the Bridge. He seemed to expand, in body and in sheer presence, such was the power and authority he put into the words: "We prepare this vessel: we offer it to hold fire, as the world was readied to receive the Fire of Arna at creation. *Ai va kherūl; ai dheir lūth'ha shi.*"

His voice boomed and echoed round the square. The guards, normally uninterested in the rite looked up, wondering with an unexpected thrill what had happened to the old nightly routine.

"We declare this gate blessed and warded; we affirm protecting fire against all harm, against all realities that may be but shall not be against this city. *Vah'hurthan kherūlishta shi.*"

527

Azhur faced the helpers as his words rolled once more around the square, his back now turned to Mardokhal. "I thank you for your assistance," he said quietly. "Arna shine on you."

The priests and novices stared, both awed and uplifted.

The bald-headed priest was the first to break the silence. "Magnificent, Anthu."

"Not at all," replied Azhur, looking wide-eyed into the distance. "Just my calling." He sighed. "Well, good night." He walked slowly and a little unsteadily towards his horse.

"Never heard it spoken like *that* before," said a whisper behind him.

"Something wrong there," muttered an older voice.

Azhur permitted himself, not a smile exactly, but a strange, expressionless calm, for he was all right and nothing at all was wrong. Had he not faced Mardokhal for the first time in what seemed an age and defiantly remembered? Had he not beaten the memories down by bold assertion of his priestly self?

The Rite of Protection had scoured Azhur's head of its noise and pain. Glad of it, he leaned quietly against his saddle before mounting, stroking the horse's neck and murmuring to it. With a sigh, he glanced towards Val-Nhakh'hant'than's ugly statue. Near its base stood a woman he hadn't noticed when he entered the square. He wondered what she had made of his delivery of the Rite. She faced him and inclined her head. He took in the veil across her face, realising with a start it was Lady Aia Djtenga. He had not seen the princess since her discovery of Tyr's visions in Galdtchav's chamber. Azhur bowed deeply, arms crossed on his chest.

Lady Aia stood motionless for a moment before turning abruptly and striding across the square. Wrapped in the shadows at the edge of the square, her attendants waited with their horses. *Did she not recognise him?*

He mounted his horse and guided it to the long street that rose from the square towards the upper levels. The gates were rumbling shut for the night and the novices were packing up the Rite's equipment. They watched him go. The bald priest and one novice performed the formal bow. Azhur smiled and nodded to them. He must keep speaking the Rite as he had that evening. He felt a strange elation, a powerful awareness, as if he were expanding to fill himself. It occurred to him he had not wound his fingers together for some time. Nothing amiss, then, he told himself. He was who he was meant to be, and all was well.

He let the horse amble past Second Level then up to the Third, arriving at the complex of buildings grouped around the massive base of the King's Tower. He gave his mount to an attendant and made for the stairway that led to the chambers used by the Loremasters. The stone arteries of the Tower led him to a point where the ways diverged. One of them opened onto steps that led to an arched entrance to the Shrine Court, its doors still open revealing the pale evening sky beyond. Azhur hesitated briefly, then made for the arch. He would go to the Court and bow before Arna's image on the Tower before he retired. It would be a fine acknowledgement of the overwhelming success of the Rite of Protection.

The Loremaster's elated mood carried him rapidly up the steps and into the Shrine Court. The huge space was quiet and reverent as the day faded into dusk. Azhur sat among the tiered seats and listened to a priest sing the Evening Song, the farewell to the Sun as he descends to the western horizon. The events of Renewal Night were still fresh in his mind, but Azhur dispelled them by concentrating on the gigantic Arna figure whose shimmering wings seemed spread out to shield the Court from further harm.

The last light of day gathered into a long fringe hanging from the hem of the sky behind the Shrine. Beyond was Holy Fyrieg and the western Sea, and far, far beyond, the Deep Fire that burned beneath the waves at the heart of the world. Azhur rose and stood facing Arna. He spread out his hands on either side to show he was consciously present, then crossed his arms on his chest and bowed deeply and reverently. It was said that when a priest bowed to Arna, the kingdom became stronger, and so he stayed in the respectful stance for a while to make his contribution to the Northlands' security. When he stood straight again, the sun had set and the priests and populace making use of the holy space were making their way to the gates and doors like beetles on the sacred stones. Only Lady Aia moved against this tide, having entered by the door Azhur had used.

"Lady Aia! A happy meeting!"

The princess stopped, silence trailing after her, and settling round her. Azhur felt her strong, invisible stare. "That is your thinking?" she said at last.

"I saw you by the statue at the Gate," Azhur said, not knowing how to reply. "I—I felt sure it was you. I thought perhaps you did not recognise me."

"I was with the statue," replied Lady Aia. "This was important." She remained still, watching Azhur through her veils with what could only be an intense stare: tight-clasped hands, imperious body, head held high.

Azhur felt that, if he could see these eyes, they would wither him. All at once he felt trapped. She would not go and he could not. His hands were creeping towards each other. "Well, I—I hope your time there was, ah, was good. Perhaps you came to hear the Rite of Protection." At once, he regretted the vanity.

"The Rite is not for me," said Aia in a sudden, hard voice. "It was not a good time."

"Lady, I feel—your voice, your, ah, demeanour—you seem troubled. Have you any need of comfort? Of help, perhaps?" His peace had slipped by him, and he could not stop his hands coming together.

A tremor stirred Lady Aia's robes. "I looked for comfort," she said with a restrained fierceness. "It was not there."

Azhur surveyed every inch of the stones around his feet, "I see. Well, I am most sorry. I hope you find your… comfort. Have you come to bow before Arna?"

"I have not," said Aia, fury and grief overlapping in her tone.

Azhur felt assailed, his fingers now in violent combat. "Then... then what... why…?"

Lady Aia aggressively stepped towards him, "Bow?" she said, her pain palpable now. "Bow to Arna? I am here to… to… what is the word?" She threw out her arms, her usual serenity forgotten. "I have come to scold Arna!"

Azhur gasped. *Scold?* That was what women did to children and lazy husbands. It was what children did to kittens and each other. How could one scold Arna?

"I will tell you, red priest," Aia said even though Azhur had stayed silent in his shock. Her hands clenched into fists by her side, her wrath throwing a burning light about her. "I spoke with your Galdtchav. I learned of nov-is Tyr-shan, that he had seen the beautiful spirit by the statue in the Gate Square. It is the spirit that came to my ancient sister Borukini. Now it is in this city again, and I am here too—where can I see it? The voice in my heart-palace is crying to welcome the beauty—where can I meet it? It was not seen in this Shrine by me, not in the halls of the palace-tower, not in the house of your scrolls. No! Do not speak, red priest! I have the right of words! Hear what I say to you! Here is a great place with priests and the sacred houses and the great holy gem, and in the all-place of this there is not a one that has seen the beautiful spirit. Not a one but my ancient sister and a boy who is turning hearts of the priests away. Is it not a fight of things?"

Azhur was feeling unaccountably guilty. Her complaint seemed aimed at him, and he could not understand why.

"Shrine Court is the world's most safe place at your Renewal," said Aia. "You have told me this, yes?"

"I told you, yes," he said. "We have always...." his reflexive answer died on his lips and fell on to the death-stained stones.

"We were not safe!" she forced out. "You told us Arna made us safe, so we came here. We feared the evil Harrach-man, we wished to be with all-other in our house and you said no, go to Arna's court, and Arna was no shield to us!"

Azhur groped among his thoughts for some kind of apology or restitution for Lady Aia, even as he cringed inside at the words being spoken in this holy place. He glanced desperately around the Shrine Court, seeing again in his mind's eye, the flames whirling around the unstoppable sorcerer. The Rite of Protection's surge of elation was being leeched out of his body. At length, he managed: "But you survived, Lady Aia. I thank the gods you have come through, though others did not. It was a terrible thing to endure and I do not understand it; but you have borne it without loss—"

"Without loss?" cried Aia. "Oh, red priest, you do not know!"

She stood directly in front of Azhur. The Loremaster stared desperately at her swaying veils. A thought he was afraid to understand rose in his mind. Aia's hands came up to take hold of her veil.

"I will show you my loss! You will see how Arna failed me!"

Then, with a wail of pain, she ripped her veil away and Azhur saw where her matchless face had been. He was glad of the failing light.

"What am I without my beauty?" she said. "The devil-fire has torn me away."

Struck by this terrible sequel to the Rite of Protection, Azhur stood in shock. A terrible confusion had fallen on him, freezing even his battling fingers.

"I went to the Statue Square to see the beautiful spirit," said Aia. "I learned also that Tyr-shan had seen it by the statue, and I learned that it stood with a beggar-woman and her child and a love came out from the heart-palace of the spirit, and a com... com..., I cannot say it!"

"Compassion," whispered Azhur.

Aia seemed to find even the word a promise of hope. "What is the com-pa-shon?"

"It is a kind of pain we experience when we see another suffering," Azhur told her. "We say it comes when love births within us a desire to ease a person's pain."

"Then this is in the heart-palace of the beautiful one," said Aia through tears. "I hoped I would receive it for myself. I hoped to see the beautiful one by the statue and have his love-pain for myself. But it was not there. How can I find him, red priest?"

Azhur tried to reply but could only shake his head and look down. Aia stepped back. "Ah, I should know. You are Arna's man!" Then she whirled around and threw up her arms towards the giant, glimmering figure of the hovering god. "Arna! Look at your failing! Look at what happened because you had no strength in your own house! I have anger to you! May the gods punish you! May you do penance to Mūlakē, our Watcher-lady! I will come to your house no more."

Aia fell silent. Her outburst had left her cleansed and shaking. Slowly, she replaced her veils, then turned to face Azhur. Again, he felt the invisible glare, all the worse because he had seen.

"Goodnight red priest," she said. "I hope he will treat you better." She went quickly down to the passageway arch, draperies fluttering like terrible banners, and was gone.

The darkness thickened round Azhur, as if to cushion the blow of Aia's story. He swayed, feeling a child's desire to curl up on the terrace and protect himself. He would have liked to weep, but doing so here would not be appropriate.

"I heard it all," said a sudden laconic voice. "I saw her going around in those draperies and wondered what it was about. I thought it might be something... like that." Bal-jarrak stepped out of a shadow beside a plinth.

Azhur acknowledged him with an alarmed nod. "My lord. You come to bow before Arna?" Bal-jarrak was the least likely source of the comfort Azhur longed for.

"I come to take a short-cut home," replied Bal-jarrak drily. "Back to my chambers after an evening's supper." Azhur marvelled at the man's ability to wring unpleasantness even from the matter of veneration. "They're all talking already about tonight's Rite of Protection," the priest continued. "You've made quite a stir with your rendering: much more of an assertion than the usual mumble. People seem to think it'll actually work."

"Why, of course," said Azhur, anxiety rising. "The sacred words of protection, my lord."

Bal-jarrak raised his eyebrows and sighed. "Well, yes, of course. Not much protection in here though, as our poor little darling found out. I caught a glimpse. Shame. I wonder if they have physicians in Murinde who could do something."

Azhur's shock deepened, his head swimming as first Lady Aia's pain and then Bal-jarrak's dearth of compassion challenged his sacred store of knowledge.

Bal-jarrak found his thread again. "Yes, it was a fine recital. We're all very grateful, I'm sure." But the praise was a sly blade. The priest looked down at his ringed fingers. "I wondered if it was the sight of Mardokhal that inspired you. Did you know you can just see it past the Bridge?" It was no coincidence and both men knew it. "Your mother would have been so proud of you," said Bal-jarrak in a voice that showed he cared nothing for her feelings. "Such a shame she could not see this day." His eyes slid across to Azhur.

A force began to rage in Azhur's body that he struggled to keep in. Through gritted teeth he said, "My mother saw my true calling."

Anyone else would have read the warning signs, but this was Bal-jarrak and he continued on obliviously. "Oh, yes, yes, of course. Your father, now… I knew him when I was a young fellow and I thought he had the right idea: discipline, dedication, a man of action. You'd have done so well in his regiment if your mother hadn't, well…"

Azhur roared, seized Bal-jarrak's robe and pulled him close, his fist back.

Bal-jarrak almost smiled. "Oh, it still hurts, I see. So sorry. But do me the favour of striking me and ending your career. Right under Arna too. Go on, disappoint mother."

Azhur held still, then thrust the cruel man away. The voice that had boomed at the Rite of Protection rose again, "This I am. I serve Arna in his ancient cult."

Bal-jarrak straightened his robes, a lizard-look in his eyes. "Of course you do. We all play with fires, say the proper words for him: it's all he wants. Myself, I say religion be damned; I have a kingdom to run. You'll find out. Goodnight, Loremaster. Remember to bow before you leave." He went briskly away to the passage.

Shock upon shock. Left alone, Azhur tottered, then slumped upon the terrace steps. Thoughts span in his head so fast he could scarcely see them. He might have dozed, but at last he pulled himself to his feet with no thought of the huge, ghostly form above him and shambled from the house of Arna.

Once in his chambers he fell onto the bed. As sleep claimed him, he could not blank out the awareness that V'karra's fires had left one perfect eye in the ravaged terrain of Aia Djetenga's beautiful face.

~

AUTHRAN'S DREAMS AND DRAWINGS were quite forgotten by the time he and Tyr ambled down to Second Level many days afterwards.

"Have they got statues up to what's his name? Tharsjhad?" asked Tyr. "They didn't just forget him when he got booted off out east?"

"Oh, yes," said Authran, "but not that many. He's not what you'd call distinguished. I mean, he hasn't really done anything apart from being a prince and running Amouch Arna. He'll have loads of statues *there*."

"Well, that's somethin', isn't it? Keepin' all that end of the kingdom goin'?"

"Absolutely, a very important thing to do, but other people make the *real* decisions. Nobody believes Tharsjhad's doing it. Everybody knows he's not capable. Jarthastra approves all decisions anyway."

"I'd chuck it if it were me," said Tyr. "Bloody embarrassin'."

"Very, very well summed up. I think he would chuck it, if it wasn't for the comforts and the money."

"Blessin's of day, young masters," said a woman, giving the lads a little nod as she passed by.

"Arna shine on you, lady," replied Authran, with the crossed-arms bow. The woman smiled and hurried on. "And what a figure to shine on!" he shouted after her. She gave a shocked, shrill laugh, stifled it, then went on her way, smiling and tittering.

"Didn't know novices got a bow," said Tyr when he had calmed down.

"They don't usually, not unless you cut a very impressive figure. Or she might just have been in a good mood."

Tyr grinned massively. "She's in a better mood now."

Thus, they arrived at the Potters' Square. *The Cure* was waiting for them, looking as inviting as an inn can when placed beneath hundreds of feet of granite. Despite regular visits during his brief time in Valderthaan, Tyr was still unaccustomed to eating at tables that sat beneath the sheer cliff that soared straight up to the third level. Even sitting in the common room of the building tucked right against the very foot of the rock face was disconcerting. There was no logical *reason* for the cliff suddenly falling on them, but it didn't *feel* right, regardless. Everything about the arrangement said, *Ominous*. Authran, of course, didn't care. Valderthaan was crammed onto a single island after all, so he merely expected this kind of thing. He indulged in a relaxed appreciation of the various ceramics stacked outside the potters' workshops as he strolled past the spot where he and Tyr were to meet Azhur.

"Well, that is *nice!* Look Tyr, the figure of Djorobos. My mother has a soft spot for him, pious old darling, and her birthday's coming up. I don't know how they get that blue-green colour so uniform. It never runs in the kiln. Um…, Tyr, do you know a sort of sweet old rustic couple?" Tyr stared at his friend.

"Aye, hundreds."

"Well, do you know *that* one?"

"What one?"

"The one waving madly in our direction."

Tyr looked at where Authran was looking and yelped in amazement. Seated at a table outside *The Cure* were Veshren and Naida, the old couple he'd met with Azhur on the morning his friend had shown him Valderthaan from the watchtower on the Mardhoran. He trotted over to them.

"Isn't that a wonder, Vesh! He's got the black on!" cried Naida. "You have come here to be a priest as well, then?"

"It is a wonder, my dearest. After y' askin' him too!" said Veshren. "Eh, young Tyr!" He reached out and slapped Tyr's arm in welcome.

"Oh, I'm that pleased for you!" She stood up and threw her thin arms round Tyr and kissed him on the cheek.

"Aye," said Tyr. "Black on me back, like they say."

"Now, take a seat. What decided y'?" asked Veshren. "It's a big step, is that."

"Oh, I, eh, I met some priests and… well, they sort of give us an invite, and I thought, well, why not?"

"Invited!" crooned Naida. "Well, eh? Must have thought a lot of you! And is this your friend? He's got the black on as well, I see!"

"Oh. Aye, this is—"

"Authran va-Saweré, at your service." Authran gave the couple a formal bow.

"Here's me good friends, Veshren and Naida. Known them for years, I have!" declared Tyr.

"Get away," trilled old Naida. "We've only met him once, not long ago with young Azhur."

"Oh, I say," exclaimed Authran sitting down at their table. "You know Twister?"

"Eh?" said Naida.

"Azhur," explained Tyr. "Aye," he told Authran, "They do and all. Known him since he were a sprog. Vesh used to be quartermaster for his dad."

"Oh my, I thought he was born reciting the Scrolls. You mean he had a childhood?" Tyr and Authran laughed, but a brief, serious shadow seemed to fall over the old couple.

"Aye, well," said Veshren, rubbing his coarse, white beard. "Ey, well, we've come to see me goodwife's cousin. She's got a house on first level, not bad for down there. We comes and has a break, to see the sights, sort of thing."

"Will you have a bite with us, boys?" asked Naida. "Celebrate Tyr bein' a novice?"

"Aye, we will," Tyr told her, missing the way the conversation had lurched in a new direction. "If y' can put up with Ran here."

"Well, what makes you celebrate Tyr being a novice?" asked Authran.

"Don't mind him, he's a cheeky bugger. He can't help it. They're all like that in his family."

"I think we'll do all right," said Veshren, chortling. "Ey, lass, will y' give them poor starved lads some vittles?"

Sazhura, thus summoned, came to the table, a tray full of mugs and dirty plates wedged on one hip.

"Ey, country boy," she said pleasantly. "Back again? Right scroungers, them novices. They don't feed them in that Tower."

"I'll make me own soup then," shot back Tyr. "I'm right good at it!" Sazhura tilted her head and wrinkled her nose as though a little child had shown her a toy. "Ahhh. Learned it at your mother's knee, did you?"

"I did not! Our healer showed me. He could make—" Tyr stopped, a lump in his throat refusing to let his voice work.

"What's up, love?" asked Sazhura.

Authran, who knew, leaned on his shoulder. "Tyr? It's all right."

Naida reached out and took his hand. "What's wrong, lovey? You can tell us."

Tyr drew a hand across one eye. "Nothin', it's all right. Just me friend, the healer. He died not long ago."

"Oh, I'm that sorry," crooned Naida. "Was he not well?"

"Wolf," said Tyr tightly. He closed his eyes as Naida gasped. It had been wonderful for a brief moment to talk as if Wyrdha were still alive, before the deep ache in his heart welled up again. A little gift with a sting in its tail. He opened his eyes and coughed very loudly.

"I'm right sorry, love," said Sazhura, and she did seem to have an unexpected distress of her own. "You're all right, though? You—you're managin'?"

"Aye, aye, I'm all right," Tyr told her. "Y' get on with it, don't y'? Ran keeps me goin' though, when sometimes... y' know." He jerked his head towards Authran.

"Do I really?" said Authran, arm draped round Tyr's neck.

"Aye. Aye, y' do." He dropped his voice. "Y' just don't know." Authran tightened his arm for a moment, then sat back.

"Well," said Sazhura, "long's you're all right. Aye, some nice bowls of soup here, I think. You just give me a few minutes." She went off quickly towards the door of *The Cure*.

Tyr noticed her wipe her face and was glad of her sympathy. Naida and Veshren were still looking distinctly awkward.

Authran leaned forward, hands on the table, and changed the subject. "The novices called Azhur, *Twister*, because of the fingers." He produced an exaggerated but effective impersonation of Azhur's inevitable response to difficult moments. "Ah," he muttered, "um... er... well, ah, I suppose..."

Veshren roared with laughter. "That's him, that's him!"

"Oh, he were always right sensitive about that," said Naida, unable to forbear a giggle nonetheless. "The other lads ribbed him somethin' awful. Don't call him that in front of him, will y'?"

"But if he doesn't like it..." said Authran.

"Don't think he knew he were doin' it, half the time," remarked Veshren. "Ey, never mind that, soup's here!"

Sazhura had appeared from *The Cure* like a bountiful goddess from her shrine. She bore steaming bowls of her celestial soup for the gracious nurture of mortal stomachs. Indeed, that wonderful potage was almost a sacrament of the good and true, the worth of life. The four ate and talked, bound by the power of sharing food, their bowls miraculously replenished by the cordial sprite that attended them till all were content with full stomachs, sitting delighted in the warm daze of friendship. Veshren, in fact, sagged into his chair and was soon asleep.

They chatted on for some time, the dangers of humiliating fingers forgotten. At last, Authran said, "Your husband was quartermaster for Tw—for Azhur's father, then?"

"Aye," said Naida briefly. "Is Azhur still in the black? Haven't seen him for ages. Not a proper priest yet, is he?" Tyr informed her of his friend's meteoric ascent to the Second Circle and when her ecstasy of amazement had died down, she asked, "And does he still see that nice girl in the city?"

"Marrying her very soon," said Authran. "He hopes, anyway. Her father's very high up now, you know."

"Well! Oh, that's lovely! It's just lovely!"

"Hasn't snogged her yet, though," observed Tyr.

"That's all you know," said Authran.

"No, boys, that's very proper," said Naida through the sniggering. "You wait till near the weddin' and you make a nice ceremony of it. That's how they do it in high-up families."

"How they don't do it, you mean."

"You're a cheeky pair, you are," said Naida, giggling in spite of her scruples. "Our Azhur's from a right respectable family, you know."

"Well, no, I don't know," Tyr told her. "I'd have not known he were respectable except he talks posh."

"Do you know, that's right," Authran remarked. "I don't think I've ever heard him say more than two words about his family."

"Oh, he's right close about it," agreed Tyr. "I know his mam died—he told me that—but he wouldn't say nowt about his dad. Ey! Naida! Y' upset?"

The old woman was staring down at her hands as they twisted a fold in her dress, frowning hard like someone longing to change the subject. "I'm all right, I'm all right," she said, revealing she was not.

"Did I say somethin'?"

"Oh, well, I suppose it's obvious," conceded Naida. "It's just… well, I get right upset when I remember Azhur's family. His poor mother! Oh, what a hard time she had, and such a nice woman."

Authran sat up, "I'm so terribly sorry. Oh, Lady's mercy! Was she ill?"

"No, no," faltered Naida. "Well, she was, but… well, it wasn't good at home, you see. Oh, dear, dear, what can I say?"

"Azhur's dad not much help then?" ventured Tyr. "Old Kherzir?"

Naida examined her hands again. "Master Kherzir was… well, he could be a little bit difficult sometimes."

"He were a miserable, gripin' old sod," said Veshren without opening his eyes. "Never gave that lad a day's peace or a word of praise. I would have wrung Kherzir's neck for him, if I could have. Go on then, my love."

"Go on what?" asked Naida.

"Y' usually tell me to shush when I say that."

Naida sighed. "No, Vesh, lovey, not today. It's got to be said sometimes. We both feel better when it is. When did you wake up?"

"About five minutes ago."

"But… I mean, what happened?" demanded Tyr. He and Authran were astonished by the revelations. "What were he like that for?"

Naida hesitated, "Oh…, I don't know if I should."

"Might as well, my love," Veshren told her. "Might be a good thing if somebody else knows. That's one more as might help, y' see. Understandin', like." He leaned forward, resting his elbows on the table. "Y' see, lads, us did our best when Azhur were younger. Had him round the house, had a lot of chats, that sort of thing. But it's different now after we moved away and he took the black. Don't y' go lettin' on to him, mind."

"No, no!" cried Tyr. "Ey, I'm right cut up."

"Rather taken aback myself," added Authran. "Such a nice fellow. You'd never think… but of course my lips are sealed. Painful memories and all."

"Well, I suppose it's all right," sighed Naida. She took a breath and began, emphasising her words with both hands like a schoolmistress.

"You see boys, Lady Ulië, Azhur's mam, she'd never been strong. When she married Kherzir folk said as she'd never keep up with him. Big, strappin' feller, always rushin' about, more energy than a warhorse with his plans and ambitions. He'd talk for hours and not stop for a breath or an answer. His mind just kept goin' and goin'. Folk got wore out just listenin' to him."

"And it were all about him: what he thought, what he wanted," added Veshren. "I don't think he knew there was other folk in the world apart from him." He shook his head grimly as Naida continued.

"Lady Ulië got tireder and tireder, all pale and sad. I thought I could look through her sometimes. Got so she'd just sit like she weren't really there."

"She weren't, far's that bugger were concerned."

"Well, that's not far wrong, Vesh. I think he forgot she were in the house, he were that taken up with things. He were pleased when she gave him Azhur, of course. Nearly killed her, mind, but I don't think Kherzir knew that. I helped deliver the babby. He were lovely, and I loved seein' his mam so happy. But with Kherzir, it were all: *my son, my heir, what I say he's goin' to be*. He had the poor thing down for a soldier. A High Commander at least. The lad was like a horse gettin' trained for a big race. Kherzir'd been a soldier himself, you see, then became somethin' with the Governor at Lachresh, where Azhur were born, right high up. Anyroad, poor Ulië starts gettin' sicknesses, one thing after the other, so she couldn't go to banquets and things with Kherzir and she were in bed half the time. When she couldn't go places and appearin' at things with him, he started sayin' she were holdin' him back and she didn't care about his career and she were tryin' to take Azhur away from him. Oh, terrible stuff it was. He'd get so angry at her. He really went queer, he did."

"He were always angry," said Veshren.

"Aye, he was. I think that's what kept him goin', but it really came out at Ulië. Some folk used to say he hit her."

"He did, I saw him."

"Well, I wasn't goin' to say, but you see what sort of feller he was, boys?"

In the horrid silence, Tyr tried to imagine what it would feel like to see Tyrmar strike his mother and found he could not. The very idea chilled him.

"Lady's mercy," murmured Authran.

Naida braced herself for the rest of the story, "You keep me right then; keep me right, Vesh."

"Y' doin' all right, lass, keep on."

"Aye, well, come the time it were obvious Azhur weren't cut out for a soldier, his dad just got angrier. Never mind the lad were brilliant and knew more than a shrine full of Loremasters. Never mind he were a lovely, quiet feller, who everybody loved and trusted. Didn't suit Kherzir."

"He were the exact opposite of his dad," explained Veshren. "You could see he were able for great things, but they wasn't the great things his dad fancied, so the old sod took it out on him."

Naida nodded emphatically, "He did and all. Everythin' any normal dad would have praised his lad for, Kherzir criticised him. He were soft, he were stupid, he were a pansy, not a proper man, he'd shamed his dad, he'd never get anywhere—oh, what a list I could make!"

"Oh, please don't, Mistress Naida," Authran begged. "You've—well, you've explained a lot already."

Tyr said nothing but wiped an eye.

"Well," Naida continued, "the worst of it was, Kherzir got this job as court Ambassador in Sarvien."

"Arna's wings!" gasped Authran. "Graavesh? He didn't deserve it!"

"That's as may be, but he was to live at the capital down at the south—"

"They gave him the Meira palace?"

"Whatever it is. Now, will you shush? He'd stay in that place in Sarvien and be somethin' in all the countries round the Woundsea. He'd have had these great big estates in Sarvien and he'd have been in charge of some land we had over the water at Dhar."

"Well!" said Authran, marvelling at the injustice of it all. "He was a capable man, then! Outside the family, alas. But that's a tremendous crown to a career."

"Aye, well, that's what he kept sayin'. Azhur were talkin' about bein' a priest and a Loremaster by then, but Kherzir were pushin' him to go to Sarvien and work under him. Couldn't just let him be himself."

"Proud old bugger," remarked Veshren. "His head were nearly burstin'. I'd have burst it for him if I could."

"Well, you didn't have to, did you lovey? Anyroad, they was all set to go south and Ulië took ill."

"I can guess this," muttered Authran.

"Well, listen. They got the physician, and he says to Kherzir she shouldn't be goin' to Sarvien. Even if she can manage the travellin'—and she probably couldn't have—she'd not survive the hot and dusty climate down there. *You take her down there*, says the physician, *and she'll just be an invalid and dead in two years. That's if she's lucky.*"

"Well, Kherzir should have done her a favour and gone by himself," Authran declared. Tyr nodded.

"Oh, not him. It would look bad, you see. Wonderful Kherzir abandonin' his wife to make his name down south. And it weren't just that. He knew folk would say he'd done her a favour with clearin' off. Two blows to his pride! He couldn't take that, so he stayed and made do with bein' governor of miserable little Mardokhal."

"And turned into the bitterest, angriest feller in all the north," Veshren summed up. "Ulië and Azhur's lives wasn't worth livin'."

"Took it out on them, he did. We went into his service when he were at Lachresh and we stayed with the family when he got Mardokhal. We'd have cleared off when we saw what he were like, but we hung on for Ulië and Azhur's sake. We was friends by then, you see. Glad we stayed because we saw Azhur grow up."

"Did his mam get better, then?" asked Tyr.

"Yes and no. She picked up a bit, but she weren't never quite right, not really. And she were feelin' it were her fault about Kherzir's job. Anyroad, time went on and he got her pregnant, even when the physicians said she shouldn't have another babby. She'd lost three, you see, after Azhur; just not able for it."

"Kherzir tryin' for his bloody soldier boy."

"Aye, Vesh, he probably was. Anyroad, nobody thought she'd carry it all the way, it were that difficult. But then, when she were about five months gone, one day we hears shoutin' from upstairs. Well, we knew what that meant. Kherzir were roarin' at her again, but this time we heard her as well and all us servants was delighted: she were shoutin' back at him! *Wonderful,* we said, *about time.* Then there were this scream and us all ran through with Azhur and there were Ulië layin' at the bottom of the stairs moanin' and holdin' her stomach. She lost the babby, and she died the next night in Azhur's arms. Kherzir were at an important banquet. *How were I to know she'd die?* he told us, *I'm not a physician.*"

"What happened?" asked Tyr, fearing to know.

"Well, she… fell," said Naida vaguely.

"I know, but what *happened?*"

An expression of great grief appeared on Naida's face. She turned towards Veshren.

"Might as well," he said.

"All right," said his wife. She fixed the novices with a severe stare. They were frozen still, hardly breathing lest they provoked her into changing her mind. "It don't go past you boys, you know that?"

The lads both nodded, with Tyr in an agony of wondering.

The old woman continued, "After the funeral, Azhur comes to our house. He wants to know what we saw when his mother fell. *I've got to know,* he says to us. Well, we couldn't lie to our Azhur, could we?"

"What?" said Tyr, alarmed now. "Lie about what?"

Veshren reached out to Naida, patted her arm, then took her hand. "I'll do it, Naida my love, don't worry. Tyr, lad, this is what happened. Me and the missus got to Ulië first when she fell. We both looked up the narrow staircase she'd just fallen down, like y' do, and we sees somebody turnin' away into the shadows."

"We saw enough," said Naida, curt and hard.

"Kherzir?" blurted out Authran.

"Course it was," said the old woman. "Never saw his face, but it were him all right."

"Aye, it were him," said Veshren sadly. "Saw him just for a second, but it were his coat—nobody had one like it, sent up from Sarvien it was. And it were his long hair—right colour, and the braid down the back

544

that he had."

"And we heard feet goin' away along the corridor," added Naida. "It were his stride, and you could tell the noise of them fancy boots he always wore."

Authran could barely speak, Tyr did not try. "And—but... what are you saying?"

"What do you think, lad?" barked Veshren. "We're sayin' he bloody shoved her!"

"No! Oh, no. Surely...."

"Well, look. If your standin' beside your wife—pregnant wife, mind—and she trips and falls down twenty steps, what do y' do? Eh?"

"I'd run down after her, see if she was... Oh!" said Authran.

"Precisely, my lad. And did he? No. And he were up there all right, we'd all heard him shoutin'."

Tyr was crying quietly. Authran was trying not to believe, "But what did he—I mean, he must have... said something. Later."

"Oh, aye," Veshren said. "He gives this big speech about how she yelled at him, then ran away along the upstairs corridor towards the steps and he went into this room and shut the door. Said he never saw her fall or heard the scream."

"Isn't that possible?"

"Think about it, lad. They was arguin' at the *top* of the steps. That's how we heard them. Plus, we saw Kherzir."

"He *had* to have seen her fall, then?"

"Aye, and if they was at the far end of the upstairs corridor—and it were a long one—we'd never have heard them arguin' so clearly."

"And you said the scream came *during* the argument, so there was no interval when she was running along the corridor towards the stairs. Oh, Lady's mercy!" Authran clapped his hands against his cheeks, squashing his face into a narrow mask of dismay. "And Azhur...."

"He heard us talkin' about it after the funeral." Veshren explained. "He'd come round to our house, and the door were open. We didn't know he were outside, so we was sayin' all sorts. He caught enough to give him a shock. He demanded to hear the whole story."

"We told him everythin' we saw and heard," Naida put in. "Had to, or

545

he'd have wondered all his life."

"And then?" asked Authran. "How did he take it?"

Tyr still sat in round-eyed silence.

"He shot out of our house like a hunted hare," declared Veshren. "I knew where he were goin', so I rushed after him. I knew he'd be headin' straight for the Governor's Residence."

"Never seen him like that afore," Naida said, shaking her head.

"It were a now or never thing. He'd never stood up to his dad in his life, but I thought, if he can do it now it'll be the makin' of him. And Kherzir deserved it, the bugger. Well, when I got inside the residence, I could hear them shoutin' in the big hall. I put me head round the door and there were Azhur like a wild thing. He'd found all this strength and pluck and he weren't scared of Kherzir at all. He were yellin' about how his dad hated him and his mam, and how he had made her ill and ruined her life. Kherzir didn't know what to do. He'd had Azhur actin' like a little dog all his life, and now he'd turned on him. It were grand to see! But Kherzir just did what he did best: humiliation.

"*Who do you think you are?* he says. *You're a weakling. You'd be nothing if I didn't tolerate you. You're an ungrateful boy.* Well, it usually worked, but not this time.

"*Give me something to be grateful for!* shouts Azhur. *You think insults and curses all my life put me in your debt?*

"*Yes, I do!* roars Kherzir. *It was more than you deserved. I doubted if a weakling like you could ever be my son!*"

Authran gasped, Tyr lowered his head.

"He were a cruel bugger," said Veshren. "Anythin' but be wrong. Anythin'. Anyroad, Azhur stands like he had a spear in him, all white and shakin', and says: *Why d'you think that, father? Because you sired three that hadn't the strength to live? Were they all you were capable of?*

"Well, Kherzir went into such a rage he could hardly breathe. I never saw the like. He flung his self at Azhur and I knew he were goin' to try to beat him senseless. But Azhur surprised me. He defended his self and whacks his dad on the jaw. He shoves him back, and Kherzir yells, *Oh, you attack me now? Then you're no son of mine! I name you bastard!*

"Well, it were too much. Azhur yells, *You admit it then, you can only sire stillborns! Three in a row from mother and probably a fourth. Is that why you pushed her? You couldn't stand to see one more from your watery loins? Is that why you killed her, father?*

"I think Kherzir just went mad then. He howled and threw his self at Azhur with his hands out like claws. Azhur dodges, and his dad smashes on the floor. He stood back up and grabbed this big heavy chair, throwing it at his son. He misses, and then starts goin' for Azhur with everythin' he can lay his hands on. But he's a big, heavy feller out of trainin' and Azhur's keepin' out of his way no trouble.

"*Stop it, father,* he shouts. *You've made your confession, so just stop. You're not a soldier anymore. You've lost the strength, you've lost the honour, so just stop!*

"Kherzir were like a beast, face all purple, mouth all spit. He makes a noise like he's bein' strangled and pulls this big bronze axe off the wall—massive decorative thing.

"*Don't show off, father,* says Azhur. *Your fighting days are over, you can't control me anymore.* Kherzir swings the axe above his head and runs at Azhur. The lad jumps back and even laughs. *I'm going to be a priest, father,* he says. *It was mother's dying wish. I'm going to be free of you at last.*

"Kherzir roars and spits with the axe in the air and tries to throw it, but it smashes at his feet and he's grabbin' his chest in terrible pain. Then he's against the wall and slides down to the floor. I runs in then to help and we're both bendin' over him, me and Azhur, but he's holdin' his chest and starin' at the lad, still mad with hate, his eyes bulgin' out. *Bastard!* he says to him. *Bastard!* And then…"

All four of them sat, poised on the terrible, silent memory.

"Then he died," said Veshren, closing the door on the vault of the past. "He died, and that were his last words to his son." He took a piece of bread, savagely tore off a mouthful with his teeth, and began to chew. The others sat quietly, as though guilty for knowing.

Tyr looked up at the huge cliff that lowered over *The Cure*. Above it, he knew, was the upper city, the third level that contained the Shrine and the King's Tower. Azhur spent most of his time up there, safe in his parchment cocoon of words and thoughts, where the red robe on his back separated him from the demands and cruelty of his father, daily proclaiming his revenge. Now it all made such good sense: the uncertainty, the hesitancy, the difficulty with people, the nervous, interlocking fingers, simultaneously fighting and protecting, the constant insistence on priestly knowledge, priestly function, priestly identity. Azhur va-Kherzir was a priest and Loremaster through and through. He had to be.

It seemed to Tyr that the young man he'd met at Falakhoth had turned out to be a character in one of Eorthas' plays. A character who looked like his friend, but who was less complex, less layered, less known than the real man. Azhur was much closer now, yet because Azhur hadn't told him this tale himself much further away too. This left Tyr deeply unsettled. His heart ached for the double pain of learning about Azhur's loss and doing so behind his back. He longed for something easy, something ordinary and comfortingly familiar.

Suddenly, his ankle flared with pain, jolting him from his thoughts. Authran had kicked him and was jerking his head toward the entrance to the Potters' Square. There was Azhur, striding breathlessly past the rows of pots and jars, dodging people as he made his way towards *The Cure*.

"Well," sighed Veshren, "got to say I'm feelin' better for sayin' all that. Builds up in y', sort of thing—"

"Shut up!" hissed Tyr, before he could think. Azhur had seen them and was waving.

"Eh? What did you—?"

"Vesh, shush!" said Naida.

"Why should—oh, hell."

Azhur came striding up, beaming and pushing the hair out of his red-ringed eyes. "Oh, how marvellous! Who'd have thought it! It's been ages. Are you seeing your cousin?" He kissed Naida and shook Veshren's hand warmly.

"Aye, we're just havin' a little break," said Naida.

"Seein' the sights," added Veshren, nodding and grinning too widely. "Oh, aye, that's it."

"Sorry I'm late lads," said Azhur. He dragged a chair from a neighbouring table and threw himself onto it.

"All right are y' lad?' asked Veshren. "You look right wrung out."

Azhur seemed to wander for a moment, "Ah… last-minute things. I had to put a seal on a parchment. I've given permission for something, but I'm not sure what."

"It's all right," said Tyr as normally as he could.

"Oh, don't worry," chimed in Authran, "my father—" he stumbled over the word — "he does that all the time. It's a complete bore."

"Oh, yes, but I'd better pay attention in the future. Have you had soup or something, lads?"

"Aye," said Tyr briefly. He knew his façade was crumbling. "It was nice."

"Oh, good. Well, you don't mind if I, ah—" Azhur could not avoid what was before him. "Tyr? What on earth is it? Look, I'm sorry for being late, I honestly couldn't help it—"

"No," protested Tyr. "No, y're all right."

"But you're not." Azhur took his friend's arm. "Oh, Tyr, tell me. Naida, do you know what—Naida! You're crying! What's going on?"

And then Tyr's country honesty took over him. Used to the open frankness of his home, he thought nothing of the consequences. "I'm that sorry about y' mam, Azhur," he said, tears on his cheeks. "I never thought somebody like you could have a rotten sod like that for a dad."

Azhur stared at him, frozen in place.

Authran gave him another warning kick under the table, but Tyr couldn't keep his new knowledge secret. "I'm right upset for y'. Imagine him sayin' that to y' when he died! I don't—"

Azhur jerked back as though stabbed. He lurched suddenly to his feet, the chair flying backwards on the flags. He stood like a statue, breathing hard, eyes fixed on Tyr, hands clenching and unclenching. "You told him!" he said at last, as if he could hardly speak. "You told him!"

"I'm sorry, lad," said Veshren, staring at the table.

"It just came out!" cried Naida. "We didn't—we was feelin'—"

"You promised! Nobody!"

Naida buried her face in her hands.

"Lad," said Veshren. "Listen, lad—"

"I trusted you!" cried Azhur. "The only people I ever trusted, you two and mother! I thought you'd contain it, I thought you'd hide the shame!"

"It were eatin' us up! Sometimes it got like that. It's hard to carry—"

"Sometimes? And what did you do when it did? Who else have you told?"

"Nobody! Just... just friends. People as don't know you."

"Everybody knows me! Everyone knew my family! The whole city knows about it now for all I know!"

"Azhur, love," said Naida through her tears, "folk's lookin', don't shout, lovey. We're sorry."

Tyr moved to Azhur to comfort him, "Azhur, it's all right. I'm not worried, neither's Ran. Y're our friend."

"You shouldn't have listened! You shouldn't have let them!"

"What do y' mean? I can't just go deaf!"

"I didn't want you to know! I was starting to forget! You should have stopped them!"

"Ey, don't blame me! I didn't know what was comin'!"

"Oh, nobody's to blame, nobody's to blame! Too much to carry, can't go deaf! It is too much—*far* too much! And I have carried it, the weight in my stomach, iron bands on my chest, the fire in my head, the pressure—the pressure and the noise, always the noise!" He staggered, grasping at the air.

"Lad, sit down!" said Veshren.

"Look at the colour of him," said Naida. "Come here, Azhur, lovey!"

"You had no right!" Azhur told her. "How many know? How many are laughing at me now? How many of these people here?"

"Nobody's laughin' at y'!" snapped Tyr. He found he was becoming angry.

Azhur stood trembling, both hands clasped to his head as if trying to hold it together. "How do you know?" he rasped. "I carried the shame, I let it crawl on my skin: my father's shame, my mother's shame, my own. I thought it was ebbing away, I thought I was losing it. I wanted to bury it, thought I was managing. Now it's all there again. All back, all the venom. What would you know about it?"

"Don't be bloody stupid!" yelled Tyr. "Y' dad were a wicked bugger, that's not y' fault!" Now there was an audible buzz in the square. Sazhura appeared at the door of the inn, hands over her mouth. The secret was spreading further.

"Yes, tell the world," hissed Azhur, dismayed. "Tell them, *friend!*"

"Sorry, I didn't mean—"

"No, of course you didn't," groaned Azhur. His body sagged, a dangerous dark colouring spread round his eyes. "You couldn't. These things don't happen in fields, in nice families."

Tyr was stung: his countryman's temper broke, the pain of Azhur's long absence bursting out. "Ey, don't y' dare! Don't you look down on me because—"

"I'm not. I'm stating a fact! You've no idea about this because you've been spared! You don't need any *songs*." Azhur began to walk away.

"Y' callin' me ignorant?" Tyr roared at Azhur's back. "Stupid country lad don't get it? Well, I get it. Y' jealous of me dad, because yours were a swine! Y' were stuck with that mad bugger and y're takin' it out on me!"

Azhur whirled round, rushed up to Tyr and seized his coat, his fist drawn back. Tyr was truly afraid. His friend was hidden under a wildness Tyr had never seen in Azhur before. They stood like this for a few dreadful moments, noses almost touching, Azhur's breath on his face, his fist trembling with anger.

The priest lowered his arm, releasing Tyr with a furious little flourish, pushing him away as he stepped back.

"I will not be like him," Azhur said through his teeth. "But you have no idea. Remember that." He turned unsteadily and paced away, head down.

CHAPTER 25

A Messenger at the Tower

"THAT WERE BLOODY QUEER," said Tyr. He sat on the floor by his bunk, hugging his drawn-up knees.

"It was awful," said Authran, sprawled on his own bunk and still half in shock. "Worse than queer, just awful."

Tyr made a distressed snorting sound, "No, I mean, do y' think somebody'd worked it all out and writ it down like the players do and we was just actin' it out."

"How so?"

"Well, I mean, first Azhur says he's goin' to meet us, and the day he says just happens to be the day Naida wants to see her cousin—"

"Oh dear, yes, poor old things. Hope they're all right."

"Ran, will y' shut up? And they arrive in Valderthaan they just happen to fancy a bit of scran at *The Cure*—I mean, bloody hell, why *The Cure*? And it's exactly the same time we turn up, and it's one of the days they're burstin' to talk about Azhur's dad and when they do the man himself walks in and nobody's able to cover it up and... and... it's that bloody... I don't know—*timed* or *rehearsed*. Like somebody'd been gettin' it ready for weeks!"

"Feeling better now?"

Tyr began to bump his forehead rhythmically on his bent knees, "Not much. Ey, I were that stupid! It's a rotten, stupid temper I've got!"

"Oh, it's not something you've *got*," said Authran. "It's *you*." He clasped his hands behind his head. "Think of it as a gift."

"A *gift*?"

"We are gifts from the gods to ourselves. The Holy Mvraurgh'harth of the Unexpected Perspicacity said, *Anger is given to us to enable us to fight injustice, bad spirits, and evil generally.* Got a point, you know. Who ever heard of a great moral crusade being led by some spineless weed? Anyway, you'll do all that."

"Better do it quick afore I lose any more friends."

Authran reached down from the bunk and patted Tyr's head. "You won't, and you haven't. Just let him cool down."

Forehead-thumping wasn't helping, so Tyr stopped and rested his chin on his knees instead. "Don't know if he will. Ran, I were that scared! I never seen nobody act like that afore, especially not Azhur. I thought he was goin' to rip the square up."

"Yes, he did let a bit of steam off. Glad no novices saw it. His life wouldn't be worth living."

"What were he about though? Iron bands, fire in his head... what's that supposed to mean?"

"I don't know. He might not be awfully well."

Tyr looked up, alarmed. "Y' mean he's mad? Like Jarthastra?"

"Oh, no, he obviously isn't. But we had someone at Ceor once who used to say things like that. He used to get terribly ill and couldn't work for weeks at a time. The physicians had terrible trouble treating him. But he wasn't mad."

Now Tyr found another use for his knees and began pounding his fists on them. "Bugger it! Bugger! Oh, I can't settle, I need to—I need— ey, what about y' drawin'?"

"Oh, Tyr, sorry, I really don't feel like drawing."

"No, y' daft nellie, the one y' was doin' of y' dream. The feller sat on the grass. Did y' finish it?"

"Oh. Yes, I did, actually."

"Let's see it then. That'll take me mind off things."

"Oh, right." Authran lowered himself down from his bunk. "One of my better ones, if I do say so myself. I can see that fellow's face as if I'd met him." He went to his providential cupboard, pulled out a wad of papers, then sat himself beside Tyr. "Now then. Look, I did the view again, made a better job of you the second time too."

Tyr took the sheet, "Me legs aren't that long!"

"You're a growing boy. Now here's the fellow I said wouldn't go. I spent quite a bit of time on him—"

Tyr laughed, "Ran, give over. I'm not daft."

"No, but the connection escapes me."

"Well, y' give it away, didn't y'? When was y' there?"

"Where?"

"Falakhoth. All this time y've been to Falakhoth and never let on."

"Tyr... Tyr, look—"

"Y' must've knew Thal well and all. That's a crackin' picture."

Authran gripped Tyr's arm and made him lower the paper. "Tyr," he said as evenly as he could, "I swear to you by Arna's image I've never been within twenty miles of Falakhoth." They stared at each other.

"Then how?"

"I've no idea." They stared at each other once more.

"Galdtchav?" said Tyr.

"Yes, I think so." They sprang up and bolted from the dormitory, clutching the drawing.

~

GALDTCHAV RUBBED HIS EYES and leaned on his desk.

"The Senior Loremaster does *not*, as a rule, grant audiences to the novitiate at this hour of the afternoon." He clasped his fingers together and hazily regarded Tyr and Authran like an irascible, somnolent turtle.

"Did we wake y' up?" asked Tyr. "Sorry."

"Inappropriately insistent, Anthu," chirped the anxious, flustered attendant. "The degree of importunity. Please forgive—"

"Dreadfully important, Anthu," blurted Authran, then bowed—twice—being more in awe of Galdtchav than Tyr was. "A unique thing, astounding and alarming. There was no-one else to whom to turn."

"Oh, *unique*, is it? Oh, well, better carry on then. You see, Sharn? They've reached me through my vanity: the Senior Loremaster corrupted by a pair of novices. Very promising start to their careers. Breathe not a word of this."

"If you wish, Anthu, I can—"

"I don't think I do wish, Sharn. Thank you, you may go."

Sharn backed out of the chamber and closed the double doors on the novices' unique alarm.

"This had better be very good indeed, my lads," declared Galdtchav. "I was dreaming of strolling through the palace gardens with the first love of my life, a charming, green-eyed Ceorthan girl."

Authran bowed again, "We do regret, Anthu—"

"But not very much, and not as much as I do. But I don't believe we've met, young sir."

"He's me best mate," offered Tyr. "Auth—"

"Authran va-Saweré," finished the Loremaster. "And no doubt at my service."

"I surely am, Anthu. Your servant forever."

"Aye, well, he sleeps—" began Tyr.

"In the bunk above you." Galdtchav interrupted him again. "I do make it my business to be *fully* informed about the novices in whose training I find such joy, young Tyr. Now, I would rather like to return to the palace gardens with she of the emerald eyes, so if you could get to the point."

"Certainly, Anthu," said Authran smartly. "Well, the point is, I had the most amazing dream—"

"Oh, dear," said Galdtchav.

"No, he did," insisted Tyr. "He dreamt about this feller, and he drew him when he woke up. That's him." He snatched the drawing from Authran and thrust it under Galdtchav's nose. The Loremaster peered at it intently. "He saw him in the dream and he remembered him like as like, and—"

"And he was sitting on the ground saying, *I'm not going, I'm not going*," said Galdtchav.

Shock shot through the lads like an arrow.

"I caught a glimpse of his face when they brought his body into the square at Falakhoth," continued the Loremaster. "And unless I'm mistaken, Tyr, this is your innkeeper fellow whose funeral I attended."

Tyr's mouth made silent shapes for a while and when at last words emerged he said, "Aye, it's Thal, but—but how?"

"I've had exactly the same dream for the last three nights," said Galdtchav. "You were in it too. Running along a road by the river. Not nearly so fetching as my Ceorthan lady, I fear."

"But Anthu," stammered Authran, "What can—where could it possibly...?"

The Loremaster tossed the sketch onto his table. "Oh, I recognised it easily. It's the little burial ground outside Falakhoth. This fellow's sitting on his own grave."

In the silence that followed this, Tyr felt himself breathing very hard. The room seemed to be circling around the Loremaster while he looked into the serious, old blue eyes.

"But Anthu," he heard Authran saying, "how—how could...?"

"I haven't the ghost of an idea," said Galdtchav, "but I think we'd better find out about this, don't you?" The novices nodded: there was little else to do. "Oh," said the Loremaster suddenly. "Well, you are thorough, aren't you?" He glanced up at Authran.

"Am I?" said that youth.

"Yes, you've even got the amulet."

"The amulet?"

"I believe I said that. Look, you've drawn it in the corner here." The lads stared at the end of Galdtchav's finger as it tapped on the drawing. Beside the sketch of Thaljhaz, Authran had drawn a shape like a decorated oval cut in half. On the curve and on the straight edge were eyelets, where what looked like a leather thong was threaded through. The surface bore elongated lines and curving, jagged shapes.

"Er," ventured the artist, "he was holding that, Anthu. In the dream."

"Yes, I know. I gave it to his wife; she dropped it in the grave."

"*You* gave it to her?"

"You do repeat people. Yes, it's the Senior Loremaster's amulet. Passed from each to the next since the kingdom began, that sort of thing.

Ar-ven's supposed to have worn it, but nobody believes that any more. Usually just lies in a drawer. I only had it on that day because I'd been at the Regional Overseers' gathering at Arcorath and I decided I'd wear something traditional. Nobody bothers with the thing any more so I thought I'd make a gesture of sympathy and gave it to the wife. But into the grave it went, which seemed to comfort the poor dear."

"Is that what I've drawn?"

"Certainly looks like it. Dream in colour, do you? Good, tell me the colours."

"Oh. Well, these shapes are red and pale yellow—it's enamel in a raised motif—and the long shapes are white on lapis lazuli."

"You don't miss much, that's it exactly."

"Very visual mind, Anthu."

"Certainly is. And you never saw me wearing it?"

"Oh, no, Anthu, never been close enough before."

"And I've hardly ever worn it, anyway. Well, we do have a mystery. Fortunately, my Assistant Loremaster should be arriving any moment."

The double doors thudded open, then closed. Azhur entered the room unannounced. A thundercloud was on his brow and the glow of rekindled embers in his eyes. He was looking ahead in an unfocussed way, as if he did not know why he was there.

"The very man!" said Galdtchav.

Azhur's head jerked round. He saw the novices and looked down at the floor as if he could burn a hole in it.

"No scroll-work just now, Azhur," continued Galdtchav. "My young friends and I have a most pressing conundrum that requires your knowledge."

Azhur said nothing, but straightened his back and looked at the two novices as if from a great distance.

"Sorry," said Tyr.

"Quite all right," said Azhur, showing it was no such thing. Galdtchav's eyes darted from one to the other.

"And I also, Anthu," added Authran. "Had I known—"

"No need to mention it. What's this conundrum?"

"Oh, yes. Well, I had a dream about somebody sitting on their own

557

grave saying, *I won't go*. Can't think what—"

"Well, where do you go when you're dead?" said Azhur tersely.

"Oh. Not terribly sure. You... you wait...."

"Everybody knows that. And then?"

"Well, Ardhruthak comes: him and his daughters. So they say."

"That's it, the lord of the dead, the collector," said Azhur, in a voice that was beginning to sound somewhat alarming. "Drives them down to the deadlands. The cattle-whip and the ox-goad. All in the Misery Scroll—oh, I forgot, they don't give that to novices till their fifth year. Rather a lot to swallow."

Galdtchav leaned forward, "Azhur, are you all right?"

"Perfectly, thank you, my lord. Some difficult circumstances today, that's all."

"Ah," said the Loremaster, and his eye flicked towards Tyr.

"Weren't all my fault," muttered Tyr.

"Not at first," snapped Azhur, not looking at him. "Now, Authran, people wait by their graves because they can't go home: they don't belong there. Their home's under the earth and they don't know the way, so they wait for the Dreadful Guide. They need to avoid the Gulta and her tricks if they want to get to Arna. Those that can."

The young Loremaster moved about the chamber, as his senior watched keenly and the novices' anxiety grew. He did not seem to move because he wished to, but because a contained fury drove his limbs.

"Azhur," said Galdtchav quietly, "you seem to be revisiting..." Azhur waved a hand. "Later, perhaps? The lads..."

"Please don't worry, my lord. The *lads* are well aware of *that* story."

"I see. But that would mean...."

"Yes, it would. They told them. Very remiss, I felt."

Galdtchav examined his fingertips, "I understand, Azhur. Shall we speak later?"

Azhur snapped round, trembling, "Frankly, Lord Galdtchav, I feel very much like speaking *now*. Out of character I know, but things... surface and must out."

"All the same, Azhur—boys, would you mind...?"

"Oh, let them stay, they've heard it all!" Azhur's hands were not twisting together now: they moved emphatically but helplessly, as though he could not express what burned inside. Every sweep of his arm seemed to release a furious thought, a world of pain. "I feel... betrayed. People I trusted all my life, and my newest friend, have torn the wound wide open again, and I do not know who will rub salt and grime in it next."

"Not I, my friend," said Galdtchav softly.

Azhur wavered at this, but did not reply.

Tyr attempted to step into the space in his friend's wrath, "What's a Misery Scroll?"

Azhur planted his fists on his hips and glared at the floor. "Oh, a dire thing: a compendium of fear and confusion, the record of exalted ignorance." He said this with a strange feel of savage regret that threw Tyr into a dumb confusion.

Galdtchav tried to rescue the moment, "Azhur refers, Tyr, to the Eighty-fifth thousand and third Scroll," he said evenly. "A rather bleak document, I'm afraid."

Authran's eyes suddenly widened, and he raised a hand to his mouth.

"What's in it?" asked Tyr.

"Its formal title is The Scroll of Uncertain Hope," said the Loremaster. "A collection of many thoughts about what takes place after one... departs."

Tyr was taken aback. *Why should such a thing be necessary?* "But the Guide, Ardhruthak, comes for y', don't he?"

Azhur made an angry snorting sound.

Galdtchav sighed and said, "Some say yes, some say no. Some put forward many ideas and versions of the story. Others offer maps of the regions under the earth, detailed descriptions of the path to Arna, or whatever destination. There is elaborate advice and instruction, hopes, possible despairs, recompense, leniency, life, nothingness, simple clarity, and bizarre scenario. I know people at Falakhoth are clear in their own minds about this, enviously clear, bless them, but the Misery Scroll offers and withholds, declares and confuses, builds uncertainty from its contradictions."

"I rather like it," said Azhur forcefully. "Parts of it."

"I know," said Galdtchav gently, "and I'm concerned you may return to that preoccupation again. Can we speak about things ourselves, as we usually—"

"It says *some* people get dragged off by their hair with the ox-goad through them and the Five Daughters throw them down to Arahoth."

"Azhur, please, you're not helping yourself."

Azhur strode up to the Loremaster's table, leaned on it with his fists so he and Galdtchav were almost face to face. "I hope he's there," he said. "He ought to be. He ought to be in Arahoth. I hope the parts about everyone reaching peace aren't true. These damn contradictions torture me, but some parts let me think he's there. May his heart burst for ever."

And with that, Tyr understood. "It's y' dad, isn't it? Look, don't be horrible. The Guide just comes and they go to Arna!"

Azhur glared at him, grim and silent.

Galdtchav raised his wrinkled hand, "Arna's cult is very much for this existence, Tyr," he said hesitantly as though he were apologising. "Our lives on the world's hide, the maintenance of his realm. In truth, it has little clarity to offer about what we are after passing."

"Except a little about Arahoth," said Azhur relishing in it. "That vein of thought gives some of us comfort: such justice consoles."

Tyr shuddered. Folk in Falakhoth spoke little about dire fates under the earth and kept the immensely wicked for fireside tales. Why quiet, gentle Azhur should dwell on such horrible ideas was beyond him. But it was all too profound. Tyr's temper and country sense rose up. "Azhur! Y' great nellie, can't y' just forget about y' dad?"

"*No!*" roared Azhur. He stood for a moment as though someone had struck him. He fumbled with the buttons of his tunic. "Do you know why?" he said breathlessly. "Shall I tell you why?" The tunic was undone. Azhur unfastened his shirt, then came up to Tyr and pulled it open. "There, that's why. He made sure I wouldn't forget!" There on the right side of Azhur's chest was an old, savage scar. The figure of a rearing horse had long ago been burned into the flesh. "The emblem of his regiment: all his men had it. It was to be the sign that one day I'd be a great captain in his command!"

"But… if they all had it," stammered Tyr, bewildered, "if everybody had it when they joined...."

"I was eight," said Azhur. His eyes were full of wild grief. "He dragged me out onto the parade ground in front of the regiment and named me their future commander. Then he pulled my shirt off and branded me. Most of the men tried not to look, but some of them were laughing. Because I knew what would happen later and because I wouldn't be shamed, I didn't scream. I still can't." He looked away, breathing hard. "Love didn't tell me who I was that day, that monster told me." Tyr remembered his mother's song before the Conclave. He put his hand over his face and felt tears roll over his fingers. Once more he saw Azhur standing in the square at Falakhoth with the gaping wound in his chest, now understanding it was not simply a wound to the body. "I'm sorry," he whispered, "I'm sorry."

Azhur refastened his shirt and tunic. He was calmer, but the hatred still burned in his eyes. "It is right that Arahoth is there," he said. "It must be, or the debt to my mother and myself will be unpaid forever. If I knew a place where it lies under the earth I would drag him there, dig till my back broke and throw him down myself. It would be right." He turned, trembling, and pushed open the glass-panelled door that led to the balcony outside. Going out, he stood leaning on the parapet, looking down on the city to recover from his wrath.

"He has so much held inside," said Galdtchav quietly. "Sometimes a touch opens a door, and it overwhelms him."

"It were horrible," said Tyr, wiping his face. "Like somebody I didn't know."

"That is exactly what it was," the Loremaster replied. "And yet that furious young man is Azhur. As is the gentle student you know well. They are one and the same, but you have met only certain aspects of your friend. Do not be too shocked. You have not lost him."

Tyr did not entirely understand but managed a smile at the reassurance.

"Well," said Authran rather desperately. "I think we'll get back to the dorm."

"Eh?" said Tyr. "What about—?"

Authran hit him on the arm. "Really should be getting along. It'll soon be tea-time. Thank you, Anthu, another time…"

"Yes, I think so, lads. Come back tomorrow."

The two novices gathered up their embarrassment and shock as they edged towards the door, leaving things in Galdtchav's fatherly hands.

Azhur came shattering through the glazed outer door and smashed against Galdtchav's table in a shower of glass and splinters. A man came in from the balcony, stepping through the ruined door. He was lithe and naked, his nails black and curved, a sharp, feral glitter dancing in his yellow eyes.

"Some climb that was," he said, showing grotesque, jagged teeth. "Worth it for what I'll get." He stood recovering his breath, leering in his triumph.

"And who will reward you for this?" asked Galdtchav, stooping over Azhur. The young man lay hunched on the floor, blood running from his head.

"Feller as wants him punished. He was rude to somebody important, and he's got to take what's coming."

The Loremaster dabbed at his assistant's wound with a corner of the tablecloth. "Ah," he said. "I am indeed impressed. Truly a great and powerful man if he sends one who can not only scale this tower but break the enchantments that guard this room."

Tyr and Authran glanced at each other. What enchantments?

The feral man was also puzzled for a moment, but then decided to wallow in the praise. His back arched, his chest swelled. He began to strut about with loping strides, relishing his power. "He don't just send anybody on these jobs. I'm the strongest, the fastest. I can take a bear down. Nobody never got away from me!" He raised his arms and flexed his clawed fingers.

"Then I must beg you for mercy!" stammered Galdtchav. "But if you are the messenger, what a master must honour you!"

The man laughed, a deep, guttural sound. "He's the greatest master there is. He's the best, the oldest, the strongest, the only one that's not afraid down below."

"What awesome riddles!" gasped the Loremaster. "I too would bow before such a one if he would allow me. If I could share… *your* honours."

Another savage, liquid laugh. "Not you, grandad! Not y' stinking, red-coat sun-servers!"

"Oh!" said Galdtchav as he half-cradled the groggy Azhur. "Do you and your master not serve the sun? Are you and he so great you can afford—you can *dare*—not to? Oh, you are in a powerful circle indeed!"

"Too right I am!" snarled the monstrous man. "And you priests'll know it when the real sun comes up." He tensed his muscles in a proud display. "You'll see what a sad little candle you've been serving."

"I marvel! A brighter sun yet?"

The intruder rounded on the old man. "Not brighter, you stupid bastard! Y' think I'd just waste me time on a bigger version of what y' got?" He stabbed at his chest with a clawed finger. "Our sun's different! But y'll find out."

To the shock and dismay of the novices, Galdtchav knelt abjectly, Azhur's head in his lap, and raised an imploring hand. "I beg you, ask your great master to reveal these things to me! How can I have power like his?"

"Don't you insult him! Nobody's got power like him. I don't hang about with small fry. Nothing could ever touch him, not even in the desert, not even under the desert."

"Then tell me of your sun!" begged Galdtchav. "Even I do not know this lore! Tell me, when will this wonder rise to bless us?"

The man smiled horribly and his chest swelled again, then he checked himself, uncertain, his breathing quickening. "No!" he barked, leaping at Galdtchav, he seized his left wrist and peered at it as the black nails dug in. "Where is it?" he demanded. "Where is it?"

"I don't understand," said the Loremaster. "What do you want?"

"The amulet! Where's your amulet?"

"That? Lost long ago; a boating accident. Search the Lake if you want it."

The feral man gave a howl of rage and swung his barbed fist against the old man's face. Galdtchav fell across the table on Authran's sketch.

"Bleedin' hell!" the intruder hissed, snatching at the paper. "That's that bugger we got down at Braldhach Falls! He saw! We had a game with him. I was right up close. Took his throat out meself!" His yellow eyes fixed on Tyr. "Buried him, didn't you, sonny? Put him in a hole at Falak-hoth, *we* know!" He glanced at the paper again, then howled like a beast. "That's it! You drew it! You drew the amulet!" He looked about, tensed as if to spring. "What's it doing there? Why's it next to him?" He jolted with the realisation. "It's in his grave! It's his grave-gift! You lying bastard! I'll have your throat for that!" He spread his arms to leap at Galdtchav, but instead screamed and fell. Azhur, conscious again, had seized the Loremaster's long paper-knife and plunged it into the at-tacker's leg. The shrieking man writhed away, pulling out the knife. "You now!" he bayed. "Punishment!"

"For what?" yelled Azhur, furious and terrified.

"Somebody you insulted. He marked you at the Renewal party and I've found you."

"Found me? How?"

"The hate, you stupid bugger! That hate in you set the mark off, took me straight to you, so take your licks!" He coiled himself up then sprang across the room like a beast. Jaws seizing on Azhur's neck, claws ripping at chest and shoulder. The sheer mass of writhing muscle was far beyond him.

And then Tyr did the bravest, stupidest thing he could have done and flung himself on the human beast. Authran followed, trying to grip the powerful flanks before being kicked away. Tyr hung on, hitting at the evil head, trying to tear it away, scratching at the eyes and face. There seemed to be a flash of light and words entered his mind from far away. An ancient phrase Azhur had spoken to the foreigner under the trees at Falakhoth that had terrified the man.

Tha sh'herakh tha ai'vel! Tha sh'herakh tha ai'vel!

He yelled it out now, hardly knowing why, like a spell, like a rite, like a battle-cry. He thought of the Fire-spirit as if the words could somehow reach it and find help.

A scream like no beast he had ever heard. The feral man whipped away from Azhur, writhing violently across the room. His body lashed and flailed, gouging and bruising himself against chairs and scroll-racks. Broken glass sliced at him, splintered wood tore him, stone walls scraped and pounded him, but nothing mattered save escape from the deadly, holy words. Authran flung a chair at him and missed, but the ravaged, naked figure, glistening with blood and sweat, flung itself somehow through the jagged ruins of the doorway and leapt over the balcony.

Tyr kept a firm hold on Azhur, hugging him and sobbing. "Look at the blood! All that blood! He's not—he won't—"

"No, no," said Galdtchav. "Those wounds aren't as deep as they look, I think. But deep enough. We must be swift." He turned to find his attendant standing horrified at the inner doorway. "Sharn! The Master Physician, quickly!" The attendant turned and raced away as Galdtchav sagged back against the legs of his chair. "*Grauhamurshi!*" he said desperately, as if to himself. "He was right, he was right! The old Scrolls!"

"Who's right?" said Tyr, inquisitive even now, as Authran helped him staunch his friend's wounds with torn tablecloth.

"A wise man," said Galdtchav. "A man of experience. Ah, the terrors this realm has seen. But lads, I think I guess who we are up against."

"What do y' mean?"

"There's that southerner you met, the one who attacked Jarthastra at Renewal, but I fear he's not the worst. That fanged fool told me more than he thought."

"Ey! Y' was stringin' him along!"

"Oh, perspicacious, Tyr. Yes, I can think as well as read, and I wormed a lot out of him."

"Tell us, Anthu," said Authran as he tended Azhur.

"That beast's master wants the amulet—he must believe it has some kind of power.... And their sun, not bright like ours, will rise. We must assume there will be dire consequences if it does."

Azhur stirred and opened his eyes. "Lord Arna's the sun," he said weakly. "Priest of Arna."

"Of course you are," said Galdtchav, stroking Azhur's head and gripping his hand. "A fine priest you were meant to be."

Tyr finished fastening a makeshift bandage with crimson hands. "How can a sun not be bright?" he said, as much to keep himself going as anything. "It's stupid."

"I don't know," replied the Loremaster. "Is there a sun that radiates darkness?"

"Can't be," insisted Tyr. "But this master feller's not even scared of nothin' underground. Ey!" He stopped his work for an instant.

"Tell us, Tyr," said Galdtchav.

"*Lady give you happy death, save you from the one beneath.* We sing that at home."

"The one beneath," repeated Galdtchav. "The terrors under the earth, the evil, banished things that crept back from the dark and buried themselves in the heart of the new-made world, beneath its hide. So many stories and legends, so much lore. Azhur named them at the Coming Forth. Could it be true?" He gazed horrified into far possibilities, then shook himself. "Lads, this *different sun* will appear soon, I am convinced. The fellow gave it away. I asked him when and he checked himself and would not answer. Something is imminent, I know it. An immensely powerful man, unafraid of the worst terrors of history, still wants my amulet, and wants it now."

"Don't give it him," groaned Azhur. "Won't be punished! No punishment."

"Imminent, Anthu?" asked Authran, "Are you sure?"

"Not entirely, but that is how it falls together in my mind. I must chase the clues through certain Scrolls, but have I time?"

"What about y' amulet?" asked Tyr.

Galdtchav shook his head. "I don't understand its importance. But your Thaljhaz seems to think he's guarding it and refuses to go from the living world with Ardhruthak. And then there's the hugely powerful monster who desires it." A horrid thought stopped him. "What if it enables this *different sun* to appear?"

"Y' don't even know what that is."

"No, but be sure it is very bad."

There was the briefest pause, then Tyr got to his feet. "I'll go for y' amulet. I'll go to Falakhoth now. Best not wait."

"Oh, dear," said Authran. "Well, I suppose I'd better go with you. You'll never manage it by yourself."

"Oh, my dear lads," said Galdtchav. "Bless you both, but you—" He stopped and held them in his gaze as if he had forgotten what to say. "Yes, I think you must. Give me the writing-board! Paper!" And, cradling Azhur, the Loremaster scribbled as Authran held the board for him. "Wax! Quick!" He pressed his seal on two papers and handed them over. "Take these to the royal stables, no-one will argue with that seal. They authorise you to use the horses of the Imperial Post: the relays of these mounts can cover a continent in two days. Now go! At once! Do not stop till you reach Falakhoth! Bring me the amulet! We do not know what depends on this! *Go!*"

They rushed to the door as the Master Physician and his attendants came in. Tyr's last backward glance caught Azhur lying in his blood, reaching weakly towards him, but he dared not wait.

As they flew down stairway and passageway, Tyr found his mind fixed absurdly on Sharn, Galdtchav's attendant: he had such a short name.

CHAPTER 26

The Dark Sun

THE FIRST FIGURES ENTERED Val-zajjhak's hall. A far-off door closed softly, two pairs of boots grated on the stone flags. Ilissos glanced over at the sunken area before the dais where he was sitting and thought in brighter days it would have made a charming pool about the depth of a man's waist. There, the eager fish would have darted under the floating blooms of waterlilies, and the gracious sunlight would have been flung against the walls and ceiling by the endless ripples. Now, the Syrgan watched the two men, cloaked and shapeless, hesitate by the arid, empty space, the afternoon light squeezing through shuttered windows.

Val-zajjhak sat at the edge of the raised dais. He was leaning forward in his chair, gripping the staff against his shoulder, utterly still. Ilissos could feel the immense watchfulness, the palpable waiting. He sensed also how the vraakhin's mind reached out towards the two men. Through the thoughts of his captor he touched their anticipation and fear, their surprise at seeing him. He even caught the echo of their names, but he felt nothing of their purpose. Instead, he sensed a hostility deflecting his thought. They were wary of him.

The vraakhin spoke with a horrid deadness that Ilissos was learning to pity. "You are the first. Come you by sun or moon? Light they your way in the earth?"

A heavy, throaty voice mumbled the reply, "In the strength of the Dark Sun we are here. We need not flame nor shining; our power is our own."

"And it is very great," said Val-zajjhak, and Ilissos sensed something like a thrill beneath his heaviness. "It is much that there are still two with such power in Ceor."

Feet scuffed, one gave a cough, "We, ah… we heard about Gurdjatt. Got word from the city. They said the Shrine boys or Bel-ghirá's apes got him. We're sorry about it."

"We knew what Vardresh might mean," replied Val-zajjhak flatly.

Ilissos felt something deep and painful stir, sensing the force that held it in check. A barrier lifted, and the Syrgan knew how deeply moved the vraakhin was behind his colourless eyes, how much he wanted to tell the man from Ceor about his loss.

Instead, Val-zajjhak said firmly, "Gurdjatt is honoured by your words." The barrier fell back into place and the only exchange approaching mutual warmth that Ilissos had seen among the vraakhin was over.

"Started the minute we heard," the man continued. "Kharhalkhar came, says there'll be enough and it'll really happen."

Val-zajjhak nodded.

"Ahh," said the other in a wheezing voice. "We've won after tonight!" He laughed with an unpleasant happiness.

"We won long ages ago," said Val-zajjhak with drab menace. "We now see the fruition. What we do now will be done in victory."

"Ah. Well, I knew that, you know what I mean."

There was no answer.

"He's here, is he?" asked the first man. "V'karra? He's here?" His voice echoed disturbingly. It was too loud and eager for the heaviness of that room.

Val-zajjhak let the silence settle again. "He is here."

"Good. That's good, then. He ought to tell us some things. I've got questions."

Val-zajjhak drew in his breath. "You may tell Lord V'karra yourself what he ought to do."

Ilissos felt the cold fear this passionless statement created.

"Didn't mean that, exactly. Was speaking generally. But Kharhalkhar says we really will do it at last. That's... that's marvellous but assure me again: we really can trust him? I mean, he's not—"

Val-zajjhak moved very slightly. "I gave him his message."

"Oh, *you*—well, that settles that, of course, yes, but can I just ask: will we have that boy? Everybody knows, great anticipation—"

"Murghjhash has been sent for him. He will pay his dues."

"Murghjhash? Well, that's a strong one, I hear. No trouble there, eh?"

"He travels the Plain at this moment: the mark will lead him."

"Mind you," said the self-important vraakhin, rambling with nervous enthusiasm, "I've got some thoughts there. Why, tell me, do we have Karhalkhar and Murghjhash and all that pack? I mean, they're not *like* us, they're not natural. So why do we bother with—"

"It pleases the Lord Gehrava."

Now Ilissos sensed a lance of real terror in the man.

"Gehrava? Then... then...."

"He will honour us today. He will come among us."

The two men were frozen with fear. The less talkative one edged away.

"You will need to rest," said Val-zajjhak softly. "You may sit, and you may wait."

Ilissos felt rather than saw the baleful light in the vraakhin's eyes as he watched the two figures move past the empty pool and into the deeper shadows. The Syrgan had no idea who Murghjhash was hunting or what mark would lead him, but he whispered a prayer for them non-etheless as he hunched up against the wall.

Outside, the daylight thinned. Inside, the shadows in the hall drew together into dark pools. The vraakhin of Ceor became blurred shapes. Ilissos felt that he was seeing the room through a grey web in which the pale sky-frame of the window hung like a panel painted with the faint likeness of heaven. Val-zajjhak scarcely moved.

At last the door scraped open again and a big man in a long coat with a black bear's pelt about the shoulders strode into the hall. He pulled off his fur hat and snapped a question to Val-zajjhak instead of a greeting. "Who's that?" he demanded in a deep, angry voice, waving his hat at Ilissos.

Val-zajjhak shifted a little and Ilissos became aware of him raising a mental shield against the probing thoughts of the new arrival. He sensed his own mind was likewise protected, given how it echoed that of Val-zajjhak's.

"You will discover who he is when the time comes, but know that it pleases the Lord Gehrava and Lord V'karra that he is here."

"Gehrava's here? The real thing, then? About time."

"Come you by sun or moon? Light they your way in the earth?"

"In the strength of the Dark Sun I am here. I need not flame nor shining: my power is my own." The big man snorted and stamped away to a corner. A ripple of hostility ran across the hall.

More arrived. Alone or in twos and threes, they stood before the empty pool and rejected the powers of the sun and moon in favour of their own. Ilissos realised how fitting it was that these words should be said in darkness. On a bright Syrgan hillside they would fade into the air and be lost.

He saw too how far-reaching V'karra's influence was, how great the strength that must be ranged against the Valgraav's realm. In the words Val-zajjhak exchanged with each new arrival, Ilissos recognized many names. From the memory of the crumpled map in his saddle-bag, he placed Ceorthas, the ancient land by the Western Sea; Ngal, that rock in the dark waters among the whale-ways where the rulers of the islands near the Northern ice-fields had their seat; Harrokaan, the Harrak's ancient home in exile; Amouchraan, watcher of the mountain-passes to and from the Great Plain; Nerthald by the great Southern ranges; Amouch Arna, guardian of the Valgraav's eastern shores, her face towards the sunrise. There were more, many more, but still they came, and Ilissos' horror grew, for he heard names and tongues from far lands: Eirva, scarce three hundred miles from his own land, seaport of quiet Sarvien; Mahour, the mountainous land by the Southern coast; Burdaz, Hirbaz, and Ravin, cities of strange Lachir that thrust itself greedily into the Woundsea; Kherosh and Zirribh, alien, dusty places that sat under a fierce sun; and then places unknown to him such as Vel Charig and Nervashi. Until there came a name that struck him like a blow, for through the shadows came the voice of one who had journeyed from

571

Labanei, by the House of Life, on the Third Hill of Syrga.

Ilissos, sick with dismay, cared no more what he heard, for he knew that if the vraakhin were in Cynathé's land he needed no more proof of their creeping strength. Had Syrga's name alone been mentioned he would have known and now, what could he do? What could anybody do? Weary and horrified, he sank back into himself, trying to shield his mind from the terrible knowledge. Would the incomparable land of the Green Jewel suffer the horrors of the rape of Vardresh? He dared not think it.

~

TYR AND AUTHRAN IMAGINED they sat upon eagles as the splendid horses of the Imperial Post, bred for generations to speed and endurance, carried them swiftly down the Lakeside road. Still, it was a desperate race, knowing how at that very moment a dreadful, unknown foe was seeking what they did and perhaps pursuing it with equal haste. They clung on grimly, hands still red with Azhur's blood, and prayed they were fast enough. Perhaps the beast-like man had already reported the where-abouts of the amulet and they were already too late. Their foe, knowing they realised the amulet lay in Thaljhaz's grave, would surely anticipate their next move, and if he had more servants like the one he had sent for Azhur it was not a happy thought.

On they flew as dusk deepened. Travellers and livestock fled as they blurred past, yelling, "Imperial Post! Imperial Post!" at the pitch of their lungs. As the road curved left of the Lakeside, the lights of Lukar came into view far off to their right. Tyr wondered briefly how Yauva was, and if his leg was still all right, but they were past the town before he knew it and his mind returned to the spiral of how much time they had.

Could Galdtchav be wrong? Did the dreams mean something else? They only had Galdtchav's intuition to go on, and while the master was the kind of man you listened to, would it be enough? Tyr remembered the care-free morning—years ago it seemed to him now—when he had tried to outrun the storm cloud above Falakhoth. Was a more terrible storm brewing? Could he outrun *this* one?

On and on. Fading sky, blackening land, empty road. Tyr began to feel a dullness seep through him. He found he could not maintain fever-pitch excitement or coherency of thought. All that was left was the feeling of travelling: the flexing horse-muscles against his legs, the wind in his face, the drumming of hooves beneath him. In the dark there was little consciousness of progress. He had only to sit on a horse and wait, powerless against the forces that conspired to beat him to Falakhoth.

~

THE BAREST SMEAR OF RED lingered in the sky and the hall was almost dark when, with the sound of feet, came the thud and scrape of wood on stone. Even before the coarse voice grated through the darkness, Ilissos knew Gaur-van had arrived.

"Save your breath, Crow. You know about me: power's me own, and no mistake, eh?"

Though the old man was hardly visible, Ilissos could see his leering grin clear in his thoughts. He glanced towards Val-zajjhak and his eyes went wide with surprise. Around the faint outline of Val-zajjhak's head, angry red shapes glowed and pulsed. The vraakhin did not move or speak, and no-one else seemed to see them, not even Gaur-van who was looking straight at the vraakhin too. It took Ilissos a moment to surmise he was seeing a form of the man's inner rage. Were their minds joined so directly?

Gaur-van, at least, sounded as garrulously cheerful as before. "Big night, Crow, eh?" He gave a slurred cackle. "Well, I've brought our new boy. I reckon he's up to it, eh? He's got power, all right. Them Shrine priests found out and no mistake. Arna and his Valgraav got no use for him, so he's one of us."

"Don't say that!" snapped a deep voice. Ilissos could hear the man's laboured breathing over the length of the hall. "Don't say these names here! It's not safe."

"Oh, excuse *me*," sneered Gaur-van. "If I'd known the great Brughar of the Forests got scared of *names*, I'd have watched my tongue!"

"Power in names," said Brughar. "They're weapons or don't you know?"

"Power's in *me*," said Gaur-van dangerously. "Or don't you know *that?*"

Silence, then the sound of Brughar moving away. Hatred shuddered in the air. Gaur-van chuckled quietly.

Val-zajjhak, the red lights gone, struck the floor with his staff and spoke into the darkness. "Let our new brother speak."

Gaur-van's companion scuffed forward. Ilissos wondered briefly why every arrival stopped before the sunken area in the floor. Why did no-one approach Val-zajjhak?

"Come you by Sun or Moon? Light they your way in the earth?" Val-zajjhak asked the latest newcomer.

"In... in the strength of the... the, ah, Dark Sun I am here."

Ilissos felt a wave of fear break against him as he recognised the voice of the speaker: Gizhurthra. Pain twisted around his memories as his mind forced him to relive the anxiety and humiliation from the night he first heard those ominous words, as Val-zajjhak stood outside Gizhurthra's door in Falakhoth.

A breath, a gulp, then more loudly, "I... I..."

"Need not flame," growled Gaur-van quietly.

"I need not flame—flame nor shining."

Silence. Ilissos wondered if Gizhurthra could continue. Through Val-zajjhak's mind, Ilissos perceived him as scarcely more than a whirling bundle of emotions, held together by the driving need to win the acceptance of the brotherhood of the sorcerers.

In a shout he said, "My power... is... *my own!*" Great surges of relief and release came from him, and Gaur-van laughed quietly as he slapped him on the back. No-one else made any kind of acknowledgement of Gizhurthra. The air felt sullen and heavy. Both men moved away to the edge of the room, accompanied by the sound of Gizhurthra's muffled sobbing.

Ilissos hadn't realised he'd fallen asleep until the sound of a slamming door pulled him awake. Lamps had been lit, and the hall was filled with murmuring and movement. Val-zajjhak was on his feet, beside him was the dark-swathed figure of V'karra. The very air felt deadly with the southerner now present.

A figure was limping past the sunken pool. He was naked and terrified, blood streaming down his leg from a wound in his thigh. The southerner raised his hand, and the wretched man stopped in touching distance of the dais. The other sorcerers shrunk closer to the walls, leaving him alone in the vast empty space. Ilissos could hear the man's rapid breathing.

"Well, now, Murghjhash," said V'karra. "Did you punish the Shrine-beetle?"

"I did: mauled him bad."

"Dead, then?"

"No. Not dead, but hurt very bad. Might die yet."

"Not dead," repeated V'karra slowly. "Well. The boy then, where is he? Do not say you are alone."

Murghjhash trembled. "Couldn't get him," he whispered.

"Why not?" asked V'karra. He spoke with an infinite softness, tilting his hawk's head, his predatory eyes fixed firmly on the man before him.

"I... I had my teeth in the other one and the boy jumped on me—"

"We gave you this honour for your strength."

"Wasn't that. He grabbed me.... and he said—he said...."

"Tell us, Murghjhash. Did he... *frighten* you?" The other sorcerers gave an anxious laugh. V'karra raised a hand to silence them. "Come now, what did he say?"

"He said—he said—what the other one said to you. In the village."

V'karra remained silent for a long time as the man writhed under his stare. "So," he said at last. "But why have you not brought him?"

"I... I... I don't know. I had to get out. When he said... *that*, it was like my body went mad, like it couldn't stand hearing the mention of the shining—oh!" A long, horrified moan went up. "No, no, I'm sorry, I didn't mean—"

"You mention that to me?" said V'karra, descending from the dais.

"Sorry, sorry, it just came out! Forgive me, it's a terrible word, terrible! What it does to you, you'll understand—"

But this was a worse error still. "*I* will understand?" V'karra said, voice rising. "*I* will understand what that crude sound does to a cur like *you?* How dare you! There are those who have slain themselves rather than

575

speak to me of failure! I myself crafted the shield around you, I myself set the mark on those two. Lord Gehrava himself told you what part the boy was to play tonight, and still you *failed!* Very well, I have done with you. You shall answer to Lord Gehrava."

"No!" shrieked frantic Murghjhash. "I can't! I can't face him, nobody can! You tell him, my lord! I beg you. He'll take it from you. You tell him and ask him to forgive me." Murghjhash's terror was palpable. A gasp went up from his audience when he reached out to snatch at V'karra's cloak. He pulled his hand away, barely in time. Hardly able to stand for fear, he staggered away, searching the hall for a sign of support. Every eye that looked upon him was full of fire, save for Val-zajjhak's, whose eyes were bitterly cold. The victim's panic mounted. "All right, I'll grovel to him, I will, I'll beg forgiveness, I'll do anything he wants. I'll lick his feet if I—"

"Do not dare," said V'karra, in a voice like slow millstones.

Murghjhash's legs gave way from fear and he sank to the floor, moaning and clutching his head. A creaking, grinding sound began, a trembling in the earth. The floor shuddered beneath the sorcerers' feet; they cried out and backed against the walls. A metallic noise echoed throughout the hall as great machines turned and laboured in the depths. With the clamour of keening, scraping metal, the floor of the empty pool began to inch upwards, moving on massive hinges as the broad, solid stonework rose on an ancient iron frame moving against an unseen counterweight. The great stone slab grated upward, exposing a black pit beneath. Murghjhash turned to watch as smoke and vapour of filthy air issued from the exposed chasm, together with a stink so intense that the watchers recoiled and turned away. A metal staircase swung rasping into place, a pathway to the world above for who knew what below.

The great, invisible engines keened and thudded to a stop with a moan of metal. The sound of slow, dragging footsteps and a trailing, whispering robe replaced the shreiking metal. More ominously, remote, unguessable sounds wound up from the pit amid the reeking vapours. The figure reached the top of the stair and stepped over the lip of the pool into the hall before the dais. All around him the vraakhin huddled down or threw themselves on the floor in frightened, awestruck homage: they knew, or guessed, who had appeared. Only V'karra and Val-zajjhak stood erect to greet the visitor from the depths.

"Lord Gehrava. Welcome." Even V'karra inclined his hawk's head and bowed his regal shoulders.

Ilissos peered at Gehrava. The man was swathed in trailing robes of no colour, as if their hues had been burned to nothing by the sun, and he leaned heavily on a staff, stooping his curved back like an ancient tree and thrusting his head far forward like the desert-birds that seek for carrion. The pit itself was strangely dark and his head was labouring under a sudden heaviness, a weighing, a muffling of his thoughts. There was the sensation of dryness, a strong, brittle will, a dust-laden wind sifting through caverns immense and ancient, a tremor of vast power, the constant straining of unguessable sinews. The grinding and scraping began again as the stone slab once more became the floor of the abandoned pool and the horrid portal was closed. A gnarled hand pulled down the wrappings that concealed the features and Ilissos, looking into the face of Gehrava, caught his breath. The sorcerer was old, older than he expected any man could be; but this age was not only visible in the bent body, the parchment skin, and the ringed, deep-sunken eyes. Gehrava lived not only in the present moment, but carried all his years with him, had drawn them into himself, clinging to them so that all the past was a vast, invisible burden of time, a weight of days that spread out from him and pressed on the spirits of everyone in the hall.

"You see, my brothers?" he said in an unexpectedly powerful voice that echoed over the heads of the prostrate vraakhin. "I walk fearless and unharmed under the earth. The One Beneath is friend to me, such is the majesty that protects you. I cannot show you the Great One, not yet, but when our sun is risen, the world will be fit for him. Wait a little while and you shall see what no man but I has seen."

Gehrava began to pace round the empty pool, taking in the circle of men who cowered at the edges of the hall. His threadbare robe whispered over the floor and his staff made a sharp *clack* as though an executioner's axe fell with every stride. On the further side of the pool, he stopped. After a moment he placed his staff under the chin of the man before him and made him raise his head. It was Gizhurthra.

"Men tremble when I do this," said Gehrava quietly, almost with a gentle curiosity. "Some vomit, some open their bowels, some faint. None can simply look at me, as you do."

"Ah," said Gizhurthra with an exalted tone to his voice. "Well, I'm vraakhin, you see, and I can see you're master here—I know these things—but apart from that, I don't know who you are, sir. I know you were at Lukar, but I missed you. I was very sorry about that—"

"Enough," said Gehrava. He withdrew the staff and peered long into Gizhurthra's round eyes as if wondering whether the man was stupid, powerful, brave, or ignorant.

Gizhurthra made the most of the attention and held his face up proudly with an ecstatic little smile.

"Well," said Gehrava at last, "this new one is right. We will use him at Lukar." He planted the staff on the floor—*clack*—and resumed his pacing.

At last he completed his circle and stopped by Murghjhash. The wretched man was huddled on the floor, shaking with fear.

"Up," said Gehrava. His hapless servant instantly obeyed. "Murghjhash, what is this? You appear before me in this uncovered form?"

"Came straight here, my Lord. No time—"

"Would you not make time for *me?*" asked Gehrava, sounding genuinely pained. "Oh, look at you: blood, sweat, dirt, every muscle obvious. And *hair!* You flaunt this vile, physical thing, you emphasise it, accentuate it! Why, even the smell of you!" The ancient man turned away in distaste. "Do I not teach our brotherhood to cover and despise this base shell they must inhabit: this low, corporeal, animal thing. This prison? Pains, fluids, stink, a weight upon the mind with its corrupted needs and instincts!" The sorcerer's voice grew higher as he looked around the vraakhin's circle. "I have subdued my body these long years, my brothers, as I prepare for the release of the real self, the exact self, when this thing that grew in my mother will be consumed and I shall rule you as true, pure spirit, unfettered mind, on the day that I create myself anew. The day which our gathering hastens!" His last, shrill words went echoing

"Well," said Gehrava at last, "this new one is right. We will use him at Lukar."

round the hall and Gehrava made a disgusted little sound between his teeth, then remembered Murghjhash and rounded on him. "Well: no boy, no amulet. Where are they?"

"Forgive, Lord. The boy said a terrible thing—"

"I am aware. And the amulet?"

"He didn't have it, said he'd lost it, but I worked it out, I worked it out for you, my Lord."

"Then I shall reward you, Murghjhash. How did you do this?"

"They had a picture of somebody I killed. He's buried at Falakhoth, and the amulet was on the picture and that's how I knew. They made the amulet his grave-gift. He's buried with it, so I came as fast as I could to tell y'."

"That is very good, Murghjhash. We will find it. I am pleased."

"I praised you to them, my Lord."

"Did you? Well, so you ought, that is fitting."

"I said my master was the strongest, the oldest, he wasn't afraid of nothing in the deserts or under the deserts and when our sun rose they'd all know it, all the filthy priests and sun-servers and y'—"

Gehrava raised a hand to stop him. "It appears you have failed all the same. You did not do what I told you."

Murghjhash's reborn hope died at once. "Mercy, my Lord! I was—I truly thought it was there—that horrible word. Oh, mercy, please!"

Gehrava turned to V'karra, "Give him a light."

The tone of these four words filled Ilissos' mind with images of bones scattered white in the dead wadis, of hard, splintering earth, and of crumbled cities borne away on the wind. It was the voice of drought, famine, the merciless years, and but that living man spoke, the voice of death.

V'karra stepped forward, gave Murghjhash his lamp, and withdrew. Murghjhash shook violently as one of Gehrava's skeletal hands reached out to him.

"Yes, your mind is open—no, do not speak, there is nothing to say. You are quite right. You depend on my mercy. Now, raise the lamp and let me see your face."

"Lord Gehrava, your mercy! I thank you. I praise you."

"Do not lower the lamp." There was a dreadful silence. No indication of Gehrava's thoughts showed in his face or voice. He let more tortured moments pass. "Are you truly sorry?" he said at last.

"Oh, yes, Lord, yes! If only y' knew—"

"I do know. I wanted to hear it from your lips. You have not disappointed me." The ancient man stepped back and looked Murghjhash up and down like a proud father. "So, I will have mercy. Bow your head and I will speak over you."

The man's limbs trembled. He almost collapsed from relief as he bowed.

Gehrava raised his hand, held it aloft. Then the hand sliced down as the sorcerer spoke one terrible word. There was a fragment of time for Murghjhash to realise before the lamp in his hand burst into a gout of flame that covered him like a wave. He staggered back, screaming even then for some merciful charm to save him. His feet landed on the edge of the empty pool and he fell backwards, his arms flailing like burning wings.

The vraakhin were thrown into a frenzy. Wails of terror and exultation went up in the chamber. Some raised their arms or waved their hands, casting spells for their own safety. Several voices even sang: deep, snarling threat-filled chants or wild, deep songs. Some ran about the hall distracted and a few turned on each other. Their faces were that of beasts: hungry, round-eyed, and filled with instinct, all thought gone. A wave of animal desire came howling through Ilissos's thoughts as Murghjhash writhed and screamed.

Gehrava ignored the mad spectacle as he made his way slowly around the hall. The vraakhin edged away from him or simply fled. They knew what was among them, and there was no more pretence at formality. Murghjhash's unnaturally long torment was evidence enough. Still the man thrashed. Flames leapt above the lip of the pool as his agonised cries continued to fill the air. From Ilissos' vantage point he could see how the fire burned but did not consume anywhere near as fast as it should.

All at once Gehrava stopped. He looked around him, then raised a hand. A blistering bolt of energy burned across the hall above the insane gathering like an indoor storm. The men ceased their cacophony and threw themselves down panting, groaning, or quietly whining. Even Murghjhash's tortured utterances quieted to a low murmur. Supremely indifferent, Gehrava listened to the comparative quiet for a while, before calmly asking, "Where is Karhalkhar?"

A red-haired man loped over to him and knelt, eyes fixed on Gehrava's bony feet. To Ilissos, it looked as if the man would paw them like a dog.

"Here, me Lord," said Karhalkhar.

"Where are the packs, Karhalkhar? Are any of your brothers near Falakhoth?"

"Yes, me Lord. There's the pack at Braldhach Tor."

"Braldhach, that pleases me. Fix your mind upon the pack leader. Keep your head bowed." Gehrava's wizened hand fastened on the man's head, his fingers clawing amongst the man's red hair. "Ah, I have him. Send him your thoughts: tell him to go at once to the Falakhoth burial ground and seize the boy. Bring him here with the amulet. They must dig it up themselves if need be. Tell them Lord V'karra has marked him and he is to keep him alive. I will repay my servant's insult." The two stayed poised for a while, then Gehrava withdrew his hand and Karhalkhar fell limply on his side. The sorcerer ignored him. "They may even now be trying to retrieve the amulet. They may even know what it is for since Murghjhash gave them many clues. They may even guess who I am and what we do." The sorcerer turned to V'karra. "We will be safer still if I locate the boy. V'karra, most honoured servant, come close and help me. Which hand did you use to mark him?" The southerner held out his left hand to him. "Good, good. You understand how I must use you?"

"It is my honour," replied V'karra as Gehrava clasped his hand in both of his and closed his eyes. V'karra bowed his head. His breathing became laboured, and sweat ran down his face.

"I have him!" exclaimed Gehrava. "He is on King's Road with one other. Yes, bound for Falakhoth! But the pack may miss him." He moved his head as though looking around the hall, though his eyes were tight shut. "Ah. There is someone nearby I could use, what shall I do with her?"

"My Lord," said V'karra suddenly, "I would ask you something."

"What, my son?" said Gehrava, eyes still closed.

"You take such pains for me. If the pack slays the boy, I am content: my honour will be upheld. Why do you wish to have him here?"

Gehrava's eyes snapped open. "My son, do you not know? He has seen our enemy."

~

LUKAR WAS FAR BEHIND THEM, the road running almost straight in the long valley next to the river. Trees, land, and stone rushed by, hazy shapes in concealing darkness. A spur of rock jutted out ahead and forced the river to make its one major bend. The racing horses threw themselves round the spur, then skidded and reared as the lads yelled and heaved on the reins. In the dark it took them a moment to see a woman had stepped out onto the road in front of them.

"What the hell y' doin', missus? Couldn't y' hear us coming?" roared Tyr. "Get off the road, we're in a hurry!"

"Nearly trampled you!" called Authran. "Do be careful!"

The woman came up to them, smiling. "Oh, Tyr!" she said. "How amazing! Oh, I'm so glad."

"Aienna?" gasped Tyr as he peered at the woman in the moonlight. "That's never you?" But Aienna it was: beautiful yellow hair, nightingale voice, marvellous dress that shimmered green in the dark and made the stark night road a garden with a single lovely flower. "What y' doin' out here on your own?" demanded Tyr. "Where's y' horse?"

"Oh, the stupid thing bolted. A fox or something ran across the road, and it threw me. No damage done, fortunately, but *look* at this dress!" She showed them where the left arm of her dress had been badly ripped, and mud and blood had ruined the fabric.

"Ey! Y're bleedin'!" exclaimed Tyr, dismounting.

"Don't worry, it's not too bad. Oh, mother will be *insane* over this! It's beyond our seamstress' skill!"

"What y' doin' here anyway?"

"Well, actually I came to visit Veshren and Naida after—you know what this afternoon. I thought I'd pour a little oil on troubled waters."

583

"Somebody had to. That were nice of y'."

"Oh, yes, but look, a message came—by carrier bird—and it said Azhur's all right. I don't know what that means, but that's what it said."

"Ey, that's brilliant! I were worried sick!"

"The message said I was to set off home and if I met you on the way I was to tell you Galdtchav made a mistake about the amulet and you mustn't go to Falakhoth. Just stay here and people from the Shrine will come and meet you. And here you are!"

Tyr sagged with relief and leaned on his sweating horse, letting the tension drain away.

"I hope all that makes sense to you," continued Aienna, "because I've no idea what it's about. Anyway, I did meet you. Isn't it amazing?"

"Well, bugger that, beggin' y' pardon. I didn't fancy diggin' in no graveyard."

"Graveyard? Whatever are you up to, Tyr?"

"It's a long story, Aienna. Well, that's it, then. Me and Ran'll wait for them Shrine fellers and give y' a lift back. Can't wait to see if Azhur's ok."

Aienna smiled. "Yes, what was that about? Has he had an accident?"

"Aye, well, y' could say that."

Authran coughed politely. "And, er, if I could just put a word in, lady, you don't seem awfully bothered."

Aienna smiled brightly. "Well, of course I am. Whatever do you mean?"

Authran dismounted, looking rather cautious. "Well, lady, you've just found out something's happened to your beloved that's worth a special reassurance, you meet us riding like maniacs with blood up to our elbows, and you don't look the tiniest bit upset. You don't even seem terribly bothered about what happened. In fact, you look so bright and cheerful you could be at a court masque. It's all a bit odd, really."

"But Azhur's all right," trilled Aienna.

"Yes, but—well, any normal woman would at least be wondering what happened. Don't you think?" Authran raised his blood-caked hands and waggled his fingers to underline his point. "And anyway, Veshren and Naida aren't at home, they're staying in the city."

A little pause, as Aienna continued to smile beautifully.

Tyr began to look very puzzled. "Well, now Ran mentions it..."

"Oh, Tyr, what on earth are you worried about? Look, I haven't seen you for ages. Let me have a hug and a kiss."

She raised her arms and stepped forward.

"Aaaaarrh! No, yer don't!" All at once there was a scuff of boots on the road and a figure appeared between Tyr and Aienna. A sturdy, bearded little man was making extremely threatening gestures at the gentle girl, who simply continued to smile. "That's enough of yer tricks, yer great rotten slag!" he roared.

"Ey!" yelled Tyr. "Watch y' mouth!"

"Tricks? Tricks?" said Aienna. "Whatever are you talking about? Never mind him, Tyr, where's my kiss?" She leaned forward over the little man, who immediately rammed his fist into Tyr's stomach. The lad tottered back, winded, and the fellow dodged round and deliberately tripped him. Tyr landed on his back on the road, clutching his middle.

"Oh, well, really," exclaimed Authran. "That's not very nice!"

The midget glared at him, "Oh, yer think so?" he snapped. He turned on Aienna, who was still smiling.

"Oh, dear," she said brightly.

"I'll give yer oh dear, yer mould-scab! You leave him alone, d'yer hear? Go on, bugger off!"

"I will do no such thing," exclaimed Aienna cheerfully. "Tyr is my friend and I shall have my kiss, oh yes, I shall indeed."

"Right, that's it," snarled her small enemy. "The Shining on yer! White Shining on yer! White Shining!" And with that, Aienna shrieked and seemed to melt rapidly into one shape after another: faces, limbs, trees, bones, black smears of formlessness.

"You filthy little bastard!" she howled. "Leave me alone! I was sent for him! He's my business!"

"Not if I make it mine," bellowed the man. "Ahh, yer stupid hag-bag, yer can't even do it properly: standin' there grinnin' like a loony! Get back ter yer cave, you're finished! White Shining on yer!"

The thing that was trying to be Aienna gave a foul, guttural belch and collapsed into the form it truly owned. Where the fair girl had stood, a grotesque creature of vaguely female shape lay writhing on the road. Tyr yelled and scrabbled away backwards. Authran hauled him to his feet, and they watched horrified as long, glistening limbs flailed about. A head like a stretched-out skull bobbed and swayed, the mottled, oily skin stretched and sagged. A stink like rotten vegetables smote them.

"Bloody hell!" shrieked Tyr. "That was tryin' to kiss me!"

"Aye, and imagine what would've happened then. Had ter get yer away from it. Go on, Gulta, sod off back ter yer cave!"

The creature whined and bubbled. "You always spoil it for me! What'll I say to him now? Why don't you stick to your own side of the river?"

"Yer great stupid fungus!" said her little adversary. "Yer think yer matter enough ter even get near him, never mind speak ter him? Don't flatter yerself!"

"Miserable little bastards!" hissed the Gulta. "What you got against me?"

"If I told yer, we'd be here all night. Now, do yer want me ter say it again?"

"No, no, I'm going! But you'll catch it, you will. Just you wait till the sun's up. Not long now afore he does it! I felt it in the ground I have, under my cave! He's started!"

"Yer slimeys like ter think so."

"Well, how do you think I knew to be here, eh?"

"Right: White—"

The thing screeched in terror and leapt away on its gangly legs. A splash came back through the darkness. Tyr and Authran stared in disgust at a smear of slime across the road.

"Well, yer fell for that all right," said the little man. "Thought you pair was smart."

"What was it?" gasped Tyr.

"Oh, it's a Gulta. They change shape, yer see, or make yer think they have, but they never get it right. That one there, now, she can't do the emotions. Doesn't realise people have more than one feeling. She thinks lovely ladies just stand around smiling all day. Stupid great bint."

"But it knew things," said Authran, "about people we care for."

"They pull things out of yer thoughts so's they can make up stories to fool yer. Yer did well, though, young sir. Kept her waiting long enough fer me ter wade in."

"Never have thought, never have thought," Authran said, shaking his head. "You read things in Scrolls and, well...."

Stunned, the two novices stared hard at their rescuer and wondered how someone so diminutive could be so aggressive. He was stocky and short—very, very short—and seemed to have a brown, tough skin like tanned leather. His eyes were small, bright, and wise, and sat deep among many lines and creases. His beard was thick, coarse, and stiff. He looked around him and scratched his nose with one of his long fingers.

"That's the last of her, I reckon. She won't try that again. Lady Aienna too, bloody cheek." He turned and called into the roadside bushes. "Right lads, let's be havin yer!" Three more like himself appeared, two with buckets. "Just give yer horses a drink of that, my lads."

"What is it?" asked Authran.

"Something fer horses. Get on with it."

"I never heard of them things afore," said Tyr as he took the bucket and let his horse drink. "We don't talk about them at home."

"That's because they've not been about much. But things is waking up: all sorts of things. She has; we have. There's things being shook awake that should be left to lie till the end, but that's how it is. We'll do what we can."

"She won't like it," said one of the others. "She won't like it at all."

"Who won't?" asked Authran, but as he spoke there was a tiny thrill of energy under their feet, as if some ancient stratum far below had moved in its sleep. The four small men were alert at once.

"Gulta told the truth fer once!" said one. "She felt it under her cave right enough!"

"Can't tell how far."

"No, but movin' all the same. Never know the minute, do yer?"

"Yer right there, we was sent just in time!" They snatched their buckets and were gone.

"Come here!" called Tyr. "What's goin' on? Who sent y'?"

"And where's your etiquette?" said Authran. "Don't rush off! I mean, now what?"

A bearded face appeared among the bushes. "Now what? Yer get on them bloody horses and get to Falakhoth, that's now what!"

And so they did. They never knew what had been in the buckets, but they could barely hang on as the horses ran like lightning bolts.

~

THE FLAMES IN THE sunken space continued to burn with no sign of abating; ancient tile-work cracked and split. Ilissos watched the black reek, felt its stink in his nostrils, and wondered if the North would end thus, with darkness and devouring fire. Would the Valgraav's halls become like this awful room, filled with red light and ruined men?

Gehrava gasped and released V'karra's hand, tearing Ilissos' eyes from Murghjhash's slowly burning figure.

"You reached her, my Lord?" asked V'karra. "She has obeyed you?"

"Useless!" spat the sorcerer. "Foolish, mindless thing! Useless! But no matter, the pack will bring me joy." He raised his voice. "Brothers! We will begin!"

Val-zajjhak rose and brought his staff down sharply on the floor. "Close the shutters!" he called. "She must not look upon us!"

Through the hall's broad windows, the bright rising moon was visible. As oaken shutters swung into place, Ilissos understood: they had assembled while the sun declined, denying the powers of heaven while darkness grew. Now the clean light of Iathena's moon must not be exposed to them either. And Cynathé, where was she? Did she know the evil in her land? But what could his goddess do, so far away in the South? Were these men now irresistible?

Suddenly, he was looking up at V'karra's face. The southerner stepped forward, grasped Ilissos's hair, and hauled him to his feet. He was dragged past Val-zajjhak's chair as Gehrava ascended to the dais. V'karra swung him forward, then held him from behind, with one hand fastened on his throat, the other gripping his shoulder. The ancient man approached to a background of baying, jeering laughter.

"He is here for you, my Lord: the servant of the gods!" said V'karra.

The talon hands held Ilissos forward like a broken toy, and he looked into the face of Gehrava. Such a wave of desolation smote him he recoiled against V'karra's chest. Shuddering and retching, he could hardly stay conscious.

"Down!" rasped the southerner. "Do the gods save you now?" The southerner's cruel grip forced Ilissos to bow before the ancient sorcerer. V'karra pressed him onto his knees, forced him to hold a palm inward before his face, then hauled him erect once more. If this gave Gehrava any pleasure, he showed it not at all. Ilissos was vaguely aware of the yells of the vraakhin, but the horror of the ancient enchanter numbed his mind and confused him. "Again!" roared V'karra, and thrust him down, smashing his knees against the stone. Again he was hauled up, again flung down, until he could no longer feel his legs or tell up from down. He was a broken doll in V'karra's grasp.

"The one that served the gods is ours. We have never yet wrested anything from them, from their very hands, so devious are they." The old man moved forward. "Serve *me!* Serve *me!* See what I make you! Feel this, a little grain of my power." One hand reached forward—parchment skin, protruding bone, thick blue vein—and brushed Ilissos' forehead.

The Syrgan's body recoiled, lashed like a whip, his head cracked against V'karra's face. The grip loosened, and he jerked forward to vomit on Gehrava's robes. With an outraged howl the sorcerer swung his fist against Ilissos' head. A stronger arm would have killed him, but Gehrava tottered and almost fell from the effort. Through the blood that ran across his eyes, Ilissos saw how he swayed like a desert snake.

"He is yours now, my great Lord," spat V'karra, blood on his lips. "They have lost him. See, I hold him for you. *Qadza, geb'hanir! Qadza!*"

Gehrava lurched forward. With a cry, he swung his fist of bones against Ilissos' mouth. Again the blow fell, a jarring counterpoint to the screaming of the crackling voice. "You send your slaves against *me,* do you? *That* to your puppet! There! I can break him without a spell! There! My own hands! Ha! I'll destroy your abandoned failure, not you! I'll take the whole world from you!"

The voice and the beating went on until Ilissos hardly knew of either. The last time he had suffered at the hands of the vraakhin he had called on the gods and cried out in a tongue he did not know. Could he do it again, frighten them again? He tried to mumble a prayer to Arna, to the goddess—what was the name of the goddess? But his lips could not move, nor his mind hold thoughts. Darkness took control, and all fell away.

~

THE DISTANT BHANIRAN HAD BROKEN the horizon many hours earlier, its snowy peak a ghostly beacon to follow. Before it, Falakhoth's hill had come upon them with a hurried greeting. Tyr tried not to look at his home. Within the shadows of the hills were people he loved, Wyrdha's empty house, and the stage for most of his life. It was an agony to race past the little street that led up to the square, even worse to glance up and see the red-lit rear windows of the forge where his father must have been working late. Even a brief visit was unthinkable. They did not know what time they had, and for all they knew they would draw some pursuing horror down on anyone they met.

They raced past and in minutes were dismounting at the town's burial ground. Trembling, they got their breath.

"We're actually here, mad as it is. We made it," gasped Authran.

"Let's get this over with," said Tyr. "Before anything else *wakes*."

"Don't need to tell me twice. Let's get that thing and get away. Perhaps your mother can make us tea," Authran said hopefully.

Hastily they moved up the path, not even stopping to bow at the Lady's statue at the entrance. They began an anxious search among the tree-ringed grassy mounds. There were so many stones, figures, and poles with mementoes. The dark made it hard to identify each one until the boys were nearly on top of them.

"It were here," said Tyr. "I'm sure that beech tree to the left of the willow were at the head." He stopped as his heart jolted into his throat. Under the willow lay Wyrdha. All the facts of loss and severance came hammering back. He steadied himself.

"What is it?" asked Authran.

"Me friend, the healer. He's over there."

"Oh. So sorry."

"It's all right. Better carry on with it."

"Right, well, we're the first. Nothing's disturbed."

"Y' sure?"

"Don't think they'd be the sort to tidy up." They moved to the grave at the foot of the beech tree. "You sure that grave's the one?"

And suddenly Tyr wasn't. "Er—oh, bugger, it's dark, it's all different. I'm not sure." He whirled, stamped about, peered at the memorials. The wan light of the moon painted in sharp, black shadows that had not been there at the funeral, it's light glittering confusingly on the dark river, changing shapes, changing colours, and casting a disturbing unreality over a place that was unsettling enough already. Tyr reminded himself that the moon must help, because it was the Lady's sign, but this agitated him more. Then he halted, heart pounding and icy dread trickling down his back.

"What?" whispered Authran. "What's wrong?"

"Ran, y' don't think—I mean, what if... what if it's dead folk tryin' to mix us up?"

"Oh, rubbish. Why should they?"

"They might not like us trampin' about."

"Everybody here's dead. They're not interested."

"Thal's not dead, not properly."

"Well, he's different, apparently. He's dead, he just hasn't... you know... gone."

"That's the sort of thing I mean."

"Look, nothing can happen, just apply yourself."

"There's a lot we thought couldn't happen. What about the Gulta? What about the dreams and that feller with claws?"

"What about your Fire-spirit?" Authran asked.

"Oh. Aye, well, right enough."

"Wouldn't profess to know about these things but, um, could it help? Or be helping? I mean, could you ask it?"

"Dunno. Never thought of talkin' to it. Dunno if it's here, even."

"Neither do I, but time's moving on and, you know, nothing ventured and all that. I would personally be very grateful to it if a bit of help was forthcoming."

"Do y' think it'd come to a graveyard?"

"Haven't a blessed clue, but from what you say, it just does what it likes—oh, *Arna's wings!*"

Both lads howled and stepped back, then stared and stared.

There was Thaljhaz, sitting on his grave, glowering at them. "It's this one," he said. "Y' had it right the first time, Tyr, y' great nellie."

Horrific, frozen silence. Sheer, utter shock.

Thaljhaz glared more severely, "What's the matter with y'?" he said. "Y' haven't got all night."

After a long time, Tyr managed to get his voice working again, "Thal?"

"Aye, Thal," said the man on the grave. "Who do y' think?" He tilted his head back and ran a finger along his throat where the great raw tear that killed him was held closed by Wyrdha's careful stitches.

"Oh, Thal, did it hurt?" asked Tyr, feeling extremely foolish as soon as the words left his mouth.

"Course it bloody hurt!" said Thaljhaz. "It were quick, though, I'll say that. Everythin' mixed with mercy." He shook his head grimly. "Verdje all right? And Utha?"

"Aye," stammered Tyr. "Aye. Sold the inn, gone up to her sister's."

"Aye, good move to start again." Thaljhaz did not ask after Bardcha and Tyr felt disinclined to offer information. "Y'll be after this, then," said Thaljhaz, and held up an object on a leather thong. The novices gaped. Was it really going to be that easy?

"Aye, we are," said Tyr simply. He could not understand how Thaljhaz could be so matter-of-fact. How could a dead man behave so like a living one? "Can we have it then?" said Tyr, nodding at the amulet.

"Do y' know what it's for?"

"Not really, but it'll be safer if we've got it. We worked it out from the dreams."

"What dreams?"

"Y' never did the dreams?"

"Don't be daft. I can't do dreams, I'm an innkeeper. Well, was."

"Well folk, good folk like Ran here, dreamed y' was here with it, and we found out some bad feller wants it, so it's right important. That's why we're here." Despite being true, this sounded horribly lame when you said it quickly.

But Thaljhaz nodded thoughtfully. "Thought it'd be somethin' like that. Have it and welcome, but y'll have to dig it up."

"Y've got it in y' hand!"

"Aye, but it's still in the ground."

"*You're* up here!" Authran said.

"Aye, *and* I'm in the ground."

"That's daft."

"No, that's how it works. All that with places and distances and times and where y' are, that's not how y' do things when y're, y'know..."

"Why not?"

"I dunno, I didn't arrange it. That stuff just don't work like it used to."

"What's it like, sir?" said Authran suddenly.

"What's what like? Oh, y' mean—?"

"If you don't mind me asking, sir."

"No, lad, no. Ask away."

"It's just—well, I've never met a... um... what you are, and it's fascinating. No offence."

"None taken, none taken. Well, it's hard to say. I'm not right used to it, if y' follow me. I mean, I've been sat here since they put me in—oh, and that were a right nice few words that feller Azhur said, by the way. Mind and tell him for me, Tyr, will y'?"

"Oh, aye," said Tyr.

"So, let's see. Y' know things. Y're aware of more. I mean, I knew about this amulet thing straight off. Very nice of that old feller givin' it. Mind, I thought it were queer him wearin' just half an amulet."

"*Half* an amulet?"

"Aye. Oh, I knew it weren't complete soon's it went in me grave. I could feel the energy cracklin' out lookin' for the other half."

Authran and Tyr both looked at each other.

"So it's... it's powerful?" said Authran at last.

"It is that. I reckon if y' put both halves together y'd have—well, I don't know what, but by gum it'd be powerful, all right. That's part of the awareness business: y' feel all kinds of things about the world y' never knew when y' was alive. It's like y're a bit *more* alive even though y're dead. I could feel the energy strainin' away southward out of that thing."

"*Southward?*" said Tyr. "Is that where the other half is? Can y' tell?"

"Well, I'd say so. There's like a little feel of somethin' answerin' back. That and the other thing."

The novices exchanged apprehensive looks.

"The other thing?" gulped Authran.

"Y' see," continued Thaljhaz, warming to his subject, "there's like a kind of feelin' of somethin' movin' through things, goin' here an'd there like a wind blowin' underground, if y' follow me."

"Not really, sir."

"Thought not, it's a bit hard to describe. Y'd understand if y' was dead, though."

"I'm sure I would, sir. I'm certainly a bit of an outsider to that state of affairs at the moment."

"Aye, I suppose so. Anyroad, it's been roamin' around kind of thing, all over the north. Started not long after they put me in here. But the queer thing is, I can feel it movin' down this way now. It's really strong. I can even tell where it's comin' from: sort of north-east, round about the Plain."

"Well, if that's the case Thal, I think we'll get diggin' if that's all right," said Tyr. "Hope y' don't mind us messin' up y'... er... place."

"Got to be done," said Thaljhaz, as practical in death as in life. "There's a little place past the willow there where they keeps spades and that."

"Right," said Tyr. "Oh."

"What, lad?"

"I think I know," said Authran. "The willow, yes? I'll get the spades." And he picked his way to the spot, weaving his way among the soft, moonlit mounds and remembering to bow respectfully at the one that so affected Tyr.

"I see," said Thaljhaz. "Wyrdha's place is over there. Is that it?"

"Aye," Tyr told him. "I just—I can't just now."

"Very understandable. It's not been long."

A thought struck Tyr. "Thal? Can y'—I mean, do y' ever...?"

"No, lad, can't say anythin' about him over there, sorry. Would it make any difference?"

"Suppose not. Do y' think I could ever see him, like I can y'?"

"Dunno. Doubt it, though. He's probably gone by now. Anyroad, I think we're havin' this chat for a very particular reason, like y' want that amulet and I'm lookin' after it."

"Exactly why are you looking after it, sir?" asked Authran, arriving with two spades. "I mean, you're very tenacious about it."

"Very what?"

"You're, um, you're holding on, you won't go to Arna with the Guide and I thought everybody had to. I never thought there'd be an option."

"Inquisitive feller, aren't y'?" said Thaljhaz.

"He's a crackin' student," said Tyr. "I'm a novice at the Shrine now, and he's me best mate. Knows all sorts he does."

"Y' never are! Well, fancy our little Tyr a novice! All right, I'll better explain to y' mate, then."

"You don't know if it's in a Scroll, I suppose?" asked Authran.

"Haven't a clue. Anyroad, that amulet's me grave-gift. Y' know how folk drop things in graves as a sort of goodbye present? Well that's mine, and it's special to me, just me. It'll be there with me till the very end, and when all's put right, I'll still have it. It's nearly a part of me now, so I'm sort of protective of it, y' might say."

"And you're letting us dig it up?"

"There's so much power in this thing, I thought, I can't just go on and leave it, anythin' could happen. I don't want it in the wrong hands or getting' mixed up in somethin' not right. I figured somethin' this powerful means there's probably somebody or other goin' to be after a thing like this. Y' understand?"

"And if somebody—the wrong person, a thief or something, tried to take it, could you—I mean, what could you actually do about it?"

Thaljhaz looked very hard at Authran through the dark. There was the faintest phosphorescence in his eyes. "I don't think I want to go into that just at the moment," he said in a voice that carried oceans of meaning.

"Y'll not even go with the Guide?" gasped Tyr, awestruck.

"Not even him. I'm stoppin'."

"But he's death," said Authran. "How can you refuse death?"

"Don't be daft, he's not death. I'm dead already with no help from him. He'll try again, I suspect."

"Ey! Y' mean he's been already?"

"Oh, aye. Very persuasive too, him and his five daughters. *You're not supposed to stay here, come on now,* he says. But I explained, and he were very respectful."

"Bugger it, Thal!" gasped Tyr. "That's the Dreadful Guide. He don't talk like that!"

"Are you absolutely sure about this, sir?" said Authran. "I've never heard—I mean, nobody—oh, look, no offence, but could your, er, recent, very traumatic experience..." he drew a finger across his throat, "possibly have, er, skewed your perceptions a little?"

Thaljhaz glared at him.

"Just a theory of course. Entirely speculative."

"Please y'selves," said Thaljhaz. "Get diggin'."

"Yes, of course, sir," said Authran, "but, really, I'd like to be quite clear. We're very grateful, very honoured, but why are you letting *us* take your grave-gift?"

"Because it's important, like I said," explained Thaljhaz quietly, "and because I know it's safe for Tyr-shan, son of my mate Tyrmar, to have it." He looked sternly at them both. "I'll ask one thing of y', though. Promise me, when y've done whatever y' do with it, y'll come here and put it back."

"We will, Thal," said Tyr, with tears on his face. "We'll do that for y', we will."

Thaljhaz sighed. "Right then, lads. In that case, call it a loan."

~

WHEN ILISSOS BECAME ALERT AGAIN, he found himself looking down at the sorcerers. V'karra was holding him up to the yelling crowd like a trophy.

"I have told you how the gods abandoned their servant to me at Falakhoth! This is the first thing our power has taken from them. A gift to the brotherhood from the gods!" The men reached up, clawing at Ilissos' feet. V'karra, laughing, snatched him away, dangling him just beyond their reach. "Wait! Wait, my brothers! We must savour this!"

Ilissos could not remember what prayer he should say. He raised his head to look over at the pool where Murghjhash's body somehow still lay twitching as it burned. He supposed they would fling his dead or dying body to join him soon. The reek of it swirled about the hall and he felt himself floating, about to be borne away on the black billows.

And then there was air on his face, parting the drifting pall before him. A man was standing beneath him, ignoring the frenzied wizards all around him. He was as still and calm as they were wild, as composed and intent as they were mad with instinct. They could have been in different rooms. He was looking earnestly up into Ilissos' face with an expression of determination and compassion. His long hair and beard were a reddish brown, with a tribal scar on his cheek. In the eyes under his level brows something shone. He stood with hardly a movement, surrounded by the rabble but not a part of them. Ilissos took him in as V'karra roared out his hate.

"Think, my brothers, think! Make this moment last! Consider, then do what you will!"

As the howls of the sorcerers went up, the face of the silent man became bruised and disfigured, as though he had suffered the very beating that Ilissos had. He turned and thrust out a hand towards Val-zajjhak.

"Lord V'karra, wait!" Val-zajjhak said, a hand outstretched.

The southerner's head snapped round. "Wait?" barked V'karra. "I let him live at Falakhoth to wrest him from the gods. Why should we wait?"

Through the bond that had formed with Val-zajjhak's mind, Ilissos heard the thoughts that the three sorcerers hid from their slaves.

It is said the gods never truly release one of their own, Val-zajjhak said. *If he is still theirs and we destroy him, may not wrath break out against us?*

Wrath? came Gehrava's bitter thought. *What could they do? We have one of the oldest gods beneath us now; he left them at the beginning.*

My masters know the lore: it is also from the beginning, or so we under-stand. Whether it be true is for your judgement. You permit me my thoughts,

597

may I be wrong, but if the gods are deceitful, as you say, how can we know they have abandoned the Syrgan? Might they have given us their servant so we destroy what is truly theirs and so break the ancient laws of high conflict? Might we be duped into opening a channel for destruction? Forgive, I speak only for your honour and our cause. Val-zajjhak bowed, drew back a step.

Val-zajjhak begins to be afraid of the gods, Ilissos thought. *Does he want to save me?* He pushed his mind towards Val-zajjhak's, probing for an opening. He felt the sorcerer's mind swell and break open from the pressure of the thoughts within him, and Ilissos slipped into a memory of their earliest meetings in that very place. The references to the glorious beauty, the scenes of the threatening woman, the longing for recognition, and the words that he, Ilissos, had spoken over the smouldering, broken staff: *You are known, Val-zajjhak. We will not give up.* He knew then he had touched a place so deep within Val-zajjhak that something had changed. Suddenly their eyes met, and he realised that running through the sorcerer's fear was a vein of hope, the tiny dawn of an idea that the words were in fact an exhortation whereby the power he had met might be for him, not against him. That the beauty might, by an undreamed wonder, possibly shine on him. Yet such hope filled him with an anticipation of threat and dislocation. Fear closed the doors of Val-zajjhak's mind.

They'll know, thought Ilissos at once. *They'll see it, they'll kill him.*

Another mind spoke, *No, I shield him.*

Ilissos found himself looking into the stern, sad face of the stranger. Why didn't the others see him?

A trembling uncertainty moved between Gehrava and V'karra. They had apparently reached a tenuous agreement while Ilissos travelled Val-zajjhak memories, for V'karra now dragged him away from the edge of the dais and the blood-hungry men, to let him fall nearby. The sorcerers' thoughts came to him again through a haze, as they debated. *Your wisdom grows... but still a triumph: defy them... not enough to be powerful... greater guile than theirs... give them no opening... keep him... a badge, yes, a hostage, wrest him to our use... great power that way... tell them we keep him as a sign of victory, a pledge...*

V'karra began shouting to the gathering again.

Ilissos' body refused to respond to his commands after being dropped by V'karra. By the time he pushed himself up into a position to search for the man whose thoughts he had heard, the man was lost in the mob. Ilissos slumped to the ground, grateful he had been momentarily forgotten.

~

"REALLY DECENT OF YOU, SIR," said Authran as he straightened to rest his back from digging, "considering we don't know what we need this amulet for."

"Shut it, y'," said Tyr. He wiped his brow. "Just keep diggin'. We don't know how much time we've got." He shoved his spade in the earth again.

"I think it's more to that side," said Thaljhaz helpfully. He had thoughtfully moved up his grave a little to make the excavations easier. Both novices were grateful for this. The prospect of digging through Thaljhaz's presumably corporeal form had filled them both with dread. "Like I said, I knew it were important it don't stay here."

Authran gave a mighty thrust with the spade.

"Here, go carefully. Don't chop it in half!"

"Sorry. You know, whoever wants it thought our Loremaster had it— you know, the priest who gave it to your late wife... I mean, former wife... no, I mean..."

"Did he think that really? He a priest then?"

"Doubt it, but he sent this dreadful chap for it. Never seen anything like him: hairy, fanged, claws like a beast."

"Claws?" said Thaljhaz, in a voice that made Authran stop digging.

"Ran! Will y' get on with it!"

"Y' saw this feller, young Tyr?" asked Thaljhaz.

"Aye, and I don't want to see no more, so move y' arse, Ran!"

"Bit of the wolf about him, would y' say?" said Thaljhaz.

"I would that. And he went for Azhur like a wolf as well," said Tyr.

"Yes, very wolfish, now you say it," said Authran. "I thought—"

"It were one of them that killed me."

Now Tyr stopped digging, "I thought it were a wolf!"

"Everybody did, that's what it looked like."

"Then how...?"

"I'll tell y'. Keep diggin' now. Y' remember I went to the falls at Braldhach to try and shoot that wolf as were causin' havoc? Well, I gets there and suddenly this whole pack comes out the woods round the Tor with this massive red one in the lead."

"Ey, never heard of a red wolf afore. Keep on, Ran."

"Nor had I, but red it was. Anyhow, the pack gets round me and one of them comes right up to me, and then it weren't a wolf, it were a feller: claws, teeth, like y' said. *Did y' like that?* he says. *Surprise, wasn't it? Here's another one.* And he went for me throat and that was it."

Authran paused in his digging and raised a finger.

"And before y' ask, aye, it were very interestin'. There I was stood lookin' at meself and all me blood pourin' down to the river. *Bugger!* I thought, *I'm dead!* And then the whole pack changes and there's all these fellers standin' about laughin'."

"There's more, then," said Authran.

"Oh, plenty. I can feel them. All over the north they are, but mostly round about Valderthaan and the Plain. And them buggers is still at Braldhach—oh no, wait, they've moved off. Anyroad, there's them, and all sorts of things y'd not have thought of appearin', all strange, all busy. Then, y' know, sometimes I can feel things as are really big—"

"Not as big's y' mouth," grunted Tyr, labouring hard. "Y' don't half talk a lot for somebody dead."

Thaljhaz waved a finger, "Now then, young Tyr, talk nice to y' elders."

"It's improved y' temper, anyroad. I'd have had me head in me hands if I'd said that when y' was livin'."

"Aye, but there's a lot to learn, y' know. Y'll need it someday."

"I'll manage, thanks. Let's get this bloody amulet and get away, not that it's not nice seein' y' and all."

"Quite understand. What were I sayin'? Aye, I can feel these things as are really *big*, really—well, I don't know what— powerful y' could say, but *different*, like they was from some other place all together. There's one or two I can feel sometimes and they're marvellous, just marvellous, and

"And before y' ask, aye, it were very interestin'."

there's some as gives me the willies. Everythin's wrong when I feel them, like there's somethin' mucky about them, like they was never meant to exist."

"I am *so* fascinated," said Authran.

"Ran, don't be: *dig!*"

"But no, I mean, oh dear, hope there aren't many of the big mucky ones about, sir."

"Ah, well, there's a big one over by the Plain just now. And I know what them wolf-man packs feel like: they're all over the place. Wouldn't have felt them afore I were dead, mind."

"Oh, bugger!" said Tyr.

"Have I upset y', lad?"

Tyr had frozen in mid-heave with a spadeful of earth. "I just had a thought. The one as sent that beasty feller to get the amulet from Galdtchav, he must have somethin' to do with the packs, and what you felt comin' down from the Plain, I bet that's him lookin' about for the amulet."

Authran dropped his spade. "Oh gosh, yes. Tyr, remember the clues: something under the earth, something evil; another sun that's going to rise."

"Ey, and the Gulta felt somethin' under her cave and she were goin' on about sunrise."

"I thought she just meant dawn."

"And she said somebody sent her! Ran, somethin's happenin' tonight! Now!"

"I think so, Tyr," gasped Authran. "I think so."

"What the hell are y' pair goin' on about?" asked Thaljhaz.

"Master Thaljhaz, sir, what do you feel from the Plain now?"

Thaljhaz listened, if listening with your dead body could be called such. "Somethin' goin' on there all right. Lots of energy and disturbance all concentrated and swillin' around together, and some feller bang in the middle of it that's right old and strong. Don't know who it is though."

Authran knelt down. "What about under the earth?" he asked, fearing the answer.

Thaljhaz listened again, then jolted back, "Bloody hell! That's a big 'un! And it's brim-full of right horrible clout!"

"Are they together?"

"It's right close to him! One up here, one down below. There's somethin' happenin' on that Plain!"

~

Ilissos opened his swollen eyes. They had left him where he had fallen to gather around the pool where the dreadful fire still flickered. How long had Murghjhash been burning? The upper air was thick with fumes, and the light was dull and red. The hall was filled with black moving shapes that turned into people whenever they came near the horrid glare of the flames. They were swaying and shifting to the broken, violent rhythm of a slow, deep chant. Quick, pale lights ran among them as they shuffled and whirled; a colourless glow twined in the air. Ilissos was past fear; he tried to rise but could not. He gingerly put a hand to his face to trace the swellings and cuts. Did they believe they could come so close to murder and not provoke the gods? Or could it really be that the gods had selected the trader of Agoras to be their agent in this vile company? The thoughts were too large to manage. He let them go, able only to watch.

Gehrava was standing at the edge of the sunken pool, staring down like a mourner at a burning grave. Beside him were V'karra and Val-za-jjhak. Nearby, Gizhurthra's tear-streaked face was staring blindly into the fire. He moved limply from side to side, utterly given up to the rhythm of the voices.

"My brothers!" called Gehrava over the chant, voice impossibly loud for his withered frame. "Only a few of you know where we stand. Before you is one of the few ancient portals to the world below. This very building was the Great One's northern temple in the earliest days. Here he will join the forces of his might with ours as we call our Dark Sun over the horizon of being. Aeons crept past as I waited; now the moment is here. The magnificent beams of our Sun—which the ignorant call dark—will make the earth a place that the Great One below may inhabit. Very soon, he shall walk unconquerable upon the world's hide, and we shall see our reward and fulfilment in the fruition of our cause. The gods shall fall, and with our splendid champion we shall rule. Prepare your powers!"

New words entered the chant, and the rhythm slowed. Long, groaning syllables shuddered in the grimy air; shouts and wails broke out. Gehrava turned, beckoning abruptly to the shadows. The chanting faltered at the drawn-out moans of a beast, horribly bizarre among the human voices. Once more the awful baying came, then the circle broke as a huge wolf loped up to the edge of the pool. Ilissos would have fled if he could, spells or no, but he could only watch in terror as the beast looked about it then crept, head lowered, along the side of the pit like a grotesque cat on a window-ledge. It reached Gehrava, and the sorcerer ruffled the animal's fur in a parody of proud affection. The beast sat by his side, panting and showing its fangs.

"You shall have your reward tonight, Karhalkhar," said the sorcerer. "Faithful servant!" As though this completed some insane scenario, Gehrava raised his hand. "Now!" he called. "This is the time! Your powers are your own, my brothers. Join them and let the Dark Sun rise!"

Lights and twisted shapes slid and moved as Gehrava spoke terrible, foul utterances, words the air was never meant to carry. Over their heads black smoke shifted in a slow, swirling eddy that descended dark and heavy towards the pool. Murghjhash was finally no more, and the fire took on a life of its own, moving lazily to cover the bottom of the pool even though there was nothing for it to burn. Above the flames, the darting lights formed the outline of a sphere.

"Nearer!" roared Gehrava. "Do not break the chant!"

The vraakhin thrust out their hands towards the sphere, howling the words that released their power. The orb drew in their energies, filling with a writhing glow, a colourless imitation of light, thin and soiled; a light that illuminated nothing.

Ilissos stared with the fascination of disgust. The flames in the pool took on a new intensity, glowing red as they danced upwards towards the orb. Suddenly, the colour left the fire, and all true light in the hall was devoured. Ilissos clutched at his chest as the pulsing orb snatched at the energies of his life.

"Your powers are your own, my brothers. Join them and let the Dark Sun rise!"

"Now, my son!" cried Gehrava. "Take your gift!"

There was a dreadful howl, and the wolf ran and launched itself in an immense leap over the pool and into the unlight at the heart of the orb.

For dreadful moments there was nothing, the arc of the leap cut short. Ilisos felt his heart beat three times before the wolf burst free. It trailed deathly fire as it landed, snarling and clawing among screaming wizards at the farther end of the sunken pool. Under their feet came the vile bellowing echo of the underworld exulting in its own power and hate. A howl for the utter end of being from a thing craving that only itself should exist.

Blackness came again, with a confused and muffled silence.

Sounding breathless, Gehrava spoke out of the darkness. "We hear your voice, Great One! Lord G'chraada, we feel your power! The Dark Sun has risen!"

~

"Y' should get a move on," said Thaljhaz helpfully. "Use y' hands in case y' miss it."

"Plain's miles away," said Tyr.

"Aye, but I can feel that Braldhach pack. They're near the river above Falakhoth."

"That's miles away and all."

"Well, not that I'm worried personally. I mean, why bother if y' dead? Did anybody funny put their hand on y' right shoulder recently?"

"Eh? Why?"

"I can see a sort of glowin' hand print thing on it."

Tyr remembered with a jolt V'karra's hands gripping Azhur and himself on Renewal Night: *You are marked. I will find you.* "Oh, bugger, aye! Some wizard did it."

Authran gasped as conclusions rushed together. "Whoever's on the Plain's sending the pack! It must be him! They know where you are, Tyr!"

The two novices stared horrified at each other, then threw themselves into the quarried grave. They clawed, scraped, and burrowed in the earth with their fingers.

"It's terrible, terrible!" moaned Tyr, almost weeping. "Me mam's just up the road doin' tea. She don't know! She don't know!"

"She will, Tyr, keep at it."

They carried on, their finger-ploughs making rapid furrows, questing the earth for the amulet even as they tore nails and cut their hands.

"String!" yelled Tyr at last.

"Ey, now, will y' look at that?" said Thaljhaz. "Timed that well."

"Oh, Arna, more string!" exclaimed Authran.

"No, it's leather!"

"Oh, it's the thong! Timed what well?"

"The Guide," said Thaljhaz matter-of-factly. "Don't give up, does he?"

The lads whipped round, terror-numbed. Over by the willow, the night-shapes of the burial ground were boiling and melting, moving aside as a door opened in reality. In the abyss beyond, a figure formed. It stepped slowly across the worlds, holding out the ox-goad and the cattle-whip that drove the dead down under the earth. It glared at the novices with huge, burning, empty eyes and opened its devouring mouth. It was a terrible thing of mists and vapours, bones and parchment skin, decked in a tarnished crown and regal, rotten, fluttering grave clothes. Thaljhaz had been dismally, abysmally wrong, his understanding fractured by his own violent death, and now here was the monster that towered over every fear and would take them before their time.

Tyr and Authran scrabbled out from the grave. Still they held ends of the amulet's thong; the muddied little thing bobbed between them. Five other stalking shapes emerged from the void, the sight of the pale daughters of Ardhruthak paralysing the novices with dread. The daughters held out their hands, grasping and cajoling, staring from cavern-eyes, speaking seductive reassurances from their thin, crimson lips. Black, cobwebbed hair floated and twined. No tale Tyr and Authran had ever heard allowed them to imagine the Lord of the Dead would not take them.

Authran was the first to pry his mind from the sight. The Guide had come for Thaljhaz; they were the living. He seized Tyr and with an effort that used all his store of life, he hauled him away from the grave. If only they could reach the horses at the roadside below, they could be mounted and away within moments. He dragged Tyr toward the slope, but one of the ghastly women moved ahead of them towards the road, cutting them off from the horses. Hope nearly died, but he heaved wildly, causing Tyr to stumble and fall into him. Tangled, they rolled down the slope, past the ghoul-woman, and on to the road.

This shocked Tyr out of his fearful stupor. He was the first onto his knees, onto his feet, and grasping for a bridle. A dazed Authran had had his breath knocked from him during the tumble and had let go of the amulet's thong. He moved his hands over the dirt, desperately trying to find it.

"I got it, Ran," Tyr said, holding the amulet up. "Let's go." He put it on over his head and reached out a hand to help Authran to his feet. The horses were neighing and fidgeting at the danger they could sense, but their rigorous training held them fast. Tyr allowed himself to believe they would escape.

A sound of insane baying and half-human howling cut through the air.

Behind Tyr and Authran was the devouring King of the Grave, his daughters gliding down the slope, and before them, racing round the bend in the road, moments away, were the servants who would surely send them to his realm.

The Braldhach pack had arrived.

THE END OF BOOK ONE

ACKNOWLEDGEMENTS

A MASSIVE THANK YOU to all who have encouraged and supported me in the writing of this book. An honourable mention must go to Steve Hall, my publisher and editor, who somehow found the time and energy to apply his considerable skills to everything that was needed to get me to publication, when I myself lacked the wherewithal. No easy task, I know. Thanks hugely, Steve.

I also have to thank those who brought the book along in its various metamorphoses from a pile of handwritten sheets to dot-matrix printout of a steam-driven Amstrad PCW8256 to final form on the hard drive of a gleaming PC. I must praise the friendship and flying fingers of John Wallace, who dedicated himself to transforming thousands of words into their present incarnation. Thanks so much, John.

It would be ungrateful to pass by the wonderful institution of *Gusto and Relish*, Glasgow, which is simply the best bistro in the world. Over the years, their premises were the scene of much composition and illustration, with much appreciated advice and encouragement for the latter from Martyn McKenzie. I still have a bottle of ambience that the manager gave me. Thanks loads, guys.

The last mention by name must go to the intrepid Steve Downs, my erstwhile landlord, for help above and beyond the call of proprietorship. What can one say of the man who endured a thundering mechanical typewriter (yes, I had one of those) in the room above his bedroom at two in the morning? For that and more, thanks, Steve.

Now I must pause and extend my gratitude to those many people who consistently provided that love and encouragement without which creative persons are unlikely to flourish. You know who you are, and your powerful and gracious lives will not be forgotten. Thank you.

G. Ian Smith, Glasgow, July 2020

AUTHOR BIO

G. IAN SMITH WAS BORN in Glasgow and is still there. He enjoys being creative, which is just is well, as he's an artist, a writer, and has dabbled in theatre. He also made a video recording of Princess Anne from only six feet away. Ian wrote and recorded a play for radio, *Herod's Last Night*, and his modernised re-telling of the Gospels, *JOSH*, was published in 2010. He has illustrated about twenty books, but as far as he knows, nobody's coloured them in. However, one of them can be found in the library of Iona Abbey. He also has the distinction of impersonating Charles Dickens in his solo performance of *A Christmas Carol.* To cap all this, for several years Ian studied theology, which is far more exciting than most people think, and resulted in him ghost-writing a recent work on Eschatology (look it up). He also has a strong interest in mental health and likes cats, especially his Bengal cat Saffy.

PRONUNCIATION GUIDE

THIS IS A GUIDE to how to pronounce the names of main characters and places. Ian encourages you to work out your own pronunciation from the *look* of the word or in line with what you enjoy saying or hearing, but knows others prefer the authenticity of how the author would say it. This is for the latter.

Aia Djetenga   *Aa-yah Je-teng-ga*

Aienna   *Ay-en-na*

Authran   *Ow-thran*

Azhur   *Az-oor*

Bal-jarrak   *Bal-ja-rak*

Bel-ghirá   *Bel-gee-ra*

G'chraada   *Gi-kra-da*

Galdtchav   *Gald-chav*

Gaur-van   *Gow-van*

Gehrava   *Geh-ra-va*

Gizhurthra   *Giz-hoorth-ra*

Iathena   *Ya-thay-na*

Iera   *Yay-ra*

Iethen   *Yeh-then*

Ilissos   *Ill-i-soss*

Jarthastra   *Jar-thas-tra*

Karhalkhar   *Kar-hal-kar*

Meinze   *Mine-zay*

Naida   *Ny-da*

Shar-ra'ul   *Shar-ra-ool*

Shivara   *Shi-va-ra*

Tyr   *Tirr*

Tyrmar   *Tirr-mar*

Utha   *Oo-tha*

V'karra   *Vih-ka-ra*

Val-zajjhak   *Val-za-jak*

Vraakhin   *Vra-keen*

Wyrdha   *Wird-ha*

Yauva   *Yow-va*

Archraad   *Arh-chrad*

Ceorthas   *Kay-or-thas*

Dhar   *Dar*

Falakhoth   *Fal-a-koth*

Fyrieg   *Fir-i-eg*

Lachresh   *La-chresh*

Lukar   *Loo-kar*

Murinde   *Moo-rin-day*

Syrga   *Sir-ga*

Valderthaan   *Val-der-than*

ALSO AVAILABLE

Available now or coming soon from Cookies and Oxygen Publishing.
Find out more at www.cookiesandoxygen.co.uk.

EAGLE'S GUARD by Lindsey Stirling

Seventeen year old Aiden has done the unheard of: he has taught himself to wield the eighteen magical runes.

When the Eagle Riders—the elite magical guardians of the kingdom—go missing, Aiden embarks on a dangerous journey in an attempt to rescue them.

EAGLE'S PATH by Lindsey Stirling

The dark wizard Sorcier has returned. As Aiden and his friends fight to reunite their people, the path ahead remains unclear. Aiden is forbidden to fly again, Tristan finds his heart rebelling against his orders, and Branwyn contends for her place in a world of warriors and wizards.

LAMENT FORGIVE by Steve Hall

Time is a terrible healer. Our memories of the disloyalty, betrayal, or abuse we've suffered keep the pain fresh and the consequences ongoing. No wonder forgiving is so hard.

God wants to heal our memories, but for you and I to believe that, we need to reframe what it means to forgive.

HELP! OK. by Richard O. Morgan with Steve Hall

Why does every form of therapy meet with a certain degree of success to change people's lives?

Perhaps magic happens not because of the therapy we choose but by our cry for help being met by someone willing to listen. So where do we find the right listener?